D0587222

Malcolm Ross was born in 1932, the eldest of three brothers. While he was growing up, his family lived in Shropshire and South Africa, but they eventually settled in Cornwall. After school he studied fine art and then travelled, doing a variety of jobs including teaching, farming, mining and tunnelling. His first novel was published in 1961 and he has written several non-fiction works, radio plays and historical novels under a different name. His novels written as Malcolm Ross include *Tomorrow's Tide*, *Crissy's Family*, *Kernow & Daughter*, *An Innocent Woman*, *Mistress of Pallas*, *A Notorious Woman*, *To The End of Her Days*, *A Woman Alone* and *A Woman Possessed* (all published by Piatkus).

The Carringtons of Helston

Also by Malcolm Ross:

THE DUKES
MISTRESS OF PALLAS
A NOTORIOUS WOMAN
AN INNOCENT WOMAN
A WOMAN ALONE
A WOMAN POSSESSED
TO THE END OF HER DAYS
KERNOW & DAUGHTER
CRISSY'S FAMILY
TOMORROW'S TIDE

writing as Malcolm Macdonald:
WORLD FROM ROUGH STONES
THE RICH ARE WITH YOU ALWAYS
SONS OF FORTUNE
ABIGAIL
GOLDENEYE
TESSA D'ARBLAY
IN LOVE AND WAR
THE SILVER HIGHWAYS
THE SKY WITH DIAMONDS
HIS FATHER'S SON
THE CAPTAIN'S WIVES
DANCING ON SNOWFLAKES

writing as M. R. O'Donnell
HELL HATH NO FURY
A WOMAN SCORNED
ALL DESIRES KNOWN
FOR I HAVE SINNED

The Carringtons of Helston

Malcolm Ross

PIATKUS

The Carringtons of Helston © 1997 by Malcolm Ross
Tamsin Harte © 2000 by Malcolm Ross-Macdonald

This combined edition first published in Great Britain
in 2002 by Judy Piatkus (Publishers) Ltd,
5 Windmill Street, London W1T 2JA
Email: info@piatkus.co.uk
Website: www.piatkus.co.uk

The moral right of the author has been asserted

A catalogue record for this book is available from the British Library

ISBN 0 7499 3050 0

Printed and bound in Great Britain by
Mackays of Chatham Ltd, Chatham, Kent

for

'Deirdre'

who turned out to be

Fiona

to our overwhelming joy

Contents

PART ONE
The Enchanted Well 1

PART TWO
Ghosts of the Past 147

PART THREE
Shades of the Future 219

Part One

The Enchanted Well

1 After Truthall Halt the branch line veers briefly northward, threading its way along the hillside among tiny, stone-hedged fields, meandering lanes, and wind-bowed copses. At the head of the valley it turns southeast again, leaps across a tall viaduct of Cornish granite, and completes its journey to Helston up a short and none-too-gentle slope, which always brings out a fine display of steam from the little saddle-tank engines that serve the line. From time to time the stolid square tower of Sithney church can be seen, a mile and more away, just breaking above the skyline of Sithney Common Hill.

"Is that it?" Leah asked the first time she noticed it, jabbing her gloved finger against the rain-streaked, smut-mottled window of their compartment. "Our church? Or it will be if we go ahead and buy this farm."

"We!" her brother echoed scornfully. "I like that! *You* won't be buying it." He looked to their father for support.

Their father raised a sympathetic eyebrow at his daughter. Since their mother's death in 1910, four years ago now, Leah had taken over the distaff side of the household, making all the decisions and undertaking all the public duties that would have fallen upon her mother. At eighteen it had seemed a heavy burden; now, at twenty-two, she shouldered it as if it had been hers from birth. He would never buy the Old Glebe Farm without her approval — and they all knew it. But William, two years younger than his sister, chafed at every show of her authority, no matter how slight or casual.

"I might, too," she said airily. "It depends on the price."

He did not rise to it. He was getting better at not rising to her more obvious provocations.

"Helston," their father said, leaning back from the other window to allow them a better view.

How often he had heard his old man speak of the little town, even though he, too, had never seen it; in fact, he had been passing on *his* old man's boyhood memories of the place, before he took the emigrant boat to America, back in the 1830s.

"I'm all discombobulated now, sir," William drawled. "Is Helston our old home town? Or is it Leedstown?"

Leah, who had noticed, since their arrival in Cornwall the previous week, how her brother's rather jocose Americanisms grated on local people, had to restrain herself from speaking out sharply. She, too, was getting much better at not rising to obvious provocations.

"A bit of both, son," their father replied. "Gran'pappy Carrington called himself 'William Carrington of Leedstown' when he first set foot in America. But he had all his schooling right there in Helston and did his early courting there, too. Or 'couranting' he called it. So I guess his heart was there."

"Home is where the heart is," Leah murmured. And though her gaze was on Helston still, her inner vision dwelled more fondly on a certain quiet street in far-away East Haven, Connecticut, where stood the dearest little clapboard house in the Cape Cod style …

She closed her eyes then, to see it more clearly. *Oh, Tom,* she thought, holding her breath so that no sudden sigh might give her away, *will I ever see you again?*

"You okay, sis?"

She opened her eyes once more and found William grinning at her. He knew very well what had been going through her mind — and that the old man's talk of courting had provoked it. She lowered her eyes and waited for him to tease.

But no words came.

She glanced at him again and was met with an ambiguous expression — almost, one might say, a gaze of sympathy. She looked away hastily, having no means — that is, no experience — of dealing with such a novel emotion from him toward her.

"'Course, in those days," their father said, "his only way of getting about was on foot. They didn't even have bicycles. So 'home' was a few acres. But *our* home, I guess, will be the whole of Cornwall. Or West Penwith, anyway, when we get an auto."

"Where's West Penwith?" Leah asked.

"Clear to Land's End from here," he told her. "A couple o' dozen miles, mebbe."

"What sort of car are we gonna get ourselves, sir?" William asked eagerly.

Leah let their conversation drift off into the background as she turned her face to the grimy window once more. The train thundered over the viaduct and began its energetic final haul up to the station; it was only two coaches long, so each thrust of the pistons could be felt as a little nudge of the seat against her. They were like the nudges a parent might give a reluctant child: Go on! Go on! Go on!

Do I like this Cornwall? she asked herself, running her eye this way and that, tracing a path as random as the hedges and lanes out there.

Certainly the county was doing nothing to present itself in a good light on this particular day. February-filldyke, the nursery rhyme said, so the month knew how to behave. Today, a steady, almost invisible rain fell from a sky of uniform gray. Away to the west, crowning Trigonning Hill — the tallest in the district — one long streak of silver relieved that uniformity. But it was not wide enough to promise any improvement; it merely gleamed off every slate roof, every puddled byway, and each bare branch among the nearer trees, revealing something more profound than simple wetness. Soaking, sodden, sopping wetness. A wetness she could feel in her very bones, even here in the warmth of their first-class compartment. As if to confirm it, the cattle stood up to their bellies in mud, patiently steaming as they awaited their dole of hay.

Her dad once said Gran'pappy William told him he'd felt colder in Cornwall on a wet February day (just like today, in fact) than in New England at ten below. She thought of the crisp, snow-blanketed landscape they'd left behind them three weeks earlier and, this time, permitted herself a sigh. Never another summer on the remote, wild, untramelled foreshores of Cape Cod ... never another motor ride upstate to picnic by the beaver lake above Bashbish Falls ... never another Thanksgiving with all the ...

Well, at least they *could* have Thanksgiving — anywhere in the world. Did they have turkeys in England? Never mind. They could get one shipped.

The train clattered beneath the bridge, just before the station, and the sudden noise jolted her out of her reverie. The brakes were already beginning to bite. *Baggage,* she thought automatically — and then remembered that today was just an outing, to look at this farm in Sithney. Their baggage was all at the White Hart in Redruth, only partly unpacked, waiting a permanent ... yes, she'd soon have to start calling it 'home.'

Freed from responsibility for counting trunks and carpet bags and valises, she rose to her feet and punched her gloved fists alternately into their opposing palms, trying to get some warmth back into her fingers.

"There's our man, I guess." Her father had let down the window and, shielding his eye against smuts from the engine, was scanning the platform as they juddered to a halt. "Mister Coad?" he called. "Over here."

Steam from worn couplings rose around them as they stepped out of their carriage.

"Mister Carrington. I'm glad to make your acquaintance, sir." The auctioneer shook hands all round as the old man introduced his offspring. "I'm sorry Helston can't put on a better welcome." He shot an accusing glance at the rainclouds above, which had just opened in a new downpour.

Although the canopy protected them from direct assault, it could not shield them from that which splashed obliquely off the curved roofs of the carriages.

"It'll pass," Coad assured them. "At least, it did yesterday — eventually — and the day before. And the days before that. Shall we have a cup of tea while we wait?" He nodded toward the tea-room at the end of the building.

"What are all these?" William asked, tapping his cane on the nearer of two large stacks of crates, which impeded their progress along the platform.

"Winter greens, dead rabbits, daffodils ..." Coad said. "They'll all be in Covent Garden or Smithfield by this time tomorrow." He grinned. "If you think the price of land in these parts is outrageous, *there's* one explanation for it, right before your eyes." He jerked a thumb at the stacks of crates. "We can now get all our produce fresh into the London markets — within a day of harvesting, in fact."

"Well, I won't be *farming* the Old Glebe," John Carrington said. "As I explained in my letter, I want to make a garden of it. A garden on the grand scale ... a return to Eden, if that doesn't sound like blasphemy."

Coad went first through the tea-room door and held it ajar, first for them and then for a rather fussy, middle-aged couple who had been tormenting a porter all the way along the platform behind them.

"There's something in all of us that yearns for such a return," Coad said.

"I *beg* your pardon, sir?" the fussy gentleman exclaimed.

By gesture alone Coad managed to convey a petty apology to him, along with the explanation that he was actually talking to the Carringtons.

"Furriners!" he murmured as he joined the three Americans.

"Oh?" Leah was surprised. "They sounded very English to me. 'Veddy' English, as we say."

"Yes, they are."

"You call English people 'foreigners'?"

He chuckled. "You bet! — as you also say."

"What does that make *us*, then?" William asked.

"Oh, but you're Cornish, of course — by seed and breed. The Carringtons of Leedstown."

They stared at him in disbelief, suspecting a bit of salesman's persiflage. But he was clearly sincere.

The waitress interrupted at that moment to take their order — tea for four and toasted teacakes all round.

"You'll meet scores of people who still remember William Carrington of Leedstown," Coad said when she withdrew. "Not all of them kindly, I have to warn you. Celtic memories are long — as I'm sure you know. Even death will hardly make them fade." He smiled at each in turn, ending with his eyes on Leah.

She had taken an instant liking to him, not just because he was both presentable and easygoing but also because he had an air of culture about him. His demeanour suggested he was an auctioneer and realtor only to earn money for more important ends. Not 'realtor' — estate agent. Much grander-sounding.

"Oh?" Carrington had caught something in Coad's tone when he said that not all local people would remember his gran'pappy kindly. "Something I ought to know about?"

Coad stared briefly out of the window, marshalling his words. "I don't suppose William himself made too many enemies ..." he began.

"Hardly old enough," Carrington put in.

"Just so. But his family did, I'm afraid. There's one incident in particular that I have in mind, and it's pertinent to our present business. His uncle — who would be your great-great-uncle, sir — 'Honourable' Carrington ... his real name was Hannibal ..."

"Right." Carrington nodded.

"But schoolboy humour traded it for 'Honourable,' so it stuck to him for life. Anyway, he was a clerk to the Pallas venturers, who had a group of tin mines between Sithney and Carleen. I'll point them out to you. They're all abandoned now but that was their heyday. He lived in Sithney, not far from the Old Glebe, in fact. And he was one of the leading lights of the parish council. Indeed, he was its chairman in the year in question — the year of eighteen and forty — when the Old Glebe was declared redundant by the church and they put it up for sale. And Honourable Carrington insisted on a covenant to the title deeds, ensuring, in effect, that the farm never fell into the hands of dissenters and nonconformists. Of course, it has been voided since then, but it remained in force for about twenty years. No Methodists — primitive or otherwise — no Baptists, no Christadelphians …"

"No Methodists!" Carrington exclaimed. "I can imagine how popular that must have been down here!"

"And the others I mentioned. There's a fair sprinkling hereabouts. But one family in particular took great offence at it — the Liddicoats. Staunch Methodists to the last man, woman, and child. They saw the covenant as a device to exclude them in particular. I think James Liddicoat, especially, was very keen to buy. And Honourable knew it. So of course Liddicoat took it personally. Who wouldn't!"

"But all that was more than sixty years back," Carrington protested. "D'you mean to say …"

"Remember what I told you about Celtic memories?"

"Sixty years, though!" He shook his head in amazement.

"Is this James Liddicoat still alive, then?" Leah inquired.

Coad smiled as if he'd just been waiting for someone to ask it. "His son is. Clifford Liddicoat."

"Drop the other boot," William said. "He still lives in Sithney. Am I right?"

Coad nodded. "At Grankum Farm. The farm across the valley from the Old Glebe. In fact, he has the renting of the Old Glebe fields until Midsummer Day."

"Don't tell me!" Carrington exclaimed. "Now it's on the market again, he's interested."

Coad grinned. "You bet!" he said again.

2 They stood in a small group, leaning on the gate at the lower end of the cobbled yard of the Old Glebe. Ben Coad swept an arm across the western view from there. "When old William Carrington of Leedstown last set eyes on this," he said, "he'd have seen many more trees. The mines have pretty well denuded the landscape since then. The only surviving woodlands now are clustered around the big houses. Or they're preserved as game covert. Like that." He pointed to a sliver of the woods around Godolphin Hall on the Duke of Leeds's estate, which was just visible now that the rain had eased off. "Of course, Grankum Wood, just below us here, is too steep to farm."

"Oak?" John Carrington guessed from the bare trunks and branches.

Coad nodded. "And ash and hawthorn. There's an abandoned quarry down among them. Also a well, whose waters are said to be enchanted. They have magical powers."

"To cure what?" Leah asked.

"Loneliness, I suppose, Miss Carrington." He chuckled. "They say that if a spinster or bachelor has an eye on a possible partner and can induce him or her to drink of its waters without knowing it, love will follow almost instantaneously. But, against that, a couple of dozen families draw their daily water supply from that same spring, and there's no detectable increase in the infatuation rate of the two parishes."

She raised her binoculars to her eyes and surveyed the wood.

"It's near the upper end," he told her. "But I doubt you'll see it. It's below the flank of the hill from here."

"Are you married, Mister Coad?" Carrington asked with a twinkle in his eye.

"I have so far evaded ... I mean, I do not yet have that honour, sir," he replied.

"Then perhaps you will one day conduct the definitive experiment."

"Or be the victim of one," Leah added, lowering the glasses again and smiling sweetly at him.

Her eyes and Coad's dwelled in each other's for a moment. Then he said, "I walk in fear and dread already, sir."

"You mentioned two parishes?" she prompted.

"Ah, yes. Breage and Sithney." He pointed out the tower of Breage church on the skyline, a mile distant as the crow flies but almost twice as much on foot. It stood on the long southern flank of Trigonning Hill, which towered above the landscape. The narrow streak of brightness they had observed from the train had meanwhile expanded to fill half the sky.

Between the two parishes lay a Y-shaped valley, though from where they stood only the V-end of the 'Y' was visible. The Old Glebe was about halfway up the eastern arm of the 'V.' The ground between the two arms was not so high as where they stood so they were able to look obliquely down upon it — and to see over it to even more distant parishes, beyond Breage.

"What a curious mixture of landscapes," William remarked. "It's almost like a history diagram. I mean Grankum Wood, I guess, is the nearest thing to the primeval forest that once covered the whole of Cornwall. Right?"

Coad dipped his head.

"Then you've got all these lovely little patchwork fields with their stone walls all around ..."

"Hedges." Coad corrected him. "I know they *are* walls but we call them hedges in Cornwall. *English* people call them walls."

He made being *English* sound quite dreadful. Leah tried to imagine some remote part of America where people would talk of *Americans* with similar contempt; it was impossible. Except for an Indian reservation, maybe. Perhaps the Cornish were England's redskins?

"Okay, hedges," William continued. "Farms and fields and hedges — which is like Nature being *controlled* by us. Humans in control of Nature, right? Cooperating, you could say. But then you get *that!*" Like a courtroom lawyer producing some especially damning piece of evidence he waved his hand at the central portion of the scene before them. "Humans in contempt of Nature."

No one could disagree. A century and more of the steam engine, coupled with the skills of the Cornish miner, had produced a landscape of utter devastation: open quarries, mine buildings — all deserted and many already derelict — and heaps of poisonous spoil on which nothing would grow. 'Spoil' was the word for them all right.

Ben Coad reeled off some of the names, pointing each out as he went: "Wheal Fortune, Wheal Metal, Scott's, Wheal Vreah, Deepwork, Wheal Anchor ..."

When they asked where all the wheels had gone he explained that a 'wheal' was a working or, specifically, a mine working.

"But so much waste rock!" Leah said. Once again she was surveying the scene through her binoculars. "Couldn't they have left it underground and just taken out the tin?"

He laughed. "I'm sure they'd love to be able to do that. But veins of tin ore are only *inches* wide at best. You'd have to train mice as miners. However, in some places the veins themselves are as close-packed as they are on a drunkard's nose. See Wheal Vor over there? By Godolphin Woods?"

"Where the entire hillside is covered with waste stone?" She passed the glasses, unasked, to her brother, who accepted them with pleased surprise.

"That's the place. The waste stone — *halvans* we call it — is all that's left now of the famous Great Lode of Wheal Vor. When it was fully mined out, about thirty years ago, the space it left was big enough to build two churches the size of Sithney's, one on top of the other!" He swept his hand once more across the scene. "It's five hundred acres of devastation now, but fifty years ago the land between here and Trigonning Hill was the richest thousand-acre spread on earth — richer than the Klondyke or California, richer than the Rand or any of the Australian goldfields."

"And where has it all gone?" Carrington asked, for they had seen little evidence of such wealth so far, and certainly not in the countryside immediately around them now.

"You're not the only Cornish people who'd like to know the answer to *that* question," he replied darkly. "Shall we look at the farmland while the rain holds off? Perhaps Miss Carrington would like to inspect the house meanwhile ..."

"Not a bit! I came prepared, see?" Leah lifted the hem of her dress enough to show her toecaps. "Gum boots," she said.

"Ah, gum boots. Interesting. 'Wellingtons' we call them. I noticed a couple of spare pairs in the barn last time I was here — if either of you gentlemen are interested?"

The men decided their everyday boots would be stout enough if they kept to the less-wet parts of the land. The plan worked well enough except at the gates between fields, where Liddicoat's cattle had poached the land to a quagmire. There they had to hug one of the granite gateposts and inch their way around the strip of solid ground at its base.

"There's your southern neighbour," Coad said. "George Gosling of Trelissick." He pointed out the small group of trees among which nested the farmhouse.

"We should have saddled up those horses in the stables," Leah said, nudging her brother to return the binoculars. "Are they Mister Liddicoat's, too?"

"No, they belong to the rector, Reverend Langham. Despite his age, he's a keen member of the Fourborough, which is our local hunt, or one of them. The Cury is the other. Are any of you keen on hunting?"

"Not I!" William said at once.

"I am," Leah said. "As long as they don't catch too many foxes. I enjoy 'steeplechasing,' I think you call it? Why did you grin like that when I suggested saddling up those horses?"

Ben Coad was a little taken aback; he was not aware she had been watching him so closely. "Oh," he said diffidently, "nothing really. I showed an *American* over a farm the other side of Helston last week." He stressed the word as if to imply that they were not Americans, or not for the purposes of this particular story. "He told me about his 'spread' back home. He said he could saddle up in the morning and ride his horse all day and still not reach his boundary by sunset. Unfortunately I misunderstood him." His mischievous grin told them he had done no such thing. "I told him I'd owned a horse like that once. There was nothing to do but shoot it."

They were still chuckling when they reached the boundary of this particular spread — the stone hedge that separated the Old Glebe from Trelissick.

"Does this valley run all the way down to the ocean?" William asked as he followed its sweep with his eye.

"You could say so," Coad replied. "It curves round and joins up with the other one. Then they both broaden out and run down to Porthleven, which is behind this flank of the hill to our left, about a mile and a half away. Strictly speaking, it's not really ocean there, either. It's the English Channel. The ocean begins at Land's End."

"It all looks so rural," Leah said, "apart from the mines and the waste. You'd never think we were just over a mile from the ocean — or Channel."

"You can see it from the upstairs windows of the Old Glebe, though. With a good pair of glasses like those, you can even pick out the different kinds of ship — clippers, dreadnoughts, luggers, coasters … It's a pretty busy horizon, you know. I'd guess there'd be at least one vessel in sight at any given moment, day or night."

While he spoke he was watching John Carrington's eyes traverse the fifty acres of the Old Glebe, back and forth, forth and back. "What d'you think of it so far, sir?" he asked at length.

"Morning sun," Carrington replied at once. "When there's any sun at all, that is — and we have yet to be convinced of that, I may say."

As if to answer him, a single narrow beam of sunlight poked through the clouds, over beyond Godolphin. Small as it was, it transformed the entire scene and lifted everyone's hopes of a brighter afternoon.

"What, may I ask, is the significance of morning sun, sir?" Coad asked next.

"I don't suppose it affects too many farm crops but a lot of garden plants that are allegedly damaged by frost are actually damaged by going straight from frost to full, early-morning sunlight. Still, that's not a point against it. We'd just have to be judicious in our planting."

"Which is Grankum Farm?" Leah asked, training her glasses up the valley once more.

"The one immediately above the wood," Ben Coad replied. "The house is bigger than it appears from here. There's a sort of annexe among the trees."

She only half heard him. Most of her attention was on a figure who had just emerged from among the trees Coad mentioned. It was Clifford Liddicoat, no doubt — their rival contender for the Old Glebe.

A tall, bareheaded man with a lithe spring in his step, he crossed the yard in a dozen easy strides and then vaulted the gate, pivoting with one hand on its topmost rail. It surprised her. Coad had said he was the son of that James Liddicoat who had been thwarted by Honourable Carrington's exclusion clause, sixty years back, so she had assumed he'd be much older — certainly too old to go vaulting gates one-handed. With that same agile step he strode halfway up the field, making for a calf lying among the rough tussocks of grass. It rose and trotted off as he drew near and this apparently satisfied him it needed no help. He stopped then and stared uncertainly about him — which was how he came to notice the party of four, standing at the farther end of the Old Glebe's fields.

Now that he was facing them Leah moved to the nearest gatepost and rested her glasses against its flank, to steady the view they provided. He stood like a colossus, feet apart, hands on hips, jacket open. His waistcoat buttons were out of step, she noticed, with a spare hole at the top and a spare button at the bottom. He was about her own age she guessed — lean, athletic, and devilish good looking, with his tight blond curls and his strong line of jaw.

He fished in one of his pockets and pulled out something dark and compact — a hipflask, she supposed, from the way he raised it at once to his lips.

Or no — not to his lips but to his eyes. He must have had her in clear focus by the time it dawned on her that he, too, was using a pair of binoculars.

Panic!

He must surely see her staring at him. True, his glasses were smaller and probably less powerful, but what did that matter over less than four hundred paces? Fortunately at that moment a bird of prey of some description — a peregrine, perhaps — rose from the hedge behind him and she gratefully followed its ascent with her glasses. Now he'd think that she'd been birding all along, not spying on him and his farm.

To complete the deception she passed the glasses to William again and pointed out the bird, which was now soaring high above them.

Coad and her father were already strolling back across the fields toward the farmhouse.

When her brother returned the glasses she risked a further peep, beginning high in the sky and slowly coming down, as if following some bird's descent. When she found him again, he was standing exactly as he had been a couple of minutes earlier — legs apart, glasses to his eyes, staring straight at her.

It pleased her far more than she could easily have explained.

Experimentally she raised a hand and waved it — not with the grand, semaphoring gestures she'd have made if neither had had binoculars, but with the hesitant, petite sort of greeting she might use across a room.

After a moment's hesitation he let go of his glasses with his right hand and responded with a breezy little salute, dipping his hand halfway and finishing with a flourish.

"What's this?" William asked.

"Oh, I'm just being friendly to our new neighbour," she replied offhandedly.

"Oh, so you've decided to buy, then!"

"Yes, I rather think I have," she said, still keeping the glasses to her eyes.

3 The Old Glebe had been built in early-Georgian times. In Cornwall, where builders' pattern books lingered on until no one could read them for thumbprints, the date meant that its style was from an even earlier monarchy: William and Mary. The Dutch influence was most obvious in the red-brick curlicues of the gable ends — a semicircular apex with little horizontal parapets on either side, yielding to concave quarter-circles down to the level of the gutters. It was pretty, but two centuries of Cornish weather had taken its toll of the brickwork, which was now spalled by frosts and cracked from movements of the roof timbers. The cracks had been repointed, along with the rest of the bricks, but their outlines were still alarmingly visible.

"That doesn't look too healthy," John Carrington commented as he surveyed the façade through binoculars. "I see several glass telltales there. When were they put in?"

"When they did the repointing — almost a year ago," Coad replied. "They were all still intact up to New Year's Day this year, which is when I last inspected them. So the movement is probably ancient. It's visible in photographs from the seventies, which I can show you back in the office."

Carrington's only reply was a sardonic grunt. He was laying the grounds for cheapening the price from the presently outrageous £600. "How old is the barn?" he asked.

"Medieval," Coad answered proudly. "It's the original tithe barn, built with a cruck frame, which you can see exposed in the end wall."

"That's where I'd be putting my glasshouses," Carrington murmured, more to himself than to them.

"Dad!" Leah was shocked. "You can't tear down a building that's stood for four hundred years!"

"Six hundred," Coad corrected her. "Possibly longer. It's about as old as the church building itself. Some of the timbers have the same carver's initials."

"There!" she said.

"If a building has outlived its time and utility, honey, there's no sense in preserving it." He turned to the estate agent. "Surely you agree, sir?"

"Well…" The man scratched the back of his neck awkwardly. "Six or seven hundred years is a long time."

"Long enough, I say. There's some sense in preserving royal palaces and town halls and other buildings of historical interest, but you start preserving stuff like that — old barns — and where do you stop? Factories? Those derelict mine buildings over there? Labourers' cottages? Pigsties? Why, you'd turn the whole of England into one great open-air museum. Life would be all pomp and no circumstance, to twist *Othello*. Is that what you want?"

Coad gave a baffled laugh. "Well, sir — to twist *Much Ado*, I can see a hobby horse — by daylight — so I'll say no more. Except for this: People might begin to think you more American than Cornish if you demolished such a fine old building."

Carrington had to accept that point — which, in any case, suited his purpose just as neatly. "Well," he sighed, "it reduces the value of the property to me. I hope that's understood."

Leah, who had seen that point even while Coad was still speaking, wondered why he had given the warning at all. Everyone knew that a realtor's business was to sell real estate. Whether the purchasers did popular or unpopular things after parting with their cash was none of his affair. So maybe 'estate agents' were subtly different from 'realtors,' after all.

Coad, too, was somewhat taken aback to realize he had spoken out so bluntly. The professional side of him was mildly annoyed, for obvious reasons; but the man himself, the private individual, was more than mildly surprised. It made him realize that, in the space of less than an hour, the Carringtons had come to mean much more to him than mere customers — or potential customers. If they did settle in the Helston area, he hoped to cultivate their friendship. He and the old fellow had 'clicked' from the first. And, to be sure, there was Miss Leah, too — charming, bright, open, capable, self-assured, and decidedly good looking. The boy also had his points, no doubt.

Coad could not deny that he would never have articulated such thoughts so forcefully, not even to himself, if he had not noticed how Miss Leah had kept her binoculars trained on young Harvey Liddicoat, across the valley at Grankum. For some reason he had omitted to mention that old Liddicoat had a son — two sons, in fact — when he had described the historical but still tender animosity between the two families, so Miss Leah had probably mistaken Harvey for his father, Clifford.

In short, the professional Coad, who was desperate to find at least one other interested buyer for the Old Glebe — to stop old Liddicoat from naming his own price — was at war with the private Coad, who was already lining up properties on the far side of Helston to tempt the Carringtons away from Sithney and the two young Liddicoat males.

"Well," he said genially in response to Carrington's latest comment, "I have even more attractive properties than this on my books at the moment. Over toward the Lizard. Good hunting country, too," he added by way of encouragement to Miss Leah.

But she pulled a face and said, "Lizard — what a name! I saw it on the map. It doesn't sound very ... you know ... attractive." She took the glasses from her father and inspected the patched-up cracks for herself.

"It means 'high field' in Cornish," he explained. "*Ard* is 'high' and *les* or *lis* is 'field' or 'enclosure'." He tried not to look at the line of her bosom, which her action had accentuated into a different sort of high enclosure.

"So," William put in, "instead of *les-ard* becoming 'Lizard' *ard-les* might have become 'Artless'!"

Coad laughed dutifully. "It would have been even more of a misnomer, sir," he replied. "Several artists have settled there, in fact. Some of considerable renown." He was about to qualify this rather bold assertion, admitting that the number was not as great as had settled in St Ives or Newlyn, when he noticed Miss Leah's interest prick up.

"Really?" she asked, letting the glasses fall to her breast. "Who, for example?"

"A Scotchman called Dougal MacKay?" He made a question of it, to suggest she'd surely heard the name. "Glasgow School?" He turned to the old fellow. "And the climate is even milder there than here, though it's only eight miles away. Water on all three sides, you see."

"I suppose you speak Cornish, do you, Mister Coad?" Carrington asked. He thought Coad was being rather clever, mentioning other properties instead of discussing the price of the Old Glebe.

The man shook his head. "The tongue itself is dead — has been for more than a century now. But dictionaries and texts have survived."

"What does Helston mean?" William asked.

Before Coad could reply they were distracted by the sound of an unoiled gate shrieking on rusted hinges. It was the gate at the lower end of the yard, where they had first stood and looked out over the hills and halvans to the west of Sithney. And there, silhouetted in the gap, stood what they took to be some species of wild man — tall, barrel-chested, gaitered like a bishop, and wearing over his head a four-bushel corn sack. He had tucked one of its closed corners into the other to make a kind of monkish cowl against the rain; but, there being no rain at that moment, he drew it off as he approached, revealing a mane of uncombed hair. Long but rather thinned by the years, it stood out in all directions, the way young children draw the rays of the sun on their older siblings' school slates. His face was grim and yet, looking at him closely, Leah could believe that a smile from him would be grimmer still.

"Mister Liddicoat!" Coad called out; his tone suggested that this was a pleasant surprise, indeed.

"Coad," was the dour reply. He did not take his eyes off John Carrington's face all the way up the yard. "Who's this-here, then?" he added as he reached their scattered circle.

"Cousin Jacks who've come back home," the man replied. Then, seeing no way of dodging the revelation, added, "Mister John Carrington."

The farmer bristled at the name, showing that Coad had been right when he warned them of the length of Celtic memories.

To Carrington he said, "This is Mister Clifford Liddicoat, who farms Grankum, across the valley."

In the corner of his eye he saw an *Aha!* light up Miss Leah's face and he knew she had earlier mistaken Harvey for his father. A moment later, when her father presented Liddicoat to her, she confirmed it, saying, "I believe I saw your son — or it could have been one of your labourers, maybe? — out in the fields just now, Mister Liddicoat."

Something in her words, or perhaps just in her tone, struck a chord in Liddicoat and made him change from whatever course he had intended to adopt in dealing with these interlopers, these competitors for a property he already regarded as his but for the ink on the deed. He was shaking her hand with perfunctory speed, and would surely have let go a second later, when her words penetrated the hairy thickets that sprang from his ears and made him slow down. He kept her hand between his but held it still, pumping it up and down very occasionally, as he stared deep into her eyes. The effect on her was hypnotic.

"Seen 'n, did 'ee?" he asked.

"Quite clearly. Through these binoculars." She patted them with her free hand.

He glanced at them and then looked her up and down slowly. She could not remember being subjected to so blatant an appraisal before.

"'Es," he said at last and in a tone of evident approval. Then, turning to shake William by the hand, he said, casually, "Fond of farming, then, are 'ee, young master?"

"I a farmer? Jee-willikin, *no,* sir! True's preachin' I'm not."

Still holding William's hand he stared into his face, hoping to embarrass him into saying more.

In the end his father spoke. "The boy's interested in mining, Mister Liddicoat — like his great-gran'pappy, you know?"

Ponderously the farmer let go of the son's hand as he turned to face his informant. "That'd be William Carrington of Leedstown, I daresay?" he commented evenly.

"The same, sir. And I gather your family has no cause to remember him — or my great-uncle Honourable — with any particular affection."

The man stared at him in amazement. Directness does not come easy to any Celt.

"See here!" Carrington went on. "No sense in beating about the bush. If apologies might serve a purpose, I'd tender a whole book of etiquette this very minute. But the fact that we're both interested in buying this place shouldn't …"

"Me?" Liddicoat was scandalized. "Who says I be interested?"

Carrington glanced at Coad.

"Aha!" the farmer exclaimed. "Told 'ee I was interested, did 'e? Well, I aren't. So there!" He challenged Coad to dispute the assertion and, when the man said nothing, added, "I told 'n if no one else *wanted* the place, I'd take it off his hands. More out of kindness than good sense …"

"Mister Liddicoat is a noted local philanthropist," Coad put in, absolutely straight-faced.

The man looked daggers at him. " 'E've been on the market more'n a year now," he said.

Coad poured on the salt and rubbed it in: "And Mister Liddicoat must be telling the truth when he declares himself uninterested in the property — he has let so many chances slip by him, to put in his bid."

The man's lips vanished inward. Deep, weather-etched cracks in his skin marked the remnant furrow. "The place is haunted," he said angrily.

Coad folded his arms, as men do when bracing into the wind. "Haunted with the spirits of men who failed to bid for it in time," he said evenly.

Carrington decided to put his oar in then. "I'm not at all certain I like the place, Coad," he said. "I prefer the sound of those properties you mentioned — on the Lizard, despite my daughter's aversion to the name."

This did not suit the auctioneer's tactics at all, so, while he still had some slight advantage of the farmer's stubbornness, he challenged the man: "Can I take it those are your last words, then, Mister Liddicoat? In no circumstances are you interested in buying the Old Glebe?"

Liddicoat reined in his anger at that, annoyed he had let it gallop him so far from the path of his own best welfare. "I'm interested in *any* property — at the right price. But six hundred pounds is daylight robbery."

Carrington cleared his throat with a chuckle. "The more I hear of you, Mister Liddicoat," he said, "the more I believe you to be the most sensible man in the whole of Cornwall. Six hundred pounds *is* daylight robbery. I never heard a sentiment with which I could agree more wholeheartedly."

The auctioneer stood his ground and beamed at them — a lighthouse that had withstood many a gale from this particular quarter. "Those are my instructions, gentlemen, and I have no power to vary them — nor inclination to, either. We will surely get our price in the end."

"But how long will you wait meanwhile?" Carrington asked.

"As long as it takes. The property is in the estate of a minor, who will have no need to realize its value for many years yet — if ever. The trustees are happy enough with the existing rents, I gather. In short, six hundred is both the asking price and the sticking point." He turned exclusively to Carrington. "Shall we go inside, sir? I think the interior may improve your opinion of the Old Glebe — as a man of taste and refinement. It is one of the few houses in the area that is *fitting* for a gentleman." He studiously avoided Liddicoat's eye.

The tactic bore fruit. The farmer nodded curtly to each and stalked off the way he had come. After a dozen paces he turned and shouted angrily at Coad: "You do think I can't pay six hundred, do 'ee?"

Coad bet everything on one final gamble. "On the contrary, Mister Liddicoat. I know full well you can. But I'm equally sure you won't."

"How?" the man asked — which, in Cornwall, means 'why?'.

"Because it's not a house in which *you* would feel comfortable."

If looks could kill, there would have been three witnesses to murder at the Old Glebe that morning.

"I think you've lost one party to this sale, Mister Coad," Carrington murmured as they watched the man stamp his way back to the creaking gate.

"We'll see about that," the agent replied, with more confidence than he actually felt. He took out the key and offered it to Carrington, as if to suggest he was already the proprietor.

"I have to tell you," Carrington said, "that the thought of making an enemy of such a neighbour as that, gives me a mighty disinclination to make any offer at all."

But Leah, who was watching the old farmer through her binoculars, was of a different opinion. Halfway down the field, just before his head vanished from view, he turned and stared at them. He was obviously not aware she was using her glasses again for, instead of the expected scowl on his face, she saw a self-satisfied grin — as if he thought he had carried off some triumph from their encounter. Friend or foe, she thought, he would make a most interesting neighbour. And anyway, what could he actually *do* that might harm them?

4   The house had been untenanted for more than three years and, what with the scandalous price of servants, even on board wages, it had been left unoccupied, too — a fate that had overtaken many houses of late, including mansions far grander than the Old Glebe. So Coad's description of it as a 'gentleman's house' needed to be taken along with liberal doses of imagination. Rooks had fallen down at least two of the chimneys, dislodging volumes of soot that carpeted the floor and half buried their decomposed and mummified bodies. Even the rats had shunned them, though they seemed to have chewed at almost everything else in sight. And, most horrid of all in Leah's opinion, a colony of some fifteen bats was hibernating in the passage outside the scullery door, which she was exploring on her own.

She fled in a panic to rejoin the others, took a wrong turning, and almost fell into an earth closet at the opposite end of the passage. She wrinkled her nose at it for someone had certainly been making use of the convenience, it being easily accessible from the side yard. She took a grip on herself and, containing her fear of those squeaky, flea-ridden balls of flying fur, found her way back into the main part of the house. She joined the others as they were making their way up the servants' stair.

"Watch out for bats," she told William, clutching her bonnet tightly around her hair.

"What's wrong with bats?" he asked with tendentious, manly scorn. "Lovely little velvety creatures."

Ignoring him, she turned to Coad and asked if the house was on town water; earth closets were intolerably primitive to her.

"Mains water?" he replied. "It's promised for this year, for the whole of Sithney, that is. There's electricity in the village already, from the Helston Power Company, but the Old Glebe isn't yet connected. You could site a septic tank … you know what I mean?"

"Yes," Carrington said. "Americans call it that, too — in mixed company."

"You could site one just to the left of that gate at the bottom of the yard. I don't suppose gas will ever come out this far, but there's an ironfounder in Helston called Toy who makes excellent cooking ranges. They heat water, too — all you could want."

"And how about steam heat?" William asked. "For the rooms and passages, you know. Do you have steam heat here?"

Coad shook his head. "I've seen it in hospitals and one or two large public buildings. But really, you know, I think our winters here must be much milder than yours. There are very few days in a year when a simple coal fire would be inadequate. You could count them on those fingers. And that's the truth." He held up one hand, noticed a tear in his glove, and turned it quickly round.

He saw Leah grinning at him and smiled ruefully back.

"It is a truth universally acknowledged …" she murmured to him as they passed into the first of the servants' rooms.

He looked at the hole in his glove, taking no care to hide it now, and added, "… that a bachelor with holes in his clothes must be in need of a wife? Yes indeed, Miss Carrington."

"How many servants board in?" Carrington asked. "I mean how many used to?"

"In the good old days? When the Daveys were here, which was around the time of the Boer War, there were eight maids, a butler, housekeeper, valet-cum-coachman, cook, three living-out kitchen and scullery maids, four in the stables, a gardener, and a boy. And anything from eight to twenty farm labourers, depending on the season."

"Why, this house must have been quite a little village in itself!" Carrington remarked.

Coad looked about the tiny room with its low-hung ceiling and said, almost apologetically, "They got four maids into this room and four next door. But girls wouldn't put up with such conditions nowadays."

"But the Boer War ..." William began. "I mean, that was only, what? Ten years back?"

Coad agreed. "Yet it seems much longer. A whole generation, almost. I don't know what people thought about it in America, but here ..."

"Oh," Carrington replied, "we ... that is, *they* ... thought it an absolute scandal. Naked English imperialism ... which is understandable when you remember the history of England's involvement with America."

"There were plenty of the same mind in England, too," Coad said. "There were disturbances in every town. It almost brought about a second civil war. Neighbours who'd lived together amicably for years were suddenly at daggers drawn — especially down here in Cornwall, where the Liberal-nonconformist traditions are so strong. And it's still going on, too. Newcomers to the county join this or that social circle according to where they stand on the Boer question."

"And the two don't mix? Never?"

"Not socially. Of course, pros and antis work side by side on charity committees, the Red Cross, the RNLI, and so on. And they obviously have to mingle at big social occasions — Helston Furry Dance, the church fête, and events like that. But that's the limit. A stiff nod of the head is all the recognition they'll give each other in the street."

"Extraordinary!"

"It even divided families. Take Clifford Liddicoat just now. His brother, Frank Liddicoat, who's an auctioneer in Camborne, hasn't spoken to him in years. Come to that, I've only just patched up relations with my own father." He frowned. "How did we get on to this? Oh yes! Servants and changes in attitudes and so on. It seems that a vast social upheaval of that kind brings other, unexpected changes in its wake. The sight of the ruling class tearing itself to shreds gave the servant class ideas, too." He laughed. "And to think that, by fighting the Boer and the Zulu for four years, we produced a new generation of servant girls who will refuse to sleep four-to-a-room when the room is the size of this one!"

"It'll hardly matter in our case." Leah looked at her father. "I don't suppose *we* will be employing a household on anything like that grand scale."

The old man nodded. Then, to Coad, he added, "It's not that we couldn't afford it, mind, and nor are we close-fisted. It's just not our style. I'm here to create a wonderful garden. He's here to study mine engineering." He nodded at William. "And she's to make a good match and raise a new dynasty."

He didn't even glance at his daughter. But Coad did. And the fleeting annoyance he saw in her eyes made him realize that her notions did not entirely coincide with her father's.

5   The Carringtons were so taken with the Helston area that they moved to the Angel Hôtel and set about inspecting several other houses, both in the town itself and farther afield. Their choice was plentiful because the collapse of tin mining had left many once-rich families with establishments no longer suited to their incomes. Only a handful of mines were left working now — near Land's End, at Porkellis, and in the Camborne — Redruth area. There were none at all in that part of the country which Coad had called the richest thousand acres in the world, once upon a time. At several of those fine houses they came within an ace of making a firm offer, but the same thing always held them back: their memory of the Old Glebe at Sithney.

Its grip on their imaginations was hard to explain. The house needed considerable work before it would be habitable, and the fact that a third of its acreage faced slightly north of west made it less attractive to John Carrington as a potential garden. As for his two children, there were several other suitable houses, nearer not only to Helston but also to other young people — which ought to have commended them more to Leah and her brother. And yet all three Carringtons felt their preference drawn to the Old Glebe instead, though not always for identical reasons.

For William, it was the landscape itself and those elements he had noticed on their visit to Sithney — the rich and contradictory mixture of ancient and modern, the struggle between the despoiled earth and that inexorable cleansing power of nature which was already showing its fringes and would one day reclaim its very heart.

This subtle fascination drew him back, alone, one afternoon toward the end of that same February. His father and sister were intending to visit yet another house, over near Gweek, which lies at the head of the Helford River estuary on the Falmouth side of Helston. William had long since tired of these inspections and, in any case, he felt in his bones that they, too, had already decided on the Old Glebe and were simply being prudent New Englanders in looking at other possible homes. So he cried off joining them and, while they boarded the horse-drawn bus for Gweek, he took one of the new motor charabancs travelling in the opposite direction, toward Penzance.

He sat behind Billy Trim, the driver, and marvelled at the skill with which he changed gears, hardly ever making a clash. It was especially noticeable at the start of the journey from Helston, where the road ran pretty well level through the market at St Johns, past the gasworks and the yards of the quaintly named Kernow & Daughter; but then, at the bottom of Sithney Common Hill, it suddenly rose at an angle that had defeated many a horse and cart down the years.

Billy Trim went down through the gearbox like a maestro — click, snick, slick! But the racket from the motor itself was quite another matter. Even in bottom gear, the cogs groaned like the damned and clouds of blue-white smoke belched from the exhaust. Old Frank Trevose, the miller, came out of his store and stood in the thick of it, provocatively holding his nose and flapping his flour-sack apron uselessly at the fumes.

"That's another letter to the *Helston Vindicator,*" Trim said over his shoulder. "How he don't just shut his doors till 'tis gone away, I don't know. Th'ole fool!"

"In America they make the exhaust tubes point at the sky," William told him.

"We'd have the bird lovers writing in then," Trim said. "Different class of letter but the same old complaint. Some people don't want progress at no price. Old Trevose has forgotten the number of horses he's seen put out of their misery, right there where he's standing now. Terrible sights. I've seen the blood running down that hill in rivers. People do forget, see?"

"It is a very steep hill, that bit," William agreed.

" 'Tis often worse going down. 'Specially on a frosty day. The sun don't hardly ever reach there and I seen horses slip going down and the cart run on and break the shafts and roll over them. Terrible sights." His eyes gleamed as he repeated himself: "Blood everywhere. People do forget, see?"

The bus reached the point where the steepest part of the hill gave way to something gentler. He moved up a gear or two, with the same enviable skill, and advanced the ignition a couple of clicks; the belching fumes turned thinner and paler. All the while he kept a nervous eye on the thermometer, out there on top of the radiator filler cap.

"You from North Cornwall, are you?" Trim asked. "You don't talk like we round here."

"I grew up in America," William explained. He went on to introduce himself properly, which was when he learned Billy Trim's name and parish, too — Godolphin, which stands at the northern end of Trigonning Hill. The man added that the village was named after the Godolphin family, great courtiers in the days of Jacobites and Williamites. He added that the Angel Hôtel, from where the buses departed, had once been the Godolphins' town house. "You interested in history, are you?" he asked.

William replied tactfully that he hoped to learn the English slant on things now that they were going to live here.

"Ah, the English!" Trim mused. "We've seen bloody times down here on their account."

The name of Godolphin reminded William that Coad had pointed out the woodlands of the Hall, on the skyline as seen from the Old Glebe. "Godolphin's near where I'm headed today," he said. "I want to walk through all that old mining country between Sithney and Carleen. Carnmeal Downs, it's called on the map. Where's the nearest you go to that?"

"The stop gate," Trim replied. "That's where they belonged to take the tolls, backalong in the good old turnpike days. I'll set you down there."

Three Jersey cows, which had been standing placidly against the hedge on the upper side of the road, suddenly panicked as the bus drew level and ran off, kicking wildly, their udders flapping like laundry in a gale.

"At least they can't write letters to the papers," William said.

"The farmers can, though," Trim answered morosely. "You related to Harold Carrington of Releath, then, are you?"

"I don't know. I suppose all Cornish Carringtons must be related, if you go far enough back. We must call on him."

The driver chuckled grimly. "You'll need one of they ouija boards, then. He's in his box in Wendron churchyard now. But his daughter, Gwen, she married Hugh Thomas of Trenear. She'd tell you, I daresay."

William stored the names in memory and then watched the man closely for any reaction as he said, "I'm directly descended from William Carrington of Leedstown — I was named for him, in fact."

But Trim just shook his head. "I never heard tell of he. A Cousin Jack, was he?"

William obliged with a potted family history, which prompted the further question: "Just over here on a visit, are you?" — which led to a few more revelations. However, William was careful to say nothing of the old enmity between the Carringtons and the Liddicoats. He wanted to know how widespread the knowledge of it was in the immediate neighbourhood. After all, Godolphin was only three miles or so from Sithney, so, if Trim knew nothing of it, the feud could hardly be a living issue for anyone but the Liddicoats themselves.

He came as close as he dared by letting slip that they were possibly interested in buying the Old Glebe. When he saw the sudden interest in the driver's face, he supposed his words had provoked a memory of the Liddicoat—Carrington story at last. But it was not so.

"The haunted house!" Trim said with ghoulish glee. "Who's got the sale of that ole place — Coad, is it? I'll be he never told you 'tis haunted!"

"Really?" William laughed dismissively. "By what, may I ask? Or by whom?"

" 'Tisn't no laughing matter, young feller," the other said in a slow, lugubrious manner.

"If it's haunted by anything, it's by the spirits of all those birds that fell down the chimneys and died trying to get back out."

"Ah! Not the house. I'm not talking about the house. The house isn't haunted, as such. 'Tweren't even built when the murder happened, which was in that ole barn. Been inside there, have you? The ole tithe barn."

"I know the one. Yes, we had a quick look inside, but ..."

"That's all you'd want, too — a quick look." With a sigh and a shake of his head he implied that even so brief a contact with the ghost that haunted the place was perilous.

They had reached the top of Sithney Common Hill by now and Sithney church tower itself was in sight — also the chimney-pots of the Old Glebe and the ridge tiles of the allegedly haunted tithe barn. Billy Trim wagged a finger in their direction before slipping into top gear and advancing the ignition fully. The motor responded with a satisfactory backfire that sent up flocks of gulls and rooks from the neighbouring fields. The thermometer steadied and from there on began to fall. "Stay clear of there after night has fallen, young fellow," he warned, "if you do value your peace of mind."

"At least tell me the story," William said, doing his best to conceal his incredulity.

The man cleared his throat impressively and resettled himself in his seat. "Ever see that play, *Murder in the Red Barn,* did you?" he asked.

"The old Maria Marten melodrama?. Yes, I saw that in summer stock at …"

" 'Tisn't no melodrama, boy. That's a true story, that is. Maria Marten was as real and 'live as what you and me are. So was her betrayer and murderer, a feller called Corder, the squire's son. And 'twas the same story in the Old Glebe, backalong in the days of Oliver Cromwell."

William frowned. "You mean the Maria Marten business really happened down here in Cornwall?"

"No," Trim said patiently. "Same story, different names. The maid's name was Catherine. Catherine Geach. That's an old Cornish name, Geach. You'll find her grave in Sithney church-yard, near the west door. And there's a memorial on the wall inside, too. 'Foully murdered,' it do say. Anyway, her father was land agent to the first Earl of Godolphin in the times after Oliver Cromwell. He belonged to live in Sithney, but the house has now gone."

They stopped to pick up passengers from Antron, and, of course, to exchange the gossip of the day; so it was several minutes before the driver resumed his tale. And then, realizing that the stop gate was now less than a mile away, he reluctantly reduced it to its barest bones:

Catherine Geach, daughter of Edward Geach of Sithney, was, in her twentieth year, courted, deceived, and ruined by the son of the rector, who, when the baby was almost come to term, ripped it from her living womb and so murdered her. And this 'murder most foul' had taken place in the grounds of the Old Glebe, under the roof of the even older tithe barn. Several doctors declared the young man insane but the wrath of the mob was such that they broke into the Helston jail, whipped him at the tail of a cart all the way back to the very scene of his crime, and there killed him by the same barbarous means — that is, by docking his genitals and opening his belly while he hung by the neck from a beam.

"And at times," Trim concluded with mournful glee, "when the wind do howl among the tops of the trees, and the storms do lift the seas above the cliffs down to Porthleven, they belong to pick their old quarrel all over again — he and she. He do curse she to the blackest pits of hell. And she do scream again as he do rip her open and take two lives with a single cut. So just you mind you stay snug and warm indoors on stormy nights, young fellow." He raised his voice and shouted out the impending stop: "Roseladden!" Then, to William again: "Now this here's the stop gate. See the cottage, there? That's the old tollkeeper's. And the road you do want, up to Wheal Fortune, is right beside of it."

And what was the wretched youth's name? William wondered. The answer, spoken over the constant roar of the engine and the sudden screech of the brakes, gave him quite a start.

"Did you say Liddicoat?" he asked in amazement as they lurched to a halt. "Are you sure of that?"

"No, not Liddicoat," came the reply. "Lidgeycot. John Lidgeycot. That's another old Cornish name. There's a place called Lidgey, up Saint Gluvias, on the far side of Truro." Then another thought struck him. "Though, now you do mention it, there *is* a Liddicoat living to this day in Sithney parish. I never thought of that, afore. Clifford Liddicoat. Farms over to Grankum. He'd be neighbour to you if you do buy the Old Glebe. Liddicoat … Lidgeycot. We-ell! I wonder?"

"Food for thought," William agreed as he closed the charabanc door and waved farewell. He could not, however, imagine what bearing a murder committed over two centuries ago might have on the present day, even if this John Lidgeycot proved to be a direct forebear of the Liddicoats of Grankum.

He heard the exhaust roar deepen as the driver retarded the ignition to pull away up the hill to Breage. The old toll-keeper's cottage was just about the tiniest dwelling he had ever seen — tiny even by Cornish standards. An old crone stood within, leaning on the half door, smoking a clay pipe. If she stretched one foot out behind her, he thought, she could probably touch the back wall with it.

"How are 'ee keepin', my lover?" she called out cheerily as he strode back down the road toward her. "You goin' up Wheal Fortune, are 'ee?"

He glanced at his map, the Ordnance Survey's geological survey of the area. "I'm going past it and on over Carnmeal Downs to Carleen. Why? May I carry a message for you?"

A 'message' to her was what 'messenger boys' delivered by bicycle from butchers, grocers, and other tradesmen. So, delighted in her misunderstanding of his offer, she said, "Why, 'es. Bring I a quarter-pound o' butter and two eggs back from Wheal Fortune Farm if you mind to. That's Mrs Rogers up there. Tell she 'tis for Mrs Oliver down stop gate. And I'll pay she when me Lloyd-George do come at the end of the week."

Willy-nilly, he had to accept.

"Where you from then?" she asked as he passed her door. "You aren't from round here."

So there went another five minutes while various genealogies were sorted out, followed by a more worthwhile conversation (to William) in which she described the scene of industry this tranquil valley had been in her girlhood. Then the little stream beside her cottage, which ran only a mile and a half, from an adit in Wheal Vor to the sea at Porthleven, was so rich in tin 'waste' that at least a dozen people made a living vanning the metal from the man-made sand it bore toward the sea.

Vanning.

He stored the word away. Separating grains of metal ore from ordinary sand, presumably by some water-washing process. Cornish. Could be dialect for 'fanning'? Or a corruption of 'panning,' perhaps?

"A thousand souls once lived 'tween here and Carleen, my lover," she said. "Now there aren't but two dozen. See that field there?" She pointed across the road. "There was a mine there — the Hanson Mine. And in the next field there. Antron Consols. And another one up the hill here. Wheal Rib. Yet you could search a year and not find a trace of them now. All gone. And the men as worked them. Your grandfather, maybe."

When she came out of her cottage to show him where Roseladden Stamps had stood, he saw she was barefoot and wearing flour sacks for a skirt.

"There now!" She pointed to a vast expanse of gray sand in which nothing seemed willing to grow — which was a decided contrast to the rich, fertile green of the rest of the valley, including the fields where she said the mines had once stood. "When they stamps was roaring away, full blast, you'd sit in that cottage and fear for the slates on the roof. Yet she've stood the test of time and they haven't. Not a splinter left. But there's another set still standing up Wheal Fortune, if you mind to see it — stamps, buddles, and vanning floors, just like the ones as was here, backalong."

"I certainly will." He stared back at the fields across the road. "Were there no buildings? No steam engines? How did they drain them? We're only ... what? Ten, twenty feet above sea level here?"

She shook her head. "No need. They never went down, see? But flat." She moved her hand horizontally. "Straight into the hill, following the lode. Not like the mines where you'm going, round Carnmeal. Now they went down *hundreds* of feet below sea level. Wheal Vor was the deepest. My father told me they had a Cornish engine there could lift ten ton o' water each stroke. Her cylinder was over a hundred inches across. And afore they put her in steam, eight gentlemen dined at a table inside her — there now! That's as true as we're standing here. 'Course, they'm all flooded now, they mines. Filled up to the adit — which is where this here stream do come out, up by Carleen Flow. Beyond Scott's Mine. If you do want to see good old granite buildings and fancy-brick chimbleys, that's the best you'll find in this valley — Scott's."

He spoke a little longer with old Mrs Oliver, asking her about the other ruined mines he'd be seeing up on Carnmeal Downs, but she knew nothing of the technical details that interested him. All she could recall were fantastical tales. For instance, she said that when the old mines were exhausted, their passages and adits were all interconnected — which would be a natural consequence of removing the ore, of course; the fantastical part came when she said that the old miners used to get drunk and bet each other on which champion could get from, for instance, the ten-fathom stope in Wheal Fortune to the abandoned crosscut, three fathoms below grass at Pallas Consols. And, she said, they would then run two or three miles underground, leaping narrow chasms several hundred feet deep at times — all drunk as lords and with nothing to show the way but a lighted tallow candle in their helmets (or 'hemlets,' as she called them).

He laughed in dutiful amazement, shook his head at the folly and courage of the human race, and bade her farewell as he set off along the goodish macadam road that ran up the valley beside the stream.

"Doan 'ee forget my messages," she called after him.

It was a moment or two before he recalled the butter and eggs. "Right!" He waved back to her and promptly forgot them yet again.

6   A short way up the road he passed a small quarry, abandoned for some years and already partly overgrown. And there he became aware for the first time that the rock strata in Cornwall do not, as in most parts of the world, lie one upon another in neat, more-or-less horizontal bands. Strata there were, all right — of quartz and shale and a crumbly sort of mudstone full of iridescent flakes that suggested mineral wealth to his as yet untrained eye — but they were closer to vertical than horizontal. Ten degrees off the perpendicular, he guessed. But what titanic forces could have lifted the earth's crust like that and left it in such disarray? It was surely beyond the reach of man's most fevered imagination. Yet there they stood, those wrenched-up layers, so calm and still now, damp with winter and caged behind tendrils of briar and traveller's joy. The deep tranquillity made their violent origins even harder to imagine.

Only the promise of even greater geological marvels ahead let him tear himself away from the spot. A hundred paces later the road crossed the stream and continued on, now along its eastern bank. He squatted on the bridge and stared into the rippling water, a mere two feet beneath his boots. The brook itself was only three feet wide and no more than a foot deep; he estimated it passed about thirty thousand gallons an hour — American gallons, of course. That would be ... his eyes vanished inside their sockets as he did a swift calculation ... twenty-four thousand imperial gallons. He must get used to thinking that way now. He dipped his hand into the water and lifted a fistful of sand. My, but it was heavy! Heavier than just any old wet sand. Perhaps one man could still make a living out of this brook — where twelve had once thrived?

He swilled it away again, rose, and resumed his walk. The valley sides were now closing in. They had been two or three hundred paces apart at the stop gate; but here the gap was a mere twenty, and the slopes were almost too precipitous to till — though the farmers on either side were obviously managing it. This was that part of the valley which had lain just out of sight from the end field of the Old Glebe on the first day they had visited it. So the farm to his right, he guessed, would be Trelissick, farmed by George Gosling. He wondered if that was the man himself, with a turnip-lifting gang in one of the top fields.

A moment later his guess was confirmed when he reached the point of division of the Y-shaped valley. The eastern branch, which ran round to Grankum, opened up to his right and the Old Glebe itself came briefly into view. From this vantage the old tithe barn obscured half the house. Only then did he recall the strange tale the bus driver had told him; he had put it from his mind the moment the serious — that is, geological — business of the day had begun. But now, what with the old barn so prominently silhouetted on the distant skyline and with Billy Trim's tale still fresh enough to curdle the blood, he found it less easy to forget a second time.

Here, too, the road turned right and led steeply, tortuously uphill, toward the northeast, as if heading for Grankum. Halfway up this rise he came to another road, which led off to his left, continuing along the western branch of the valley. He hesitated, not knowing which to take. Had he bothered to unfold his map again, he would have seen that the winding road on which he stood turned right, then left, then right again ... and so up to the farm at Wheal Fortune, which was his immediate destination.

Instead, he guessed that the branch road, which led along the western valley — though now some fifty feet above the level of the stream — was the one to take him there.

And so it did, in a way — that is, it took him to Wheal Fortune but not to the farm. Instead, it led to the abandoned workings of one of the most extraordinary tin mines in the country — indeed, in the world. He got the first intimations of it when he was about five hundred paces from the parting of the two roads, where he came to a stone-lined water course cut into the side of the valley. It was filled with running water, which poured in a smooth green arc over the top of the wooden sluice that barred its end. It was a recently made sluice, too, with the wood still pale and fresh. From there the water splashed and complained down a rocky gully it had eaten for itself in the hillside and eventually joined the stream below.

Indeed, it *was* the stream below, for, although the track of the ancient watercourse was still visible among the reeds and tussocks of marram grass upstream from that junction, William could see, even from a distance, that little water now flowed along it. And from this he guessed that somewhere farther up the valley — half a mile or so farther on and round the bend, to judge by the shallow slope of the valley floor — that same stream had been diverted out of its ancient course and forced along this man-made conduit instead — probably to power those stamps Mrs Oliver had mentioned. With renewed eagerness he set off up the path beside the conduit; once it had been a road as wide as the one he had just left, but already the brambles and bracken were reclaiming it for the great green world.

Excited as he was, though, he could not now forget the old tithe barn and its grisly history. He had, in fact, done more than just poke his nose inside the door, as he had claimed when talking to Trim; he had wandered all over it and climbed a stack of straw bales to take a closer look at the old mortice-and-peg joints of the timber frame. But of unquiet spirits and foul deeds he had felt not the slightest intimation. Of course, any old building must have been a silent witness to the whole gamut of human activities and emotions. And he had, indeed, tried to imagine the harvest suppers, the bucolic dances, the romantic assignations, the fist fights, and the conspiracies that must surely have taken place in so venerable a building. And, to be sure, some vaguely nostalgic whiff of them had stirred his senses — enough to amuse the rationalist young man within. But nothing had hinted at the agonies and bestialities of the Geach-Lidgeycot saga, so that same rationalist young man decided to pooh-pooh the whole tale, taking it to be a feverish embroidery of some very commonplace little murder and a subsequent act of revenge.

Unfortunately, as in all of us, his rationalism was not large enough to light his soul entirely, and its darker corners remained filled with an uneasiness that, he knew, would not go away until he had followed up the bus driver's tale and laid it to rest — or, of course, confirmed it.

"Concentrate now!" he urged himself aloud. "Mines. Minerals. Geology. Metamorphic rocks."

"Aaaieee!" came a scream from somewhere up ahead. A man's voice, he thought.

The hair stiffened on the back of his neck and a shiver ran from his scalp to the soles of his feet, for there was no one in sight, though the caller was clearly in some distress. He opened his mouth to shout back, but no sound came. His tongue was dry and he began to shiver with fear.

This is stupid! he told himself. *You're letting your imagination run away with itself — just because of some idiotic tale told by a ...*

"Hallo?" The cry came again, and this time a note of inquiry was laid over the distress. And it was definitely a man's.

William found his tongue at last. "Hallo?" he called back. "I'm coming."

"Quick! For pity's sake!"

The voice was now clearly coming from beyond a little spur that projected from the slope on his side of the valley. In fact, as he reached the foot of it, he realized it was not a natural feature at all but was composed of rubble, the waste of some mine, no doubt. Loose rock and shale skittered away beneath his boots as he clambered up its steeply sloping side. And, as he gained the crest, he almost tripped over the rails of a narrow dram line running out, not from a mine but from a quarry about twenty times larger than the one he had seen earlier on that walk.

But he had little time to examine it for there, in a sort of amphitheatre of rock and waste below him, stood the stamps Mrs Oliver had mentioned — six wrought-iron pounding heads, each of which must weigh a couple of hundredweight. They were held on stout wooden rods the thickness of telegraph poles, and, when the machine was working, they would be raised by eight-inch cams fixed to a drive train that was ultimately powered by an overshot wheel in the diverted stream. Fortunately it was not turning at that moment because, as William saw at once, the distressed caller, a young man of about his own age, was lying awkwardly across a stretch of smooth concrete on the downstream side of the stamps with one of his legs trapped beneath the nearest of those massive pounding heads.

"Hold on!" William called out, somewhat redundantly, as he ran along the dram line to a point where any stones he might dislodge in his descent would not fall upon the young man — and he dislodged plenty, and severely risked his own safety, as he leaped and slid down to the level of the stamps. Once there, he ran back to help the man.

"There's a crowbar against the wall behind you," the fellow called out. "You won't lift it by hand. Hurry!"

In turning round to seek the tool William's eye fell on the waterwheel and drive train, part of which was secured on the wall where the crowbar lay. He glanced back at the stamps and saw that the head nearest the top of its lift (and therefore due to fall next in sequence) was the third one away from the trapped victim. The fourth one away would be next, then the fifth and final one — by which time the one trapping the young man's leg ought to be raised halfway up its lift.

"What if I just turn this?" he suggested, grasping the largest of the cogwheels. "Keep your hands clear of the one that's just about to fall."

"Oh, thanks for that warning!" The fellow laughed. "Go on — good thinking!"

Gingerly William tugged at the wheel. There was a squeak from one of the centre cams and then the head it was lifting fell off the end and crashed to the bed with a ringing clangour.

"Jee-hoshephat!" William exclaimed. He remembered what Mrs Oliver had said about fearing for the house when the Roseladden stamps were in operation. "Can you feel any movement yet?"

"I'm not sure I'm going to *feel* anything," was the glum reply. "But go on."

There were more screeches from the next cam as the head it was lifting came near the trip point.

"It *is* moving, by George!" the man cried out joyfully. "And I *can* feel it, too!"

"Can you move the leg itself?"

"Not yet. Go on."

The fall of the next head was just as loud, but somehow less startling now that William knew what to expect.

"Another turn will do it," the man called out. "Keep going!"

One full turn of the big cogwheel turned the camshaft a mere ten degrees, which brought the final head to the point where it was about to be tripped. And the first head, the one pinning the young man down, would be next. William decided to leave that much margin of safety between such a catastrophe and the present state of the machine. "Can you move it now?" he asked, walking swiftly to where the other lay.

"Maybe. If you could just pull some rock out from under it?" the man suggested.

William squatted beside the stamps and saw that the wounded leg was half buried among crushed rock. It was curious because the bed beneath the other stamps was entirely free from rock — hence the ringing clang the heads had made when they fell. He scrabbled some of the fragments away until the leg was low enough to pull out from under the suspended head without scraping on it, but still he continued until all the fragments were gone and the bed was smooth from end to end.

Wincing, the man scooped them into a pile, as if they had some sentimental value for him.

"Now!" William said, changing his position to where he could get a hand to the leg both above and below the injury. "I hope this doesn't hurt too much. I'm going to try to pull it out evenly this way, toward me. I suggest you don't try to do anything yourself — in case the foot is no longer joined to ... well, you know what I mean."

"Cheerful bugger, aren't you!" the other exclaimed.

William hesitated a moment and glanced at him. "You're saying it's not as serious as it seemed before? Actually, there's no blood visible."

"Well, it doesn't feel so painful now the pressure's off. More numb than anything."

"Okay. Well — here goes!" Privately, William thought that numbness might not be such a good sign but, having already been accused of 'cheerfulness,' he held his tongue. However, when he slowly withdrew the leg and foot from beneath the overhanging head, inch by slow inch, he could feel that the whole limb moved as one. So, though the bone might well be fractured, it certainly was not broken in two.

He said as much to the fellow and added, "That rock probably saved it from being crushed completely. How did it happen?"

The man pulled a face and raised himself on one elbow, reaching out the other arm for William to help him sit right up.

"Whoa-back!" William cautioned him. "Let's just see how bad it really is first. Can you move your toes?"

He gripped the man's boot over the top of his instep. A moment later he felt sinews flexing beneath the stout leather — and heard an *ouch!* from the man himself. "Good!" he said. "Nerves intact and no bleeding. Can I take off your gaiters and look at the skin? The name's Carrington, by the way. William Carrington." He reached out a hand.

The other gripped it as best he could. "I guessed as much from the accent," he said. "And I'm Nicholas Liddicoat. I think you've met my father."

"To put it mildly," William replied as he set about easing the gaiter buttons out of their eyes. "And I think I saw your brother through a pair of binoculars on that same day. Sorry!" he added as Liddicoat winced. "Tell me how it happened — take your mind off what I'm doing."

"My brother saw your sister, too," the fellow replied. "You're not the only one with binoculars, you know. He's hardly stopped talking about her since. Says she's the most beautiful creature ever to flutter down gently to earth."

William grunted. "He must have been looking through the wrong end, then." He freed the last of the buttons and eased the gaiter off. It was stiff with age and want of greasing. When he tapped it with his knuckles it rang like thin plywood. "That might yet prove to have been the saving of your leg," he said as he began to ease up the knickerbocker leg. "You didn't say how it happened?"

Liddicoat pulled the same self-deprecating face as before. "I noticed that head was almost off its cam, so I put a bit of rock under it and tried to shake it off. I just wanted to see what damage it could do — to the rock, I mean. But it wouldn't drop. So I shook harder ... slipped ... got one leg under ... the other leg hit the side-stay there ... and bang! Down she came." After a pause he added, "Grin away! I agree."

"I wasn't grinning *at* you, Liddicoat, but at the thought that it could so easily have happened to me if you hadn't got here first. It sounds pretty much the damfool-numskull sort of thing I might try."

"Well, thanks for the rescue, anyway." Liddicoat managed to sit up on his own now, the better to see his leg for himself. "What does Doctor Carrington say?"

Now that the gaiter was off, the potential swelling became actual and, even as they watched, the inward side of his shinbone swelled until it looked as if a smallish tennis ball had materialized under his skin.

"I think that if you could stand soaking this in water for ten minutes or so, while I go up to the farm and borrow or fashion a crutch out of something, that bruise might last only two months instead of four. If you leaned on me, d'you think you could hobble over to the stream?"

Five minutes later, with his 'thornproof' tweeds torn in several little triangles, he trotted into the yard at Wheal Fortune, where he found Jethro Rogers, the farmer, turning the handle of a mangle-worzel cutter while one of his labourers topped and tailed mangles and turnips and threw them into the hopper. The mushy-sickly smell from the chopped roots told him where the taint he had noticed in his breakfast milk this past week had come from.

When he explained what had happened Rogers turned to the labourer and crowed: "Jarge! What did I tell 'ee? Gusson now, boy — go get 'n!"

And when 'Jarge' limped away, William saw he was wearing an almost circular boot, more suited to the hoof of a large shire horse than to a human foot. The farmer explained that the man had been badly trampled by a horse two years back, and that while it was mending — even though in a badly deformed shape — he had hobbled around the farm on a crutch. "And only yesterday we looked at 'n, in the rafters in the cowshouse, and

Jarge said to throw 'n away, but I said we'd have need of 'n agin, soon 'nuff. So there now!" He took the crutch from Jarge, who returned as if on cue, and presented it to William like a trophy. "Go on down and see if Liddicoat can walk with that. Us'll follow with a stretcher in case he can't."

William set off without arguing, though he was sure no stretcher bearers would ever make it through the thickets that had delayed him on the way up. At the yard gate he turned and called out, "If you hear me whistle" — he put his little fingers to his tongue and gave an ear-splitting example — "you needn't bother to come."

Rogers waved back. "Kettle's boiling, anyway," he called out in reply.

On making his way back down the slope, William noticed a well-worn path leading obliquely across the direct line to the stamps and, by following its zigzag trail, he came unhindered to the spot in half the time.

"I think it's fractured, all right," Liddicoat called out cheerfully as soon as he caught sight of his rescuer returning. "But thankfully not broken."

To prove it, he swirled his leg about in the water when William drew close enough to see. "Hurts like hell but shows no tendency to float away on its own," he added. "I say! Is that one of Jarge's old crutches?"

"Think you can manage it? That bruise has gone down quite a bit. Perhaps you ought to bathe it longer yet?"

"If I do, I think my leg will freeze and drop off. Help us up, there's a good chap."

In looking round to check that nothing of value was being accidentally left behind in all the excitement, William noticed that the little pile of crushed rock by the offending stamp had been cleared away — the pile young Liddicoat had so carefully scraped together earlier.

"What now?" the man asked with jocular weariness, suggesting that William was the world's fussiest.

Behind it, however, William thought he detected a note of genuine anxiety. But for that, he would have said straight out, 'You've cleared all the crushed rock away.' Instead, he replied, "I thought I had a map with me. Didn't I?"

"This?" Liddicoat tugged at the edge that protruded from his, William's own, pocket.

William thumped his forehead with the butt of his hand and, carrying one of Liddicoat's boots, walked on his downhill side, ready to buttress him in case he fell.

After a few paces he was satisfied Liddicoat would make it all the way on his crutch, so he gave the promised whistle, which he then explained to the man.

"Seriously," the fellow replied, "I am more grateful than I can say …"

"Stow it, you oaf!" William had read enough English school yarns to know the right words for such embarrassing moments.

"No. If you hadn't happened along just when you did, it could have been pretty nasty."

"Why were you trying to crush the rock anyway — if I may ask? You've lived here all your life, surely?"

"Yes?" Liddicoat made a question of the word, implying he didn't see that the point had any relevance.

"Well, judging by their condition, those stamps have been working until very recently. You must have watched them many a time. With me, it would have been out of curiosity — to see how well they crushed the stone."

"Oh, well … I suppose it was just the sight of that thing, hanging there by the thickness of a hair. I mean …" Inspiration struck him and he gushed suddenly: "Any child could have wandered down there and been maimed for life. Or even killed, my God."

It sounded a pretty thin sort of excuse but William pretended to accept this 'logic.'

Then, apropos nothing, Liddicoat added: "I only put the stone there to cushion its drop."

Now it sounded thinner than ever but William did not press the point. Instead he resolved to be assiduous in his study of Cornish mineralogy — and then to return here to see what had excited young Liddicoat into making such a stupid blunder.

7   That evening at the Angel, when the Carringtons assembled
       for dinner, the old man and Leah announced that they
had finally settled on — and would soon settle in — the Old
Glebe. "Not without some degree of reluctance," John Carrington added. "I don't know what it is about that place. Maybe
it's just because we saw it first and it stole our hearts away …"

"I just felt we belonged there in a way I haven't felt in any
other house we've seen," Leah put in. "It felt like … I don't
know — somewhere we once lived and have forgotten about. I
mean, if we looked through the old deeds and saw the name
Carrington there, it wouldn't surprise me."

After a brief silence her father turned to William and said,
"You're mighty quiet on the subject, my boy."

He cleared his throat awkwardly. "I wonder if the two of you
will still feel so all kiln-fired enthusiastic when I tell you the tale I
heard this morning."

The serving maid came to their table, picked up the butter
dish, sniffed it, put it back, and called out, "No. This one's all
right, Martha."

William stared at the butter and said, "Shoot! I forgot."

"What?" Leah asked impatiently.

"I promised Mrs Oliver I'd … oh, never mind. I'll take her
some butter and eggs myself tomorrow."

"Hark at the big butter-and-egg man!" Leah said to her
father, jerking her head toward her brother.

The old man did not think it quite so amusing. "Son," he said,
"I hope you aren't going around the district giving out the
impression that *I* am a big butter-and-egg man. Everyone here
thinks all Americans are dollar millionaires and good-sense
paupers. I've been very careful to …"

"It's nothing like that," the young man said wearily, and with
a baleful look at his sister. "Anyway, suppose I was to tell you a
foul murder was once committed in …"

"Whoa-back!" his father interrupted. "One thing at a time.
What is it with butter and eggs, anyway?"

"Nothing!" William sank his head in his hands. "I asked an
old lady, a Mrs Oliver, the way to Wheal Fortune, meaning the

mine, and she thought I meant the farm of the same name. Anyway, it didn't matter, because they're cheek-by-jowl. And she mentioned the farmer's wife's name, Mrs Rogers. And I asked if I could carry any message. And it seems that 'message' down here is like 'errand' — so ..."

"What has this got to do with murder?" Leah asked.

"Nix. But I was told to take one thing at a time."

"And you're not even making sense of that," his father said. William let out a short, hopeless sigh and said, "No."

"Well?" Leah asked after another short silence.

"It doesn't matter. It was all probably hokum, anyway."

"What was?"

He sat up, squared his shoulders, gave them a rather brittle smile, and said, "I had a splendid day, thank you. I saw an abandoned mine where the tin lode was so rich they *quarried* it. I heaved rocks down abandoned shafts and heard reverberations and splashes that would chill your blood. I saw a mine chimney with the fanciest brickwork. And there's enough abandoned plant and machinery out there to make you think an overnight plague swept through the place."

"All very productive, I'm sure," Leah commented, being envious of her brother's freedom to roam where he liked.

A splendid steak-and-kidney pie rescued them from further profitless discussion; but when they pushed their empty plates away, the awkward silences returned. At length William announced that he had no stomach for pudding and begged permission to leave them. "I'll just go for a stroll down to the bowling green and back and then turn in," he said. "I must have walked miles today."

It was, indeed, true that he had no stomach for the pudding for he had eaten so many pieces of Mrs Rogers's 'fuggan' — a sort of lard-rich plum bun — while she put cold compresses on young Liddicoat's damaged foot. And oh! the things he'd heard — the things he could have told his father and sister if they didn't keep putting him down like this!

His father, misunderstanding his son yet again, followed him out to the passage where he gave him a sovereign. "Don't do anything I wouldn't do," he said with a wink.

William was too astonished to make any reply, other than to stammer his embarrassed thanks — an embarrassment his father, yet again, misunderstood. "We've all been there, son," he said as he went back to rejoin his daughter.

"I worry about him," she said as her father resumed his seat. "D'you think his brain is going soft or something?"

The old man, still believing he knew precisely what was distracting his son — and knowing he could not possibly discuss it with Leah — dismissed the idea. "He got good grades at school," he said. "And the Camborne School of Mines seems keen enough to accept him."

"But he's so scatterbrained, Pa. He can't even retell a simple story or stick to a single train of thought."

"Maybe he's got other things on his mind."

"I'd like to know what!"

Carrington cleared his throat. "It's different for you and me, honey. I've made my way in the world." He grinned and lowered his voice. "Tell it not in Gath but I've got all the butter and eggs we'll ever need. And as for you, well, a woman's place is the same in the Old World as it is in the New. But young William is still a little fish in a big pond — and a *new* pond, too. Don't let's forget that. Old World, maybe, but new challenges, new rules. And he's competing against people who grew up here, who know it all in their very bones. Indeed, it would be surprising, not to say alarming, if he weren't a little … unsettled, shall we call it?"

He smiled with relief, thinking he had buried *that* subject most satisfactorily. He thought of his son, out there somewhere, going through the 'Hallo, Charley — looking for a bit of fun?' ritual with some pretty little drab under a street lamp, and felt a twinge of envy himself.

Leah, who had a puritan distaste for wasted food, eschewed the 'polite' habit of always leaving a morsel on the plate. She swallowed the last mouthful of a rather stodgy plum pudding. Then, as if asking the most casual of questions, said, "I wonder if they take women at the Camborne School of Mines?"

Her father laughed. "No such luck for young William, I fear. He'll have to sail on wider seas to find his bride to be."

But his smile vanished when she responded, "Actually, Pa, I wasn't thinking of him."

He frowned. "Who, then?"

"Me."

He laughed again, though not quite so wholeheartedly as before, she noticed.

"I'm serious," she persisted.

"Yes, honey. So is measles, but it passes."

"Why shouldn't I have the same chance as William?"

He looked about the room as if he hoped for rescue from some quarter. "The answer's too obvious even to need stating," he replied.

"Those gardens we saw this afternoon," she said.

"What about them?"

"Mrs Scawen made those terraces herself. She blasted them with dynamite out of bare cliff."

"Not herself."

"Pardon me but she did. Mrs Curnow told me — while you were talking to Mister Petifer, I think. She said Jane Scawen was the first person, man or woman, to use dynamite in Cornwall. She learned dynamiting in Camborne solely in order to ..."

"At the School of Mines?"

Leah hesitated. "Well, that was implied."

He smiled dismissively. "Maybe one of the instructors there taught her privately. She was a rich lady even then by all accounts, so that's possible. But as for lady pupils at the school itself ... ha!" He raised his hands as if inviting laughter to fall from heaven. "Where would be the point of allowing them in, anyway? Women aren't allowed to work down mines in these enlightened days."

"If I learned dynamiting, I could help you terrace the fields at the Old Glebe."

He reached across and patted her hand. "At least you tried, honey," he said soothingly. "You've got spirit. I'll yield to none in my admiration of you for that. But dynamite will not be necessary at the Old Glebe — except maybe to get rid of that ugly old barn. For the rest, a gentle steam shovel and good old elbow grease will accomplish all the landscaping I intend doing, thank you very much."

At least I tried! Leah echoed the words angrily in her mind. *Well, Pa — don't imagine I'm giving up this easily.* But she smiled sweetly as she said, "Tell me about them — your plans — now that we've decided at last. We have decided, haven't we?"

"One hundred per cent," he replied.

8 William seethed with frustration as he set out into the Helston night. Why did they never let him get out more than half a sentence before they jumped down his throat like that? Well, it was their loss. They'd chosen ignorance and now they'd have to suffer for it. A smile returned to his face as he thought of one item of ignorance for which they probably *would* pay, and in extreme discomfort.

When he'd mentioned Coad's romantic tale about the love-potion powers of the Grankum well, young Liddicoat and the Rogerses had almost burst a blood vessel laughing; and later, after they had left the farm, Liddicoat had explained: "It's beautiful, clear, tasty water," he said, "and people who've drunk it all their lives aren't affected by it. But the first few times that newcomers drink it, until they're accustomed, well, it's better than epsom salts, cascara, and the number nines all rolled into one. In short, it gives you the backdoor trots."

Well, let them find out the hard way now — then they'd be smiling on the other sides of their faces!

He was halfway down Coinagehall Street before he realized what his father had been talking about. 'Don't do anything I wouldn't do'! My God, he meant *that!* The very thought of it stopped him in his tracks. He felt his face flush with embarrassment and was glad of the darkness, which the flickering gas lamps barely penetrated. Unfortunately that same darkness prevented the man behind him from noticing that he had stopped. His eyes were not yet accustomed to the dark for he had only just emerged from the house that fronted the footpath. The resulting collision almost sent both of them into the Helston River — which was a rather grand name for the insignificant brook that ran in open granite kennels on either side of the street. In the ensuing dustings-down and hearty apologies, the stranger heard the American accent and said, "Have I the honour of bumping into Mister Carrington, then?"

William replied that he didn't know so much about the honour but the rest of the surmise was true.

"And is it Carrington *père* or Carrington *fils?* Forgive me — and allow me to present myself. Frank Kernow — your servant."

"William Carrington — yours."

As they shook hands, William glanced up at the darkened window of the house the man had just vacated and saw there, in black-edged letters of gold: *Francis Kernow, Solicitor and Commissioner for Oaths*. "The lawyer!" he said, as if he'd already heard of him from half a dozen sources.

Kernow laughed. "Well observed, young man! May I buy you a drink to show there are no hard feelings? Have you dined, by the way?"

"Just. But let me do the buying. After all, I was the one who stopped so abruptly."

"The night is yet young. We'll *both* buy," the other decided, putting a hand to William's shoulder and propelling him toward the saloon-bar door of the Blue Anchor. "Me first. Age before beauty, as they say."

Kernow's youthful voice and manner had led William to believe the lawyer was joking, that he was at most two or three years older — which he would have had to be in order to qualify. But when they reached the lighted passage of the inn he saw that the man must be in his early thirties.

"Whisky?" Kernow suggested. "No bourbon or rye, I'm afraid, but they do Scotch or Irish."

"Jee willikin!" William had never tasted either and said so. Indeed, he had only once tasted rye — an occasion that nobody cared to mention nowadays.

"Irish," Kernow decided. "It's smoother. They distil it twice, you know. The Scotch only distil once." He held up two fingers to the barmaid and nodded. "Let's go and sit over there."

He led William to a table for two in the inglenook, where he stretched his hands gratefully toward the fire. "Glorious!" he exclaimed. "I sometimes think Scrooge could return and live happily in my office — except that in my case it's the clerk who dictates to the master. My clerk cannot abide a warm room. Indeed, he cannot abide a cold one, either, but must have it as frigid as the North Pole."

"And if you ignore him and stoke up the fire?"

"He falls asleep and blames me."

The barmaid brought their whiskies and did not wait for payment, from which William assumed his companion had an account there.

"Did that brother of yours get his back-pay yet?" Kernow called after her.

She turned and smiled. "All thanks to you, Mister Kernow," she said.

He waved away her gratitude. "It was pure pleasure, Eileen." He pushed William's glass a token inch across the little table. "Cheerioh, me dearioh!"

"Cheer-ho!" William took a sip and gasped at the fiery bite of it. And this was supposed to be the *milder* of the two whiskies?

"Tell me true, now," Kernow went on. "Had you really heard of me before our fortuitous meeting outside just now?"

William wondered what was 'fortuitous' about it but he replied, diplomatically, "Kernow's quite an important name in Helston — so I gather."

"Ah! You're thinking of Giles Curnow, no doubt. But he spells his name quite differently."

He was about to spell it when William answered, "No, I was thinking of Kernow and Daughter, actually. I've noticed the shingle several times."

"Yes," the other snapped. "One can hardly avoid it."

"I saw it from the bus this morning. Are you related to them, by any chance?"

"The 'Kernow' is my father and the 'Daughter' is thus my sister. Let's speak of something more congenial."

"Than sisters?" William responded. "Hear hear! I'll gladly drink to that!"

"Oh?" Kernow raised an interested eyebrow. "Is yours older or younger?"

"Older, by two years."

"Mine's younger by one. Makes no difference, I suppose. They're all as fickle as opal. You help them all you can. You put your life and career in the balance. And what do they do — once they've got what they want? Turn round and kick you in the teeth! Don't tell me." He laughed to show that his vehemence was largely theatrical. "Actually, *do* tell me! A misery shared ... you know."

William sighed. "Everything was fine between us — give or take the odd attempted murder — until our mother died. Almost four years ago now. And since then Leah, that's my sister ..."

"Yes, I've heard of her. Come to think of it, I'm almost sure I've seen her — now I know who *you* are. Short, dark, curly hair? Petite? And strikingly good-looking?"

"Matter of opinion," William said coldly. "Anyway, she's assumed the maternal mantle with a vengeance." He took another sip and again gasped at the sting in it.

"I wish whisky still did that to me," Kernow said as he matched him, sip for sip.

"I can't help it that I enjoy freedoms she doesn't," William complained. "I didn't make the world the way it is."

"Oh, familiar ground!" Kernow exclaimed. "You know my sister is the founder and owner of the local electricity company? Did you ever hear of such a thing? A woman! She did it entirely to spite our father, who only wanted her to behave like every other sensible girl in the land and make a good marriage. *She* chose electricity because *he* owned the local gas company! Pure spite, as I said. And who helped her? Who did all the legal spadework and got in the subscriptions?" He tapped his breastbone. "Juggins here! And would you like to see my shares in the company today?" He reached forth an empty hand, palm up. "There they are — count 'em!"

"I say! Hard cheese!" William drew once again on the schoolboy yarns.

Both men stared at the flames in an easy, ruminative silence, which was punctuated only by sips and William's gasps at the spirituous afterburn.

"You're buying a house in the district," Kernow prompted, not making a question of it.

"The Old Glebe in Sithney," William vouchsafed. "They've made their minds up today. They went to see a house in Gweek and decided against it. And that was the last of the other possibles. So the Old Glebe it is."

"You don't sound too keen."

"Oh, I'm keen enough. It's very handy for me. I'm going to the Camborne School of Mines, you see."

Kernow nodded.

William continued, "Is it true there was once a rather gruesome murder there? I was told something of the sort this morning. They say a John Lidgeycot seduced and then murdered a girl called Catherine Geach in the old tithe barn."

Kernow nodded. "True enough — though I doubt it was as grisly as the popular tongue has since made it."

"They say the old barn is haunted."

The other laughed. "But surely you don't believe in such rubbish! Haunted, indeed! It's strange — there's a murder in Cornwall almost every week. Certainly one a month. In short, there have been at least two *thousand* murders down here since that particular one. So what makes it special? Why does only Catherine whatsername's ghost haunt her place of death? Where are the rest of those two thousand victims? I have no patience with it." He chuckled. "Mind you, as a bargaining point to abate the price ... *then* I believe! Whoever your lawyer is, he should certainly make a strong point of it."

"Yes," William said decisively. "You're right. That's the way to approach it."

"Who is your lawyer, by the way?"

William shrugged. "I don't believe we have one yet. When the time comes, my father will probably seek Coad's advice — the estate agent, you know."

"Oh, I know young Coad!" the lawyer said heavily. "Did he think to tell you about the bad blood between the Carringtons and the Liddicoats?"

"Oh, yes — even before he showed us the house."

"Did he, now!" The answer clearly surprised Kernow but he recovered swiftly. "He must have had some other property he preferred to sell you."

"Or he fell in love at first sight with my sister, and didn't want her to think ill of him if we bought the place and only *then* learned of it."

"You're a shrewd fellow, aren't you!" Kernow eyed him with approval. "Did Coad tell you about the ghosts, too?"

William shook his head. "Perhaps he didn't want to appear ridiculous. Look how scornful *you* were just now."

"True." The lawyer nodded. "But someone has obviously told you. What do your father and sister think about it?"

"That's the trouble." He sighed. "I'm the only one who's heard the tale. I tried to tell them tonight — I mean, I only heard it myself this morning — so I tried to tell them tonight and they both ... I don't know ... made it impossible."

"Sat on you?"

"Yes! A very good way of putting it. They utterly squashed me." He looked at his companion's glass. "I say. You've finished your drink."

"So have you."

William held up his own glass and stared at it in surprise. "So I have! Let me do the honours this time."

Kernow raised his hand again and, when Eileen came over, William handed her his sovereign and said, "You may serve me the same again, miss."

"Similar," the woman said with a grin at Kernow.

"She's passing on my pedantry, I'm afraid, old chap," the lawyer said. "It can't be the *same* again because we've already drunk it."

"Same *substance*," William objected.

"Ah, now we're into theology — how much does the deity weigh before and after all those millions of people eat and drink Him at the Communion table?"

William decided he wasn't getting light-headed; it was just an effect of Kernow's strangely haphazard conversation.

"And why aren't the mines haunted?" the man continued. "You wouldn't believe the number of disasters there have been in that area. You go up Trigonning Hill and look down on it and you'd think it's all solid land. Not a bit! It's riddled with great empty spaces beneath the surface. And almost every one of them has been the scene of some disaster or other — some within living memory. Carnmeal Downs should be 'standing room only' for spectres and elementals."

Like so many of the lawyer's comments, this did not seem to invite further development. How they train to be judges, William supposed — sprinkle an air of finality over everything.

Eileen returned with their whiskies. "And nineteen shillings," she said as she handed William his change. He wondered whether it was gentlemanly to count it and decided it probably wasn't; so he mentally photographed it as he slipped it into his pocket. "We won't be able to move into the Old Glebe at once," he said as he totted up the coins in his mind. "So I suppose we'll be at the Angel for most of the spring. Cheer-ho!" The whisky hardly burned now.

"Cheers!" Kernow looked thoughtful. "I wonder …"

"What?"

"That never occurred to me. Is there a lot that needs doing out there?"

"By the time my sister has finished drawing up her wishing list, yes!"

"Well, it so happens that I own an apartment house down in Cross Street, Helston's most salubrious suburb — if a single street can be called a suburb. It was once a gentleman's town house but it was divided into four very pleasant apartments about twenty years ago. And, it so happens, one of my tenants is leaving at the end of next week. I wonder — d'you think your father and sister might be interested?"

"I'm sure they will be. I'll ask them."

"May I ask you something?" He raised his glass and toasted the young man silently.

"Fire away!" William raised his glass in response.

"Can you tell me what coins you have in your pocket?"

"Easily." William laughed. "Why?"

"I'm just curious about people. Did you actually count it that quickly, in the blink of an eye, or are you so rich you don't bother with such trifles?"

"I'm certainly not rich," he replied vehemently. "I only got given that sovereign because my father supposed …" His voice trailed off in embarrassment. "Anyway, Eileen gave me six half-crowns, two florins, a sixpence, a threepenny bit, and three pennies. Nineteen shillings, I believe?"

"Bravo!" Kernow was genuinely impressed.

They sipped in easy silence awhile, smiling into the flames, crossing and uncrossing their ankles, watching the steam curl off the soles of their boots.

"So!" Kernow said at length. "Your father must imagine Helston boasts some exquisite courtesans if he gave you a whole pound for that special purpose. A shilling would easily get most of 'em. Still, since it's now paying for a much more reliable pleasure" — he held up his almost empty glass — "we ought to drink an appropriate toast, eh? So here's to both ends of the corset!"

They laughed and drained their glasses.

"One more for the road, eh?" Kernow said, clapping and rubbing his hands. "On such a bitterly mild night as this I think we deserve it."

9   Frank Kernow pulled his gig into the stable yard of the Angel. He had raised the hood just in case anyone might be around, even at that late hour, and might notice the young man sprawling unconscious in the body of the vehicle. But only a single light burned in the empty yard. The stable lads, kitchen staff, and sundry loafers and scroungers had all gone. One lone scullerymaid was finishing up for the night, down on her knees, scrubbing the floor. She rose painfully to see who the visitor might be and buried her hands in her armpits, partly to thaw her fingers, but mostly out of shame for their soda-cracked, water-wrinkled skin. "Sir?" she said. Then, as he stepped beneath that single lamp, "Oh, 'tis you, Mister Kernow."

"'Tis me, Mary. And here's a penny for you if you'll slip upstairs without alerting anybody and let Mister Carrington know he's wanted down here. D'you think you can do that?"

"And if 'e do ask why, sir?"

Kernow smiled. "I'm sure he'll guess why. Cut along now, there's a good girl."

She certainly earned her penny for, within a remarkably short time, she returned with a half-anxious, half-angry John Carrington in tow.

"Permit me — Frank Kernow, sir." The lawyer extended a hand. "At your service."

When he learned why he had been summoned in such secrecy, Carrington gave the girl sixpence and said, "Not a word about this to anyone, eh?"

Between them, and in silence, they got the stupefied William up the back stairs to his room, where they removed his boots and tie and left him to sleep it off.

"May I offer you a nightcap, sir?" Carrington asked the lawyer. "I'm sure mine host has not yet retired for the night."

"That's remarkably civil of you, sir," he replied.

"Not at all — the very least I could do in the circumstances. I hope you've not been put to any, er, financial …"

"Not a bit. But a modest glass of mild ale would be most acceptable. I'm delighted to make your acquaintance, anyway. I'm only sorry the circumstances are so disagreeable."

"I hoped the boy would have learned his lesson after the last little episode, back in the States," Carrington said as they made their way down to the landlord's quarters. "Apparently not. Did you find him in that condition or what?"

Walter Blackwell had been proprietor and landlord of the Angel too long to show his true feelings at having to reopen the bar so late at night, but he returned to his bed nonetheless and left the two men to their ale when they assured him they would not require a refill.

"You asked how I found him, Mister Carrington," Kernow said as they settled by the embers of the fire. "In fact, we bumped into each other — quite literally — in the dark. I, being mostly at fault, invited him to a convivial jar at the Blue Anchor, which was at hand, and, well … I chiefly blame myself for his condition. He did not, in fact, drink very much. I suspect he has no head for it, that's all."

"He has no head for *anything*, it seems to me," Carrington said. "I hope he pulled his weight tonight — paid his way? He had the resources. I made sure of that before he went out." With a cautious glance at his companion he added, "Though it was not to finance a drunken spree, I may say."

The lawyer ostentatiously hid a smile behind his hand.

"Told you about it, did he?" Carrington asked.

"In a way, sir. I don't believe he quite understood the impulse behind your splendid generosity. At least, not at once."

"Impulse, eh! I don't believe that critter *has* any impulses — except to stun himself with hard liquor. But what can *I* do, except keep him short of the price of a drink? Which is no answer at all. May I ask if you're married, Mister Kernow?"

"I've successfully evaded my responsibilities in that line. So far, anyway." He smirked.

"It seems to be quite a general custom down here. Coad said almost the identical words. Anyway, you'll see the difficulties when you have to raise a boy of William's age — larn him the facts of life, as we say. It's hard for a father to maintain a scrupulous respect for morality while, at the same time, recognizing that young men are full of wild oats. And wild oats demand to be sown *somewhere* — and with as little damage to decent society as possible." He smiled gloomily and added, "*Some* young men, anyway."

"Oh, I'm sure your son is … how may I put it? Not *different* from others in that respect, sir."

Carrington glanced up hopefully. "You have evidence of it, sir? I have no wish to pry into the details of your evening together, but I don't mind telling you I have often worried on that score."

Kernow shrugged. "I confess I have no direct evidence, Mister Carrington. We spent our evening in light, convivial conversation around the fire at the Blue Anchor. His collapse into his present condition was quite sudden. However, to address your fears, there is one infallible way to set them at rest."

"Yes," Carrington mused as he scratched the day's stubble on his chin. "It's what my own father did, after all. But he took me to a sporting house in another town. In another state, in fact. But where's the equivalent here? Is Falmouth far enough away? Will an American accent mark me out there, and so bring the tale back here? Do I have to go as far as Plymouth, then? And how can I possibly leave my daughter unguarded here?" He chuckled. "I could hardly take her with us! And what reason would I give her?"

Kernow looked up sharply. "She would require *reasons?*"

"Yes, siree!" The other shrugged hopelessly. "American girls are, well, American girls."

"Well," the lawyer said soothingly, "Cornish ones are little better these days. Ask my father — no one knows it better than *that* poor man!"

"The 'Kernow' of 'Kernow and Daughter'? It is an eye-catching shingle. Yes, I've heard the story. And so has Leah, *my* daughter. She's avid to meet your sister." He sighed.

Frank Kernow thought it significant that, while the son had known nothing of Jessie Kernow's waywardness, his father and sister had not only heard of it but had obviously discussed it, too. "That would be very easy to arrange," he said lightly. "Or *not* to arrange, just as you wish!"

Carrington dipped his head in gratitude but soon was gloomy again. "As to the other little matter, Mister Kernow, may I ask what you would advise?"

The man bit his lips and licked them nervously. "I hesitate to trespass upon an acquaintance so brief and fragile, sir …" he said diffidently.

"Oh, come!" Carrington broke in with bluff embarrassment. "Brief, I grant, but fragile? Surely not. I'm a man of the world, sir, used to dealing with all sorts and conditions of men, both socially and in the way of business. And I pride myself on being able to judge a man by more than the cut of his cloth and the superiority of his sentiments. And at the risk of embarrassing you, Mister Kernow, I'd say you're no 'squirtish sort of a feller,' as we say. I'll stake my veracity on it. Come to think of it, I'll be in need of a good lawyer soon enough. Is there a page for me in your books?"

Kernow raised his glass and smiled. "Mum's the word," he said. "It's not the custom here to discuss business in a bar — except for the one marked 'private bar' — I'm sure you're unaware of that. But if you'll call upon me at my office tomorrow, we may happily conclude the business. And as to the other little matter — the sowing of wild oats ..."

"Yes?"

"Would you think me presumptuous if I volunteered my services ... mind you, I do not speak of service in a professional sense ..."

"More in a veterinary sense, what?" Carrington guffawed.

"Quite. Yes, very good — I must remember that."

"I would be indebted to you for ever, man. You do see my predicament, I hope."

"I do indeed, sir. And in stating it you reveal yourself to be a man of infinite refinement. As for me, while I do not frequent such houses as you mentioned ..."

"Oh, well, in that case, look here ..." His voice trailed off as the lawyer raised his hand.

"The fact is, I have made my own private arrangements with one particular young female — I mention it merely to reassure you that I am not 'different' in that sense you employed earlier." He snickered. "I may have my own wild oats to sow, like any man, but they are not *Oscar* Wilde oats!"

"Good! Good!" Carrington rubbed his hands. "And *I* must remember that one."

"However, like all lawyers with a courtroom practice, I am inevitably kept informed of goings-on among the *demi-monde*. And I think you may safely leave me to guide your son in his ventures into this particular *passage* of life."

10 Leah and her father descended from the bus at the Sithney turn, just over the brow of Sithney Common Hill. He carried a postman's satchel filled with notebooks, measuring tape, binoculars, and a packed lunch, for they intended spending the best part of the day at the Old Glebe.

They watched the vehicle draw away, looked at each other, and smiled a slightly baffled smile. "What a preposterous tale, eh!" Carrington said.

In the corner of her eye Leah caught sight of a plume of smoke and steam away on the northwestern skyline, beyond Mellangoose. "There goes William's train to Camborne," she said. "I wonder what sort of day he'll have?"

Her father grunted but said nothing. The train vanished between the high banks before Truthall Halt.

"I'd hate to join a course that had already been running half a year," she said. "But they seem to think he'll have no difficulty catching up."

He sighed. "They see things in that boy which certainly escape us." Turning again to watch the departing bus, he went on, "What did you make of that driver's tale?"

"Ghosts? Ha!" She took his arm and started to cross the road. "Come on — this sun may not last."

"No, but the fact that he told that same tale to William — and the boy didn't even mention it to us. And then that business Coad told us yesterday — about how William rescued the Liddicoat lad from being trapped in some old mining machinery. Two dramatic happenings in one day — and yet what did *he* think was the most important thing to tell us about? Remember? Some garbled tale about an old woman and forgetting her butter and eggs!"

"And a mine chimney with some fancy brickwork." Leah sighed, too. "I do see what you mean."

"So where is this smart-as-a-lick-o'-paint young man Coad and Kernow claim to see in him — not to mention the absolute genius they found in him at the Camborne School of Mines? It beats me." He grunted and shook his head, the way a dog shakes off water. "Anyway, what about our bus-driver's tale?"

His tone was less scornful now. "You don't set much store by g-g-ghosts?"

"Do you?" She was surprised.

"I don't know," he replied awkwardly. "Somehow, it's much easier to believe such things when you know the building is at least five hundred years old. I took against it from the start."

She chuckled. "That's only because it's standing on the best site for your beloved glasshouse. Anyway, we won't be able to do a thing there for months and months yet — not until the place is ours."

"Can you believe that? The church has owned it since time immemorial — or until a couple of generations back — and yet it's going to take Kernow *two months* to do all these *searches!* Just to establish clear title 'in fee simple' and to make sure it's not encumbered with liens and mortgages. I'll bet the fee will be anything *but* simple! And then, Kernow says, if, one week after buying the place, we decided to sell it again, the new purchaser's lawyer would have to go through the whole idiotic business all over again! 'I don't know how they manage in the States,' I told him, 'but I do know that if any lawyer took the best part of two months to convey a piece of real estate, he'd be run out of town.' Times like this I'm happier to be American than Cornish. I'm sure he thinks we're the most impatient people ever."

At the next bend in the road, where it forked to the right for Sithney and to the left for Breage, a rather fine two-storey house came into view. They paused a moment to admire it. "Parc-an-Ython," Carrington said. "According to Kernow, Mrs Vosper Scawen used to live there — that woman who dynamited those gardens out of the cliffs at Helford. She lived there before she married Scawen."

"Oh?" Leah looked at it with renewed interest. "I thought she lived out in that big house we saw beyond Breage — Montpelier, was it?"

"Sure. That was before her father died — back in the eighteen-fifties. She was unmarried then and, of course, having inherited his considerable fortune, she could not possibly live there unchaperoned. So the mistress of Parc-an-Ython — whose name I've forgotten — gathered her under her wing."

They took the Sithney turn and halted again, briefly, as they passed the house. "Bricks and mortar don't care about us at all, do they," Leah mused aloud. "Think of all the arguments that must have gone on under that roof. And the murders in the old tithe barn, too. All those overwhelming emotions! Yet how serene both buildings are now!"

"Arguments?" her father echoed, frowning at Parc-an-Ython as if he had missed something.

"Well — use your imagination. A rich young heiress with the world at her feet — a woman of some spirit, quite obviously — and a fussy old chaperon telling her she couldn't do this and mustn't do that and 'no, dear, it would be utterly reckless to have *two* dances with young so-and-so' … All I can say is thank heavens *we* live in this much more enlightened age!"

"Er … yes." Her father cleared his throat uncomfortably as they walked on. Then, hoping to get back on safer ground, he said, "D'you know, even *after* we've signed the contract — which has all the outward appearances of a legally binding document — it turns out to be no such thing. Either party can withdraw right up to the moment of the sale. Kernow cheerfully agrees that 'something ought to be done about it,' but it would probably take five years of parliamentary time — and since they're all lawyers up there, anyway, they have no interest in changing a law that lines their pockets so warmly."

"Well, at least we have 'reasonable access' to the property for our architect, builder, surveyor, and so on. Did Mister Kernow get the surveyor's report back yet?"

"Oh, yes. I forgot to tell you amid all the excitement of getting William off to college. The cracks are nothing to worry about. They're almost as old as the building itself. They used green timbers, apparently, because the navy took all the seasoned oak. You just can't get away from history, here!"

"It's not subsidence?"

He shook his head. "There are no mine workings under the property, except for the corner of one field down near Grankum Wood …"

"Oh! Speaking of the wood — may we go down there today? If it doesn't rain?"

"We'll see. What do you think of young Kernow, by the way?"

"We could eat our sandwiches down there perhaps — and drink the water from this well, which is supposed to bring on attacks of love at first sight."

Her father shifted the satchel onto his other shoulder but said nothing. She knew he was waiting for an answer to his question. "Kernow's probably a good lawyer," she said carefully. "He would need to be. There's so much competition in Helston. The town's crawling with them. I don't think a bad one would survive. So he must be quite good."

"Well, thank you, honey, but you know that's not what I meant. I can make up my own mind about him as a lawyer."

"As a man, then? Well, I guess I'd trust him as long as he stayed in plain view. I sure would like to meet his sister, though — Mrs Trelawney. Did you ask him?"

"What about Coad, then?"

Now she held her silence until he was forced to say, "Mrs Trelawney is away with her husband, visiting his people in Leeds. Kernow says she goes up there every now and then to mend their generators but I think that's just a family joke. So what about Coad — and I don't mean as an estate agent?"

"He's amiable … enjoyable to talk with … well read. What more can I say? He'll make some lucky girl an admirable husband one day, I guess."

"And do you also guess that the lucky girl has a name?"

"Pa — stop it! I am not on the *qui vive* for a beau right now. Much less a husband. I'll find one when I'm good and ready. And he'll probably be someone we haven't even cast eyes on yet." She took his arm again, briefly, and squeezed it. "I know I'm getting awful long in the tooth but … patience, huh?"

Shortly after that they entered Sithney itself. The road through the village followed a tight oxbow loop, making an almost complete circuit of the church and the new glebe house. At the bottom end of the loop, in the middle of the village, a macadamized farm track led slightly downhill to the Old Glebe — and then swung right to join up with the Carleen road. The junction itself was called Boase's Burnthouse, presumably because a house belonging to one Boase was burned down there once upon a time. However, all trace of it had long since gone.

"Now in *that* house," Carrington said as they passed a dainty little cottage with roses — at present flowerless — rambling around the porch, "there once lived a widow woman. She was the wife of a penniless nobleman who died and left her with nothing in the bank and four nubile daughters in need of husbands. And she managed it! And — tarnation! — I've forgotten *her* name, too."

Leah chuckled. "How d'you know these things anyway?"

"I asked Coad. I figured that, since we're going to settle here, we might as well know the recent history and background of the parish. I hate walking past a place and seeing just a heap of stone and mortar, don't you? That's why graveyards are so dismal. It's not the thought of death — which we know very well is inevitable — but all the histories that died with them. All the stories we'll never know."

Leah's immediate thought was that her father had acquired these sentiments in conversation with some woman; they seemed too feminine for him to have arrived at them spontaneously. Then she realized that, even so, he was not wearing them as he might wear a woman's dress for a masquerade. He truly meant what he had said. Was he, in fact, revealing a part of his nature he had been concealing all these years?

"Doesn't it bother you?" he asked.

She decided not to agree too readily, to make him talk about it and, perhaps, reveal more. "Not until now," she said.

"When you see a gravestone, d'you just say, 'Oh, that's the site of a mouldering corpse.'? You've never yearned to know their histories?"

"If I want histories, I can always read Sir Walter Scott. Or Charles Reade. Or Jane Austen — if it's a woman troubled by unmarried daughters."

"But that's not *real!*" He hammered his brow at the seeming impossibility of making her understand his point. "I'm talking about *real* stories. Stories with no contrived endings — they just stop when the grim reaper reaps. But the loose ends trail on in the flowing river of time until they snag on other people's lives. Get woven in. Into yours and mine, now we're going to live down here. Don't you realize we're going to get caught up in all sorts of loose ends of dead lives — things we don't even know about. Come on, Leah! You're not so detached you can't follow me here."

She was amazed. With every word he revealed a man she had not met before. If a stranger had asked her to describe her father, she'd have said he was a no-nonsense man of business who, whether or not he had been born with more than his share of down-to-earth common sense, had certainly acquired it in his dealings with his fellow man. But on the question of his imagination — certainly of the sort of imagination he was now revealing — she would have passed rather than rate him low.

"You should make them up, Pa," she said. "All these unknown or elusive stories — just invent them. Show Scott and Jane Austen where they go wrong!"

"You still don't understand," he said in disappointment. "Think of the tale Coad told us the day we arrived. If he'd kept his mouth shut, we'd have behaved very differently when old Liddicoat came charging across the valley. But because we *did* know, even as he came striding up the field, all sorts of cogs and gears in our brains were going clickety-click! And when he started speaking, we knew exactly what was behind it all. *That's* what I'm talking about. These people who've lived here all their lives — they see each other and little cogs go clickety-click! inside their brains all the time. And when any one of them opens his mouth, everyone else knows what's behind it. But we won't. That's what we're missing. That's why I want to know all these human histories. It has nothing to do with Sir Walter Scott and Jane Austen. Now d'you see?"

She did, of course. But what he had just said did not sit quite square with his interest in the prenuptial life of Mrs Scawen and in the fate of the anonymous widow and her four undowried daughters. That was in a different category to the history of ill-will between the Carringtons and the Liddicoats. She suspected her father was now cloaking a curiosity that was essentially romantic and feminine in justifications more utilitarian and masculine. But was he aware of it?

"You do see," he said, taking her silence for agreement. He held the garden gate of the Old Glebe open for her; it squeaked and fell off one of its hinges. "Good start!" he commented.

"I see a difference between the Liddicoat feud and the widow-with-four-daughters tale," she said. "In terms of value to us."

But he was not to be drawn again. "If you ain't the most cantankarest female!" he exclaimed. "It's like picking houses — or stocks — or hiring hands. Until you've looked them *all* over, you can't talk 'in terms of value to us'!"

"The same with husbands, I guess," she added lightly.

"Hmph!" was all he said to that.

11 With New England thoroughness they measured and remeasured every room in the Old Glebe, and not just the principal dimensions but into every niche and alcove, too. They also compared the two main diagonals, to check that the rooms were square. Only one was — the room where four maidservants had once been crammed. "So their accuracy here was probably an accident," Carrington said.

"Coad told me that Truro Cathedral, which was built in living memory, is twenty feet shorter at one end than the other — which was deliberate, because that's the way they used to build back in medieval days. Just by eye."

"That man!" Her father shook his head admiringly. "He comes up with the excuses before we've even lodged the complaints! I'll bet he knew we were going to find everything here out of plumb."

"Does it make the building less safe?"

"No. Just more ... more ..." He hunted for a word and settled on, "... *quaint.*"

She sniffed the air. "I'll tell you this — after only a morning with the windows open and the sun pouring in, it sure smells a lot less musty. Can we go down Grankum Wood to eat?"

"'Go down Grankum Wood'!" he echoed in amusement. "You're starting to talk like a local, my girl."

"'Es!" she replied, relishing her talent for mimicry. "Proper job, my 'ansum! Can us?"

He laughed. "I guess so. And when we come back we'll discover if it really does smell less musty or if we've just gotten used to it."

He emptied the satchel of everything but the two packed lunches, which were wrapped in greaseproof paper and tied with thin white string in such a way as to furnish a small carrying loop. When Leah pointed this out, he left the bag, too, and they sauntered out into the back garden, each dangling lunch from one crooked finger.

The first thing they saw, naturally, was the old tithe barn, which almost dwarfed the house. Their eyes met and a wordless question flashed between them.

"Why not?" Carrington said, turning his steps toward the barn door.

But disappointment faced them when they arrived at its threshold, for a new galvanized padlock secured the bolt.

"Liddicoat doesn't trust us, it seems," he commented.

But Leah discovered that by lifting the padlock up and pressing it flat against the door, she could ease the crook-end of the bolt past it. "The old boat house for the Yale Rowing Club was like that," she remarked.

"Oh?" His tone begged her to tell him more — until he recalled that Tom O'Leary had been a leading light of that club. Then his repeated, "Oh!" closed off further discussion. Before they left East Haven he'd had enough of Tom-O'Leary-this and Tom-O'Leary-that to last a good while yet.

But when he saw the sadness in his daughter's eyes as she stood there, absently holding the padlock and staring through it at infinity, he could not help giving her arm a little squeeze and asking, "How is it now?"

She came back to the present moment with a little start. "Oh," she said. "Not so bad, I guess."

She opened the bolt to the full and pulled at the door with the toe of her boot. "Who's going to brave it first?"

Chuckling, he stepped past her into the gloom.

Dust motes hung in the shafts of sunlight that fell aslant the lofts and ladders, mocking the insignificant hoards of hay and straw they held. Leah followed her father and then overtook him, arriving at the heart of the barn first. Birds fluttered up in panic — two pigeons at one end and a jackdaw at the other. As her eyes grew accustomed to the gloom, she noticed an unflustered barn owl squatting on the wall plate above the door.

"Could that be the beam they hanged him from?" Carrington asked, pointing to the central rafter and prodding the air beneath it as a blind man in a forest might test the way before him. "Was this the space that once caged his insane but dying presence?" Then, assuming a comic-sepulchral voice, he boomed: "O, unquiet spirit of John Lidgeycot, if such thou art, I charge thee! Come forth and …"

"Pop!" Leah shrieked in horror.

"Ha!" he cackled and stabbed an accusing finger toward her. "So you *do* believe after all! Where's your fine skepticism now!"

Realizing he had just been trying to trap her she was quick witted enough to keep the look of horror on her face and whisper, "No! No! Look behind you!"

The blood drained from his face as he spun round and saw ... nothing!

Now it was her bright, mocking laughter that turned the tables on him.

"Okay!" He held up his hands in surrender but added in a steely voice: "Even so, I guess that, skeptics or not, neither of us is going to volunteer to come out here upon a midnight hour if the fire needs another log!"

They stood there a moment in silence, trying to feel any sort of presence or atmosphere that could be called supernatural — an unprovoked tingling of the skin, the stirring of hair roots in the scalp, a vague frisson up and down the spine. But nothing of that sort lingered in the quiet air; no host of phantom listeners, ready to oblige.

"I guess we're not such stuff as hauntings are made on," Leah said at last. "Also, I'm starving."

He looked up into the ancient rafters, shook his head sadly, and said, "What on earth are we going to do with all this useless empty space?"

As they reached the door he took two old horse blankets from a peg beside it.

Outside again she reversed the trick with the lock. Her father stared at the result in amazement. "You'd swear that was impossible," he said.

In the gateway at the bottom of the yard they paused again, this time to take in the panorama. It was the same half-wild, half-polluted landscape as before but now it was made cheerful by the sun.

"D'you think we could have inherited some memory of this scene, Pa?" Leah asked.

"Why, honey?"

"Because it looks so familiar. Even that first day it looked like something I'd seen once, long ago, and forgotten. Didn't you feel it, too?"

"Mm-hmm," he agreed vaguely. "But then Coad had already told us that tale about the place."

"How would that make a difference?"

"Well, we knew the Carringtons — or one of us — had been remarkably possessive about the Old Glebe, even before we set eyes on it. Coad made sure of that!"

"You think it was deliberate?"

"I'd take a note on it." He chuckled. "Smart fellow, Coad."

"Okay, Pa," she said wearily. "I hear you." She set off into the field, forcing him to follow.

"A woman's no different from any other female in creation," he said. "They all want a good, secure nest for their cubs."

She halted and turned to face him. "And you?" she asked. "What do you want?"

"By happy coincidence, my dear, men also want a good, secure nest ..."

"No. *You!* Just you. What do *you* want?"

"To see William launched into life and you secure in *your* nest, of course."

"Right!" she exclaimed, as if he had fallen into her trap. "And what then?"

"What d'you mean — then?"

"I mean *then!* Look at that house!" She spun him by the shoulders and spoke to the back of his head. "Look at the size of it! With William gone and me gone ... just you and the help rattling around inside there. What d'you want then?"

He faced her again, frowning in bewilderment. "Are you saying we shouldn't buy the place after all?"

"Of course not!" She set off once more for Grankum Wood, whose uphill margin was now a mere hundred paces distant. "What I *am* saying is that sauce for the gander is sauce for the goose. If *this* gander has to be looking out for a goose to nest with, then there's another goose, not a thousand miles from here, who ought to be thinking of a gander to share *that* huge nest with him." She jerked a thumb back toward the Old Glebe.

"Ho-ho-ho!" he responded with ironic joviality. "I see your game, young miss. Every time I mention husbands from now on, you'll respond with talk of wives, for my benefit — yeah?"

"Don't you think it's a point worth considering?"

"Sure," he replied complacently. "And I have, too, considered it — so there!"

It was her turn for bewilderment. "Who?" she asked, cudgelling her brains for one likely name.

"Not in particular, my dear, but in general. The obvious thing to do is to hire a housekeeper."

They had reached the fringe of the wood by now. Its beauty and stillness silenced them, held them in awe. Spring was still some way off, yet all the buds were there, tight on their twigs and branches — minute pinholes of green that combined to lend a subliminal shimmer to the scene, a greenness that trembled at the very threshold of being. Just for a moment they had an intimation of some mighty force in the dark earth underfoot, stirring itself, reaching up into the lichen-mottled trunks all about them, building up the pressures that would, one day soon, erupt in a riot of new foliage.

"No birds sing," she whispered.

"Midday," he replied.

Rooks cawed far off, in the elms around the church and the Old Glebe.

He sniffed the air. "Fox," he said. "D'you get it, too?"

She moved upwind of him and said, "Oh, yes!"

They tried to follow it but lost the line within very few paces.

But the spell of the woods was broken and Leah returned to their earlier conversation. "Why is hiring a housekeeper so obvious?" she asked.

"Because a wife can say, 'Go back outside and wipe those boots this minute!' and you've got to knuckle under. But a housekeeper ..."

She interrupted, continuing his sentence for him: "... will tell you if you're going to walk mud all over the house like that, she'll want better wages!"

"Right, honey," he said. "My train of thought exactly!"

"Oh." She felt deflated.

"Only a fool hires a woman," he went on. "It's smarter to hire her husband — then you get her labour for free!"

"Good luck!" she said, abandoning any attempt to speak seriously with him on this particular topic. At least he'd know what to expect in future, any time he started in on his hobby horse about her finding a husband.

The slope of the valley grew steeper as it neared the bottom and it was soon impossible to go directly down. Instead, the hillside was criss-crossed by a maze of narrow paths that alternated between horizontal and gently sloping. Leah picked one a yard uphill from his, which brought their heads almost on a par.

She was now the same height as her mother had been. Their similarity, which was less obvious when she stood at her normal height, eight or nine inches below his eyeline, brought a sharp pang to his chest — so much so that he had to pause awhile and pretend he was out of breath.

She relieved him of the horse blankets and continued along the path. "There's the enchanted well," she cried out when she had gone a couple of dozen paces. Then, "It's not a well at all. It's a three-sided cutting into the rock. With a shallow pool at the bottom. I could walk right into it from here."

"Man made?" he asked, coming to join her. "Yep!" he answered himself, running an appreciative hand up the smooth-carved walls. "Looks like good water, too. Silvery and clear. Must be a spring."

"It's all we have for drinking right now," she said. "Are you going to risk its enchantment?"

"Risk?" he asked.

"Well, some hideous old crone might come along right after you've drunk your fill — and it'd be love at first sight!"

"Oh, that old tale!" he replied wearily. "Hand me one of those blankets."

He passed her his cap in return and, holding back his forelock in one hand, knelt and slaked his thirst. If he had not just seen her likeness to his late wife, he would have joshed with her on rising — pretending to have fallen under the spell of the waters and with her as the object.

And she, being his daughter, would have played the same joke on him after she had drunk her fill — if they hadn't heard the sounds of someone approaching.

They moved back onto the path and saw him at once — a good-looking young man, dark-haired and wiry, striding with easy grace along well-known paths, making no effort at silence. When he saw that they had noticed him he stopped, being still twenty or more paces away. "Mister Carrington?" he called out. "And Miss Carrington?"

"The same," her father called back. "Have we met?"

The fellow resumed his approach. "I've met your son, sir," he replied. "In fact, he saved me from a most unpleasant situation

— involving an encounter with some abandoned mining machinery over at Wheal Fortune, in which I had come off second-best. Nicholas Liddicoat," he added, being now close enough to offer his hand.

But Carrington could hardly take his eyes off Leah — and from the light that danced in her eyes he was almost ready to swear there was something in that old wives' tale after all.

12   He had two bloodied rabbits and a pheasant dangling from his belt. Slung over one shoulder was a short bow; over the other, a quiver with half a dozen arrows; he divested himself of both and laid them carefully on the ground beside him. John Carrington looked on with amusement. "If you hadn't told us your name, young man," he said, "I'd have guessed at Robin Hood."

Nicholas Liddicoat shook his head solemnly. "Robin Hood used the long bow," he replied.

"Sure." Carrington could not tell whether he was making a straight-faced joke or a serious point.

"Also Robin Hood is dead," Leah put in, as solemnly as the young man.

"Ah!" His tone suggested he could say a great deal more on that particular subject.

"Have you eaten, Mister Liddicoat?" Carrington asked. "May we invite you to share our humble ..."

"I have eaten, thank you."

"Then you don't object if we ..."

"Please do! Did William tell you about our meeting?"

"He saved your life — at least, that's the way they're telling it all over Helston."

Liddicoat laughed at the exaggeration. "I bruised my leg, that's all. However, he certainly saved me a great deal of discomfort and boredom. I could have been trapped there for days. In which case, come to think of it, he would have saved my life. Did he say that?"

Father and daughter munched their sandwiches and exchanged awkward glances, aware that, between them, they had perhaps not given William much chance to account for his day.

"He's not usually the most communicative of persons. Not to us." Carrington explained.

"Really?" Liddicoat was surprised. "Oh, well." He nodded toward the Grankum well. "Did he tell you about the danger that lurks in those waters?" He grinned knowingly.

"Coad told us," Leah said. "The very first day we came here." She spoke coolly, not wishing him to get any ideas.

"Ah," he replied. His eyes did a quick scan of their meagre rations. "And yet I see no flask of water, no pop, no ginger beer? Did you risk a drink despite the warning?" He grinned again.

The nerve of the man! Leah thought. He must imagine that, just because he was pretty good-looking (she could not deny him that), he could hang around the spring, posing as Robin Hood, and bamboozle credulous damsels with that old wives' tale! Who did he think she was? "We don't believe *everything* we hear, Mister Liddicoat," she said loftily.

His grin only broadened. "Faith is not necessary in this case," he told her. "It's a simple physiological reaction. You don't feel anything yet?"

For brazen effrontery, this took the gold medal. She replied in her coldest, most off-putting tone, "I believe my constitution is proof against whatever *spell*" — she spoke the word with contempt — "those waters may cast upon me."

"Amen to that, Miss Carrington," he said sympathetically. "I trust it is so. And for you, too, Mister Carrington."

"I?" he responded with surprise, looking around for a female object of this supposed witchcraft. "I feel quite safe so far." Then, wishing to change the subject, he went on, "Tell me, why did you say 'Ah' in that tone just now — when my daughter pointed out that Robin Hood is dead? Were you going to tell us that death does not stop the unquiet spirit from roaming abroad in these parts? Because, if so, we've heard *that* old tale, too."

Liddicoat, thinking that the sight of his bloody trophies was putting Miss Carrington off and making her so snooty, hid them behind a clump of wild garlic. At the same time he replied, "So William told me. But I don't believe in anything supernatural like that, do you?" Being turned away from them, he did not catch their mystified expressions. "This is a rational universe, in my book. Ghouls and spectres belong to the age of, well, of Robin Hood, I suppose."

Leah was now convinced he was that shallow sort of young man who talked in scribble, saying the first thing that came into his head — and no doubt thinking it mighty clever because it came from *his* head.

"And what of chalybeate waters that act as love potions?" Carrington teased him.

He flapped his hand as if wafting the thought into oblivion. "You heard that old tale, too, did you? Love at first sight! Well, I've drunk from that well since childhood and, I can assure you, it never had *that* effect on me."

"I wouldn't be so sure," Leah said acidly. "I noticed just now, when I drank from it myself, that the first living creature I saw — reflected in the surface, of course — was myself!"

Their eyes met and locked. It took him a second or so to grasp her meaning. Then his face darkened with anger. "Then you *do* believe that old nonsense," he said. "Well, it puts you on a par with most of the women hereabouts. And now they clamour for the vote! Hah!"

Leah was momentarily speechless. Her jaw clamped so tight it hurt the muscles at her temples; her nostrils flared as she drew a deep breath to reply.

"Now, now ..." her father began, but he had left his intervention too late.

"We have the vote in Spain," she said. "In Norway. In Australia. In New Zealand. And in at least three states of America. And — it may interest you to know, Mister Liddicoat — in none of these enlightened places has the world come crashing down around men's ears."

"Yet," he replied calmly. "You are obviously a bit of a suffragist yourself, Miss Carrington."

Her father moved his hand up and down as if seeking to cut the invisible rays of hostility that flashed between them. "Come, come!" he exclaimed. "Young man, you have catapulted yourself into tiger country."

"What d'you mean 'yet'?" Leah asked. "D'you mean the world *will* come to an end in those places — and any others that may follow?"

"Absolutely!" He chuckled happily, the way a teacher might chuckle when a dim pupil grasps a difficult point at last. "The world as *I* know it, anyway."

"Aha! Aha!" she crowed. "There we have it! The world as *you* know it."

"You'll get on famously with my brother Harvey," he told her. "He was arrested, along with a whole gaggle of the shrieking sisterhood, in Camborne last year."

"In that case, I think I will," she said.

"I'm quite sure of it!" He laughed sarcastically. "His head's 'crammed with louch,' too — as we say."

"May I ask ..." Carrington tried again.

"I like him better by the minute," Leah said.

"He'll be delighted to hear that, Miss Carrington. He already feels pretty *hurrisome* about you — there's another Cornish word for you." He turned to her father. "I'm sorry, sir. You were interrupted just now."

Carrington sighed. "I merely wished to ask if you had any particular reason for stopping and talking with us?"

"Oh. Just to be neighbourly, actually." The young fellow laughed at the incongruity of the remark. "To be precise, I hoped to discover if we *were* neighbours. Or are about to become neighbours, sir."

"In other words, spying for your father!" Leah suggested.

"He'd like to see *that* day!" was the enigmatic reply.

"Well, let me *spy* in my own behalf." Carrington hoped his humour would rob the word of its sting. "Is your father intending to put in a bid on the Old Glebe? Coad is rather surprised not to have heard from him already."

"Surprised and disappointed, I imagine," Liddicoat said.

"So he won't be bidding? I'll be frank with you, young man. We *have* put in a bid, and it has been accepted — though, as I've also learned, it means nothing in law. Another, higher, bid could be entered even now, and we'd be right back where we started." He paused and waited for a reply.

Liddicoat squirmed a little before he responded. "Let's just say that my father is, after all, a farmer."

"Meaning?"

"Meaning he's quite happy to sow seed in the fall and see no result until next spring. I also intended — whether we are to be neighbours or not — to offer to take you over the old mines, show you the things I showed William last week. I suppose he told you about that?"

It was their turn to squirm — again. "As I said, he's not the world's leading conversationalist," Carrington responded.

"Yes," Liddicoat went on. "That surprised me the first time you said it."

The implication that it no longer surprised him, now that he had met them and got to know them slightly, was not lost on either father or daughter. To Leah it was just one more example of the fellow's arrogance; she just wished he'd go away. But her father took it in quite the opposite spirit. The jibe made him eager to continue in young Liddicoat's company, if only to show him how wrong he was.

"Why, that's mighty civil of you, sir. Isn't it, Leah. We'll be happy to accept."

Liddicoat grinned triumphantly at her. She knew what he was thinking — the fiery suffragist was being forced to submit to the patriarch's will. There was no warmth, no spark of friendship, in that smile at all.

Actually, come to think of it, that was what made the suggestion at all acceptable. If she'd thought for one moment that he was truly aiming at a friendship with her, she'd have risen without a word and left them to it. Even so, she did not yield without a protest. "We left the house unlocked," she reminded her father.

"Grankum Farm has no locks," Liddicoat put in. "I don't think any house does in these parts."

"Besides," Carrington said, "what's there to steal?"

Liddicoat strung his game from an overhanging branch, beyond the reach of foxes, and rested his bow and quiver against the tree itself. The other two stuffed the paper wrappings and string down a rabbit hole and prepared to follow young Liddicoat on his tour of discovery.

"One more sip before we set off?" he suggested mischievously as they passed the entrance to the well.

"I will!" Leah could not resist the challenge.

"Good," he said as she emerged from the narrow cleft again, wiping her lips.

"Why so?" she asked.

"I'm keen to see this constitution in action — the one that can withstand the effects of Grankum's 'chalybeate waters'." He smiled at Carrington as he quoted the words. "You'll be the first in my experience, let me say."

"Such airs!" she said, pushing past him. "Are we going that way?" She pointed down the valley.

"Anywhere that's close to a hedge," he replied. "Such would be my recommendation, anyway. Right along the floor of the valley to the end of the wood."

"There's no such thing as poison ivy in Cornwall, is that right?" Carrington asked nervously.

"Only stinging nettles," he replied.

"Yeah, we learned about stinging nettles — the hard way."

The trickle of water that spilled over the basin of the well joined a small brook that drained the upper part of the Grankum valley. Paths led downstream along either bank.

"If we cross up here, we won't have to leap across it lower down," he added. "You'd not want to do too much leaping for the next day or so."

"This stream looks man-made," Carrington commented as he helped Leah cross to the path on the farther bank.

"Man-improved," Liddicoat agreed. "In my grandfather's time, the area where we were just sitting was one big marsh. When they started quarrying stone there — did you see the quarry up there?"

"We glimpsed it."

"That was when they dug this deep channel for the stream — and hewed out the sides of the well."

Walking in single file and picking their way carefully among brambles and fallen branches made conversation difficult. Mostly they listened to a monologue from young Liddicoat — pointing out a spot where they would see orchids later in the year, describing the 'one carpet of blue' that covered the ground in bluebell time, warning them of a badger's 'set' — a word new to them, meaning 'earth.'

"D'you say 'set' for foxes, too?" Leah asked.

"No — it's 'den' for foxes. 'Form' for hares. 'Burrow' for rabbits. 'Nest' for birds ..."

"Yes. Thank you, Mister Liddicoat. I didn't want the whole encyclopedia. I only asked about foxes."

He could not do the simplest thing, it seemed, without trying to annoy her. It even annoyed her that she had let him go ahead because it would allow him to imagine her eyes were upon him all the way. But when she tried ostentatiously looking to one side or the other, just in case he should turn round to check, she ran into trees and stumbled over roots. She thought of sidling past him on one of his frequent lecture-stops but then, she realized, she'd be giving him the chance to ogle her from behind. So, that wouldn't do, either. Therefore, whenever the path divided into two or three parallel trails, she chose one that would bring her abreast of him, where she could look ahead without letting him think she had eyes for him.

Chalybeate waters, indeed!

A similar dilemma occurred at the end of the wood, where they were obliged to leap from the top of a stone hedge down into a field, about a hundred paces from the very bottom of the valley. The drop was a mere thirty inches, which she would normally have done without a pause; but here, near the foot of the valley, the field sloped at a giddy angle and she was afraid of turning her ankle. Only the thought that she would then have to rely on his support until they came to the nearest dwelling made her steel herself to accept his outstretched hands. He clasped her by the waist and, with what seemed like no effort at all, lifted her down to the grass.

"Thistledown!" he said, not letting go of her waist. "May I call you Thistle?"

Behind her she heard her father laugh. "Hang me if that ain't *le mot juste,* young feller!" he said. "Come on, daughter — what d'you say to that?"

Fastidiously she peeled his hands away, saying, "If he calls me Thistle, I'll call him Nark — short for Narcissus."

The reference to the youth in the Greek legend who fell in love with his own reflection in a pool of water and pined away at his unattainability was not lost on him, coming as it did on the heels of her jibe about his drinking at the Grankum well. "I reckon Miss Carrington knows best," he said quietly. "Well now!" He pointed along the valley. "We can go that way and pick up the path William took last week. Or we can go arrow-flight, straight up the hill here, over the brow, and down to where he found me." He indicated the land rearing above them to their right.

Carrington stared up the punishing slope and echoed him ironically. "Arrow flight! I'm for the horizontal walk. It may be longer but it looks lovelier."

They went diagonally down to the very bottom of the valley. There at last they were able to amble side by side. The jests about Thistle and Narcissus, barbed though they were, had eased the tension a little — enough to let Leah ask, in a most reasonable tone, "Why d'you say that women's suffrage will end the world as you know it, Mister Liddicoat?"

He chuckled defensively. "D'you want a long argument or a short one? We've time enough for both."

"I don't wish for an argument at all," she replied. "But I suspect that, even with all eternity before us, I should never find reasons enough to change *your* mind."

"Any more than you'd find herrings enough to feed us in the middle of the Sahara."

"You imply there are none."

John Carrington, who knew everything his daughter might say on this topic, listened with only half an ear. He spent most of his time gazing into the fields at their left — the Old Glebe lands — daydreaming their conversion into one of the great gardens of Cornwall. Exotic trees that would not break the skyline until his grandson was an old man waved their fronds in his mind's eye and gladdened his heart.

"I *assert* there are none, Miss Carrington," Liddicoat told her. "And it is not open to question, either, since all I assert is that *my* world, or the world as *I* know it, would be changed for ever by the granting of female suffrage. Who can gainsay it?"

"And what is so wonderful about your world — if I am not guilty of *lèse majesté* in asking?"

He marshalled his thoughts before responding. "If it were merely a matter of granting the vote, I'd yield it this minute. Gladly. For me, that's not the problem."

"Problem?"

"Threat, then. If women ever get the vote — which will be over my dead body, let me say — it won't take them long to discover what men discovered when manhood franchise was granted back in ... eighteen ... whenever it was ..."

He looked to see if she would jeer at his ignorance.

She kept her eyes fixed on the path ahead.

"So there are some things that even you don't know!" he remarked. "Interesting!"

"Eighteen eighty-four," she said flatly.

"I shouldn't have asked." He sighed.

"You didn't ask. You jeered."

"I shouldn't have jeered."

"Quite. What did men discover back then, anyway?"

"Not all men. Just those without economic power. They discovered how useless political power is without economic power to back it."

"Ah — and you're afraid that disillusioned women will start demanding economic power, too?"

"You know very well they will. *I* certainly would — and I don't think I'm any brighter than most of you lot."

"And what about fairness?"

"What about it?"

They had arrived at a gate. The next field marked the lower end of the Grankum valley, where it curved round to their right and joined the valley William had followed up from the stop gate. It was well stocked with cows, some too close for Leah's liking. "Do they ...?" She hesitated.

"Bite?" he suggested.

"No!" She withered him with a glance. "But they won't charge us or something? Their horns look fearsome."

"The breed is called dairy shorthorn, funnily enough."

"They may be short but they look wickedly sharp to me." She turned to her father. "What about changing our mind and going up the hill?"

He smiled tolerantly and opened the gate. "They won't dare harm either of us, honey," he said, winking at Liddicoat to show who 'us' included. "Not with you here to protect us."

Half angry, half terrified still, she followed them through and, taking her father's left arm, placed him firmly between her and the bulk of the herd. And as a shield against stragglers on her other side, she walked rather closer to young Liddicoat than she would normally have wished.

"What about fairness?" he asked again as soon as their walk was resumed.

This time she saw to it that they marched rather than ambled.

"You imply that men have all the economic power," she said. "Don't you think it would be only fair to share it?"

"Yes," he replied.

"Well, then!" she said. "Why not do it?"

"Because fairness doesn't come into it. If we all went around being *fair*, civilization would grind to a halt."

"Oh!" she exclaimed. "'You're just enjoying being perverse for the sake of it. I'm sorry I started this."

"I'm not," he went on in that same infuriatingly 'reasonable' tone. "I'm neither sorry you started it nor am I simply enjoying being perverse. Look — my family owns Grankum Farm. Yours owns the Old Glebe — or soon will. I could introduce you to a hundred people, living in this very parish, who think that arrangement is most *un*fair. And they're very probably right. Follow the history of ownership back to its roots — in time immemorial, I mean — and you'll find it was almost always taken at the point of a sword. What we call theft nowadays. Just imagine for a moment that you own the Old Glebe. It's yours — freehold. You can do anything you like with it. What does your sense of *fairness* tell you to do?"

Angrily she probed this argument for weaknesses. It must have some, but none was immediately apparent — which merely angered her more.

"See?" he concluded calmly. "That's why people like me — men — will never give you the vote if we can avoid it. Most of us have only a fraction of the economic power we feel entitled to. So we're never going to dilute our share by heeding your cries of 'Fair Play!' And such cries would follow the suffrage as sure as moon follows sun."

"Well," she replied, wishing she could find something more crushing to say. "We must just agree to differ on the topic. That's all. One day the constitution will be amended and we *will* get the vote."

"Talking of constitutions, how is yours holding out?"

She did not deign to reply.

Half an hour later he repeated the question, after he had shown them the stamps and explained how William had 'saved his life.' She answered him with the same withering glance — except that, this time, she was showing distinct signs of uneasiness. So was her father.

He showed them all over the old mine workings, then, beginning with the quarry at Wheal Fortune where the stamps stood abandoned. "Wheal means 'mine'," he said. "But here the different veins of the lode were so tight-packed — and so close to the surface — that the workings collapsed into each other and turned into this quarry." He waved a hand at the fractured stone walls all around.

"That tunnel I can see up ahead," Leah said awkwardly. "Is it, er, still in use?"

"Only by bats," he assured her. "It's an adit, actually."

"Bats?" She cried out in dismay. "Well, what about the other one? Is that an adit, too?"

"Why?" He guessed, of course, but he wasn't going to show any sympathy, not after all her boasting.

"Oh …" She flushed with embarrassment. "I find I need to … to pay a call of nature."

He waved toward the second adit, whose mouth was about seven feet high by three feet wide. "That only goes in about six yards. They started to …"

"No bats?" she asked urgently, already walking in that direction. "You promise?"

"No bats. I'll wait back there by the stamps."

"Actually, young fellow," her father said apologetically, tearing up handfuls of dry grass as he spoke. "I'm in a similar predicament. The summer scour. There must have been something in those sandwiches. I'll see you by the stamps, too."

While he stood by the old machinery, Nicholas Liddicoat ran his mind back to that odd remark: 'Must be something in the sandwiches.' Surely, if they knew all about the aperient power of the water in Grankum well, they had no need to suspect the sandwiches? Therefore they did *not* know about it. Not at all. Therefore … and therefore …

And so, step by logical step — for, as he had told them, his was a rational world — he worked out that while he had been referring to the aperient influence of the water upon the bowels, the Carringtons had been talking about … something quite different. About what?

He began to laugh.

About the old wives' tale of falling in love at first sight! Even more confusingly, they had assumed *he* was talking about that old legend, too.

And so he understood very well why Leah was so affronted to find him laughing his head off when she rejoined him at the stamps. But that only made it worse.

13 The signing of the contract to buy the Old Glebe might have had little legal standing but it was an adequate sign to local society that the Carringtons were now committed to the district. It was therefore time for that same local society to determine their fitness as new members. The newcomers had already leaped one hurdle: John Carrington was clearly well-to-do. And any rich man with a young bachelor son and a nubile spinster daughter would be welcome in a society brought to the verge of ruin, first by the collapse of tin mining, then, more recently, by a decade of agricultural depression.

But old ways die hard in old country towns. It was rumoured that Carrington's father had made his fortune in something called 'hog trading' in Chicago and that Carrington himself had worked in the business until he was fortyish. It did not sound too auspicious. However, no one was sure whether the American 'hog' meant exactly the same as the English 'pig.' And then there was that other word, 'trading' — had it been respectably wholesale or undesirably retail?

Fenella Compton, who dabbled in oils, knew that the best brushes were made of hog bristle, which proved, she said, that the hog trade had a genteel side to it and so they should give Mr Carrington the benefit of the doubt. She was not alone in profound commentary of that sort. But the acknowledged authority in this particular field had to be Jimmy Troy, himself an American, and rich, and the third-generation descendant of a Cousin Jack. His wife, Elizabeth, was the heiress of the Pallas estate, one of the biggest in West Penwith; so the word of either would count for something. And Jimmy Troy's word was that hog trading at the Carrington level involved tens if not hundreds of thousands of carcases. So it was all paperwork — and thus eminently respectable.

He was one of the first to call on his compatriot, who was his junior by a mere six years. The leaders of local society imagined it was to appraise him; in fact, Troy's purpose was to *apprise* him of the forthcoming ordeal of Trial by Scrutiny and Sneer, which he, too, had once endured, back in the nineties. His method of 'calling' was hardly orthodox, except by the mores of that commercial society in which both men had been raised. Troy walked straight up to him in the saloon bar at the Angel, slapped him on the back, gave out his own name, and proffered a Havana cigar. His accent revealed his origins and so, within minutes, they were agreeing about English beer, crazy plumbing, and lunatic systems of property conveyance.

When Troy got round to his warning, Carrington took it with a laugh. "I'm well used to that, ol' feller," he said. "America isn't so different. Why, I've known men whose fathers made a fortune selling bad whiskey to Injuns yet their wives would claim to sniff pork when they just heard my voice in the next room. Society cultivates and refines, they say. Well, I'm just amazed at the speed of the operation."

Jimmy chuckled. "Yessirree! We sure do things quicker in America. Here in Cornwall, if your ancestor was a farmhand, it takes at least three generations to forget him. But in New York the putting-on of mourning is an universal way to forget an inconvenient ancestor. And in Pittsburgh they go one better. Why, I knew ancestors who were still slaving daily at the board of trade, but who were already completely forgotten by their own sons and daughters across the river in Allegheny. By the way, a 'board of trade' is called a 'commodity exchange' over here. But I wouldn't bother to translate. 'Board of trade' sounds much more respectable." He winked.

The two men, starting with so much in common, got on famously. As John told his daughter later that evening, "I took to him like a Yankee takes to pie, honey. Anyway, the long and short of it is that he and his wife, Elizabeth, are hiring the old Coinage Hall for the night, just up the street here, and giving a ball to welcome us and introduce us to local society. Isn't that swell of them?"

"When?" Leah asked.

"Oh, he didn't say exactly. Sometime next week, I guess."

"Next *week?*" she echoed in horror. "But I haven't a thing to wear. Oh, my lord!"

"Nothing to wear?" he protested. "You have trunks full of gowns you haven't even opened yet."

"Yes, and all in last year's American fashions — or older. Very appropriate!"

"Well, why did we bring them at all?"

"It's only *four* ballgowns, Pa. You make it sound like …"

"Correction! Why did we bring even four ballgowns if not one of them is good enough?"

Having no answer to that, Leah simply stared balefully at him and told him he didn't understand.

"Can't one of them be made over?" he asked. "Your mother was a regular dab at that."

"There won't be time to do anything else, will there!" she replied angrily. "I do think he could give us a bit more notice."

Elizabeth Troy agreed but, since Jimmy had gone directly to the town clerk's office and hired the hall for the following Friday, the 20th of March, which was a week to the day after his conversation with John Carrington, there was nothing she could do about it. She accordingly left her card at the Angel, desiring Leah to call on her at Pallas Home Farm at her earliest convenience. Her telephone number — Tregathennan 1 — was scribbled on the back of the card, so Leah called her and arranged to take tea that very afternoon. She was to catch the early-afternoon train to Pallas Halt, which was the next stop beyond Truthall, where Mrs Troy would meet her. She was also to bring one or more of the ballgowns, suitable for alteration, and Mrs Troy would see what her maids and 'a little lady she knew' could manage between them.

It was all very bewildering to Leah, who had so far received no more than the usual courtesies due to a visitor, a mere tourist. That is, people she had met casually in shops and tea-rooms were friendly and interested; but the friendliness stopped short of friendship and the interest ceased at their parting. An intimate meeting like this one with Elizabeth Troy, in her own home, too, had never before been suggested. She just prayed she would do nothing, even inadvertently, to start a bad report circulating in the district. At times like this, as she prepared herself for that teatime ordeal, she missed her mother more keenly than ever.

She spread out her four ballgowns and stared at them ruefully. Even for East Haven they were out of date. She knew very well why she had insisted on bringing them, just these four — because at one time or another Tom O'Leary had danced with her while she had been wearing them. That one at the sophomores' ball, that one for inauguration, that one last Thanksgiving, and that one ... she couldn't remember. But he had touched them all. She lifted one, of pink bolting cloth over black and gold brocade, and pressed it to her cheek, choosing the part that would have covered the small of her back, where his hand had rested.

Oh, Tom ... She surrendered to a dear and familiar yearning. But she had to shake her head and throw the dress back on her bed before it brought on real tears, which would leave her looking a sight.

Why all this fuss about a pip-squeak ball in a boondock town like ... no, she mustn't start thinking like that. People are people the world over. The same value everywhere. But why all the fuss about the eligible young men who would be introduced to her ... when there was only one truly eligible young man in all the world? No question of same value there.

She returned to the practical business of discarding the gowns that might prove least adaptable to the prevailing fashion. In the end, curiously enough, she picked the oldest, the one that had started life as her mother's, back in those prehistoric days when they still wore bustles — all of ten years ago! Since the banish-the-bustle revolution came in, the only real change had been in the position of the waistline, which had now crept up almost to where it had been in the days of the American Revolution, right up under the bosom. This particular ballgown, made of blue, watered-silk, had no waist at all; so a band, suggestive of a waist, could be sewn in at any level. And with as many, or as few, tucks and folds as fashion now required. Even so, and despite such practical considerations, she knew she really picked it because its elegantly faded blue, with just a hint of green, would bring out the dark blue of her eyes perfectly. And while these part-vain, part-practical thoughts milled around in her mind, a nagging little doubt crept in at the edge — harking back to her undiminished love for Tom O'Leary.

Since it was highly unlikely they would ever meet again, why did she, who had always been praised for her robust practicality and good sense, continue to hanker after him? Could it be a convenient way of shutting out thoughts of Coad and Kernow and Harvey Liddicoat — not to mention all those yet unknown young men whom Mrs Troy was about to add to her dance programme? And even Nicholas Liddicoat, perhaps? No. She had to laugh at that. Nark Liddicoat (as she now called him on those few — those very, very few — occasions when thoughts of him flitted across her mind) needed no phantom beau to keep him at bay; his own odious personality was quite sufficient for *that* task!

In the end she decided that, whether her feelings for Tom were a true embodiment of undying love, or were a convenient 'hedge,' as her father would say, against a precipitate romance on this side of the Atlantic, they had their practical uses in her life; and for that reason, if no other, she would do nothing to dispel them.

In good heart, therefore, she took the train from Helston and, thirteen minutes later, alighted at Pallas Halt. The single platform stood in a shallow cutting on the slope of Tregathennan Hill, a near-rival to mighty Trigonning, on the skyline to the west. Her first impression, as the train pulled away in swirls of leaking steam, was that she had got off at the wrong place. Only the word PALLAS in flaking paint on a rickety old board reassured her it was not so. But the platform was a mere ten paces long, which was hardly the length of a single carriage, and there was not even the most rudimentary shelter against the elements.

A cow, which had been standing with its head over the hedge, chewing the cud and staring impassively at the little branch-line train, suddenly seemed to notice her. It threw up its head in fright and galloped away down the field. Elizabeth Troy appeared at the top of the embankment at that same moment and said as she walked down the gravel path, "It probably never saw a human being alighting here, you know. Usually the only things that get on and off are our milk churns. You must be Miss Carrington. I'm Elizabeth Troy. How'd'you do? And welcome to Pallas." She waved her hand vaguely about. "Such as it is!"

Leah shook the proferred hand and bobbed a curtsey.

"My, my!" Elizabeth said, slightly embarrassed. "There's really no need for that."

To be honest, Leah was a little disappointed in Mrs Troy's appearance. She owned one of the biggest farms in West Penwith, if not the biggest, and was certainly the doyenne of local society. Yet here she was in boots and gaiters, a plain dress of dark gray denim that didn't reach her ankles even, a tweed hacking jacket, and an alpine sort of trilby hat with a pheasant feather stuck in its band. She wasn't even wearing gloves! Against that, however, she had the most wonderful auburn hair, silky and lustrous, and plaited in a single long tail; also the merriest eyes, light brown in colour and brimming with promises of fun and secrets to share. And her complexion would be the envy of a woman half her age — which Leah (who *was* that woman and did, indeed, envy it) guessed to be forty-five-ish.

The road was little more than one carriage wide, moist at its verges, dry and dusty along the middle. It rolled over the smaller ridges and meandered around the larger ones skirting the flank of Tregathennan. The high stony hedges on either side often shut out the view, lending their walk an air of privacy.

"It's very good of you to spare me your time, Mrs Troy," Leah began.

"Not at all. Forgive my appearance, by the way. Saturday is my day to share the milking — which is also a way of keeping a check on my herdsmen without making it too obvious. Have you ever milked a cow?"

Leah shook her head in amazement. In every way Mrs Troy was turning out to be the opposite of the sort of woman she had expected to find. Her own fears of proving socially inadequate were evaporating fast, only to be replaced by fears of a subtler nature — the fear of being dull, of seeming too conventional.

"You might have a try later," Mrs Troy said. "It's not too difficult. I can lend you some suitable clothes." She stopped and stood alongside Leah, measuring herself by eye. "Give or take an inch, we're pretty well matched," she said. "You could look through my ballgowns, if you prefer. It might save a lot of panic-work on yours."

Leah, now eager not to appear conventional, said, "May I ask, Mrs Troy — are you a suffragist?"

The woman chuckled as they walked on. "You mean, do I go around slashing pictures of nude women in public galleries?" Mary Richardson's notorious axe-job in the National Gallery, on the Rokeby Venus by Velasquez, had occurred the previous Tuesday, four days earlier, and was naturally on everyone's lips. "I don't think I'd have the courage for that," she concluded. "Would you?"

Leah had at first deplored the action, but the sneers and contempt of the men around her, and the vicious tone taken by the newspapers, had led her to defend it as, at worst, noble but misguided. Now she did not know what to say. So, when an apposite thought popped into her head, she spoke it without pausing to think where it might have come from. She said, "I salute Polly Dick" — Miss Richardson's nickname — "but I think political power on its own will prove a delusion to women."

Mrs Troy stopped again, this time to stare at her in frank admiration. "How extraordinary!" she exclaimed. "May I ask how old you are?"

"Twenty-two," Leah replied, pleased to have excited this admiration but annoyed, too, for — of course — she now remembered from whose odious lips she had recently heard these sentiments.

"I share your opinion precisely," Mrs Troy said. "But then I was married to a member of parliament for several years — my second husband. In fact, he still is our local MP. But I had to observe the Westminster Follies at close hand for some time before I reached that same conclusion. Is it your own? How did you come by it?"

Leah pursed her lips.

"I'm sorry," Mrs Troy began.

"I'm annoyed with myself," Leah told her. "For speaking without thinking. I suppose it *is* my opinion, but I heard it from a person I despise so heartily that I still feel it to be tainted."

"Ah, yes! I often had the same difficulty with the opinions of my second husband, whom I, too, despised most heartily. Alas, he was often right, though." She smiled engagingly. "Isn't it *maddening* when that happens? Who, may I ask … oh, dear, I seem to be presuming rather a lot upon an acquaintance that has hardly yet …"

"Nicholas Liddicoat," Leah said — and from her tone of voice there was no doubting the depth of her dislike. Nor its length and its breadth, either.

"Mmm," was all the other replied to that. Then she said, "Here, let me take your valise a while."

After a polite struggle they agreed to take a handle each — a symbolic linking that somehow made possible a greater intimacy than so brief an acquaintance might otherwise sanction.

"Is that *your* opinion of Nicholas Liddicoat?" Leah asked. "Just 'mmm'?"

"Oh dear!" Mrs Troy sighed. "I asked for it, I suppose. I know exactly what infuriates you so about that arrogant, opinionated, pig-headed, contemptible young man. Many's the time I have only just managed to stop myself from sending for an axe to sink between those supercilious eyes. And yet … and yet …"

"Yes?" Leah prompted eagerly.

"Well, loath though I am to admit it, he is one of the few men I know who will argue with a woman and take her seriously. True, his arguments themselves are odious in the extreme, but he expects you to refute them if you can, and to do so as robustly as he advances them. And he does *listen!*" Her laughter was more baffled than amused. "Perhaps that's the most annoying thing about him. Other men — who may be much 'nicer' in the conventional sense — politer, more considerate, et cetera — argue with one hand ostentatiously tied behind their backs, if you see what I mean. They sort of verbally pat us on the heads, as if to say that any *real* display of their mighty intellects would pass right over us. So they say yes and we 'may be right' and 'there's something in that' and you know they're really thinking 'poor, dear, muddled, creatures but God bless 'em all the same!' — d'you know what I mean, my dear?"

"Only too well!" Leah replied.

"But not Mister Liddicoat the younger — alas." After a brief silence she murmured, "I wonder?" and fell silent again.

"What?" Leah asked.

"Tell me, what is it about him that infuriates you? Precisely."

"Precisely?" Leah echoed, as if that were a tall order. "All the things you said, I suppose. Arrogance …"

"Yes," Mrs Troy interrupted. "But what is the precise nature of that arrogance?"

Again Leah hesitated. Her companion, who had a shrewd idea what the difficulty might be, said — as if changing the subject — "Suppose he were to lose his heart!" From the way Leah's eyes suddenly fixed upon her she knew she had struck a chord. "I don't just mean lose his heart. I mean lose it *utterly.* Become besotted … possessed … head-over-heels! Not able to eat or sleep! Be turned into a 'wretched wight, alone and palely loitering'! Wouldn't that fetch him down off his high horse! And wouldn't it be a sight worth seeing?"

"Yes!" Leah gasped, not realizing until then that she had been holding her breath with excitement at the thoughts and images Mrs Troy had been conjuring up. "You've put your finger on it. Ever since I met him — which was only last Tuesday, actually — the same day as the Rokeby Venus attack, funnily enough! — ever since then I've been thinking he was filled with contempt for me. I mean for women in general. But actually, it's not quite that, is it. He's contemptuous of the notion that he might one day be bewitched by one of us. He's so *sure* he's immune." She gave a deep sigh of satisfaction. "Oh, yes! It *would* be a sight worth seeing."

Their eyes met. A silent proposition flashed between them.

"Well," Mrs Troy said, "*I'm* a little long in the tooth for that sort of thing. Besides, I'm rather satisfied with my present husband, even though I've had him for nearly twenty years now. I'm thinking of keeping him, anyway."

Challenged, Leah, who enjoyed the fantasy far more than the prospect of its realization, said, "I don't know …"

"Afraid it might backfire? That you might suffer the fate intended for our victim?"

"Never!" Her eyes flashed.

"Well then!" Mrs Troy said.

14 No more was said about Nicholas Liddicoat for the time being. The notion floated by Elizabeth Troy and half taken up by Leah sank into a kind of limbo, neither pleasant fantasy nor fully hatched plot. Their conversation turned to other things. After a time Leah began speaking of her father's impossible desire to know the history every stone would speak if only it had the power of utterance. The notion seemed to fascinate Elizabeth Troy. They happened to be approaching the derelict gate lodge of Pallas House at the time.

"I think I know what he means," she said. "I remember feeling it myself when I first came to Cornwall. Walking along this very lane, in fact!"

"Aren't you Cornish, then?" Leah asked in surprise.

She shook her head and smiled. "I'll be a furriner till the day I die, my dear. I only *married* a Cornishman — the man who owned this estate." She waved vaguely at the trees to their right. "You'll already be considered more Cornish than me. My present husband, who's as Yankee as they come, is much more accepted then me — because his grandfather was Cornish. Don't ask me to explain the Celtic mind to you — just take it that it's so. Besides, I've ruffled too many feathers ..." Her voice trailed off as if she would like to say more.

Leah gave a little tug at her handle of the valise, hinting that she wanted to change hands.

But Mrs Troy had stopped and was staring at the roofless gate lodge. "If stones could speak, eh? Zakky Gilbert — the man who built those stones into a wall — was sacked from the Clowance estate for being *too* good. True! He was on piecework and they said he was earning too much money. So I snapped him up and put him to work here. I didn't care how much he earned as long as he truly earned it — which he did. You never saw such a worker. Now he's one of the biggest highway contractors in Cornwall. Now *there's* a story to gladden a Yankee heart!" Her tone was merry but a sadness crept into her eyes as she went on. "And when that lodge was finished, my mother moved into it, God rest her, and she went about the county stealing silver and knicknacks from friends' houses — which I had to return in great embarrassment. Oh, yes — these stones could regale him for many an hour!" She laughed as she added, "And bore him to tears, I'm sure."

"No!" Leah said fervently. It was the first moment she truly understood her father's fascination for such gossip. Coad's stories and Kernow's had seemed as unreal as any 'true' story told at second hand. But Mrs Troy was not just telling a tale for the sake of it, she was reliving it, too — and making it seem like hers, even when it wasn't.

"D'you want to know the *most* astonishing thing that happened along here — that *I* know of, anyway? You've seen these brewers' drays going around with 'Rosewarne Ales' on their sides? Of course you have. Well, that huge firm was founded more than sixty years ago by a certain Johanna Rosewarne, who started brewing in an outhouse up in Ashton — the far side of Breage from here. She did it to make a living when no one else would give her work. And the reason they wouldn't give her work was that she'd had a baby out of wedlock. And that baby

— a little girl she called Hannah — was born in this very lane, just a couple of hundred yards from here — in a howling gale with the rain falling in stair rods. I'll show you when we pass it."

"Is she still alive? Hardly." Leah set down the valise at last and stared into the tree-girt gloom that had once been a gravelled front drive.

Mrs Troy laughed. "Yes, you *are* Cornish — asking questions and answering them like that. Hannah is still alive — getting on for seventy now. She married into the Fox clan, who own the Falmouth shipyards. If you're ever over there and you see a Rolls-Royce landaulet with a little old lady in the back, you can smile to yourself and say, 'I know the ditch where you were born — you grand old thing!'" She laughed at her own fantasy. "But how will it profit your father to know these things?"

"I don't know. I don't really understand it — not in his case. I mean, I understand the desire to know all this gossip but not why *he* feels it."

Mrs Troy followed her gaze into the gloom beyond the gateless gateway. "Would you like to see the house into which I was married? Pallas House. It's a ruin now, like this lodge. But *there* are some stones that could talk, for those with ears to listen. Leave the bag there. No harm'll come to it."

Leah bit her lip uncertainly. "We mustn't forget my ballgown ..." she said hesitantly.

"I've got lashings," Mrs Troy said. "Don't worry." She looked at her quizzically. "You're a bit of a puritan in matters of duty and pleasure, aren't you. Now that's *not* Cornish!"

"Really?" Leah closed the small gap between them and they set off along what had once been the drive, leading a serpentine trail through ten acres of fox covert to Pallas House. "I thought nonconformism held great sway down here. That's the puritan tradition, surely?"

"It's like the safety valve on a Cornish steam engine. Beneath that tight, iron-banded exterior you've no idea what passions are stirring the Celtic spirit. They're like the Irish — the other branch of the Celts. On the outside it's all humble submission to religious authority. But inside they're seething with fervour and wild emotions of every kind. Especially where land is concerned. You tell your father to keep a sharp eye out for the Liddicoats — especially the old man, Clifford. His family have had their hearts set on that place for ... well, at least a hundred years. Ever since they farmed at Grankum."

After a pause Leah said, "It's no use warning my father about threats like that. They only make him more stubborn. I mean, we do *like* the Old Glebe, but we saw lots of other places where we'd have been equally happy ..."

"Yes, I'm afraid there *are* rather a lot of them on the market just at present!"

"But I think he took the Old Glebe *because* of the threat, not in spite of it."

"He's a Celt, then," Mrs Troy said firmly. A moment later she clutched at Leah's arm and froze in what looked like horror.

Leah followed her gaze, which was fixed on the path ahead of them, but she saw nothing, apart from some fairly recent horse droppings. "What?" she asked.

Mrs Troy shook herself and relaxed, but not enough to let go completely. "Extraordinary," she murmured. "D'you ever get that feeling called *déjà vu* — where you're convinced that everything you're experiencing has happened before?"

"Yes?"

"Well, the really odd thing about it this time is that I *know* this has happened before — finding horse apples here in the drive — exactly here. And I know exactly when it happened, too — a day I'll never forget — the day of my first arriving at this house. That was in the September of eighteen eighty-nine. I'm hopeless at sums. What's that?"

"Getting on for twenty-five years ago," Leah said at once — and thus realized that Mrs Troy must have gone through her first two husbands in five years or less.

"Don't think me silly, dear." She let go of Leah's arm at last. "But would you mind going up to that ridge and seeing if the house truly is derelict — you'll see it in the hollow below you. I just get these premonitions sometimes."

The ridge was a mere twenty paces away and Leah was there almost before the woman had finished speaking.

The house was derelict, all right. It must have been beautiful in its day — plain, simple Georgian, a style just coming back into vogue. Like high waistlines, indeed. That connection had never occurred to her, oddly enough.

"Well?" Mrs Troy prompted.

"I'll bet it was beautiful," she said, returning to the drive. "Why did you never rebuild it? I presume it was fire?"

"Too many cross-currents. Too many ghosts."

Leah knew the woman was staring at her, to see if the word had any effect. She steeled herself and suppressed the obvious response. "Funnily enough," she said, "going back to the Liddicoats, my father asked Nicholas Liddicoat directly if *his* father intended any mischief to us if we bought the Old Glebe."

"And?"

"Well, it was quite strange. He got very uncomfortable. He wouldn't say yes and he wouldn't say no. When we pressed him, all he said was, 'He's a farmer'!"

"Meaning?"

"That's what my father asked. And Liddicoat said it meant he was used to sowing his seed in the fall and seeing nothing happen until the spring."

"Playing a waiting game, as they say."

"Yes," Leah agreed. "But waiting for what? For an earthquake to move the Old Glebe bodily onto Grankum?"

Mrs Troy made no reply but sank into thought for the next hundred yards or so, until another bend in the drive, or ex-drive, brought them below the ridge and in sight of the elegant ruins once again. Then she said, "Are you going to inherit the farm or your brother? I'm sorry. That sounds brutal, put like that. Of course, we hope it'll be a long time yet — but that's what we're talking about, isn't it: waiting a long time!"

Leah half glimpsed the conclusion of this train of thought. "You mean ..." she said, hoping to prompt Mrs Troy to spell it out. "Oh, but it won't be a farm by then. My father has plans for a garden to rival Trengwainton."

But Mrs Troy waved away the objection. "Trengwainton could be turned back into farmland inside a year, trees and all. How does your father intend to leave it? Tell me it's none of my business if you wish."

"No, no. He's going to leave it to me, I think. And the money and stocks and things to William. But he might marry again — which would change everything. I've tried suggesting it to him — remarriage, I mean. After all, it's more than four years since our mother died. Or even just hiring a housekeeper because ... you know ... I've got my own life to lead — which he doesn't seem to appreciate yet. But anyway, that's the present arrangement. House and land to me, the rest to William. Why?"

"And might he have told anyone of it?"

Leah had to concede the possibility. "It's not a secret. He's almost certainly told lawyer Kernow because of having to make a new will. An American will cannot dispose of English property. Not in an English court, anyway. He probably told Coad, too."

"So it's not hard to see how such a story could have reached Clifford Liddicoat's ears. And he has two bachelor sons — two arrows to the bow. And you're an only daughter and an heiress — just one target to aim at. Now *that* fits in pretty well with the idea of a waiting game, wouldn't you say?"

15 In open countryside Leah's mild unease about cows would lead her to take long detours through empty fields rather than risk a shorter walk across one with a herd in it. At close quarters, however, that same unease grew into something like terror. The creatures seemed so much bigger when they stood only a yard or two away. Out in the open you might even admit there was something appealing in their eyes, so large and dark and uncomplaining; but here in the gloom of the cowshouse they seemed black, watchful, and menacing. How Mrs Troy could serve such an elegant tea and converse in such civilized tones and then immediately transform herself into a blustering milkmaid, hollering at the cows, getting them into their stalls with knee-thrusts and elbow-jabs that would fell a heavyweight wrestler was beyond comprehension. Half excited and half repelled, and still wholly terrified, Leah shrank against the milking parlour wall and watched.

The parlour had only four stalls, divided into two pairs by a low brick wall, to which the two middle cows were tethered. A narrow passage ran the full length of the back of the parlour, along which a milkmaid — a real everyday one called Martha — carried hay and chopped roots to each cow as it came in. She then took up her pail and joined Mrs Troy at the business end of a cow — not the same one, of course — and soon the jets of steamy-hot milk were pouring in a continuous stream. The sound of it was high and tinkly when the pail was empty but, pull by pull, it turned to a rich foamy thud as it slowly filled up toward the brim.

So that was the system; Leah watched with interest despite herself. There were always two cows feeding while they waited to be milked and two others finishing off their feed while Mrs Troy and Martha milked them. Leah worked out that, since there were still sixteen milkers out in the yard, the parlour would see five complete changes of the four before this ordeal was over. Her heart fell when she realized that, at the present rate of progress, it would take almost an hour and a half. Ninety minutes, trapped in this dangerous purgatory among huge, unsteady beasts with shiny black tips to their horns — beasts that slithered and stumbled over cobbles and concrete in their eagerness to get at their food. It was ghastly. Not even the thought of the beautiful ballgown in blue watered silk and the jewelled wrap in sea-green satin could compensate for *this!* Not even when she remembered that Mrs Troy had told her it was hers to keep.

It did not take Leah long to realize that the safest place in the parlour was in the feeding passage at the back, where only a cow with the blood of a mountain goat would dream of trying to go. The decision to suggest it to Mrs Troy — that she should be allowed to take over Martha's feeding chores — came right after one of the cows had lifted her tail and, coincidentally, coughed. The product of these activities only just missed Leah, though she was standing almost ten feet away; a large greeny-brown blob slithering down the limewashed wall at her side showed her what she had so narrowly avoided.

The laughter of the other two suggested it would have been even louder had the cow's aim been more accurate — which at last emboldened Leah to make her suggestion.

"They don't all get the same ration of roots," Mrs Troy warned her. "The heaviest yielders get more. I'll tell you how many scoops for each one as she comes in. But you can shake out the hay ad lib."

Leah's sense of relief was enormous. Safe behind the barriers of the mangers she could afford to relax and observe. She had to get at least one scoop of roots into the manger before the next cow came in, because the first thing it did was put its head down into the trough — and that gave Martha or Mrs Troy the chance to close the wooden vee-shaped structure that secured the cow by the head while it was being milked. The vee, when closed, was wide enough to leave the neck free but too narrow to allow the head to get out, especially with the span of those wicked-looking horns.

She noticed how they treated each cow as an individual, and not just in the matter of food. One liked to have her ears tickled and stroked as soon as she was in her stall. "It do help she to let down 'er milk, see?" Martha said. Another, for the same reason, preferred to have the point of the drover's stick rubbed up and down beside her spine with enough pressure to have made any human beg for mercy. Others would have none of these inducements but would let down their milk *too* early — at the first touch of the warm water in which their udders were cleaned immediately before milking.

Then even Mrs Troy would shriek, "Not yet! Not yet, you heller!" and smile at the shock on Leah's face. "It's the only language they understand, I'm afraid," she added.

Every now and then Martha would slip into song — the same song, so that by the end of the milking, Leah knew it off pat:

> *As I went walking to London town*
> *I met a young man who was singing a song.*
> *And although 'e was singing, 'e wished 'isself dead.*
> *You could tell by 'is faace that 'e wanted for bread.*
> *Cold blew the blast, down come the snaw.*
> *No plaace to shelter, no plaace to go.*
> *No mother to guide 'im, no friend to turn to.*
> *Cast out upon the wide world was Poor Old Joe!*

"Don't you know any others?" she asked the woman after the tenth recital of this dirge.

"Only sad ones, my lover," the woman replied.

"It's Saturday," Mrs Troy explained. "There's a different song for each day. The cows like strict routines, so if you want to hear the others, you'll have to come back."

"Thanks," Leah said, insincerely heartfelt.

As cow followed cow into the stalls, she gradually conquered her fear, or the worst of it — sufficiently, at least, for her to bend down and give the beast a few hesitant pats, or a rub between the ears, or even, on the one at the end, beside the gangway leading to the feeding passage, a stroke up and down the spine with a stick.

"That's the idea," Mrs Troy said encouragingly. Then she undid all Leah's progress by adding, "Actually, this one's a bit of a kicker." She broke off and yelled "No!" at the cow in a tone that would have made even a guardsman take notice. Then, gentle again, "Would you mind just lifting her tail onto her back? Like this."

She put the milking pail beyond reach of the creature's kick and, standing up, grasped the tail about fifteen inches down. Then she brought her hand round and up, resting it on the spine, which bent the tail a full half circle. "No tighter than that," she said, "or it will hurt her."

Swallowing her distaste as best she could, Leah grasped the thick, hairy, gristly *thing*, which did not feel truly alive, and said, "What does that do?"

"It keeps her legs where I want them. If she lifts one to kick, her tail *will* hurt. You know the motto with cows?"

"No?"

"Cows may be dumb, but they're not stupid. Isn't that right, Blackeye?" She butted the cow's flank with her head. The cow went on munching her roots with that peculiar, rotatory motion of the jaws.

The milk thundered, thick and creamy, into the pail and Martha's voice rose among the rafters yet again: "As I went walking to London town …"

And for the first time that afternoon Leah, in absolute control of Blackeye's movements, felt that here was something she might even get to enjoy.

But her flimsy confidence was shaken yet again when Mrs Troy said, as she came to wash the last cow of the day, "D'you want to go home and *really* surprise them all? Tell them you've milked a cow and there's nothing to it?"

When the challenge was posed in such terms, how could Leah possibly refuse!

All the same she approached the hind quarters of the animal with great reluctance.

"Old Celandine's the mother of the herd," Mrs Troy said encouragingly. "And grandmother. She wouldn't kick out if you had nails like a Chinese mandarin. Give her a little scratch in the small of her back."

Celandine stirred as Leah obeyed. The parlour door creaked — or so she imagined; but when she looked she saw it was still closed. "What was that?" she asked.

"Rheumatics," Mrs Troy told her.

"In cows?" Leah stared in amazement at the bony knobs beneath her fingers.

"It happens to us all, my dear. That's enough mollycoddling — or Celandine-coddling. Sit down on the stool, make a valley of your skirt between your knees, and stick this pail there."

Keeping a wary eye on the nearer hind leg, Leah did as she was bid and then reached a tentative hand toward the nearest teat. She wished now that she'd volunteered to milk one of the heifers, who had small, neat udders and smooth pink teats. Celandine, a veteran of seventeen calves and an equal number of lactations, had warty old things made even less inviting by huge melanic freckles the size of a half-crown. "You're sure she won't kick?"

"Well, as the horse dealer said when the farmer came back and complained that the mare died as soon as he got her home, 'She never done that before'!" And with that reassurance she squatted beside Leah and reached her left hand past her to grab the hind teat. "Like this," she said, nipping it high up between her thumb and the ball of her index finger. "The teat is full of little channels down which the milk flows. They're full of milk now, so trap it at the top to stop it all flowing back up into the udder when you squeeze. And then squeeze from the top down. No — don't pull. That makes them uncomfortable. Squeeze progressively from the top down. D'you know the names of fingers? Start with Minnie Milton, then Long Lauder, Davy Gravy, and end with Little Dido Bone. There!" she exclaimed with delight as, both from her teat and from Leah's, two thick jets of milk went pinging against the silver bottom of the pail.

Leah laughed with incredulous delight and made to stand up again, glad beyond measure that it was all over.

"What are you doing?" Mrs Troy asked.

"Well, I've done it. I got milk from a cow!"

"And now you'll finish the job," the other commanded with jocular severity. "It's not everybody who can do what you've just done — and at the very first squeeze, too — so you just sit down and make a proper job of it." Her vowels broadened as she added, "Praaper jaab, as we do say."

Leah steeled herself to resume her position on the stool and reach again for one of those repulsive teats. But the reward of a rich stream of milk was more than recompense for that unpleasantness and soon the warts felt like old friends as she squeezed away.

"Now try with both hands," Mrs Troy advised. "Alternately, the way you saw us doing it."

Leah amazed herself. Celandine's teats were so old and slack — and thus so copious — that it took a full second to squeeze each one empty, during which time the other refilled itself to capacity, too. So, by slightly overlapping her squeezes, she was able to make the milk fill the pail in what sounded like a single, unbroken jet, tinkling at first but soon thundering into a creamy froth that swiftly filled it.

When the froth rose to the level of the brim, the actual milk about three-quarters filled the pail. Then, though the cow still had some milk left to yield, Leah rose without bidding and, as she had seen the others do, carried the heavy pail across to the diary. This little ante-room was built 'foreanenst' the cowhouse (as she had heard Coad describe a lean-to) and was reached by a door at the start of the gangway to the feeding passage. There she tipped it slowly into a big, wide tundish, or funnel, as she would have called it. It had a muslin filter over the hole at the bottom — 'to keep back the horns and tails,' as the joke went.

"Well done!" Mrs Troy said as she returned. "Shall I just finish her off?"

"Not by a jugful — nothing doing!" Leah squeezed her hostess aside and sat down with as much eagerness as she had earlier shown reluctance for the selfsame task. After a while she broke spontaneously into song — "The lambs on the green hills they sport and they play-ay …" Its elegaic rhythm fitted well with the pace of her work.

As the flow of milk began to dwindle she started giving the udder a light upward prod, first with one hand, then with the other, every fourth or fifth squeeze.

"Who taught you that?" Mrs Troy asked admiringly.

"An old Irish maid we had back in East Haven."

"No! I mean who taught you to pummel the udder like that when the flow starts to die?"

"Oh, you did. I watched you. And Martha."

"You're a quick study, Miss Carrington. You know why we do that? Because it's the way a calf will persuade its mother to let down her milk when it wants to suckle. You may think there's nothing more unnatural than modern farming — yet we always try to work *with* nature wherever we can."

What with these and other excitements Leah missed the evening train home, so Mrs Troy drove her back to Helston in her car — an experience, Leah later said, she would not repeat even if the alternative were to pass the entire night in a field full of cows and every one a bull. The car was sound enough — a six-cylinder Thorneycroft of 45 h.p. only three years old — but its driver seemed to think it should spend as much time as possible with all four wheels in the air. Also that it would be a kindness to the parish hedgecutters to do half their work for them. They came to a screeching, skidding halt outside the Angel and, if it had not been for the granite cover to the kerbside river at that point, to allow coaches to get to the stable yard, she would surely have ended with one wheel down in the water.

It had obviously happened on previous occasions because, as they descended, Mrs Troy looked at the nearside front wheel, saw it was mere inches from disaster, and said blithely, "Not this time — jolly good!"

"You drive with great ... er, sort of ..." Leah wished she had not started the sentence.

"With great panache?" Mrs Troy rescued her. "I know. You're not the first to say so. I took to it like you took to milking — immediately. As if born to it, you know. And I've only ever had one accident — or one that I regard as entirely my fault — and that was in my first ten minutes, right after I bought my very first car, in nineteen-oh-three."

"What happened?" Leah was beginning to gather her wits.

Mrs Troy bit her lip and grinned. "I ran over a policemen's foot. Even then, you know, it was partly his fault for springing out into the road like that. Fancy thinking he could stop a car at *that* speed! That was a Thorneycroft, too. We've always stuck with them. Wonderful cars! Pity they've stopped making them." She jerked her head toward the vehicle she had so nearly wrecked a dozen times over the previous fifteen minutes. "She was one of the last of the line. Nineteen-eleven. There won't be another so we must try to make her last."

At supper that night Carrington asked his daughter what sort of day she'd had. "Oh, you know ..." she replied vaguely. "We strolled around and chatted about this and that, and ... picked a super-dooper gown for me to wear."

Somehow she didn't think it would please her father to know she had the makings of a pretty good milkmaid, too. Instead, she regaled him with all the if-stones-could-talk stories Mrs Troy had told her — which left him pretty satisfied that the day had not been wasted.

Later, alone in her bedroom, she drew the curtains tight, spread her dressing gown over the cracks in the old oak door, hung her nightcap over the keyhole of the connecting door to her father's room, and than sat down before her looking glass to examine her breasts in the light of today's discoveries. The nipple was like the teat, that was clear enough, but if there were tubes and channels and things like that behind it — like the milk-collecting tubes in the cow — she could not find them.

Then, growing bored at finding so little correspondence, she fell into a more abstract reverie, wondering what it would be like, one day, to have a baby of her own suckling there. Would it pummel at her breast when the flow began to give out? Would its tongue squeeze from the top down, the way she had to squeeze the cow's teat with her fingers?

These questions, too, being unanswerable — at least by her — soon palled. Then she thought of all the steps that must inevitably come between that moment and this — the balls, the picnics, the dinners, the theatre outings, the shy advances, the letters, the first kisses, the first tame intimacies, the Question, the Engagement ... oh, the long *longueur* of the Engagement ... She could not even complete the list in her mind, much less contemplate its application to her life over the years to come.

"There should be an annual lottery and we should make do with whatever we get," she told her image in the mirror.

The image shook her head in fervent agreement.

"Except that one might then end up with ..." She had intended saying 'Nicholas Liddicoat' but the name that popped out — to the obvious surprise of her image — was "Frank Kernow."

16 The weather the Carringtons had expected to find in Cornwall in January finally turned up in March. It lasted most of that week before the welcoming ball. It came not with snow but with subzero temperatures and a dry, biting wind that blew steadily out of the east, day and night. It dried the land as fast as any summer zephyr and what it didn't dry it froze. Even the stems of the grasses seemed frozen for they did not ripple and bend as eddies of wind plucked at them but rather vibrated, like stiff rods on strong springs. Farm labourers wore three potato sacks where normally one would do, and the animals in the fields huddled forlornly in the lee of the nearest hedge. Down in Porthleven the fishermen spat at the ripples and declared the seas too rough for fishing that day. Nobody went abroad who did not have to.

Except the Carringtons, for whom such prolonged spells of cold were annually expected. Only weeks earlier they had laughed at their ignorance in bringing their fine beaver coats and coonskin caps. And as for those skates …! But now they were the envy of all who saw them, even of Jimmy Troy. Only last year, after a long succession of more typical Cornish winters, he had been persuaded to give away all his fur gear to visiting American cousins. By midweek the Carringtons were not just the envy of Helston, they were the talk of it, too — because of the ice. Before the cold had set in, the River Cober, which runs through the bottom of the town, had followed its usual winter habit and flooded the Lower Green to a depth of several inches, which was shallow enough to freeze right through after several days of subzero wind chill. Then their most laughable imports of all — the ice skates — gave Leah and her father a chance to display skills that most local people had seen only in exhibitions of motion pictures at the cinema. William would have joined in, too, except that he was still going daily to the School of Mines. It would take more than a cold wind to halt the railways.

John Carrington was a skilled skater, if rather dull. Back in his former home he liked to do five steady miles upriver and then five miles back again. Here, with only an acre of frozen pond on which to disport, he just clasped his hands behind his back and did umpteen stolid circuits; people could have checked their clocks by timing his transits. For Leah, by contrast, to be skating again was a bitter-sweet pleasure. She had almost always skated with a beau, and usually with one particular beau, at that. So the air at her side was not just an empty space but an aching void. Her hands would instinctively reach across to clasp his, left to left, right to right, and her body would long for those accidental but exciting touches between parts that otherwise never touched at all.

All in all, though, it was an exhilarating time and when, on the Friday morning — the morning of the ball — a drop in the wind and a rise in the temperature brought hints of a thaw, she realized how much she had missed not just Tom but the company of young men in general. It was a joyous discovery to make, with relief so near at hand! She could hardly contain her impatience for seven o'clock to strike. And when it did, she was standing there with her father and brother, bright-eyed and eager at Elizabeth Troy's side, ready to welcome each new arrival to the old Coinage Hall.

To be honest, when she had first seen the inside of the place, earlier that day, she had been hard put to hide her disappointment. The chamber was so small. She couldn't imagine how more than twenty couples could dance there — two dozen at most, depending on the size of the band. But disappointment turned to bewilderment when Mrs Troy said that she had invited close on a hundred guests. When Leah asked how so many would be able to take the floor, *and* the musicians, *and* a buffet table, she explained that both the dancing and the buffet supper would take place in the much larger Market Hall, just across the way. She had rented the smaller Coinage Hall so as to try out a social innovation that, having crossed the Atlantic from America, was just beginning to take hold in London — a 'cocktail party,' as it was called.

"Oh, I've heard of those," Leah said. "You stand about informally like at a garden party — except that it's indoors — and all you do is talk, while the waiters bring around trays with little glasses of drink and delicacies and things ..."

"And the drinks are all blends of spirits and fruit juices with outlandish names like Harvard Sling and Bushwhacker ..."

"*Yale* Sling, if you please!" Leah chided.

"Of course, dear." Mrs Troy feigned contrition. "Too insensitive of me! I wonder how Helston will take to this transatlantic innovation? But I couldn't imagine a better occasion on which to introduce it."

She and Leah permitted themselves one secret Yale Sling each (just to be sure it wasn't too, too awful) before the first of the guests arrived. And then, it seemed, they all came at once: Mrs Chinnor, Mr and Mrs Tresidder, Mr Barney Kernow and Miss Pym, Mrs Gilbert, Mr and Mrs Giles Curnow … soon the names began to merge and then Leah realized she had no hope of remembering them all. Her father, however, had a system and was more sanguine; it let him down only once, when he later addressed Mrs Hastings as Mrs Battle. However, he did not practise it upon everybody there, so the true failure rate might have been a great deal higher.

One name they did not need to memorize: Liddicoat.

Mrs Troy had debated back and forth with the Carringtons about inviting them. They were 'not on her usual list.' Back in 1891, when she had just inherited the Pallas estate and was striving with her late husband's sister, Morwenna Troy, for control of it, Clifford Liddicoat, though not a tenant of the estate, had gone about stirring up people against her. On the other hand, to exclude them when so many others were invited might, in the eyes of some local people, give them carte blanche for the mean little tricks they no doubt planned to carry out against the Carringtons after they settled in at the Old Glebe. To invite them, by contrast, would deprive them of any such justification and, simultaneously, bind them more tightly to the codes of civilized behaviour.

And so here they were, creaking in unaccustomed dance pumps, shining like weather-bronzed pippins: Clifford Liddicoat and his sons Harvey and Nicholas. Also, trying to hide herself behind them, their sister Adelaide, whom none of the Carringtons had so much as glimpsed before, not even through their high-powered binoculars.

"Oh, do call me Adèle, please!" she murmured in agonies of embarrassment as Leah shook her moist, trembling hand. "Adelaide is so fustian, don't you think?"

Her heart went out to the poor girl at once. She was rather short, rather plain, and dressed rather for Sunday chapel than for a Friday-night ball — and she was, obviously, squirmingly aware of these deficiencies.

"I've been *so* looking forward to meeting you," said Leah (who had not until that moment even heard of her existence). "You must keep some time free for me so we can have a nice long chinwag. Don't give every dance away." She tapped her programme and pointed out the table where Adèle could pick up a blank one.

The girl was embarrasingly grateful for the suggestion that she might get more than half a dozen names on her programme. But Harvey's manner was quite different. He was trying to mask his unease behind a cloak of insecure jocularity. "Talking of giving dances away, Miss Carrington," he said, "I hope you have one left for me, you know?" He glanced not at her but at his father, for approval.

"Why, you are the very first to ask it, Mister Liddicoat!" She smiled her most engaging smile at him. "Take your pick." She turned to include his father in her delight.

If Mrs Troy had been right, then the price of keeping old-man Liddicoat from playing any silly tricks on them was now clear: It was to take his obviously gauche young daughter under her more cosmopolitan wing and to fan his elder son's hopes of an alliance. Well, fate had dealt worse hands to better-deserving girls than she. And Harvey was quite handsome. And she could spin out the game for as long as she liked. Also a pointless flirtation with Harvey would be a way to keep Nicholas at more than arm's length. There were advantages all round.

"Oh!" Harvey was now mortified to discover how forward he had been. "Put me down for the first polka, perhaps?" he said, choosing one he hoped would be safely in the middle of the evening — not too conspicuous either way. This lack of spirit did not please his father.

"What a tease you are!" she replied, mainly to wipe the scowl off the old man's face. "The first dance is a two-step and I shall put you down for that — as a reward for honouring me first. I hope you *do* think it a reward?"

"Oh … yes," he replied lamely. "Thank you."

Nicholas, who had been standing impatiently at the end of the Liddicoat queue all this while, smiled apologetically at the next couple in line, as if to say that their delay had not been of his making, nor had it been to his liking, either. Then he shook her hand, once, and briefly, and muttered something indecipherable before moving swiftly away.

As Leah was being introduced to that next couple — a Mr and Mrs Trelawney — she saw in the corner of her eye a suppressed altercation between Nicholas Liddicoat and his father. Then the young man came stamping back to her and, hardly waiting for the Trelawneys to move on, said, "I don't suppose you've got a dance for me, too, then?"

"You don't have to, you know," she told him.

"Oh yes I do." He gazed balefully after his father. "Still" — he turned to her with a smile of relief — "if your programme's full, then ..." He made to withdraw.

"Not at all," she replied before she bit her tongue off. "I mean, I suppose ... if you *insist,* I could *just* squeeze you in."

"It's not me who's insisting. Still, put me down for something near the end. I'll enjoy as much of the evening as I can."

An imp made her say, "I'll put you down for the last waltz, Mister Liddicoat. Since your brother (whom I find much more agreeable, by the way) has the first dance, there's a pleasing symmetry to it, don't you think? And I, too, shall be able to enjoy the evening until we get to its very dregs." Ostentatiously she wrote 'Nark' in the space beside the last waltz.

"Well, Thistle," he said, "on behalf of my father I thank you. Dregs at the bottom. Scum at the top. And nobody knows what's in between, eh?"

"In between?" she echoed. "It will be an otherwise agreeable evening, I trust."

He would have come back with more if others were not waiting to be presented to her. When they, too, had gone in search of cocktails and little things in aspic, Mrs Troy turned to her and said, "I had no idea you and Nicholas Liddicoat got on so well!"

"I can't *bear* him," she said vehemently. "He's quite ruined my evening now."

"Oh ... quite!" The woman beat an amused retreat. "Yes, I quite see that."

Only then did Leah remember that the Mrs Trelawney to whom she had just been introduced was, in fact, the 'Daughter' of the firm whose billboard intrigued her every time she passed it: Kernow & Daughter. So now, having let them go with no more than a polite platitude, she had even more reason to be annoyed with Nark Liddicoat

When the stragglers were arriving at roughly minute intervals, Mrs Troy said they could fend for themselves and so she began circulating her new friends among her old ones. To Leah's delight almost the first people she spoke to were the Trelawneys — Cornwallis and Jessica. He almost immediately plunged into conversation with her father about his plan to create a grand garden at the Old Glebe. Mrs Troy, who had had little chance to talk to William as yet, asked him how he was getting on at the School of Mines — which was a daily topic for Leah and her father and thus of little interest to her. She and Mrs Trelawney exchanged slightly awkward smiles.

"I don't envy you the work that lies ahead at your new home, Miss Carrington," the woman said. "It's a beautiful old house — I do envy you that — but I'd balk at the labour of restoring it to its old glory."

"Oh, Mrs Trelawney!" Leah said fervently. "If you have *any* ideas along those lines, I would so welcome them."

"*My* ideas on home decoration?" She glanced at her husband with some amusement in case he had overheard — which, it seemed, he hadn't. "Well that's something that no one has *ever* thought of consulting *me* upon."

Mrs Troy, who had every good hostess's ability to conduct one intense conversation while eavesdropping on two or three others nearby, laid an apologetic hand briefly on William's arm and put in, "You should know, Miss Carrington, that Jessica Trelawney, it is universally agreed, would prefer to live in a dry, south-facing cave whose one concession to comfort would be glass over the opening."

"And electricity," Mrs Trelawney said equably. "As long as it had electricity, too, I see nothing wrong with that."

"Well," Leah said, "so you think simplicity is the keynote to a successful ..."

"I don't know about keynotes, Miss Carrington, but I have one simple rule. If nobody uses a particular item for a week, it goes up into the attic. If it gathers dust there for a month, it goes to an outhouse. If after a year out there, no one has touched it, it goes to the next jumble sale."

"That's three rules," her husband said over his shoulder, with hardly a break in his own conversation.

"It's certainly worth the wages of three housemaids," she replied at once.

Leah tried another tack. "I'd also love to hear how you came to found the Helston Power Company. I've heard a little bit about it from your brother Frank, who is my father's lawyer, as you may know."

She saw the woman's lips tighten at this mention but no comment followed. Leah went on: "It sounds such an exciting thing for a woman to have done. I'm sure you have most interesting views on the suffrage question?"

"What suffrage question?" Mrs Trelawney asked at once. "There *is* no suffrage question. It's a chimæra, a false rainbow, a mare's nest."

"You think so, too?" Leah said.

"Too?" the other echoed, almost as if she were annoyed to find that her views were not unique. "Who else, may I ask ...?"

"Mister Liddicoat the younger — or youngest, I suppose. I mean Nicholas."

Mrs Trelawney relaxed and chuckled. "How gratifying!" she said with more than a tinge of sarcasm. "Last month I spent the best part of an hour convincing him that ..."

Leah interrupted: "... that political power without economic power is useless?"

"My words exactly." A smile of understanding spread across her features. "Why? Have you and he been discussing the same question? And did he put forward those views as his own?"

"He did — most forcefully, too. Most sneeringly. I very nearly hit him, I can tell you."

The two older women — for Mrs Troy had continued speaking in one direction and listening in two — laughed at her vehemence.

"Well, he certainly deserves a lesson, Miss Carrington," Mrs Trelawney said. "He cannot be allowed to go about the district, stealing opinions like that and brazenly passing them off as his own. Perhaps you'll come to tea one day next week and we'll discuss the possibilities? I'm At Home to all the world each Wednesday, so shall we say ... Thursday? Now I mustn't monopolize you tonight, there are so many people here just dying to meet you!"

She did not say *'other* people,' as politeness might have suggested. Leah had the impression that Mrs Trelawney would only really be happy at the centre of attention. She had smiled with satisfaction and made little preening movements at the mention of the Helston Power Company and she clearly enjoyed her reputation as a woman whose opinions ran contrary to those of the general herd, whether the subject was domestic decoration or suffrage for women. Still, if she had ideas about taking Nicholas Liddicoat down a peg or two, she was well worth cultivating.

With the help of one more cocktail — which would have been two if Mrs Troy had not caught her eye — the rest of the evening turned into a pleasant, if rather kaleidoscopic blur. If she wanted a good portrait taken, she learned, she should go to Gillot's in Penzance. No, said another, Collett and Trevarton were better. As for medical attendance, Doctor Reeves in Helston was very good. Yes, Reeves was pretty good, but she might find Doctor Moore of Godolphin just as skilled — and quite a bit closer to the Old Glebe. He had a daughter of about eighteen, whom Leah might find it agreeable to know. (Some people, Leah realized, did not appreciate the gulf between eighteen and twenty-two, especially when the twenty-two-year-old was mistress of her own household! But she thanked them for their information.) Had she heard about the ghost of the old rector who had murdered his housekeeper in the tithe barn? She had? Oh, dear — and wouldn't she be afraid to go abroad at night? Did she think the business in Haiti would lead America into war? Martha Richardson had gone on hunger strike in Holloway and had released a splendid (or disgraceful) letter explaining her vandalism in the National Gallery. Would the House of Lords reject the Women's Enfranchisement Bill when it came up in May? Mrs Trevaskis, who kept the milliner's shop up Meneage Street, had a brother in Madras who sent her the most gorgeous silks and calicoes and her prices were very reasonable — don't look too obviously, but that was her over there. If they needed horses for the farm, Johnny Tyacke in Carleen was the man to see. The latest kitchen ranges from Toy's Foundry were really very good — lashings of hot water and a very good pasty oven. The French and Germans were up to their old tricks over the Baghdad Railway. You should never put carrots in a pasty. Did anybody hear the rumour that there was going to be a *coiffeuse* in Penzance (a sort of lady-barber, dear — no, for ladies, of course)? Had she heard about the plague pit beneath the floor of the old tithe barn? The spirits of the poor victims were said to walk abroad when the moon was full ... or was it the new moon?

John Carrington caught Jimmy Troy's eye, toasted him laconically, and said, "Well?"

"One of these things goes a long way," Troy said. "There used to be a swell restaurant near the Blue Island Avenue Station, where the self-styled élite of Chicago liked to dine. Before Lincoln got fashionable. People wondered why they never saw me there, but I'd tell them I met too many stray fools by day to want to hang around the watering hole and catch the main herd at night."

17 At nine-thirty they cleared away most of the tables. Six of the tops were relocated on beer crates to form a stage for the band — Charlie Straws and his Ambrosians. It was a sign of the times that, only a year ago, the same seven men had been known as Karl Strauss and his Vienna Players. Karl or Charlie, his real name was Fred Thomas and he had never been farther east than London; the rest of his band had never been farther east than Plymouth. They still played with the same old Viennese gusto, though.

"They remind me," Elizabeth Troy told Leah, "of a story about the Germoe church choir, who heard a famous adjudicator was staying in the neighbourhood and so put on a special performance for him. And the poor man, who had heard some of the best choirs in England, hardly knew what to say — until inspiration came to his rescue. 'Well,' he told them, 'I've heard sweeter, but never louder!' And they repeated it for years as one of the highest compliments anyone had ever paid them!"

Others around them joined in their laughter, for, though they might have heard but a snippet of the conversation, they knew the rest of the tale well. "Yes," one woman said, "I've heard sweeter, but never louder." And a second, more subdued wave of laughter followed.

"I've just noticed something," Leah told Harvey Liddicoat when he claimed her for the first dance. "Cornish jokes are all about real people being shown up in some way. And when a person tells the joke, they tell it, and everyone laughs, and then they — or someone — repeats the actual funny line, and they laugh all over again but not quite so much as the first time. Also, it doesn't matter if it's a joke they all know already."

He thought it over and then said, "I'd never noticed that, but I suppose we do. Call it good housekeeping — roast meat on Sunday, cold cuts on Monday. Nothing wasted." He laughed and seemed about to tell her more but then thought better of it.

"What?" she urged. He was a good dancer. Not a leg-maniac, as they say, full of brilliant, flashy steps, but an easy mover who made the gyrations seem natural.

"Nothing," he replied. "The words 'nothing wasted' brought another joke to mind but it's not repeatable."

"It can't be a *Cornish* joke, then."

He shook his head. "It is but it's also rather … what shall I say? Rather agricultural."

Other young men she had known, even Tom O'Leary in the early days, would by now be desperate with embarrassment and looking for any excuse to change the subject. But not Harvey, it seemed. The way he told her it was not suitable was as calm as if he'd said it would take rather too long to tell on this occasion. She was annoyed at being excluded, of course, and yet she also admired his calm manner and sense of authority, which, in a subtle way, did *not* exclude her. She could not say how, but it made her feel a party to his decision.

At any rate, it emboldened her to say, "I'm not as easily shocked as you may suppose, Mister Liddicoat. And we are living in the twentieth century, after all."

"Well," he said jovially, "it's a true story about local people. A couple of farmers living in Sithney parish." She thought he was going to relent and tell her after all, but he went on, "So it won't spoil for keeping and it'll be funnier when you know them. Anyway, we're supposed to be talking about the weather, the season, the last hunt, this wonderful music, and other important things like that."

"Oh — *important* things, eh?" she said. "So tell me about your brother, then." She was pleased to see that this change of subject — or this *particular* change of subject — did not amuse him. "Is he an universal misogynist or has he a particular down on me?"

There was a long, thoughtful pause before he replied, "I've known Nicholas for twenty-three years — naturally — and I still don't understand him."

"Well, that's not much of an answer. In any case, I didn't ask for a complete litany of his character — just whether he's down on all women or only little old me?"

Another pause for thought. "I think he sees women as a threat," he said awkwardly. "All women. I really feel disloyal, talking about him like this. Why don't you ask him directly? Did you put him down for a dance?"

"Yes. Didn't he tell you?"

"No. He seemed pretty indignant to me. I thought you'd probably said no."

"Well, I didn't. I couldn't. Not once he'd made it quite clear how much it cost him and his pride even to ask for it. What *did* he say to you, then — I noticed he said *something?* Or is that also quite unrepeatable?"

He chuckled. "It is, I'm afraid. May I ask — what dance did you give him?"

Rather than answer him, she took up his earlier remark: "He sees women as a threat to *what?*"

"To his life."

"Good heavens!" She stared at him in shocked amazement. He was *very* handsome. It was going to be easy to keep his father contented with the progress of an imagined affaire.

"I don't mean to his physical life, but to his plans. To the way he's planned his own life. He's a great admirer of Jimmy Troy — and of your father, too, I may say."

"Something about Americans?"

"No. Something about self-made men. Nicholas wants to be rich, too, one day — self-made rich."

"But my father *inherited* money from his father. So did Mister Troy, I believe."

"Yes, but they didn't just sit back and spend it. Whatever they inherited, they doubled and doubled and doubled again. Nicholas won't inherit a bean, but he still thinks he can make his fortune. And women offer him nothing but distraction, he believes.

There now! I don't think I'm being disloyal because he makes no secret of that much."

"What's he going to make his fortune *at?*" she asked next.

"Who?"

"Nicholas."

"Good heavens!" He made his surprise seem genuine. "Are we *still* talking about him?"

"Okay!" She laughed, and butted his shoulder with her forehead — an unladylike gesture that did not go unnoticed by others in that assembly.

Especially not by Harvey's father, who had hardly taken his eyes off the young couple since they had stepped onto the floor. William, who had not yet engaged himself for any among the first set of dances, was standing at his side, watching Nicholas, who was dancing with his sister, Adèle. They seemed to be getting on so well together, like true friends, the way a brother and sister ought to get on once they'd passed out of their argumentative teens. Of course, Adèle, being the youngest, had never taken over the role of mother to the family when Mrs Liddicoat died, which was eight years ago now. She'd have been only ten then. Ten or eleven.

"Proper 'ansum couple," Liddicoat said, still watching Leah and his son.

"Yes," William agreed.

"How isn't your old man sending you to farming college, then?" he went on.

"*Farming* college?" The abruptness of the question took William by surprise.

" 'Es. Mining won't be no good to 'ee over to the Old Glebe. There's no minerals left under they lands. But I suppose you do already know that?"

"I don't suppose there's much left under Grankum, either, sir," William replied. "But it doesn't seem to impede Nicholas in his studies."

" 'Es, but then he isn't going to farm Grankum, is he!" the old man said.

"Ah!" William pretended the point left him baffled, though he knew very well what the other was angling to be told. "Talking of Nicholas, sir — I was wondering … where does he hope to find employment in mining?"

"Why, anywhere. Australey, Americay, Russia ... there's deep mining all over the world."

"He seems to spend a lot of time much closer to home than that — on the old halvans around Wheal Fortune."

"Oh?" Liddicoat's focus was suddenly vague. "I never noticed."

"Almost every spare moment, I'd say."

The man sniffed. "Studying rocks and that, I s'pose."

"Inside as well as outside!" William laughed.

"Well, what's inside a rock — that's what mining's all about."

"Mmh." William nodded but said nothing.

"Surely they taught you that?"

"Well, the way they *taught* us is to tap the rock with a hammer — not try to get an abandoned set of stamps going again and then use them to crush the rock to dust. That's for mineral extraction, not mineral study."

At that point Liddicoat spotted a man who owed him money, so he said, and went to bend his ear.

William noticed a rather pretty girl, a latecomer he guessed, not dancing, and went to ask her for the next one, a quickstep. Her name was Blanche Curnow. Her mother gave the nod and she accepted. He introduced himself to the woman, expecting her to ask him a few questions, but she merely suggested that he and her daughter should go and stand near the edge of the floor, ready for their dance to begin.

Blanche was eighteen. She lived at Chynoweth Hall, near Culdrose Downs, to the southeast of Helston. Her father was one of Cornwall's biggest wholesalers, mostly in groceries, fresh vegetables, and meat. She was the fourth of five brothers and sisters. Her younger sister, Phillippa, was in disgrace this evening because, being only fifteen, she was too young to attend tonight, and she had kicked a panel out of the door in her anger. Phillippa had the most ferocious temper though she was an awfully sweet girl, really. One shouldn't say 'awfully' ... Was she talking too much? Her elder sister, Gillian, who would be ... well, one shouldn't be too-too exact after twenty-one, should one ... anyway, she'd got married two years ago and was expecting a happy event quite soon. Honestly, you'd think she was the only woman who ever managed it! She'd be furious at missing this ball, which was going to be the event of the season. She *was* talking too much, wasn't she!

William assured her it was not so.

"You go to the Camborne School of Mines, don't you," she said. "My elder brother, Maurice, left there last summer, you know. He did electrical engineering and now he works for the North Cornwall Power Company. How d'you like Cornwall? A bit of a change after America, I should think."

"I like the School of Mines. Cornish mining still leads the world, you know."

Their dance began. They took to the floor at once.

"What about Sithney and the Old Glebe?" Blanche asked.

"I'm fond of that, too," he told her. "It's like a textbook of Cornish geology for me — the landscape at our doorstep. But I can't understand why my father and sister are so keen. The landscape on your side of Helston is much prettier." When she pulled a face he added, "It cuts no ice with you?"

"The scenery's all right but there aren't enough young people there," she said. "Only Meredith Johnson, and I've known him since the nursery. Besides, he's so belligerent."

"Is he here tonight?"

"Yes, worse luck! That's him arguing with your neighbour, old man Liddicoat. Talking of whom — Harvey Liddicoat seemed to be getting on very well with your sister in the first dance. That was your sister, wasn't it?"

"Yes."

"And the *first* dance, too! She must have made a conquest there. He's usually too shy to open his mouth until three sets have gone. I say — you're a good dancer, you know. Are all Americans as good?"

He laughed. "I'm Cornish, really — or trying to be."

"I know. But you know what I mean. You were reared there. Anyway, what d'you think of your neighbours, the Liddicoats? The girl's a bit of a shrinking violet, but what about the boys?"

"I can't understand how a bluff old farmer like him can have such cultivated ..."

"Don't you believe that about 'bluff old farmer.' Old man Liddicoat may talk like one, and act like one most of the time, but ... have you seen his library? He's one of the best read men in Cornwall, so my father says. Always got his nose in a book. And not just religious books, like his fellow ranters. You know he's a Methodist?"

"Yes, and we know the story, too — how my great-uncle, Honourable Carrington, banned his grandfather from buying the Old Glebe backalong. And now here we are, shouldering the Liddicoats aside again. The whole district's talking about it, I suppose?"

She grinned and nodded. "Even I've heard about it — and I make it a point *never* to pry into other people's affairs. I detest gossips, don't you?"

"Only when they stop talking about me."

"You!" She nipped his wrist jovially. She was very pretty when her eyes flashed like that — even in pretend outrage. "I hope you're thinking of asking me for another dance later. It's fun talking with you. Most of these men here — I know *exactly* what they're going to say."

"What d'you think about Nicholas Liddicoat?" he asked. "Rum chap?"

She hesitated — for the first time since they had struck up this conversation. "There's a tale going about Helston," she said at last, "that you saved his life."

"It was hardly as dramatic as all that," he protested. "Though he was well and truly trapped under those stamps. I still don't know what he was doing."

She gave a single, ironic laugh. "That goes for almost everything else he does. No one can fathom him, and no one with any sense would want to. Although ..." She hesitated again.

"He was quite rude to my sister ..."

"Oh, I'd love to meet her. Would you present me to her after this set?"

"Sure. Shall we dance the whole set together, then? It's only two dances after this."

Her expression was both pleased and alarmed. "I think that might cause comment," she said.

"Would that worry you? Do say yes, Miss Curnow. You don't strike me as that sort of worrier. And, besides, I enjoy talking to you, too. And — like you — I detest gossips. I prefer to listen to someone like you, who can dish out good, straightforward, factual information on all my new neighbours, unvarnished and by the bucketful."

She drew a little apart and eyed him warily. "Are you pulling my leg, Mister Carrington?" she asked.

"I wouldn't dream of anything so forward, Miss Curnow. But a little genial rib-tickling, perhaps?"

She pouted. "Then I *do* talk too much. I know I do. My mother always tells me so."

"Not too much for my liking, I assure you. Still, if dancing the whole set with me would cause comment, and comment would cause you distress, then ..."

"All right," she said suddenly. "I'll be killed by looks — and I've never done such a thing before in my life — but if you'll tell me you believe that, I'll put you down for the other two dances as well. There!"

"Good!" he exclaimed. "So now there's no hurry and we can relax ... and so forth."

"No hurry for what?" she asked archly.

"Oh ... to ask you to tea? To suggest we might go to the local movie theatre one evening? Or make up a picnic party of friends if the weather improves a bit? That sort of thing. But now I needn't even mention it for at least ten minutes, need I?"

She laughed and promised to be utterly flabbergasted when he did finally speak of such things.

"And meanwhile," he said evenly, "you can tell me what you know about young Liddicoat. Not gossip, of course, just the simple facts."

Her grip tightened on his wrist. "It'll be the Chinese burns next time," she warned. "Just for that, I'm not going to tell you a thing about anybody."

But her smile challenged him to make something clever out of that.

"I'm sorry." He hung his head penitently and then, brightening, said, "But see here — I won't know how severe a punishment that is unless you let me know what you're intending to withhold."

She frowned. "How can I do that?"

"Just tell me what you're determined to keep back — to rub the salt into the wound. Then I'll know better than to tickle you in the ribs next time."

"How can I refuse?" she asked. He felt that, if they'd known each other ever so slightly better, she'd have stuck out the tip of her tongue at him.

The dance ended but they stood their ground, lke a tennis pair whose opponents were hunting for the ball. William saw that they were, indeed, attracting some attention. Blanche ignored it and continued speaking. "What I think of Master Nicholas Liddicoat" — she mimed rather than spoke the name, because so many people were watching — "could not be properly expressed in polite company. He is a boor. An arrogant, utterly conceited …" She broke off and stared across the emptying floor. "D'you know who that person is — the man who's about to dance with your sister?"

He followed her gaze. "Frank Kernow," he said. "No relation of yours, I suppose?"

She shook her head. "Different spelling. My father calls them the upstart Kernows — but don't ever tell Frank that. Actually, he has a lot of admiration for Jessica Kernow, as was. She's Mrs Cornwallis Trelawney now."

"Yes. We've mumbled our how-de-dos. She was talking to my sister over in the Coinage Hall earlier."

"I missed that — or, rather, I wasn't allowed to go. My father says I'm too young for cocktails. But I could have just stood there and talked, couldn't I?"

"I'm sure you could have! But you needn't worry about my sister and Frank Kernow. I've heard her say she'd trust him about half as far as she could throw him — and only then in broad daylight."

"He was a much nicer man when he was younger. Of course, I was only just beginning to move into my teens then, so I'd be no judge. But my sister Gillian said so, too. He's become very selfish and scheming, like his father. My father says it happens in all small towns. Big fish in little ponds want to be big fish in big ponds. But they can't be. So they get all frustrated and start nibbling at the edges of the law and good business practice and things like that. Isn't it a pity!"

"It's greed," he said.

The word was a new trigger to her. "You say such sensible things, Mister Carrington! Can I call you William? You can call me Blanche, if you like. I hate greed, don't you? The only thing I'm greedy for is life. I want some life before … I mean, I don't think Gillian has a life at all. She's …"

"She has one inside her," William said.

Blanche stopped dead and his momentum almost pushed her over. She picked up the rhythm again quickly enough but the lobes of her ears had turned bright pink. "Oh, dear! I'm so sorry," he said. "I thought from the casual way you spoke about it earlier that you wouldn't ..."

"I just said 'a happy event.' I didn't mean to imply anything so ... so agricultural."

"It offends you?"

She glanced all about them and then murmured, "No. Of course not."

"Why d'you say your sister Gillian's life is nothing to envy?"

"Because she went straight from school into nursing, which is just like school, mostly, and then she married the surgeon — the first man who ever asked her seriously. And that's three different cocoons and no fresh air in between."

"What d'you call 'fresh air'?"

"I want to study art. I want to live in Paris. And travel all over Europe — not staying in posh hotels but in ordinary homes. And" — she smiled archly again — "America, too. What d'you call those flat-top mountains?"

"Mesas? Buttes?"

"I want to sleep on top of one of them, with nothing but the stars above. Does the Oregon Trail still exist? I want to ride that from Council Bluffs to the Pacific, right up over the Continental Divide, like my great uncle did — Byron Curnow. He was a Cousin Jack, too, you know. The family tradition is that Lord Byron was his real father but I don't suppose there's any truth in it, do you? I want to roam the world till I'm too old to walk another mile. Thirty, say."

"You'll be old enough for cocktails then, too."

She laughed dutifully. "But seriously. Wouldn't you love to do something like that?"

"Seriously, Blanche? I think you should ask me the same question — seriously — in about two years' time."

Her face fell. "Why?"

"Because we'll know each other pretty well by then — I hope. Also, you'll be of age and no one could stop you. Also I shall have a profession by then — one of the most transportable professions in the world, as it happens."

"But I didn't mean with ..." she began. Then she paused, looking him first in one eye, then in the other. "Well, come to think of it, maybe I did," she said.

18 A hundred times that evening Leah wished she had not engaged the last dance to Nicholas Liddicoat. What a stupid, *so-there* sort of act it had been — as childish as sticking your tongue out at a neighbour in class. And it did her reputation no good, either. To open the ball with one of her neighbour's bachelor sons and to close it with the other ... well, it was rather blatant. Especially as many people there knew of the ancient hostility between an earlier generation of Liddicoats and Carringtons; and those who hadn't known of it at the beginning of the evening had certainly caught up by its end.

But there it was. The deed was done. The name *Nark* sat four-square in the last box on her programme and to change it now or to plead a fit of nausea (which would not have been too difficult to simulate) would only have increased the attention and interest of the populace.

"Do you think there's anywhere in the world," she asked Mrs Troy as the awful moment drew near, "where one can be truly anonymous — just be *oneself*, you know?"

"It all depends on whether you wish to return, at some future date, to a place where you are known," she replied. "Don't look now but you see that tall lady over there — under the middle window, in the mauve dress?"

"I know who you mean," Leah said. "I've noticed her a couple of times. Once, I'm almost sure, she was going to speak to me. But she didn't. There's something remote about her."

"That's the Honourable Consuela Grenfell. Very well con-nected. A cousin of Lord Desborough. She's probably the only *real* aristocrat here tonight. She was a débutante back in the eighties but she never finished the season. She was packed home in disgrace. Such a pretty girl — and d'you know what her crime was?"

Leah shook her head.

"She vanished for two hours one afternoon *without her maid!* There now! They tried to hush it up but you know how servants talk and how censorious they are when judging their betters. Word got round and she became completely unmarriageable — not worth spending another penny on. So they packed her off home, and that's where she's been ever since. Languishing in spinsterhood, as they say."

"How awful!" Leah at last dared to look at the woman. The 'something remote' she had seen earlier was now translated into something very sad. To have one's whole life ruined by a mere two hours' indiscretion — what a terrible age to have lived in! "Was it an assignation?" she asked.

"No. That's what made it even worse. It was an act of charity. She'd gone out *with* her maid for some little shopping expedition — all right and proper. And on their way back she noticed a little cripple girl begging and crying. So she stopped to help but the maid told her they had to get home and then there was an argument and she told the maid to go home by herself if it was so important. And she spent those two hours — *alone* — getting the girl into a charity home."

"And couldn't she just explain that?"

"She did, of course. But in a way it only made matters worse. Who wants a wife or a daughter-in-law, no matter how well connected, who gives way to foolish and self-willed impulses like that!"

"But what on earth do they imagine she ought to have done, for heaven's sake?"

"What she ought to have done was to hand the girl a card from the Mendicity Society — to which her parents subscribed — and tell her to apply to them for relief."

Mrs Troy spoke with such uncharacteristic primness that Leah could not tell whether she was being sincere or ironic. "And what has she done with her life since?" she asked.

"Been a good aunt to her sisters' children … a shoulder for the sisters themselves to cry on … a grown-up nanny to her brothers-in-law … a nurse to her dying mother (who has been dying for twenty luxurious years, I may add) … and a tireless worker for charity. Not what you could call a wasted life by any means — and yet there is that look in her eyes."

Leah stared at the woman openly now, willing her to return the stare. But it did not happen.

"And what does that look in *your* eyes mean, young lady?" a more familiar Mrs Troy asked next.

Leah gave up with a sigh. "I was thinking it must have been a dreadful fate in *those* days but now …" She broke off and said,

"Don't think me rude but, may I ask — weren't you a débutante in those times, too? Didn't you go through all that?"

"Hardly, dear!" The woman laughed. "I was a working girl. D'you mean no kind neighbour has told you of my humble origins — my rags-to-riches story?"

"No!" Leah rubbed her hands with relish.

"Don't get too excited," Mrs Troy warned. "My father was a horse doctor. A vet. He died when I was eighteen, four years before I got married. He left us with very little money so I went to train as a nurse — at Guy's, which is one of the big London teaching hospitals. My husband-to-be, Captain Bill Troy, was in the army; he was also, of course, the heir to the Pallas estate. I nursed him through an illness. We fell in love and got married. In Brighton. On our way back from the church, immediately after the wedding, he was driving me in a gig, the horses bolted, the gig overturned, and poor Bill died."

"So you didn't …" Leah began hesitantly.

"No, dear. The marriage was never *consumed*, as my maid once put it. It led to a fine old legal argument when his family learned he had left the entire estate to me, I can tell you! The Settled Lands Act of eighteen-eighty-eight will be found engraved on my heart when I die."

"What's that?"

"Don't!" She closed her eyes and shook her head vigorously. "Basically it allows a woman to keep land she has inherited."

"Yes, I had heard he left you the estate. But not the rest of it."

"Really? Well, that is encouraging. People must be changing. After my second husband divorced me — David Troy, the MP — people wouldn't even talk to me. Most of these people here would simply pass me by in the street back in those days. And I sometimes think it wouldn't take much to make them do it all over again."

Leah gazed over the throng of guests and said, "That's hard to believe — looking at them now."

"Aha!" She laughed. "I did two wise things — three, in fact. First I sold the Pallas estate to its tenant farmers, thus creating landowners who were on my side. Second, I married a rich man — Jimmy Troy — too rich to be ignored. Third — we went off round the world and stayed away for ten years, which was time enough to let things settle. Still, I'm surprised they've settled to such an extent that no kind friend of mine has told you the scandal. As I say, people must be changing."

Leah cleared her throat delicately and said, "Bill Troy, David Troy, and now Jimmy Troy ..."

"Oh, you have heard that one, then!" she said with amused weariness. "My supposed motto: If at first you don't succeed ...! Yes, I have to admit that it was quite funny when Jimmy first said it *twenty years ago!*"

"Sorry!" Leah laughed.

"What were you about to say earlier?" Mrs Troy asked.

"When?"

"Oh!" The woman raised her eyes to the ceiling. "Young gels these days — such scatterbrains! You said that the poor Honourable Miss G's fate must have been dreadful *then,* but nowadays ... what? Not so dreadful? Even worse?"

"Oh. Not so dreadful. Perhaps not dreadful at all. I think it would be wonderful if one could just come to a ball like this and enjoy the dancing for dancing's sake — without everybody looking at you with this man or that man and thinking, would she do for him or would he suit her? Dancing still isn't really just for fun, is it. It's still just a way of finding out if a young man has bad breath or is incapable of conversing for three minutes without boring one to death. It's hardly a basis for deciding to marry someone, is it!"

"Well," Mrs Troy replied — being more aware than Leah that the last waltz was almost upon them — "at least you can devote yourself *entirely* to enjoyment of the dance for what remains of the evening!"

"But there's only the ... oh! I see what you mean — I think."

"I mean that, since the question of marriage — or, indeed, of any tender association between you and the younger Liddicoat — is out of the question, there is nothing left for you but to ... how did you put it? 'Enjoy the dancing for dancing's sake'! Go on with you, now — here he comes."

"For this encouragement, much thanks," Leah said grimly. "Well, Nark," she went on, turning to face her opponent for the last waltz, "I'll say it again — you don't *have* to go through with it if you'd rather not. I'd hate to *force* you. There'll be no tears on this side of the house, I promise. We could blame the bruise on your leg."

"Well, Thistle!" He stood with arms ready to hold her body as far away from his as anatomically possible. *"I'll* say it again, too: I do have to go through with it. And that's an end to the matter. My leg is completely better, but thanks for asking."

She joined him to dance in the old style, with one arm at her side and the other just resting on his hand by her fingertips. And a moment later they were off.

She already knew he was a good dancer, from having watched him earlier that evening with other girls. He was even more graceful and confident than his brother — though, lacking his height, he had to put more energy into it. After just a few twiddles and turns she lost a good part of her nervousness — that part which arose from her fear that he might be deliberately wooden and unresponsive.

"Actually," he began, "I have a proposition to put to you. Not a proposal," he added on seeing the alarm in her eyes. "A simple, humble proposition."

"Go on," she replied guardedly.

"It only struck me during the evening, so it may still be a little unpolished around the edges. So kindly bear with me if you will. Hear me out to the end. It starts from the fact that my father, for whom I have very little time — nor he for me, as you may have noticed — intends to make life as difficult for you Carringtons as only he knows how ..."

"Then he'd better look to his locks — is all I can say."

"Goodness!" he said wearily. "What a civilized and intelligent response! I'm trembling with fear!"

Her hackles rose. "Are you trying to provoke me into stopping this dance?"

"D'you want to?" he asked. "It's all right by me."

"No," she admitted angrily, annoyed at her cowardice.

"Why not?" he asked in quite a different tone, as if her answer truly interested him.

"Because I don't want a scene," she snapped.

"Oh." His disappointment seemed genuine, too. Against her better judgement it prompted her to add, "Also you don't dance *too* badly, I suppose."

She realized that the distraction of their argument and her annoyance had allowed them to get dangerously close — bodily, that is. Quickly she moved away from him again but, in doing so, wrong-footed him on the turn so that they almost fell. Then, of course, she had to apologize and put herself in the wrong.

"You only needed to ask," he said stiffly, holding her at maximum distance again. Clearly he did not intend any further conversation between them.

But he wasn't tall enough to act in that aloof manner and carry it off. If his head had been above hers, he could have stared directly ahead like that, into empty space, and pretended not to notice she was looking at him; but as things were he had to gaze over her shoulder — or look away so pointedly that he would appear ridiculous.

"All right," she said after the silence had lasted long enough. "What is this proposition of yours? We might as well talk about something. What sort of annoyances has your father in mind?"

"He'll commit every nuisance short of an action that would lay him open to a claim in court. It shouldn't need much imagination to realize that the annoyance could be considerable. Sheep could strip a prize shrub in minutes. Pigs can root up ..."

"But if they were his animals ..." Leah started to object.

"Ah, but what if they weren't! Animals stray all the time. Not everyone can afford wire. One tap with a stick where it wouldn't blind them could be enough to make sure someone else's strays took a wrong turn into the Old Glebe."

"Lord — so childish!"

"Indeed, Miss Carrington. So my proposal is ..."

"Proposition."

"My proposition is equally childish but, for that very reason, it may work."

"Go on then. I meant what I said about your not dancing too badly, by the way."

"Do you think we could dance just eighteen inches apart, then? This chasm between us has become rather tiring."

She did as he asked and then, thinking that rather curmudgeonly, closed the gap to the usual few inches that currently ruled in even the best ballrooms. He passed no comment on it.

"The only thing that would hinder my father is the thought that one of his sons might marry one of your father's daughters."

She frowned. "But there's only ... oh, I see! All right. But even then the son wouldn't automatically get the land."

"Is that American law?"

"No. Well, yes, it is. But it's also English law now. The Settled Lands Act of eighteen-eighty-eight, you know." She had never seen such a self-satisfied smirk on the face of any man. "You *did* know!" she accused.

"Of course I did. But I'm interested that you know, too. You must have looked it up. I wonder why?"

She wasn't going to demean herself by arguing. "Go on," she said tiredly. "You were talking about your father's wish to see one of you waiting for me to walk up the aisle. It'll be a long wait, I can tell you!"

"I know. The longer, the better as far as I'm concerned! However, to get back to him — his dearest wish would be for Harvey to be the chosen one. What d'you think about that?"

She gasped. "I certainly wouldn't tell *you!*"

"Very well," he said calmly. "I'll tell you. There's no hope whatever of any such thing."

"Oh! You know that, do you!"

"Yes." His self-confidence was so infuriating. "I watched you and him dancing this evening. You beguiled Harvey and you duped my father but you didn't deceive me!"

She had to tense her muscles to stop herself from slapping him and walking off the floor. In an insistent whisper, while she forced a smile and tried to look as if they were exchanging the usual pleasantries, she said, "You are just about the most arrogant, insufferable, detestable ..."

"Good!" he interrupted. "That's precisely why my proposal — proposition — might work. Because I, for my part, think you are just about the most vain, most smug, least self-critical young lady *I* have ever met. In short, the chances that we might ever fall in love with each other must be close to the minus-infinity side of zero. Therefore there would be no risk whatever in *pretending* to an interest we both know can never develop into anything that might threaten the independence we both cherish."

"That's preposterous!" she said at once. "Do let's talk about something else."

"Very well. I'll talk about my brother. If you have any idea of 'playing him,' as anglers say, forget it! He's interested in you all right. You probably don't need me to tell you he's nuts on you. But he's not a patient man. The Cornish for 'nuts on' is 'hurrisome.' You keep it up with Harvey and you'll soon find out why! And you'll begin to wish you'd paid me more attention here tonight — in every sense of the phrase."

He relapsed again into silence.

Once again it was all she could do to stop herself from striking him, or something equally silly. How dare he call her smug and vain and un-self-critical, when he was all of those things himself, only a hundred times worse!

"Anyway," she said when she could hold her tongue no longer, "it's more risky than you think. Frank Kernow told my brother that his sister made a similar bargain with Cornwallis Trelawney, and just look …"

"Quite right," he said. "It was at a dance in this very room, so legend has it."

"And just look where it got them!"

"You miss the point entirely," he said.

"Well, I'm sure you'll find a sledgehammer to drive it home."

"The point is that, with them, it was an *amicable* arrangement."

19 On the day the Carringtons moved into the Old Glebe — Monday, 4th May, 1914 — the prophecy Nicholas Liddicoat had uttered came true. Old Man Liddicoat chose that very morning to 'put the land in good heart,' as he waggishly explained it later. He had a contract with the Helston municipal sewage works and he exercised it vigorously, all over the fields he rented and would continue to rent until 21st June, Midsummer Day. Farmyard manure would have been bad enough — and quite adequate to his purpose, which was to fire a warning shot across their bows; but the sludge from the town works was insufferable. The stink of it was, as he intended, almost the only topic of conversation at the Old Glebe.

" 'E done just the same the day 'is sister tied the knot," Dolly Cory, the new kitchen maid, told Leah. " 'I aren't goin' to 'ave none of that old fussin an' fadgin', 'e said. And 'e went in special-early to the sewage farm. And the whole wedding party had to pass by 'is fields smelling like that."

The new cook, Sarah Gundry, gave an ironic snort. "You aren't hardly old enough to mind the day he got married hisself. Poor Olwen! Olwen Jones, she was. You know they Joneses who do live up Leedstown, by the Horsedowns turn? He's her brother — Billy Jones. Anyway, he wouldn't put up his wedding suit and go to chapel until evening milking was done. The whole family had to argue with him three weeks till he agreed to do it early — three in the afternoon. And then he said the yield was down and Billy Jones had to pay him sixpence compensation."

"But surely the yield was up extra next morning?" Dolly said.

"Course t'was! Course t'was! But that's old man Liddicoat for 'ee. He belong to go on until everyone else do give in, see. He bought a horse once, in Helston market, and when he got 'n home he found two nails missing in one shoe so he put the creature back to the dealer and got fourpence knocked off the price! Cute as a pet crocodile, he is!"

"Can you milk a cow, Dolly?" Leah asked.

The girl laughed at the question. "I shouldn't think there's many round these parts as couldn't, Miss," she said.

"Good," Leah told her.

Maid and cook exchanged puzzled glances.

Leah left them to get on with lighting the range and setting out the kitchen. "I think I'll put on some gumboots and go out and help old man Liddicoat," she said.

"Where are you off to?" her father asked as she passed his library. "Some of these books haven't travelled too well. The damp has got into them."

"Oh, dear. Perhaps if you spread them out on the windowsills? I'm going to help Mister Liddicoat."

"What?" He was aghast.

"I'm going to show him he doesn't intimidate us. I presume that, as landlord, you have the right to tell him when he's not doing something properly?"

He bit his lip uncertainly. "Don't do anything to antagonize him, dear."

"There's bound to be a clause in the lease that lets us take back the land if he doesn't practise proper husbandry — don't you imagine?"

"Oh, dear!" He set down the book, which was now the least of his problems, he suspected. "What's on your mind now? I know that look in your eye, honey."

"The trouble with old Clifford Liddicoat is that people around him have been saying that sort of thing all his life — don't do anything to antagonize him. He now thinks if you ring a doorbell long enough in an empty house, *someone* will answer it."

She went out to the old barn and pulled on her gumboots; she was already wearing her drabbest, oldest clothes for the moving-in, so there was no need to change them. As a bit of theatre, though, she took an old flour sack and tied it round her waist with baler twine.

"Why don't you go over there and haunt *him?*" she called out loud to the ghosts. On their many visits to the Old Glebe, preparing for this moving-in day, she had taken to addressing them directly in a challenging or truculent fashion — as a way of quelling a fear she was ashamed to acknowledge. "Make yourselves useful for a change!"

On her way out she grabbed a four-tyne yard fork, locally known as an eeval. She had some vague idea of helping them at their work, which would not only make him realize that his shot across their bows was ineffective, but would also encourage him in his hopes of an alliance between her and Harvey. She hadn't done too much encouraging of that sort lately, mainly because the Nark had proved correct in predicting that his elder brother would grow 'hurrisome.'

Walking down over the yard, with the eeval resting on her shoulder and her arm curled comfortably around it, she knew that this, too, should feel more theatrical than genuine. And yet it didn't. In a curious way it felt like something she might have done in another life and could just dimly remember. It felt *right*.

Until then her only agricultural flirtation had been at hay-making on Tom O'Leary's cousin's farm below Sleeping Giant Mountain. And that had been little more than an excuse, a token fee, paid to enjoy horsing around in the hay and not-quite-skinny-dipping in the creek afterward. But this was real. This put a spring in her stride and made her heart sing. Mrs Troy had said, after milking the cows that day, "I sometimes think that if I didn't do this once a week, I'd slowly fade away — like the Cheshire Cat in *Alice*." It had seemed a charming fancy at the time but now Leah understood what she had meant. There's something of a farmer in everyone.

She kept a watchful eye on the Liddicoats, father and Harvey, as she walked. They had not noticed her yet. The horse and cart stood horizontally across the slope; no brake was needed. The tailgate was down, so that all Harvey had to do was pull a couple of cubic feet of sludge out of the cart with a hooked rake, whereupon his father, who stood at the horse's head, would walk the creature on a yard or so. Then, after covering a few dozen yards in this way, both men would attack the claggy lumps with eevals and attempt to scatter the fragments evenly over several square yards around the track of the cart. Some of the fragments, she noted once she entered the field, were still pretty large.

The old man was the first to spot her, and then only because he looked around as he went to the horse's head. "Well, maid," he called out. "You do look a fright, I must say!"

"What are you doing?" she shouted back. Thoughts of lending a hand were beginning to fade.

That was when he spoke his piece about 'putting fresh heart into the land.' He was, of course, delighted that his disgusting prank had — seemingly — caused enough consternation at the Old Glebe to bring her out here, though the sack round her waist and the eeval over her shoulder were a bit of a puzzler. "You look like some old bal maiden," he added.

She didn't know what he meant but she wasn't going to pass the initiative to him by asking. And that was when thoughts of pitching in with them vanished entirely.

"Never mind that," she snapped. "You say you're putting fresh heart in the land but look at it! The one thing hearts don't like is clots."

"Clots?" he echoed, taken aback.

"Clots! Clods! Lumps! Look at this!" She prodded the largest with her eeval and twisted so that it fell in two. She was relieved to see how easily it did so. "Even those two bits are too large. The sun and the wind will turn them into prairie chips. *Then* how long d'you think it'll take for rain and weather to break them down? Christmas, I shouldn't wonder."

"He won't have no smell by then," he told her.

"The smell doesn't bother us at all. But we have a saying in our family — if you're going to do a job, do it *properly*." She prodded one of the halves and broke it in two yet again. Then she mashed it with the tynes of her eeval and shook the bits that stuck away again, spreading them over a square yard or two. "Like that," she said.

Recovering from his surprise he laughed at her energetic seriousness. "Why, maid, I've been muckspreading more years than you've got teeth and toes, and if you ..."

"Then you've grown slack and careless," she interrupted him. "Come on now. Don't leave it all to me. Do it properly. I want all these clods broken up and scattered." She continued to break up the larger ones as she spoke. "You say the smell will be gone by Christmas. It'll be gone by next week — and all the value will be gone with it. Don't you know *anything* about the *science* of muck and muckspreading?"

"My dear soul!" he exclaimed, breathless now with rage — and a rage that was more than tinged with alarm. He could not remember the last time anyone had dared speak to him in that fashion. And in front of his elder son, too. "Go on, boy!" He rounded on Harvey. "Pull away! Pay no heed to her."

With the eye his father couldn't see Harvey winked at her and pulled another clod off the cart. He started to break it up but the old man clucked the horse forward and called out, "More, boy! Just keep pulling. Never mind she."

The game had turned sour and he wanted to get away as soon as he could.

She ran to a point some five paces in front of the horse and there stood her ground, one hand resting on the top of the eeval handle. He would have gone on, forcing her to leap aside, but the horse jibbed and threatened to put the cart on a potentially disastrous downhill slant.

"What now?" he asked angrily.

"You may not have bothered to read it, Mister Liddicoat, but there is a clause in your lease that allows us immediate repossession of the land if you fail to practise proper husbandry. Leaving huge lumps of sludge to encumber a ploughed field is not good husbandry by anybody's standards. I just don't want you to be in any doubt about our intention to exercise that right if those clods are not broken up by this evening."

If there had been no witnesses, he might have run his eeval through her then and there. As it was, a trapped and frightened animal, he just stood there, breathing furiously, staring at her, and shivering.

"Come!" she laughed. "You tried to play us a trick and it failed. That's all. But you'll think of better ones, Mister Liddicoat.

You'll make us smile on the other sides of our faces yet. Isn't that the idea?"

She stepped aside then and he continued on his way without a word. He also continued to traverse the field at a slow walk while Harvey was obliged to rake great lumps of the sludge out over the tail.

Her spirit sank.

She realized that he had won. He was gambling that, no matter what she might say, her father would not exercise the right to repossess the lands — even if it was in the lease, which he couldn't remember. And even if he should exercise it, the lease was up in seven weeks — long before the law would have lumbered into action.

She changed her tack then. "I'll give you a hand," she called out as they passed her on the return leg. "Just to show there are no hard feelings." And she set to, breaking up the lumps with her eeval.

It proved an even bigger blunder. The old man had probably intended to fetch and spread no more than a single load. The stink off a second and subsequent loads would add little nuisance to that of the first. But when he saw her systematically breaking the clods, beginning with the very first they had dropped that morning, he went directly back to the sewage-farm, down beyond the power station in Helston, and came back with a load of fresher, smellier, even claggier stuff. The journey took about an hour, there and back.

Leah, who had just finished what she imagined would be the entire task, almost broke down and wept when she saw a grinning old man Liddicoat and his desperately apologetic but enforcedly silent son return with the same again.

Except that it was not the same, for by now her hands, unused to the toil, were red to the point of blistering, her arms ached, her shoulders ached, her back ached, and her feet throbbed inside gumboots that were half a size too small for her though they felt fine when worn for only half an hour or so. Not that she allowed any sign of wilting to show while they were in the field. "My father has asked me to tell you how grateful he is," she called out to the old man. "He says this is a fine, neighbourly act and he won't forget it."

But that bravado, too, proved an act of folly for it must have set that cunning little brain to work even harder. As he left the field for a second time he gave her a cheery wave and hollered out, "Leave it if you mind to, maid. Us'll come back and help 'ee tomorrow." Over the other shoulder, after he turned at the gate, he added, "Or the next day." His dying laughter told her how much trust she should put in these promises.

But they did lure her into a false sense of relief — that she had only that second cartload to disperse and then her torment would be over. So she *did* weep when, an hour later, he returned with the third load, for by then the redness had turned to blisters, as yet unbroken, and all her aches were screaming pains. But she turned her face from the Liddicoats and mastered her distress.

"Getting tired, are 'ee, maid?" the old fellow cackled as he and Harvey started raking out the next load. "You haven't done half so much as what you done afore."

She could not trust herself to reply. All she knew was that she would not yield. Every last clod would be broken into the smallest possible pieces. She was resolved that he should not be able to crow over her defeat at the market next Monday — for all the farmers there today would surely have seen him carrying the sludge and the story would soon have spread throughout the district. With grim determination, therefore, she fought her tears, screamed back at every pain, and continued her toil.

She had never battled pain in that way before — never set herself against a challenge so great that, at the outset, she would have given herself no chance at all of winning. And what did 'winning' mean in this context? It no longer meant getting the better of old Liddicoat. She had set a trap for him and walked straight into it herself. Now 'winning' meant getting the better of herself, her own weakness — her bodily frailty on the one hand and, on the other, her almost overwhelming desire to throw her eeval into the nearest hedge and crawl home to her bed. She wondered if she even dared to break for lunch, suspecting that she'd never be able to pick up the eeval again if she did.

But in a curious way it was her hunger — that gnawing emptiness in her vitals — which helped her win. Hunger is allied to pain and yet is different from it. Had it been just one more pain heaped on all the rest, it might have overwhelmed her; but its differences were marked enough for it to push her pain into the background. There came a point, when she reached the farther hedge, at the end of one of those now interminable rows of scraped-out sludge, when she looked back and realized she had been working almost unconsciously for the past twenty minutes. In all that time she had been obsessed by her hunger. Only her hunger. The pains in her back, her shoulders, her neck, her arms — all had ceased to trouble her. Even now, when she was consciously aware of the fact, they did not come crowding back. Gingerly she tested herself, sending careful mental feelers out into those once-screaming joints, and felt — she could hardly believe it — something like exhilaration there.

There is an unsurprising border between pleasure and pain that anyone can explore. Just try scratching an itch harder and longer than its relief requires. No matter what the affliction — from the minor discomfort of the itch to the pain that threatens consciousness itself — that border travels with it, raising the stakes as it goes. Leah had now discovered it at that upper extreme, though her senses moved in the opposite direction, that is, from pain into something curiously like pleasure.

It was doubly curious because her muscles were no less tired, her joints were no less afflicted, and yet they almost sang with joy as they obeyed each new command to perform. She knew then that she could do it. She might pay for it in days of uncomfortable convalescence, tomorrow and beyond, but she could get through *this* day; and that was all that mattered. She could accomplish this task; she could make old Liddicoat's chuckle choke him yet. In other words, she could safely take a break for lunch; she owed that debt of gratitude to her hunger, for showing her how to ignore and overcome pain.

She stabbed her eeval into a particularly large clump of sludge. "Don't go away," she promised it. "I'll be back."

The first person she met, on returning to the yard, was William. "Why aren't you at the School of Mines?" she asked.

"Half day," he replied. "Or practical day, rather. We have to turn up tomorrow with interesting geological samples. Nick Liddicoat and I are going over Wheal Fortune this afternoon."

"Nick?" She was puzzled. "Why should he help you?"

"He's not. He's collecting for himself. We're in the same group. There are places where it'll need two men and a rope."

"Hang on! Same group? What same group? D'you mean he's at the School of Mines, too?"

"Yes!" He applauded her ironically. Then, seeing her continuing puzzlement, he added, "D'you mean you didn't know that?"

"No, William, I didn't know."

She started walking again, toward the old barn, dying to get out of her gumboots.

"You mean I never told you?" he asked, following her.

"William — you never tell us *anything*. Not that I'm the least bit interested in what the Nark does with his days — except that it'll be a relief to know he isn't across the valley most of the time. I can go out safely without the risk of meeting him."

"I'm sure I told you," he grumbled. "Anyway, why were you looking so pleased when you came into the yard just now? If the risk of meeting him was weighing so heavily on you?"

"Was I?" she asked airily. "I don't know, I'm sure."

"You looked as if you'd lost a penny and found a shilling."

"I found shillings all right!" She laughed and proudly showed him her blistered hands. The blisters were large and white as silver. "All alive-oh!"

"Oh God, Leah!" He was appalled. He grasped her upturned hands in his and stared at them in disbelief. "What ever came over you?"

"Nothing came over me — and nothing will overcome me, either. Especially not old man Liddicoat. He thinks he's so smart, spreading this sewage on the day we move in — just to let us know he can make life pretty unpleasant for us every time the west wind blows!" She broke from his grasp. "These gumboots are killing me. I'm going to put on walking boots this afternoon."

"This afternoon?" He followed her into the barn. "You're going back for *more?* What are you doing, anyway? Putting it all back in a cart and dumping it on his side of the valley?"

"No! I'm putting heart into the land." And she explained briefly about breaking it into small, easily incorporated lumps. "And, by jiminy, I'll finish the job today, too, no matter if he brings another load after lunch. Two loads. Let him bring as much as he likes, he won't beat me!"

William cottoned on at once that there must have been more to it than she was saying. Somehow a few heated words had intensified into this battle of wills. "I'd better help you," he said reluctantly. "I can probably find some interesting minerals in any old hedge stone ..."

"You'll do no such thing! Oh, blessed relief!" She wiggled her toes in their new freedom.

"You've got blisters there, too," he said.

"I have not. They're just holes in my stockings."

"Pardon me but they are blisters. You're mad."

"I'm mad at the Liddicoats, I can tell you that!" She laughed. "Tell me, William — have you ever felt pain to the point where it stops being painful? Where it's almost pleasure, instead."

"Every Saturday," he replied calmly. "Let me go and get some goose-grease to rub into those toes."

"You can do it when we get indoors. I'll just slip on my shoes and ... ouch!" She hobbled a few steps toward the door.

He caught up with her and offered his shoulder to lean on.

"Thanks," she said. "What's special about Saturday? Why d'you get pains then and ..."

"That's when I play rugby with the colts."

Again she stopped and stared at him, baffled. "What is the point," she asked, "of living under the same roof as you? What are the colts, anyway?"

"Sort of junior side. I play there because I never played before. Rugby's like American football only not nearly so gentle. They say I may soon be good enough to go into the reserves. Didn't I tell you?"

"Don't keep asking that. You know very well — you never tell us anything."

He sighed but did not speak.

"Do you!" she challenged him.

"Maybe it has something to do with the way you and Dad jump down my throat every time I try."

"We do not!"

"Well, your imitation's perfect."

"Anyway, I thought you spent every Saturday afternoon with Frank Kernow."

"No thank *you*!" he said vehemently.

"Why not? Is this something else you haven't told us?"

"I've told Dad." He held open the back garden gate for her to pass through.

"Well?" she prompted, waiting for him to tell her, too.

He shook his head. "It's not suitable for a young lady's ears."

"Oh?" Now, of course, she was doubly intrigued. She hopped through the gate and turned expectantly to him again.

"It really is unsuitable," he assured her.

"I say!" She grinned knowingly. "Did he make unnatural advances to you?"

He faltered in his stride and his jaw fell open. "He's a *man*," he said.

"I know all about *that*," she responded. "Was it that?"

"I'm starving," he said, brushing past her.

"Was it?" she insisted, hobbling after him.

"No," he snapped.

"Worse?"

"I'm not going to tell you."

"Then it was worse. I can see I shall just have to ask Dad."

He spun round and gripped her by the wrist. "No!"

"Or I could ask Mrs Trelawney to ask her brother Frank."

He relaxed and smiled. "Okay — go ahead. I wouldn't object to that."

It forced her to smile, too. "Dear, oh dear," she said amiably as they went indoors. "It seems to be my day for having my bluff called."

20 Fortified by a good farmhouse lunch of bread and cheese and pickles, Leah put on her stoutest walking boots and returned to the sludge-strewn field. Her father was proud of what she was doing but thought her mad for doing it; he understood why she turned down all offers of help, both from himself and from others he might easily have hired. The honour of the Carringtons was at stake and only she could champion it in these circumstances of her own making. And she did not doubt she could do it. The sharp, stabbing pains in her back, neck, and arms had dwindled to a dull, all-over ache. Her blistered hands and toes were soothed and reinforced by goose grease and bandages. She was in good heart.

It lasted until the moment she reached the gate. For there, halfway down the field, with *her* eeval in his hands, stood the

Nark, breaking up the sludge and spreading it with expert little flicks of the arms and wrists, making it look as if a toddler could do it.

"Get out!" she yelled. "Scram! Vamoose! Go home!"

He looked up, gave no sign of seeing her, and continued.

"You're trespassing!" She started down the field in long, loping strides, scattering loose tilth before her. "Give me my eeval," she demanded when she drew close. "You've got no right to come over here and do this."

"You're an idiot," he said quietly.

"Coming from you, that's a compliment."

"Thinking you can tackle my old man head-on!"

A wicked thought crossed her mind. *If I were to burst into tears now, I could really make him squirm!* But, greatly though it would please her to see him reduced to that, the realization that he might try to make it up by *comforting* her was enough to banish the thought.

"Besides," he went on, "you're the one who has no right here. *He* rents these fields."

She realized that just by standing there, saying nothing, she could make him feel uncomfortable, so she continued to stand there, saying nothing for a little while longer.

He said, "I couldn't believe my eyes when I came cycling down the hill to Grankum — seeing you all dressed up like the miller's daughter, making a complete jannacks of it — a simple job like this."

"Oh?" she felt provoked into saying. "I thought I was managing rather well."

"I think you did miracles but so did the saint who baled out Loe Pool with a whelkshell. You must be in agony. Walking *along* a steep slope like this one to spread dung! One leg up, the other down. One shoulder up, the other down. One arm short, the other stretching all the time. I couldn't believe anyone would be so wiffle-headed."

She noticed then that he had been standing facing the slope all this while, walking backwards while breaking up the lumps above and in front of him. She had assumed that was merely to keep his eye on the gate, to mark her approach. But now she saw at once how evenly balanced his body was. And how he didn't have to reach so far down because the slope, as it were, lifted the lumps up nearer him. She could have shot herself for not working out something so elementary on her own. Just because the horse and cart went across the field, she didn't have to follow it.

"That's my eeval," she said rather lamely.

"He's gone in Helston for another load," young Liddicoat replied. "I'll make myself scarce when he comes. We'll hear the wheels on the cobbles, which will give us plenty of warning." When she made no reply, he added, "What I mean is, you can go and get another eeval if you like."

All this time he had not looked at her. It galled her, that.

"Why didn't you bring one of your own?" she asked.

"Oh, the old man would *never* have recognized it, would he!" he replied sarcastically.

"So how am I going to explain bringing two of mine here?" she asked without thinking.

"You could offer one to Harvey — say you brought it for him. Force him to stand up to the old man for once. It'd be interesting to see if he'd take the challenge." He sniffed — and looked at her for the first time. And he even smiled.

She had to admit that he was ... well, not exactly pleasant ... not even tolerable ... but less objectionable when he smiled.

"It'd be even more interesting," he added, "to see if the old man would *allow* him the challenge."

"Oh?" she replied offhandedly. "It would be interesting to some, I suppose. Why?"

"Well, if it's not interesting to you, there's no point in explaining myself, is there."

He had finished to the bottom of their final dung-spreading sweep by now. He slung the eeval easily over his shoulder and set off for the top of the slope again, seemingly not caring whether she followed or not.

"All right — why would it be interesting?" she asked, lifting her skirts and striding up the loose soil after him. "You have broken it up very well," she added. "And you make it look so effortless, too."

"It is effortless," he replied impatiently. "As you'd find out soon enough if you went and fetched another eeval."

She ran, all the way to the barn and back, as if she feared the thread of their conversation might break if she were away too long. "Okay," she said breathlessly as she settled to work at his side, "why would it be interesting — to see if Harvey would challenge your father?"

"And to see if the old man would allow him to do it," he reminded her. "Isn't that easier now?"

"Oh, shut up!" she snapped. Then, after a pause: "Yes."

"A challenge from Harvey would tell you how hurrisome he is. And the degree to which my father accepted it would tell you how hot or cold he still is on the idea of acquiring the Old Glebe by way of marriage."

"Ha!" she exclaimed. "Well, I said it would be interesting to *some.*" When he failed to rise to it she said, "Can I ask why you're helping me, Nark?"

"Because, Thistle, *he* would be insufferable if he won this idiotic challenge you issued."

"D'you really think I wouldn't have gone on till I dropped? Even doing it all the wrong way and suffering the most awful pains — you were quite right about that, of course — but d'you think I should ever have given in and let him win?"

He was silent so long that she had to prompt him. "Well?"

"No," he admitted at last.

"Then the question remains," she said. "Since you knew I would never let your father win anyway, why are you stepping in and helping me?"

Again he was silent.

"You could have sat at home and watched me through your binoculars, suffering the torments of the damned up here, *and* have had the additional satisfaction of knowing I'd still beat your father at this game."

"I couldn't," he grumbled.

"Why not?"

"Because I'm supposed to be out collecting specimens."

"Oh, yes — that's another thing. Why did you never mention you're at the Camborne School of Mines, too?"

He was surprised enough to stop, momentarily, before he remembered he wasn't going to react to anything she might say. Respond, yes — react, no.

"William never tells us anything," she said. "He never told us about rescuing you by the stamps that day, nor about hearing the story of the old tithe-barn murder, nor about having tea with you and the Rogerses at Wheal Fortune. As I say, he never tells us anything."

"Perhaps he's afraid that …"

"No, don't say anything smart, Nark. He simply *forgets* to tell us. That's all. His favourite phrase is, 'Oh, didn't I tell you that?' He's said it twice to me already today. D'you know why he's fallen out with Frank Kernow?"

He shot her a frightened glance. Or was it something more than simple fright? Alarmed, perhaps — also a touch amused. Ambiguous, anyway.

"I'm a big girl," she said by way of encouragement. "I thought it might be because Kernow tried a touch of the Oscar Wilde."

He coughed and covered it with an explosive laugh. "You're in the right area, anyway."

"I durn well know I am. I could tell by the way he blushed when I asked."

This time the laugh was both explosive and genuine. "I wish you'd waited for me," he said. "I'd love to have seen his face. He didn't answer you, I take it. Or are you just seeking corroboration from me?"

"If you don't tell me, I'll tell him you did. Then he'll challenge you to a fight — which he'll probably win. However, if you *do* tell me, I promise I'll …"

"You never learn, do you!" he shouted angrily at her. "We Liddicoats do not yield to threats."

His anger excited her as much as ever but this time, for some reason — perhaps because she was desperate to know — she swallowed her pride and apologized. "I should realize that you *are* different from your father," she said.

"I know I am," he replied, softening somewhat. "But how d'you mean it? Not as a compliment, I'm sure."

"I do. Your father never gave me a *second* chance."

He saw how he had allowed her to back him into that one, and he could not help smiling at her cunning. "All right," he said. *"One* second chance coming up."

"Will you please tell me why William has fallen out with Frank Kernow?"

"No," he answered simply, his eyes brimming over with amusement. Then, as she drew breath to argue and tell him he was being unfair, he added, "Yes, of course I will. It seems it all began with your father. He, being uncertain as to how he should go about the business himself — that is, not being a local man, familiar with the local geography, shall we say — he asked Kernow if *he* would kindly undertake the dreaded chore of completing your brother's education. The transition from theory to practice. Am I putting it delicately enough?"

"In other words, he asked Kernow to take William to a sporting house," Leah said.

He laughed. "Admirable." Then he looked at her. "You mean William couldn't tell you that?"

"Could you tell Adèle?"

"She's only nineteen. You're an old woman — almost past it as far as marriage is concerned. Besides ..."

"What?"

"Never mind. Oh, well, why not? The fact is I wouldn't even know where to start *looking* for the nearest 'sporting house.' Good name for it, by the way. I'll bet Kernow knows a hundred. There's something rather" — he shuddered for want of a word — "about that man."

When she said nothing he added, "You agree with me but would just hate to admit it, eh!"

"I'll shake this clump over *you* in a minute," she warned him.

He chuckled and for a while they fell into silence, an easy one surprisingly enough. Then she said, "Can I ask you something?"

"It's a free country," he replied.

"You remember that 'proposition' you made at the ball?"

"Ye-es?" His tone was guarded.

"Why did you make it?"

"I told you at the time."

"Yes, but why did you *really* make it?"

After a brief pause he gave a little sigh and said, "I don't have much time for women."

"*Really?*" she asked sarcastically. "Are you sure they have any time at all for you?"

"Either way, it doesn't matter. I can have the most wonderful, easy conversations with Adèle, and ..."

"On *most* topics."

"Just shut up and listen. God, you do think you're so smart! Always putting in some smart little ... just listen. You asked a question and I'm answering it. D'you want to hear it or not?"

"Oh, Nark, you're so right. Lordy but I'm so sorry. I'm *awful!* Will you ever be able to …"

"And you can stop *that,* too." He laughed against his will.

"Okay. I will just listen. I promise. You were saying you can have the most wonderful, easy conversations with your sister, and that …?"

"… and I keep thinking why not with other young females? She cannot be unique."

"And have you tried? Sorry, I'm not interrupting or seeking to be provocative …"

"Yes, well, that's it, you see. Provocative! You don't need to *try* to be provocative, Thistle. It's as natural to you as breathing. 'Have I tried'! For heaven's sake! It seems that no association is possible between young males and young females that is not either aimed at holy wedlock or at that disreputable union which has caused William to fall out with Kernow. 'Have I tried'! I try all the time. I try talking to women as I'd talk to any man, and what do they do? They either go all coy and simper and flutter their eyelashes — as if they hope I'm taking the first of ten thousand weary steps to the altar — or, like you, Thistle, they go all prickly and aloof and suffragist, as if I don't really have any right to walk on the same earth where their dainty feet have trod."

"Well!" She plunged her eeval into a large clump of sludge, lifted her skirt three or four inches — enough to reveal her stout walking boots — and exclaimed like a Southern belle, "Well, fan mah brow! Jess look at mah dayunty feet!"

And she went on showing her boots while he stared at them and tried not to laugh. "Wrong foot," he said at last.

"Which one? I'll have it amputated at once."

"No — the one we got off on. I knew it, you see. I had this feeling that you might be the girl of my dreams — the one I could talk to who … I mean, the one I could talk *with.* And there'd be no distant ring of matrimonial bells. And you'd put out no signs saying keep off the grass, beware of mantraps, stick no bills, trespassers will be prosecuted, and all that daw-brained nonsense."

She worked in silence for a while. He did nothing to break it.

"Suppose …" she said at last … and then fell back into silence yet again.

After a while, still with no help from him, she tried again. "Suppose we could start on the right foot? Start again?"

"Why?"

She laughed with astonishment. "God, you are suspicious!"

"D'you wonder?"

Her laughter relapsed into a sigh. "All right. Let it pass. Either you're a most cunning and devious rogue or, just by a million-to-one chance — of a kind I do *not* believe in, really — you would suit me down to the ground. I mean, your *proposition* would suit me down to the ground. Even *this* ground here!"

He sniffed. "At the risk of repetition, I'll ask again: Why?"

"I *was* going to marry … I mean, I was sort of unofficially engaged … I mean, nothing was announced or anything but it was always *somewhat* understood that this young man — back in Connecticut — and me … that we would sort of annexe up to each other one day. So I never had that pressure all round me that makes a girl … what did you say? Simper and coo and get all desperate about wedding bells. Incidentally, you should try putting yourself in their shoes one day. Not just thinking *about* it and talking *about* it but actually imagine yourself *being* like that. But don't let's get diverted into that argument. I was saying I never felt under those pressures myself — until I came here. But now my father, and Mrs Troy, and Mrs Trelawney, and just about everybody … they don't necessarily *say* anything — and they certainly don't beat my brains out with it — but there's that insidious idea there all the time. She's got to find a husband. We must find her a partner. They just all *assume* I'll get married. That that's what I'm *for!*"

"And what *are* you for?"

"Me. To just be me. People say poor Miss Grenfell! I say *lucky* Miss Grenfell! *She* may not think so, because she was brought up in a different world … different expectations … but I think she's had a pretty good life. I wouldn't mind it. I just wish it was as easy as vanishing for two hours without a chaperone these days!"

"And the alternative is what I proposed?"

"Yes, but not for the reasons you gave — to keep your old man and mine happy."

"But I was lying, of course." He laughed. "If I'd only known you feel like *this* …"

They had worked their way to the bottom of the hill, or the part that had been spread. They surveyed their work with pride before setting off for the top again. But at that moment they heard the rumble of an iron-tyred cart on the cobblestones of the yard. Nicholas turned at once and made for the cover of Grankum Wood, taking the eeval with him. "Something to think about, eh?" he called back over his shoulder. "See you when they've gone."

She was sure he had taken the eeval deliberately — so that she wouldn't after all be able to offer it to Harvey. Interesting, she thought.

Singing loudly enough to make sure the old man heard her as soon as he came into the field, she strode back to the top and started shaking out another downhill swath. When she 'noticed' him at last, she gave a cheery wave and called out, "I've found a much better way to do it. Come and see."

Old Liddicoat halted the cart in the gateway, where, clearly, he told Harvey to wait. He climbed down and strode toward her, radiating a sort of hesitant suspicion that could turn to anger or scorn, as required.

"See!" she said, demonstrating as she spoke. "You work backwards, downhill. Not back and forth across the field. It's so much easier."

He paid her next to no attention, surveying instead the herculean area she had apparently spread. "I'll bid 'ee good day, Miss Carrington," he said curtly. Then he called out to Harvey to turn the cart round.

"Aren't you going to give us that load, too?" she asked as he walked away. "No, actually, you're probably right. The rain will wash enough of this down to make it unnecessary." As he reached the cart and climbed aboard she added at the top of her voice, "Thanks very much for today, Mister Liddicoat. You couldn't have welcomed us in better style!"

Part Two

Ghosts of the Past

21 Away from Nicholas's persuasive tongue Leah became less sure that his proposition offered a way out of her dilemma. Two words hovered around it in her mind: deceit and defeat. The element of deceit was obvious. In a curious way it was akin to the deceit in which the two parties to an arranged marriage must connive: to parade before the world a love that has no basis and which, in their heart of hearts, they know does not exist. She did not feel she could do it, or not for long — and nor, she suspected, could he. Sooner or later something would give. She felt sure that had happened with Jessica Kernow and Cornwallis Trelawney when they had hatched up a similar plot; something had given way and, despite her cleverness, she had ended up as Mrs Trelawney. For Leah to end up as Mrs Liddicoat would be a defeat, all right!

But even if she and the Nark avoided such a dreadful fate, the very arrangement itself would represent a kind of defeat for her. The battle was to remain herself. Sure, she wanted to avoid the treadmill on which she saw so many others trapped — marriage, children, and domesticity — but not by subterfuge. Even to pretend to be engaged or, more loosely, spoken for, would be a partial surrender while the guns were still bright and the powder dry. Yet what was her alternative? What did she hanker after? She could not say. She felt great affinity for the suffragists but could not imagine herself a fulltime disciple. For the same reason a life devoted to charities and good works, though equally praiseworthy, did not attract. She was not so singleminded. She craved variety.

The only truly contented woman she knew was Mrs Troy, whose children had grown up and left; well, Trevanion, at twenty-one, was under tutelage in barristers' chambers in London, and Zelah, a year younger, was at a finishing school in Switzerland. "Not off my hands yet," she said, "but out from under my feet!" She was convinced that the best years of her life lay ahead.

But Leah's trouble, she realized, was that she was convinced of nothing so positive. In fact, all her convictions seemed negative; she knew what she did *not* want but was vague as to what she *did* want. It changed from day to day. At the height of planning and rearranging the Old Glebe, she knew she wanted to be an architect. An hour spent helping Walter Blackwell check the stocks at the Angel convinced her that hotels and catering offered the most interesting and varied life of all. Tea and a chat with Mrs Kernow, and playing with the typewriting machine down in her office at St John's, were enough to sweep all that aside and assure her that the hurly-burly of business would be the most satisfying of all. But a summer-evening stroll about the lanes, chaperoning William and Blanche Curnow, provided final proof that the wholesale trade in farm produce offered the richest and most fulfilling life imaginable. It was a merry-go-round.

Blanche Curnow, she discovered, was of a similar mind. Her father had taken her around with him for as long as she could remember. He had invented the system whereby local hoteliers could be supplied with local produce, from fish to french beans, for no greater effort than picking up the telephone. During the early years of the scheme it had involved visits to dozens of hotels and hundreds of farmers. And Blanche, not then in her teens, had often accompanied him. She had thus seen a world that was normally closed to women. But even then she had seen a few farms, and hotels, where a woman ruled the roost. Usually she was a widow; sometimes she'd be an orphan daughter left with a bit of capital, too small for her to simply invest and live off the income.

"But what I think," she said one evening when Leah was driving her back home, "is that any girl should be able to get a bit of capital out of her father — if he can afford it, which mine certainly can — to start her own business. Just like a son can."

"What about your beautiful dream of sleeping on top of a mesa?" Leah asked.

She was shocked. "Did William tell you about that?"

"No. I've heard you say it myself. More than once."

"Oh, dear!" She bit her lip in consternation. "I do seem to prattle on sometimes. Not that I'm aware of it, mind. It's just that once I get going, I seem to …"

"But what about that dream?"

"Well, I want that, too, of course, but not at the same time as I want a bit of capital. Sometimes I want one thing, sometimes another. Don't you find that?"

Leah chuckled. "Who was it in *Alice* who tried to believe two impossible things before breakfast? You want two impossible dreams before supper!"

"They're not impossible," Blanche protested. "My mother says nothing's impossible if you really try." After a pause she added, "But she also says there's a sting in the tail. Because if you can achieve anything you want by trying hard enough, you'd better be jolly sure you *do* want it. Because by the time you get it, you may have changed your mind completely."

"She sounds a very wise woman, your mother," Leah said. She hammered the rubber bulb on the car horn. Some chickens were taking an evening dust bath in the middle of the main road. "Get out of our way!" she shouted at them, too. The horn protested and emitted no more than a squawk. "Like a dying duck in a thunderstorm," she said and pressed it more gently.

The resulting *parp!* startled the hens into flight and soon the car was mobile once more.

"D'you know what I think she was referring to?" Blanche went on. "Promise you won't tell anyone I told you?"

"Sure. Go ahead."

"Though, actually, I'm sure almost everyone knows the tale," she added.

Considering the girl's facility, both at making public utterances and at forgetting them, Leah thought it highly probable.

"She was very much in love with a young ne'er-do-well," Blanche said. "A 'scape-grace, as they called them then. And her parents refused to let her marry him. So he emigrated to South Africa and died. And then she married my father, even though I don't think she really loved him at that time. He was thoroughly approved of by my grandparents, though."

"Have you ever spoken about it with them?"

"No, they're both dead. Why?"

"Well, my grandfather's dead, too, but my gran is still alive, back in America. I found her much more forthcoming than my own mother. But I'm sorry, I interrupted ..."

"Yes, well, the irony was that her first love *hadn't* died out in the Cape — this was before the Boer War and all that. In fact, he'd made a fortune in gold out there. And he came back to Cornwall, hoping to find Mummy still waiting for him. But of course, by then, she had ..."

"You know that for a fact?"

"What? Mind that haycart. Oh, don't you just *love* the smell of fresh hay?"

"*Was* he still expecting to find your mother waiting for him?"

"I don't know. He wasn't married — though it later turned out he had been and he'd lost his family in some epidemic. Anyway, does it matter? The point is everyone *thought* he'd come back hoping to claim her."

"And had he? Who is this man, anyway?"

"I'm coming to that. He's our next-door neighbour now, at Culdrose. My Uncle Maurice — Maurice Pettifer."

"Oh, yes, I've met them — at Mrs Troy's. His wife is that big, bony, bonny woman. Mrs Troy said he hitched her to the plough once, for a joke. Sorry! I'm interrupting again. It's a dreadful habit. I can't think *who* I got it from."

Blanche dug her with her elbow. "I shan't tell you if you're just going to insult me. Actually, you've made me forget the point, anyway."

The brakes screeched as Leah negotiated the bottom of Sithney Common Hill, the steepest part of it, by the mill. Frank Trevose, the miller, came to his door and stared after them balefully. It was another lost skirmish in his unending war with what he called the infernal combustion engine.

Leah said, "You were saying something about being careful what you wished for when young because you'd surely get it later. I think I can see the point. Your Uncle Maurice came back and your mother wondered what she ever saw in him. Is that it?"

Blanche screwed up her face, trying to square this gloss with the version she had been about to give. "It wasn't quite that simple," she said at last. "That's the way it is now, I'm sure. But I think it caused a lot of upheaval at the time. Of course, children live in a world of their own. We weren't aware of any of this. I saw Uncle Maurice crying once and I suppose I wondered why for as long as five whole minutes. And I remember an evening when my mother smashed everything in the drawing room."

"Everything?"

"Bookcases. The piano. Little whatnots. Every bit of glass. I don't know why. It was never explained. But I'm sure it had to do with her and Uncle Maurice in some way. But they're all the best of friends now — though when my father beats him at archery you can tell it means more than beating any of the others. There's still a rivalry there."

Leah had to drive carefully among the summer strollers, all along St John's, from the disused toll house below the mill to the weighbridge by the Porthleven turn at the bottom of Coinagehall Street.

"There's rivalry between all men," she said. "They don't need reasons. Even my father and Jimmy Troy. They're both retired from business. They've become bosom pals. They've got no *cause* for rivalry, yet you should see them throwing horseshoes or playing skittles! You'd think they were five, not fifty."

"Isn't it funny to think of our parents having tantrums and emotional storms, just like us. Can you imagine it?"

Leah laughed. "Do you have emotional storms, Blanche?"

"All the time. Don't you?"

"I try not to."

"Oh, so do I. But it doesn't work. Perhaps you've never been in love yet. I tried so hard — I really did — not to be in love with William. But it was no good. Haven't you ever felt like that?"

"Yes," Leah replied.

"And?"

"And what?"

"Well!" Blanche gave a baffled laugh. "You can't just leave it like that. What happened? Is it someone here? Or someone you left behind?"

"Someone I left behind."

"Oh, Leah!" The girl touched her arm. "I feel so dreadful for you. Does it ache all the time? Are you going to be true to him for ever and never look at another? Will he come to Cornwall one day and ..."

"Hold it! Hold it!" Leah laughed. "It's not as neat as any of that. Life is messy, full of loose ends that never get tied up."

"Do you write to him? Does he send you the most wonderful letters, full of ..."

"Nothing like that. I haven't written to him. He's not written to me."

Understanding dawned on Blanche. Solemnly she said, "You made a pact. No intercourse of any kind for a year and a day — a test of your devotion. How wonderful!"

"I haven't written to him," Leah said wearily, "because ... well, what's there to say? We probably won't ever meet again. He'll start teaching at Yale next September. He'll meet some nice young college girl. They'll marry, settle, and raise a family. If ever we do meet, it'll probably be like your mother and Mister Pettifer — we'll wonder what all the fuss was about. In fact, I already do at times."

"Because of meeting Harvey Liddicoat?"

Leah laughed, sighed, and shook her head, all in one. "For someone who told me, not a month since, that she'd rather be an intrepid lady traveller in a cannibal's cooking pot than the happiest married woman on earth, you've certainly learned to sing a different tune! Why must every important change in one's life and thinking be tied to a man?"

"You're right. I must give up William at once." She glanced nervously at her friend. "Will you tell him?"

Leah shook her head. "I think he'd rather hear it from you, my dear — well, you know what I mean. If he must hear it at all."

The ensuing silence between them was filled by the groaning of gears as the car wound its way up Coinagehall Street. When they turned into Meneague Street, where the uphill slope was much gentler, conversation became possible again.

"D'you miss him already?" Leah asked.

Blanche nodded. "I must break it to him gently," she decided. "And take my time about it. I don't want to get a reputation as a breaker of hearts. I hate those girls who just go around deliberately breaking men's hearts to satisfy their own vanity, don't you?"

Leah nodded. "Scalp-hunters, we used to call them. It always seemed a pointless hobby to me."

"Perhaps William and I could just be the best of friends. D'you think he could accept that? I do enjoy talking to him. He can be very interesting, don't you think? D'you think it's possible just to be friends with a man — the way you and I are friends, for instance, or William and Nicholas Liddicoat? What would be really good would be if you could be friends like that with Nicholas Liddicoat and I could be friends with William. Then we could be a foursome. What fun we could have!"

Leah smiled. "What makes you think Nicholas Liddicoat would welcome such an arrangement?"

"Oh …" Blanche was airily arch all of a sudden. "Just the way I've seen him looking at you when we've met out walking. And things he's said to William. And I hear he's taken to attending church on Sundays — to the scandal of the whole chapel. The Liddicoats have been elders there for …"

"What has he been saying to William?" Leah asked.

"You mean William hasn't told you?"

"William never tells us *anything* — as well you know! Come on — stop teasing, or I shall think you just said the whole thing for a tease."

"Nicholas told him you're the only woman he knows — the only woman on earth, probably — whom he'd ever dream of marrying. And even then it would take wild horses to drag him to the altar."

"Oh, how big-hearted of him!" Leah was both pleased and angered at the thought that the Nark was going about the place saying such things. And to William, of all people. Quite why it pleased her, though, she couldn't say.

"I feel sorry for men, don't you," Blanche was saying.

Leah gave up trying to follow a consistent train of thought — even her own — and said, "Why — in particular? Is this your turning, by the way?"

"No. The next. And mind the potholes in the drive, remember."

"Why d'you feel sorry for men?"

"Because of the way we're changing. Women, I mean. We've been one thing for centuries and now, just when they've got used to it, we're turning into something else. We've been like cats, don't you think? If you read our mothers' diaries — women of that generation — which I do whenever they're foolish enough to leave me alone in the house — and our grandmothers' — you'll find very little faithfulness in them. Only a catlike sort of belongingness. Feed them properly and provide a nice warm home and they'd purr and have huge litters of kittens, et cetera. But they weren't faithful like dogs. If Mummy had felt a real doglike devotion for Uncle Maurice, she wouldn't have behaved like that when he turned up after all those years. This is the drive. Remember …"

"… the potholes. Okay. And we're no longer like cats?"

"I don't think we are. Do you? *I* don't want to be pampered. *I* don't want a husband at any cost. I don't want to faint with gratitude when a man asks me to have his litters. I want to do the asking — if I feel like it. I want to do things for myself — lots of things. Daddy's going to have tarmac put down in front of one of his warehouses and he's going to order extra to put down on this drive. Won't that be swell?"

"Swell? Now where did you get that word?" Leah laughed as the car swept to a halt before the front door.

And there *was* her father, Giles Curnow, standing on the front steps, staring vacantly across the lawn. Blanche leaped from the car before it stopped rolling. She ran to her father and started pouring out her customary excited account of the day's happenings. But, as Leah noticed when she had parked the car and alighted, he must have said something to silence her.

"Hallo, Mister Curnow," she called out. "What a splendid evening it's turned out to be!"

"Mmm." He nodded and stared back across the lawn, where long fingers of evening sunlight were reaching into the dark beneath the trees at its edge. "We must make the best we can of them," he added. "These days of summer. The news from Europe, I fear, is grave."

"Oh?" She halted a few paces from them.

"Yes. Two days ago, it seems, a member of the Austrian royal family was assassinated by anarchists in Sarajevo."

"Why is that bad?" Blanche asked.

"It's a spark among tinder, my dear. There's no knowing where the conflagration will end."

22 From the moment the Archduke Ferdinand and his wife were shot dead in Sarajevo, on 28th June, everyone knew that war was inevitable. The surprise was that its actual declaration took so long — until 4th August in the case of the British Empire. Throughout that July people expected daily to wake up and find those stark headlines facing them across the breakfast table; but all that the papers contained were tales of increasing tension — hurried conferences here, agreements there (torn up, of course, before the ink was dry), and ultimatums everywhere. And mobilization everywhere. And jingoism everywhere.

The long days of that fretful month gave the Carringtons time — only too much time — to reassess their positions. William was the first to voice the thought that had occurred to all of them: "We're Cornish, of course," he said, "but we're not English. Remember what Coad said when he met us at the station that very first time? About the Cornish and the English? So, if we're not English, we're certainly not British — okay? It's not *our* war."

"Therefore?" his father pressed.

"Therefore we should go back to America until it's over — and we should go now, before they start torpedoing the liners."

"They'll never do that," the old man said. "That's just scaremongering. The papers are full of it. You shouldn't believe a half of what you read. Not even a tenth."

"What about your studies?" Leah asked. She knew she ought to leap at the chance of going back to America and wondered why she didn't. If both his children wanted it, their father would not insist on staying.

William shrugged and spoke to his father, as if he had asked the question. "I can do mineralogy at Yale for a year. It can't last more than a year, surely? Then come back and continue the practical stuff. And Leah could see Tom again." He smiled at her, expecting to recruit her support if, indeed, he did not already have it.

"And Pa's garden project?" she said.

"Right!" her father added.

William stared at them in amazement. "Well, you surely couldn't go ahead with *that*, even if we stayed."

"I couldn't?" The point had not occurred to him.

Leah's heart began to beat a little faster. Some part of her brain comprehended her brother's argument before she knew it consciously.

"You saw it in the papers," William said. "And some things you *can* believe. Island race … horses and other livestock eat half the cereals we grow here … grain ships will be sunk … all the grain in the Empire will be no help at all. Starvation stares the nation in the face, et cetera. We must cultivate every inch of arable land we have. Patriotic duty. They'll pass laws forbidding good farmland to be taken out of use. Your project's canned, sir, until the war's over."

Leah remembered something Mister Curnow had said — which was perhaps why she had seen William's argument before he actually made it. "Blanche's father says they'll set up committees to take over badly farmed land even. They almost did it in the Boer War. They would have done if the Germans had come in on the Boers' side — because of the submarines, you see. Everyone was talking about it."

Carrington was aghast. "You mean they'd push a man off his own land? They'd just expropriate it?"

"No ..." Leah tried desperately to remember what Mr Curnow had said. "They'd force him to rent it to them. They'd pay him market rent but they'd do the ..."

"Who's *they?*"

"The government. Or some official committee — the 'war agricultural committee' or something like that. A committee of local farmers and inspectors from the department of agriculture or whatever they call it here. Something like that. I don't recall the details. But they certainly don't intend to let land lie fallow or go out of production."

"It's no longer a free country, sir," William added, trying not to crow, for, with Leah weighing in with all these depressing facts, it looked as if she were on his side, too.

But she wasn't. She knew now why she was so excited. The Old Glebe would remain a farm for the foreseeable future — a real, live proper farm! And, since the tenants had departed two or three weeks since, it was now wholly and inalienably theirs. At least, it would remain inalienable for as long as they farmed it diligently, wasting no cranny where corn might grow or cow might graze. For her it was the crowning of all her unspoken desires, her unconscious dreams, ever since they had arrived in the old country.

"Leah?" her father said.

Curbing her enthusiasm she tried to sound judicious — on the one hand, on the other, looking at it all round, and so on. "Will's right," she said. He had always hated being called Will in America, because of taunts of 'whip-poor-will!'; but no one said that here and all his new friends thought Will smarter than William. "We're not British and it isn't our fight and it's not going to be too pleasant while it lasts. On the other hand, we are Cornish, and lots of good Cornish boys are going to get caught up in it. And nurses, too, no doubt. I'm just wondering what it'll be like for us if we run back to America now and stay there until it's safe again. How will it be when we come back and … for instance, face Mister and Mrs Troy with Trevanion buried on some distant battlefield in Europe?"

"Leah!" The two men were scandalized at her frankness.

"God forbid it should happen, of course," she said. "But we'd be fools not to consider the possibility. *All* possibilities. Everyone says the war would be over very swiftly, and they're probably right. But they said that about the Boer War, too. Suppose they're wrong once again? Suppose it goes on and on until both sides have fought each other to exhaustion? Suppose we came back to find that half our new friends were missing at least one of their loved ones? Would they even shake hands with us — the ones who turned tail and ran?"

They were reluctant to admit she had a point but they could think of no effective answer.

"So what are you suggesting?" Will asked. "You say I'm right — which means we should go back. But then you say we can't go back because …"

"I'm not saying that at all," she said calmly. "I'm saying go back by all means, but face the *possible* consequences. And I only say they're possible, but we have to face them. It may all be over very quickly, with little loss of life — in which case, we can return here with little risk of accusing glances from those who stayed and faced the peril. Or it may drag on for years and lead to the most appalling slaughter — in which case we could not possibly come back and look our friends in the eye. Ever!"

Will looked at their father, saw he was all but won over, and let out a sigh of exasperation. "Now who's scaremongering!" he said bitterly.

"Quiet, son," his father said. "Your sister's right — as she almost always is. This requires some thought."

"We were happy in America," Leah pointed out — knowing she'd won and that she'd have fences to mend with Will before long. "And we can be happy again. You could buy that plot in Hamden, Pa, and create your garden there instead. Maybe some dreams just aren't meant to be. We got close but History had other plans. That's not dishonourable …"

"You be quiet, too," he growled.

23 In all the negotiations leading up to the purchase of the Old Glebe, Ben Coad had almost always come to the Angel or the farm itself. On the few occasions when some of the business had been conducted at his offices in Coinagehall Street — two doors up from Frank Kernow's office — Leah had, by chance, been engaged elsewhere. So she had never seen the man on his own ground before. Today, however — two days after the official declaration of the war — she had urgent business that could not wait on a visit from him at his convenience. Besides, she was in the town, anyway, taking up a kind offer from Blanche's father to stock up on sugar, rice, flour, and all the tinned foods she could manage. One sight of the Curnows' own larders — and cellars and lofts — had convinced her the situation was grave. If a wholesaler of food felt he had to take such precautions …

She was shown in to Coad's office, which was little larger than a cubbyhole, straight away. He was standing at the open window trying vainly to fan away the cigar smoke and introduce some fresh air.

"Good afternoon, Mister Coad," she said. "Please don't go to that trouble on *my* account. I quite like the manly smell of a good cigar."

"So do I, Miss Carrington," he replied, climbing down off his footstool and coming round his desk to help her into a seat. "But I was dealing with *these.*" He grimaced as he took out a pack of cheap cheroots, no larger than cigarettes. "One step above chewing 'baccy. Ghastly gaspers, I call them, but they're kind to the purse." Then, seeing her eye them curiously, he added, "Care to try one?"

She recoiled with an embarrassed laugh, sat down, had second thoughts, and, reaching forth a hand, said, "Yes, well, why not? As they come so highly recommended!"

He was as surprised as she but he lit hers — and relit his — without comment.

"I do smoke a very occasional cigarette," she admitted as he went back to his side of the desk. "But never one of these things." She held her mouth open and let the blue, acrid smoke curl its way up her face. It stung her tongue and made the saliva pour. But the aroma, once it was diluted with enough air, was pleasantly stimulating to her.

It created the right atmosphere in the metaphorical sense, too, for this was a business call if ever there was one — the most important call of her life, she calculated. "Haven't seen much of you lately," she said, knowing that, in business, one never got directly to the point.

"Well ..." He seemed surprised she should comment on it. "The sale went through some time ago. Your tenants vacated without fuss — I'm surprised old Liddicoat went so quietly, but there it is. Not that I'd set too much store by it." He chuckled. "I heard about the incident with the sewage sludge, by the way. I knew he'd play that card once too often. You trumped him pretty well."

"I simply called his bluff," she said modestly. "He didn't know it, thank heavens, but he should have raised the bid instead of folding. My hand was pretty ..." She took off her gloves, looked at her hands, and changed the sense of what she had started to say. "In fact, my hands weren't at all pretty. They've only just recovered. Feel that callus!"

He looked at her askance.

"Go on!" she urged. "I'm not ashamed of it. I earned it."

Gingerly he felt the hardened circle of skin where blisters had once wept. "Impressive," he said.

"I daresay I'll earn a good many more in the months to come," she added casually.

"Oh?"

"Yes. There's no question of turning the Old Glebe into a garden now. We'll be farming every square inch of it."

"Ah!" Understanding dawned in his eyes. "You want me to draw up new leases for your tenants — or your former tenants. Is that it?"

She shook her head. "We shall be farming it ourselves."

He tried to say something but no words came, except a cautious: "Yes?"

"Yes. We could either put it all under wheat and barley. Or half of it, with store cattle on the other half. Or a small dairy herd — up to a dozen milkers and their followers. Would we need to keep a bull for that number?"

This deluge of possibilities took him aback. He answered the easy one first: "There are lots of bulls all around you. Good ones, too — the ones that are at stud, anyway. There's John Carter down to Gwavas. Or Harold ..."

"So you think dairying is the thing?" she broke in eagerly.

"Ho-back! I didn't say that."

"It would be the *selfish* thing," she mused, as if talking more to herself than to him.

"How so?"

"Well, if we went in for cereals, we'd have to spread fertilizer to keep the land in good heart — because my father does want to create this garden, as soon as we've won the war. Or done our bit to help win it."

He scratched his chin. "Which you wouldn't have to do with cattle on pasture — except for lime. You'd still have to spread lime or the land would turn acidic."

"Quite," she said confidently. "We've still got some left over from the rebuilding."

He laughed, thinking she was joking.

She laughed too, pretending she was joking; she also made a note to look up this 'lime' stuff as soon as possible. It was obviously not the same as what the builders used.

"I thought you might go back to America," he said. "Wouldn't that be the sensible thing to do? You could let the farm again, just until it's over. It'll only last a few months they say."

"It never even crossed our minds," she told him unblinkingly. "How could we look each other in the face if we turned tail and ran like that — let alone all our good friends here once we did return. No — we're Cornish and we'll stand shoulder-to-shoulder with our fellows."

"Is Will going to volunteer?" he asked.

The question floored her. In all the permutations and possibilities she had considered since threats of war had started to loom, that had — truthfully, this time — never even crossed her mind.

"What would he do, I wonder?" she asked — meaning what would be his choice?

Coad took it more literally. "Miners ... sappers," he said. "He could join the Royal Engineers — dig tunnels under enemy strongholds, fill them with explosives, *bang!*" He laughed.

The world was full of overnight military savants.

"I'd go myself," he said, "like a shot — if only my father were well enough to come out of retirement and take up the reins once more. Poor old man!"

The world was also full of people with excellent reasons for doing everything possible to help win the war, except enlist. And now, if she had anything to do with it, Will would be among them, too. Staying here and farming the Old Glebe, when they could so easily go back 'home' to America, was sacrifice enough for the Carringtons to make. But what a coward she would think poor Ben Coad, if she had no brother herself!

"We must keep the home fires burning," he said.

"And the home fields growing," she put in. "And the home herds milking. Wellington said the war against France was won on the playing fields of Eton. Well, I think this war against Germany and Austria will be quite different. It'll be won on the *working* fields of Cornwall!"

"That's good!" he said admiringly and he took up a pencil to write it down.

"So we'll be looking to build up a milking herd at the Old Glebe," she went on. "I hope we can count on your skill as an auctioneer, Mister Coad — your ability to judge a good heifer from a bad one? Perhaps waiving your usual commission?"

He laughed and shook his head. "I'd be the most *un*skilled auctioneer in Cornwall if I did that, Miss Carrington."

"Well ..." She grinned. "Perhaps waiving it altogether *is* asking a bit much."

Still he shook his head. "Tell you what I will do, though," he said, "as long as you'll give me your word you'll never breathe it to a living soul?"

She nodded. "You have it."

"It's in your own interest not to tell, anyway," he added. "If you do as I suggest, you'll start off with a high reputation as a judge of good dairy cattle."

She stubbed out the remaining half-inch of her cheroot and rubbed her hands eagerly. "I can't wait!"

"You'll have to, I'm afraid — till next Wednesday, anyway. You just missed yesterday's auctions. But you come to the market at about eleven next Wednesday. That's when we sell first-and second-calf heifers with their calves still on them. There should be five or six to go in the ring. And I'll tip you the wink if there's anything good coming up in the cow sales after."

"What's before eleven?" she asked.

"Pigs and sheep, mostly for slaughter. You'll probably want a pig or two later, but build the dairy herd first — that's my advice. Anyway, when I'm selling the heifers, I'll …"

"What about sheep?"

He shook his head. "Not with a neighbour like old Liddicoat. The possibilities for mischief are just too enormous."

"Why not just a few sheep?"

He chuckled. "My old father always said of sheep, 'Keep five and you might just so well keep fifty — or five hundred.' Ever go to a sheepdog trial? They only pit eight or ten sheep against a dog but you should see the mess they can get into sometimes. No, my advice is steer clear of sheep until you're happy with cows, pigs, and chicken."

"Why couldn't old Liddicoat be just as 'ockard' with cows?"

"Because he's got his own herd to think of. If yours go mysteriously straying one dark night, then so can his — and there are a lot more open, unfenced mine shafts on his side of the Grankum than there are on yours!"

"Are there *any* on ours?" she asked in alarm.

He shook his head and chuckled. "That's the beauty of it. But there's at least a couple of dozen on his. He'll think twice before he messes around with cows. Straying sheep are a nuisance without falling down mine shafts. Anyway, as I was about to explain — when you come to the auction on Wednesday, if you see me doing this with my pencil" — he grasped it by the eraser end and dotted it on his blotter, so that his fingertips ran down to the writing end, whereupon he turned it over and did the same again, running his fingers down to the eraser end — "if you see me twiddling like this, it means keep bidding. If you see me tapping it like this" — he demonstrated — "it means make one more bid only. You can bid early on any of them, because we always start ridiculously low, so there's no danger of being landed with one you don't want. And someone just might twig what we're at if you only ever bid when I'm twiddling or tapping. So, bid early on any of them but don't stay in unless I give the signal, right?"

"Okay. How do I know how much to bid?"

"I'll tell you. I do that in any case. I say something like" — he drew breath and spoke in an artificially deep voice to simulate loudness — "Five pounds I'm bid. Do I hear guineas? Will anyone bid me five guineas? Come on now, gentlemen, surely? Half-a-crown, then, for daylight robbery!' and so on. And I'll glance your way when I name a price you should bid. I hope we get away with it!"

She drew on her gloves and rose to go. "I can't tell you how grateful I am, Mister Coad," she said.

"There is just one thing more. I may have to make a joke or two — a mild one — but at your expense. It isn't often we get a lady bidding in the ring, see? The occasional farmer's wife or daughter when the man himself is ill, but even then there's comment. I'll have to do it, I'm afraid, or someone will be sure to shout collusion."

"You don't know me very well, Mister Coad," she replied, "if you think a little thing like that would put me off my stride. There's no harm in names, as they say."

He hesitated, biting his lips, while a slow smile spread across his face. "Well, Miss Carrington," he said hesitantly, "it is true — I do wish I knew you better."

She could hardly complain if he saw an open gate and ran straight through it — especially as she had so unthinkingly opened it for him. "It's a free country," she told him. "And I'm sure you have my address in your files somewhere?"

He grinned again. "Till Wednesday," he said.

"Till Wednesday."

24 Leah arrived home from her highly succesful meeting with Ben Coad, only to find William with a face as long as a dull sermon on a wet Sunday. "You look as if you lost a shilling and found a penny," she told him, reversing a saying he had once used on her.

"Nick's enlisted," he said.

"What?" For a moment the words made no sense ... Nixon listed? Who was Nixon — and who listed him? Then she realized what he'd said. "Nicholas Liddicoat? The Nark?"

"Enlisted. Joined up. Signed up. Gone for a soldier."

"When? I've not seen him for absolutely ages. Well, not for some days, anyway."

"Yesterday. They told us at the school today. I couldn't tell whether they were proud or angry. Bit of both, maybe."

"Well, I know what *I* am," she responded without thought.

"What?" He grinned.

"Relieved!" she snapped. "I wish him well, of course — that is, I wish him no harm — but it'll be easier not having to ..." She gave up trying to patch insincere words over her distress.

Not that she had any reason to resent his enlisting. There was no arrangement between them — not of the kind he had suggested, anyway — nothing to oblige him to tell her he was even thinking of doing it.

"Not having to what?" William asked.

"Oh, shut up! Come and help me and Pansy unload the jingle before it gets dark."

"Didn't you go in the motor? Unload what?"

"We're saving petrol for emergencies. I got twenty two-gallon cans and there won't be any more. Most people are putting theirs up on blocks until the war's over."

"Unload what?" he repeated as he followed her out.

"Pansy!" she shouted as they passed the side door.

A moment later the maid appeared, wiping floury hands into her apron. "Yes, Miss Leah?"

"Bring the two big baskets from the old tack room and come and help us unload the jingle."

Leah watched her brother's eyes as they followed the maid back indoors. She had a most attractive figure; one could not deny it. But Leah believed her stays were laced more for display than for comfort. She made a mental note to have a word with the girl about it. She also wanted to drop a hint to her brother but could not quite think what to say — something light and subtle but not ambiguous.

The body of the jingle was full of the tinned food she had bought from Curnow's — "At wholesale rates, let me add," she told William when his eyes went wide at her apparent extravagance. "Come on! I want to give that horse a rub-down and get on with preparing the store indoors."

When Pansy joined them she, too, gawped at the little mountain of tins.

"This is only part of it," Leah warned her. "Curnow's delivery van is bringing out the rest. We've got a busy week ahead."

"What d'you mean by 'preparing the stores'?" William asked.

"Can you solder zinc?"

"I can braze it. Why?"

"We need patches soldered, or brazed, over the holes in the liners to the old bins in the scullery, or the rats will get in. I've got several sacks of flour coming. Plus rolled oats for the hens. Could you get some more zinc sheet from somewhere and make up four or five containers for the sugar? It'll be to take half a hundredweight each."

"Half a *hundredweight?*" he echoed. "You know the English hundredweight is heavier than ours?"

"That's pints and gallons, dear brother," she sneered. "Pounds are the same."

"Pounds are the same but hundredweights aren't."

"A hundred is a hundred wherever you are." She looked at Pansy and said, "Men! They think they know it all!"

"How many pounds in a hundredweight, Pansy?" he asked.

"A hundred and twelve, of course. Eight stone." To Leah she added, "A stone is fourteen pound."

"I did know that, thank you, Pansy," she said wearily. "I might have guessed it. Where else but in England would a hundred and twelve equal a hundred!"

"You can divide their hundredweight by seven — and eight — which is more than you can do to ours," he pointed out.

"Oh, good," she said sarcastically. "That's going to be so useful here."

"We'm seven under this roof, miss," Pansy pointed out as she added the last tin the basket could safely carry. "Where shall us put these?"

"I'll come in with you. We'll clear a space." To William she said, "Can you fill the other basket and follow us?"

"I'll help Pansy if you like," he said, leaping beyond her on the path and taking up the basket.

"I do not like," she said. But she said it under her breath as she watched them wander away.

25 The postponement of his life's dream, the grand garden project, took its toll of John Carrington's spirit. He spoke little; he lost some of his appetite for food; and he took to going on long, solitary walks. The moment Leah had sorted out the stores, a job she completed after their dinner that evening, she went looking for him. She thought it odd that he hadn't come to help her and the maids, or even to see what bounty his money had bought. At the back of her mind, too, was the thought that even if she didn't find him about the farm, she could go on through Grankum Wood to learn whether this rumour about the Nark were true.

She hadn't seen much of that young man recently. Nor had she taken up his suggestion, but her thoughts had turned to him more and more as the days had passed. The idea of knowing a man, not as a beau but just as a friend — a dear, close friend who could talk to her as to a sister, as he clearly talked to Adèle — was becoming increasingly attractive to her. Indeed, by that evening it almost amounted to an obsession — something she simply *had* to talk with him about. So the news that he'd 'gone for a soldier' was doubly disquieting, both for his safety and for her frustrations.

She saw her father as soon as she entered the yard. He was leaning on the gate at the farther end, gazing out over the field that old man Liddicoat, and she, had so liberally fertilized three months earlier. Now the new-sown grass of the ley, which John Carrington had intended to plough in as green manure for his garden, stood tall and lush. A feast for any herd of cows. She knew, just from the hunch of his shoulders, that he was standing there, rehearsing his ancient dream and mourning its death. *She* knew it was not dead, of course, but in the infinite wisdom of her twenty-two years she also knew that anyone at the ripe old age of fifty-two must daily ponder his own mortality and nightly wonder if he would rise to greet the dawn.

"Penny for 'em," she said as she came up close. "Tuppence if they're bright."

"Ha!" he chuckled as he turned to welcome her. "Where did you hear that one?"

"Local saying." She took his arm and turned him back to face the field and the mellow evening sun. "The days are drawing in quite fast."

"Full moon tonight. The rector told me the ghosts of Catherine Geach and John Lidgeycot are supposed to walk at full moon."

"For a man who says he finds it hard, sometimes, to believe in God, he's mighty ready to believe in ghosts! Anyway, it's the soldiers one thinks of when the moon is full nowadays. The snipers have no need for those flares and things. It must be dreadful for them."

She felt his arm go tense. "You heard about Nicholas Liddicoat, I guess?" he ventured.

"I was thinking of going down there to see if it's true."

"That's all, is it?" he asked. "Quite sure?" There was a jocular edge to his tone.

"What d'you mean?"

"I mean it is *Nicholas* you want to hear about?"

"Why — has Harvey volunteered, too?"

"No!" It irritated him that she did not (or would not?) understand his tease. "They'd not take him, anyway — a farmer's eldest boy. If the farm were bigger, they wouldn't take Nicholas, either. I was just thinking — if we rented these fields back to them again, maybe they wouldn't take the boy. Fifty more acres could tip the balance."

The thought tore her in two. On the one hand she could possibly save his life by giving up her own ambitions to farm the Old Glebe; so then there would be *two* thwarted Carringtons moping about the place. On the other, it was the only thing she had ever really wanted in all her life — not just to farm the place but to make a brilliant success of it, too. Just lately her mind had been crowded with exciting images. Herself at the plough with two great shire horses responding to every click and whistle, every tug of the rein. And herself stooping to pick up the rich tilth and let it run through her hand. Herself chopping mangles on a frosty morn. And herself burying her head in the warm flank of a restive cow with an udder full of rich, creamy milk, and relieving her distress. She knew how absurd and romantic those images were, how cussed a draft horse can be in the wind and rain, how her hands would freeze before the third mangle was in the hopper of the chopping machine, and how a restive cow can lash out with one hoof and spill the whole pail before you could blink an eye. But even so it felt so *right* for her. And now, to save the Nark's life, she'd have to give it all up!

"We could run the place ourselves and hire him as farm manager," she suggested on an inspiration born of despair.

"Well now there's a thought," he said gloomily.

"Oh, Pa!" She hugged his arm. "I'm sorry."

"It's not your fault, honey."

"I'm not apologizing. I'm just saying I'm sorry this dream of yours got stopped the wrong side of the grade crossing."

"*Level* crossing they call it here. But you're right. A couple more months and I'd at least have made a start."

"I think you still could."

"Huh?" He stared at her incredulously.

"And I think you might actually end up with an even finer garden, despite the delay."

He reached over and pinched her wrist gently. "Yup!" he said. "You're real enough. But did you really say that?"

She nodded confidently. "You know the long two-acre that stretches from our entrance along the hill to Bose's Burnthouse? It's never been much good for farming. A herd would trample it flat and graze it out inside two days. It's too long and narrow to work easily for cereals. About all it's good for is truck farming — I mean market gardening. If the hedge weren't so stout, I think it would have been incorporated in the ten-acre years back. But that same stout hedge will keep it safe from marauding cattle."

"For a market garden?"

"No. For a nursery. You could plough a patch of it and stick cuttings for your hardiest shrubs up there, where they'd root over winter. And meanwhile you could build a glasshouse 'foreanenst' the end of the tithe barn, as they say, and sow the seeds of your more tender or exotic shrubs and things. They'd be up by next spring, all ready to plant out next summer and harden off in the fall. The war will surely be over by then, but even if it's not, you could still be bringing on every shrub and herbaceous perennial you'll one day move to its permanent site. How about it?"

He went on staring across the valley. The sun bronzed his skin and she was reminded of a redskin chief she'd once met, massive in his silent dignity.

"Well?" she prompted.

"I'm just realizing I ought to have stuck to pork trading, honey. You're so right — why didn't I think of it? I had this picture of teams ploughing the whole farm and setting out paths, building walls, erecting pergolas, designing little temples ... fountains ... sunken gardens with ponds ... the *architecture* of it, you know ..."

"You didn't think of the plants at all? I don't believe that."

"Well, of course I *thought* of them. I saw them as little bushes and saplings that would steadily grow bigger and burgeon into" — he sculpted something massive in the air in front of them — "luxuriance." Then he pointed at the greensward. "It wouldn't take all that long, either. Just look at that! Did you ever see such verdant growth? If only we could have gotten such fertility back in New England!"

"It will be better, won't it?" she asked. "Letting the plants grow sturdy and acclimatize themselves up there? It'll be an even better garden in the end?"

"Sure, sure — I said it. It's a great idea. I'll get to see their habit, too, before I set them out permanently. How can I repay you, honey?"

"Well ..." she began cautiously.

"Talking of which," he went on, "I haven't forgotten it's your birthday the day after tomorrow. What d'you want? More linen for the bottom drawer?"

"Not this time," she said, wondering if she dared.

"What then?"

"Something rather big, rather expensive?"

"Your own automobile? Oh, no — stupid! Okay, I give up. What is your heart's desire?"

"Something to eat this grass."

"Your own horse!"

"No — a herd of cattle?"

He laughed, as if he thought she were joking. Then he stopped abruptly. "By jiminy, you mean it!"

She nodded and held her breath.

He looked away, down across the field again.

"It's a lot of grass," she murmured.

"And then, I suppose, the idea is we'd hire Nicholas to manage the outfit?"

"Well," she said reluctantly, "one thing at a time, eh? Maybe we won't have to go that far. Maybe they'll turn him down. Flat feet or something. I don't know. Let's just wait, huh?"

"A herd of cattle, eh?" He cleared his throat and she knew he was about to tease again. "Well now, honey, I've seen herds in Texas that stretched from ..."

She laughed and dug him with her elbow. "Ten milch cows and followers," she said. "That's the limit of my ambitions. And capabilities, too, come to think of it. If we bought first- and second-calf heifers, we'd get them cheaper than cows."

He looked at her sharply. "You had this all worked out!" he said accusingly. "When they declared war and we had that confab about going back to East Haven or staying here — you already had this in mind!"

She bit her lip and lolled her head submissively. "But then," she murmured, "whose daughter am I? How long have you had your grand gardens in mind?"

"Okay!" He nodded, and now the submission was on his side. "You know what you're doing, I guess. Shall I ask Coad to buy in a good little nucleus of a herd for us?"

She silently blessed him for that 'us' but she said, "I think I can manage the buying, Pa. I know exactly what I'm looking for."

"Yeah ... but how ... I mean, what'll you do? Just go round from farm to farm making offers?"

"No. I'll bid at auction, just like any other farmer."

"They'll walk all over you! They'll bless the day you entered the ring."

"I think not. I think they'll bless the hour I *left* the ring."

He stared into the darks of her eyes and a little shudder ran through him. "It's what you want?" he asked. "Truly?"

She nodded. "There's a cattle market in Helston next Wednesday. Camborne's is on this Saturday. Penzance has one a week today — we've missed today's ..."

"Oh, dear!" he said ironically.

"Let's go to Camborne on Saturday? You could see Will's teachers before term ends and I could at least get a feel for prices and suchlike." She slapped him on the back. "Whaddya say, Pop?"

He laughed and threw his hands in the air. "I say I know when I'm being railroaded!" Then, serious again, "Are you going down to Grankum Farm — see if it's true about Nicholas?"

"Oh, why not?" she answered casually. "There's an hour to go before dark. Just one more thing ..." She put out a hand to stop him for he had already turned to go. "I think we'll have to find some *occupation* for Will during this summer vacation."

"On the farm, I guess," he suggested.

"No. Most decidedly not on the farm."

"You don't think he could work with you as the boss?"

"There's that," she conceded. "But there's more." She bit her lip. "I don't want to fire Pansy just for being so pretty, but ..."

"Oh!" He tugged at his chin. "I see."

"It's not her fault, after all."

"No."

"Nor is she to blame if Will's a little, what shall I say — free and easy with his familiarity."

He nodded again. "So what had you in mind?"

"Jimmy Troy was in the mining industry, wasn't he?"

"He still is. Or his company is. Though he has no part in the day-to-day ..."

"But he would know people in the mining industry?"

"In the States?"

"And here?"

"I guess he would, why?"

"If he could talk someone into getting Will a job as dogsbody to some mine captain in Camborne or Redruth, just for the vacation — with instructions to make sure he's well and truly *exhausted* — and I mean drained of all energy — by the weekend ... it would add a practical dimension to his studies and ... er ..."

"... *remove* all risk of a practical dimension to his leisure pursuits, eh?"

"Quite."

"Leave it with me. I'll see what can be done."

He opened the gate for her. "Shan't be long," she said as she set off down the field. "Hup, Buttercup! Hup, Daisy! Come on — it's milking time!"

To John Carrington it felt as if his heart turned over in his chest. She was so like her mother at times. He missed Hannah now more than ever, more even than in those awful months after her death, when he imagined no man could miss a loved one more.

26 Leah met Adèle in Grankum Wood; the girl had a broad wooden yoke over her shoulders and a bright, galvanized pail swinging at either end. "Gone to fetch water from the well," the girl called out. "The rainwater's all but finished in the tank."

"Can I give you a hand?" Leah shouted back, branching from her path so as to meet her at the well.

"Not really." They were within speaking distance now. "The yoke balances, see?"

At the edge of the well she did a curious kind of corkscrew-curtsey, which dipped the pail in the water, filled it, and lifted it out, all in one. She turned a half-circle and did the same with the other pail, rather more ponderously. Then she smiled at Leah and raised herself a couple of times on tiptoe. "See? 'Tis easy if the balance is right. You coming up our place, are you?" She set off at a sedate walk, picking her way carefully among the trees.

"Just to say hallo."

"They're out after rabbits. Setting snares. There's a plague of them in the top meadow."

"Yes, I noticed some damage in our new grass along the edge of the wood just now. They don't seem to like the new grass as much as the old permanent pasture, though. I wonder if the new varieties of grass aren't as nutritious?"

"Cows with colic," Adèle said over her shoulder, "you put them on old pasture and they'll mend themselves in half the time. Everyone knows that."

Except guess who! Leah thought. "Will the men stay out till it gets dark?" she asked.

"Depends how many runs they find. But I shouldn't hardly think so tonight. They've been gone an hour now. You heard the good news about Nick, did you?"

"About joining the army? Yes."

"No — about *not* joining up. He'll tell you himself, I'm sure."

"You mean ... are you saying he's at home now?"

"No. He's out setting snares for rabbits. Like I said."

They reached the edge of the wood, where the path broadened out to the full width of a lane. Adèle paused for a rest, setting the pails down in a gateway to their right. She turned and leaned on the gate, which was tied to its post with baler twine. It seemed to be a rule in Cornwall that you could not talk face-to-face with someone if there happened to be a gate nearby; you both had to lean on it and face out into the field. Leah often thought that if there were such a thing as a gate shaped like a bay window, they'd stand happily at it, talking away at ninety degrees to each other.

"We're going to grub up those anemones and violets, put this field down to winter cabbage," Adèle said. "There'll be more profit in vegetables now than flowers, the old man reckons."

"What does Harvey think?"

"Ha!" was all the answer she gave to that.

"He doesn't agree?" Leah guessed.

"He doesn't even care. All he wants is to go off and fight the beastly Boche."

"But …" Leah did not quite know how to frame the question.

"They won't take him either, of course. He says he's going to run away to Plymouth and join the navy — lie about being a farmer's son. We can leave the daffodil bulbs in here. They'll hardly interfere with the cabbage, see."

"You could follow with onions," Leah suggested. "Cabbage root fly doesn't care for land where onions grew."

"That's not a bad idea." Adèle broke the rule and actually looked at her — admiringly. "You're becoming quite the farmer's … girl."

Leah was sure she had been going to say 'wife' — and wondered why she hadn't. "When you say the army turned Harvey down *too* — d'you mean they actually turned Nick down? Rejected him outright?" she asked.

"No." She wouldn't explain any further. "Like I said, he'll probably tell you himself. They said that what he's doing now could be more valuable."

"Studying mining?"

"I don't know. It must be, I suppose. He said he wants a word with your Will."

Leah chuckled. "That shouldn't be too hard to arrange. They see each other every day, just about."

Adèle sniffed and then asked casually, "Is he still couranting with that Blanche Curnow?"

"He sees quite a bit of her," Leah replied guardedly. "Rather less now that he can't just hop in the car and tootle off. A bicycle gives one a different outlook. Coinagehall Street going, and Sithney Common Hill coming back, would make any bicyclist think twice about the absolute necessity for making the journey between us and Chynoweth Hall."

The suggestion that a mere hill could dampen Will's ardour seemed to encourage the girl, Leah noticed. She felt sorry for Adèle if she was harbouring romantic illusions about William — not only because she'd feel sorry for *any* girl who behaved so foolishly, but also because, in her particular case, she knew Adèle would stand no chance. "Can I try your yoke?" she asked.

"There's nothing to it," Adèle replied, helping her fit the thing across her shoulders.

"Hey!" Leah said as she stood to her full height again.

"Straw!" Adèle put in. Then, seing Leah's bewilderment, "You said hay — 'hay, straw, donkey manure' — it's a saying."

"Oh. You're right, anyway — it is wonderfully easy."

They ambled slowly uphill in easeful silence until Clifford Liddicoat's voice rang out on the evening air, crying, "You heller!" It was followed by a bovine bellow and the ringing clang of a gate.

"He's missed her time again, then," Adèle said in disgust.

"Who? What?" Leah asked.

"One of our cows. She was troublesome two days ago and I said we should get her to Johnny Carter's bull, down to Gwavas. Because we missed her three weeks ago, too. She's quick in and out, see. But no. He's fallen out with Carter so he had to go and bring Johnny Meagor's bull from down Scott's. And now he's missed her time again." She shook her head in exasperation.

Leah digested this awhile before she said, hesitantly, "How, actually, do you tell when ... you know ... a cow is, er, trouble-some? Does that mean the same as on heat with dogs?"

"Yes. Bitches, we say."

"Yes. I meant bitches."

"You can't tell, not easily. Well, you can if you know what to look for. When you milk them. Of course, if it's a virgin heifer, she won't be in milk ... but with the others. When you wash her tids you grab a-hold of her tail and curl it round on her back ..."

"Yes, I've seen that done at Pallas Home Farm."

"Well, if she stands very still, stiff and still, with a little arch to her back, and pricked-up ears and staring eyes — as if she's looking for the bull to jump aboard … that's it. When you know the way they stand, you can't mistake it. But out in the field the other cows know. They call the bull over."

"How?"

Adèle giggled. "They say, 'Come on, Bully-Boy! There's one here a-waiting for you!'"

Leah laughed dutifully. "No, but seriously?"

"Seriously, they do. Not in words, of course. They jump up as if they were the bull. 'Bulling' we call it. And the bull sees it, of course — if you're running a bull out there with the herd — and he thinks, 'How's this? Someone trying to steal one of my young ladies from me?' and off he charges to do the job properly. The advantage of that is you don't miss the chance to serve a cow or heifer. But the disadvantage is you don't always know the day when he served her, so you don't know the day when she's going to fall due."

"Is that why you don't run a bull with the herd?"

"Yes and no. Why are you asking all this, anyway?"

"I'm thinking of taking up farming myself, actually."

Adèle ran a pace or two to get ahead of her and then, because Leah's head was bowed with the effort, bent forward to look up into her face. "You're not joking," she said.

Leah shook her head. "If there's a war, every acre will count. Whoo! These may be easy to carry but this is quite a hill!"

"Here! I'm used to it." Adèle resumed the yoke. "Are you looking for a cowhand?"

"Don't you call them dairymaids?"

The girl laughed dismissively. "You'll need something more than a dairymaid, Leah."

"Tell me why you don't run a bull with your herd."

"Because a ten-cow herd is too small. The bull doesn't work enough and he eats too much. So that's the advantage of not having one — you don't have to feed him. The disadvantage is you've only got two or three days to notice when a cow is troublesome. If you miss it — like my father's just missed it with Onehorn — that's a cow with one horn, see …"

"I'd never have guessed!"

Adèle pulled a face. "I'll swing one of these pails at you."

"You'd have to go back and refill it."

"Then I'd chuck the other over you, too — it'd be worth it. Anyway, if you miss her time, you've got to wait three weeks till she comes in again. So her next lactation is three weeks late, too — which is three weeks you're feeding her, and no milk to pay for her keep. If you're going to keep cows ..."

"Yes?"

"You're going to need someone who knows things like this. And more — much, much more. What d'you do for bloat? Two hours and the cow will be dead — what d'you do? If the calf scours after the colostrum, how d'you stop it? How d'you make a calf drink from a bucket — head downwards, see — when it's never drunk but head-upwards, from the udder, all its days? If you smell the smell of mice on a cow's breath, how d'you save her life? If a cow gets mastitis in the first flush ..."

"All right, Adèle, the point is taken." She raked the darkling sky with her gaze. "Now I just wonder where I would find a cowhand like that?"

"On your bended knees," Adèle replied haughtily.

They both laughed and nothing more was said on the subject that evening.

They arrived at the farm just as Harvey and Nicholas were coming in from setting their snares. The brothers formed two dark-purple silhouettes against the flaming red of the twilit sky, just minutes after sundown.

"He's missed Onehorn's time again," Adèle said angrily.

"My fault," Harvey admitted ruefully. "I thought I'd told him and ... oh, hallo, Miss Leah, I didn't see you there."

"Head full of tunes of glory!" Adèle said scornfully over Leah's response. "Come-us on in," she said to Leah. "You've not been inside before, have you. Mind your head."

"Hallo, Nark," she said over her shoulder as she followed Adèle indoors.

"Hallo, Thistle." He came in behind her, trying to tread the shoes off her heels.

"You just stop that," she said angrily. "You do that once again and I'll kick."

He laughed. "You know how to stop a horse kicking, don't you? Stallion or mare?"

"Tie her tail to a rafter?" She thought of Mrs Troy's cows.

"No. You do this." He ran to her side and pressed his legs tight against hers — as tight as he could without falling over. "Try and kick me now," he challenged.

"Nick!" Adèle said angrily. "That's no way to behave."

"Go on!" he challenged Leah, ignoring his sister's rebuke.

Leah, trying to think of some way to embarrass him — as he was clearly trying to embarrass her — stood her ground, relaxed, smiled, and said, "Mmm!" It was the sort of noise she'd have made if she'd picked a fruit, expecting it to be sour, and had found it sweet and palatable instead.

And it certainly embarrassed him! He leaped back as if she had stung him — which, in a sense, she had. He turned away from her and called out to Harvey, "Haven't you sorted out those snares yet?"

"Sorry." Harvey came in reading the newspaper. "Mrs Gilbert must have left this in. It says our troops are going to France tomorrow." He looked at the date, which was yesterday's. "So that's today." He glanced up. "They're landing today!"

The light in his eye made Leah shiver. In one way she admired him — his bravery, his burning passion to serve — yet in every other way she wanted him to stay. Not that she loved him but she wanted him to be there. She wanted him not to be killed.

"Will you have a dish of tea, Leah?" Adèle asked. "Or maybe you'd prefer a glass of ale?"

"Oh …" Leah could not decide. "You have to carry all your water up from Grankum now?"

"It's the same either way, tea or ale, we brew them both."

"Ale, then, please — just a small glass."

Adèle drew glasses for them all, and one for her father, who had not yet returned from dealing with Onehorn. Leah looked around her and saw that what Blanche had told Will about old man Liddicoat being an avid reader was true. There were books everywhere — on shelves, on cupboards and sideboards, and in piles against the wall.

"Nothing exciting," Nicholas said, following her eyes. "No novels or scandalous biographies. Just lives of great men, sermons, philosophers, Milton, Bunyan … stuff like that. Bowdler's Shakespeare."

"A German officer has killed a French corporal in the Jura," Harvey said. "The German cavalry is out scavenging for horses around Belfort — you see, they're not even *prepared* for war! The French are going to wipe the floor with them. It's going to be all over before we can get there."

"Let us hope so," Leah murmured.

He looked daggers at her. "And America will do nothing — except sell to both sides and take its profit."

"Harvey!" Adèle snapped. She looked angrily at Nicholas for holding back.

"America will do what's right for America," Leah replied, calmly sipping her ale. "And it's nothing to do with me. I live in England now. This is my country and I shall play my part here — whatever I'm called on to do."

Adèle, seeing Harvey's lip curl in a sneer, said, "Careful, you! They're not going to turn the Old Glebe into a garden. Leah's going to farm it and grow food for England. So there!"

Harvey stared at Leah in amazement. Nicholas began to laugh. "Farm it?" he asked. "You?" He laughed again.

"And what will *you* be doing?" she asked him coldly. "I gather the army turned you down?"

He stared at her as if he wondered if she was worth an explanation — and decided she wasn't. "Is Will at home tonight?" was all he said. "I want a word with him."

"Will is one of those immature young men who think it smart to have secrets from those around them," she replied. "You're familiar with the type, I'm sure. So you'll just have to walk over there and take your chance, won't you."

He opened his eyes wide in simulated terror. "Not on the night of a full moon!" he exclaimed.

She turned to Adèle. "Is your father likely to come home soon? I shouldn't like him to think me rude. But I really ought to be …"

"He'll stay out as long as he dares," she replied. "He knows what I'll say about missing Onehorn's time again."

"The navy's going to engage the German fleet if they attack the French coast," Harvey said bitterly. "They'll pulverize them. It's going to be over at sea before we know it, too."

"I'll go, then." Leah squeezed Adèle's hand. "That thing we were talking about — I'll think it over. Would you like to come to Helston market with me next Wednesday?"

"What's this?" Nicholas asked truculently.

They both rounded on him. "Mind your own business" — "Nothing to do with you," they said simultaneously, uniting in thought if not in their choice of words.

Leah got as far as the lane when she heard someone running behind her. She knew it was the Nark before she turned round. "You don't have to," she said wearily. "I don't believe all that rubbish about ghosts."

"I do. But I also want to see Will rather urgently."

"You could wait ten minutes, surely? You don't have to accompany me."

"Very well." He folded his arms and sat down on a large stone that had fallen out of the hedge.

She walked on ten paces before turning round again. "Oh, come on, then! This is absurd."

"Mine not to reason why," he said lugubriously as he joined her. "Mine but to do and die — or not, as the case may be. Talking of doing and dying — what d'you think of Harvey, eh? Can't wait to get killed or injured!"

"He's your own brother, for heaven's sake!"

"I know. It's even more worrying. Suppose it's infectious!" After a silence he went on, "Still, that's enough about him. What about you? Are you serious about farming?"

She kept her eyes fixed ahead. "I'm not going to provide you with yet more ammo for your quips. What d'you want to see Will about? What's this news that just can't wait?"

He became serious at once. "Actually, Thistle, it's you I want to tell. Then I'd be grateful if you'd advise me."

"About what?"

"About whether I should tell Will anything or not."

She thought a while and then said, "Okay."

"It's confidential," he went on. "I haven't told any of my family and I don't intend to for some time. You'll be the only one who knows, and I'd rather like it to stay that way. So tell me now if you'd rather I kept silent."

"Why me?" she asked.

"Brutal truth?"

"If you must."

"Because your opinion would mean a lot but also — I must admit — because you wouldn't be able to exploit what I'm going to tell you."

They entered the wood, where twilight had already turned to darkness. Over Sithney, no doubt, a full moon was rising, but down here in the valley bottom all was stygian gloom. Somehow that made it easier for her to say, "All right. Go ahead and tell me. I shan't tell anyone."

Now she felt him at her side but saw him only as a darker shade against the dark. "You remember the day Will met me first?" he asked.

"Saved your life?"

He laughed. "If you like. I was trying to crush some rocks for an assay. I was looking specifically for wolframite, which is the ore of tungsten. Does the name mean anything — tungsten?"

"A very hard metal?"

"Good. The thing about it is that it retains its hardness even when white hot — filaments in electric lamps, for instance. Mix it with steel and it still keeps its hardness when red hot. It therefore makes excellent machine tools. Are you beginning to see …"

"Did you find it?" she interrupted. "This wolframite?"

"Yes. What's more, I think there's enough there to make commercial extraction profitable."

"Who has the mineral rights?" she asked.

He emitted something between a gasp and a laugh. "You don't believe in holding back, do you!" he said.

"It's the obvious question."

"Yes, well, I suppose it is. I own them — or I will, shortly — which is why I don't want anyone else to know just yet."

"Not even your own family?"

"If the white-feather fever grips people the way it did in the Boer War, and if people started taunting my family about me not enlisting, they couldn't resist blurting something out. That's all. I'm protecting them — and me. It's nothing underhand."

She laughed. "Whereas you're absolutely sure I'd never blurt out a word in defence of you!"

He fumbled in the dark and nudged her jocularly. "You read my mind, Thistle. Anyway, I've put a down-payment on the surface mineral rights. They're owned by a widow over near Cury. She thinks I'm mad, so I'll be getting them quite cheap — which is another reason for secrecy just at the moment."

"And is that why the army turned you down?"

"Something like that," he said vaguely. "I saw a man at the Ministry of Supply — who arranged for me not to be eligible for enlistment. That's the outline of it, anyway."

After a moment's thought she asked, "What do you want to see Will about?"

"I wondered if he'd like to spend the summer vacation helping me set up the extraction plant."

"Would it be hard work?"

"Backbreaking."

"Take all his energy?"

"Every last ounce. Why this interest in …"

"Then I think you should ask him the very moment you own the rights," she said firmly.

They emerged from the wood into the field where he had helped her put one in the eye of his father. "This grass came on well," he said innocently.

"Yes, I wonder why!"

"Oh, my God!" He stopped dead and stared up the hill in consternation. "Look!"

"What?"

"The moon! The full moon! I said it — and then forgot. I should never have come."

"Don't be so stupid!" She turned on her heel and continued up the slope.

"And yet I can't leave you," he whined. "Oh dear, oh dear, what am I to do?"

"Grow up," she shouted.

He ran to catch up with her. "You really don't believe in ghosts?" he asked.

"Of course not — and nor do you. You're just being very childish and silly."

"Prove it!" he challenged.

"How?" She knew it was a mistake as soon as the word was out of her mouth.

"Go and stand alone in that old tithe barn for one minute. Sixty seconds, that's all. I dare you."

She saw at once that she had but two choices — to weasel her way out of it or to accept. "Okay," she said. "If it amuses you."

But her heart was already beating double — and it had little to do with the exertion of walking up the hill.

27 Leah began dragging her feet the moment the barn door came in sight. She stared at it, hoping against hope to discover a sign saying *Danger! Keep out! Unsafe structure!* But there was no such easy luck. The door had an ethereal quality in the moonlight, as if the wood of which it was made were half dissolved in some kind of mist ... or — the thought struck a chill into her — as if the barn were dissolving away to become a ghost of its mundane self. Perhaps it had been plucked back through the centuries by the ferocity of the passions that had once played themselves out to such a grisly end within its confines. *Confines!* The very word was like a judgement knell. In less than a minute, if she persisted in this tomfoolery, she would be within those *confines*.

"You needn't go through with it, Thistle," Nicholas said with a grin. "No one knows but me, and I shan't tell."

"And me," she replied. "Besides, I'm not going to fail a challenge from *you*, of all people."

"Ooh!" he said, as if she had paid him a compliment.

"I don't mean you're *important,*" she sneered. "I mean that for me to refuse a challenge from you would be like a horse refusing a fence twelve inches high." She peeled a flake from the wood around the locking bar and murmured, "It needs a new coat of paint before winter comes."

He pulled his 'alderman' from his waistcoat pocket. "D'you want me to call out every ten seconds or what?"

"Or nothing!" She spoke with more daring than she felt. "I'll stay in there until I get bored — or until you do. Yes — that's it! You come in and get me when you get bored. Let's see how much *you* dare!"

He backed away from her in horror, putting up his hands to ward off her words as if they had physical weight. "I already told you. No power on earth, or anywhere else for that matter, would get me inside there when the full moon shines. The last person who tried it came out looking like an old man, with hair as white as snow."

"Stop it! Hair is dead. How can it change colour in minutes?"

"It's true. I swear it — an old man with hair like the driven snow. And stark, staring mad. On my honour." He came back to her side. "Please — this joke has gone far enough. Turn your face from this madcap venture."

"Who was it, anyway?" she asked, aware that she was playing for time.

"Reverend Langham."

"But he *is* an old man — and his hair is already as ... oh, *you!*" She punched him hard in the chest but he rode with it.

"I didn't say what he looked like *before* he went in," he said. "Anyway, he's not stark, staring mad."

"You haven't been paying attention to his recent sermons. 'God is in every English bullet and the Devil in every German one' — that's not the talk of a madman?" He looked up at the moon. "All the same — quite seriously — I wouldn't monkey around with the spirits on a night like this. Let's get Will and go for a walk, eh? We might find some lovers to sneer at — safely living ones, I mean."

Annoyed with him, first for challenging her then for making it sound so easy to go back on her acceptance, she put her hand to the bar. "Now don't you dare lock this again," she said — or she would have said it if an eldritch shriek from within had not frozen the last few words on her lips.

Nicholas laughed but swiftly turned it into a whimper of fear. He ran to the far side of the yard, shouting in a stagey rural accent, "Come away, mistress! This be not for mortal eyes."

"I'll come over there and hit you if you don't stop it," she told him. "It was only the spindle thing or whatever you call it — the thing the bar spins round. Probably. It needs oil."

She gave the door a tentative push with one boot. If the spindle of the bar needed oil, the hinges needed a whole oil well. It amazed her that she had never noticed their rusty state by day. The door did not swing far. The hinges were deliberately set at a slight diagonal to ensure that the door would shut by gravity, which it now did, again with a chorus of shrieks.

"Enough to waken the dead," Nicholas said in a sepulchral voice, almost in her ear.

"Oh!" she snapped at him. "You gave me the fright of my life. How d'you move so quietly?"

"You'll never 'ear no footsteps," he said in the same voice, "from the likes of we."

She cried out in frustration, "God give me strength! Now listen, you — just let that door close by itself. Understand?"

He gave up his play-acting. "Look, Thistle," he said, all reasonable again. "If you're determined to see it through, good luck to you. Take my hat off and all that. I shan't touch a thing. But if you think that door is going to close *by itself* on such a night as this …" He laughed at her naïvety.

She longed to link arms with him and force him to go in there with her, though whether that was out of anger or fear she was not sure. A bit of both, most likely. "If you play any tricks," she said, "I'll come back out and murder you."

"And I, for my part, will come in at the very first scream," he promised with a grin.

It was the grin that finally determined her; it said, 'We both know you're not going through with it so why not give up now?' She pushed open the door again and stepped inside. It closed with a shriek and she was left in total darkness. Her annoyance had been a magnificent spur to action, but the courage it had given her evaporated the moment she was alone …

… if, indeed, she was alone.

Had the Nark slipped inside with her? No doubt he'd think that very funny — to watch her cope with her terror. She flailed about her in the blackness, hoping to catch him. Part of her longed to catch him, to feel the touch of another human being … to hold him …

No! She shook off such weakness. "Nark?" she called out.

His voice came through the door. "Are you giving up already? It's only been fifteen seconds."

"No. I was just checking you hadn't slipped inside with me."

To her surprise his chuckle sent a thrill of pleasure through her. "Curses! I never thought of that. What's it like in there?"

"Oh, it's a blaze of light and they're dancing to a fiddle band and drinking cider … what d'you *think* it's like?"

"Sorry!" After a pause he said, "Thistle?"

"What now?"

"I think you're pretty good to go through with this. You can come out, if you like. I was lying just now. It's actually coming up to the full minute."

"Not on your life, Nark! The challenge was to stand alone in the middle in the dark — not to play Pyramus and Thisbe through a crack in the door. Start counting again." She stepped out confidently into the dark, hoping to end up somewhere near the middle of the open space between the hay, the straw, and the old farm carts.

The night was suddenly full of sounds — the creaking of ancient timbers, the soughing of a wind that had not even been apparent outside ... the thunderous beating of her heart, the shivering of her breath ... and little rustling noises from living creatures of unknown variety. Never mind spectres and phantasms, this place was filled with *living* terrors — how could she have forgotten it? Mice. Spiders. Rats. *Bats!* Oh, dear God — bats! She could actually hear their squeaks now, and that was no product of a fevered imagination. Those high-pitched explosions of sound, set at the very limits of human hearing, now over there, now over here ... they were unmistakable.

A moment later one brushed her face, or came close enough to fan her cheek with the breath of its wings. Only a superhuman effort on her part, aided by the knowledge that the Nark was out there just waiting for some sign of her weakness, prevented her from shrieking out the horror that now gripped her; for among the many creatures that render the night terrible, bats were the most frightening of all to her. No matter that she was wearing a bonnet and that it was tied tight around her head, there was still plenty of loose hair for a bat to get caught up in. It took little imagination to think how one of those squeaky, furry, flea-ridden creatures would writhe there and scratch her with its sharp little claws and bite her neck with those needle-teeth.

Her flesh crawled. She cringed from the dark, yet the only space into which she might escape was deeper into another dark, full of terrors as yet unimagined. Nothing else but that knowledge could have made her do what she did next, which was to crouch down, catch up the hem of her skirt at the back and draw it up, up around her waist, up over her shoulders, over her bonnet, where at last she pulled it down like a shawl all around her head.

"Two minutes," Nicholas called out but she didn't even hear.

She stayed there, crouching down, flinching from the bats, not comfortable but no longer in abject terror — until she remembered the rats. To say she remembered them is too mild. She actually *saw* one crouching stock still not a yard from her.

For, now that her eyes were growing used to the dark, enough moonlight stole through a myriad small cracks between the roof tiles and around the doors and window shutters to reveal the foul creature. Or the shape of it, at least, if not the texture of hair or the colour of dread. Nor, in this case, the gleam of its beady eyes. In a way that was more horrifying yet — the thought that the brute was watching her through hooded eyes.

Why didn't it move?

Then she thought of it moving … crawling toward her where she crouched … disappearing under her petticoats … Her flesh crawled with loathing for it. But if she stood up again — never mind the bats — it might make a run at her and her petticoats would fall around her ankles and it would be trapped underneath. Sharp little claws making ladders in her stockings and then climbing them … She froze in an agony of indecision.

There was a stick nearby. It would fall just within her grasp if she stretched to her utmost. Slowly, painfully slowly, she reached out her arm, never for one moment taking her eyes off the malevolent little rodent.

It still did not move.

She almost overbalanced but she got the tips of her fingers beyond the stick and, after resting on them for a moment, managed to tweak it toward her. By and by she manipulated it close enough both to recover her balance and to get her fingers around it. Then she wasted no time but raised it above her head and brought it down with an almighty thwack on the rat.

It did not run. It did not even flinch. It made no sound. Instead it clung to the stick and flew up in the air when she raised it for a possible second strike. It had no weight. It vanished, literally into thin air — into the dark, thin air. She stood there, shoulders hunched, eyes closed, shivering as she waited for it to fall upon her from out of that same thin air.

"Thistle?" Nicholas called from outside, from another world, from a time she had almost forgotten.

She heard a voice call from her throat: "Yes?"

"That's five minutes. I think you've proved your point. Also I'm getting cold."

She laughed, feebly — or sounds she dimly remembered as laughter came out of her.

"May I come in?"

She looked to see if her skirts were back in place — an everyday action that brought her to her everyday self at last.

"No one's stopping you," she called out.

He thrust open the door and kicked a stone in place to hold it ajar. The hinges complained again but the sound evoked no terrors now. The sight of him, however, was enough to rekindle more than a little frisson. He stood there, uncertain of her mood, unwilling to move until more sure of it. With his legs braced apart he looked as if he were carved in anthracite; the moonlight upon him was silver-blue and brilliant enough to burn; his long black shadow reached into the barn, across the silvered floor, all the way to where she stood.

The scene was sinister enough to recall for her, and for the first time since she had stepped inside the barn, the unquiet dead who had been supposed to terrify her. She wondered if Catherine Geach had stood just there, where her feet were now planted, and had seen the black shape of her erstwhile lover, John Lidgeycot, standing there at the door with his long moonshadow reaching out toward her …

Her fear was rather contrived but it prickled at the back of her neck like the real thing. Then, as her eyes scanned the length of the Nark's shadow, she saw the piece of rag she had mistaken for a rat. She began to laugh.

Relieved, too, he started to walk toward her. Her laughter might even have become a touch hysterical if at that moment a barn owl, annoyed at her intrusion and infuriated at his, had not swept down between them. It swooped as silently as only an owl may swoop, so that it seemed to materialize from nothing, and it hooted as it rose again to its nest.

Without thought she uttered a cry, sprang to him, and flung her arms about him. Instinctively his arms enfolded her. "It's all right, Thistle," he said. "It was only an owl."

She just clung to him and shivered. He began to understand something of the torments she had just endured. "Why should we fear the dead?" she asked. "When the world of the living has terrors enough!"

It really was very pleasant to be held in a man's arms again, even the Nark's.

"It's all right," he said again, patting her awkwardly on the back. "It's over."

"I thought I saw a rat." She looked up at him.

Their eyes dwelled in each other's, unreadable in the moonlight. Slowly, hesitantly he lowered his lips to hers. They met. It was as if she were brushed with something glowing, alive, electrical, unearthly. Her senses ached at it. She vaguely recalled similar feelings, as if in another life, but they had been mere harbingers of this.

It did not last. In the very act of surrender some other part of her, a part that did not welcome this at all, asserted itself and made her pull away. "No," she murmured. "No! It wasn't as ... I didn't mean ... that wasn't the ... Let me go!"

She wriggled free but continued to hold him by the arms.

He pulled himself together with obvious effort. He looked about guiltily, even though he knew that no one else could have been watching. "You're right," he said. His voice was thin and shivery. "Bad mistake. Shouldn't have happened. In fact it didn't happen — right?" He took a different grip on her and began to hop up and down on the spot, dancing to some tune in his head. "The fiddlers are striking up again. What a jolly tune!" He began to sing it: "Oh, I'm a proper country chap, Me family come from Fareham, At 'ome they got some more like I, And they well knows 'ow to rear 'em!" And as he sang he spun her away in a frenzied twostep, round and round and round ...

"What on earth is going on!" Will's cry halted them at last.

They spun down to a halt and turned, breathless and panting, to face him.

He was standing in the doorway just as Nicholas had stood a few minutes earlier. Nick froze, seeing in Will what Leah's imagination had made of him in that same stance. "Why, 'tis John Lidgeycot, mistress!" he whispered in simulated terror.

She shook him and said, "We did all that — remember?"

"Oh, yes." He was chastened.

William laughed. "Are you both mad?"

"No," she replied lightly. "Just dancing. The Nark challenged me to be alone in here, in the dark, with these supposed ghosts."

"And?"

"She stayed in five minutes," Nicholas said.

"And?" William insisted.

Leah smiled at Nicholas. "Nothing happened — did it."

"No," he admitted ruefully. "Nothing happened."

28 The cattle market was within strolling distance of the Camborne School of Mines, so Will escorted his sister there while their father spoke with his tutors. His head was full of the plans to extract tungsten from the wulframite Nicholas had discovered at several sites around Wheal Fortune, for young Liddicoat had told him all about it. He could hardly wait to get started. The little tableau he had interrupted in the barn on the night of the full moon also intrigued him, of course.

"Are you really going to buy cattle today, Sis?" he asked.

"If I see a real bargain, sure," she replied, though in truth she had not the slightest intention of doing so. She just wanted to see how people behaved at cattle auctions so she wouldn't make a complete fool of herself next Wednesday.

"How will you know?" he asked.

"Oh," she said vaguely, "I haven't wasted my time when visiting Mrs Troy, you know."

"Ben Coad is sweet on you."

"So?"

"So make use of it. Get him to help you. He could tip you the wink when to bid and when not to."

She halted and stared at him. For a moment she wondered if Coad had spilled the beans; but Will was so pleased at his own cleverness that it seemed unlikely. "You really have the most devious, underhand spirit, Will," she said. "I wouldn't dream of putting myself under such an obligation to him." But the uncomfortable thought that she had done precisely that now began to nag at her.

"He'd do it anyway. He's been sweet on you since the day we came. He'd do it without expecting anything …" He clapped a hand to his mouth and spun a full circle on one toe. "I shouldn't be telling you this."

"Oh, Will!" She pinched him playfully. "What game is this?" His all-too-accurate analysis of her actions and motives continued to disturb her, though.

"It's no game," he assured her. "Or it's the oldest game of all. It's not a good idea for young females to know what havoc they can wreak with the male psyche. Nor should they know how absurdly monomaniacal — is that the word? Like Ahab and the White Whale? — how monomaniac it ..."

"It doesn't matter. It's all rubbish anyway — what you're trying to say. Can women possess men's minds? Nonsense! Men find it only too easy *not* to think of us for ninety-nine percent of the time. Whether they're hauling fish from the sea or tin from the earth ... or hunting the fox or mauling each other to death in the boxing ring — when do you think of us *then?*"

"Ha!" He raised his hands to the skies, inviting all heaven to bear witness. "About every ten minutes, if you want to know."

Something despairing in his tone made her withhold the scornful reply she had been about to make. "Truly?" she asked.

He nodded glumly. "Maybe not if someone were trying to punch me senseless in the ring. But at all other times — take it from me!"

"You think of Blanche Curnow every ten minutes — is that what you're claiming?"

He hesitated and then said, "Yes."

"How?" she challenged. *"What* d'you think of? Just her face? Or kissing her? Or ... what?"

"You know," he said awkwardly.

"No I don't."

"Well, what do you think about when you think of Nicholas?"

"Nicholas?" She hoped her alarm sounded like surprise. It was true that she had been thinking about him quite a lot these past few days. Not every ten minutes, but more often than she wished. She didn't want to think of him at all but somehow he kept intruding around the edges of her consciousness and then, before she could stop herself, there he was, right in the centre of things. And not just his face, either. She could still feel his lips on hers and the sweet, burning sensation that had filled her ...

But then, within moments, she was usually able to shrug it off again. It had been the merest lapse, a few seconds only ... she had been so emotionally stirred by her ordeal ... and then the surprise of that owl swooping down on them like that ... and the Nark taking advantage of her weakness ... it meant nothing.

So had Will read it in her face?

"I *saw* you," he said when it became clear she was not going to deny it openly.

"Dancing in the barn! So?"

"No, Sis, I saw you kiss him. I didn't deliberately set out to spy but I was crossing the yard and the door was wide open and the moonlight …"

"Okay, okay — I was there, too, remember. And *I* didn't kiss *him* — just for your information. On the contrary, he kissed me and I stopped him."

"Sure!" he said superciliously.

"I did too!"

He shrugged. "If that's the way you want to gloss it, I won't argue with you."

His attitude annoyed her so much that she blurted out, "Anyway, it's not Blanche Curnow's face that distracts you every ten minutes, is it! It's that Pansy Tregear's. You don't fool me, Jackson!"

She thought he would respond angrily — indeed, she rather hoped for it, so that they could agree to change the subject. But instead he sighed and said, "I know. Isn't it stupid?"

The response took her aback for a moment but she saw it was a chance she could not waste. "Yes, Will, it *is* stupid. It's just about the stupidest thing you could ever embark on. There can be absolutely no question of an alliance between you and her. She's a pleasant enough girl, I grant …"

"Oh, but she has no idea of marrying. Not me. Not anyone. Not just yet, anyway, she says."

Leah did not know what to say to this; all the arguments she had begun marshalling in her mind evaporated. "You've discussed such things with her?" was all she could ask.

"First thing. I mean it was the first thing *she* said."

"What? You mean to say she just walked up to you and said, out of the blue …"

"No!" He lolled his head wearily. "If you must know, I tried to steal a kiss — only to have her turn round and hand it me on a plate. On a great big silver chafing dish, in fact. Bowled me over, I can tell you. I've never known such a passionate kiss. So I got embarrassed and started apologizing — but she just laughed and said it was all right but if I wanted more, I should pick my moments more carefully."

The market lay a quarter of a mile beyond the level crossing, which closed as they approached it. So they had to wait for a train to pass through.

"What on earth did she mean by that?" Leah asked with sinking heart.

"Well, without repeating the whole conversation, the upshot was — or is — that she doesn't want marriage or even a steady beau but she's not averse to a little flutter. Or even a big flutter. And she says I'm not to get downhearted if she sparks with other lads, too."

"Indeed!" Leah was astounded, not just at the girl's effrontery, but at her brother's calm acceptance of it. "The baggage will clearly have to go."

"I know." His tone was neutral.

"Well, you seem to take it calmly enough!"

"It won't stop us meeting. She's expecting it, anyway. She thought she'd get her marching orders last Thursday. You saw at once, didn't you — that there was something going on."

'Yes, but I didn't think it was as serious as this."

A big locomotive, all valves closed, went hissing through the crossing and pulled up in the station with a screech of brakes. It was the express from Paddington, Will said. The signalman cranked a wheel up in his box overlooking the crossing and the gate swung open again in a series of lazy jerks. Leah opened and closed her parasol smartly to throw off the smuts. "You've got some on your collar," she said. "Don't move."

She took off her glove and delicately lifted the soot away on her little fingernail. He smiled at her and said, "It's getting harder and harder to play momma, huh?"

"Only because it *ought* to be less and less necessary. Doesn't Pansy mind about losing her place? She was keen enough to get it." She pulled on her glove again and they resumed their stroll.

"She'll be sorry, of course. She thinks the world of you. You're a sort of heroine to her. But she won't have any difficulty getting another place. The naval stores in Plymouth are crying out for hands, male or female. And the munitions factories in London, Birmingham … all over. Girls can easily earn double what they'd get in service."

Leah's heart sank at these words. If the men were going to volunteer all over the place and the women could be enticed away like that by high wages, she could see herself trying to run the farm single-handed — which wasn't at all what she'd had in mind. "And they'd take her? Just like that?"

"They'd take her. And she wouldn't stay down on the workbench for long, either. She's too bright. She can read and write with ease and her mind's as sharp as any blade."

"Hmm." Leah decided that sacking the girl was no answer. Something more subtle, more cooperative, more female, was called for here. "And you're really stuck on her, eh?"

"Seems so." He nodded grimly. "More than she is on me. Maybe that's why. Wounded pride."

After some thought Leah said, "It would be ridiculous to talk of love after so short a while but, er, these feelings you have for her, would they be strong enough to make you *respect* her? You know what I'm referring to, I'm sure."

"On my side, yes. But she doesn't particularly welcome that sort of respect. She says she wakes up each morning and thinks, 'I'll never be as young again as I was yesterday!' She says time is short and we could all be killed in the war, and ..."

"But that's crazy! As if the Germans are ever going to overrun the whole of England!"

"No — we *men*. She thinks all the young men could get killed and then she'd spend the rest of her life thinking of all the chances she missed."

They turned in at the gate of the market.

"Okay," Leah said. "We'll have to talk about this again. But now it's business."

There was no doubting where the cattle were being auctioned. The almost unintelligible singsong — which sounded like '*Hat* four five *hat* four five I'm-bid can-I-hear ten *surely!*' — was coming from a circle of iron stanchions capped by an iron-honeycomb roof clad in lead sheet. The horizontal tubes between the stanchions supported a motley of ragged boys and farmers in leggings and gaiters. Gnarled sticks were everywhere, clutched in equally gnarled hands that prodded the ground or the cattle with indifference. One farmer who passed them as they stood there, uncertain as to how closely they dared approach, brought his stick down with metronome regularity on the back of the cow he was driving. He did not even seem to know he was doing it, for he was engaged in earnest conversation with the man at his side all that while. To Leah's surprise the cow did not seem to notice it, either; he might as well have been swatting flies on her back for all the response she made.

"Want to see a bit closer, do 'ee?" the man's companion called out after he had passed them.

"We wouldn't be in the way?" Leah asked.

With an expansive sweep of his arm he waved them to join him, peeling away from his companion at the same time. "I'll warrant you not," he said. "On holidays, are you? George is the name. Henry George of Copperhouse." He held out a clean but weatherbeaten hand.

When they shook it and introduced themselves he placed them at once. "My wife's aunt had a half-sister who married a nephew to your great-grandfather, William Carrington of Leedstown," he said.

Leah felt awful that she couldn't bring herself to care all that much about such tenuous links, despite their importance to Cornish folk. "Isn't that amazing!" she said brightly.

"Not really," he replied. "Why, I daresay half the people you can see would be able to find *some* connection with you. Hardly so strong as mine, of course, but there'd be something there. So" — he smiled genially at what he considered to be his fairly close if long-lost relations — "you do want to see how we belong to buy and sell bullocks, eh?"

"Oh, is it bullocks today?" Leah was disappointed. "I thought it was milch cows."

"Why, so 'tis, maid. We do call all cattle 'bullocks' down here in Cornwall, see?"

"Except calves and yarlings," a nearby farmer put in.

"Except they," he agreed. "Whoo-up, Tregembo!" He patted a ringside farmer on the shoulder. "There's two Carringtons of Leedstown came all the way from Americay to learn how we do buy and sell bullocks."

Leah, feeling dreadful, started telling the man she had not the faintest wish to deprive him of his place at the ringside. But he grinned and almost pushed her in, saying, " 'Tis nothing but wisht and jealous stock, anyway."

When Leah, rather than William, took the vacant place, Farmer George asked the youth if he wasn't interested in farming. William explained about being at the School of Mines. "Wise man!" was the reply. "There's still more money underground in Cornwall than ever there will be over it, and that's a fact, my son."

Then he noticed how keenly Leah was watching the proceedings and transferred his attention to her.

"You might think she a'n't got much milk," he said of a first-calf heifer in the ring. "'Cos her bag is so small. But you won't see no bag at all on a mare, yet she'll yield four gallon a day to her foal. That's more'n what that heifer'll give. You can't tell nothing from the size o' the bag, see."

And he went on doling out a nugget for each 'bullock' that entered the ring. He told her what sort of backbone she should look for — straight as a ruler — what arrangement of the hips, what slope of breastbone, what smell on the breath, what thickness of milk-stream … and half-a-dozen other pointers to a good or bad cow. In between times she watched the farmers and dealers who were actively bidding — how they hardly ever looked at the auctioneer (and yet never let their eyes stray too far from him, either), how they prodded the cattle and, now and then, climbed into the ring to feel their bags. All the cows had been left deliberately unmilked that morning and so they were distended to a painful degree. Many of them spontaneously let down their milk at the slightest touch. The floor of the ring was spotted white and slippery with it.

Above all, she noted how they managed to bid, some by the merest glance up at the auctioneer, some by a diagonal tilt of the head, some by a barely perceptible nod. The most placid of all folded their hands around the knobs of their sticks and lifted one finger in a single wag.

"Blink your eyes at the wrong moment," Farmer George said, "and you could end up on Carey Street!"

She thanked him when the auctions were done and hoped they might meet again at some other market — to which he replied that they surely would.

As they went away another farmer who had been standing nearby, listening to Henry George's good advice, caught up with them and said, "I'll tell 'ee one thing, maid — how *I* do buy a cow. I don't care if she's got five legs of different sizes and horns all down her backbone — if she'll yield ten gallon a day, I'll buy her!" Laughing at his own wit, he went away without waiting for her reply.

"I thought *you* were going to buy something," William said accusingly as they started retracing their steps back into town.

"No," she replied scornfully. "'Twas nothing but wisht and jealous stock today — or so I'm informed! I wonder what jealous means in that context?"

"Huh!" he exclaimed in a hollow tone. "Jealous is jealous is jealous! Take it from one who knows!"

"Oh, Will!" She rubbed his arm tenderly, anxiously. "I'm sorry — truly, I am."

"Will you sack her?"

"No. That would be too easy. I mean, as you pointed out, it wouldn't solve anything."

"There *is* no solution," he said glumly.

"Don't be so defeatist. There's *always* a solution."

"Yeah! Lock her up in a tall tower!"

She stared at him in bewilderment.

"Well," he said, "it would keep the other fellows at bay."

Leah, catching his drift, laughed at the idea. "She'd only grow her hair long enough for them to climb up."

" She'd do it overnight, too!" he agreed.

"But little changes can achieve big results. Remember what Pa always told us — 'A ten-cent shave and a five-cent shoeshine can turn a thousand-dollar deal'? We've just got to find those little buttons to press that will make Pansy ..."

"You don't understand the problem," he complained.

"Okay. You tell me, then."

He checked all about them before he replied: "I love her enough to *respect* her — as you put it. Keep my hands to myself, in other words. Her honour is like my own. Now girls are supposed to swoon with gratitude when they meet such a man. But that's not what Pansy wants at all." He groaned and mimed the tearing-out of hair.

"Go on," she urged.

"In all those penny dreadfuls they read down in the kitchen it's always the young master who has his wicked way with the poor innocent maid. Often, one of his arguments is that if she doesn't yield to his demands, he'll transfer his affections elsewhere and some other lucky girl will get him. I'm looking for the story where it's the maid who tells the master that if he doesn't have *her* wicked way with her, she'll find some other lucky — and willing — man. I want to know how *that* tale ends."

"Mmh," Leah replied. "You're not the only one."

29 The last of the fatstock was sold at ten-thirty. There was a little ritual in which Ben Coad put away one set of books and took out another; it was matched by a ringside ritual, too, in which butchers withdrew and farmers took their place. Butchers wore gumboots; farmers leather and gaiters. Butchers ran their hands along the backs of the cattle and squeezed their flanks; farmers stood back and appraised the shape, or they bent and felt the udder. Butchers hardly ever looked a beast in the eye.

On Adèle's advice Leah had dressed in a plain suit of brown serge with a skirt that finished several inches above the ankle — not that her stout leather boots made for much of a revelation. She wore very little underneath it — a corset and one petticoat — for the day would have been hot even for a naturist. Her father, who came with them to make sure she did not disgrace the family, was the only man dressed for the occasion — in a thin suit of unbleached linen and a straw hat. Farmers in their summer-and-winter tweeds looked at him with envy and wondered if they'd ever dare put up anything so sensible.

Though the old man kept in the background, his presence dampened that spirit which might otherwise have led to many a ribald comment around the ring as his daughter made clear her intention to bid. She saw farmers going up to Coad, one by one, to remind him how they would signal their bids or to tell him of a change to their usual system. The others stayed back a respectful distance meanwhile, like customers in a bank. Leah waited patiently and apart from them. When the last had had his little say, she made her approach.

There was a ripple of surprise, which she affected to ignore.

Coad ignored it, too. "I've thought out a tactic," he told her. "There's no time to explain it now. Just trust me. You remember my signal?"

"With the pencil — yes. But how do I signal *my* bids?"

"Just call out yes or put it in plain English. Make every bid obvious. That's part of the tactics. It'll unsettle them — a bit of openness and honesty always does." He chuckled and pretended to be laughing *at* her.

"Is it okay if I feel their bags outside the ring? I can hardly climb over to go into it. Not in this skirt."

He said that would be fine and so, with dry mouth and mounting excitement, she and Adèle went to the gangway leading into the ring, where the first bullock was waiting. She was a second-calf heifer with her calf at her heel, a little bull just ready for weaning. The gangway was about eight feet wide, between posts of cast iron that time and a thousand hands had burnished. The two women made minuscule additions to that polish as they stooped and climbed between the middle and upper bars — to cries of 'Oh my eye!' and 'Here comes the Light Brigade!'

"Do we want a bull calf?" Leah asked Adèle, ignoring the rabble as she stooped to feel the heifer's bag.

"You've got enough grass," she replied. "You could neuter him, bring him on to six months, and then put him back here in the fatstock sale as a yarling store."

"What's this on her bag? High up on this side — can you feel it?" Leah stood back to let Adèle have a go.

"Just a vein," was the verdict.

"Sure it's not mastitis?"

"No. Mastitis feels like a cuttlefish bone under the skin. That's just a vein. A milk vein, they do call it."

"And it's not going to burst or anything horrid?"

Adèle just laughed. "D'you think you're really cut out for this-here farming, maid?" she asked.

"I just want to get everything absolutely right, that's all."

"Ready, gentlemen!" Coad called out, adding as an after-thought, "And *ladies!*"

There was a universal whoop at that and those few who had not noticed the two females craned their necks and followed the pointing sticks and pipestems. With excess gallantry the farmers near the entrance to the ring made way for them.

"Now, first off the mark today," Coad began, "is a fine dairy shorthorn, second-calf heifer. She gave five hundred and thirty gallons in her first lactation. Her mother belongs to give over seven hundred. Look at that conformation! She'd be a credit to any herd so what do I hear for a starter? Twelve pounds? Who'll start me at twelve now surely?"

To Leah's amazement she saw him making the pencil signal.

Panic seized her. Had she got it wrong? Was she to bid when he *wasn't* making the signal? No. She was sure that the signal meant bid. But, even if she had not been at Camborne market the previous Saturday, she'd have known that you *never* accept the auctioneer's opening call — not in any sort of auction.

But she also remembered his final injunction: 'Trust me!'

It was asking the moon of her but she decided to do just that.

"Come on, now. Twelve pounds surely?" Coad asked in long-practised desperation that fooled nobody. "She'll go for double, so you might as well."

"Yes!" Leah called out in a voice twice as shrill as she would have wished. "Twelve pounds!"

"Are you mad?" Adèle whispered at her side.

A stunned silence fell. Coad's mouth dropped. Heads turned between them as if watching a pingpong match. Coad should have been teaching at drama school, Leah thought. His surprise was absolute and his recovery from it a masterpiece. "We have twelve pounds, my lords! Who'll make it guineas?"

The pencil was held quite still in his hand; Leah waited.

One or two farmers began to look more closely at the heifer. They had seen Adèle earlier and now began to suspect she'd seen something they had missed — for twelve pounds was close to the expected finishing price for even a good second-calf heifer. Two of them climbed into the ring and felt her bag. One gave a barely perceptible nod.

"Guineas I'm bid!" Coad crowed. "Do I hear thirteen surely?"

He was fiddling with the pencil again. This time Leah had no hesitation. "Yes," she called out.

"You're mad," Adèle hissed even more furiously.

Leah had not told her of the arrangement. In her pride she wanted her friend to think the day's triumph was — or would be, when it was done — all her own work. "I know what I'm doing," she told her. "Just wait and see."

"Thirteen," Coad announced. "Thirteen on my left. I'll take guineas surely. Will anyone give me thirteen guineas?"

Someone gave a signal. Leah did not see who, but someone had clearly decided he was missing something that others could see. He wasn't going to be left out.

Coad asked for fourteen pounds — and gave Leah the signal. She bid fourteen.

Then guineas. Then fifteen ... sixteen ... until the bid reached an astronomical seventeen pounds — the price of a good, mature cow. And that bid was hers.

At that ridiculous point the rest dropped out. "Will someone give me guineas?" Coad asked with a knowing smile. And once again he gave her the signal.

She was now so committed to following him that she called out her yes without a thought.

Everyone laughed. She looked around in bewilderment, for if Coad could act his head off, so could she. The auctioneer laid down his pencil and smiled at her. With infinite patience and kindliness he said, "The bid is already with you, Miss Carrington. If you *insist* on paying guineas, I'll accept them, of course, but if we're all done" — he surveyed the others with comically raised eyebrows — "she's yours for seventeen pounds. And a bargain at that, if I may say so!" He banged the stone that doubled as gavel and paperweight.

Roars of laughter surrounded her, and her blushes owed nothing to her acting skill, such as it was.

Adèle stared at her miserably and John Carrington came up behind them, trembling with anger. "I think we'll go home now," he hissed in her ear, "and pay Ben Coad to select a good starter herd for us."

For a moment Leah did not move. She knew this was one of those big moments in her life, when a choice in any direction would affect everything she did thereafter. She gathered her feelings, drew a deep breath, and turned to look her father in the eye. "This is my money I'm spending," she reminded him. "My birthday present."

Her sudden calm disconcerted him, but he came back quickly enough. "Squandering," he said. "And it's my pride and self-respect you're squandering along with it."

"You said you'd trust me."

"I said I'd trust you to make a good bargain — which you're clearly incapable of doing. All you seem able to make is monkeys — out of both of us."

"You said you'd trust me to the end and I'm going to hold you to it," she replied, still in that icy-calm voice.

Inside herself, however, she was anything but calm. Her interior voice was shrieking out a prayer that Coad knew what he was doing, or it would be a long time before she'd be able to walk through Helston without giving rise to sniggers all down the street behind her.

The next bullock was in the ring by now, a big friesland in her sixth lactation; her calf had already been weaned from her. Coad knew his clientèle better than they knew themselves. He knew they had scented blood and that, since all Cornish humour is centred on people and their foibles and follies, they saw the chance of a tale that would regale many a bar and hearth down the years. The cow was worth, at most, fifteen pounds but, through signals to her, Coad pushed the bids up beyond that. The farmers cooperated with hearty fervour. When one of them bid eighteen-ten in hope of pushing her higher yet, Coad stopped signalling to her. It did more than leave the poor farmer out on a limb; it did more than ensure that the butt of those jokes round hearth and bar would be him rather than Leah Carrington; most important of all, it cleared the way for Leah's uncrowded bidding for the rest of the auction. From then on, no sensible man was going to risk running her up above a reasonable price for any bullock.

Over the following hour, out of twenty-three put up in the ring, she bought six — for a grand total of eighty-five pounds. All, except the first, were bargains by any measure. And if you looked at the thing in a wider context, that had been a worthwhile bargain, too, in its way.

Leah, with Adèle still in tow, joined her father and the three of them leaned against the railings round the stall she'd hired for her purchases. "Well?" she said.

"A motley lot," he replied.

"I don't care if they've got five legs each of different sizes and horns growing out of their spines, if their yield is good, they'll do me. But that wasn't the point of my asking."

He shifted uneasily and said, "Okay, they look pretty good to me. I grant you that."

"I don't think any farmer here could claim to have done better," Adèle put in.

"That's still not what I asked," Leah insisted.

"I know," he said ruefully. "Tell me, did you *plan* that little coup right at the beginning?"

"Or what?" she asked cautiously.

"Or did you realize you'd dug yourself in a hole and so then you improvised your way out of it?"

Briefly Leah wondered which would reflect more glory. The second, probably. She was just about to confess to it when caution overruled her; after all, Ben Coad just might let something slip one day. "It was sort of planned," she admitted. "You can't map out every little move but you can set up the general shape of the thing."

She hoped that was vague enough.

Carrington shook his head sadly. "I think I retired at just the wrong time," he said. "Never mind Kernow and Daughter — Carrington and Daughter would have made one heck of a team at a pork-belly auction."

Leah grabbed his arm and laughed as she hugged it. "Oh, Pa!" she said, blushing in her confusion.

"*Mea culpa!* I should have had more faith in my own bloodline." He leaned forward and addressed Adèle past his daughter. "Well, young lady, is your brother going to make a fortune at Wheal Fortune?"

"*He* thinks so," she said dismissively.

"It's not an idle question," he continued. "If I'm not going to squander a small fortune on my planned garden, I shall have to put that money somewhere. Wars have made lots of men rich but they've never increased the value of idle cash. That was true in Ancient Egypt and it's true today. So is Nicholas Liddicoat a good investment?"

Adèle, realizing at last that he was serious, despite the joking edge to his question, gave an answer whose seeming naïvety surprised him. She said, "Maybe it's just what he needs."

"Everyone needs capital," he remarked.

"Yes, but Nick needs it in a different way. He needs to know that someone believes in him — and believes in him enough to put up the capital."

Now it was Leah's turn to be surprised. It had never occurred to her that the Nark might be lacking in self-confidence.

Carrington made no immediate reply. He stared at Adèle as if seeing her in a new light, then at his daughter — ditto — then at the heavens.

Later, when they had driven the cattle home and baptized the brand new galvanized pails with their milk, he joined Leah at the field gate and said, "Well?" in the precise tone she had used earlier, back at the market.

"Look at them," she said. "They don't know which one is boss. It's more important than food."

"It's all about food, actually. Who gets the lion's share. Nature red in tooth and claw!"

"We're the same — humanity. We're worse, in fact. Cattle fight for a bit of the field. We fight to divide the whole world. And yet …" She sighed.

"And yet what?"

She leaned her head on his shoulder and said, "I think this is probably the happiest day of my life, Pa."

"It can only go downhill from here on in, eh?"

She chuckled. "You didn't come out here to gloat. When you said 'well?' just now — what are you asking, really?"

"About Adèle?"

"What about her?"

"About what she said this morning. That was pretty astute, don't you think?"

"She is astute. I've never thought her anything else."

"I was watching the new girl — Pansy — while she was running the milk through the cooler. Talking with her about this and that. She's convinced herself that all the young men hereabout are going to be taken by this war. She doesn't think it'll be over by Christmas."

"Has this anything to do with, you know, what we were talking about before?"

"In a way. If Pansy's fears are right — and one can't rule them out — the world is going to need young women who can do what you did to those farmers this morning and what Adèle almost did to me."

"Why?" Leah's laughter was slightly bewildered. "What did she *almost* do to you today?"

"She almost got me signing a cheque there and then, on the spot. She turned a casual, rather vague inquiry into a notion I'm now taking very seriously."

"You could set up a partnership," Leah suggested. "Young Liddicoat's know-how — and mineral rights — plus Will's enthusiasm and muscle power plus your capital."

"Just so," he said.

30 Over the next few weeks there were more bovine skirmishes in the fields of the Old Glebe as Leah brought her herd up to a dozen milkers and the newcomers contended for their place in the pecking order. She became a well-known and ultimately accepted figure in the market and, although she could not go into the pubs, there were plenty of farmers who had signed the pledge and who therefore congregated round the Band of Hope's mobile tea canteen, which toured all the markets to cater for them. 'The cup that cheers but not inebriates!' was its motto, painted in a rainbow arch over the serving hatch.

In sober conversations over many such cups Leah picked up much useful farming lore; but the main thing she learned was that farmers are a maddeningly reticent lot. They'd admit to keeping pigs but if she asked how many, they'd reply, 'a few' or 'quite a few' or 'some' or 'it do vary.' All her particular questions elicited the same sort of response; they were generous with generalities, parsimonious with the particular. She could have asked Mrs Troy and got a direct answer at once, of course — which was what her father had advised when she first thought of building the dairy herd — but pride made her want to go it alone as far as she could.

Eventually, however, she found the answer. She hired a labourer called John Hamden, who came with Ben Coad's recommendation. He was then working as a hedge-trimmer for the county council. Though he wore an old-fashioned frock coat and a battered top hat, both green with age, he looked like a wild man, with his pale blue, staring eyes set deep in their sockets, and his hair like a lion's mane. A bit like old-man Liddicoat, in fact. Because his county-council job took him through many parishes at a time when most husbands were away at work, he was rumoured to have sired a large number of children in the district. But he acknowledged only seven, all by his wife. Because of his reputation the maids giggled when he spoke to them and they treated him with a half-comic, half-serious awe. But he certainly knew about farming and farm animals. If a cow were off her food, he'd know at once if it was a matter for the vet or whether she'd find the right herb and cure her colic by herself. He could tie knots that would never come undone of their own accord, yet they'd fall apart with a single tug at the loose end. He knew when a cow would 'come in troublesome' before her behaviour made it obvious. He taught Leah how to toss a sheaf of corn twice as high for half the effort.

All his help was over little things like that. When she asked general questions — should she get in a few pigs, or some chicken, or what catch crops would be best for this or that field, and so on — he would shrug and say, "That's your caper, missiz." It was so frustrating that, while the farmers would never be specific, and Hamden would never be general, there was still a large area in the middle where neither would tread.

Salvation came when, one day in the market, the stress became too much and she said, "Hamden thinks I should get in a dozen sows and keep my own boar." She chose the figure at random, just to put down a marker somewhere and see if anyone laughed. It was a stroke of accidental genius. For the farmer who would keep his own counsel all the way to the grave if she asked a direct question would feel his own honour imperilled if he let such ridiculous advice from a jumped-up hedge-trimmer pass him by without comment.

"That Hamden," one farmer said, "do know more about breeding and less about pigs than any man west of Plymouth!"

And thus she learned that four to six sows would be a more reasonable number. And since John Carter of Gwavas kept not only a stud bull but two stud boars as well, she could save the expense — and danger — of keeping a boar herself.

Soon Leah was crediting John Hamden with the most surprising opinions across the entire range of twentieth-century agriculture. In response to which she went on to learn that a couple of hundred chicken would bring in a useful weekly income. Also she'd missed the season now but if she could put up a long glasshouse by January, she could get a tomato crop next year; tomatoes were doing very well since it had been proved they weren't poisonous — and she could overwinter the same beds with lettuce and spring onions, which Giles Curnow was always looking for.

She discussed each of these ideas with her father but his attitude was that she'd learn more, and learn it better, if she made her own mistakes. Anyway, he was all fired up again with the idea of a sleeping partnership in Nicholas Liddicoat's tungsten business; he and Jimmy Troy were thinking of putting up the £5,000 jointly.

At last Leah felt she had acquired enough knowledge to try her tentative plans out on Mrs Troy. She drove over to Pallas Home Farm one Saturday in September, when she knew the woman would be doing the milking. By then she could milk as well as any maid who'd been reared to the business, so she took an extra pail and stool and between them they finished the job in record time. Mrs Troy linked arms with her as they drove the cattle back into the field. "I think, dear," she said, "that it's time we dropped the formalities and called each other Elizabeth and Leah, don't you?"

Leah's heart swelled with pride. Nothing could have done more to make her feel she had *arrived* than to be on such terms with one of the leaders of local society. She stammered her thanks and added that, back in America, she'd always been told the English were such stuffed shirts.

"Well, so we are," Elizabeth agreed. "But we do make exceptions for exceptional people. I heard all about your début at the auction ring. Quite a coup."

"And quite undeserved, I'm afraid. I'll tell you what really happened if you promise it won't go further ..." And she explained how Ben Coad had set the whole thing up and guided her every step of the way to 'her' coup. "Don't even tell Mister Troy," she begged. "Because he might let something slip to my pa, and then ..."

"You didn't tell him?"

Leah shook her head. "I ought to have, I know. But he weighed in so proudly, speaking about our bloodline and all, I just couldn't do it."

"Yes," Elizabeth said, tapping the rump of the last yearling through the gate. "Those moments when the moving finger writes ... and you can't go back and cancel half a line! One gathers so many of them on one's journey through life."

"What's your worst?" Leah asked impulsively, spurred on by their new first-name intimacy.

"Oh, my dear girl!" Elizabeth bridled. "That is close to asking the impossible."

"Sorry!" Leah wished the ground would open. Then, to show willing herself, she said, "I'll tell you mine. It's very fresh in my mind so it's easy." And she described the night of the full moon, back in early August, when the Nark had dared her to go alone into the old barn. Her voice broke when she came to the moment of their kiss but she drew a deep breath and, mastering her emotions, said, "And for some reason I pulled away and said no ..."

"Fear?" Elizabeth suggested.

"I don't know? Maybe. Deep down, perhaps, but not on the surface. It was all so sudden, you see. Too much. One minute we were looking in each other's eyes and next minute we were kissing. And everything inside me just screamed out *yes!* It was like, I don't know — coming home? It was like it was the rightest thing I ever did. The whole of my life was a straight arrow zooming toward that one moment. Bullseye! And that just scared me, you know?"

"Why? Don't you trust your certainties?"

"No. I remember in school once saying 'nine nines are seventy-two'! And when I said it I was *absolutely* sure I was right. I mean, I'd have staked my life on it, I was that certain. And then when the teacher frowned and everyone else started laughing and I heard in my mind's ear an echo of what I'd just said ... well, I was so mortified I can't tell you. Look — are my ears turning red now? They feel like they are. And that's how awful I still feel. Not because of the mistake, because anyone can have a slip of the tongue like that, but at my certainty and that shocking, hideous laughter. I'll hear it till I die. And so whenever I get that feeling of *absolute* rightness I just shrivel away from it. I back off. I say no. Go away. Stop!"

"And that's what you said to young Mister Liddicoat that night — stop? Go away?"

"Mmh-hmm. Poor man. His face!" Her tone changed. "Of course, he's too proud and stiff-necked to *do* anything about it. His brother won't take no for an answer — worse luck. I mean, Nicholas could try and push just a *little,* don't you think?"

"I've never heard you call him Nicholas before."

Leah breathed hard a couple of times and then thumped the top bar of the gate with her fist. "He's just so infuriating."

"Many have found him so."

"I mean, I don't want to *marry* him or anything. I don't want to marry anyone just at the moment. I don't want a deep and solemn affair. But what's wrong with a kiss now and then? And a cuddle. And saying sweet nothings in each other's ears. And just having someone who's a little bit more than a friend — why can't he see that?"

"I wonder what he's saying about you?" Elizabeth murmured. "Of course, with your brother working alongside him every day, it wouldn't be impossible for you to find out, would it? How do you and Will get on these days?"

Leah considered this possibility but the pessimist within her rejected it. "Men don't talk like that. Nick could be breaking his heart over what happened, and yet he could work alongside Will for ten years and he'd never breathe a word of it."

Elizabeth took her arm again and turned her homeward. "You're half right, anyway," she said. "He'd never confess to a broken heart, but men aren't as good at hiding their feelings as they'd like to believe. Nicholas might bring you into the conversation rather often. Or there might be a little hesitation when he speaks your name. Or a certain look in his eyes when Will tells of something you've done. The man who even *knows* he's giving himself away in such subtle clues is as rare as hens' teeth. The man who can actually suppress them is twice as rare again. I think Will could be your ally in this — though men have such funny ideas of loyalty. If Nicholas does the usual thing and pokes fun at your efforts to farm the Old Glebe and generally gives the impression he finds you comical and beneath his contempt, Will might easily think he truly means it. And then he would regard it as disloyal to his partner to help you achieve your purpose here."

There was quite a lengthy silence while Leah absorbed all the implications of this advice. "Suppose …" she said at last. "Just suppose I were to do the same? If I spoke rather too often about Nicholas …"

"The Nark," Elizabeth reminded her.

"Of course! Suppose I were to speak rather often about him but — in the same breath — make it clear how little I cared about the answer …" She let the rest of the idea hang; although she could see the general strategy of the thing, she could not grasp its precise tactics.

Elizabeth finished the thought for her: "Then if it just so happens that the Nark is doing the same thing at work all day, your brother would have to be a monster of unheeding ... unperceiving ... what's the word?"

"He'd have to be a simp, a real punkin-head, not to put two and two together."

"Quite so! And that would make him feel immensely superior. You're both ... what? Three or four years older than him but you're behaving like children. It would bring out the altruism in him, don't you think? Having put two and two together he would feel it his duty to do the same with one and one — one Nicholas and one Leah! Oh, I do hope it works, Leah! It's such a pity that men can't be simple and straightforward and honest about these things!"

31   The new farmer at the Old Glebe soon became a fanatical student of the almanac, particularly of the hours of sunrise and sunset. Soon after the first of each month she could reel them off for all its remaining days. They were the hours that ruled her life, especially as the mornings and evenings drew in and each hour of dwindling daylight became correspondingly more precious. "I'll bet there's something you didn't know," she said to Will one evening when she and he were sitting by the fire after supper. "I'll bet you thought that as the days get shorter they lose an equal number of minutes at dawn and dusk. Well, it ain't so! Sunset at the end of this month is fifty-seven minutes earlier than at the beginning. But sunrise is only forty-three minutes later. I wonder why that is?"

"Everyone knows *that!*" he replied scornfully. "The sun likes to lie in of a morning, just like everyone else."

She flung the almanac at his head but missed. Then she said, "Anyway, you've got it the wrong way around — as usual."

To her surprise he picked the book up and returned it to her. She asked if he was feeling quite well.

He grinned, stretched his boots toward the fire, and said, "It's been a pretty good day, one way and another. You know Pa and Mister Troy were having second thoughts about their investment in the ...?"

"D'you mean they've now had third thoughts and said yes?" she asked excitedly.

"Wait!" He held up a finger. "It gets better yet. Jimmy Troy came and looked at our samples. He knew the assay was good but he was worried there might not be enough of the stuff just lying around — and he had a very good reason to worry, as you'll hear. He was afraid we'd have to reopen some of the mines — and then, of course, we wouldn't be talking about a measly five grand."

"Ho ho! 'A measly five grand,' indeed!"

"Well, that's picayunish compared with what you'd need to reopen any of those mines. Anyway, the reason he got so cautious is that he once tried to extract tungsten from the halvans around Pallas Home Farm …"

"*Tried* to?" she interrupted. "When was this?"

"Well, succeeded for a while. Twenty years ago, when he first came here. But the assay wasn't so good and the market fell and … anyway, it didn't last too long. So it's once-bitten, twice-shy for him."

"That's good, surely?"

"Yes, but it's why he and Pa had second thoughts. Of course, the market is way up now, with the war and all. So, when Nick got a much better assay than he ever had, old Troy fell to thinking. And that's where the men who make money differ from the men who make a living. You or I would simply have thought, 'Oh good — we've got enough without reopening any of the old mines, so now we can go ahead'! But not good ol' Jimmy Troy."

"Nor not me neither," she put in.

"What would you do?" He eyed her suspiciously.

'I'd say to myself, 'If it's just lying around the place at Wheal Fortune, why not at Scott's, too — and Deepwork, Wheal Vor?' I'd look over all the other halvans in the district, too. I'd find out the limit of the mineral …"

"Okay, okay!" he said with weary disgust.

"… and I'd buy up all the rights to stop anyone else muscling in on the claim."

He heaved a sigh and stared at the flames.

"Sorry if I spoil your tale," she said. "Is that what Pa and Mister Troy have been doing?"

He nodded. "I don't know why you never ran for president, Sis. You'd have been a shoo-in."

"I really am sorry, Will." She rose and came to sit on the sofa next to him. "I honestly didn't mean to spoil your story but" — she rubbed a finger lightly up and down his forearm — "it *is* rather an elementary precaution, don't you think?"

He continued staring at the fire. "I'm never going to be rich, am I."

"Does it matter?"

He laughed at last. "I guess not." Then, as if it were apropos, he added, "I'm going to suspend my tuition at the Camborne School of Mines. Pa agrees. I can go back when LCT no longer need me. That's the firm of Liddicoat, Carrington, and Troy, in case you were wondering."

When she made no reply he said, "You disapprove?"

"No." She stirred. "You and the Nark get on all right together, do you?"

"Of course we do. Otherwise I'd hardly be going to sign ..."

"Oh, well, that's all right then. I just wondered."

"Wondered what? What are you suggesting?"

"Nothing! It's just that some people get on and others don't. Two people working side by side all day ... you obviously *do* get on. So that's fine."

He chuckled. "You mean you and he wouldn't. Well, I can *certainly* believe *that!*"

She said nothing, for fear of giving away her interest.

"Do I ever complain about him?" he asked.

"Do I ever complain about John Hamden? But I find his conversation quite tedious at times. Especially this morning."

"Talking of John Hamden ..." He rose and put another couple of logs in the fire. "What's come over him today? He hardly had a word to say when we passed in the lane."

She sniffed and avoided his eye. "It was something I said."

He returned to his place at her side. "Was it something repeatable?" he asked.

"I guess it is — to you, anyway. Don't tell Pa. It might shock him. One of the sows I bought from John Carter, down Gwavas — which he swore was already in pig — returned this morning. So ..."

"Returned?"

"Came in heat again. So I went down with John Hamden to make sure we wouldn't be charged for another service. And anyway, while it was happening, old Hamden sort of moved closer to me …"

"You mean you were watching?"

"Will!" she chided gently.

"I mean …" he said.

"Yes? You mean what? Go on!"

"Nothing. I suppose you have to. Anyway, what did Hamden say? Or do?"

"He sidled up to me and said *he'd* like to be doing that." She laughed to show him she hadn't been shocked.

But it only added to her brother's fury. "The devil he did! I'll punch his head in next time I see him."

"You'll do no such thing. Do grow up!"

"And *he* has the nerve to be shocked at something *you* said!" he exclaimed. Then the implications of her words struck him and, in an altogether more cautious tone, he asked, "What *did* you say to him?"

"I asked him at least to let the boar finish with her first."

She only just managed to keep a straight face. Will tried to recover his anger but the thought of Hamden's response, which he could not help picturing in his mind's eye, carried the day, and once his laughter broke through there was no curbing it. He laughed until the tears ran.

"He spoke not a single word all the way back," Leah added when her brother had calmed down somewhat. "It was a blessèd silence. Somehow I don't think I'll be bothered with smutty remarks and *doubles-entendres* from him in the future. But just think — if I'd blushed and stammered out some embarrassed rebuke, he'd have been cock-a-hoop and he'd never stop insinuating things. You see that, don't you?"

He nodded unhappily. "Guess so."

"But you'd still prefer it if I sat in an ivory tower doing needlework with my maids, eh? Oh, Will!" She laughed. "What d'you think women talk about when we're alone together?"

He stared up at her, mouth agape. "No!"

"Yes. I know, for instance, that you have not heeded my advice in the matter of Pansy Tregear."

He bridled at that. "I don't recall *getting* any advice, actually."

It was a fair point and, for a moment, Leah did not know what to say.

He leaped into the silence. "And what has she been blabbing about me, anyway?"

"Not she. The other maids. Maria Vose and Dolly Cory — they claim to be shocked, of course. I think Dolly is, quite genuinely, but Maria is just jealous."

"I can't think what about. Pansy seems to have cooled off lately. Off *me,* anyway."

His emphasis struck a chord within her. She remembered her father telling her about watching Pansy cooling the milk that time. And on several occasions since then she had come across them together — never in a compromising situation or anything like that. And, to be sure, when two people live under the same roof and one is there to serve the other, it is highly likely that they will find themselves in the same room on numerous occasions, even several times a day. And it was true that Pansy was a bright, nimble-witted girl who learned fast and was not afraid of responsibility; she had made herself indispensable about the house and farm in the few short weeks she had been there. All the same, the old man had taken to singing her praises rather loud and rather often.

"Suits me," Will added. "I find Blanche Curnow more interesting — and more attractive."

The strong whiff of sour grapes in this remark only added to Leah's disquiet. "Has Pa ever spoken to you about marrying again?" she asked.

The sudden fear in his eyes told her he was worried, too, but also that he did not want to talk frankly about it — not yet, anyway. She realized she had to steer toward safer waters. "The reason I ask is that, now the Grand Garden scheme is on ice ... well, you know what energy he has ..."

William bit his lip thoughtfully. "I never looked at it that way," he said.

"Looked at what?" she asked shrewdly.

"Oh ... nothing. Just, you know, the general situation."

"Will!" she challenged.

"What?" He was all hurt innocence.

"You know. It's worried you, too — the reason why Pansy may have put *you* on ice lately."

His head slumped between his shoulders. "I guess so," he said. "But there ain't much we can do — is there?"

"Oh, we can do a lot."

Her blithe confidence heartened him, at least to the point where he'd argue a case. "Such as?" he asked. "If you fire her, first of all he might not let you, and secondly ... well, like I said about me, it wouldn't stop any meetings."

"But that would cause such a scandal. It would even have caused a scandal in East Haven, which is part of a city. Imagine it down here!"

He shook his head stubbornly but did not argue.

She went on. "I know they say there's no fool like an old fool, but Pa's not old. He's only just turned fifty-three."

"Exactly!" He gave a hollow laugh.

"What does *that* mean?" she asked when he volunteered nothing further. "Look — are you going to tell me or not? Surely you're not still trying to shelter my blushing, maiden ears — not after what I've told you tonight! Don't you think I ought to know what you know? Or don't you care?"

He shook his head and stared into the fire at the impossibility of explaining such things to her. But he tried. "What I know?" He echoed her words. "What I know is *me*. I know the absurd, ridiculous things *I* was planning when she knocked me off my feet like that. Even though I knew I hadn't the money ... nor the opportunity ..."

"Ridiculous things like what?"

"It doesn't matter. Use your imagination and stop embarrassing me! The point is, Pa *does* have the money. And the opportunity. And he *is* young, like you say. He still has plenty of that same youth which got me so kiboshed over that girl." He tapped his forehead to show where the affliction had struck him. Then he looked her level in the eye for the first time since this conversation had started. "Do I really need to lay it all out for you?"

"I guess not," she replied wearily.

In silence they stared into the flames for a while, glad of some small distraction.

Then Leah said, "We don't know too many widows, do we! Nice, comfortable, middle-aged, middle-class ladies past childbearing ..."

"... who would share a passion for gardening without having strong ideas of their own ..."

"... and who wouldn't object to a stepdaughter who fondly imagines herself a farmer ..."

"... nor a stepson who comes home covered in rock dust every evening ..."

They relapsed into silence again.

Then he said, "No, we don't know too many like that."

After another, shorter silence, she said, "But we can agree on one thing."

"Such as?"

"Such as: There's no such thing as *too many* widows like that!"

Part Three

Shades of the Future

32 Like a wolf on a sheepfold Philomena Liddicoat descended on Helston, all unannounced, on the morning of the last day of September. She was short, slender, pretty, and deadly. Those who knew her and witnessed her grim march from the railway station down to the Angel raised their hats or dipped their heads and held their breath until she had safely passed. She carried with her the aura of an old woodensides man-o'-war under full sail. How one so spare and slight could do so was a mystery, but it was the sort of mystery they would rather observe than investigate.

Sergeant Daws watched her passing from the police station window and murmured, "I've been wondering how long 'twould be afore *she* turned up."

Henry Plum, the town clerk, saw her five minutes later, coming down the steeper part of Wendron Street. He stood well back from his window, to avoid catching her eye, and pointed her out unobtrusively to his assistant, Claude Werry, who murmured, as quietly as if she had been in the room with them, "Poor old Clifford Liddicoat, eh! He must have thought he'd seen the last of her."

Only old Bassett, the tobacconist near the bottom of Wendron Street, had a smiling welcome for her. He spotted her about the same time as Henry Plum, when she was still some thirty grim marching paces away. He dashed back into his little emporium and returned to stand at his threshold proffering one of Miss Philomena's favourite cigars. He was smiling from ear to ear — as well he might, for they were an expensive brand and she had always been an excellent customer. In fact, he still had a whole, unbroken box of them left over from her last visit home, five years earlier.

"Welcome home, Miss Liddicoat," he cried. "Allow me the honour of presenting you with this small token of our delight at seeing you here among us again."

She accepted it with her most radiant smile and he breathed once more. "You may put me down for a box, Bassett," she said. "I think I'm going to need them. If certain reports that have reached me are true."

"By the greatest good fortune, modom," he replied, "I have one that arrived only yesterday."

She puffed the cigar alight. She had nothing but contempt for ladies who smoked cigarettes in the street but cigars were altogether different. Anyway, nobody had ever criticized her for the habit. Not to her face. "You can show me the invoice, of course?" she said casually.

"Ah ..." Bassett was nonplussed. "I had to return it. There were two errors. But they will post me an emended copy." His flat tone signalled his defeat plainly enough and she did not press him further.

"Tell me if these disturbing rumours are true," she said. "About the Old Glebe."

"The Old Glebe?" he asked uncertainly, for there were, of course, many glebes, old and new, in the district. "You mean the one up Sithney?"

"Where else, man? Mrs Kelynack, my cousin in Wadebridge, wrote to tell me it has been sold — and to a Carrington, of all people. I hope it is not so?"

Bassett tilted his head apologetically. "Will you come in and take a seat, Miss Liddicoat?" he asked. "The news on *that* subject is as grim as could be, I fear."

She accepted his invitation and seated herself regally before his counter. "So it's true," she said grimly.

A gentleman entered to make a small purchase, saw her there, recognized her, and beetled off again. She appeared not to notice. "Tell me about these Carringtons," she said in a voice that would ripen green mustard.

Ten minutes later, grimmer than ever, she stomped into the Angel and sought out Walter Blackwell, the proprietor.

Even Walter Blackwell, implacable scourge of those who drank too much or paid too little, quailed at the sight of her.

"Are they still here?" she demanded without preliminary.

"Why, Miss Liddicoat!" he exclaimed with every show of delight. "How very pleasant to see you in Helston again! May I ask whether ..."

"Yes, yes!" She cut him short. "All well and good. You'd better let me have a room until I see the lie of the land. I don't think the atmosphere at Grankum will be too congenial for the time being."

Blackwell, who did not doubt her opinion, was wise enough not to say so.

"*Not* the room these Carringtons occupied," she added. "If, that is, they have already gone."

"Ah!" He was crestfallen. "All our other rooms are occupied, I fear." It was not true but he was trying to keep the other rooms clear for refurbishment.

"Then move someone," she told him, as one tells a child something utterly obvious. "My bags are at the station."

Blackwell mumbled that he'd see what could be done.

"I shall be staying in the district for a year or so at the very least," she said. "Until this war is over. They have requisitioned my house."

The slight stress she laid on the word 'my' would have alerted an attentive stranger to the possibility that the ownership of the house was, or had recently been, in question. Blackwell noticed it, of course, but then he was no stranger to the story. It had been whispered all over Helston at the time — about a year earlier — when Colonel Jellicoe's family had disputed his will, which left the house and a thousand a year to his 'dearest housekeeper and companion,' Miss Philomena Liddicoat. The most scurrilous inferences had been drawn from that careless use of the word, *dearest* and from the unheard-of generosity of the annual bequest.

Blackwell did a quick calculation. If her house were only half as grand as the descriptions of it that had appeared in the press at the time of the trial, it would easily command a rent of £150 a year, even from a parsimonious war office. Then again, the war was surely going to depress his regular trade as quotas and rationing made travelling salesmen unnecessary. He had only that week decided that a few long-term residents on *en-pension* terms would not come amiss.

"I can offer you full-board *en pension* at one pound, nineteen-and-six a week, Miss Liddicoat," he said, manfully resisting an impulse to duck once the words were out.

It did not take her long to trim three-and-six from the offer.

"I shall start from this minute with breakfast," she said. "And you may sit with me and tell me what you know of this Cousin Jack Carrington who has dared to steal Sithney Old Glebe from under our noses."

Blackwell organized her breakfast while she went for a wash and brush-up. He also sent a pot-boy down to Frank Kernow and Ben Coad with the news that Philomena Liddicoat was back in town, this time for the foreseeable future. He also told Jenny Tregellas, the head barmaid, to rescue him in five minutes with some sort of emergency.

Miss Liddicoat's manner of handling a knife and fork was not in the least inelegant; indeed, objectively observed, she was more ladylike than many who claimed the title of lady would objectively deserve. Yet there was something about it that chilled Blackwell to the marrow as he sat to her table and tried *not* to observe — objectively or in any other way.

"He's a decent sort of fellow," he began.

"Describe him. What's he look like?" She drew her knife across the egg. Euclid himself could not have bisected the yolk more neatly. As the yellow spilled out she stemmed it with equally perfect squares of fried bread. "You still put up the best breakfast in Cornwall," she added.

He wondered why the compliment did not put him more at ease. "Fiftyish," he said. "Indeed, I know for a fact he turned fifty-two this month now gone. He stands about five-foot-nine. Dark hair turning gray. Wavy. Proper handsome. They're a good-looking family, all three."

"Husband, wife, and … son? Or daughter?" She speared a small pyramid on her fork — the firm yolk on top, underpinned by white, bacon, kidney, and fried bread.

It was her eye-teeth, he decided. If Dracula had a daughter, she would have such teeth as that — subtly larger than most but not enough to detract from her general prettiness. "Widower, daughter, and son," he replied, "in order of age. The daughter, Leah, is just turned twenty-two. The son, William, comes of age next January. Will I describe them, too?"

She nodded, swallowed, and said, "Everything."

"Leah would be about five-four, with short, dark, curly hair and dark, piercing sort of eyes …"

"Twenty-two, you said? And pretty? And not yet engaged even?" Philomena listed the facts as if they were contradictory. When Blackwell hesitated she added, "Tell me the worst, man. Something is obviously amiss if *she's* still a miss! If my nephews are both besotted by her, I need to know."

He looked away and shifted uncomfortably. " I hardly ever see them. Your brother's no drinking man, Miss Liddicoat, as well you know. And your niece Adèle, she …"

"Adelaide! I have no niece called Adèle."

"She brews her own ale, which she and her brothers …"

"Stop this flannel, man," she interrupted. "I know very well what sort of gossip is exchanged over your public bar of a market day. And I know you're quite able to overhear three conversations at once. So — *are* my nephews besotted by the Carrington creature?"

"William Carrington is said to be sparking with Blanche Curnow of Chynoweth."

"Giles Curnow's daughter? Good heavens is she … yes," she sighed, "I suppose she is. Last I saw of her she was a spotty little thing in pinafores. I've been away too long." She delivered the last sentiment with an ominous lightness. Few in Helston would have agreed though none would openly disagree.

"And as for Leah Carrington," Blackwell put in before she could goad him, "she is sparking with no one. Instead, she's taken pattern from Roseanne Kitto — remember? Farmed Wheal Fortune on her own before she married Stephen Morvah? Well, Miss Carrington's farming the Old Glebe now."

"Farming?" The toast shattered in two jagged halves under the sudden pressure of her knife. "My cousin, Mrs Kelynack, gave me to understand that this Carrington man intends to turn the whole of the Old Glebe into some kind of ornamental *garden?"* Her question implied she hoped it was not true. Blackwell assumed she was expressing a contempt for gardening that was common among Cornish farming folk, whose motto was, 'If you can't put it either on your own table or on the train to Covent Garden, dig it up by the roots and burn it."

"No. She's farming the place and she's the farmer, too. She bought her herd down Saint John's market backalong in August, or the foundation of it. Turned a neat trick on Sam Hocking, too, when he tried to run her up — she left him with a sour bid."

"And the father's taking no part in this farming nonsense?" She buttered her toast and daubed it with marmalade.

Blackwell eased his collar. "Well," he replied hesitantly, "he's thick as thieves with Jimmy Troy these days — which is hardly surprising. Them both being Cousin Jacks and …"

"Why should that prevent him from farming? I don't follow. The Troys still have Pallas Home Farm, surely?"

"Why, that's more *Mrs* Troy than her man. The thing is, Troy and Carrington are what you might call venturers now."

"In tin?" she asked incredulously as she popped a sliver of toast and marmalade into her mouth.

Blackwell wondered if any man had ever had the temerity to seek a kiss from those lips. Colonel Thaddeus Jellicoe had, if the rumours were true. The innkeeper took advantage of her eating to get it all out quickly: "They've put up the capital for young Nicholas, your nephew, to extract wolframite from the old halvans round Wheal Fortune."

"Have they, indeed," she said calmly as she prepared another sliver to follow the first. "We shall soon put a stop to that! What sort of capital is involved?"

Blackwell stared unhappily at the door. Where was that Tregellas girl? "I heard tell as the first payment was five thousand pounds, Miss Liddicoat."

She blanched at the sum. "*First* payment?" she echoed. "Are they reopening a mine as well or what?"

"It seems they found wolframite in several old halvans between Wheal Fortune and the Flow at Carleen. So they had to buy up all the surface mineral rights — and word leaked out."

"Even so — five thou' for … what is it, man? Why d'you keep looking at the door?"

"Oh … er, I thought I heard a commotion in the kitchen. I'm sorry — you were saying? Five thousand for … what?"

"For a one-man operation — it seems quite an excessive amount of capital."

"Oh, it's bigger than a one-man operation, Miss Liddicoat." He rose and went to the door. "Jenny? What on earth is going on down there?"

"A lot bigger?"

"No — not a lot. *Jenny?*"

"How much bigger then? Do stop fussing and come back here — I've not done with you yet. There's nothing happening out there, quite obviously."

"It's a two-man operation, in fact," he replied, dithering between obeying her summons and giving Jenny Tregellas one chance.

"Your reluctance on this point is not inspiring, Blackwell," she said sharply. "I begin to fear the worst. Who is the second person?"

At long last Jenny came running up the passage. "Oh, please, Mister Blackwell, sir, come quick, sir! Cook's been and gone and got her foot caught in the drain and she thinks it's broke."

He stared at her in utter dismay and asked in a fierce whisper, "Is that really the best you can come up with?"

"What is his name?" Philomena thundered.

"No, sir. Honest, sir. 'Tis true, sir. Martha lost a scouring brush down there, see, and ..."

He turned back to his latest guest. "I fear I have to go, Miss Liddicoat," he said, struggling to keep his relief out of his voice. This was a *genuine* emergency! He had never been so glad to hear of one.

"His name?" she insisted.

"Oh — that. His partner is William Carrington."

He ducked from imaginary blows as he beetled off down the passage in Jenny's wake. But no explosion of wrath pursued him. In its way, that was the most spine-chilling feature of all.

33 The stamps at Wheal Fortune and their numerous predecessors back over the years had been crushing ore to a fine sand for the best part of a century before the whole venture was abandoned. The resulting sandy waste, once the heavier tin ore had been vanned out of it, had been left to wash down into the valley until it threatened to choke the stream on which the entire operation depended for motive power. So every few years, teams of mules with drag-shovels had been brought in to scrape the sand into carts and carry it farther up the hillside. There the ever-growing piles eventually formed sandbanks twenty and more feet deep. And now, for Nicholas and Will, those banks had proved to be the richest source of wolframite among all the ready-mined ore.

Certainly it was the most get-at-able and the easiest to load and cart back down to the stamps for a second vanning — this time to separate a lighter fraction than the original cassiterite, or tin ore. Nicholas and Will divided their days between loading a hand cart up at the sandbanks and adjusting the vanning tables to give the maximum yield. The slope of the table, the rate of vibration, and the flow of the water across it all played a part and it was a matter of trial and error — of many trials and many errors — before they got the right combination. They achieved it on the last day of September that year, the day Aunt Philomena arrived in Helston.

They worked till sunset when, weary but happy, they trudged homeward up the path from the bottom Blueborough field. As they went they sang 'Belgium Put the Kibosh on the Kaiser' and dreamed of the patriotic riches their venture was going to bring in. The song petered out when, as they reached the bend by the Blueborough whim shaft, which was part of the old Wheal Fortune deep mine, they saw Adèle hastening toward them.

"You look as if you lost France and found Belgium!" Will called out cheerily. It had become a game among them to think up ever more bizarre variants of the catch phrase.

"Something wrong?" Nicholas shouted more seriously, he being more experienced at reading his sister's expressions, especially at a distance.

"You may well say so," she shouted back.

"Germany won the war?" Will was determined to stay cheerful. It had been too good a day for any little domestic upset over at Grankum to disturb him. Of every hundred shovelfuls he humped from now on, one would be pure tungsten ore!

"Worse!" Adèle replied. They were close enough now not to shout. "Aunt Philomena's house has been requisitioned by the war office."

Was *that* all? Will turned to Nicholas, expecting him to laugh. Nicholas did not laugh. Indeed, he did not even smile. "And they don't want her to stay on as housekeeper?" he asked.

"Would you?" she replied.

From the very tone of his friend's question Will knew that something serious was afoot. "Who on earth is this Aunt Philomena?" he asked.

"The Eighth Plague of Egypt," was the reply. "The one God never needed to use. The merest hint was enough to make Pharaoh cave in and let the Israelites go." To Adèle he said, "I ⸱pose she's come back here for the duration, then? Is she at ⸱kum now?"

"She may be. I came to warn you, anyway. She came down on the night sleeper and took breakfast at the Angel. Walter Blackwell got word to Ben Coad, who got word to the Old Glebe and then to us. The old man vanished at once, to buy new moleskins in Truro, he said. We shan't see him until late tonight, I'm sure. I don't know where Harvey is. I've spent the afternoon in fear and trembling but so far there's been neither sight nor smell of her."

"Jee willikins!" Will was impressed at last. "She sounds quite a lady. Is she your late mother's sister or your dad's?"

"Father's sister," Nicholas said. "She's the only person who ever persuaded Arthur Godden, the old station master at Helston, that her watch was more accurate than the Great Western Railway's timepiece."

"She got the train brought all the way back from Pallas Halt," Adèle added.

"And the main-line express was held for her at Gwinear Road." With a tinge of admiration in his voice Nicholas went on to tell his new partner about the aunt's generous inheritance from the late Colonel Thaddeus Jellicoe.

Adèle capped it by adding, "They say he didn't dare *not* leave her the place and the income — otherwise she'd have dug him up and given him a hot enough helping of tongue pie to awaken the dead."

Nicholas cleared his throat.

"They did!" Adèle protested.

"Yes, well, that was *one* of the reasons advanced at the time."

"Tskoh!" Adèle punched him slightly harder than playfully. "That was just scurrilous talk put about by the Jellicoe clan."

"So — have you come out and left the farmhouse empty?" Nicholas asked her.

"Eileen's there, buttering eggs. And Sampson's in the yard."

"Oh! I wonder how much dung will be turned and how many eggs buttered by the time we get back!"

"D'you mean I shouldn't have come to warn you?"

"No." He slipped an arm around her shoulders and gave her a quick hug. "You were absolutely right."

"All the same," she said, "I think we should go back directly over the croft. Not round by the road. You'll have to help me over the hedge."

The hedge in question was on the Grankum side of what they called a 'croft' though it was, in fact, an eleven-acre patch of poisoned land — a dump for ash and waste from the calciner, whose rusting firebox and oven still dominated the hillcrest above Wheal Fortune. Nothing grew there but a feeble carpet of ling and a dry sedge that struggled to turn from yellow to green. It had been walled about to keep the cattle out rather than in. Few birds sang there in winter but in summer it was a haven of skylarks, nightjars, and one ever-returning family of kites. Its near-dead surface offered an easier path than the winding, rutted lanes, but the farther hedge, with a six-foot fall on its Grankum side, was a formidable obstacle. Generations of Liddicoats, of whom Nicholas was the latest, had vowed to build stepping stones into the face of it. He repeated his pledge now, as they approached it. Neither of his listeners bothered to reply.

Will went over first, finding convenient footholds in the furze or among the stone, where the binding earth had been dug out by rabbits or rats. The drop on the far side looked daunting but, with Adèle's eyes upon him, he did not care to hesitate. If he had not been wearing stout boots, he would have turned his ankle on the tussocky grass.

When Adèle stood on the top he could reach no higher than her thighs — which, naturally, he did not even attempt.

"Can you sort of sit and slide off?" he suggested. "Or maybe I could lift you off, if you were sitting."

"I'm quite capable of getting down by myself," she said, contradicting her earlier request for assistance. "So, if you'll just turn your back a mo ..."

"No — come on." He stretched out his hands. "Just sit down. Or squat. As long as I've got hold of you ..."

"Oh, for God's sake!" Nicholas gave her a push from behind and she fell off the wall with a shriek, moving her arms like a swimmer starting a swallow-dive.

Fortunately Will had his hands raised high already and so he caught her round the waist close to the start of her fall, before she had gathered enough momentum to overwhelm him. The effort needed to brake her descent and turn it into a controlled movement was at the very limit of his muscular power but his muscular power had increased greatly since the start of their operation and, to his own great surprise, he managed it.

He became the circus strongman to whom she was a mere feather. Showing off at last he set her down among the tussocks in ultra-slow motion, making it look as if her feet were sinking through thick treacle.

"Oh, Will!" she murmured breathlessly, looking up at him with such devoted admiration that he was spellbound by it, unable either to speak or to let go of her waist. It was the very last thing he expected to happen.

She lifted her chin an inch or so. If they had been alone they would have kissed. He knew it. She knew it. Their eyes, dwelling deep in each other's, flashed their knowing back and forth. He had never seen such inner beauty in a face so plain. He did not know what to do about it.

"Come on — she's not hurt!" Nicholas grabbed Will by the arm and hauled him away downhill, past Adèle.

Will pulled himself free and turned back to Adèle, who was still standing as he had left her. She had her back to him so he could not read her expression. "Adèle?" he ventured.

She snapped out of her reverie and turned round. "Yes," she said flatly. "Home."

Before he could stop himself, Will held out his hand to her. "You might still fall," he said solemnly.

She hesitated briefly and then took it with a smile. "So I might," she said.

"Ohmigawd!" Nicholas exclaimed wearily.

They hardly heard him. They were both rather stunned by what had just happened — by what was still happening. For Adèle it was something she had not even permitted herself to daydream about — an impossibility too painful to indulge in, even in moments of fancy. For Will it was something more complex — something he had never remotely imagined and yet, now it had happened, something that did not greatly surprise him, either. It was almost as if some secret part of his mind had been contemplating such a thing without even hinting about it to the rest of him, which went on its merry way, alternately obsessed by Blanche Curnow and Pansy Tregear, whom he had imagined as aspects of sacred and profane love.

He tried to think of them now — one after the other, for he had never been able to think of them both in the same sweep of fantasy — and in both cases the image was of someone rece

— vanishing at the stern of an invisible boat on dimly glimpsed waters in a dark, subterranean lake.

Part of him — the part that had been taken by surprise just now — rebelled at the loss. It would rather have added Adèle to his pantheon of goddesses in some third category, somewhere between sacred and profane. But Adèle was not and never could become a category. She was that warm hand clenched so tight in his — how could mere fingers and knuckles feel so utterly precious? She was that wondering, incredulous smile, provoked by him and him alone — aimed at him and him alone. She was that remembered look of adoration when luck and muscles held just now. In her short, bonny, buxom person she embodied so much sense, such a wealth of good humour, such an abundance of calm judgment that now he wondered that he could ever have thought of another girl.

Nicholas was saying something about building a lockable shed in which to store their wolframite ... and how they must be careful not to undermine the road ... or should they perhaps build a new exit, avoiding the sandbanks altogether? And Will went on saying "Yes" and "Uh-hunh" and "Okay" until Nicholas said, "What d'you mean, 'yes'? I asked shall we or shan't we?"

But the new idyll between Will and Adèle — and the questioning from Nicholas — came to an abrupt end when Adèle, the only one looking directly in front of them at that moment, said, "Well, I'll go to hell! What *does* he think he's doing?"

Nicholas stopped in his tracks and said, "I thought you told us he'd gone to Truro?"

"He did," she asserted. "He must have realized it was only postponing the evil hour."

"But *that's* no answer!"

By 'that' Nicholas was referring to the unbroken shotgun their father was carrying at the slope while he paced up and down the yard like a sentry at the barracks gate. No doubt it was cocked and loaded, too.

"Father!" Nicholas called out reproachfully.

"Never you mind for me, mister!" he shouted back. "I know I'm about. You go on in and have your supper, all of 'ee. u — young Carrington — you duck your head down he hedge and go on home. This isn't no business of family."

They leaned against the yard gate and watched him in dismay. "Really, Father! What good is that gun going to do anybody?" Nicholas asked.

"You'll see," he replied darkly, and would say no more.

A moment later they saw — at least, they saw why he had come out into the yard to pace up and down in that menacing manner. A gig, which he must have spotted the moment it passed Boase's Burnthouse, came down the lane from the junction by Merther Cottage. Without hesitation it turned into the Grankum yard.

No one was more surprised at the sight of the lady at the reins than Will. From what her nephew and niece had said of her, he expected to see a grim, ugly, implacable female, carved in granite and dressed in Bible black. This petite and pretty lady, elegantly and expensively dressed, did not at all accord with those guided preconceptions. He thought they could not possibly have remembered her correctly — or that her inheritance had transformed her beyond recognition.

But the moment she opened her mouth and barked the one word, "Clifford!" at her brother, his doubts fled. It was enough. If old man Liddicoat were the barrack sentry, his sister was the most feared sergeant major who ever paralyzed an entire regiment with a single word. Already Will wished he had obeyed the order to get his head down behind the parapet and, by trench and sap, scurry for the safety of the rear echelon as fast as his legs could carry him.

"Don't 'ee come no closer, woman!" The old man lowered his gun and aimed it at her. "You've no business here. You aren't wanted here. You turn about and go back where you come from, and us'll not fall out."

She flung the reins at Sampson, who had come forward to assist her but who was now skulking behind the horse. "See to him, man," she said as she climbed down. He took the traces and raced the horse and gig over to one side of the yard, well out of the line of fire.

"I'm a-warning of 'ee!" Liddicoat said.

"Oh, Father!" Adèle whispered, beating her forehead gently against the top bar of the gate.

Will slipped an arm around her shoulders but she hissed "Don't!" at him urgently.

"I'm not afraid of her," he replied with more confidence than he felt. "What can she do?"

"Make life not worth living," she told him grimly.

Aunt Philomena walked straight toward her brother and took the gun from him without even pausing on her royal progress toward the house. "Come on in, you three," she called out, shielding her eyes against the evening twilight sky. "Who's the third fellow? It's not Harvey."

"Ohmigawd!" Nicholas said again — this time with absolutely no comic or satirical overtones.

"Cheer up!" Will clapped him on the back. "You look as if you lost a brother and found an aunt!"

Even at that he did not smile. Then Will, with all the courage of the ignorant — the fools who step in where angels fear even to *look* — vaulted the gate and opened it for the other two to enter. Leaving them to close it, he strode out, smiling, toward the woman, hand outstretched to greet her. "Good evening, ma'am," he said. "Miz Liddicoat — am I right? I am William Carrington, the son of your brother's neighbour …"

"Are you, indeed!" The slight smile of provisional welcome vanished. "I know my brother's *neighbour!*" She ignored his outstretched hand. "I've heard all about my brother's *neighbour.*" She turned to her brother, who had meanwhile come up from behind, and thrust the gun back into his hand. "*Now* you can shoot," she said.

For an awful moment the old man looked as if he were actually considering the possibility.

Will felt a squirt of fear threaten to sink his empty stomach even as his mind rebelled. It was no longer a tussle between him and this allegedly formidable woman. In fact, there was no 'allegedly' about it. Her steely eye, her coldly belligerent manner, her utter sense of self-possession, even when making the most outrageous proposal — all confirmed that she was, indeed, a most formidable woman. Yet, as he had begun to realize, it was no longer a tussle between him and her but a three-cornered ⸻ in which his body and his mind were at odds with each ⸻ His body wished to yield while his mind rebelled at the ⸻ght of doing so.

⸻ hose juices of terror could fill his veins and render ⸻ ss he laughed and said, "Don't be ridiculous!"

The word, spoken with his American twang, cracked like a whiplash among the other four. A few moments later it stung him that way, too; but by then he was committed.

"Will!" Adèle plucked at his sleeve from behind. "Don't! Honestly, just don't."

It was too late. Aunt Philomena turned to him with a smile. "Ridiculous?" she repeated quietly. It was a long time since anybody had stood up to her — only chaff and riffraff like railway servants and cabmen. Her last real opponents had been poor dear Taddy's relations, who had taken her on without realizing what they were letting themselves in for. Her real opponent would, of course, be the father of this rash and callow youth but if she could send him back to the Old Glebe as a bruised sort of emissary, it would be a good day's work, after all.

"Well now …" Will said in a tolerant, cajoling tone. "What would you call it, Miz Liddicoat? You'd be appalled if your brother took you at your word."

He looked about him, trying to recruit the other three with a laugh. The father regarded him with anger, Nicholas with apology, Adèle with tender concern. "It *is* ridiculous," he asserted, wishing he sounded more convinced of it himself.

In desperation he even contemplated taking the gun from the old man and thrusting it into the woman's hands, telling her to do the thing herself. But a debater's instinct — something he was hardly aware of possessing as yet — saved him. He saw — or *it* saw — that such a gesture would degrade 'ridiculous' into 'farcical.' And, if he was ever to assuage this lady's anger and bring her to accept the Carringtons in a spirit of surly neutrality (anything warmer was too much to hope for), he would have to avoid pushing her into corners where she would appear farcical. Even to show her up as ridiculous — which she clearly was being — was risky.

But that same instinct then pushed him too far in the opposite direction. Apropos nothing he said, "But what the heck! We've only just met and we haven't even shaken hands." He pointedly did not offer his a second time. Instead he said, "At the risk of annoying you all over again, Miz Liddicoat, may I say that I think that is one of the most strikingly beautiful hats I have ever seen. Do you have them made especially for you?"

"Will!" Adèle cried out in a voice of despair.

He was about to turn and pacify her when Aunt Philomena bridled at his insolence — as she saw it. "How dare you!" she cried. Her nostrils flared. Her entire body trembled with rage. For two farthings, he thought, she'd have grabbed the gun from her brother and done the deed herself. And yet ... and yet ... If he'd turned to Adèle as his new-found feelings for her urged him to do, he'd have missed it — that momentary flicker of fear in the older woman's eyes. Fear and ... something else. Doubt, by golly! Self-doubt. He could tell how rare a moment it was for her by the surprise that soon effaced it.

A brasher young man would have pressed in on this fleeting advantage, would have challenged her to face him — *and* her fear, and her self-doubt — all at once. But he still had that instinct which told him that, in facing him like that, she'd master the fear and uncertainty in passing. And so all future advantage would be gone.

"I'm sorry," he said in his humblest, friendliest manner. "Truly I am. I guess the sort of compliments we learned to pay to beautiful ladies in America don't go down too well over here. But I meant no disrespect, Miz Liddicoat. And I truly do think it is a *gorgeous* hat."

Her doubt, and the fear it brought in its wake, intensified. Her massive armoury of aggression had no weapons against flattery, still less against sincere compliments. The last man to call her beautiful had been her dear, darling Taddy. And now ... this damned little whippersnapper ... She held her peace and put on her grimmest countenance rather than reveal the slightest hint of her confusion.

Or so she imagined.

"I see I am the fly in the ointment here," Will said. "So, by your leave, ladies ..." He bowed at Miss Liddicoat, winked at Adèle and her brother, nodded at their father, and walked past him toward the lower gate.

"Young man!" Aunt Philomena called after him.

He turned round.

"...t ever come back here to Grankum!"

"...hed. "That will be rather difficult, Miz Liddicoat. But ...happy to explain it to you, no doubt." He waved ...he other three as he turned again and resumed his ...k.

34 Darkness gathered in the foot of the valley long before it laid its pall over the crests of the surrounding hills. Will was grateful for it, though on any other night he would have been a little wary — especially of that transition from the deep gloom of twilight's final minutes to the stygian night which already filled Grankum Wood. Then the rustle of leaves in the canopy above, the underfoot stirrings of creatures of the dark, and the rising-swooping shrill of bats from the abandoned quarry's cavelets, all combined to people the woodland with phantasms of the mind — on any other night but this.

Now the only image before him, behind him, beside him, was the dear, sweet face of Adèle, forever frozen in his mind in that moment of surprise when their eyes met and dwelled deep in each other's, when her plainness was transfigured for him into something holy and beautiful beyond bearing. Now he went out of his way to walk where she had walked, not diagonally up the long hillside to the Old Glebe but keeping to the valley floor, which was her daily path to the well when their rain tanks dried or turned an unpalatable green.

The enchanted well!

The well of enchantment!

She has been here! his spirit sang. And she was there yet, for the damp earth, the moss, the ferns, the very stones beside her path still caged something of the rare magic of her presence; they joined with him in that ecstatic cry. A line from Oscar Wilde, which had always puzzled him before, puzzled him no longer: *She hardly knew she was a woman, So sweetly did she grow.* That was Adèle. Of all the women on earth that was Adèle — more person than woman.

Pansy was woman. Blanche was woman, or soon would be. They were two fish in the big pool of interchangeable women (as he and other men were interchangeable to them, no doubt). There in that pool all young bachelors, and many a widower, too, could trawl by licence — at dances, chapel picnics, harvest suppers, and At Homes — keeping or returning their catch as head or heart might dictate. But not Adèle. Adèle was sud[den]ly interchangeable with none. Adèle was now uniqu[e]

Adèle, Adèle ... he thought his heart would burst right out of his breast at the sweet repetition of her name. It had mysterious, magic powers to move him now, and especially here in the dark of her own wood.

And most mysterious and magical of all was the fact that it had taken so long to happen. He had first seen her in March, at the ball where Blanche Curnow had so taken his fancy. He had seen her every week, and latterly every day, since then. Yet the love for her that was in him, and which must have been in him from that very first day, had taken all this time to emerge. Did that not prove how profound it was, how deep it must have lain all these weeks while he worked those other silly infatuations out of his system!

He drank at the well — her well — for its chalybeate waters no longer had their amusingly aperient effect on any of the Carringtons. And he breathed deep draughts of the air that had bathed her and which lingered here, craving, like him, one more brush with her ineffable sweetness. Then, with long, manly strides that she would surely admire if she were truly at his side, he set off up the hill for home. As he wound his way among the trees and across the fields he sang, 'It was a comely young lay-a-dee-eee fair ...' — which tells of a love, unrequited for seven long years, but rewarded at last. Pansy had taught it him but he did not think it disloyal to Adèle, nor, indeed, to Pansy, to sing it now. Love not only conquers all, it sanctifies all, too.

To his dismay, however, his singing of the final lines: 'For a dark-eyed morning, Brings forth a shining day' was joined by an all-too-familiar voice from somewhere up ahead — indeed, by the very voice that had first taught him those words and the accompanying tune.

"Pansy!" he called out; his surprise was genuine enough but the happiness of his delivery was forced.

She was leaning on the lower yard gate, silhouetted for a moment against the rising moon, which was still a couple of days short of full. Her long, fair hair, freed from its everyday knot, framed her in a veil of silver.

"... have 'ee?" she asked gleefully.

... start, thinking she meant Adèle; he had quite ... allegedly fearsome Aunt Philomena, having put ... nd the moment he left Grankum Farm.

"I'll wager she fell on they other poor Liddicoats like a sky of lead!" she added.

"Oh — Miz Philomena. Yeah. She did."

Her tone became curious. "Of course Miss Philomena. Who did you think I meant, then?"

"Nobody. I couldn't think *who* you meant. I'd forgotten all about her. What are you doing out here?"

"Waiting for a kiss," she replied. Her eyes danced merrily. Her head was resting at a slight angle on her folded arms, which rested on the top bar of the gate. Although the moon was behind her, his night-accustomed eyes could see her features clearly — especially the two full breasts that strained against her blouse as they thrust out beneath that bar. She knew, of course. No woman with her endowments — and attitude — could fail to know what havoc she was wreaking among all his pure and high-minded resolutions.

"Oh, dear!" he exclaimed, disguising the shiver in his voice as lack of breath after his stiff climb. "Am I scaring some young feller off? I'll be gone in a trice."

In a trice she grabbed the hand he intended for the top bar of the gate and carried it to her breast. He felt the firm flesh beneath the cotton of her blouse, the swelling bud of her nipple. She let out a shivery gasp at his touch. He willed his muscles to pluck his hand away; she pressed it even tighter to her. She closed her eyes and lifted her face, reaching her lips toward his. Until then he had not realized how close they were. Nor, until it closed around the full, ripe softness of her other breast, did he realize what his other hand was doing. And then he could not stop it.

Everything within him that was capable of forming words cried out that this was wrong, wrong, wrong! His lips melted in the soft sweetness of hers. They flowed together. *Wrong!* Her nipples swelled like miniature breasts in their own right. *Wrong!* Instincts he did not know he possessed guided his palms, his fingers, his fingertips, his nails, to actions he had never imagined, much less rehearsed. *Wrong!* In all this he was spurred on by the rewards she offered, her feeble moans, her helpless whimpers, her fighting for breath, her hot, delectable tongue as it boldly claimed the freedom of his mouth and shared with him the ~~r~~ she had been chewing just before she joined his song~~.~~

To his surprise she suddenly broke free from him and laughed. The woman who, a mere second or so earlier, had seemed abandoned beyond all hope of self-control, or any other control, either, broke free and laughed! "That was some mistake," she said gaily.

"Yes!" he agreed eagerly, relief flooding through him. "We must …"

"Starting with you one side of the gate and me the other," she went on. "Here! I got an idea …"

His heart fell.

"Put your arms through the gate … no — *under* the second bar. That's it!"

Then he saw it had been no 'mistake' at all. The bars of the gate could have been made for her purpose there that evening. For the second bar, the one she told him to slip his hands beneath, was so aligned that, if she stood a mere six inches back, the only place he could embrace her was by the hips. If she were pressed tight to the gate, of course, he could hold her more decently round the waist. But, since she seemed unwilling to make that little journey on her own, he had to grope around her hips, get his hands to her buttocks, and pull her to him.

As he did so his nobler self gritted its teeth at such wanton intimacy; the remaining ninety-five percent of him shivered with ecstasy and went weak at the knees as he felt those normally untouchable parts of her anatomy come alive between his eager hands and wriggle snakelike toward him. She was surely wearing no more than a single petticoat (if that, indeed) beneath the loose-gathered folds of her linen skirt.

Reluctantly, yet knowing it was his duty as a gentleman, he lifted his hands to her waist as soon as he physically could.

At once she retreated a few inches, knocking his hands back down to their earlier, more voluptuous hold around the lithe and lively fullness of her bottom. And now it was she who squee___d herself in against the gate, making his hands follow ___ to be forcing her do so. He pressed against her, too ___as when he discovered that the third bar down was ___inst the tops of his thighs — and hers — thus ___most forbidden and untouchable parts of all into ___ngry contact. Her mound was like a darning ___ sock, hard yet delectably supple.

Wrong!

"Here!" she giggled. "You got something for me down there, haven't 'ee! I can feel 'n, so big as a bull."

She massaged her body against his and at once he began to ejaculate. She felt that, too, and wriggled all the more ecstatically, laughing now.

He was more surprised than pleasured by it; indeed, it was the most mechanical, least erotic climax he had ever experienced. Disjointed phrases of shame and apology began assembling in his throat … and died there, too, as it dawned on him that she was laughing and happy. "Now us'll have to wait a bitty while, eh?" she said, withdrawing slightly and looking up at him with a winsome accusation in her gaze. "Still, we shan't be so hasty then, shall us, my lover. We'll have some sport that lasts."

She opened the gate to let him through. She took his arm as they sauntered back up the yard. "I'll be waiting for 'ee 'bout half-past-lemm tonight," she said matter-of-factly. "In th'ole tithe barn. You bring a blanket and some cigarettes and port wine, can 'ee?"

He composed himself to explain why — or, at least, *that* — he could not honourably comply with her suggestions. But the palms of his hands recalled the adorable fullness of her breasts and the voice that had cried *wrong!* now cautioned him to break it gently to her; it reminded him that hell hath no fury … et cetera. And the other voice, the one that was incapable of crying *wrong!* — the weasel voice that spoke aloud — now said, "I don't … you know, Pansy … I mean, my true feelings … I … that is …"

"You don't love me," she put in gaily. "That's what you're trying to say, innit? Not now. Not ever. You never could. Your heart is engaged to Miss Curnow … or someone." A wave of her hand consigned the actual object of his true affections to the realms of triviality. "Well, Master Will, if I thought you had *that* much love for me" — her right hand grasped her left little finger and showed him no more than its nail — "I'd no more open up for you than I would for a six-foot quilkin."

"Quilkin?"

She imitated the croaking of a frog. He shuddered at the picture her words now conjured in his mind's eye.

In case he still hadn't grasped the meaning, she freed her hand from his to imitate a frog's leaping, too, all up his arm.

Even that much contact sent a new shiver of lust up his spine, travelling from where lust has its seat to where it is normally controlled. Despairing now of that control, he made one last desperate throw of the die: "Aren't you afraid of … you know — breaking a leg?"

"Lord!" She gave an inconsequential laugh. "Don't you worry your pretty little head about the likes o' that, boy," she said, parodying advice that must often have made her grit her teeth. "You leave all they worries to them as do understand such things." She took his hand again but then, seeing they were about to come within view from the upstairs windows of the house, she let go and leaned instead against the wall of one of the farrowing sties. "Half-past-lemm, then," she repeated.

Her eyes gleamed at him out of the coal-black moonshadow. *I won't go,* he promised himself.

On the other hand, since he'd made it absolutely clear that there was no question of a romantic attachment …

But it would still be treachery to Adèle. He shrank now from relishing her name. How swiftly had the purity of his love been tarnished! Thoughts of her still filled him with an overwhelming ache of happiness but he now felt even more remote from her than ever. The virtue she had every right to expect of any man who aspired to love her seemed vanishingly unattainable.

For a dozen blissful paces his mind was a blank, void of shame, criticism, self-doubt. He glanced over his shoulder and saw Pansy hasten across the gap in which she would be visible to anyone looking out from the house, trotting toward the kitchen door. He saw her for less than a second but the image burned on when the gap was empty once again. She held her hands to her unsupported breasts to stop them whanging about, and her fine, fair hair streamed out behind her like silvered gossamer.

What was he to do?

If he didn't show at half-past 'lemm,' she'd turn into a hell-cat, spitting fury; she had that spirit, he suspected. She could spread scandal that would hurt Adèle more than one trifling infidelity — of which Adèle would never get to hear, anyway.

So one could almost put one's hand on one's heart and say that keeping this assignation was in Adèle's best interests, too. Of course he ought to have had the presence of mind — and strength of character — to say 'no, no, a thousand times no,' at once. But he hadn't, and now the damage was done, and the only way out was to limit its scope as much as possible.

Also, if there was absolutely no romantic interest on either side, could one brief assignation fairly be called by so portentous a name as 'infidelity'? Surely the word ought to be kept for *important* betrayals? Otherwise its currency was devalued. You could say that he owed it to the very *idea* of fidelity not to relate it in any way to a hasty coupling in the hay. Loyalty and devotion were truly grand elements in the human soul. His loyalty and his devotion to Adèle soared so high above the sordid plane of earth and all things earthy that to measure this night's casual and frivolous encounter by so noble and lofty a yardstick would be ... yes, well, there was no need to argue it to the last dot and comma. Case closed.

He would keep the appointment ... do whatever was required of him to content her ... then ... what?

Well, certainly refuse all future assignations!

Actually, it would be better if he could do something to make sure she'd never even ask for one. Act all clumsy and hurt her? He couldn't do that. Finish so swiftly he'd leave her unsatisfied? Ha ha — she'd already taken care of that disaster! Weep, beat his breast, tear out his hair, indulge in a cataract of remorse and self-vilification? That was the best idea so far but he wasn't sure he was actor enough to carry it off. Or, to put it another way, he *was* sure he wasn't.

Ah, well, something would turn up. He'd find a way to touch her heart and make sure this first time would also be the last.

"Hallo!" Leah greeted him as he crossed the threshold. "You look as if you've lost Blanche and found Pansy!"

"I *beg* your pardon?" He hoped his guilt came out sounding more like astonishment.

"Don't bother trying to pretend." She stepped back to let him pass. "I saw you embrace her at the gate."

But he stood his ground. "You watched?" he asked accusingly.

"That's not what I said. I said I *saw* you — just before she opened the gate for you. But it was quite clear you had been embracing. If the gate had not been between you I should have something much sharper to say."

He pushed past her then, brushing against her with unnecessary brusqueness. "You're not my mother," he grumbled.

She ran two paces and caught him by the arm. "Nor do I speak as your mother. Not even as your sister. I speak as any friend would speak to you, Will. And any *good* friend will tell you it won't do. I'm sure your own conscience is telling you the same — it simply will not *do!*"

He pulled free of her and took a pace or two up the stairs. "Is there hot water for a bath?" he asked.

"Of course." She stood and watched his progress all the way to the landing.

There he turned and asked, "Are you spying on me?"

"Of course," she said again.

35　The moment the Carringtons took their seats at dinner that evening the old man said, "Well, son, don't keep us all on tenterhooks like this. Spit it out! Did you see her?"

Will started guiltily — and only just managed to avoid looking at Pansy, who was passing round the soup plates. "See who?"

"See *who?*" his father echoed. "Why, Mrs Gundry says she saw something very like a dragon go flying over the hedges with the sparks flashing from …"

"Oh!" Will waved a weary hand, not quite in his direction. "You mean Miz Philomena, I suppose? Well, there's no harm in her at all. People have …"

"No harm?" Leah chimed in scornfully. Then, seeing Pansy hanging around, she thanked her and said she could go back to the kitchen and wait for a ring for the next course.

His father, meanwhile, said to Will, "If you'd seen the gleam in Mrs Gundry's eye earlier, you wouldn't say there was no harm in her."

"Okay." Will, as always, gave up the struggle to tell his father and sister *anything*. Placidly he took a spoonful of soup and said, "Mmmh! It's good. There's nothing like a day's shovelling and vanning to get a man's appetite up."

"Is that what did it?" Leah said lightly.

"Oh? How did that go today?" his father asked — to Leah's annoyance, for the last thing she wanted to discuss was the LCT venture. It was clear that Will had actually seen the dragon-woman and she wanted to hear all about that, instead.

Will droned on, deliberately spinning out the technical detail until even his father, who had money riding on it, grew bored. "So then," he concluded, "just about sunset, we downed tools, opened the sluice, and set off for Sithney, home, and beauty." Then, remembering what Leah had witnessed, he changed it to, "Home and the beauty *cure* of a bath, I mean." He grinned at her as if he had scored a point.

"It didn't work, dear brother," she informed him sadly.

Ignoring her he continued, "But then Adèle came running to meet us and she was in such a bate I thought they must at least have been struck down with cattle plague or something. But it was seemingly worse than that. Apparently, Aunt Philomena — old Clifford Liddicoat's younger sister ..."

"Younger sister?" their father asked in amazement. "Are you sure of that? From the descriptions I've been given ..."

"Father!" Leah cried, holding her fingertips to her temples. "Something awful is happening here!"

"What?" he asked in alarm.

"Will is telling us a story. And he's starting at the beginning. And every word of it, so far, is making perfect sense! I don't think I can take much more of it."

"Ha ha!" Will tried not to laugh. "D'you want to know what happened or don't you?"

She hung her head contritely.

"We want to know," the old man said calmly. "Tell us about her. How much younger is she?"

"I guess she's got to be all of forty-five — but she sure doesn't look it. She's a real fashion plate — peaches-and-cream complexion and dressed right out of *Modern Modes*. I complimented her particularly on her hat — which you would have *adored,* Sis."

They could only stare at him. Disbelief was mounting. Either he was unobservant to the point of imbecility or he was pulling their legs. Or, it was beginning to dawn on them, this was a show of perverse bravado — the whole world walks in dread of Miss Philomena, so the bold, brave Will puts his head in her mouth and lives to tell the tale. Meanwhile the tales *they* had been told of the aunt's ferocity coloured everything he said.

"I don't know why they're so scared of her — which they obviously are." He laughed. "The moment old man Liddicoat heard she'd arrived he invented some excuse to go to Truro for the day!"

"So he wasn't there?"

"No — I mean he *was* there. He must have realized that slinking off to Truro was only postponing the evil hour, so he wound his courage to the sticking place and came back to face her." Now his laughter quarrelled with the soup and he had to drink a whole tumbler of water. Even so he had to take several runs at the sentence. "He stood there ... he stood there ... holding ... he stood there in the yard holding a gun — which he actually aimed at her when she arrived."

Now his family did not know what to think. The behaviour of the Liddicoats bore out all they had been told about the old — or, it now appeared, not so old — woman; only Will's responses clashed with the general opinion.

"What did she do?" Leah asked.

"She ignored him, of course. She just walked straight toward him and pushed the barrel aside. Told him not to make such an idiot of himself — and quite right, too. I ask you! He's going to shoot his own sister dead, right there in his own yard, with half a dozen witnesses? Oh, yeah! Of course she called his bluff. What they don't understand is that *she's* all bluff, too. What can she do? Okay, she's all kiln-fired sore at us Carringtons for stealing this place — as she sees it. And I guess she'll foam at the mouth when she hears about Nick and me and LCT — if she hasn't already." He almost mentioned Adèle, too, but wisely held his tongue. "But what can she actually *do?*" he repeated.

"Make life a misery for them?" his father suggested.

"Only if they let her. I don't understand them. They're pretty much in awe of her — and she *is* awesome, I'll grant her that. She's a little spitfire. But she has no real power. Can she stop people calling on us? Stop tradesmen and shopkeepers serving us? Prevent servants from applying for places? Forbid the steel barons to buy our tungsten?"

Father and daughter exchanged glances. This was a 'baby of the family' they had never seen before. It seemed that he was not simply putting on muscle over at Wheal Fortune but the lineaments of manhood at last.

"You're right, son," his father said thoughtfully. "That's quite a list there. However, even without meeting your little spitfire, I get the feeling that she won't let a little thing like impossibility stand in her way. She'll try! Maybe not with the steel barons but the rest will look attainable to her — to some degree, at least. So, while it may be brave and commendable and all that to dismiss her as ultimately powerless, we must also recognize that she could inflict a lot of hurt on us before she acknowledges defeat. There was never any doubt about the fate of hogs on their way to the slaughterhouse but you should have seen the damage one or two rogues could do on their way there!"

"So it's thinking-cap time," Leah said, taking cue from her father. "The first thing to ask ourselves is where she has the greatest influence."

"Leverage — it's always the key to situations like this." Her father rubbed his hands. Memories of commercial and personal skirmishes were stirring — hard fought and enjoyable times. Life had, indeed, been somewhat bland of late. Now he was actually looking forward to meeting this spitfire of a Liddicoat. "She'll fight a woman's war, honey," he said. "With woman's weapons and a woman's guile. So you tell us — where's she gonna strike first?"

"Well, her greatest *leverage*" — she used her father's word with emphasis — "is on her brother and his children. Was Harvey there, by the way?"

"No," Will told her. "He'd gone off without telling anyone. The old man must have been pretty steamed about that, too."

"To try to join the navy, d'you think?"

He shrugged. "No one will say it out loud but you can see that's what they're all afraid of. I didn't say anything."

"So she'll try every which way she can to drive a wedge between us and the Liddicoats, huh?" their father said. "She'll try to unravel LCT, I guess." He scratched his chin thoughtfully and eventually said, "She can't. It's Troy's money and mine. True, young Liddicoat has the Wheal Fortune mineral rights but we own the rest. If she prevailed on him to kick Will out and cut loose from us, we've got the rights to ten times as much wolframite as he does …"

"A hundred times," Will said. "He wouldn't just be cutting off his *nose* to spite his face … it'd be like cutting off his whole *head*. The fact is, LCT only works because it's a cartel of three. In effect, you and Troy have agreed to leave your rights unexploited until we've exhausted the Wheal Fortune halvans — and that's how we keep the price up. Cutting loose and going into competition would be suicide for Nick."

"How did he respond to his aunt's sudden appearance among them?" Leah asked.

Will stirred uneasily. "Very quiet ... subdued. Most un-Nick-like. Maybe *she's* why he's got this bee in his bonnet about strident women and suffragists?"

"Okay," his father said. "We put a tick in the worry column for LCT. And someone" — he looked at Leah — "has to put a little backbone into young Nicholas."

"But I never thought he lacked it," she replied defensively — though why she should have to defend him, of all people, she could not say.

"Well, let's just lock this stable door *before* the horse decides to bolt, eh?" He turned to Will. "And as for you, son — I know we've raised you *not* to trifle with the affections of respectable young females, so I wouldn't wish you to do any such thing with poor Adèle. God knows she's a homely little creature but how close a line d'you think you might tread there, *without*, as I say ..." His voice trailed off as he saw the expression on Will's face. "Have I said something wrong?"

Tell them! Will screamed in the silence of his mind. But something stubborn refused to give them that hostage; father and sister had spent too many years putting him down and poo-poohing his hopes and ambitions.

"There's no need for that," he said nervously, slipping his hands beneath the table so that they would not notice the tremor of his excitement. "As a matter of fact, we already get on extremely well."

Leah grinned. "Adèle's nuts on him, Pa. For her, the sun rises and sets with his day." She, too, saw the expression on his face and said, "Didn't you know?"

All he could do was shake his head. "It's not true."

Of course, he desperately wanted it to be true. He longed for Leah to offer a hundred proofs of it, all at once — and still he'd ask for more.

"It is, too," she assured him.

"Has she told you? I'll bet she hasn't said anything. You're just trying to tease."

Leah went on grinning.

"It's cruel to toy with people's affections," he went on. Where was her weak point? Where could he lash out at her? Provoke her into letting something slip? "The way you do with poor Nick, for instance," he blurted out.

"The Nark?" She laughed uncomfortably. "The *poor* Nark? Spare me!"

"Well ..." he said, catching his breath and letting it out in little gasps, as if there were so much he could tell her if only he were not bound by word and loyalty to say nothing at all.

"The Nark?" she asked again; but now she was more incredulous than scornful.

"Forget I said it," he told her uneasily though secretly exultant to have achieved so much for saying so little — indeed, for saying nothing that could be dragged up later.

"Really?" she asked. And now she was more worried than incredulous.

"I said nothing," he reminded her. "I say nothing now. And I'll say nothing in future, no matter how hard you pester. Nothing! I shouldn't have lashed out like that. One day, I'll grow up, I suppose."

"No fear on that score, son," the old man said laconically. "I think you already did. So you reckon you're already friendly enough with young Adèle?"

"Reckon so, Pa." He nodded sagely. " 'Course ... if it's war, I could sort of annexe up to her a bit further. All's fair in ... er, war, they say."

"All's fair in *love* and war," Leah corrected him.

Their eyes met and, hard though he tried to hold her gaze — her cool, penetrating gaze — he had to look away first. He knew that she now suspected him of some duplicity, though whether it was over his attitude toward Adèle or over what he had hinted at between her and Nicholas he could not tell. Already he mourned the days of his innocence, now lost — the days when they thought him too simple for anything like that.

Pansy came flouncing into the room just at that moment. "Mrs Gundry says does anybody want their joint tonight, else she might just so well go on home."

"Sorry!" Leah gave the bell a token ring and made a token effort at stacking their soup plates.

Her father, who had heard from Fenella Compton that 'gentry don't stack,' frowned at her but was soon distracted by Pansy's lithe, provocative young body as she sashayed around the table, making twice as many movements as a factory efficiency manager would recommend for the purpose — at least, for the purpose of clearing the table.

Leah watched her father's eyes as they followed the girl around the room and the problem of Miss Philomena Liddicoat suddenly became quite trivial. The girl did not seem to be wearing a corset; her movements were so lithe and easy. Well, she would simply have to go. It was not, of course, the first time the thought had crossed her mind, nor even the hundred-and-first; but she always came up against the thought that, while Pansy was a servant under their roof, the constraints of society were there to rule him in their most powerful form. Once she was just a girl 'out there,' she was a free agent — and they hardly came more free in their ways than Pansy! She would be open to any sort of arrangement and Leah's father would suffer little in the way of social contumely as long as the business remained discreet. It was more than the hundredth time she'd rehearsed *that* argument, too. Perhaps, she thought, if any Carrington were to be bewitched by the girl, it had better be Will. Maybe she had been a little hasty in her earlier warning.

"Okay," their father said as Pansy placed the joint before him to carve. "The dragon can't break up LCT but she can — or so it would seem — make life pretty nigh intolerable for the other four Liddicoats."

"She do want a *man,*" Pansy said as she waited, holding Leah's plate for the first slices off the joint. "My dear soul — that's some 'ansum beef, that is!"

Leah wanted to tell her to hold her tongue at table but her father had already tolerated — indeed, chuckled at — too many such outbursts for her to be able to do that. Instead she laughed, not at all warmly, and said, "Dear me, Pansy, is that your answer to *every* feminine difficulty? Get a man?"

"She do," Pansy replied calmly as she walked round the table with Leah's plate. "Look at that lovely blood!"

"On what do you base this diagnosis, Pansy?" Will asked. "Is it a general observation on the plight of the female sex or does it relate to Miz Philomena in particular?"

"Stands to reason," Pansy said. She refused to let herself be provoked by his banter.

"Tell us," the old man said, quite serious now, for he suspected she had something significant to say.

" 'Course you wasn't here when 'twas in all the papers — how that Colonel ... what was his name? Jelly bean? Gelatine — something like that."

"Jellicoe," Will said.

The others looked at him in surprise.

"Nick told me," he explained. Then, to Pansy, "I think I know what you're driving at. They said she did more than simply keep house for the old boy."

She nodded and smiled at him saucily. " 'Twas in all the papers. Everyone down here do know it. They do say as she made sure he died smiling."

The old man almost dropped the carving fork in his surprise. "They actually put that into cold print? I mean — in so may words? 'He died smiling'?"

"Well ... no," she admitted grudgingly. "But that's what they meant. 'Cos he wrote about his *dearest* housekeeper in his will. They put that in big black letters at the top of the words — *dearest* housekeeper. 'Twas a nine-day wonder, though, 'cos the suffragettes went and put that time-bomb under the dean of Saint Paul's, to give him a bit of a surprise, like, and everyone forgot the dearest housekeeper — 'cepting down here, of course. Last year sometime it was."

The Carringtons looked at one another. "We never heard about that," Leah said. "Did the suffragettes actually go so far as to blow up the dean?"

"No. A cleaning lady found it and poured water on it. 'Twasn't under him, 'twas under his seat — the one they said was carved by a gibbon. But 'twas lovely carving. Anyway, that's Miss Philomena Liddicoat's trouble, if you ask me. She's missing old jelly — whatsizname."

After she had gone — with the old man's eyes following her to the last flounce of her skirt as the door closed behind her — Leah risked saying, "Well, Paw, you're so keen for me to annexe up to the Nark and for Will to annexe up to Adèle — looks like *this* one's for you!"

He laughed good-naturedly and said, "That'll be the day!"

36 Leah heard Will's bedroom door open and close. She had been expecting it. In fact, she had waited up, fully dressed, glad of the chance to put her household accounts into order. All that evening, whenever Pansy had entered the room — to tend the fire, bring a shawl, or carry out the cups and glasses — she and Will had struggled valiantly to ignore each other, to arouse not a wisp of a suspicion in Leah or the old man. But that in itself was give-away enough, for on any other evening there was plenty of mild flirtation between them, of an amiable or facetious kind. She had to strain her ears to catch the sound of Will's clandestine exit from the house because a strong wind had sprung up during the evening. Indeed, Maria Vose's father had said, when he called to fetch her home, that south cones had been hoisted down in Porthleven and the harbour-master had let down the 'bock,' or bulwark, to close the inner harbour against the approaching storm.

She didn't hear the front door either open or close. She began to wonder if Will had gone up to Pansy's room in the attic, instead. The thought filled her with horror. A little spooning by the light of the moon was something to reprimand, but a furtive visit to a servant girl's bedroom at dead of night would call for instant dismissal. And, despite her earlier thoughts on the subject, Leah did not want to lose Pansy, who was the brightest and most efficient maid she'd ever known. How many other girls could lay a full silver service when called for, wait impeccably at table, invisibly mend the finest lace, milk a cow, and muck out a byre — all with the same infectious, if rather cheeky, good cheer?

Leah would almost turn a blind eye to any shenanigans, rather than lose her. Almost but not quite. She focused her attention upwards, listening out for a creak on the stair, or the complaint of a bedspring from Pansy's room. But then a sudden movement of the air, a rise and fall in its pressure, told her that Will had, in fact, opened and closed an outside door. She gave a sigh of relief and slipped downstairs as swiftly as she could. In the porch she paused only to slip into her galoshes before she followed him out.

The wind, streaming inland off hundreds of miles of ocean, was strong and steady. It was a merciful wind for lovers; there was not a cloud in the sky and, without it, the night would have laid a sharp frost over the land. Indeed, the wind must have been coming up out of Africa. It would have been warm at any time of year but was especially so for the start of October — which it would be in half an hour's time. Despite the warmth, however, there was really only one place for an assignation in such a gale: the tithe barn. Leah reached the back-garden gate just in time to see her brother take the last few paces up to the barn door. He was in his dressing gown, carrying a blanket draped over his arm and a basket, which banged against his leg and made him walk lopsided.

For an absurd moment her childhood memories overcame the grown-up in Leah and she supposed that her brother and Pansy were bent on nothing more reprehensible than a midnight feast. She even thought of calling out to ask if she could join them. The fantasy lasted no longer than the sour laugh it provoked in her as cold good sense returned and, with it, her baleful vigilance.

When Will reached the barn door he leaned toward it, his attitude attentive. He was probably calling out to see if Pansy were already there but not even a shout would carry crosswind to the house in that gale. Fortunately, it cut both ways — Leah heard Pansy coming round from the servants' entrance and was able to dive into a clump of false nutmeg before she might be seen; she made enough noise to rouse the dead, downwind, but did not catch Pansy's attention at all. By the time she emerged from the thicket and returned to her vigil at the gate, Pansy was halfway to the barn. She was wearing a dressing gown, tightly wrapped about her body, and her long fair hair streamed away from her. She was not so much walking as wiggling. Leah stood transfixed, never having seen anything quite like it; she had thought the girl's movements around the house provocative enough but they were the mere gliding of a nun when set beside this coquettish display.

It was so raw, so energetic, so self-enthralled, that it spoke without the need for words. It opened Leah's eyes at last, telling her that her brother and this maid were intent on something much heavier than mere spooning in the moonlight. They were going to do *It* — make the beast with two backs ... go all the way! Her mouth went dry and the blood drained from her limbs. She had to reach out and find a handhold on the gatepost to support herself for a while. Her mind raced as she revised her tactics in the light of this appalling realization. It was worse than simply creeping up to her room — which could, after all, be the impulse of a moment. This was premeditated, planned in detail. The blankets, the prepared basket, the congruence of meeting-place and time — all confirmed it.

And she, Leah, had formed no plan at all to act against this monstrous contingency. She had intended watching them spoon for a while and then she would intervene and play some jape upon them — pretending to be a ghost, say, or a poacher ... make a noise to scare them into giving up and going back home.

But *this!* They must be mad even to think of such a thing. And ten times madder still to carry it through.

She couldn't possibly allow them to start on such madness — no, not even to start.

Not that she had any very clear idea what 'starting' might entail. She had only the vaguest idea of what men and women actually did in those most intimate circumstances. She'd several times seen a boar with a sow but she didn't think it offered much help for understanding humans. The boar butted the sow here and there with his head and foamed a bit at the mouth. A strange corkscrew-thing twisted in and out underneath his belly. And the sow just stood there until he did a piggyback. Then they both grunted a bit, shuddered a bit, and, finally, the boar fell off again, still foaming at the mouth. Leah blushed to think how innocently she had used the term 'piggyback' all her life but she hardly supposed it told her anything about humans. After all humans did not gobble from a trough at dinner time.

As soon as the two lovers had kissed and vanished into the tithe barn she slipped out by the gate and ran across the dusty cobbles to its door. The wind masked any sound she made. Unfortunately it also masked any sound they might be making inside. She was just about to apply her eyes to one of the cracks when she realized that the moon, though almost overhead, was shining inward through that same crack and the sudden darkness would very likely betray her. She stepped hastily backward, a single pace that plucked her shadow off the outer wall, and then she hastened round to the far side of the barn, which was still entirely in shadow.

Even as she ran, though, she knew she was shirking her duty. She ought to go right up to that door, throw it wide, and ... well, a single 'No!' should be enough. She stopped halfway to her new vantage and ordered herself to go back and do the right thing. She would have done it, too, if the most shameful scene had not risen in her mind, even as she hesitated. In it she stood there, having said her 'No!' and Will just replied, 'Go home, Sis. This is none of your business' — leaving her looking the perfect dummy. What would she say to him then? 'I'll go and tell Pa'? Well, she ought to, of course, but she wouldn't. The less Pa got personally involved in any question concerning Pansy, the better — and Will knew it. 'Okay, but don't forget to wipe your feet when you come back indoors' — that would be just about the most authoritative thing she could say if Will got all truculent.

Morally defeated, she resumed her walk round to the back of the barn, though now she had no good reason to prolong this vigil. Unless you counted simple human curiosity. Well, it could hardly be called a *good* reason but it undoubtedly was powerful. At last she was going to witness — in a sense, to share in — the last of life's great mysteries. The compulsion she felt was greater than all the arguments against it.

As she approached the farther corner of the building she heard a regular bang-bang-bang, as if someone were hammering at the wood. Indeed, for a moment, she half expected to find John Hamden out there with a lump hammer in his hand and a mouth full of nails, securing loose planks against the gale. But it was just a loose plank, of course — about twenty feet long, secured at the top but shaken free from about halfway down. The gale continually peeled it back until its own elasticity made it return and slap against its framing again.

It gave her an idea, though, about getting inside rather than simply peeking through a crack in the wood. The bangs were not as regular as a metronome, so a longer-than-average interval would not be especially noticeable. She chose a moment when the wind had pulled it out to the maximum and, praying it would not split if she opened it just a little bit wider — enough for her to squeeze inside — she tugged at its edge and more or less rolled herself vertically through the opening.

She paused in the dark and listened hard, but the resumed banging from the plank would have masked anything quieter than a silver band playing Old Hundred. And the light-dark-light-dark it created, just where she stood, was as if some child were playing with a lampwick, turning it up and down, up and down. However, it allowed her to see that she was standing in a narrow and accidental passage between the outer wall and the stack of hay they had been forced to buy in, since Liddicoat had cut and carried every blade before Midsummer Day. She knew the pile was high, so there was no fear of being observed.

That still left her with the fear of observing. Every decent impulse within her urged her to return now, before it was too late, before she did that most despicable thing — the Peeping Tom. Or Tomasina. But impulses are as chaff in the gales of instinct, and her instincts impelled her onward, to watch, to *know* at last this great and, as yet, unrevealed mystery — unrevealed to her, at least: the mystery of life itself.

She edged cautiously away from the clatter of the loose board, still having no idea precisely where she was in relation to what she remembered of that load of hay — nor where Will and Pansy were, either. They could even have climbed a ladder to lie in one of the lofts, this side of the central open space or that. She froze. They could be above her now, looking down with amusement, having heard her come in. Slowly she raised her gaze to the rafters, ready to call out, 'Good heavens! Did you hear that noise as well?' and spin some yarn about fancying she heard slates peeling off in the gale. But no one looked down. No thing looked down — not even the resident owl. She breathed again, and again sidled toward the centre of the barn. Wherever they were now, they must have started from there.

She edged her way cautiously from the intermittent light toward the dark. But she went slowly enough for the dark to lighten perceptibly as she moved into it; there were plenty of cracks in the walls and the moon was very nearly full. The end of the hay pile (one could not call it a proper stack) appeared as a dark, ragged silhouette against dozens of moonlit dots and dashes — the perforations in the opposite wall. The doorway showed as a recurrent streak of moon-lightning — with appropriately simultaneous thunderclaps as the gale plucked the door open a fraction and slammed it to again.

Between those bangs she heard the two lovers. And then, by that light, she saw them — not eight feet away. They were lying on a blanket spread out on a pile of hay on her side of the open space. She went rigid with terror. Pansy seemed to be looking directly at her. Only the fact that she did not start up with a cry and clutch some shred of clothing about her revealed that Leah was, thus far, invisible. A short while later — fifteen seconds by the clock, perhaps, but an eternity measured by heartbeats — Pansy's continuing lack of response reassured her of her invisibility and she was able to relax. Enough, at least, to begin to take in the extraordinary scene before her.

For a start, they were both naked. The only nakedness of which she had any experience, except when skinny-dipping as a kid, was in statues and paintings. And they were no preparation at all for *this*. Will, who had his back toward her, was a dark triangle with an intermittent silver outline that showed the lithe contours of his muscles and the easy movements of his arms. He was stroking Pansy's body — her thighs, her hips, her tummy, her breasts — and occasionally running his knuckles lightly across her neck and cheeks. She was lying full stretch, staring up into his eyes, smiling placidly, occasionally reaching out a languid hand and stroking him, too — his head, his hair, neck, shoulders, chest, and ... well, lower down. They both laughed with delight when her hand went down there.

Will reached into the dark behind him and his hand returned, bearing a bottle. Port by the look of it. He filled, or refilled, a glass — which both explained the basket and emphasized the adult nature of this particular midnight 'feast.' He took a sip and then put his lips to Pansy's. She gulped and then giggled again; she had a lovely, silvery little giggle.

How did Will know to do things like that? Perhaps this was not their first-ever assignation here, though Leah felt in her bones that it was. These loving gestures had not been polished over many such occasions; they arose spontaneously between them. But how?

To her surprise she discovered that the answer was within herself. She could feel it there — a little knot of understanding which she had only to tweak for it to unravel. Not here. Not as a mere observer of others' passions. But elsewhere, some other time, as partaker herself. Her heart fluttered wildly at the thought. No, it was more than thought. It was a conviction. It *would* be. Her breath shivered. Her whole being shivered, body and soul, at this revelation. She had crept in here, expecting to see a physical act, only to discover that its mere physicality was the least important thing about it. What mattered, what spoke to her directly — and found echoes within her, too — was the tenderness of Will's caresses, the melting light in Pansy's eyes, the spontaneity of their every gesture, the utter ease they obviously felt in each other's nakedness. It was the most beautiful thing she had ever witnessed.

He stretched over Pansy to set down the glass in a beam of moonlight; it sparkled like a ruby. He did not raise his body again but snuggled himself half on top of her. She saw the girl's thighs fall apart to let his knee settle between them. They stretched luxuriously, shivering with the exertion — and with something more. She writhed gently beneath him and he began to move, too.

Leah could watch no more. Nor did she need to. Her own body had taken fire from its empathy with the lovers in their gathering ecstasy. She closed her eyes and pushed her face hard into the hay, savouring the sharp needling of its dry stalks against her cheeks and brow. It was as if she were trying to blot out these new discoveries, though she knew they would never leave her now. They were the new ghosts of the old tithe barn; they would haunt her until she found the means to lay them.

As she edged back toward the loose wallboard, she heard a cry from Pansy that stopped her dead. At first she thought Will must have done something, no doubt unwittingly, to hurt the poor girl. But then she cried out again, this time saying, "Yes! Yes!" as well. Leah stood transfixed and listened. And the final mystery of all was revealed: that this … this *thing* they were doing, this beautiful, easy, tender thing, was an ecstasy almost too sweet to bear.

Outside again (she hardly remembered getting there) she leaned against the ancient wood and closed her eyes and raised her face to the warmth of the wind and fought to still her racing heart. Everything she had ever heard, or guessed, or read between the lines, about this business was untrue.

Filthy? Furtive? Scandalous? Animal? Gross?

Untrue.

A woman's burden ... grin and bear it ... *his* right ... think of the little baby, instead? Grit your teeth and think of family, nation, race?

Untrue.

The sordid triumph of some 'lower' nature, regrettably necessary, over all that is high and pure and noble in the divine human soul?

Untrue – all untrue!

In a daze she wandered back into the house. In her room she undressed and washed almost without realizing it. Then she lay in bed and wondered how she was going to face Will tomorrow – and tomorrow, and tomorrow. What on earth would she be able to say to reveal her understanding without letting him know what she had seen?

And who was Will, anyway? Certainly not the dull, childish dimwit she and her father had always seen in him. In a way – perhaps in the most important way of all – he was streets ahead of her in the game of life. The game of growing up. Without knowing it he had pulled her down off her high horse, kicked the throne out from underneath her – however you cared to put it. In the past half-hour he had travelled a long odyssey away from her and back again, returning as a voyager who had seen too many strange sights and made too vast a discovery of the wider world to explain to a dull young stay-at-home like her.

She expected dreams that night but had none she could recall the following day. Perhaps dreams were no longer enough.

37 The wind veered westerly during the night and turned several degrees colder. The skies clouded over toward dawn and the rain was falling in big, fat drops by the time Will set out for Grankum Farm, which was now the first stop on his daily walk to Wheal Fortune. In his euphoric mood he hardly noticed the rain, though the wind almost buffeted him to the ground a couple of times on the exposed flank of the hill. To his surprise he met his father emerging from Grankum Wood. When he had gone upstairs to shave after breakfast he had naturally assumed the old man had done likewise. But there he

was, unshaven as the dawn, holding up a large, dead buck rabbit and grinning with triumph.

"Got the bugger!" he said in parody of Hamden. "Set a snare for 'n last night and got the bugger at last." Then he showed why the labourer might have been on his mind. "Hamden told me I'd never do it my way."

"Well done!" Will said, bemused. "Was he giving trouble?"

"Hamden?"

"No, the rabbit."

"He'd have devoured the seedlings I hope to be setting out in the long acre today."

"Are you going to work out in this weather?"

"Sure. You think you're the only *man* in the family?"

His stress on the word, though no doubt innocently jocular, came too soon after Pansy had, in the vulgar phrase, 'made a man of him' for Will to accept it in complete comfort. "We'll probably spend the day indoors," he replied. "Or under cover, anyway — bagging up the ore. It's grown to quite a pile and we've been waiting for weather like this to deal with it. Are you going to stick seedlings alone? Wouldn't Hamden help you once he's finished the chores?"

"Oh," his father said airily, over his shoulder as he resumed his homeward walk, "Pansy said she'd give a hand — if Leah could spare her." Very much as an afterthought he added, "Leah, too, maybe."

Full of foreboding, Will entered the wood by the gap from which his father had left it. Down here in the lee of the hill and the added shelter of the trees, the gale was reduced to a creaking, keening wind. The leaves were showing the first autumnal tints, though none was falling yet, not even on such a day as this. He could not bear to think of Pansy working beside the old man. He could just picture them. His father would stand to one side of the taut-stretched line and stamp the blade of his long-handled shovel into the ploughed and thrice-harrowed earth. He'd change his grip and pull it up three inches, pressing the soil toward him. And Pansy — lithe, supple, slender girl, bent almost double — would pop a seedling into the cleft and hold it there in her delicate fingers while he put his boot behind the blade and withdrew it, tramping the loose soil firm and closing the crack around the baby plant.

True, she'd be swathed in oilskins and a big sou'wester would cover her head, denying him the pleasure of gazing down at her adorable ears and her smooth, slender neck, but even so ... What thickness of clothing was proof against the inner eye of a man when such a nymph is bent double before him?

And what a chatter she'd keep up all the while — what country jokes and reminiscences and infectious giggles would stream out of her, banishing the storm and lightening the day! He almost turned about, to go home and warn Leah, to tell her to stick seedlings with the old man and set Hamden on to do the same with Pansy. He wouldn't object to that. Hamden couldn't stand the girl; to him she was 'that kitey giglet' — the sort of female who would benefit from 'a good fist between the eyes.'

Will knew that Pansy had warned him against falling in love with her, and he didn't think he had. Nor for one moment did he suppose she had fallen for him, not even at the height of last night's frenzy, when she had 'scratched his back to fletters,' as she said when she later bathed the blood away (and showed him the little horseshoe bruises where his teeth had bit into her back!). She relished the freedom to do such things without the constraint or excuse of love — to do them for their own sake, because they were good in and of themselves. All the same, the knowledge that she'd do the same for the old man if he ever lost his wits sufficiently to beg the Favour of her was powerfully discommoding to a fellow.

The only thing that prevented Will from turning about was the thought that, if he were late, he might miss Adèle, who often went to Penzance of a Thursday. Last night, while waiting in his bedroom for 11:30 to strike, he had wondered if he would ever be able to face Adèle again. But now he could hardly wait. His only fear was that, in some rash moment of insane honesty, he'd blurt out what he'd done — merely so that he could tell her that it didn't matter a jot! It meant nothing. It no more impinged on that new, special *thing* between him and her than would ... he tried to think of some other pleasure, just as intense but equally neutral, too. The neutral bit was easy. Eating ice-cream and strawberries ... swimming in the cold of the ocean on a blistering summer day ... Life was rich in neutral pleasures of that kind. But 'equally intense'? Honestly compelled him to admit there was nothing to match it. The first sweet plunge into the coolness of that ocean ... prolonged for an hour or more? The mind could grasp the words but not the reality they sought to convey.

He was out of the wood again before he realized he had passed the well — *her* well — without drinking of its enchantment. He didn't go back for that, either. As he approached the farm gate memories of the tableau he had left behind him last night (was it only last night?) returned. He would not have been surprised to see them all standing there, with Miz Philomena cracking the whip over them still.

But the yard was deserted and, to judge by the 'baling' from the field, as the locals called the bellowing of cattle, the milking had not even started.

"Ho there!" he called out as he swung himself in an athletic arc over the gate, hoping Adèle noticed his strength but not the way the pain from his lacerated back made him flinch.

"Come on in," Nicholas shouted as Will lifted the latch.

He found father and son trying to eat fried bread and bacon that shattered at a touch. "Roll on rationing!" Nicholas said morosely, impaling a fried egg on his fork and waving it about like a pennant.

The old man, still smarting no doubt from yesterday's humiliation, kept his eye on his plate and chewed stolidly.

"Where's Adèle?" Will asked at once.

"Good question," Nicholas replied. "She accompanied the aunt back to Helston last night and was probably sliced into tiny pieces and fed into the Helston River. Anyway, she didn't come home." He popped the egg whole into his mouth, held his nostrils tight together, and chewed as if it were a puncture-patch — which it probably resembled quite closely.

Will decided not to mention the aunt at all. Nor Harvey. He said, "We can bag up some of that stuff today, I suppose."

Nicholas washed the rubber shards down with some tea, pulled a face at its taste, too, and went over to the larder. "No pasty for my croust," he said disgustedly as he helped himself to a bag of sausage rolls and reached for his oilskins. "A fellow's got to marry these days to get a decent household about him."

Will shot a startled glance at the old man. On any other day such a statement would have provoked him to a rage, but he just went on chewing and staring at his *Methodist Weekly* without reading it — probably not even seeing it was there.

"Come on!" Nicholas picked a scabby apple off the tree beside the front door. Out in the yard he twisted a twig off the hawthorn and chewed the end of it to form a makeshift brush. Between them, the apple and the twig, he cleaned his teeth as they walked up the yard and on across the field, among the 'baling' cattle, to the wall where Adèle had fallen into Will's arms — and his heart — some twelve hours earlier.

Standing on its crest, tricing up against the wind, he glanced back, hoping at least for a sight of her returning. Instead he saw her father open the gate and cry, "Cope! Cope! Co-ope!" to cattle who, for once, needed no come-hither cry at all. Normally he swore at them and slashed furiously at the nearby hedgerow with his stick, calling them hellers and devils and every name going. Today he just stood and watched as they hastened past him into the yard.

"It's taken the wind out of his sails, eh?" Will said to Nicholas.

"You got out while the going was good last night," he replied. "What happened? How long did she stay?"

"Too long. Almost three hours. Three hours too long."

They set off across the poisoned croft. Now Will could see that the rain would probably not hold. Great ragged clouds scudded toward them across the sky but in the distance there gleamed a brighter impasto of white and blue — only flecks of blue as yet but even a single fleck was more than dawn had led him to expect.

"I suppose you just sat at home by a nice warm fire reading H.G. Wells or something shocking like that," Nicholas said.

"Something shocking like that," Will agreed. "Tell me — why are you all so scared of the old family dragon? What can she do to you, anyway?"

"I don't know," Nicholas said after a brief, morose silence. "I went to bed last night thinking, why do we let her do this to us? Just like you say — what can she do? But somehow, when she's there in the room with you ..." He sighed and gave up trying to explain it directly. "It's like watching a conjuror — but without the pleasure. You watch him as hard as you can for one false move and yet he still fools you. You *know* there's no such thing as magic — just as we know there's nothing she can really *do* to harm us — but it makes no difference. He beats you all the same. And so does she."

"Did she ever whack you as kids — or what? Did she get a hold over you then?"

"Never! God — the times I've stood there just *wishing* she'd box my ears and let me go ... instead of having to stand there being skinned by her tongue! Last night you could really hear she was Cornish."

"What does that mean?"

"Well, how d'you think she sounds?"

"Lawdydaw? Not Cornish, anyway."

"Exactly. That's what I mean. When she took up with old Jellicoe's circle she forgot every last syllable of her Cornish speech. But not last night. We were edjacks and slummocks and slumps, scadgers and bitter-weeds, eckas, gabbies, gawkuses and ... I don't know what. I didn't know we had so many words for 'idiot'." He laughed. "Of course, we do have more than our share of idiots to start with."

"Did the Old Glebe really mean so much to her?"

The question led to a long silence. They were approaching the old calciner now — or 'calla-siner,' as the dialect has it — the source of all that poison underfoot. Its rusty ribs and the hints they gave of its once-massive bulk made Will wish he were more of an artist than he was; its perverse beauty cried out to be recorded. "Didn't mean to pry," he said at last.

Nicholas spoke as if concluding some internal argument: "What do I owe her, anyway? Her anger has nothing to do with the ancient Liddicoat—Carrington feud — remember? The banning of all nonconformists from acquiring title to the Old Glebe. She *says* it has but she's just picking up any old stick to beat a dog. The *real* trouble arises because her father — my granddad — once promised her that, by hook or by crook, the place would one day be hers. You never knew him, of course. I can only just remember him but it was the sort of extravagant thing he loved to say. He was a lovely man — a local preacher, and very popular because he promised heaven to all and sundry. Very unusual in a Methodist. Anyway, he promised her the Old Glebe one day, and she ..." He hesitated.

"Swallowed it hook, line, and sinker?" Will suggested.

"I reckon so."

They took a little detour to pass by the old Wheal Fortune Number Four Wim shaft, where it was now their daily ritual to throw in a boulder or two. They listened, awestruck, to the huge, hollow roar it gave out as it ricocheted from wall to wall, fetching down loose shale as it went — all of which fell into the water at the adit level with a mighty splash. Or *splooosh*, deep and cavernous, would be more closely onomatopoeic. If they breathed in slowly through a wide-open mouth, they could actually feel the vibrations in the pit of their lungs.

When they resumed their walk down to the stamps, Will said, "In the opinion of the servants at the Old Glebe your aunt is missing the old colonel."

"Could be," Nicholas agreed.

"In every possible way," Will added.

"Ah!" He cottoned on at last. "I wonder?"

He wondered for the best part of a minute and then added, "I don't think so. Women aren't like us in that respect. Females in general. Sows just stand and wait patiently for the boar to be done. Same with cows. Hens just crouch and shudder a bit. Ewes go on eating and staring at the horizon — I've seen them. And ladies don't enjoy it at all, I'm afraid, old chap." He gave Will an apologetic grin and punched his shoulder playfully. "Think again."

Will tugged at his ear, gazed at the sky, and said nothing; after all, he himself could easily have been guilty of those sentiments a mere twenty-four hours earlier.

The rain died back to the occasional flurry as they strode down over the sandbanks and shale of the old halvans.

"We'll still bag up a ton or so, I think," Nicholas said. "Even if it stops raining completely. That pile is getting a bit unmanageable. We'll fill the hoppers first and bag it inside — rather than carry in hundredweight bags of wet ore-sand."

"We could dry it first," Will suggested. "Get a good furze fire going between rows of stones. Lay sheets of that old corrugated iron over the top — the stuff someone dumped in the quarry last month, remember? And spread the sand out on that. We could dry out a hundredweight a minute, I reckon. And then the smelters couldn't tell us we were five pounds light on every bag because it was wet."

"It would never be as much as five pounds," Nicholas said in a dubious tone.

"Try telling them that *after* it's all gone into the furnace!"

Nicholas saw the point and, grudgingly, agreed to the plan. "I'm not going to sweat inside these oilskins, though," Will said when they arrived at the stamps. "I'll put that old shirt on and keep this one in the dry."

He went into their little toolshed to change. Nicholas followed him, intending to do the same, but the moment he popped his head inside he could only stand and stare. "Dear God!" he exclaimed at last. "Did someone drag you backwards through a bramble hedge or what?"

"Something like that," Will replied casually.

"Go on!" Nicholas laughed and punched him again. "What really happened?"

"That, dear boy, is what one of your passive, bored, unfeeling females can do while granting the Favour — just to express her passivity, boredom, and general lack of feeling, you understand. A *human* female, I hasten to say." He laughed at his friend's gaping incredulity. "Care to revise your opinion of your sainted aunt's frustrations?" he asked.

38   Leah did not help her father stick seedlings and cuttings that day. Nor did she particularly mind when he asked if Pansy could help him. Knowing nothing of her brother's feelings for Adèle, nor of Pansy's unconventional ideas about granting the Favour, she assumed that her brother and the maid now 'belonged' to each other, for at least as long as such casual affairs usually endure. In any case, she was eager to see Elizabeth Troy again, not to tell her about last night but to seek her advice in dealing with Miss Philomena Liddicoat. She arranged the day with the servants, indoor and out, and drove the pony and trap into Helston.

On her way through the cattle market — deserted on a Thursday, of course — she saw Ben Coad standing outside the ring, watching Tony Allet, the local sign-painter, putting the finishing touches to a new nameboard. She turned off the highway and drew up alongside them. "What was wrong with the old sign?" she asked.

"I've got *two* telephone numbers now," he replied with feigned nonchalance. "Anyway, it needed a thorough spring clean — or a fall clean, I suppose. You looking for another couple of milkers, are you?"

She became cagey at once. "I might be. Why?"

"Mrs Pascoe, over to Tregathennan, wants a valuation for probate of her late husband's herd. She might sell, too."

"Tregathennan?" Leah said. "I'm going to Pallas Home Farm, if that's on your way."

"Tregathennan's farther on," he said. "Richard Pascoe used to manage Pallas Home Farm for Mrs Troy — so he didn't breed rubbish."

"You could take this trap and call for me on the way back."

A visit to the Pascoe farm was not particularly convenient to him at that moment but he mentally rearranged his day and gladly accepted the lift, stopping only briefly at his office to pick up some papers and let his clerk know of the change.

"I thought it was set to rain for the day," he said as he climbed back beside her.

"That's the joy of Cornwall — you never can tell. By the way, we are deeply in your debt, Mister Coad, for your warning about Miss Philomena Liddicoat."

"Did she call on you?" he asked in surprise.

"No. Only Will has seen her so far …" She hesitated, wondering how much more to tell.

"Which way are you taking?" he asked.

"I usually go out on the Wendron road and then cut back in at Coverack Bridges. That's the way Mrs Troy goes."

"Oh, but there's a much quicker way — back through Saint John's to the toll house, then up through Lower Town. It's at least two miles shorter. She only goes the other way because she can pretend she's at the motor races."

When Leah faced the horse back down the hill he added, "When you said you were on your way to the Troys, I wondered why you came in as far as the market. I thought it was to see *me*, of course. How stupid!" He laughed to assure her he was joking.

"Well, I'm glad anyway," she told him. "It's been too long."

"And you've been busy, I expect. We certainly have. The army and the navy have sent in huge requisitions for meat and the cavalry's been round several times looking for remounts. It's wonderful — they just hand you the government cheque book and say, 'Get 'em!' But it's a fearful lot of work, even so."

"I can imagine," she said.

They were repassing the auction ring by now. "A couple of inches higher!" he called out to Tony Allet, who waved cheerily back. "He won't do it, of course," Coad said under his breath to her. "Artistic genius!"

A little farther on he said, "You bought the Old Glebe at exactly the right time, you know. You could sell it for half as much again now — just the land and farm buildings."

"Oh! That will please the Liddicoats," she said glumly. *"Why* are they so obsessed with the Old Glebe, anyway? It can't just be because of what Honourable Carrington did all those years ago, surely?"

"No," he agreed. "It's also got to do with living at Grankum. For three generations they've farmed those acres. Three generations have looked across the valley and coveted your place ..."

"And didn't they have the chance?" Leah interrupted vehemently. "How long was it on the market before we put in our offer?"

"I know, I know," he replied in a placatory tone. "I lost count of the times I warned him that someone would come along and snap it up. But of course, when nobody *did* come along and snap it up, he thought he could laugh up his sleeve until we dropped the price. I'll bet he's kicked himself ever since."

They turned off the old turnpike at the toll house and took the metalled road along the valley toward Lower Town, which was actually no more than a hamlet.

"Especially ever since yesterday evening!" Leah said.

He sighed. "Yes, I missed a trick there. I should have written to her the moment the place came on the market. She wouldn't have hesitated." After a moment's thought he added, "Mind you, that was right after the scandal in the papers. I had no way of knowing what sort of mood she might be in — and no one approaches that woman voluntarily, even when she's in the best of moods."

They drove on in easeful silence under a brightening sky for a while before Leah said, "That colonel fellow ..."

"Jellicoe?"

"Yes. She obviously wasn't all that formidable to him. 'My *dearest* housekeeper' ...?"

"Oh, well, she isn't always in a bate. I've seen her as sweet as Cornish niceys. But I'd say she's even deadlier then than when she's frowning."

"Yes, but that's just being deadly-sweet. I've known people like that. But that's not what I mean. There must have been times when she was genuinely sweet — don't you think? I mean — the sort of woman who won't suffer fools gladly simply isn't capable of *pretending* to be sweet over long periods. She must have been genuinely sweet to old Colonel Jellicoe."

"Well, now!" He coughed awkwardly. "That was the rumour, to be sure."

"As well as *that*, though." Leah refused to share his embarrassment. "I'm not just referring to *that*. There must be a real gentleness in her somewhere."

"In theory," he conceded. "I'd hate to be sent in with a lantern to scout for it, though."

They rounded a corner and the railway viaduct came into view, a mile away at the upper end of the valley. As if it had been waiting for the moment, the sun came out in a single shaft that swept like a spotlight across the tall, slender arches ... and then vanished again as the clouds closed the gap.

"Doesn't it seem an age since that day!" she murmured.

He did not ask what day she meant.

"I think our first impulse to buy the Old Glebe came because *you* showed it to us, Mister Coad."

"I?" he echoed in surprise — delighted surprise.

"Yes. You were so kind to us that morning — assuring us we were almost more Cornish than yourself ... warning us about the ancient feud ... and so on. Tell me one thing — but don't answer if you'd rather not. Did you decide to be so frank before or after you met us?"

"After," he replied without hesitation. "Now, of course, you want to know why!"

She laughed as she obliged: "Why?"

He pinched his brow as if he had to think. "Looking at it all round," he said, "putting two and two together ... taking the rough with the smooth ... at the end of the day ... when all's said and done ..." He glanced slyly at her and chuckled. "I can keep that up a long time."

"I'm quite sure you can," she replied with mock severity.

"All right — penny on the drum," he said briskly. "The long and the short of it is ... I had hopes of a long and happy association with ... you ... people."

She glanced at him hastily, nervously. He had an auctioneer's gift for using pauses. "Not dashed, I trust — those hopes, I mean — not dashed?"

"By no means," he replied. Then, in the same breath, as if it were part of the same thought, he added, "Another reason why Miss Philomena may be particularly aggrieved at the loss of the Old Glebe (as she would see it) is that her father more or less promised it to her."

In her surprise she chucked the pony in the mouth and they came to a dramatic halt. "Sorry," she said, touching the creature with her whip. As they set off again she added, "You'll have to explain that."

"Well, her father, James Liddicoat — who was also Clifford's father, of course ..."

"He was the Liddicoat barred by Honourable's exclusion clause — right?"

"The same. We forget, in these enlightened days — we forget how all-consuming religion was back then. Methodists, Baptists, Christadelphians, Anglicans ... they were different *tribes*. They lived intermingled with one another so they couldn't fight pitched battles, but they fought a war of endless skirmishes with whatever weapon came to hand. The law being one of the most obvious, of course. So, in a curious way, old James Liddicoat *expected* to be excluded from the purchase. Honourable Carrington had the power, so he used it — all according to the rules of war. And when James went to the courts and got the exclusion clause annulled, he was fighting by the same rules."

"So he chalked up the final victory," Leah said.

"I don't think Miss Philomena ever saw it that way, though. The fact was, they had lost the chance to buy the Old Glebe — and that was victory to the Carringtons. She'd be spitting-mad if *anybody,* other than a Liddicoat, had bought the place last spring. But to hear that a *Carrington* had once again snatched it from under her nose — and an almost lineal descendant of old Honourable, too!"

"You were saying that her father promised the place to her?" Leah reminded him.

"Oh, yes. Old James was a preacher on the Helston circuit — but in great demand all over. There are two ways for a circuit preacher to be popular. The commoner way is to preach hellfire and eternal damnation. The more vivid the pictures, the better they like you. The rarer way is to stress God's infinite love, mercy, and forgiveness. Congregations would take seven hellfire sermons — until the children started having nightmares — then they'd send for James Liddicoat to spread a little balm. That was how it worked. The meek always inherited the earth when James was the preacher."

"He sounds a sweet man," Leah said. "Why do such traits die out in a family?"

The comment interested Ben. He stared at her to see if she meant it.

"Go on," she said.

"Well, I suppose that Miss Philomena — growing up in less tribal times — was less willing to accept that it had been a fair fight and that her father had won it in the end. She just saw the practical result — they'd won the legal principle but lost the actual acres. And old James, who promised heavenly bliss to the deepest, dyed-in-the-wool sinner ... well, could he do less than promise his darling daughter that the place would, indeed, be hers one day!"

"But *how?*" Leah was still bemused.

"Lord! James Liddicoat never let a little detail like that interfere. God's infinite love and compassion would do it all. Lean on the arms of the Lord! Leave it to Him. Patience and faith were all we require here below."

They forded the Cober at Lower Town and started a diagonal climb up through Gwavas to Pallas Halt.

Leah said, "It explains a lot about his children — Philomena and Clifford, anyway. Life with such a father must have been hell, not to mince words."

Coad laughed with surprise. "D'you think so?"

" Sure. With someone as insanely optimistic as that — and so blindly trusting in ..." She waved a hand vaguely at the sky.

"You don't believe in any kind of divine intervention then, Miss Carrington?"

"I don't believe in winning prizes without competing. My father says the only things you'll find in a pie — apart from the things you took the trouble to put there yourself — are flies and other feller's fingers. Don't you agree?"

"I do. I do. And I think that's a point on which you and Miss Philomena would wholeheartedly agree." He chuckled at this discovery. "How she would *hate* to be told she has more in common with you Carringtons than with any of her own line!"

When they had laughed at this bizarre conclusion he added, "Except, maybe, Nicholas?" He made a slight question of it to test her response.

"Well," she commented, "as for Nicholas — at last we know where he gets his fear of women from! Fortunately, it does not seem to be infectious. Will has no ..." She hesitated again and then, without completing the thought, said, "Quite the opposite, in fact. Shall we give this pony a rest? It's a stiffish climb. Also, that's part of Mrs Troy's herd in that field, I think?"

He stood and peered over the hedge. "You're right," he said.

The pony stopped rather more abruptly than she intended and he had to grab at her shoulder for support. She dropped the reins and caught his arm.

"I'm so *sorry,* Miss Carrington," he stammered when his footing was again secure. His ears turned pink, too, as he pulled his arm away.

"Don't be," she said, letting her own grip linger a second or so and releasing him with a squeeze.

The pony, still panting heavily, started grazing at the foot of the hedgerow. She set the brake and, leaving the reins loose, leaped nimbly down. A moment later she was leaning on the gate, sizing up Elizabeth's herd with a slightly more experienced eye than the one that had seen them last.

"It shows what you can do if you control the breeding for twenty years and more," Coad said as he joined her.

"You get good-looking cows," she said dismissively. "But not a penny more for their milk. That's another of my father's sayings — you can't taste a hog's pedigree but you can tear it up if the ham is sweet."

"Democracy!" Coad pretended to scorn it. "It has never caught on over here and it never will."

She laughed and dug him with her elbow. "You're good company, Mister Coad," she said. "I'm glad I started off the wrong way. This morning, I mean."

39 Pansy suspected the gig contained the two Misses Liddicoat — Adèle and Philomena — but she said nothing for the moment. Between sticking the seedlings and quicksets in their nursery beds she kept an eye on its progress through the lanes. Only when it turned in at Grankum Farm was she sure. Even then she said nothing. She didn't want to interrupt old man Carrington, who was telling her about his life as a dealer in the Pittsburgh board of trade — a world she would never be able to imagine if he did not bring it so vividly to life. But some fifteen minutes later, when she saw a single female emerge from Grankum, get back into the gig, return along the lanes, and then turn off at Boase's Burnthouse, she could not help crying out, "Oh my gidge! I do believe she's coming here!"

"Who?" John Carrington asked. He was so wrapped up in his memories he had almost forgotten who Pansy was.

"Miss Philomena Liddicoat," she said. "That's her boneshaker coming along the lane now."

Carrington straightened up and, following her pointing hand, saw in silhouette the upper half of a female torso bowling toward them along the lane. She was, indeed, making for the entrance to the Old Glebe. In a moment or two she would pass the gateway into the field where they were working. They stood and watched.

In fact, she did not pass the gateway. When she saw them in the field she reined in her pony and turned toward them. "My good man!" she called out.

He and Pansy exchanged glances. The woman's error gave him an idea. He winked at the maid. "Hold your tongue now," he said. "Us'll 'ave a bit fun wi' she!"

Pansy giggled but he pointed a finger at her and said, in his usual voice, "You'll stay here if you can't control yourself better than that, my lass."

He started to walk over to the gate in a slow, loping, labourer's pace. Pansy, taking pattern from him, slipped into the slovenly gait of a field girl as she followed. It would not deceive Miss Philomena, however, if the woman recognized her, so she didn't exaggerate it.

"I never heard you talk Cornish afore, sir," she said.

"Cut out the sir." He dropped back into dialect. "'E in't too difficult, see. West Country English is faather to American, anyway. I do often hear a man talking and I 'ave to think now is 'e Cornish or American? Hush now or she'll 'ear us."

"My good man," she called again when they were just within talking distance. "I'm looking for Mister Carrington — your master, I presume. D'you happen to know if he's at home today?" There was not a trace of Cornish on her tongue.

He scratched in the stubble of his still-unshaven chin. "Carrington," he said slowly. "Now would that me Maaster William or Maaster John?"

"The father! The father!" she replied angrily. "I know very well where the son is — more's the pity."

Carrington turned to Pansy. "Whurz th'ole bugger got to then?" he asked her in a perfect imitation of John Hamden.

Pansy stared at him in horror and then suffered a coughing fit. He sent her off to drink a 'dish o' tay' from the bottle they'd brought out with them.

"I suppose I shall just have to seek until I find," Philomena said crossly. "What does he look like?"

"Why, 'e's some tall feller," Carrington told her. "Wears a frock coat and top 'at. Fancies 'isself a farmer, 'e do — so you'll like as not find 'n with an eeval in 'is 'and, mucking out the cowshouse or turning the dungheap." He spat contemptuously into a furrow.

But she became interested in the fact that this yokel could string so many words together — and did not seem intimidated by her. "You worked for him long, have you?" she asked, letting a touch of Cornish creep into her voice.

Carrington spat another quid, as if he'd been chewing tobacco. "'E in't a bad ole feller," he replied. "'Course, 'e got 'is funny ways — like anyone, I reckon." If this went on much longer, he'd have to admit that one of his 'funny' ways was to imitate his labourers and pose as one of them.

"Come here," she said.

She descended from the gig and approached the gate. As she walked she took a sixpence from her purse and held it where he could see it. "Tell me about these 'funny' ways," she said. "You, too, girl," she added to Pansy, who had just rejoined them.

"I know you, don't I? Pansy Tregear from over Carleen? Goodness, how you've grown!"

"From Trew, Miss Liddicoat." Pansy corrected her.

"Trew, Carleen … it's all the same," she said crossly. "What are you doing working on the land?"

"This is gardening, ma'am," the girl replied in a slightly offended tone. "Not field work."

"Hmph!" was all she replied to that. "But *you*" — she frowned at Carrington — "I don't know you."

His heart fell. He had not, of course, planned any part of this practical joke but he had imagined it would run to no more than two or three exchanges. And a good laugh later. He realized, however, that he could not, in all honour, tell her a direct lie. "You aren't gwin to like it, Miss Liddicoat," he said, "but I'm a Carrington, too. Not one o' *they,* though," he added vehemently, waving his hands vaguely toward Sithney, which she could take to include the Old Glebe if she wished.

Another thought was now entering his mind: His unwillingness to give her the lie-direct implied that some part of him assumed there would be a social relationship between them in the future; otherwise, if it was to be outright war, with no social meeting of any kind, he could say what he damn well liked.

He wondered why the woman did not press him on this unlikely assertion — but that was because he did not see Pansy, behind him, gyrating a finger near her temple and pointing to the back of his head.

"I see." Philomena's tone became gentler. She smiled sympathetically at him — which only increased his bewilderment — and turned to the girl instead. "Tell me about your master," she said. "He sounds a great deal more interesting than most of the men hereabouts."

"He *is,* ma'am," Pansy said fervently. "He's the best and kindest master a maid could wish to serve. There's *nothing* what I wouldn't do for him — and I don't mind if he knows it. He can tell tales of his days in America to put all adventures in the shade. I thought Stanley and Livingstone was exciting enough, but …"

"Yes, yes," Philomena interrupted, curbing her impatience with only moderate success. "But … er …" She looked about the field as if she might find there the words to steer her inquiry away from these gushing opinions and more toward hard facts about her enemy.

Carrington, no fool, had meanwhile worked out that Pansy had rescued him earlier by suggesting he was a bit simpleminded. He fidgeted and stared at the sky, as if he could not concentrate on even the simplest topics for very long. Anything now rather than be unmasked.

In a way, Philomena did find her inspiration in her survey of the field. "Gardening, you said?" She echoed the word with more than a hint of disbelief. "What has this to do with gardening? What are you sticking over there? It looks like winter cabbage to me."

Her jaw dropped when the girl replied, "*Sorbus sibirica,* if it please you, ma'am. And *Cornus alba* 'Elegantissima' and *Philadelphus incanus* — that's a rare one, that is."

She mangled the botanical Latin but there was no doubting that the day's work was horti- rather than agri-cultural.

"I see," Philomena said thoughtfully, turning the coin over and over, *almost* as if she had forgotten it was there.

Carrington stared at the maid in amazement, which Philomena took for his simplicity. He knew, of course, that the names were on the labels round the sphagnum-wrapped bundles from the nurseryman but he had never imagined she would read them, much less remember.

"'Course, the war has stopped his plans," Pansy went on, "but 'twill be over soon 'nuff and we shall have this nursery field full of sturdy plants to set out, see?"

Philomena stared toward the Old Glebe. "I still don't quite understand," she said. "The garden is hardly what you'd call large — and is, in any case, filled with well-established …"

"Lord, ma'am!" Pansy, in her enthusiasm, dared to interrupt. "Didn't Mister Liddicoat tell 'ee? This whole farm — all fifty acres — is to become a garden to rival Trewennack and Skyburriowe and Trengwainton." She waved a hand across the landscape. "There'll be peacocks and fountains and … and they temple things with columns and bare white ladies in stone … and a shell grotto … and a wishing well … and trees …" Her invention petered out at that.

During this flight of fancy, Philomena noticed that the maid glanced at her simpleton partner a couple of times. Something about those glances, an edge of nervousness, made her inspect the old boy more closely. She was always on the qui-vive for insults, slights, injuries, shopkeepers' tricks, so she now began to notice his *un*-weatherbeaten skin, his clean ears, his well-tended hair. And when he became aware of her scrutiny he fumbled with his hands, trying to hide them. That was when the penny finally dropped.

Her biggest surprise, though, was not the realization that she was, in fact, in the presence of the man she now most detested in all the world — and a man, moreover, who had just tried to make a fool out of her — but that she was more amused than angry at it. A clumsy attempt at deception, something she would have seen through at once, *would* have infuriated her. But this was well done. It had a certain wit. And, she now recalled, he had, indeed, told her his name was Carrington.

But he was not at all the man she had expected to find ensconced at her beloved Old Glebe. She thought he would be a brash, overbearing man of the mercantile kind, for she had known several Cousin Jacks who had returned 'home' with more money than taste. They were ever-ready to brag about America's vast superiority in every field and their own cleverness at climbing the ladders over there.

This man clearly posed a greater challenge than she had bargained for. She was sorely tempted to linger there and tease them — keeping them in the prison of their imposture while she extracted every last drop of information and advantage. But she was less confident of her acting ability than old Carrington was of his. (And, she admitted grudgingly, with good reason, too; his imitation of Cornish, and specifically of John Hamden, whom, she now realized, she had almost been sent to find, was impeccable.) And so, rather than give away the fact that she had seen through them, she thought it best to beat a tactful, and tactical, retreat.

These rapid musings were not so much thoughts as feelings within her — feelings in her bones, feelings that swept through her mind in far less time than it takes to tell. So Pansy had barely finished her stumbling panegyric to the gardens of the future at the Old Glebe before Philomena said, "How very interesting, Pansy! I had no idea your master had any such thing in mind. As soon as the war is over, you say?"

"Oh, ah." Pansy was nonplussed by this apparent about-turn in the woman's attitude.

"It does rather change things," Philomena said, giving no hint as to whether it changed them for the better or for the worse. "And, talking of change, *you*, my dear, have changed rather a lot from the vain, flighty, empty-headed little giglet you were when last I saw you. You've turned into an observant, nimble-witted, and bright young woman. And a rather pretty one, too. Yes — distinctly pretty."

Pansy blushed, curtseyed, and started to stammer out some vague sort of disclaimer.

But Philomena continued, "So I was all the more surprised to hear you say just now that there was *nothing* you wouldn't do for your master. Surprised and not a little disquieted, let me say. I trust you'll *never* utter such a sentiment in his presence. That would be so foolish, you know." She gave the simpleton an apologetic smile for talking so far above his head and, leaning toward Pansy, lowered her voice confidentially. "We women know what we mean by such words. We use them in their noblest, purest sense. But men are cast from a different clay. I know you won't mind my saying this — as your old Sunday school teacher — but do strive to remember that your master is a widower. He lacks the nightly solace of the marital bed. He is also of that age when men grow desperate at their waning powers. Some feel they must grasp at every fleeting opportunity to exercise them. You do know what I'm driving at, don't you?"

Pansy swallowed heavily and nodded.

Philomena smiled at her affectionately and gave the simpleton another apologetic smile. She was delighted to find him almost beetroot-purple and exophthalmic with rage. "However," she went on briskly, "since you say you would do *anything* for him — in the sense that any dutiful servant girl would mean those words — may I prevail upon you to hand him my card? It is a small but common civility." She fished again in her bag and produced one, passing it over with the sixpence. Then she turned to Carrington and gave him, too, what he thought to be sixpence but later discovered to be half a sovereign. "And as for you, good fellow," she said, "I'm sorry for your affliction, but we cannot all be clever. Nonetheless, we can all strive to be good. Protect this maid to the best of your limited wits, eh? Oh, and buy yourself a good pair of working boots. Keep those for Sundays — they are far too good for field work, even of a horticultural nature."

And, without waiting for his thanks — which were not forthcoming, anyway — she turned about and, smiling to herself, remounted her gig and set off once more.

When John Carrington found he was clutching a half-sovereign, he dropped it in his surprise. "Bitch!" he said bitterly while Pansy picked it up. "She tumbled to me after all."

"Half a sovereign!" Pansy exclaimed, holding it up against her sixpenny piece. They were almost the same size, silver by gold. "You think she made a mistake?"

"No mistake," he said, taking the card from her. "That woman knew exactly what she was doing. The only reason she gave you this is so that I will know where to send my letter of apology: the Angel, Helston. She must have had these printed yesterday." He tried to smudge the ink but it was quite dry. "Or she even brought them from London with her. We start one-down, Pansy — no doubt about that."

"Bloody cheek!" Pansy muttered, staring after the departing gig. "Telling me what to do and what not to do like that." She rounded on him almost belligerently. "Don't you pay no attention to what she said." Belatedly she added, "Sir."

But Philomena's cruel portrait of him — of all men his age — had left an indelible mark, being far too close to the truth for his comfort. He would not even be able to go through the first stumbling motions of a pass at the girl now — not without the clown-like spectre she had raised intervening and mocking him to impotence.

Pansy, who did not mind how long they stood there and chatted, since she was not particularly keen on stooping all morning long, said, in quite a different tone, "She's some bowerly woman, though — don't 'ee think?"

"Bowerly?" he asked. He was not able to hold her eye after the outrageous things that Liddicoat woman had said.

"Eyeable," she explained. "Doxy."

"Good-looking?"

"That's what I said — she's some 'ansum woman."

"So Will said last night. I thought he was exaggerating but he wasn't. Not a bit."

"Still — beauty's only skin deep, they say."

He chuckled. "That's right where any sensible man would want to find it, Pansy." He took the gold coin from her and stared at it pensively.

"You going to send that back, are you?" she asked anxiously, wondering if she dared suggest one or two alternatives.

"No," he said, popping it in his waistcoat pocket, "I'll find some way to rub her nose in it, never fear." He started walking back toward the nursery bed, now with a master's tread again. "A gentleman should never do business with a lady, Pansy," he said. "Remind me if I ever look like forgetting it."

"How?" she asked, meaning 'why'?

"If her position's weak, she'll add in her sex and beat him to the deal. If it's strong, she'll subtract her sex while he's not looking — and *still* beat him to it."

40   Ben Coad was waiting at the gate to Pallas Home Farm when Leah left. Elizabeth Troy caught sight of him when she saw her guest to the door. "*Now* I understand why you refused my offer of a drive into Helston. I thought you'd brought Hamden or someone along as driver."

Leah was about to explain how her picking up of Ben had been pure accident when she saw that the conclusions to which Elizabeth had leaped would happily cover her real reasons for refusing the lift, namely Elizabeth's belief that she could beat Fred Karno on the open road at any time. "He's good company," she agreed.

"They're a very solid, dependable family, the Coads. Ben's father was the Troy family solicitor."

"But not yours?"

"He would have faced a conflict of interest so he very honourably advised me to go elsewhere." She laughed. "So I went to George Ivey and gave him such a horrid time that he got out of law entirely and took to painting instead."

Leah remembered her father's sadness that the Carringtons, as newcomers, would never know all those things that people need to know in order to belong to a community. Even when people told you snippets of their past, they dressed them up in jocular half-truths as Elizabeth had just done.

Ben offered her the whip as she approached but she waved it aside. "It's very kind of you," she said. "But I can look around better and see what everybody else is up to if I'm not also trying to control that creature."

"Well, was Mrs Troy much help in your perplexity?" he asked as they set off.

Leah sighed. "Yes and no. I mean, she repeated all those sensible things we've been telling ourselves since yesterday. Like, what can the woman actually *do?* She's not going to attack us physically. She can't do us much harm socially. There's no legal trouble she could stir up — as far as we can tell. And so on and so forth. But that isn't really the problem."

"What is, then?"

"Just the knowledge that she's somewhere out there, looking for a chance, waiting to pounce. From now on we've got this daily worry. We've got to guard our backs. We've got to think before we do anything — could this give her a chance to poke us in the eye?"

"Strike first?" Ben suggested.

"How? We don't wish to, anyway. My father has spent thirty years on the Chicago and the Pittsburgh boards of trade watching his back like that, guarding himself against *real* sharks — men far more formidable than Miss Philomena Liddicoat. He retired to get away from it, not leap from frying pan to fire."

Ben considered this in silence awhile and then asked, "Did he enjoy it, all that cut and thrust?"

"Of course he did. He was king of that jungle."

"Perhaps he misses it? Perhaps a polite but deadly little war with Miss Philomena is just the sauce his life has been missing — especially now his plans to build a great garden at the Old Glebe have been frustrated."

She slumped. Her head hung dejectedly between her hunched shoulders. "You're right, Ben," she said. She had not intended to use his first name; it just slipped out.

He reacted with surprise.

She smiled wanly. "Don't we know each other well enough by now — Ben?" This time the stress was deliberate.

"Well ..." He flushed. "I certainly hope so ... Leah?"

She put a hand to his arm and squeezed once, briefly. "I'll have to talk him into selling the Old Glebe again before he gets the scent of war in his nostrils. Is that house you once showed us at Gweek still up for sale?"

"No, alas. But there's a farm going at Goonhusband, about three miles the far side of Helston. It's just about to come on the market. Sixty acres facing south, overlooking the Loe Pool and Mount's Bay — breathtaking views. If I'd been able to show it to you last February, you wouldn't even have considered the Old Glebe, I can promise you."

She chuckled. "You could sell a dog kennel to a cat, Ben."

"Shall we go to see it now? We can drive straight up the hill from Lower Town and out along Clodgey Lane."

"No. Another day, perhaps. I'd better get back and start working on the old man — before he decides that a good fight with Miss Philomena will make his life complete." She shook her head and said, "People of their generation, eh! What *are* we going to do with them?"

She arrived home with fifteen minutes to spare before lunch. Her father had planted out all his seedlings and rooted cuttings and Pansy was in the scullery with her arms in hot soapy water up to her elbows, trying to get some life back into her frozen fingers. She was also bubbling over with the excitement of their encounter with Miss Liddicoat. Leah listened until the tale seemed garbled beyond belief — all that bright chatter about pretending John Hamden was the master and being given a half-sovereign in place of a sixpence. Then, halting the girl in mid-flow, she said, "But tell me what she's *like,* Pansy. Master Nicholas says she's quite pretty. Is that so?"

"Yes, miss, she's some bowerly, we do say — a goodly eyeful."

"And was she deceived, d'you think? Did my father's impersonation of John Hamden take her in?"

"Yes, miss. At least to begin with it did. But then, I don't know, she sort of tumbled to us."

"*Sort of* tumbled? She either did or she didn't."

"Well, she did, but she never showed it. Just gave a little knowing sort of smile and ... well ..." She looked away and her manner became evasive.

Leah did not let her go. "A knowing smile? And then parted with ten shillings? It doesn't add up, Pansy. She said something

— or did something — to let you know she'd tumbled to it. So let's have the full story. From the beginning."

Pansy sighed as she took the towel Leah held out for her. "I s'pose it started when the master come out with a thing no gentleman would say — just to convince her, like, that he *was* a field labourer."

"What?" Leah was both shocked and intrigued.

"I couldn't possibly repeat it, miss."

Leah went to the scullery door, looked up and down the passage, then closed it. "You can," she said with a friendly smile as she returned to the interrogation. She did not add, 'And you will,' but her eyes spoke for her.

"When Miss Liddicoat asked for the master, he turned to me and said" — her voice fell to a mumble — " 'Where's th'ole bugger got to now, then?' So there — that's what he said." The tips of her ears flushed blood red. "Oh my gidge!" she exclaimed, fanning her face and trying not to laugh.

In the end they both laughed and the tension eased. "He actually said that?" Leah asked.

The girl nodded. "I nearly had a fit. He had to send me to drink a bit tea."

"So that convinced her he was a labourer. I must admit, it would certainly convince me! The question remains, then — what *un*-convinced her? And how did she let you know she was no longer deceived?"

Pansy realized she was not going to be let go short of telling the whole tale. She tried, though. " 'Tis a bit embarrassing, miss," she offered.

"Yes? You've already made that quite clear. Go on."

"She read me a little lecture on the wicked ways of masters with pretty servant maids — how I was to keep myself pure and fight him off if he tried anything." She swallowed heavily. "And the master standing there at my side!"

"Good heavens!" Leah could understand the girl's embarrassment now. "But why? Was it just out of the blue like that?"

"Just out of the blue," Pansy affirmed, crossing her fingers behind her back.

"Dear me!" Leah sighed. "Perhaps my father noticed what triggered such an astonishing outburst. I'll ask him. She seems to be a most unpredictable lady."

The threat to quiz the old man had the desired effect on Pansy. "Maybe ..." she said hesitantly.

"Yes?"

"It *could* be ..." she went on, as if unveiling an extremely remote possibility. "It could be something I said. See — I thought, if the master's going to play tricks on Miss Liddicoat like that, why can't I play a trick on him? So when Miss Liddicoat asked if he was a good master to me, I ..." She sniffed. "I praised him to high heaven — to embarrass him like. Made out he was the *best* master who ever trod the face of the earth ..."

"And said there was *nothing* you wouldn't do for him?"

Pansy stared at her in open-mouthed dismay.

"Did you say that, Pansy?"

She half turned away. "I don't know, miss. I s'pose I might have done."

Leah grabbed her by the arms and made her face the accusation. "You did, didn't you! And you weren't playing a trick on him, you were taking the chance to tell him that if he tried any *tricks* with you — and you know durn well what I mean, I'm sure — you wouldn't put up too much resistance. Eh? *That's* what Miss Philomena heard in your tone — and *that's* what gave her the idea to read you that astonishing lecture. Eh? You little idiot! You'll have to get up a lot earlier in the morning if you want to pull the wool over *my* eyes. They see a lot more than you think."

The girl's lips were trembling and tears filled her eyes; but Leah knew she had to drive the point home. "For instance, I know very well what's going on between you and my brother," she went on.

Shock momentarily displaced the maid's embarrassment and grief; then she buried her face in her hands and yielded to tears. But after a while she realized that something more than simple contrition was expected of her and she began to mumble words to the effect that it would never happen again.

She stopped when Leah touched her gently on the shoulder. "Don't make promises you cannot possibly keep," she said. "I have to admit that my first thought was to dismiss you at once and without a character. But there are two good reasons why I did not do so."

That stopped Pansy crying between one sob and the next!

"In the first place, you're one of the best maids I've ever known." She raised a warning finger. "But don't let this go to your head. You're not out of the wood yet. And if you think you may now rest on your laurels and let your standards slip, you'll have as much chance as an egg-sucking hen at fricassee time. The second reason is that if I did dismiss you, you'd simply get employment somewhere else nearby and go on meeting my brother anyway — and I'd no longer have any control over you or him. So you'd have the last laugh anyway. There!" She smiled engagingly. "You now understand that I do *not* hold all the cards in this little poker game between us. And the ones I do have I've just laid on the table — except for *this* one." She played an imaginary card in the air between them. "Understand that, while I more or less have to tolerate what is going on between you and my brother, I absolutely will *not* tolerate anything of that kind between you and my father. One kiss ... one tiny cuddle ... and you're ..." She cudgelled her brains for some suitably appalling fate.

"Fricasseed?" Pansy suggested.

"Yes." Leah eyed her coolly. "You bounce back quickly, don't you, Pansy! Will you put all your cards on the table, too? For instance, you do realize what a risk you're running with my brother, I hope? You know there is absolutely no chance of your marrying him — if that's what's on your mind?"

"*Marry* him?" Pansy echoed. To Leah's surprise there was a touch of pity in her manner now. "That's not what I want, miss — not marriage. Nor yet for a long while, I hope. A bit of fun is all I seek — honest. Besides, Master Will's too much taken with Adèle Liddicoat ..."

"Adèle?" Leah echoed in amazement.

Pansy, seeing now that Leah knew nothing of it, quickly pulled a stupid-me face and said, "I mean that Curnow maid ... Blanche Curnow — that's who."

Leah appeared to accept the correction, though inwardly she was not convinced. A single name — Adèle — might easily have slipped out by accident. But with a surname to validate it ...? Somehow that did not ring true. "So why are you setting your cap at him — even though you know it's hopeless?"

Pansy, not *quite* looking her in the eye, replied, "I wouldn't marry him if he asked me to — and he knows it. So ask him, instead. Why is *he* setting his cap at *me* when he must know 'tis hopeless, just so well as what I do?"

Leah frowned. "But we all know why men ..." Her voice trailed off as understanding dawned.

Pansy nodded and said, "What's sauce for the gander is sauce for the goose, you might say. Now I must go and ring the gong for your lunch, if you'll excuse me, miss."

As Leah watched her go she realized that, somehow, the girl had turned the tables on her, leaving her as the one who wanted to ask questions to which she *didn't* already know the answers: Why did Pansy do it? What was it really like? How did she avoid all the usual nasty consequences?

But she swept them to the back of her mind as she joined her father for lunch. A new set of questions took their place at once.

"Well," she said as she took her seat, "I hear you met the Dragon herself this morning. Is she really as beautiful as Helen of Troy and the Queen of Sheba all rolled into one?"

It was a buffet lunch but Pansy stayed to pour out the soup and bring it to table. Leah noticed how her father glanced at the maid, as if to ask how much his daughter had been told; but Pansy's face was a perfect servant's mask.

"She is one handsome woman, right enough," he replied guardedly. "Did you hear how I fooled her I was some local yokel? I tried to fool her into taking John Hamden for me. But it wouldn't have worked because — as I ought to have guessed — she's known him most of her life."

"You say 'wouldn't have' worked — you mean she tumbled to your trick, anyway?"

"No," he said blandly, "she was obviously in haste so she just handed Pansy her card and asked her to give it to her master. In fact — and this'll show you what I mean by *haste* — she slipped me a half-sovereign under the impression it was a sixpence! Too vain to wear eyeglasses, if you ask me."

Leah frowned. "You'll send it back, surely?"

"I?" He was all innocence. "What do I, John Carrington, know of her mistaken gift to one of my labourers! No, I shall not be giving it back. I've thought of the perfect use for it."

"What? Thank you, Pansy. And there's no need to hover just outside the door. We'll ring the bell good and loud if we need anything else."

The girl lingered to see if he would think of something to keep her in the room but he just nodded agreement with his daughter.

"What 'perfect use' have you thought of for it?" Leah asked when the girl had gone.

"Never you mind," he said, relishing his secret. In fact, he relished it too much and had to blurt it out in the end. "Oh, all right!" he exclaimed after she had made some blatant attempts at banal conversation. "I'm going to put a plaque on the fountain saying that funds for its construction grew from an original and most generous donation of half a sovereign from Miss Philomena Liddicoat. And I'll have a quotation there, too — something like 'Great oaks from little acorns grow.' Eh? How about that?"

Leah made a noncommittal gesture.

"Come on!" he said. "You must have some opinion of it."

"My opinion, Father," she replied with a sigh, "is that it's a pity great minds do not from petty actions grow."

"Oh." He was crestfallen. "You think it's petty, then?"

She relented with a smile. "I know how satisfying such thoughts can be. It's not a petty *thought.*"

"As long as it stays right there! Okay, okay."

She said, "I heard some good news from Ben Coad today — two bits of good news, in fact. One is that our farm buildings and land are already worth more than we gave for the whole place. We could sell them off and be left with the house for free, plus a few pounds to spare."

He bristled. "Out of the question! Do you seriously imagine that I'd …"

"I know, Pa. I'm not suggesting it for one moment. But I'm sure it's not beyond your wit to make sure the fact trickles through to Miss Philomena, eh? *That's* why I call it good news."

He was all smiles again. "And the other — the second bit?"

"Ah, you know the money Granpaw put in trust for me?"

"Yes?" He was guarded now.

"You're now the sole trustee since Uncle Jimmy died, right?"

"Yes?" Guardedness turned to downright suspicion.

"And you're a pretty shrewd investor — or so half the state of Connecticut assured me at various times. I mean, it'd be worth a tidy penny by now?"

"Come to the point," he said. "But I warn you — I'm not going to tell you how much."

"Oh?" she said, as if his words surprised her slightly. "Oh, okay." She pushed her soup plate aside and went to serve herself from the buffet.

"What was this other good news?" he asked as he crossed the room to join her there.

"Oh, it doesn't matter now. It was just a thought." She resumed her seat at the table. "If it doesn't rain again before tomorrow, we'll have to carry a keeve of water out to the long acre and water your nursery beds. Did you mark them?"

"Come on now," he cajoled. "What was this second bit of good news?"

"Nothing — honestly. If my trust fund is absolutely secret and sacrosanct and only to be used as a dowry, then it's not good news at all — nor bad. It's not news of any kind. When I asked if you marked the beds, I meant did you mark them so that even John Hamden couldn't make a mistake?"

"No, I didn't mark them at all. And I've never said the trust fund is *exclusively* for your dowry. It's ..."

"You've always given that impression."

"I just meant it's hard to think of any *other* purpose. In fact, when something worthwhile *does* come along — like your milking herd, for instance — I'm only too happy to release some of the income."

"But not the capital?"

He started to laugh. She asked him why. "Oh, something I said to Pansy while the Dragon was driving away — one of the many pearls I used to cast before the swine on the hog-futures exchange. 'Never transact business with a woman. If her argument's light, she'll throw in her sex and beat you on the deal. If it's heavy, she'll subtract it and beat you anyway.' Words to that effect."

"That's quite a pearl," she said coldly.

"Really, Leah, honey! What d'you want to touch the capital for, anyway?"

"Nothing," she assured him. "I was just asking a general question. *If* some worthwhile project came up, would it be *possible* ... et cetera? That's all. It doesn't matter. I think I'll call on Adèle this afternoon. Ben Coad says that Mrs Pascoe, widow of a farmer at Tregathennan, has some good milkers for sale ..."

"You seem to have stopped for quite a chat with Coad."

"I didn't stop for a chat. We chatted as we drove." She explained how she had come to offer him a lift.

The news did not seem to please him. She asked why.

"I think it's maybe a little tactless just at this particular moment," he replied.

"This moment? Why is this moment any different from …"

"Because of the Dragon's sudden arrival, that's why. Think of poor Clifford Liddicoat's position."

She set down her knife and fork rather than brandish them. "*His* position?" She waved her hands in annoyance. "What *is* his position — and why *poor* Clifford Liddicoat all of a sudden?"

"You know his position, honey — from that very first day. His hopes of acquiring the Old Glebe without paying a penny on it? Have we any news of Harvey, by the way?"

She shook her head in vexation. "That's another thing I want to hear from Adèle. You mean his absurd dreams of marrying one of his sons to me?"

He closed his eyes in exasperation. "Whether *you* think it absurd or not, honey, is beside the point — which is …"

"I don't *think* it's absurd. I know it is."

"That's beside the point, too — which is that *he* believes it's the case. So just think of the situation down there at Grankum Farm. In storms his sister Philomena and chews his head off for not buying the Old Glebe — and what excuse is he going to offer? Now d'you see? It doesn't matter — not a jot — whether you or I believe it. What matters is that *he* does. And there's a fighting chance that he'll persuade his sister to the same futile hope. At least it would stop her from going berserk. You're a Carrington, honey — surely I don't have to spell out every little detail? So for you to be seen driving around with Ben Coad — even on the most legitimate sort of business — is going to undermine that whole thing. It's going to bring her down on our necks again."

He expected her to see the point, accept the argument, apologize, and promise to be more circumspect in future. She saw the point well enough but from then on her point of view veered sharply away from his. She picked up her knife and fork and resumed eating in stoic silence.

"Well?" he had to prompt her.

"Well what? I simply can't think what to say, Pa. Maybe it's something your generation just can't see. I've just spent the morning arguing the point with Elizabeth Troy — also to no avail. So I don't see much purpose in repeating the whole thing with you."

"You could try, honey. Am I leaping down your throat? Bawling your head off?"

She shook her head in reluctant agreement. "The point is that both you and Mrs Troy start from this assumption that, since she has no power over us in any direction, she can't do much harm. But *my* point is that she is already harming us, just by being here, by forcing us to wonder what she's up to, by making us ask about every little action — could she use it to our disadvantage? We're living with one eye over our shoulder all the time. She can make our life a misery without lifting a finger."

The implication of her words annoyed him. "We sure as hell aren't giving way to her," he said, adding just in time, "if you'll pardon my language."

"That's that, then," she said with resignation and returned to her meal.

"I can't believe you'd want to give way to her, either, honey."

"I can't believe it would be 'giving way' to sell land and buildings to her for more than we gave for the whole place. Who loses? She can afford it, too, by all accounts. So you've got her by the scruff of the neck — either she buys the land or she shuts up for ever — for *ever* — about us and the way we cheated her family out of it."

"And my garden project?" he asked coldly.

She pursed her lips to hide her triumph. He accepted that selling out to the Liddicoats on such advantageous terms would be no defeat. Or, at least, he did not dispute it. Being his daughter, however, she realized that to produce the farm at Goonhusband at that moment would seem far too pat. It would expose all her manipulations. So, since Ben had assured her it was not yet on the market, she decided to drop the subject for a more propitious moment. "Yes," she agreed. "That would rule it out. Still … but for that, eh, it would be a fitting way of getting her out of our lives for good."

"No doubt of that," he said easily, thinking there was little harm in such an admission.

41 Leah found Adèle up to her elbows in flour, making a beef pie for their dinner that night. Eileen, whose task it would normally have been, had not turned up that day and inquiries at her home in Carleen revealed she had not spent the previous night there, either. Nobody made the connection with Harvey's simultaneous disappearance — or not to the Liddicoats' faces, anyway — but it was naturally on everybody's mind. Even Adèle hinted at it, obliquely, when she said they'd have to hire another maid but passed none of the expected comments on Eileen's behaviour. She said she was going to Carleen after finishing the pie and asked Leah if she'd like to come along for the walk.

Leah accepted. "You look as if you could do with some cheering up," she said.

"Do I?" Adèle responded.

"Yes, you look as if you lost a lover and found an aunt."

Adèle, far from joining in her laughter, looked at Leah rather sharply. But Leah hoped the little dig would prove enough to provoke her friend into unburdening her fears a little during their walk.

The wind was now a mere half-gale. It had dried out the higher parts of the lane so the two young ladies found it possible, with care, to avoid the wet all the way to the road. Adèle's first question was, "How did Will seem to you this morning?"

Leah, whose mind was still full of last night's caper in the tithe barn, was taken aback. She played for time. "Didn't he call at Grankum for Nicholas this morning? Oh — how silly of me! You weren't there at breakfast, were you. Didn't you find the Angel noisy after the quiet of the countryside?" While she was speaking she recalled Pansy's slip of the tongue; then Adèle's interest was clear.

"I didn't sleep much," she admitted. "But that wasn't on account of the noise from the street."

"And coming up from the bar. That's what used to keep me awake. It was dreadful."

"I was wondering whether strychnine or arsenic or curare would be best — or, indeed, whether any of them would have the slightest effect on my dear, sainted aunt. She's going to ruin everything … just everything."

Leah was surprised to hear a little catch in her voice, suggesting that her humour was to mask her closeness to tears. "I've been pondering that, too," she said. "It isn't that your aunt can actually *do* anything — or not much — to harm us. My father and Will keep comforting themselves with that thought. But they miss the point — don't you agree? The point is that her reputation and her presence down here are enough to ruin our peace of mind. We now have to watch our backs the whole time. We tell ourselves she can't hurt us but we can't actually guarantee it. All the time we have to think, *could* she do this, *could* she do that?"

"That's fine for your family," Adèle said morosely. "But she *can* actually do things to us."

"For example?"

"She's got the old fellow under her thumb. He'll curse her every way to Christmas but he'll go to heel the moment she snaps her fingers at him."

"But *you* — you and Nicholas — what can she do to you? And Harvey, of course. No news of him, I suppose?"

"I'm sure he's gone to Plymouth to try to join the navy — idiot! She can make our lives so miserable we just give in. Did she see your father this morning? When she left me she said something about a scouting party into enemy territory."

Laughing, Leah told her what had happened — Pansy's version of the tale, not her father's bland, complacent gloss. She omitted, however, the lecture Aunt Philomena had delivered on how servant maids should resist the advances of hurrisome masters, young or old.

Adèle found it amusing, of course, but not for long. Her earlier gloom settled again when she said, "The more you Carringtons triumph over her, the harder it will be for the rest of us Liddicoats. I think I'll run away from home, too. I can manage a household. There must be a nice, retired, elderly clergyman somewhere who wants a capable and energetic young housekeeper …"

" 'To my *dearest* housekeeper …'," Leah quoted.

"Oh, don't!" Adèle collapsed on her arm. "You see — that's the real danger of having someone like Aunt Philomena around.

She provokes a body to such extreme actions — strychnine …
running away … anything rather than do her bidding or yield to
her will."

"Talking of Will …" Leah said — having decided to end all
this beating about the bush.

"Yes?" Adèle's sudden eagerness was heartrending.

"Penny on the drum — is there anything going on between
you and him?"

"No!" she replied at once.

Leah leaned forward and peered into her friend's face. "Look
me in the eyes and say that again," she challenged.

Adèle looked away. "It's nothing," she replied. "It's so *tiny* …
you'd only laugh if I told you."

"Try me."

Adèle turned and faced her. "Promise?" The appeal in her
eyes was poignant.

For reply, Leah took her arm and held it tight against her as
they walked. "I think I may be in a similar quandary," she said.
"So which of us goes first?"

Adèle, who had been bursting to tell *someone* ever since last
evening, before Nemesis arrived, needed no further prompting.
"It's so small," she said. "I told you it's so small. But it's one of
those things you just *know* when it happens." She described the
way she and the two men had climbed over the hedge from the
poisoned croft, how Nicholas had pushed her, how Will had
caught her and held her and set her down — light as a feather.
"And our eyes met," she said, trembling again at the memory.
"That's all. That's the little thing I warned you about. Just —
our eyes met. But something happened. It was only a moment,
but something happened. He wasn't expecting it, I'm sure of
that. But I could see it hit him like a sort of thunderbolt. He
couldn't let go my waist. He couldn't look away." She was on the
verge of tears.

Leah, to rescue her, said, "And the minutes turned to hours
as the evening slowly fell around you, and the stars came out to
marvel, and *still* …"

"No!" She laughed her way out of it. "My dear, darling
brother jeered, of course, and that broke the spell. Maybe I'll
get *two* doses of arsenic!" They both laughed and the risk of
tears subsided.

"So you want to know if Will gave any sign of this ... this epiphany — his road-to-Damascus revelation?"

"That was the idea."

Leah was now in a pickle. How do you warn a friend that she has a possible rival in another girl, but without putting it in so many words? Pansy was far prettier than Adèle, who was self-critical enough at the best of times. In present circumstances such news might drive her into the ground. She thought she saw a way — at least, she took a chance on it. "He's said nothing to me directly," she replied. "But then, I was doing my accounts last night" — and that was actually *true* she realized! — "so we hardly said more than two words to each other. And he was out this morning before I came down to breakfast."

"So you can't help," Adèle concluded glumly.

"I do, however, have some slight, indirect, evidence."

Again, the girl hung on every word.

"It's something Pansy said."

"Pansy?" There was alarm in her voice now.

"Yes, there was one thing I left out earlier — something else your aunt said." And she went on to repeat Aunt Philomena's lecture on chastity. "Pansy thought it highly amusing, of course, to be delivered such a lecture in the presence of the man your aunt was warning her against. But when Pansy repeated it all to me, I saw a chance to drive the point home, so I told her it applied equally to Master Will. At which she laughed me to scorn and said there was no fear of that because Master Will was dedicated mind, body, and soul to one Adèle Liddicoat. So there's comfort for you!"

Adèle gave a cry of joy and, slipping her arm out of Leah's, did a dance of joy in the middle of the road. But she stopped in mid-skip and, serious again, said, "You're making it up!"

"Oh, my dear!" Leah put an arm around her shoulder and gave her a quick hug. "You must *trust* yourself more. Stop thinking no man could possibly ..."

"That's not it," she replied implacably. "If Will only started feeling like that last night, how can Pansy Tregear tell you all about it this morning?"

This was the dangerous bit.

"Maybe he told her," Leah suggested.

"He discussed *me* with *her*?" Adèle was outraged.

"He discusses lots of things with her — but that's just to annoy *me*, of course."

The suggestion was intriguing enough to make Adèle rein in her anger. "Of course?" she queried.

"Yes, of course. Don't your brothers do things deliberately to annoy you? The day Pansy came to us, I saw Will's eye light up. So I told him — the slightest hint of *that* and she'd be dismissed. I told her, too. So … you know how, if you tell a little boy he's not to *touch* his brother — when they've been fighting, for instance — and he'll take you absolutely literally? He'll get so close to his brother you couldn't slip a visiting card between them. But he won't actually touch him. D'you know that sort of provocative behaviour?"

"Do I!"

"Well, I should learn to keep my mouth shut. Because now, just to annoy me, Will steers as close a line as he can to intimacy with the girl but, naturally, avoiding any trespass that might make me carry out my threat." She spoke a silent prayer, begging forgiveness for the white lie. "So it's more than possible he said something last night. You know Will! He wears his heart on his sleeve and if that same heart was bursting with a new discovery … he'd not be able to hide it. I don't imagine he said anything directly, but he must have said enough for a smart girl like Pansy to guess the lot."

"But you weren't actually there," Adèle pointed out. "So you don't really know."

"That's true." Leah bit her lip and looked worried — just enough, she hoped, to put Adèle on her mettle. "Still — it's better to know what we're up against than to live in blissful ignorance. Eh? Cheer up! Forewarned is forearmed. And faint heart never won fair gentleman."

"I just …" Adèle's lip trembled again. "I just love him so. I can't stop thinking about him day and night. Stupid things. He just fills my thoughts all the time." At last she dared glance at Leah, but what she saw in her friend's eyes surprised her. "Why that look?" she asked.

"Envy," Leah said simply. "I *long* to feel so passionately about someone but somehow I don't think I ever shall. It *almost* happened once — with Nicholas, actually — when he kissed me and I felt …"

"Nick?" Adèle shrieked in her amazement. "He actually *kissed* you?"

"Just once." Leah explained how it happened and described the feelings that had then started to work within her. "But then I ... I don't know. Perhaps I got frightened of them. I was still trying to keep alive my feelings for ... oh, just someone back in America. And this threatened them, you see. So I pulled away and said no, it was a big mistake, and we were much happier the way we were ..."

"Sparring partners."

"Exactly. And — Nicholas being Nicholas — he couldn't beg me to think again. I could feel he wanted to, but he was too proud. So he agreed with me and promised it would never happen again." She put her hand to her breast. "That cut through me like a knife!"

"So it never has happened again?" Adèle asked.

Leah shook her head. "And then — just when I'd got used to thinking the moment had gone for ever ..."

"What about this person in America?"

They were passing Benny Meagor's fields. He kept a herd of Guernseys and Jerseys, several of which were staring incuriously at them over the hedge. Channel Island milk makes the finest clotted cream. Leah made a mental note to buy some on their way back. Her nearest approach to paradise each day, straight after driving the cattle back into the fields when milking was done, was to devour a slice of bread and butter drowned in golden syrup and clotted cream, and to wash it all down with a mug of hot, sweet tea.

"Eh?" Adèle prompted.

"Oh," she sighed. "I've decided that by holding on to Tom's memory like that — Tom O'Leary was his name — I was just keeping all the *real* possibilities at bay."

"Possibili*ties* — plural?" Adèle asked coyly. "My, my!"

"That's what I was about to say just now. Just when I'd grown to accept the fact that Nicholas is too proud and independent to unbend — and anyway I've got the farm to keep me busy — just when all the dust had settled very nicely, thank you, I went into Helston this morning, on my way to see Elizabeth Troy ... bumped into Ben Coad, who was on his way to Tregathennan, offered him a lift, and ... well ..."

"It hit you like a thunderbolt!" Adèle nudged her delightedly.

"Not really," Leah had to admit. "Thunderbolts don't seem to be part of my make-up. The most I can manage is to go a bit weak at the knees."

"Well, that's *something,*" her friend said encouragingly. "Ben Coad made you go weak at the knees, eh?"

"Not quite. But I realized what wonderful company he is. I feel completely relaxed when I'm with him. I want to touch him, to be sure he's there. I long to feel his arm around me. But it's not like your thunderbolts and ... all that passion. He suggested going on to look at a farm ... Now keep this under your hat because it's not on the market yet — a farm the other side of Helston, over at Goonhusband, whatever that means. What does goon mean?"

"Down or downs — you know, like Carnmeal Downs."

Leah laughed. "Down, husband! Like, 'Down, Rover! Bad dog!' Eh? I'd better not go asking *how* it got its name. Anyway, he offered to take me there to see it and I really had to force myself to say no."

"Why did he want to show it to you? Are you looking for *more* land still? Surely not so far away?"

"Well now, that's the other thing I'd like to talk about. It's only a hazy idea as yet but I'd like to hear your opinion. How would it be if we Carringtons offered your Aunt Philomena the chance to buy the Old Glebe by private treaty? No auction. No public offer. No competing bids. She could have just the land if she prefers. Or the land and the buildings. Or the whole lot. Would she jump at it?"

They walked awhile in silence, Adèle being deep in thought. When they drew near Carleen forge, where Sam Chigwidden, the smith, was shoeing one of Will Tyacke's cart-horses, the acrid reek of burning hoof assailed them. "Poor-man's smelling salts," Leah commented.

They paused on the far side of the road to watch. A small group of loafers was gathered around the door.

"Have you discussed this with your father?" Adèle asked.

"Indirectly. I fired the first shot, anyway. I pointed out that one way to spike your aunt's guns would be to offer her the Old Glebe. The valuation has gone up quite sharply over the past few months — for most unhappy reasons, I admit, but it's a fact of life. And maybe your aunt would jib at giving any Carrington a profit — but at least she couldn't go about the place complaining we're playing dog-in-the-manger with it."

Adèle laughed. "It's brilliant, my dear! She really would have to hold her tongue, then — or buy the place. Either way, the source of all friction between our two families would be removed at a stroke." She did another few skips of happiness. The idlers round the forge watched with amusement.

Leah, who had previously considered Adèle's little displays of her feelings rather childish — something she would soon grow out of — now saw that she was, in her very nature, both demonstrative and passionate. Again she envied her, not simply for the passion but also for the easy spontaneity with which she allowed herself to show it. Will was a lucky man; she just hoped he appreciated it.

"And Downhusband isn't so very far away," she pointed out. "I think I'll call it that."

Adèle stopped dancing. "It's also just half a mile from Chynoweth Hall — and Blanche Curnow."

"Oh, I think that has all died down."

It just so happened that Chigwidden's assistant pumped the bellows at that moment. The fire that had seemed dead was blustered back into life, glowing orange, then yellow, and spitting sparks. "It can happen to any smouldering fire," Adèle commented flatly.

"Well, Blanche Curnow is not the only one with a good bellows," Leah assured her as they resumed their stroll. "But there's something else we ought to think about first, something more immediately important: Are we, the younger generation of Liddicoats and Carringtons, going to play the Martins and the Coys at our parents' sides, or ..."

"Who are the Martins and the Coys?"

"Oh, sorry. Two famous feuding clans in the Appalachian mountains. Like the Montagues and the Capulets, I guess. Are we going to play their game or stay united and play our own? I can certainly answer for Will and me. As far as we're concerned, the feud stops with us."

"With me, too," Adèle said fervently.

"No matter what devilish blandishments your aunt might yet dream up?"

"No matter what."

"And your brothers?"

Adèle hesitated.

"Not so certain, eh?" Leah guessed.

"It's not so much that," was the reply. "It's just that they could promise one thing — and mean it most sincerely — but when Aunt Philomena gets to work on them … *pfft!*"

After pondering this for a moment Leah said, "So, tell me what you know about strychnine and curare, then."

They laughed and left the discussion there for the moment.

Adèle found a suitable maid at the second attempt; the girl even agreed to come for the normal 12/6 *d* a week once she heard Miss Philomena was not to be living at Grankum.

On their return they passed Carleen Flow, a broad piece of sloping scrubland that funnelled down to the Wheal Vor adit, the source of the stream that ran down the Wheal Fortune valley, past the old stop gate, and on to Porthleven, where it emptied into a corner of the inner harbour. Adèle suggested they could follow this watercourse down as far as the stamps and see how their brothers were progressing.

They chatted about this and that, down past Scott's and on between Carnmeal Downs and Trew, where Pansy's parents lived. A little farther on, past Scott's Farm, where another adit drained yet another mine into the valley stream, they came to a neglected and now densely wooded area, which had once quite obviously been a mine halvan. The trees were stunted cork oaks whose hunched, yellowing canopy lent the place an air at once gloomy and sinister.

"We used to climb in there as children," Adèle said. "It's hard to believe there are the ruins of at least two dozen hovels in there. Only the bottoms of the walls are left, but you can see where they were — all higgledy-piggledy. No streets. No plan at all. There's also an old mineshaft."

Leah eyed a gap in the hedge, where some stones had fallen out — or, more likely, been removed by a poacher. "Could we?" she asked. "Just peep in maybe?"

They arrived at the wall to find the gap larger than it had seemed from a distance; they had no difficulty in getting through. The atmosphere inside was quite different from that in Grankum

Wood, where the trees, though slender, were tall and stately. Here the trunks looked as if they had been forced to grow among piled boulders that had since been removed, leaving them all twisted and gnarled. The brightest colour was the intense emerald green of wet moss, which grew on almost every surface and even hung in short, tattered curtains from the branches overhead.

"It's so eerie," Leah murmured. "I'd rather spend a month of nights in our allegedly haunted barn than a single midnight hour out in the open here."

"Actually," Adèle said, "it is a doom-laden place. About forty years ago this shaft was the scene of a triple murder — or what would have been a triple murder if the local people hadn't caught the murderer and saved his victims just in time. He threw them down this shaft and ..."

"But how could they survive that?"

"Have a look over the wall."

Leah obeyed and saw that the shaft, instead of falling vertically like all the others she had so far seen, sloped down at an angle. It was still pretty steep but she could just imagine that, if you dug your heels in, you could stop yourself from sliding down.

"That's the way all mineshafts used to be — before steam," Adèle said. "They followed the angle of the lode down into the ground, digging out the tin as they went. This one goes down at that angle for about half a furlong — until it meets a later shaft, the Blueborough shaft, which goes straight down. And the murderer got them down to the very edge of the vertical bit before he was stopped."

Leah stared into the dark-on-dark of the pit and shuddered. "Are any of them still alive?" she asked.

"I know two of them are. The murderer was hanged, not for that but for another murder — of a woman up Breage who was his common-law wife. One of the people he threw into that shaft was the son of that liaison, still just a little boy. He's now Mister Jake Morvah ..."

"The solicitor in Helston? The one who has chambers in the same building as Frank Kernow? Good heavens!"

"And another near-victim was his adopted mother — Mrs Kitto, who lives in that house on the headland at Rinsey and keeps a watch for German submarines — did you see that in the

West Briton — why she's allowed to keep her binoculars instead of handing them in like the rest of us?"

Leah, still lost in amazement, just shook her head. "It's so quiet and so ... overgrown now. I mean, it could have been dug back in the days of Bonnie Prince Charlie for all one knows ..."

She stopped speaking abruptly. Both girls froze. Somewhere behind them a twig snapped — several twigs, in fact. Someone — or some *thing* — was at liberty behind them. Slowly, fearfully, they turned, half expecting to see some latter-day reincarnation of the hanged man, desperate for revenge.

What they actually saw was Will, who had come through the gap in the hedge and, without bothering to check that he was alone, was desperate to pay a call of nature.

Leah stared in amazement. She had not seen that part of her brother last night. In fact, she had not seen it since they were kids, skinny-dipping out at Tom O'Leary's cousin's farm. How it had grown!

Adèle just stared — until the two girls caught each other's eyes and fought their laughter. They suppressed their giggles pretty well, but not well enough. Will spun round, away from them, leaving a fleeting semicircle of golden beads on the air around him. Then he called out over his shoulder, "Adèle?"

She swallowed heavily and croaked, "Yes?"

"You'll have to marry me now."

Silence.

"What did you say?" he asked as he shook himself and, in the quaint parlance of those notices in men's public lavatories, 'adjusted his dress.'

"She says, 'Yes, please'!" Leah called out, and put up an elbow to ward off the embarrassed blows Adèle tried to rain upon her.

The two girls walked toward him — or, rather, toward the gap, which all three of them reached at the same time. "Why," Leah asked, "with the whole of this secluded valley to make use of, did you have to come in here? I don't suppose you saw us enter by any chance?"

"Good God, no!" he protested as they went back into the bright daylight. "And this valley isn't as secluded as you might suppose. The wife of that farmer up on the hill by Trew ..." He pointed it out on the far side of the valley.

"That's Pansy's Tregear's place," Adèle said. "They're not farmers, they're only smallholders."

"Anyway, she's a small holder of very large field glasses. We should report her, really. She ought to have handed them in."

"You *were* listening to us," Leah accused him. "We've just been talking about that."

"On my honour, not. Anyway, she watches Nick and me with them any time we pay a call of nature — which is okay when we're far away, by the stamps. But up here was, I felt, a bit close. Any *more* questions?"

"You're forgiven," Leah told him.

"Am I?" He leaned forward and peered at Adèle.

"When do we call the banns?" she asked.

He pulled out his watch and said, "Well, I'm afraid we've left it a bit late *today.*"

They all laughed and a dangerously sticky moment was avoided. But his eyes met Adèle's and they both knew that what had been merely glimpsed there yesterday was now confirmed.

Suddenly he struck his forehead. "Of course!" he exclaimed. "You left Grankum before Harvey returned."

"He's come back?" Adèle asked delightedly. "Does that mean he didn't join the navy after all? How d'you know he's back, anyway?"

He shook his head. "They wouldn't have him. He's with Nick now, by the stamps, trying to cheer himself up."

"They must have found out he's a farmer's son," Leah said.

"No such luck," Will replied. "It's rather sad. They rejected him on medical grounds."

"Good heavens! ... No! ... What? ... Why?" The questions and exclamations poured from the girls' lips.

"Something to do with his heart. He's not going to die or anything like that — they told him he could live for sixty years with whatever it is but they can't accept him for fighting service. However, you just try to get *him* to believe it!"

"What did they actually say?" Adèle asked anxiously.

"They said he has a *murmur* — that's what they called it. A murmur and a *thrill.* He has a murmur on one side of his heart and a thrill on the other."

"It sounds like a lot of other hearts one could name!" Leah said quietly.

42 Harvey was just about to help his brother pull the handcart out of a rut when he spotted the others approaching. He let go of the traces and said he'd better not risk it. Will would be there soon. Nicholas reminded him that, only a week earlier, he had been carrying sacks weighing two hundredweight into the barn at Grankum, apparently without strain. Harvey replied that he had — all unwittingly — been risking death at every step.

Will was certainly not hurrying to get back to the digging and hauling — not with Adèle at his side and Leah to act as chaperon. For her part, she was amazed at her brother's apparent devotion to Adèle, when, not eighteen hours earlier, he had been locked in that ultimate intimacy with another. It was all very well for him and Pansy to protest that love played no part in their games — and that questions of fidelity did not, therefore, arise. The very fact that their meeting (or was it meetings?) had been so clandestine, and that Will would surely rather die than have them made known to Adèle, gave such *sophisticated* arguments the lie.

Or did it? No doubt Will would claim he was merely sparing Adèle's feelings. He himself knew beyond all doubt that his frolics with Pansy were mere escapades, pleasant frivolities without substance or meaning. Pansy herself regarded them in that light, so he was certainly not deceiving her. And he was not *really* deceiving Adèle, either — simply acknowledging the fact that she might not be able to see it in the same jovial light. He was merely sparing her feelings as would any decent chap.

And, Leah had to admit, Will was not a heartless man. No wicked deceiver, he; no cold-blooded trifler with Adèle's trust and devotion. Leah could easily believe that he kept Pansy and Adèle in two quite separate compartments in his mind — and, indeed, in his heart, as well — the one labelled profane, the other sacred. She was sure he believed that nothing he did with profane Pansy could impinge upon his love for sacred Adèle.

Watching the pair of them, walking at her side, talking, laughing, renewing the wonder of this strange and sudden thing that had happened between them, Leah could not help thinking of all the other couples she had seen in similar circumstances. The women had been no less radiant than Adèle, the men no less attentive and engrossed than Will. Indeed, if her own suspicions had not been aroused last night and if she had not followed him and Pansy out to the tithe barn and seen it with her own eyes, she would take Will and Adèle as a model couple, for whom the marriage vows of eternal fidelity would be the simple confirmation of ways they had practised (seemingly) from the very start.

One little accident had overturned all her perceptions. She thought back to times when she and Tom had been to each other as Will and Adèle now were. Had been ... or had only seemed to be? Adèle, looking up into Will's eyes with such credulous devotion, and seeing nothing there but a reverence to match her own, could not possibly guess it might be otherwise. So was she, Leah, any smarter? Had there been a Pansy in Tom's life, too — some feather-heeled faloosie who had taken care of him in the profane department? And was there someone like that in Ben Coad's life? Or the Nark's? You could gaze into their eyes as long and as deep as you liked but you'd never find the answer there.

Where, then? By keeping eternal vigil? By mounting watch over the body that had vowed its eternal soul to 'thee and thee only'? You'd make the whole world a jail and yourself a wardress in it.

Her mother, who had told her most things in this area of life, had not told her this. Perhaps she, too, had not known — or, knowing, had chosen to forget? Maybe women of those days, dosed with the bitter but sugar-coated medicine of *their* mothers' times, had not been able to lift the veils of romance entirely from their eyes?

"Penny for 'em, Thistle," the Nark called out as they drew near. He had abandoned his attempts to get the cart out of the rut on his own — though it would have made a splendid show for the two women to admire.

She gazed into his eyes and thought that, of all the men she knew, he was the last and least likely to have that secret faloosie tucked away somewhere. Not that she suspected his passions were weak. Quite the contrary. But his one, singular passion would override all the rest, no matter what their strength — his dread of being beholden to a female for anything. How odd that one of his worst points should also be one of his best!

"D'you really want me to tell you, Nark?" she replied.

"Oh, dear!" He pulled a face. "I should have known better. Only tell me if it's to my own undying credit or glory. You know how one tiny criticism from you can leave me absolutely shattered for days."

"I was wondering if the gift of knowledge about the nature of man is a price worth paying for female emancipation."

"Botheration!" he said. "It wasn't about me at all."

"Well, at the risk of *seeming* to criticize you, Nark, I have to tell you that my musings at the moment you accosted me (and I call them musings because I know only *men* can have actual *thoughts*) were exclusively about you. I'm sure your superior brain can work it all out."

"You've heard my news?" Harvey asked.

"Yes, I'm so sorry, Harvey. But glad, too — that it's not actually going to shorten your life, I mean."

"I just have to be very careful from now on."

Adèle put her arms around him and hugged him tight in wordless commiseration. "What is it, exactly?" she asked as she let go again.

"The heart has these two chambers, you see," he said, putting his hands together in the attitude of a praying mantis. "Called auricles. And there's a kind of wall between them called a septum. And …"

"You should have seen him carrying two-hundredweight sacks up a dozen steps into the barn last week," Nicholas cut in. "Just because Eileen was out there beating a carpet and watching him with admiring eyes!"

"And there's a defect in the septum. They call it *patent*. I don't know why."

Adèle laughed. "People were beginning to whisper that Eileen ran away *with* you!" she told her brother.

"She did — in a way. The thing is, both auricles pump blood at roughly the same pressure and in the same rhythm."

"Just a mo!" Adèle said. "What d'you mean — 'in a way'?"

"I didn't say 'in a way' — I said, 'in the same rhythm.' So there's no great flow from one auricle to the other. That's why it's not at all …"

"You said Eileen ran away with you — *in a way*. What does that mean?"

"Oh, I just meant she was on the same train to Plymouth. She's got a job in the naval stores there. Aren't you interested in my illness?" His eyes begged all of them.

They assured him they were. And Nicholas told his sister to let Harvey finish for God's sake or they'd be there all evening.

"Because there's no great flow from one auricle to the other, through this patent hole, the spent blood from the veins doesn't get mixed with the freshened blood from the lungs. It's utterly fascinating once you're in the know. The first thing I did was buy an ox heart at the butcher's and cut it open to see what on earth they were talking about it. This septum thing is about as thin as a good bit of oilcloth, you know."

Nicholas, meanwhile, had taken up a stick and was drawing a traditional Cupid's heart in the sand. He scratched an arrow through it and wrote the initials HL above it — and repeated them below it, too.

Harvey ignored him loftily.

"So where do these thrills and murmurs arise?" Leah asked.

He smiled at her gratefully. "The murmur is from the little bit that leaks across when the auricles are filling and the thrill is what you hear when they're pumping themselves empty again. The doctor put his stethoscope-thing in my ears and let me listen. It was amazing."

Adèle had meanwhile wiped out the two sets of initials with her feet. She scratched NL above the heart and was wondering what to put below it when Leah took the stick from her and scratched a circle there.

Adèle frowned. "O?" she asked.

"Zero," Leah replied. "Nil. Nought. Nothing. Nix." She grinned at the Nark, who smiled magnanimously back at her and said, "I fought with none, for none was worth my strife."

She capped him: "I loved with none, for none would make a worthy wife!"

"Anyway — that's why they turned me down for active service," Harvey said.

Adèle, wanting to end all these cross-currents of aggression, said brightly, "Wouldn't Aunt Philomena absolutely hate to see us here — all being so *friendly* and getting on so *well* together!"

They all laughed — except Nicholas, who was staring up at the rim of the sandbank they had excavated. They had, in effect, created a small, horseshoe-shaped sand quarry with walls about twenty feet high and he was staring up toward the top at the centre of the digging. "Talk of the devil!" he murmured.

They followed his gaze but saw nothing, except the ling and furze that carpeted the whole area. They laughed, thinking he was trying to pull their legs. But he swore he had seen Aunt Philomena, or the living image of her, standing up there not five seconds earlier. To prove it he turned and sprinted up a shallower part of the bank and then around the rim to where he said he had seen her. There he gazed about uncertainly, quartering the landscape like a hawk, using that technique where you gaze at a fixed point but concentrate on everything around it, hoping to spot some telltale movement. But the wind was still too strong; just about everything in view was shivering or swaying in its capricious blast.

"Well?" they shouted up.

He shrugged and launched himself into space over the rim with a cry of "Wheeee!" His heels dug in about halfway down and he braked to an elegant halt at the foot of the sand-cliff.

"Oh!" Leah exclaimed. "I want to do that."

"Me, too!" Adèle chimed in.

Harvey just sighed, implying that it was the sort of thing he'd never be able to do again.

"You were kidding us," Will accused Nicholas.

"If you mean I was jesting," he replied, "I promise you I wasn't. She was standing right there where I was."

"Then how did she vanish?" Harvey asked. "A hare couldn't have got away in that time."

"What would you have done if you'd found her waiting for you?" Adèle asked.

He laughed grimly. "That was exactly the thought that went through my mind when I was standing up there. She's there, all right, hiding behind some bush. But it dawned on me that if I had a choice between facing her and not facing her — well, it wasn't a choice at all."

"It doesn't matter if she was there or not," Leah said bitterly. "This is exactly what I mean — don't you see? Whether she's here or whether she's there, or whether she's in Timbuktoo — it doesn't matter. And whether she's plotting something deep and dark or just puzzling over a knitting pattern — it doesn't matter. She casts a pall over all our lives, *whatever* she's doing and wherever she is. Just by being Aunt Philomena, by being here in Cornwall, she ruins it all for us." She looked around at each in turn and added, *"If* we let her!"

"How do we stop her?" Nicholas asked her morosely. "Surely there's a way?"

"Just *tell* her," Will said. "Form us a posse and beard her in her den. Tell her we're happy the way things are and she can go take a long walk off a short jetty."

"Or fly to the moon," Nicholas suggested in identical tones to Will. "And paint the same message on the Man in the Moon's face. It would be easier. And safer."

"Hogwash!" Will raised his voice and cupped his hands to his mouth. "Hey! Aunt Philomena! Get your long neck out of our lives! D'you heah?"

Nicholas stuck his fingers in his ears and spun an agonized circle on one heel. Harvey sat down on the handle of the cart, panting slightly, and put his hand to his chest. Adèle plucked nervously at Will's sleeve and murmured that what he had just done was most unwise.

He looked to his sister for support but the most she would say was that they could also try something a bit more subtle.

43 For the first time in her life Philomena Liddicoat felt the lack of an ally. It frightened her, and fear was an emotion she knew little about — from her side of the fence, anyway. She realized that knowing all about it on the *other* side of the fence was of little help. People who did what you wanted them to do, but only because they were to afraid to do otherwise, were not allies. Turn your back and there they were, playing 'cat's in the cupboard and can't see me'! The sight that had met her eyes when she gazed down into that sand quarry had shaken her badly — her own niece and nephews fraternizing with the enemy in broad daylight!

And then there was Nicholas, charging up the banks like that — ready to confront her, which he had never dared do in all his life. And Adelaide, simpering like a mooncalf over the Carrington boy. The *Carrington* boy! Words failed her when she thought of him — shouting disgraceful things like that after her.

She sat in the private lounge of the Angel, nursing a glass of sherry — an indescribably shocking act for a once-staunch Methodist like her. But — like fine claret with dinner — it was a tipple she had learned from the dear colonel, though she had not made it a daily routine until after his passing-on. It had been *his* daily routine, of course; now, for her, it was part pleasure, part act of loving remembrance. On such a day as this, when she could only sit back and wonder what her world was coming to, it was indispensable.

Why should she feel this sudden need for an ally? All her life she had fought her own battles, planned her own campaigns, dictated her own terms for surrender. *Their* surrender, never hers ...

A chilling thought struck her: All that had been in the days before she met the colonel. Or had become his housekeeper. Or — be honest — had become something more than that to him. God, how she missed him — especially now! He was that ally whose lack she felt so keenly. If he were still alive, he would surely understand her bitterness at what her brother had allowed to happen. He would surely help her to undo that harm. What would he advise next?

She took another sip and faced the post mortem with the courage and honesty he always admired in her.

'You charged straight at the enemy flag, old thing,' he'd say. 'You went in with all guns blazing. But you should have done a thorough recce first.'

'But did I do *nothing* right, Colonel, dear?' she'd ask.

'You kept your temper,' he'd reply. 'That was good. When that odious Carrington man saw fit to make you the butt of his practical joke, you rose above it and you smiled. You spoke in well-modulated tones. You embarrassed him in front of his maidservant. And you rubbed salt in the wound with that half-sovereign. Now he must either return it and eat humble pie or keep it and declare himself no gentleman. All that was good. But still I return to my point: To go there like that, all unprepared, on the moment's whim — that's not like my Philly, is it! That was not well done.'

'Something would have come to me, Colonel, dear. It always does. You often admired me for that.'

'Something even better would have come if you had been better informed, my dearest. How often have I said it — one well-prepared regiment can take on the biggest unprepared army in the world and win. You *must* get information.'

'But from whom? Clifford is useless — always was. And the other brother, Frank, is not much better. Besides, he'd see it as Clifford's fight and then he wouldn't lift a finger. Harvey's gone off his chump, if you ask me. Nicholas is in cahoots with the Carrington boy — he won't tell me anything useful. He always was a perverted little liar, anyway. And as for Adelaide — she's just infatuated with that same Carrington boy, though she fondly imagines she has kept it from me. And so she might have done, if I had not met you, my darling, darling man! But now I know every earthly sign of love and loss, love and longing ... love so huge that not even the gift of all the world could requite it. And she imagines she can keep her petty infatuation from *me?* So tell me — where do I turn for this precious information?'

'Are there no servants at the Old Glebe? That Pansy Tregear — you know a thing or two about her people, surely? And what you don't know you can easily discover. She has an elder sister ... what was her name? They were all called after flowers. Violet! You also used to teach her at the Chapel Sunday School. Perhaps she's free at the moment, or would change positions for the right money? And you cannot live here at the Angel for much longer without a maid. Pansy might not be too forthcoming, but Violet would be.'

'I'll look into that tomorrow.'

'See you do, my precious. And while you're about it — does Carrington have no lawyer here in town? And what of Ben Coad, the viper who sold the place without informing you! Has he not a fence to mend with you? Could you not make him feel that obligation? Oh, there is so much you could do before your next assault!'

She closed her eyes and, in her happiness, almost spilled her sherry down her dress. That would be a fine thing to do — the next best thing to reeling down the street! Rather than risk such a spill, she tossed back what was left and breathed out the fire of its afterburn.

A maid knocked hesitantly at the door and poked her head round it. "If it please you, ma'am, your hot water jug is in your room and Mister Blackwell says you may have your dinner served there if you prefer on account of business being so slack today." She heaved a quick sigh as if she were surprised at having got out so many words without interruption.

"Come right in, maid," Philomena said. "I don't know you, do I? Are you new here?"

"No, ma'am. Please, ma'am, I'm Mary Tregear, the scullery-maid here but Mister Blackwell let Nora have the afternoon off, what with there being such little work."

"So will you be serving my dinner in my room?" Her surname, Tregear, had naturally aroused Philomena's interest, though it is not rare in Cornwall.

"Yes, ma'am." She curtseyed.

"Good. I shall be ready for it in half an hour."

Half an hour later, when Mary brought her soup, Philomena asked the maid if she had others to serve. Mary replied that there was only one other resident, a traveller, and he did not wish to dine until eight.

"So tell me," Philomena said pleasantly, "are you, by any chance, a relation to the Tregears of Trew? Take the weight off your feet, my dear."

Mary looked about her nervously.

"Go on," Philomena urged. "I'm sure you do quite enough standing all day. It's not good for a girl. You'll get horrid varicose veins — take it from one who knows."

Mary sat down and said, "My father is cousin to Aaron Tregear of Trew, ma'am."

"Ah, so you must be Noel Tregear's daughter from up Ashton. I taught your elder sister Margaret in Breage Sunday School — before you were born, probably! And your brother Benjamin."

Mary managed a shy smile. This 'old dragon' wasn't as bad as people said. Her nervousness began to subside.

"I also taught Violet and Pansy. They'd be your second cousins — and about the same age as you, if I'm not mistaken? Pansy, anyway."

"Yes, ma'am."

Philomena noticed that the maid's uneasiness returned at the mention of Pansy — because of the Carrington connection, of course. "Well, you must give my special regards to your parents when you see them next. They were the backbone of the chapel — and still are, I trust?"

"Yes, ma'am." She began to relax again.

"D'you see much of Violet, these days? Or Pansy?" She made her tone as casual as possible but even so she saw the maid's fists tighten. "You needn't worry, my dear," she added. "I know only too well where Pansy is working these days — in fact, I met her there this morning and we had quite a chat. She has grown into a very ... how can I put it ...?"

"Coxy giglet?" Mary suggested impetuously — and instantly regretted her forthrightness. She bit her lip in consternation and waited for the other's famous temper to explode.

"D'you say so?" Philomena leaned forward with interest. "Well, I would never have said this if you had not been so honest with me, Mary, but I'm sorry to admit that I formed the very same impression. We spoke for no more than ten minutes or so but she seemed to me a rather *forthy* maid, as we used to say. In fact, I felt impelled to warn her of the dangers of appearing a mite too *comfortable* — you understand me? — in a house of furriners like those Carringtons. I'm sure she's a good maid at heart ..." She watched Mary's expression carefully and saw an incipient sneer. "No?" she added. "Am I wrong?"

Mary shrugged awkwardly; the Tregears were, after all, family. Still, her father had often spoken harshly about his cousin and those preedy daughters of his. "You know what they do call she, ma'am — that there Pansy?"

Philomena shook her head.

"Manhole Tregear!" She blushed and stared at her boots.

"Dear me!" Philomena worked hard to conceal her delight. "People can be so cruel. One little slip and a maid can be branded for life."

"*One* little slip!" Mary echoed sarcastically. "One every *day*, I s'pose. And she'd never slip without a soft place to fall on." She continued to gaze at the floor until the silence compelled her to look up. Miss Liddicoat seemed lost in thought. "Ma'am?" she prompted tactfully.

The woman gave a little shake of the head and smiled a slightly rueful smile. "God forgive my want of charity," she murmured. "I was thinking that if such infection had to pollute *any* household, then it could not have found ... but no. That would be a disgraceful thing to say. What of the elder sister, Violet? Not tarred with the same brush, I hope?"

"No, ma'am," Mary said — though there had, in fact, been a whisper or two about Violet, as well. But they had amounted to no more than any passable maid could expect when she was rather choosy with her beaux and therefore tended to take up and discard them more swiftly than most. Hell hath no scourge like the tongue of the discarded male.

"I'm extremely glad to hear it. What is she doing these days? Married, I suppose?"

"No, ma'am. She's some pussivanter with men. You want another dole of soup, do 'ee? There's scats in the pot."

"I think I will, thank you, Mary. One needs the extra nourishment now, with the winter drawing on. What an attentive maid you are! I shall certainly commend you to Mister Blackwell."

Mary floated on air all the way down to the kitchen and all the way back again. As far as she was concerned, Miss Philomena Liddicoat was now sun, moon, and stars.

"So!" Philomena went on as she took the first sup of the fresh bowl. "Violet's a picker and chooser among her beaux, is she? I'm glad to hear it — glad for *your* sake, too, Mary. *Two* feather-heeled girls in a family is too many. It begins to look as if it's in the blood, you know. You didn't tell me what Violet's actually doing nowadays? Do sit down again."

"She've got work in the Helston Union, ma'am. Bathing the old cripples and putting on poultices and that."

"Hmm!" Philomena considered the news in silence for several sups. "Not too happy about it, I should think. Still, it's necessary work and Florence Nightingale herself did even less appealing tasks, I'm sure. But tell me a little more about yourself. How long have you worked here?"

While she finished her soup she let the maid prattle on about the various menial jobs she had done and how she hoped soon to go into service in a proper house. When Mary brought her main course — a sumptuous cut of prime beef — she said, "So you were here when Mister Carrington and his son and daughter arrived — before they bought the Old Glebe?"

Mary was no fool. She knew what the woman required of her — and John Carrington's generous sixpence had been spent long ago. She gave out all she knew, which was mostly hearsay, of course, since scullerymaids had little contact with visitors at the front of the house. But there was that night when the visitors had come to the back of the place and she had been there to help. She made the most of that, not just of Master William's inability to hold his drink but also of Frank Kernow's complicity in the affair.

The only other thing she knew was a bit of gossip she'd heard in the kitchen that very afternoon — about Ben Coad and Miss Carrington having been seen driving out Pallas way in her gig. She passed that on, too.

All in all, Philomena thought as she settled her head upon her pillow that night, a disastrous day had been rescued by a much more rewarding evening. Also, to her surprise, she had rather enjoyed being pleasant to the little scullerymaid; at times during their conversation she had felt almost altruistic about it, as if she had forgotten why she was being so amiable and was doing it for its own sake.

44   When Leah heard the back stairs creak that night she knew it was Pansy. She rose and, pulling the quilt around her, stood at her bedroom window. The night was overcast but the cloud was thin enough to let a fair amount of moonlight through. It was certainly enough to reveal her brother, standing at the barn door with one hand on the latch. She would almost swear she could see the grin on his lips. A moment later a movement in the back yard, immediately below her window, caught her eye. It was, of course, Pansy tripping on her way to what was obviously a nightly assignation. The girl glanced up at the window as she passed. Leah froze. Logic told her that the brightness of the cloud, the angle of sight from where Pansy was passing, and the absolute darkness of her bedroom would all combine to make discovery impossible. All the same, she had the uncomfortable feeling that the girl had seen her.

Had seen her — and had not been particularly bothered.

Well, she had her own lecture to the girl that lunchtime to blame for that; she'd as good as given them carte blanche for these clandestine meetings.

As if to rub in the salt, Pansy started wiggling and sashaying in a highly provocative manner the moment she saw Will standing there waiting. Angrily Leah returned to her bed and fell asleep pondering the unfairness of everything.

The following morning, after milking and breakfast, she put on her prettiest hat and went again into Helston, this time to tell Ben that she'd like to see the Goonhusband property, after all. His clerk, Ambrose Bowden, shook his head sadly and said Mr Coad had scats of work ahead of him that day. Ben, hearing her voice, came to the door and said that was nonsense and what did she want?

Two minutes later they left a distraught Bowden rearranging files, writing messages, and changing his master's appointments diary — yet again.

"The poor man must curse the very sight of me," Leah commented. "I ought to learn about your appointments system."

"It's extremely simple," he replied. "It rearranges itself automatically whenever you call."

"You drive," she said, handing him the reins. "You're so much better at it than me."

He looked at her askance as they set off up Coinagehall Street. "Apart from the fact that that's just not true," he said, "it's also not a sentiment one expects to hear falling from your suffragist lips."

"You know the way, then," she said. "Is that better?"

"It's the literal truth, anyway. People are still going to talk. Tongues are already wagging about our driving out together yesterday. I hope you don't mind that?"

They were nearing the Angel at that moment and, before she could reply, Walter Blackwell, having noticed their approach, hastened out to warn them that Miss Philomena had gone out not five minutes since and was walking up Meneage Street — if they were thinking of going that way. They said they were, thanked him, and drove on.

"I've not actually seen her yet," Leah said and went on to describe her father's encounter with the woman yesterday morning. Also Nicholas's conviction he had seen her on the halvans at Wheal Fortune.

"That means she hasn't seen you yet, either," Ben mused.

"Why d'you say it in that tone?"

"Because that's her on the right, looking into Pascoe's window. She's bound to see me."

"Good!" Leah exclaimed. "Will you introduce us?"

He shook his head and kept his eye on their quarry.

"Scared?" Leah asked.

"No, it would just be very irregular. People in trade do not have leave to introduce ladies and gentlemen to one another unless asked. She's spotted me!"

"Coad!" Miss Philomena called out. "The very man! I wish to call on you today."

"In what connection, Miss Liddicoat? I have a very full day, as it happens." He slowed the trap but did not quite halt it. She began to walk, to keep pace.

"Not too full to see me, I'm sure," she said. "And I think you know very well what I wish to see you about. I have a crow to pluck with you."

She stared curiously at Leah, clearly not recognizing her from that brief glimpse on the halvans.

"I'm just off to show this young lady a property over Culdrose way," he said. "I'm sorry not to stop, this pony doesn't like to start again on a hill — especially with two up."

"What property?" she asked sharply.

"A cottage near Higher Pentire." That was true, for there was such a cottage on the Goonhusband farm. Over his shoulder he added, "See my clerk, Ambrose Bowden. Tell him I said to move heaven and earth to find time for you this afternoon."

"Stop at this little flat bit up ahead," Leah said quietly.

"You want to risk it?" he asked, equally softly.

"Yes. It's not much of a risk. She's hardly likely to think we Carringtons are looking at properties again so soon. And if what you say about tradesmen is true, she won't expect an introduction, either."

"He can start again here," Ben said to Miss Philomena as she caught up with them. "It's more level. I'm sorry we can't offer you a lift."

"Not at all," she replied. "I'm only going as far as the Union." She nodded toward the entrance, which was only a hundred or so paces away. "Tell me, Coad, what reports have you of Violet Tregear, from Trew? I used to teach her at Sunday School and I hear she's working at the Union now."

"You mean Pansy's sister?" Ben said, in case Leah didn't already know it.

"Of course that's who I mean. I don't know any other Tregear girls all named after flowers, do you? Have you heard anything to Violet's discredit?"

"On the contrary, Miss Liddicoat. The complaint is that she's mighty purnick, as they say. Are you seeking a replacement for that Eileen Bersey, who ran away from Grankum?"

"My brother's family can look after themselves. *I* need a maid — someone I know and can trust."

Coad chuckled. She asked if he'd kindly share the joke. He said, "Someone with a sister at the Old Glebe, too — now that might come in handy, ma'am!"

She bridled. "You're very impertinent today, Coad."

He dipped his head in apology.

She went on, "But don't talk to me about that Pansy Tregear — what a baggage!" As she spoke a broad smile spread across her features. "But she'll wreak havoc in that household before too long — you mark my words. Haven't we all seen it happen? She's a fireship. That Carrington fellow thinks he's the cleverest creature since Plato. But she'll …"

"You've met him?" Coad mingled surprise with admiration in his question.

"I've *met* him," she replied. "Round One — ten points to me, none to him! That's what I wish to talk to you about. But don't let me hold you up now." She turned toward the Union entrance and waved them on. "He's not at all the sort of man I expected him to be."

"He has surprised quite a few people hereabouts," Ben said as he took up the reins.

"Yes," she called out as they set off again. "He's going to be a more worthy adversary than I dared hope for."

"I'll tell him that, ma'am," he called back at her.

"Tell him anything you like," she said.

Ben waited until they were so far away than not even a bat could have heard him before he said, "Well, I'm in trouble now and no mistake — letting her go on like that with you sitting beside me."

"Yes, Ben," she said. "That occurred to me, too. Why did you do it?"

"Because I want *you* to know whose side I'm on, Leah." He laughed grimly. "I'm certainly committed now!"

She reached out and stroked his arm a time or two. "It is greatly appreciated, Ben. Tell me more about Goonhusband."

"Tell me what you make of Miss Philomena, first. Is *she* what *you* expected?"

"If Will hadn't told me how good-looking she is, I'd have been more surprised. In fact, she's almost exactly what I expected her to be. And … I don't know if one can have intuitions about a person one has never met — just from hearsay, you know — but I think mine about her are correct. Especially now I've met her, even for just a moment like that."

"And what are your intuitions, if a mere male is permitted …"

"She's tough and rude and belligerent because there's a chink in her armour somewhere — a soft spot she doesn't want anyone to know about."

He laughed dismissively. "No one down here has ever seen it," he assured her.

"I can believe that. In fact, I think only one person *has* ever seen it — the man whose house she shared for so many years. You'd have to be that close for that long to manage it — back in those days, at least."

"But not now?"

"Maybe not. It's possible she had as much affection for the colonel as he obviously had for her. And once a woman yields to the luxury of being adored, it's hard to go back to the old diet."

He drew a deep breath and swallowed hard. "You speak from experience, do you?"

"Yes." She slipped her arm through his and said, "Let's give them something to talk *about*, eh, Ben?"

He looked down at her hand, then into her eyes, and said, "Are you suggesting I should ask your father if I may call upon you, Miss Carrington?"

"I'll kill you if you do, Mister Coad," she replied.

He laughed and pretended to collapse for a moment or two.

"Why d'you do that?" She joined his laughter.

"For months I've dreamed of this moment," he said. "I've tried to imagine every possible way we might arrive at it — but I never remotely imagined it would be so simple. Is that really you? Am I here?"

"And are we by any chance going to a nice empty farmhouse?" she asked archly.

His face fell. "It's not empty," he said. "That's why it's not quite on the market yet."

"Oh," she said with resignation.

"But there is an empty cottage — at Higher Pentire, just as I told the old girl back there." He grinned at her.

She reached up and gave him a quick kiss on the cheek. He smelled of shaving soap. It was wonderful to have a beau again. It was even more wonderful that the beau was Ben Coad and that it *hadn't* been love at first sight — on her side, anyway. "Have you really been thinking about it for months?" she asked. "Why didn't you say?"

"What would you have done if I had?"

She hesitated.

"See!" he said. "A man doesn't get two shots at that sort of thing. He dreams and dreams ... and he waits for the right sort of smile."

"And when did I give it you?"

"Yesterday."

"Good heavens!"

"Why? Did you imagine you'd been flashing it earlier?"

"It's been sort of on my mind," she replied vaguely. "But so have lots of other things — other responsibilities, I mean, not other people. Oh, dear — life was so much easier when we were young and fancy free, wasn't it!"

She glanced over her shoulder. The entrance to the Union was just about to pass out of sight. Miss Liddicoat was still standing there, obviously watching them until they were no longer visible. It gave Leah yet another intuition — that the woman had tumbled to what she had just done.

He was still wondering how to reply to her when she went on, "Also, I have to confess, I ... well, I have to confess two things, really. I left behind the love of my life in America, my head-over-heels, drowned-deep-in-love, only-ever-man for me ... and I had to come three thousand miles and wait several months before I discovered he was none of those things at all."

His arm, which had tensed almost unbearably when she started this confession, relaxed again — but incompletely. "And the other 'confession'?" he prompted her.

"Oh, that's a bagatelle. I did, for a week or two, imagine I might be falling for the Nark — Nicholas Liddicoat."

"But not now?"

She was silent awhile — too long a while.

"A bagatelle?" he murmured.

"It's not easy to explain. I do still feel a certain attraction to him, even though I know it's, one, absurd and, two, impossible. I mean — he *is* an impossible man. I suppose that 'growing up' means you get to recognize the existence of attractions like that but you also realize you don't have to do anything about them. If you don't plant them and water them, they don't grow."

"But you're still friends?"

"That's the only reason I'm telling you this, Ben. The Nark and I are as close as two friends could be and I don't want to have to turn it all off. At the same time I don't want to have to contend with any fits of jealousy. Oh, dear! That sounds dreadful. I don't even know if you're a jealous man or not. Are you?"

He shrugged awkwardly. "I'm not sure."

"Really? Haven't there been other girls?"

"Not like you. I've never felt like this in my life."

She gave his arm another squeeze. "Nor have I, my darling — which is why I know that my friendship with the Nark, and even the attraction I feel for him, *is* the merest bagatelle. Could we have a look at this empty cottage *before* we look at the farm? I'm absolutely *dying* to kiss you."

45 Ben Coad's eyes upon her were as caressing as any hands. Leah felt his adoration like a physical warmth, a fire, like a pressure on her skin. He trembled when his hands went lightly to her waist and pulled her to him. Too late she realized they were standing by the window, where any passing ship's officer with a good spyglass could see them from five miles away — or any sparrow in the overgrown hedge outside. It was her day for recklessness, her week … her year.

Her lips went up to seek his as his loomed down to find hers. She rose on tiptoe, holding him tight, pressing her body firmly against his and relishing the lean hardness of his muscle and bones through the linen and tweed that separated them now.

One day, she knew, it would not be so. One day they would lie together as she had seen Will and Pansy lie together the night before last, and it would be just as beautiful and just as easy. Ben was the first man she had ever considered in that light. Even with Tom, something inside her had always shied away from the thought. Was that because she had not been ready — as she was now? Or because he had he not been right — as, she knew, Ben was now?

Their lips met, melted ... fused together. She lost all sensation of weight, and even of up and down. The breath that keened in her nostrils, and his, was to keep alive not them but their earthbound carcasses; they were now two ethereal beings, twin souls who floated at liberty in and near their physical selves, held to them by the most tenuous threads yet bound to each other with ties that nothing material could now sever.

"Just every now and then ..." she murmured as their lips finally parted.

"More often than that, I hope," he said as he kissed her again.

Another timeless while later she said, "No, I mean that just every now and again life behaves as it should."

"I see," he replied slowly, in a tone that implied he didn't see at all but he wasn't going to spoil the thought by asking her to explain it.

She explained it, anyway. "I mean, one reads those descriptions of love in books — and those lurid things the servants read, which we all pretend never to look at ourselves — and it sounds absolutely wonderful and you think, why can't it *be* like that? Ever? Why is there also the milking to do and brass to clean and cows to buy and sell and bills to pay ...? And then, just occasionally, life *is* like that — the way it ought to be. Like now. Do we squander the moment luxuriously, Ben, or try to cling on to it with ever-increasing desperation until we've completely clutched it to death?"

"We squander it," he decided. "But how?"

"By telling ourselves we don't *need* to hold on to each moment, each time. By behaving as if ... Oh, I don't know!" She laughed and hugged herself tight in against his chest again, wondering if he enjoyed the pressure of her bosom as much as she did. "I'm talking garbage. What I mean is that I feel as if I've just walked through a door and closed it behind me and shut out all the hubbub and bustle … all those cares and cautions … and here we are, alone with each other, where no one can see us or reach us. And it's all snug and warm and dry in here. And everything is now up to us. We decide for us. No one else says yes or no, do or don't. D'you know what I mean?"

"Nothing like this has ever happened to me before," he said. "What about you?"

"I've had intimations of it," she admitted. "Like when you start a car and it fires once or twice and then splutters and dies. It's a genuine fire in there — the real thing — but it doesn't last. Something else was missing. And whatever it was, it just came along — just now. You brought it. It's something you've got that no other man ever had for me. So, now that the engine's ticking over as sweet as a mountain stream" — she changed her embrace and held him as if for a waltz — "where shall we let it take us, Ben? Now we've got her running nice and smooth?"

Laughing, he obliged her with a few steps, making them as flamboyant as the cramped little room would allow. "You're amazing, Leah," he told her. "I've never met another woman who gets within a mile of you."

"And what am I bid for this unique little article!" She laughed, for his tone had been so like the one he used in his ringside patter, down in the market.

"The reserve alone would break the Bank of England," he assured her with reproving solemnity. "Shall we go and look at the farmhouse itself?"

As they climbed back into the gig she said, "Do you ever get that feeling where you want to tear everything up, burn all your boats, do something so outrageous that no one you know will ever want to know you again, and then go off and start afresh? *Be* someone new."

He shook his head. "Sometimes, in the middle of an auction, there's a bit of me that sort of breaks loose and watches me — and asks what on earth I think I'm doing there."

"That's the start of it," she said.

"And the end of it," he said fervently. "D'you know George Ivey, over to Mousehole — the artist? You've seen his work, I'm sure. He's quite well known."

"Elizabeth Troy told me he was her solicitor once — oh! Talking of solicitors, by the way — my father has decided to bid farewell to Frank Kernow. I'm glad. I never quite trusted that man. Do you?"

Ben shrugged. "It takes all sorts," he replied diplomatically. "Who are you going to instead?"

"Jake Morvah. I just heard his astonishing story yesterday afternoon ..."

"He told you?" Ben asked in amazement. "It's the one thing he never speaks about."

"No. Adèle told me. We were walking near the mineshaft where it happened and she showed me. Anyway, what were you saying about George Ivey?"

"Oh, yes — he was a fine solicitor ..."

"Your father was solicitor to the Pallas estate but he pleaded a conflict of interest to Elizabeth and advised her to go to George Ivey — very honourably, she says."

"You'll find it runs in our family," he said loftily. "Anyway, young George started asking himself that sort of question — what on earth am I doing this for? — and decided to chuck it in and take up painting instead. He married Lilian Rodda, a beautiful dark-haired girl with the most amazing green eyes. She could have had her pick of Cornwall's eligible bachelors but she chose him and has stuck to him through thick and thin. And they had a *very* thin time of it for many years. If Elizabeth Troy hadn't bought some of his work, they'd have gone under. But only certain people are as singleminded as that. I don't know whether to pity them or envy them."

"You're warning me you're going to remain an auctioneer for life, eh?" She hugged his arm tight to show him she didn't mind.

"I could give it up for farming," he admitted. "For the right sort of farm."

"Or combine the two — farming and the auctioneering," she said. *With the right sort of wife,* she added mentally, though she thought it would sound too precipitate to say such things out loud just yet.

"Could be." *With the right sort of wife,* he thought, though he knew it would sound too brazen to drop hints like that just yet.

46 They both longed to make something of the name Goonhusband, as well, but again it seemed far too audacious a thing to do; one giant leap was sufficient unto the day. Leah loved the farm, of course, with its fine views over southward-sloping fields to the Loe Pool and the massive sandy bar that isolated it from the sea, but, for the moment, they both maintained the fiction that she wanted to persuade her father to move over this side of Helston and sell the Old Glebe to the Liddicoats, with or without the house.

"Back in the middle ages," he said, "that sandbar wasn't there and seagoing ships could sail right up the creek to the foot of Helston. I often think of that when I'm standing in my box above the ring. If a time machine were to transport me back seven hundred years all of a sudden, I'd be standing in the rigging of some coastal lugger. I don't know who'd be more surprised — me or half a dozen medieval peasants watching a lunatic in funny clothes asking twenty-four pounds for a cow worth fourpence!"

Meanwhile Leah was thinking that this would be *their* bedroom, with the nursery just across there, and they'd have to get rid of that wallpaper ... and *she* didn't know which of them would be more surprised if her thoughts suddenly decided to speak themselves aloud. "Damp," she said, pointing to a patch above the mantelpiece.

"Chimney needs repointing," he said. "Make a note of that — and anything else. We'll try to get the cost of it all taken off the eventual purchase price."

"*Purchase* price, Ben?" She dug him playfully in the ribs. "Don't you mean *selling* price? Which side of the fence are you squatting on now?"

"Hmm!" He sniffed. "There may be a slight conflict of interest here — I can't deny it. Mind you — looking at it as impartially as possible — even if nothing got knocked off it, today's fair price is tomorrow's bargain. As long as this war lasts, anyway. I might even buy it myself."

"And becoming a farmer would be a capital way of staying beyond the reach of snipers and dysentery!"

He shook his head. "Being able to find good remounts for the cavalry and commissariat is even better. But you're right in one way — I've no taste for guns." He eyed her evenly. "D'you think that's cowardice?"

She shook her head, implying that it was sad he should even feel it necessary to ask. "I danced all round the room when I heard that the wolfram business would keep Will safe."

He suspected she had meant to say Nicholas. "But Will would be safe anyway, surely?" he asked. "As an American?"

"Altruism knows no frontiers," she told him. "Young second-generation British-Americans are remembering their roots every day and signing up in their droves. Surely you've read about it?"

He said nothing — merely continued staring out of the window. She touched his arm, ran one finger up and down it gently. "Penny for 'em?"

He shook himself, smiled at her, and became brisk again. "A new intimacy is such a fragile thing," he replied. "You said it's like entering a room and shutting the door behind you — and so it is. But then you notice, in my case, that the room is full of beautiful and fragile-looking things. And so, although you've been longing for months to go through that door and close it behind you, you still daren't move. I mean, even to touch you like this" — he slipped his fingers into the hair behind her ear and scratched her scalp, making her shiver all over — "even that would have been *unthinkable* yesterday. Now I may do it without alarms and excursions."

"Anytime!"

"And to say the words I've longed to say to you from the day we met — 'I love you, Leah Carrington. You are all the world to me' — would have given me a heart attack yesterday. Today I can say them with impunity."

"Anytime!" she said again.

"So the summit and utmost pinnacle of yesterday's ambitions is merely the ground on which today's are stood."

Leah thought this over and said, "My mother always told us at Thanksgiving and Christmas and other times when we were set to eat more than our fill at one time ... she would say, 'Always rise from the table feeling you could eat a little bit more'." She looked at him to see if he took the point.

He chuckled. "Mine always said that, too — and no doubt *we'll* be saying it one day to ... er, the next generation ... er ..." He subsided in confusion.

She laughed and took his arm. "Come on, Ben. Back to the world of cows and counting frames."

They chatted happily about nothing in particular, the way new lovers love to do, all the way back to town. As they passed the entrance to Chynoweth, Blanche Curnow appeared, taking one of their dogs for a walk.

"I haven't seen much of Will lately," she called out to Leah. "Tell him he's a heartless wretch and it will be many minutes before I forgive him, even if he does pay us a call."

"He is a heartless wretch, too," Leah said to Ben when they were out of earshot. "There's only one woman for him in all the world now, and that's Adèle Liddicoat."

"Oh, there's a come-up! Does Miss Philomena know?"

"I'm sure she doesn't. Actually, there's something I want to ask you, to do with Will and Adèle."

"Ask away."

They were passing the Union by now. She had little time left but it might be an advantage to limit this particular conversation. "It's actually about Will and Pansy," she said. "Adèle is the love of his life but Pansy is his little bit of fluff on the side — is that the right expression?"

"Oh, dear."

"Yes, it's not exactly a pleasant thing to contemplate — still less to try and deal with. But that's my question, really — should I deal with it at all? Or shall I just let the pair of them go to hell in a handcart?"

After a moment's thought he said, "You are Pansy Tregear's mistress. Have you spoken to her about it?"

"I have — and I went completely off on the wrong trail. I thought she was setting her cap at Will. I told her there was no chance of any such union. She said she wouldn't go near him if there was. She just wants a bit of fun and no permanent ties. I can't fire her because it wouldn't stop her assignations with Will and I'd lose what minuscule control I have over her now. Besides, she's one of the best workers I've ever known. Intelligent, reliable, thorough ... a dream."

"Have you spoken to your pa about it?"

"Don't!" she answered heavily. "She's flirting with him, too, and would be quite capable of going further, just to thumb her nose at me. But I've warned her about that — one slip and she's out without a character. Not that the factories look for characters when they offer our maidservants twice what we pay them! In a way, I tolerate what's going on with Will just to stop her trying anything with Pa — isn't that awful?"

"When you say she's capable of 'going further' ... how far ... with Will, I mean?"

"All the way, Ben. And practically every night as far as I can tell. I feel just *awful* about it every time I meet Adèle, who's my best friend." She stroked his arm. "Girl friend, anyway. And then there's poor Blanche back there whom I'm also very fond of. Isn't love ruthless!"

"Blanche Curnow's young yet," he said. "Learning how to put a cheery face on rejection is valuable, too."

"I hope the young man I left behind me in America has forgotten me by now, but if he hasn't, I'd do nothing to cheer him up if it threatened our love in the smallest degree. I know I ought to feel heartless to be saying such a thing, but I don't."

They turned down into Coinagehall Street and she asked to be put off at the Angel — leaving their conversation unresolved but simmering. Ben offered to take her into the hôtel for lunch but she declined. "I want to see Miss Philomena," she said. "Alone, if you don't mind. I want to put matters straight between us and recover your good standing with her."

He laughed — a bluff, hearty laugh. "I don't give a fig for her now," he said.

"That's as maybe, but there's no point in making enemies needlessly. Besides, we may yet need her. Don't ask me to explain it — but I just have this feeling, somewhere in my bones, that she's going to play a part in solving our present difficulties. And even if I'm wrong, she and I cannot stare at each other in naked hostility for ever."

She shook his hand, giving it a squeeze that no one else would notice. She could see his eyes begging her to tell him when they'd meet next. "Don't let's start that sort of desperate caper, Ben," she said. "I'll be with you every *possible* moment — which is exactly when you want to be with me, too. Isn't that enough? That and the telephone."

"*Toute à l'heure*, then," he said jovially. "I'll put your pony in our stables. No sense in paying a day's livery at the Angel. He'll be in the end stall."

"That's right," she said solemnly. "We've got to start saving every penny now."

Walter Blackwell greeted her like a favourite niece but he was clearly anxious to shepherd her toward some part of his establishment that Philomena Liddicoat was unlikely to visit. She, however, amazed him by sending him up to her family's sworn enemy, carrying her father's card. First she scribbled her own name in pencil beneath his: Miss Carrington. The British left out the 'Leah' since she was the only daughter.

The woman kept her waiting almost twenty minutes and then greeted her coldly and without any attempt at an apology. But Leah made an oblique reference to this rudeness in her opening words: "I owe you an apology, *too*, Miss Liddicoat," she said, offering her hand — which Philomena ignored. "I regretted the little subterfuge I induced Mister Coad to play upon you the moment we met."

"It is no less than I expected of any Carrington," the older woman put in frostily. "Especially after my extraordinary encounter with your father."

"Quite! I do see your point, Miss Liddicoat. If I were less of a coward than I am, I should have owned up at once and saved myself this shameful and humiliating scene."

"Hmm!" Philomena pursed her lips and stared at the girl speculatively through narrowed eyes.

"I should have realized you are much too astute to have been deceived for long."

"Enough flattery," Philomena said severely. "Tell me what you really want."

"Your acceptance of my apology is the most I could hope for, I think."

Philomena did not believe it for one moment but, by way of a test, she snapped, "I accept, Miss Carrington," and turned on her heel to go.

"Also ..." Leah said before she reached the door.

"Also," Philomena said, "I commend your courage in coming so swiftly to make it." Again she made to leave the room.

"Also there are other matters we should discuss, I believe."

"*Should* discuss? I cannot think of one, Miss Carrington."

"But that is what I am here to tell you, Miss Liddicoat."

Still with one hand on the opened door, Philomena said, "Name one."

Leah took a deep breath and said, "For example, we both have an interest in seeing the Carringtons leave the Old Glebe — I think?"

The woman's hand fell to her side. After a moment of complete immobility she came back into the room, to where Leah was standing, and peered deep into her eyes — a chilling, raptorial scrutiny that almost put Leah to flight. "Is this some joke — another of your father's childish pranks?"

"He knows nothing of this. Indeed, he'd have a fit if he knew I was here now. He's looking forward to a battle-royal with you, which he's quite sure he'll win, of course — though, mind you, he also says you're the first opponent who's truly worthy of him — the first one he's met since leaving the old shark pond in Pittsburgh, Pennsylvania."

"Ha!" Philomena pretended to be severe though she could not entirely hide her delight at the backhanded compliment. "He has a high opinion of himself, I must say!"

"And of *you*, Miss Liddicoat. I know him when he talks like this. He's afraid he might not win, you see — even though he seems to hold all the important cards. He's already preparing the grounds on which he'll excuse his defeat at your hands."

Philomena went over to the window and stared out at the passing scene for a while, taking in nothing. Nothing in her planning could have prepared her for this. Her cautious self advised her to send the girl away, setting an appointment for another day, by which time she could have made inquiries, imagined all the things the girl might have to say, and prepared herself to answer them. But her cautious self was a midget beside the leviathan of her self-confident and pugnacious alter-ego. "Tell me, Miss Carrington," she said at length, "have you eaten luncheon yet?"

"As a matter of fact, I have not, Miss Liddicoat."

"I have taken the room next to mine for use as my private sitting room. We could have a light repast sent up there?"

When she saw that Leah still hesitated she added, "Or what had you in mind?"

"If we eat together privately, word will still get out, and eventually it will reach my father. Then the fact that we tried to conceal our meeting — or gave that appearance, anyway — will not be helpful."

"But if we dine in public, you've been here long enough, I'm sure, to realize that word will get to your father at once — and then the fur will fly, surely?"

"I hope I shall be ready for it in either case. Besides — as you will see, I hope — we do not have the luxury of time."

They were the first to arrive in the dining room. Blackwell stared at them in amazement, which the professional in him quickly suppressed. "A table for two, Miss Liddicoat — certainly. This way."

Leah watching his departing back, said, "The message is already on its way."

"Tell me, Miss Carrington," Philomena said as she spread her napkin and peered at the chalked menu on the blackboard, "why is Ben Coad showing you a property out by Helston Downs? If it's not an impertinent question?"

"Not in the least," Leah assured her. "It's the farm called Goonhusband, which I'm sure you know? Sixty-odd acres, slightly larger than the Old Glebe, and all of them facing south and with superb views of the Loe Pool and the bay. My father could make a much more spectacular garden there than ever he could in Sithney. And now, perhaps, you see the way my thoughts are running?"

The maid took their orders. Both chose leek soup and steak pudding and smiled, slightly surprised to find themselves in agreement on anything.

"The house is nothing like so impressive as the Old Glebe, though," Philomena pointed out.

"It's adequate. It could even be grandified in time. My father will put up with a lot for the sake of his beloved garden project. On the other hand ..." She sighed.

"Yes?"

"On the other hand, he also loves a challenge. The fact that a quarter of the Old Glebe faces north of west and gets less sun than the rest is just the sort of thing to set his blood racing. He's got to whip the world into line with *his* thinking. Ignorant people might gawp in wonder at an easy-to-make garden facing south on those sunny slopes at Goonhusband. But *real* gardeners, the cognoscenti whom he'd invite to the Old Glebe, would look at his verdant, flourishing north-facing acres and ask how on earth he managed it. And *that* would be worth more to him than all the ignorant praise in the world."

Watching Miss Philomena carefully during this little speech, Leah saw that she had guessed correctly; the woman was much more in sympathy with John Carrington's love of a challenge than with his daughter's preference for the easy road. Naturally, she would rather die than admit it — especially to that same daughter — but the seeds of the internal conflict were sown within her.

"Goonhusband has hazards of its own," Philomena warned. "There is a frost that forms up on the downs on windless nights under clear skies, and it spills down into all the surrounding valleys. I have seen it with my own eyes. The frosty air is perfectly clear up on the downs but as it descends, a mist forms upon it even as you watch. And soon the whole valley is like a vast lake of mist. And a cold, clammy mist it is, too, which shrivels the buds off many a shrub and blights many a garden flower. Maurice Pettifer planted a belt of cypresses to shelter his land at Culdrose from it."

"It sounds quite spectacular," Leah said. "And you describe it so vividly. I should love to witness it myself."

The maid brought their soup and some white-bread rolls.

"You'll get your chance soon enough," Philomena told her as they began their meal. "In the calm days that follow the autumn gales the same thing happens up on Carnmeal Downs — on a much smaller scale, of course. It just pours down into the Grankum valley."

"And does it affect the Old Glebe?"

"No." Philomena stared at her coldly. "Why d'you think *we* always wanted to farm on *your* side of the valley!"

Leah dipped her head as if accepting a rebuke. Then, smiling again, she said, "However, if we can only put our thinking caps on — you and I, Miss Liddicoat — we may arrive at a solution congenial to all parties, don't you think? And without a single shot being fired!"

47 John Carrington had taken to dropping in at the Angel of a Saturday, around lunchtime, to moan about English beer with Jimmy Troy and otherwise chew the fat about this and that. They called it the weekly board meeting of LCT. On that first Saturday in October, however — the day after Miss Carrington joined Miss Liddicoat for luncheon in the public dining room — there was only one topic of conversation. Poor Carrington had a hard time keeping a civil tongue after the first half dozen good-natured friends had broken the news to him, each hoping to be the first to bend his ear.

"What I can't fathom," he said to Jimmy as they retired to their usual alcove near the fire, "is why Leah didn't breathe a word of it to me. Did she think I'd never get to hear of it? She's never so naive. What's her game, anyway? What business could she and the Liddicoat woman possibly have in common? Sometimes she just baffles me."

"Wa-al," Jimmy drawled, "let's lookit this-hyar thang in a calm and collected manner ..."

"It's no laughing matter, Jimmy."

"And it's not the end of the world, either."

"The *independence* of the girl! A year ago she'd never have done such a thing — nor even dreamed of it."

"That's what growing older usually entails, John."

"Does she really think she can wave some wand behind my back and make all smooth?"

Troy merely cleared his throat in response to that.

"Well?" Carrington prompted him.

"Well, in my limited experience of these matters, when a woman starts behaving like that, she's exercising something a mite more substantial than a wand."

"For instance?"

"Intellect? A cussed propensity to be more right than wrong, more times than not? An ability to skin away mere cleverness and expose the flesh and bone of the thing — which is otherwise known as intuition? I'd say she has some intuition about Miz Philomena and she's acting on it — for your ultimate good, I'm sure. Or do you doubt even that?"

"No," Carrington conceded reluctantly. "I'm sure she *thinks* she's acting in our best interest all round. That doesn't mean she *is* so acting."

"Well, the Yankee *calculates* his conclusions, the Missourian *opinions* them, the Southerner *suspicions* them, the Hoosier *allows,* and the Buckey *reckons.* It doesn't mean they don't all agree in the end."

Carrington stared at him balefully. "Take my hat, Jimmy, if you aren't hard to follow sometimes. Speak plain, man!"

Troy sipped his warm beer with relish, though he pulled the ritual face of disgust. "Plainly spoken, John, Leah is your daughter. You raised her. You launched her. You've got to let her sail a piece on her own."

"It augurs badly, that's all," Carrington said morosely.

"Augurs?" The word surprised Troy.

"I don't think I ever told you this, Jimmy, but under the terms of her granmaw's will, Leah is all set to come into full possession of her trust at the age of twenty-three — which, heaven help us, is only ten months off now."

"No, John, you never told me that before. More to the point — did you ever tell the girl herself?"

"I was about to. Now ... I don't know. This news has fair taken the wind out of *my* sails, I can tell you. Never mind her sailing a piece on her own."

"Without mentioning any figures now — as the Irishman said — what exactly does it amount to?"

"It's enough to let her do any damfool thing she wants."

After a further ruminative silence Troy said, "Okay, but that doesn't really *change* the problem of her independent action, does it. It simply makes it more acute. The question we have to address is: What is Leah likely to have discussed with Miz Philomena? Did she attempt to apologize for your little practical joke, for instance?"

"Why should she do that?"

"To gauge how mad the lady really was? I'm only canvassing possibilities here. Did she talk of LCT at all? Probably not. Is there any spark kindling between her and one of the Liddicoat boys, I wonder? A woman in love would go into the lion's den to size up the lion's ferocity. Or lioness in this case. Now that's a sharp possibility."

"Harvey maybe," Carrington agreed. "But not Nicholas. She wouldn't let him walk where she walked last year — that's how much she likes that young man."

Troy grinned. "That's how much she *says* she likes that young man." He punched his friend playfully. "You're mighty trusting when it comes to the *word* of a female, John. Or maybe there's some little preemption between your boy and the Liddicoat girl — Adelaide."

"She likes to be called Adèle now. Yes, there may be at that."

Troy chuckled. "Of course, Leah might simply have been asking Miz Philomena how much she'd offer for the Old Glebe!"

Carrington despaired of all this speculation. "Or they were discussing quilting patterns or how to put new life into old velvet! In short, Jimmy, reasonableness ain't gonna get us out of *this* forest. I'm minded to go home and put it to her, direct. It's the only way."

He half rose to go but then, seeing his friend staring past him toward the door, he hesitated.

"I wonder?" Troy mused. "There could be an even more direct way. Are you in a mood to apologize? You'd better be or this won't work, either."

And before Carrington could say a word, he had leaped from his seat and was striding across the lounge bar to the door, where, a moment earlier, he had briefly glimpsed Miss Philomena Liddicoat. Carrington himself did not make the connection until he saw Jimmy Troy returning with the lady — who, like Carrington himself, seemed none too happy at the prospect of this meeting.

It was just as well the surprise was sprung on him like that, for a moment's thought would have confirmed his determination never to apologize to *that* woman. With no time for reflection, however, he was at the mercy of half a century's training in etiquette, in which apologies to women were *de rigueur*, no matter who was right and who was wrong.

"Miss Liddicoat," he said with a somewhat glassy smile, "can you forgive me? I was so ashamed to be found in working man's rags — which is idiotic of me, I confess — that, on the spur of the moment, I pretended to be one of my own labourers ..."

His voice trailed off when he saw the woman smiling broadly. He had expected any reaction but that. "Say not another word,

Mister Carrington," she replied. "I was annoyed for an hour or so, I admit, but I hope I can see a joke as well as the next person, even when it is at my expense."

"May I offer you something to drink, Miss Liddicoat?" Troy asked. "A cordial or some lime ..."

"A pint of Rosewarne's export ale, Mister Troy. Thank you." She took the seat he held for her and offered cigars all round.

The barmaid asked would two half-pints do as Mr Blackwell never let them serve a lady with a pint glass.

She laughed and said it would have to do, wouldn't it!

The laugh surprised John Carrington, it was so rich and warm. It also filled him with distrust. 'Beware of Greeks bearing gifts,' he cautioned himself — though he was quite prepared to play the civilized game on the surface, if that was what the lady wanted. He lit her cigar and Troy's and then, obeying a new superstition, lit his own with a fresh match.

"Well, Mister Carrington," she said as soon as they were all seated, "I presume your daughter told you of our meeting yesterday? Such a charming girl! And so full of good sense." She looked him up and down as if wondering where the girl could have got it from.

"Er ..." Carrington eyed Troy nervously. "More or less. In outline — yes. The bare bones of the thing. I wish she'd spoken to me first, though."

She was not deceived for a moment, of course. "Oh?" Her tone implied that his reply surprised her beyond words. "You mean you *don't* think it's a good idea? Well, well, well — you do astonish me. The whole ... what can one call it? Contretemps? Fracas? The whole thing is to be solved at one fell swoop — and not a shot fired in anger, as she said — and yet you don't think that's a good idea at all?"

Having taken a position, however tentative, Carrington now felt he had to defend it. He stared balefully at Jimmy Troy, silently willing him to step in. Troy could say all those things he himself could not — that they seemed to be talking about different things and perhaps Miss Liddicoat could summarize Miss Carrington's notions so that they could all agree on what was at issue.

Troy beamed at him and toasted him with a silent lift of his glass.

"Say?" Carrington challenged him directly.

"Me?" Troy asked innocently, puffing his cigar again. "I say what I always say — when a feller's done flummoxed, he's flummoxed, and salt won't save him!"

"You were *relishing* a fight!" Miss Liddicoat said suddenly, as if it were a revelation.

Carrington, his back to the wall, said, "I'll fight for any principle that's worth defending, ma'am."

"Good for you!" she replied. "I understand perfectly for I feel exactly the same way myself."

The maid brought her ale. The sight of the two glasses made Carrington aware of something the mere idea of them had failed to drive home — that the woman was going to be sitting there for another twenty minutes at the very least. He was either going to have to temper his words or leave in a huff. That was no real choice.

He was so preoccupied with these thoughts that he did not notice she was setting her drink down at the same moment as he decided to set down his. Their knuckles touched briefly. Their eyes met. A fire burned and did not die. With something of a thrill he realized that the accidental contact was a symbolic enactment of the touch between boxers' gloves before the first round begins. She had thrown down a gauntlet and he had picked it up.

But their contest was not to be a public row that divided (or entertained) the whole community; it was to be a polite, smiling affair — intimate, decorous, and deadly. So be it. They were damn fine cigars.

"My brother tells me that, before this war put paid to your plans, you intended to turn the Old Glebe into a magnificent garden, Mister Carrington — something to rival Trengwainton, he said."

He nodded gravely. "That was my plan, ma'am. Indeed, it still is — when these hostilities have ended."

"Ah, yes," she said. "These wretched hostilities! I don't wish to sound unpatriotic, but I do miss my garden. I think the only reason they requisitioned my house was that the officer in charge of that sort of thing at the war office was in the colonel's old regiment and had dined with us quite frequently before the war. He never liked me. There were many more suitable houses in the same area. And I know the garden will be a ruin by the time they hand the house back to me."

"One garden returning to a state of nature and another that cannot rise out of it!" Troy mused aloud. "Is that not an astonishing symmetry!"

Miss Liddicoat ignored him. Speaking directly to Carrington she said, "That girl, Pansy Tregear — was she inventing those names she reeled off? I can hardly think so. It sounds as if you are cultivating some interesting plants, Mister Carrington. You know that roses never do well down here? It's too wet. They succumb to mildew, black spot, rust ... everything. Though some of the species roses are quite resistant."

"Yes," Carrington said cautiously. "I've seen them thriving over at Trevivian ..."

"Jane Scawen's garden. What a woman, eh! The first person to use dynamite in Cornwall! Did she show you around?"

"She's my chief inspiration. I've always wanted to lay out a substantial garden, mind, but when I saw Trevivian ... well!"

"Quite — I do understand. And I know something of that same urge, too — though on a far more modest scale, I hasten to say. I laid out the colonel's garden in Cheam. It was five acres of grass and trees when I came to him. And I left it a ..." She closed her eyes and shook her head. "Forget it. What's done is done." She brightened and smiled again. "All the hebes thrive down here. And so does ceanothus. And I wonder about the himalayan laburnum ...?"

"*Piptanthus nepalensis?*" he said.

"You know it! It's quite a new subject."

"I've seen pictures."

"The yellow is quite astonishing, like burning sulphur. I had one in Cheam. A pod of seeds came away in my hands on a visit to Kew! They do very well from seed. Ah, me!" She sighed. "This is the time of year to be in Kew. Hardly anything's in flower so there aren't many visitors to observe one ... and *everything's* in seed!"

They all laughed at this pleasant fantasy but Carrington himself, she noticed, had a thoughtful look all the same.

She risked it. "D'you know, Mister Carrington," she said, "I would consider it the *greatest* favour if you would show me over your fields and explain to me your plans for their transformation."

"Well, ma'am ..." He scratched his head diffidently, trying to think of a way to refuse without giving offence — and then, suddenly, realizing he actually *wanted* to boast of his plans to someone — anyone — and that she would do very well indeed. Rub her nose in it. Also learn more of what she *really* intended.

"You are far too busy?" she offered. "I quite understand."

"Not at all, ma'am. I was wondering if I might invite you this afternoon — if you have nothing better to do?"

"You'll take luncheon here?" She addressed the question to both men.

"Not me," Troy said, fishing out his watch. "I'm expected back home." He smiled at Carrington.

She turned to him, too.

He had meanwhile decided it would be a fitting revenge for Leah's secrecy *not* to go home for lunch, and then to spring a 'friendly' visit from Miss Liddicoat upon her. "Indeed," he said. "May I invite you to join me?"

"The invitation is already mine, Mister Carrington," she replied firmly. "Your daughter yesterday, you today ... I wonder? Shall I book the table for your son tomorrow, in hope of completing the hat-trick?"

48 It was a pleasant lunch, considering they were sworn enemies. Philomena talked of the harshness of her early life at Grankum Farm, of the liberating power of books, of ambition, of setting oneself goals and never losing sight of them, of the virtues of hard work and persistence. John Carrington found himself in the curious position of agreeing with almost every word, even though he knew she was firing salvo after salvo across his bows, warning him that she would not yield. The goal she never mentioned was that of driving the Carringtons out of the Old Glebe for ever. The persistence she extolled was her own, in pursuing that goal.

His feelings were thus a close match to his behaviour. At a shallow level he felt warm and well disposed; he actually enjoyed her company. But deep down he knew she was deliberately fostering his delusion. Her smile was that of a tigress. The things he enjoyed in her were, in reality, the strands of a spider's web.

He had lived in conflict, surrounded by duplicity, all his adult life; yet this situation was new to him. His battles had been against the unknown — the future, the movements of the market, the success or failure of crops. Or they had been masculine conflicts, as when men of business jostle for advantage, political favours, a commercial edge. They slapped each other's backs and said things like, 'I'll lick you on this one, John — durn me if I don't!' And when it was over, they'd shake hands and swear there were no hard feelings, even if there were. It was all so open and above-board and manly and beautiful.

But this corrosively sweet warfare with Miz Philomena was something so far removed from his experience that even the most innocuous remark would leave him feeling profoundly uneasy. He felt as Gulliver must have felt when tied down upon the Lilliputian strand by a thousand flimsy threads, any one of which he could have snapped with ease but which, combined together, could hold him powerless and at their mercy. In his case those insubstantial threads were the ties of polite convention — that a smile should be answered with a smile, and a pleasing remark should not be rebuffed with a curse or a growl. And so, each time he smiled, each time he met a pleasantry from her with one of his own, he felt she was casting yet another Lilliputian thread over his supine carcase and that soon he would have lost the power of free and independent movement.

Something had to be done. Either he would bring this warfare back to those masculine levels where he could manage it, or he would be rendered powerless. 'Masculate or be emasculated,' you could say — or, in the terse language of his former commerce: 'Git or get got!'

"Civilization is a powerful thing, Miss Liddicoat," he said as he helped her into the gig. Even her physical charms — for she was still a fine figure of a woman — appeared as a threat to him, all of a piece with the seductive charm of her conversation. The elemental male within him found it hard to keep his eyes off her as she climbed aboard, but the wise man-of-the-world forced him to avert his gaze at last.

"In what way, Mister Carrington?" she asked as he leaped nimbly aboard and took his place beside her — which was also odd, because he had given up all his nimble leaping quite a few years ago.

Stretching his back to ease the twinge this particular nimble leap had caused, he reached for the reins, let off the brake, and clucked the pony to a careful walk out into the bustle of Coinagehall Street. "In that it enables a Liddicoat and a Carrington to sup at the same table, talk with amiable pleasure for the best part of an hour, and fix to spend the next hour in each other's company, walking over the very piece of land that has for so long ... I mean for which they would ..." All the images that occurred to him were either crassly belligerent or laughably feeble.

While he struggled to find something in between, she said, "I know what you're about to say, Mister Carrington, but believe me, it is not so. Not any longer."

He had to haul on the brake all the way down the hill — as well as steer the gig around street-traders' stalls, children with hoops, and two dogs and a bitch. He wished he had not started this conversation until they were down on level ground in St John's. "Of course I believe you, ma'am, since you assure me it is so. Yet I still wonder at it."

"So much has happened since last Wednesday," she said. "Was it only last Wednesday I arrived? Dear me! I was *seething* with anger that day. I have been seething with anger ever since they commandeered my house. We do not realize how intimately we are bound up with property — with land and buildings — until it is seized and taken from us."

Now that he had steered her into the one area — indeed, the only area — of legitimate debate between them he decided to play along with the line she had taken. "A house is especially important to a woman, I know," he said.

"Do you mean domesticity? Nest-building? No, I am talking about something much more profound than that. I mean the *uniqueness* of a place. Even people who live at number one-hundred-and-one in a terrace of identical homes know that their house is different from all the others. But five acres of garden that you've created yourself from nothing but grass and trees — the winding paths among borders of shrubs, the broad, lily-padded pool you enlarged from a tiny dew-pond, the rustic pergola ..." Her voice caught.

She did it very well, he thought. But to show her he was not fooled he said, "Not to mention, of course, fifty acres of prime arable land and pasture that you've coveted for as long as you can remember!"

She swallowed heavily and said, "We're still talking about last Wednesday? Yes, I admit that, having lost what was so precious to me in London, it was the last straw to discover that the Old Glebe was now in the hands of those hated Carringtons. I had indeed coveted it for as long as I can remember. And at last I had the means to acquire it, too. But instead there are those *Carringtons!*" She said the name as if it were of some third party whom they both detested. "He was an American pork whole-saler, I learned. No doubt he would be some brash, loud-mouthed, tub-thumping Yankee with more money than taste. And as for his daughter — the things I heard about her! Or, rather, the things I made out of the things I heard about her: a brazen, freethinking hussy, rising twenty-three, never been engaged, walking into Helston market and buying cattle as cool as any farmer who's been at it all his life! Well!" She smiled engagingly at him once again. "So much has happened since then, as I say."

They were down in St John's by now and he could relax a little, concentrate less on his driving. She had been so explicit about all the bad qualities she had imagined in him that he wanted to be told what pleasant surprises she had found there instead. But he also suspected that she *wanted* him to ask about it; so he held his tongue. Instead he said, "So now you wish me to believe you don't mind at all? Or you mind much less than before? Or what?"

She chuckled. "I'll tell you how much I mind — or how little — Mister Carrington, when you've told me your plans for the place. I love it still, the Old Glebe, and I always shall. But I wouldn't be the first lover in history to console herself with the knowledge that, though her love belongs to another, he could not be in better hands."

It was clever, he had to admit. Devilish clever. She was in a fortress whose walls were encased in sheer, unbreakable glass that offered him not the smallest toehold. She was frankness itself where any lie would be so obvious as to be untenable anyway; and in all other places she masked her hatred of all Carringtons and her undying ambition to own the Old Glebe behind a veneer of that same disarming frankness. Well, he was not disarmed — though perhaps it would now be wiser to appear to capitulate, to *seem* won over, to lull her into standing down the guard atop that fortress wall.

"The half-sovereign you gave me," he said.

"Yes?" She chuckled at the memory.

"You had me beaten fair and square, there," he allowed.

"But you have hit upon some way to even the honours, I make no doubt?"

"Well ... to regain a little lost ground," he admitted. "I don't know about getting even, though. I planned to have one of the stones beside my water-garden engraved with a dedication, saying that funds for the garden were begun with a generous subscription from Miss Philomena Liddicoat."

It pleased him to see the smile fade from her lips. And though she said, "I hope you still do," the words lacked the sweetness she had ladled over everything else she had said. *Yes,* he thought, *the claws are still there, underneath all this soft velvet.* And he complimented himself on his ability to make them visible whenever he needed the reminder.

She showed something of her true nature in other ways, too. As they passed one of the poorer houses near the foot of Sithney Common Hill, she called out to one of the urchins by its front door, telling her to mend that hole in her stocking before it got any bigger. To John Carrington she said, "I know the mother there — a slut from birth." She glanced back and shouted, "Now, girl! Now!" as the poor little creature tumbled over the threshold in her haste to be gone.

As they started up the long haul of the hill she became all sweetness again. "Were you always a keen gardener, Mister Carrington?" she asked.

He tapped his forehead. "In here, ma'am. But the soil in our part of Connecticut was pretty thin. Six inches down you hit stone. I had a hothouse where I grew orchids and cacti — that was my outlet then."

"Orchids?" she asked excitedly. "Did you have any of the *Cattleya* hybrids? They were first crossed in England, you know. I had a little fernery where I ..." Again her voice caught. "Never mind. Never mind," she said.

Trying to sound quite casual he said, "I had several specimens of the *Odiontioda* cross. The first cross between two genera!"

"Vuylstekeæ?" she asked in even greater excitement — and taking him completely aback. "I've seen it at Kew. Quite superb! But aren't they *terribly* difficult to grow?"

"That's what I was working on — and hope to work on again, once I have a proper place: a safe growing medium for orchids. It's so heartbreaking to lose them just when they seem to be full-grown and thriving."

"I know, I know!"

"I almost had it, too — an extract of seaweed, with the salt removed, of course. I'll lick it one day. I still have plans for a hothouse at the Old Glebe. Trouble is, the ideal location is right where that old tithe barn stands."

"Oh, I'd demolish that at once," she said. "And no regrets. It's been an eyesore for more than five hundred years — high time it went."

He stared at her in amazement. "But I was warned off doing any such thing. Ben Coad said I'd become that cultureless Yankee vandal you were talking about back there."

"Well ... yes." She nodded thoughtfully. "Perhaps *you* couldn't do it after all. It would start people talking like that — they all get so sentimental about preserving *other people's* property! I could, though. I'd like to see the person who tried to stop me."

"The Liddicoat Demolition Company ..." he mused. "I'll hire you right now."

"Ah, yes!" she replied sadly. "Anything unpleasant or unpopular — send for Philomena Liddicoat!"

"Oh, come!" He spluttered with embarrassment. "I didn't mean *that.*"

"Of course you didn't!" She patted his arm a couple of times and laughed. "I was only joking."

Yes — only probing for my vulnerable points, he thought. *Only seeing how quickly and easily I bend.* He was angry with himself — but not, curiously enough, with her. Indeed, as a seasoned warrior in this particular field of battle, he rather admired her skill. And, in the end, his admiration overcame his anger as he braced himself not to fall for the same trick twice. She was going to prove the most worthy opponent he had ever faced. Faced *down*, that is. It was going to be a real pleasure, whether he won or merely fought her to an exhausted standstill.

The remaining possibility was, of course, merely theoretical.

49 Leah was filled with consternation when, just after luncheon, Pansy came running indoors in great excitement to announce that the master and the Dragon were strolling about the fields like a pair of turtle doves. After her meeting with that same Dragon the previous day she had developed the most acute case of cold feet and had intended going back into Helston that afternoon for a further meeting with the woman, just to make sure that she had appraised her character correctly. To discover that her father — entirely without consulting her — had struck up some independent association with Philomena Liddicoat was unsettling to say the least.

How had it happened? It must have been during the weekly 'board meeting' of LCT in the bar at the Angel. She really should have foreseen that possibility. Not that she could have done anything about it — except, of course, own up honestly to what she had done.

Well, it was too late to worry about that now. The harm was done — and even more serious worries now pressed upon her: How much had Miss Liddicoat blurted out? For she, naturally, would assume that the daughter had gone straight home and told the father all. Had she mentioned Goonhusband? The outing there with Ben Coad? Had she started some campaign of her own, setting aside their common interest? Leah realized she would be riding a stormy current or two when her father and Miz Philomena came in for tea.

But they did not come in for tea, and that turned her consternation into something more like anger. The pair of them climbed back into the gig and drove straight out into the yard — presumably back to Helston. And presumably he stayed to enjoy tea with her at the Angel or in one of the town's little cafés, for it was almost dark by the time he returned. She was busy milking by then. He came laughing into the cowshouse, saying, "Guess what I was told. I was driving up past the mill at the bottom of Sithney Common Hill and the miller fellow ..."

"Frank Trevose," she said.

"That's the man. He warned me it was getting a little dark to be driving without lights — and that the cops often lurk in that side lane halfway up the hill. But, he said, if I pointed out that the pony was white, I might get away with it."

Leah's laugh was more dutiful than amused. "What were you doing, anyway, staying all that time — and with Miz Philomena of all people?"

"I'm amazed *you* should ask that," he replied coldly. But his ebullient humour broke through again. "Oh, she thinks she's so *smart!* She thinks she's got me eating out of the palm of her hand! Won't I just show her!"

"Go in and bathe, Pa," she said, nodding her head significantly toward where John Hamden was milking another cow. "We've only two more to do and then I'll come in and put some liniment on your back."

"How d'you know my back needs liniment?"

"Because of the way you're standing. You always stand like that when you've strained it."

"Oh!" he exclaimed. "If you ain't just about the cantankarest female …!"

Later, while Hamden drove the cattle out to their field and came back to muck out the cowshouse, she gave her father the promised massage. It restored his humour. The question he had intended asking quite sharply came out rather mildly instead: "What the dickens were you doing taking luncheon with that woman yesterday, honey, and why didn't you tell me?"

By now Leah was prepared with her answer: "Because I wasn't sure of her. I would have told you once I was sure. Honest, I would. Anyway, I didn't go in there to see her in the first place, I went to see Ben Coad. I just bumped into her after I'd said goodbye to him. And *she* invited *me* to lunch. I could hardly say no, could I. Did she say anything to you about Violet Tregear — Pansy's sister?"

"No?" He frowned. Mention of Pansy always put him slightly on the defensive.

"She went specially up to the Union to hire Violet yesterday, as her maid."

"Oh, I get it!" He laughed again. "She thinks she's so smart! As if Pansy's going to tell Violet anything! They've hardly spoken for years."

"Ah — you knew about this already, then?" Leah asked. "You've already spoken to Pansy?"

"Er ... no." He was defensive again. "I just knew it — already, I mean. She talked about her family when we were sticking those quicksets last Thursday. Oh, thank you. That feels so much better. I can't think how I ricked it like that. But I'll tell you one thing, honey" — he stood up, rubbing his hands gleefully — "we're going to walk small circles round that lady, who thinks she can get the better of us."

"Does she?" Leah wiped the liniment off her hands while he struggled back into his shirt. "I thought Will was right for once. Her bark is much worse than her bite. In fact, I ended up feeling rather sorry for her. Poor, lonely old woman — except that she isn't at all old, is she! She's still quite young — and pretty good-looking, too, don't you think? And desperately lonely, I'd say — since the colonel's death."

Her father was silent awhile. Then he said, "She's not as smart as she fancies she is."

"Yes, you said that before. Isn't it strange — she *loved* that house of hers in Cheam. The one the colonel left her. And the garden ..."

"She designed it and created it herself," he put in, almost as if he were proud of her. "Supervised its creation, that is — though, from the way she talks, I'll bet she got plenty of dirt under her fingernails, too."

"If the war hadn't come along, she'd be there now, happy as the day is long. I'll bet she'd almost forgotten the Old Glebe and our ancient feud. That only rekindled itself when she came back here — especially when she heard who'd bought it."

"I expect you're right, honey," he said. A lot of his earlier ebullience had gone.

"She needs another interest," Leah mused aloud. "A love affair, perhaps. Or even a husband. D'you think Ben Coad's father is too old for her? Yes, I guess so. Who else do we know? We don't want a middle-aged bachelor. He'd be too set in his ways for a strong-minded woman like her. We want a widower — a little senior to her in years and one who doesn't need her money ..." She ended with a sigh. "We just don't know enough people yet."

"I'd volunteer myself," he said, pretending to be quite serious, "except for two small impediments."

"Namely?"

"For one thing, she wouldn't have me and, for another, I'd rather marry just about any other woman in Cornwall before I'd even think of her."

He was trying to knot his bow tie but was no more successful than usual; at this point each evening he usually called for her to come and rescue him. She did it unbidden on this particular evening. "Besides," she said placatingly, "don't take offence, now, but you are just a teeny bit *old* for her — don't you think?"

He let out his breath explosively and stared at her in outrage. "I beg your pardon?" he almost roared. "Too old? Too old, d'you say?"

"I'm sorry, Pa! You don't think you are too old? Well, obviously not." She looked at him as if she hadn't conducted an inspection for quite some time. "No, I guess you're not at that," she added, as if the finding surprised her. "Still, as you say, it's entirely academic, since she probably feels just as negative about you. She'd sooner emigrate to northern Greenland than marry *you* — probably."

Again he bridled at her tone. "She could do a lot worse than me, let me tell you," he said. Then, recollecting himself, he added, "However — as you say — it *is* pretty academic."

Half an hour later, when Will had joined them for dinner, she said, as if mere seconds had intervened, "She *is* good company, though, Pa — didn't you think?"

"When she wants to be," he agreed — showing that the woman had not been out of his thoughts much during that time. "She can put herself out, all right. But so can the trapdoor spider, come to think of it."

"Who is this?" Will asked.

"That Philomena Liddicoat," Pansy told him.

"Thank you, Pansy," Leah snapped. "This is *our* conversation."

"Sorry, I'm sure," she replied, shaking her head huffily. "I just thought as you might be interested to know as she's asked our Violet to be her lady's maid at the Angel. That's all."

"Violet, eh?" Leah responded. "The sister you never talk to."

" 'Cepting when there's things to say … and things to tell."

"I see. Are we now going to be blackmailed by the Tregear sisters? Is that what this is all about? You want a rise in wages, eh? You're about to tell us how much Miss Liddicoat is paying your sister, I suppose?"

"No!" Pansy protested vehemently. "It never even crossed my mind. But — if you *must* know — 'tis twelve-and-six a week. Plus keep, pinafores, cap, and half her shoe leather. Will that be all, miss?" She tossed her head and even managed to turn a half-inch curtsey into a threat.

"It's more than enough, anyway," Leah replied. "But I don't suppose it is all."

"I say, Sis — go easy, eh?" Will murmured at her side.

"And you'll keep right out of this," she said, pointing a finger and sticking it an inch under his nose. "If you know what's good for you."

"That's right," said the unsinkable Pansy.

Will — and his father — stared at the two women in amazement. "I think we should eat this soup before it goes cold," John Carrington said at last.

They supped in silence a while. When neither of the men was looking, Leah winked at Pansy — who did not know what to make of it, of course, except to understand that she had not been reprimanded as severely as it had seemed.

"Whenever people try to be clever," John Carrington said, "they always give something away."

"For instance?" Leah answered.

"And the cleverer they try to be, the more they give away."

"You're referring to Miz Philomena?"

"Thinking it over, I don't believe this story about her magnificent garden in Cheam — not for one minute. She may have had a fernery — I accept that. And even some kind of small hothouse. She certainly knows her orchids and it's not all book learning. But everything she said about gardens was all Kew, Kew, Kew. *That's* all she knows about gardens in my opinion. See! They give themselves away."

"What can you do about it, though?" Leah asked. "You've never been to Kew. She can tell you anything she likes and you'd still have to accept it. She's still got the edge on you."

"Ha, ha!" He shook his head craftily. "If that's her game, I'll soon wipe the smile off her face!"

Leah shrugged and appeared to lose interest. "I don't see how — still, that's your ..."

"Because I intend going to Kew — that's how!"

"You?" Will asked.

"When?" Leah put in simultaneously. "This is very sudden, isn't it?"

"You bet! I decided it this very afternoon, when she let slip she's going to Wadebridge for a week's visit, starting tomorrow."

"That'd be to Mrs Kelynack, her cousin," Pansy told them. Airily she added, "There's another two females who never talk to each other, 'cepting when there's summat to say."

"Now listen! Nobody's to tell her I'm going," Carrington said. "And when I'm back, nobody's to tell her I've been. Is that understood? Pansy — you understand?"

"Yessir."

"It's rather drastic, isn't it, Pa?" Will asked. "Unless you're interested in going anyway, of course."

"I just don't like being one-down to that woman in any department. Let her try talking about Kew when she comes back!" He chuckled.

"She *has* got under your skin!" Leah said, almost admiringly.

He shook his head and grinned, not rising to it. "Besides," he added, "it's that time of year."

"What time of year?"

"Oh — you know — when hardly anything's in blossom and there aren't too many visitors to see what you're doing, and seeds and seed pods and capsules just somehow seem to stick to your hands as you pass by ... Do we have an up-to-date *Bradshaw* in the house? Or a Great Western timetable? And what was the name of that hotel in Saint James's — the one the Troys said was so good?"

50 Earl's Hôtel was the one the Troys recommended; it stood in St James's, close to the corner of Jermyn Street. Indeed, despite the fact that the manager there had once been rather rude to him, Jimmy Troy recommended it so heartily that, before he had finished listing its superior features, he decided to come along, too. They travelled up by train on the Monday, intending to stay a week. Elizabeth at first planned to accompany her husband but then she met Sibylla Petifer after evensong, who told her that Laura Curnow had told her that Leah Carrington had been seen twice recently in the company

of Ben Coad and that he had shown her over the farm at Goonhusband. Laura's daughter Blanche, who was sweet on Leah's brother, Will, had seen Coad driving Leah back into town. But Goonhusband wasn't even on the market yet — so what could it all mean? Elizabeth told Sibylla what she had seen of Leah and Ben Coad, the previous week, and they agreed that there must be a romance in the air and that that was when it had begun. So, remembering what mice do when cats depart, Elizabeth decided to stay.

The day after the men had slipped their leashes and departed, however, Jessie Trelawney brought further amusing news, which made her wish she had gone after all.

"It was the most extraordinary thing," she said. "After church on Sunday I went to tend my grandparents' grave, which is up in the top corner, by the big, straggly laurel, you know? Anyway, I've never paid much attention to the other graves around there. And even if I had, I doubt I'd have been particularly struck by the name of Jones. But I suppose you know — or maybe you don't — Clifford Liddicoat of Grankum Farm married an Olwen Jones. She was c of e, which caused a big brouhaha at the time. Even I can remember people talking about it, though I was just a child. But that's why she's buried there, with her family, rather than with the Liddicoats and the other Methodists. And who should be standing there, saying a little prayer, but ... I'm sure you've already guessed — Olwen's sister-in-law, Philomena Liddicoat!"

"On Sunday?" Elizabeth asked. "But I understood from John Carrington that she was going to her cousin in Wadebridge on Sunday."

"Ah!" Jessie's eyes promised a full budget of fun. "You're jumping the story a little. She *was* going to her cousin but an old friend telephoned her at the Angel on Saturday night ..."

"You spoke to her — obviously."

"Yes. Not at once. I said a prayer and uprooted a few weeds. The cleaver up in that corner is dreadful. I shall have words with the sexton about that. Anyway, we chatted a bit on our way back to the gate. We've known each other — distantly — for years. And she was obviously bursting with this news she'd had from this friend in Cheam."

"Where her house is? The one there was all that fuss ..."

"The very house — 'my dearest housekeeper's' house!'"

"Which was requisitioned by the army."

Jessie held up a monitory finger. "Requisitioned but not yet occupied! That was the exciting news. She said it proved what she'd always said about it. One of the colonel's old regimental comrades, who had always resented her … her … how may one put it delicately? Her *influence* over the colonel. He'd always resented it and so used his newly granted emergency powers at the war office to commandeer the place. It was a purely dog-in-the-manger act, she says. The army actually has no need for it and their failure to take up occupation proves it. Anyway, she asked her friend if they'd posted sentries or anything like that — and it seems they have not. So she intends going up to London this week, where she will hire a gang of big, burly plug-uglies and dig up every shrub and bush and baby tree she can manage. She'll wrap their roots in hessian and wet moss, or whatever they use, and bring them back here. She says she's spent five years creating that garden and she's not going to let one man's spite ruin it. What a woman, eh!"

"Indeed! But where's she going to replant them? Surely not on Grankum Farm?"

"That was the first thing I asked her, of course, but she just waved her hand and said she'd find somewhere. The main thing was to rescue them. She'd worry about replanting them later. I suppose she'd get away with two or three weeks out of the ground at this time of year."

Her eyes were still brimming with merriment. "Come on!" Elizabeth urged. "There's more, isn't there. You're still holding something back."

"The best is yet to come," Jessie promised. "She said she had only ever *lived* in London, never just visited it, you know. And she asked me if I could recommend a good little family hôtel."

"You didn't!" Elizabeth could see what was coming now. "Oh, Jessie! Jessie! Why did you not tell me this yesterday? Wild horses wouldn't have kept me back. It's too late now. They'll have met and she'll have moved out."

"It was Whittaker's Hôtel in Jermyn Street, wasn't it — the one you always recommended?"

Elizabeth slumped. "No. Earl's in Saint James's, just round the corner. Oh!" She clenched her fists and shook them in frustration. "Now we'll be on tenterhooks all week — will they, won't they meet?"

"I'm sorry!" Jessie pretended to weep. "I thought you always stayed at Whittaker's."

"Yes, dear, it's not your fault. We do — usually."

"Ever since I've known you."

"Yes. But before that we always stayed at Earl's. We stopped because the manager was rather rude to us once. But this time Jimmy just took it into his head to give them another chance. It is quite a bit more comfortable. And much more expensive. I suppose he didn't want to seem a cheapskate in Carrington's eyes — you know the petty way they compete with each other, those two! Oh, what do I *do* now? Do I go up to London and give Fate a little push? Or do we leave it all to chance?"

After a pause Jessie, speaking carefully, said, "Actually, Elizabeth, d'you think she *would* have left the hôtel the moment she discovered she was sharing it with Mister Carrington?"

Elizabeth eyed her warily. "Why d'you ask it in that tone? What else d'you know?"

The other waved a hand expansively. "I know what everyone else knows — that the Liddicoats have had their eyes on the Old Glebe lands for the best part of a century now. And that Philomena Liddicoat is the most covetous of them all. One wonders what she would *not* do to acquire them." She licked her lips daintily and stared at a fingernail. "One way or another."

"No!" Elizabeth said excitedly. "Although ..."

"What?"

"They did take luncheon together — Carrington and Miss Liddicoat — at the Angel last Saturday."

"Really? I heard that Leah had been seen dining with her. But that was on the Friday. Are you sure the story hasn't got garbled in the telling?"

Elizabeth was delighted to reverse their rôles and to impart news her friend had not yet heard. "Absolutely sure. Jimmy was there, so I got it straight from the horse's mouth. In fact, he rather pushed them into it. I don't think either was particularly keen. Also, Leah hadn't told her father about that Friday meeting — so I'd love to have been a house-martin under the eaves of the Old Glebe dining room that evening! Oh, why does everything have to happen at once? I know — why don't *you* go up to London and I'll stay here and we'll telephone each other every evening, so we'll get the best of both worlds!"

It was a pleasant fantasy but no more than that. They laughed at it and turned to other matters.

That afternoon, however, Elizabeth drove over to the Old Glebe, doing the hedge-cutter's work for him most of the way as usual. Leah heard her and came out of the dairy to greet her. As the car screeched to a halt she pulled a small branch from the bumper bar and shook her head at Elizabeth in pretend despair.

Elizabeth peered at it and said, "Sloe. Or sloan, as they call it in Cornwall. Naughty me! One shouldn't really pick the berries until after the first frost, you know."

They kissed and Leah threw the branch over the hedge. "Have you heard from Mister Troy?" she asked.

"I was about to ask the same of you and your father. Out of sight, out of mind, eh!" Elizabeth nodded toward the field at the end of the yard. "Isn't that one of Mrs Pascoe's heifers?" They started walking toward the gate.

"Yes. I bought three yesterday. Herded them over this morning. Just as well we didn't wait until this afternoon. We must have walked the same road as you've just driven!" She leaped aside with a little shriek of laughter as Elizabeth tried to pinch her arm.

"Just for that," she said, "I've a good mind not to tell you what I heard from Jessie Trelawney this morning. Did you say you bought three? Aren't you a little overstocked?"

"I'm putting two others back into Helston tomorrow."

"Where Ben Coad will get you the best price, I'm sure!"

Their eyes dwelled in each other's and Leah broke into a huge smile. "Oh, very well! You were right, Elizabeth, as usual. The Coads are a very good family and Ben is one of the best ..."

"And is the name Goon*husband* significant at all?"

Leah stopped dead and hung her head low. "One can't do a damn thing!" she said wearily.

"Is there?" Elizabeth insisted.

"Not yet." They resumed their stroll.

"But maybe?"

"I'm not saying. I'm superstitious that way." Their eyes met again and she added, "Okay — maybe. What is it you've decided not to tell me?"

They had reached the gate. She stared proudly at her three new heifers and waited for Elizabeth to compliment her on her choice. "I'm not mixing them with the rest of the herd yet. There's already been too much fighting and I want them to settle down."

"Good idea," Elizabeth said abstractedly. "Good choice, too. Tell me — I take it you knew your father and Philomena Liddicoat had luncheon together at the Angel last Saturday?"

Leah nodded. "*And* spent the rest of the afternoon walking over *my* fields, talking gardening, gardening, gardening. *And* he drove her back into town and stayed for tea."

"D'you think there's something going on between them?" She saw Leah's smile and added, "You do! Is it some plot you and she cooked up between you ..." Her voice trailed off as Leah shook her head.

"I did start out with a plan — I don't mind admitting it. At least, I don't mind admitting it to *you*, though I'd be grateful if it didn't go further."

"Of course not."

"Anyway, it's been swept away by events. The reason Ben showed me Goonhusband was that I'd asked him — last Thursday, in fact, when I came out to see you. I asked him if there was another suitable bit of land where my father could make this garden-dream of his come true."

"Well, he's right. Goonhusband is perfect. Much better than this place."

"Except that the moment I saw it, I wanted it for myself."

"Or yourself and ...?"

"Stop it, Elizabeth!" Leah laughed.

"Will your father buy it for you?"

Leah grinned. "He won't need to. You're not the only heiress in these parts, you know! I'll come into my inheritance next August, so I could easily borrow against it anytime between now and then."

"But you're not supposed to know about that — or so Jimmy told me."

"Sure. But my grandmother told me all about it, of course — when I was sixteen. She just told me not to tell Pa I knew and to act real surprised whenever he deigned to tell me, finally. Anyway — to get back to last Friday — I didn't know *what* to think when I went back into Helston." She described their meeting with Philomena on her way to the Union, which explained why she had to seek the woman out and apologize to her. "But the apology was all I intended. The notion of having lunch with her never crossed my mind. I *had* wanted to tell her about my plan — my original plan — which was to talk Pa into selling her the Old Glebe and moving to Goonhusband instead. He'd make a good profit, too, which is always a compelling reason to get him to do anything."

"Don't tell me," Elizabeth said. "I married one of them, too. So what *did* you tell her instead?"

"Well, I didn't have time to think up any other rigmarole so I stuck to my story — about persuading Pa to buy Goonhusband. I mean, we can find him *another* place over on that side of Helston. Near Goonhusband. He'll want to be near me, anyway, if … well, never mind about that."

"If you marry and have grandchildren for him to spoil! You might as well say it, Leah!"

The girl took her arm, as if for support, and leaned her head briefly on Elizabeth's shoulder. "Oh, it's so beautiful when you say it!" she murmured. "God! How I *long* for it to be!"

Elizabeth gave her hand a squeeze and said, "Anyway …?"

"Yes." Leah straightened herself and sighed. "Anyway, when we got talking about Pa's ambitions to create this grand garden, she seemed to take a different … I mean, her whole attitude changed. She'd been a bit prickly before that but then she *seemed* to be genuinely interested."

"Only seemed?"

"How can you tell? Pa thinks her gardening interest is limited to orchids and houseplants. The rest is fake — to ingratiate herself with him. He thinks she's going to lull his suspicions, get his guard down low, and then … bam!"

"Bam? What's that?"

"Exactly," Leah said scornfully. "He won't be specific — because he *can't*, of course. We keep coming back to that unanswerable question: What harm can she actually *do?* Apart from being a pest and making our lives uncomfortable from time to time. She can't *do* anything. *Bam* is just meaningless. But that's his theory, anyway. I hope Jimmy will talk some sense into him this week."

"I doubt it," Elizabeth said heavily. "He thinks the whole thing is one great sport. He agrees with you — the woman can't *do* anything, so why not milk the situation for all the fun it holds? Tell me — why does your father think her interest in gardening is all put on?"

"Because she *talks* about this magnificent garden she created in Cheam, but whenever he asks for details, she just gets close to tears and says it's all too painful to think about. The one garden she talks about forever and a day, however, is Kew. So that's why he's gone up there this week, while she's in Wadebridge. Next time she mentions Kew, he'll be able to trump her! What does that enigmatic little smile mean?"

Elizabeth told her at last.

Leah heard the tale out with mounting frustration. When she learned that Philomena was staying not a hundred yards from the two men, it was the last straw. She thumped the top bar of the gate hard enough to hurt herself slightly. While she jumped up and down, nursing it under her arm, she said, "And I *have* to take those two cows into Helston tomorrow." She turned her big, dark eyes on Elizabeth. "I don't suppose you would take them in for me? Please? Hamden would make sure he took the whole day over it. And if we don't get the cabbage hoed ..."

"Say no more," Elizabeth assured her. "Of course I will. Gladly. But just answer me this — what will you do when you get to London?"

Leah thought awhile and had to admit that she didn't know. "I just want to be *there*," she said.

"In case they go and do something foolish?"

"I suppose so."

"And you'll be able to wave a magic wand and stop them?"

Leah looked around her, for help or inspiration from any quarter. Finding none, she said, "At least I might be able to do *something*. As long as I'm stuck away down here there's absolutely nothing I can do."

"There is, you know," Elizabeth assured her calmly.

"What?"

"You can do what every son and daughter has to do sooner or later — admit that you've done the best job you can in bringing your parents up and concede that they must make their own way in life sooner or later."

51 London was exciting but Kew Gardens was, frankly, a disappointment. It was not so much a garden as a vast park with specimens of this or that liberally sprinkled about the place. It was also inhibitingly open from the point of view of any clandestine seed harvester. Time and again John Carrington would find himself standing at the edge of some bosky dell (the most interesting specimens were always planted at the edge, somehow), and the most desirable seeds would be a mere up-on-tiptoe arm's-length away, and there would be no uniformed keeper in sight ... and still he could not banish from his conscience the thought that someone was following his every move through a powerful telescope. Moreover, that unseen watcher could immediately semaphore his description to an attendant hidden in the bushes nearby. It stood to reason that, at this time of year, they were all lying in wait for people like him.

Two damp, drizzly days passed in that sort of misery. If it had not been for the theatres, the Café Royal, and the night clubs — and Jimmy Troy's determination to make him, John Carrington, seem five years the senior when he was, in fact, five years the junior — he would have returned home on Thursday. As it was, he had no further wish to explore Kew. Instead, he intended visiting the public library and going through the back numbers of the newspapers to read up on the scandal surrounding Philomena Liddicoat and the 'dearest housekeeper' bequest. He might also get the address of the place and go out there on Friday, just to see what sort of 'wonderful garden' she'd actually made there.

He awoke that morning with the sort of head that instantly made him ask what he had done the previous night; it also left him disinclined to seek the answer too assiduously. He paused at Jimmy's door on his way back from the bathroom at the end of the corridor. Loud snores were all he heard. He considered going in and waking him up with some hearty greeting but then he had a better idea. It would be much more telling to go out for a brisk walk around St James's Park and return in the pink of health, rubbing his hands, eating a hearty breakfast, and telling Jimmy what he'd missed in his senile sloth.

The hall porter told him that Green Park was nearer, if he just wanted a quick, brisk walk. Also, if he didn't want to go out and come back by the same path, he could go down to the bottom of St James's and wander through the alleys behind the palace to a little gate between Bridgewater House and the London Museum. He could then stroll through the park to Piccadilly and so come back directly to the hôtel.

He thanked the man for this information, but he was somewhat less grateful when, on arriving at the gate by the museum, he found it padlocked. What jumped-up pipsqueak of a pen-pushing civil servant had decided to do that? he fumed to himself. Then he, the man who had flinched from plucking a pod of seed from a tree at Kew, drew out his pocket-knife and selected the long, thin prong designed for piercing the butt-end of a cigar. After a little fiddling, he sprang the lock, lifted it from its hole, drew back the bolt, slipped through the gateway, and then reassembled it all, leaving the padlock looking as if no one had touched it.

As he stepped back to admire his handiwork, an oddly familiar voice behind him said, "And what, pray, are *you* doing here, Mister Carrington?"

He had been vaguely aware of a female walking down the path through the thin mist that hung over the wet grass but it took a second or two before he identified the voice.

"Miss Liddicoat!" He spun round in amazement. "Well! I think I could ask the same of you. Have you followed me to London? If so, I may tell you at once …"

"*I* followed *you!*" Her nostrils flared with anger. "How dare you even suggest …!"

"I cannot imagine what *else* you are doing here. You *told* me — or at least you told Leah — that you'd be in Wadebridge all this week. Are you surprised that I am …"

"If I change *my* mind, it is none of *your* business. As a matter of fact, I came up to carry out certain work at my house in Cheam before the army actually moves in and wrecks it. I had no idea you were in London. You said nothing about it. Your daughter said nothing about it. You must have made a very *sudden* decision to come."

"It was no more sudden than yours, ma'am. Can you wonder at my suspicions?"

His effrontery made her gasp. "And can you wonder at mine? I have given you my reasons for being here. You have given me none." She raised both hands briefly. "Judge O ye gods!"

"I came up to visit Kew Gardens," he said quietly.

It took her aback.

"Kew," he repeated.

"Yes, I know — I heard you. Why did you do that?"

He glanced at the skies. The sun was beginning to paint the clouds pink. "D'you really need to ask?" he replied.

For the first time she smiled; that was something of a sunrise, too. "Good hunting?" she asked.

He shook his head. "Miserable. I even contemplated returning to Cornwall today."

After a pause she said, "Were you out here to take a morning constitutional, may I ask?"

"Yes. We're staying at Earl's in Saint James's. Earl's Hôtel."

"We? Is Leah with you, then?"

"No. Jimmy Troy. He's the one who recommended Earl's."

"Oh, I'm at Whittaker's, just round the corner. I was going to stay the week but we made excellent progress these last two days. One more day and we'll be done."

"Are you taking a constitutional, too, Miss Liddicoat?"

"I am. I was going to do a circuit, down to The Mall, but I'll go back with you along Picadilly, if you like. I want to hear why you found Kew so disappointing."

He told her as they set off up the hill.

She said it surprised her that a man who could pick a padlock like that would balk at picking seeds that were going to fall the the ground anyway — and be chewed up by some lawnmower.

"It's just the fact that the gate is *there,*" he explained. "It's there and yet some petty clerk has decided we, the public, aren't to be allowed to use it. Seeds are different. Those people have a right to protect their trees and shrubs from marauders like me."

"Isn't that odd?" she said. "I have absolutely no qualms about raiding the plants at Kew but I would never pick a padlock the way you just did."

They walked in thoughtful silence a while and then she said, "I still cannot accept that this meeting is entirely a coincidence. I believe you when you say you had no idea I was here. I hope you believe me, too?"

"I do, ma'am — though I hope you'll understand why, at first, I leaped to …"

"Yes, yes — same here. But tell me — if your purpose was to visit Kew, why did you not choose some hôtel out Richmond way? Why here in central London? Mister Troy *steered you* toward this hôtel, you say?"

"Yes," he agreed warily. "Why? Did he also suggest it to you? Or the hôtel next door?"

"No. It was …"

"Because — pardon me for pointing this out — it's not exactly adjacent to Cheam, either."

"Oh?" She was suddenly interested. "You actually know where Cheam is, do you? Not many Americans would." She smiled sweetly.

"I looked it up," he admitted, unabashed. "To tell the truth, I had thought of going out there today and having a look at this garden of yours — having heard so much about it!"

She laughed. "Allow me to conduct you there — and Mister Troy, too, if he's interested."

"I'll make quite sure he is not! You think that steering us toward adjacent hôtels was a prank on somebody's part? In particular, Jimmy Troy?"

She shook her head. "I was recommended to Whittaker's by Mrs Trelawney — the electricity woman, you know."

"She's a friend of the Troys."

"Yes, but they didn't know I'd changed my plans. They couldn't have put her up to suggesting Whittaker's to me because they didn't know I was going to London at all. So it's still a mystery."

"How did she come to advise you at all, then?"

Philomena explained the circumstances.

"By morning service on Sunday," he pointed out, "she could quite easily have known that Jimmy Troy and I were coming to London. The prank could have been hers — on the spur of the moment — when you asked her."

"Then why didn't she direct me to Earl's? If you had not taken your walk this morning — which was the merest fluke — we'd never have met here at all."

"Yes," John Carrington had to concede with reluctance. "That bit doesn't fit."

There was a further silence before Philomena said, "What did she expect to happen, I wonder? Or they? Because if it was a prank, I'm sure she went directly to Pallas and told Elizabeth Troy all about it. Has she telephoned him?"

"Yes. The first morning." He had to admit it — she was not only a quick thinker but a thorough one, too. She covered all the possibilities and she went after them like a terrier. It was useful to know these things about one's opponent. He was grateful to the prankster, if prank it was.

"And has he mentioned Whittaker's at all ... suggested you pop round for a drink there or anything?"

"No. Maybe he's saving it. Come to think of it, he did mention Whittaker's on the night we arrived. We were just strolling round the West End and he pointed it out. He said he and Elizabeth used to stay there, for many years. Before that they always stayed at Earl's, but the manager was offensive to them once so they switched. There's a new manager now and he's giving the place another chance."

"You see — the little pieces are falling into place," she said, rubbing her hands gleefully. "Jessie Trelawney's too young to have known the Troys when they first used Earl's. She only knew about Whittaker's. The whole thing is *her* idea, then. She assumed you'd both be staying there and thought it would be the greatest joke to send me there, too — all unawares. Well, well, well, Jessie! We must think up some nice little surprise for *you* before too long."

"I have to raise my hat to you, ma'am," he said. "The way you ran that down — I declare, a Dalmatian bloodhound couldn't have done better."

But she had not quite done. "It also means that she didn't tell Elizabeth Troy at once. You're sure she hasn't telephoned him since that first morning?"

"I can check with the porter when we ... when I return."

He glanced at her for more questions but she was now deep in thought. The rumble of iron tyres and the muted roar of engines told them that Piccadilly would soon loom out of the mist. "The porter said the gate's in the corner there," he said, changing direction slightly. "What are you thinking now?"

"I was thinking that I do, after all, feel the same impulse that led you to pick that lock — the impulse to do the opposite of what someone else has decided *for* me. Jessie Trelawney has decided to force us under the same roof, to make us both feel uncomfortable ..."

Gallantry alone compelled him to interrupt. "Well now, see here — I don't allow as I'd have been so very uncomfortable about that. How about you, ma'am?"

"Well, that was quite a little shouting match we had back there at that gate — I wouldn't have enjoyed holding it in one of the public rooms at Whittaker's! And I wouldn't have enjoyed bottling it up, either! However — it's very kind of you, Mister Carrington, to say you wouldn't have felt uncomfortable to find yourself in the same hôtel as me — because I'm thinking of moving to Earl's this very day."

"Ah ..." Carrington said uncertainly.

"And I shall pay particular attention to Mister Troy's expression when he sees me there. I put you on your word of honour to say nothing to him in the meantime. Now — you'd better call for me at Whittaker's, so that he doesn't see me before I wish him to. Ten o'clock?"

52 They went by the Epsom & Leatherhead branch line as far as Ewell, where they took a cab the remaining mile to that part of Cheam where Philomena's house lay, waiting its military occupiers. The gang of hired stevedores, bummarees, and porters had been at work since sun-up, so that, by the time the cab halted at the foot of the drive, they had one dray almost loaded with bandaged and insulated shrubs, and a few small trees, as well, bare-rooted but moistened with sphagnum and thickly padded where they were most likely to abrade their tender bark.

She had said nothing of all this to John Carrington on their way to Cheam, so, for a long moment, he could only stand and stare while she prodded and pulled and directed that this be loosened or that be made a little tighter. "Cotoneasters," she said to him, pointing at one group. "That's *franchetii* and that's *hupehensis* — very graceful. And *Escallonia bifida* — that should grow against a wall somewhere. It won a medal this year. And that's *rosea* — quite common but hard to kill. It goes well with pittosporum ... there should be a dwarf red one here somewhere ..."

"Pardon me, ma'am." He found his voice at last. "What is going on here?"

"Isn't it obvious, man? I'm making sure the army doesn't ruin my garden."

"You're saving them the trouble?"

"Oh, no! They could wish they had as few casualties as we'll have with these plants!"

"But where are you taking them? Not that it's any of my business, mind."

She laughed. "Oh, but it *is* your business, Mister Carrington. They are going — immediately — to Paddington Station and thence in an enclosed wagon by passenger train to Gwinear Road and Helston."

"And then?" He broke into a grin. "Are you intending to start a rival garden across the valley?"

"Not a bit! They're all for you. I had intended it as a surprise, but dear Jessie Trelawney put paid to that. I still haven't thought of an appropriate way of thanking her. But now, perhaps, you understand why I was so angry this morning?"

He took a step back from her. "But I ... I mean, I could not possibly accept such a ..."

"Nonsense, man! Of course you can. You're a gardener, aren't you? Some gardeners I know would sell their immortal souls for a collection like this."

She turned to the men on the dray, which was just about to depart. "Remember, now — keep them as upright as possible. Plants use up a lot of energy trying to get themselves properly aligned with gravity, and these fellows don't have too much to spare." Speaking to Carrington again she added, "At least take a look at the whole thing before you turn it down." Then, without waiting for him, she turned on her heel and walked up the drive.

Shrubs and trees in various stages of readiness were lined up on each side. More were being brought from distant parts of the garden every minute. A lot of the deciduous ones had already lost their leaves, or they wore their autumnal russet and gold and were not easily identifiable. Even so, a gardener of next to no experience could have told that the variety was amazing.

Miss Philomena spouted *officinalis*-this and *variegatum*-that and *lanceolata*-the-other as they walked but it was, of course, too much for him to take in all at once.

"Well?" she asked when they had reached the top of the drive and he could see the devastation her workers had left behind them. The house was pretty splendid but he gave it not a second glance. She went on: "I believe our military friends will feel quite at home here, don't you? Certainly if the recent pictures from Picardy are anything to go by! What d'you think?"

"I think I want to kill you, of course," he replied.

She laughed. "Why?"

"Because how can I possibly turn your gift down, woman? And yet how can I possibly accept it, either?"

"Listen," she said quite seriously. "*You* will be doing *me* a favour in accepting it. My beloved plants will live and the army won't get them. Also ..." She hesitated.

"Also what?"

"Well ... John — may I call you that? We may not have known each other for long but we're old enough enemies for it, surely? In accepting this gift you'll also have to accept that I have well and truly buried the hatchet between us — and not in your skull, either. Dear man! I don't think you do believe that even now, do you?"

"If I refuse them ...?" he asked.

"I'll just abandon them in the lane outside the Old Glebe — alongside that field where you and Pansy were working. Try watching them die, then!"

He shook his head. "You couldn't do that."

"And you couldn't risk my doing it. They're going to Helston, anyway, whether you like it or not."

He turned about and looked at the plants. He sighed. Every worried atom in his body shouted that it was a big mistake but he knew he was going to accept the gift. "How will I ever thank you?" he asked morosely.

She touched his arm briefly. "Merely in accepting them you thank me enough. In giving them a second life you do more than thank me."

They filled five drays in all. It could have been cut to three if Philomena had been willing to stack the plants on top of each other. The last of them set off for Paddington just after midday.

John and Philomena went by hackney to New Malden, where they had a pie and a glass of ale at an inn before going on by train through Kingston to Kew.

On the way Philomena pointed out Hampton Court, Strawberry Hill, Sion Park, and the Old Deer Park, just south of Kew Gardens itself. "So many beautiful gardens," she said. "You could almost walk all day through one after the other."

"*You* couldn't, I'm sure," he said.

She stared at him pugnaciously. "Is that a challenge?"

"I mean your pockets would be bulging before you reached the exit of the first of them."

"Oh, that!" She laughed. "I don't only acquire seeds and little slips of twigs, you know. I also steal *ideas.*" She spoke as if that were not simply virtuous but so *very* virtuous that it made up for all her material thefts. "There's a little group of shrubs near the end of the tulip tree avenue which I duplicated perfectly at Cheam. You should see it, because you could do the same."

It was the first thing she took him to see, past the Temple of Aeolus, past the museum, the pond, the great Palm House ... right out into the centre of the gardens. On the way he was amazed to see how little bits of this and that just seemed to spirit themselves into her hands — and then, with lightning rapidity, into one or other of her voluminous pockets.

"Now *this* you *must* have," she said at one point, waving a conjuror's hand in great arcs toward a firewheel tree, distracting his eye from what the other hand was doing. "*Stenocarpus sinuatus.* It can flower at any time. And look! See? Two flowers up there actually growing out of the trunk!"

They were brilliant red and yellow tubes, three inches long, and radiating like the spokes of a wheel. "I *want* it," he murmured, captivated by its beauty.

"We have it," she said.

"On its way to Paddington?"

She patted one of her pockets. "Not just yet."

And so they passed the afternoon in happy piracy, taking nothing that Nature, in her profligate fashion, would not have wasted anyway.

"Well, that was fun, wasn't it?" she said as they passed safely beyond the last attendant who might have challenged them. Several had looked as if they intended doing so but, for some reason, they had changed their minds at the last moment. On one of those occasions John, himself burning with preparatory embarrassment, had glanced at her and understood why. There was something so solidly menacing, so implacable about her very walk. It helped him remember that, although today had, of course, been fun — indeed, he couldn't remember a more enjoyable day, certainly not in the past half-dozen years — she was still the most menacing element in his life. She was playing some highly devious game here and he had little choice but to play along until her purpose became clear. He must constantly bear in mind that she was the spider who whispers, 'Come into my parlour!'

"Yes," he replied. "Great fun. But I hope we have enough in the way of seeds and cuttings by now?"

"For this year, anyway," she assured him.

And it was 'great fun' to play along with her plotting and scheming. It produced a curious kind of intimacy between them. She was — not to mince words — throwing herself at him. In normal circumstances he would have run a mile rather than get involved — even with a woman as physically attractive and as mentally companionable as Philomena. But he knew that was not her real purpose. One day this mask of sweetness would be cast aside and the claws would be unsheathed. He knew all that very well and never ceased reminding himself of it, most particularly when he found himself wanting to touch her, take her in his arms, kiss her ... and more. It had been a long time, after all. And so, with those reminders constantly whispering away at the back of his mind, he had a licence to be as forward with her as she was with him, to match each of her advances with one of his own. Strangers, observing them, would have guessed that they were childhood sweethearts who had lately met each other after a long separation and were just beginning to rediscover all that had once held them together so dearly.

"They have a very good hothouse over at Trewennack," she said. "It's the wrong side of Helston from us, but in every other way it would be ideal. I wonder if we might beg a dozen square yards for our seeds — and share their heating bill, of course?"

"When you say it's the wrong side ...?"

"I mean it's over Goonhilly way, beyond Culdrose Farm. Incidentally, Ben Coad was showing your daughter over

Goonhusband last week. Do you know why? It isn't even on the market yet."

They boarded the bus for Piccadilly and took seats outside at the top.

"I knew nothing of this," he said slowly.

She laughed and dug him with her elbow. "Then she *didn't* discuss her plan with you — the plan I asked you about at the Angel last Saturday. I thought not."

As the bus set off he held out his hands, wrists together, as if for cuffing. "You done caught me fair and square, ma'am," he replied. "Guilty's all I can plead. So tell me."

"I think I'd better, John. Your daughter has some idea of wheedling and scheming you into accepting the notion. But she's young and idealistic still. She doesn't realize that when people reach *our* age, we've had enough of duplicity ... saying one thing and meaning another. We can take it on the chin. D'you know Goonhusband at all?"

He shook his head. "Is it an estate or what?"

"No, just a farm. It *ought* to have been an estate. The Penroses were mad to build where they did, facing north over the Loe Pool. Goonhusband is more-or-less opposite, on the farther shore and facing south."

"It must be near Giles Curnow's place — Chynoweth."

"About a mile farther south — no, less than a mile."

"I know it, then. I know the country. When we were looking for a property we all said it was a pity none was going on the shores of that lake."

"Ha — the irony of it, eh! Still, Goonhusband's going now — or it soon will be. And Leah's idea is to persuade you to sell the Old Glebe to me — since you can't do much more than build a plant nursery until the war's ended — and move over to Goonhusband. Shake the dust of the Liddicoats off your coattails for ever! That was how she outlined it to me."

"Well!" he said and, clasping his hands in an attitude of prayer, sank deep in thought. At length he asked, "Is that a roundabout way of making me an offer?"

"Not any longer," she replied. "Why d'you think I came out to the Old Glebe with you last Saturday? Do you imagine I relished the prospect of hearing *you* tell *me,* of all people, what you were going to do with the place?" She laughed.

He stirred uncomfortably. "I guess, at that ..." he mumbled.

"I intended making you an offer sometime that afternoon, of course. But then, as you unfolded your plans, as I listened to you describing the lily pond, the pergola walk, the bromeliad grove, the azalea banks ... I realized I couldn't."

"Why not? You could do all those things yourself. Much better, I'm sure."

"But I wanted *you* to do them. Did you never covet something as a child — covet it for years and years — and then, when at last you got it, you found it wasn't at all what you wanted? When I was a girl I absolutely doted on a certain man in Helston. He's dead these twenty years and more so there's no harm in telling you his name. Barry Moore. He had a one-man haulage business down in Saint John's but he drank himself to death. But when I was fourteen and he was in his prime ... oh! I trembled if I just saw him a hundred yards away. I hankered after him for years even though he had children only a few years younger than me. And then, just before my twentieth birthday, he carried some kibbled wheat out to us from Trevose's mill and he made an indelicate proposal to me. I'm sure he knew of my feelings. And, d'you know, they suddenly evaporated! Just like that."

"Waal," he drawled laconically, "thar's a warnin'!"

She looked at him sharply, as if she had never expected him to make a joke of that nature. Then she smiled, rather enigmatically, and went on, "Perhaps it's different with you? You're probably the sort who doesn't blow hot and cold once you've made up your mind to a certain course ..."

"What will you offer for the Old Glebe?" he asked.

"I told you — nothing. I *want* you to carry out your plans there — why else d'you think I've given you all my shrubs and trees, man?"

He could think of plenty of reasons but he didn't say so.

"Besides ..." she ventured when he made no reply.

"What?"

"Call me sentimental — tell me I'm that sort of twittering old maid who sees romance behind every bush — but I found myself wondering, even while Leah was telling me of her plans for getting you to move to Goonhusband, if that was what she really wanted."

"Ah!" He tugged at his lower lip.

"You follow my drift?" she asked.

"I've been aware that she has taken to dairy farming as if it's been in her blood from birth. She has a feeling for cattle that just can't be taught. So I've also been aware that, when the war's over, she's going to need a spread of her own. I just didn't think she'd be on the lookout that quickly."

Philomena smiled even more broadly. "And you can't think of anything *else* that might just possibly have tilted her thoughts in that direction?"

He frowned and waited for her to explain.

"I knew it as soon as I saw her and Ben Coad in the trap on their way out to Goonhusband — last Friday. Of course, I didn't know it was Leah Carrington then, but I said to myself at once — 'This girl's in love with this man.' She had the look in her eye that I must have had when poor old Barry Moore was around."

"My God!"

It amused her to see how pale he had become. She did not doubt that he was a shrewd man of business, that few competitors had ever been able to pull the wool over his eyes. So his blindness in matters like this, especially when it touched his nearest and dearest, was all the more remarkable. She wondered if he had the faintest inkling of what was going on between his son and Pansy Tregear — which a rather breathless Violet had told her all about.

"Leah and Ben, eh?" he mused.

"Do you approve?" she asked.

"I guess I do — though it shows how wrong a man can be when he sets himself to guess a woman's heart. She and your Nicholas were like two cats in a sack. I always thought they'd end up getting spliced."

She made no reply to that.

"You'd have put a stop to it, though," he said, to prompt her.

"Nicholas has lost his chance now," she replied. "It'll be a good lesson to him, not to be so arrogant. Not to take a woman's feelings for granted. Ben must learn the same, too — or Nicholas could become a threat to him once again."

A sudden pang seized John Carrington. Everything the woman said seemed so utterly right the moment she said it. He had never set himself up as any kind of expert on the vagaries of human emotions, especially on the distaff side, but he had never felt his ignorance as keenly as now. Leah should have someone like Philomena to tell her these things. "Would you …" He hesitated. "I mean, could you … find some way to tell her that? She'd laugh if I tried, but she'd listen to another woman — especially, I think, to you."

"Why me?" she asked in delighted surprise.

"You make it sound so … I don't know. Like a *fact*. Like a law of nature. I mean, you don't make it sound like your own opinion which you're trying to foist on her."

"Well," she said sadly, "that's very flattering — and I'm honoured you should ask. But it's hardly my place. I think she might resent it."

He sighed. She was right, of course. It was hardly her place.

When they arrived back at Earl's she came in with him to see if her bags had been moved across from Whittaker's yet. To his consternation, the desk clerk told him that Mr Troy had booked them both out. He handed John a letter that would explain all.

Jimmy Troy did not know it, of course, but it explained more than all. It revealed that Elizabeth must at last have got word to him that Philomena was staying at Whittaker's, and what a jolly jape it would be if he, Jimmy, moved the pair of them there.

He handed the letter to Philomena and, while she read it, he said to the clerk, "Well, Mister Troy may book himself into Whittaker's if he wishes. But I'm booking myself back into Earl's, right here and now."

Philomena, having read the letter, burst out laughing.

John reached for the registration book but the clerk stopped him taking up the pen. "I'm sorry, sir, but we are now full."

John's eyes narrowed. "How much did Troy pay you to tell me that? What's happened to the room I was in last night?"

"It went almost the minute Mister Troy booked you out, sir. Just after breakfast. He had a phone call from his wife and then he booked you both out. And almost immediately we received a note from a lady, who, funnily enough, was staying at Whittaker's until today."

He said more but it was drowned in their laughter.

John was selecting a banknote of a denomination which, he felt sure, would shake one more room out of the tree at Earl's when Philomena put a hand out to stop him. "Leave it this way, John. Don't you see — it's perfect! They won't *dare* say a word!"

53 One week later to the day John and Philomena ceremonially replanted the last of the uprooted trees from Cheam, a Prince Albert's Yew, in the long field at the Old Glebe. Even though John had seen the care with which Philomena prepared them for their long journey, he found it hard to believe they had survived so well. To be sure, there was still a long and possibly hard winter ahead, so they would not know the final toll until the spring, but even the most damaged of them, the ones whose roots had been impossible to separate from among the roots of established trees, still felt supple and alive. Even the clerk of the weather seemed to conspire with them, withholding the sun by day and sending a good soaking of rain almost every night.

"All that remains to do now," Philomena said as she ran a satisfied eye over the ranks of her rescued plants, "is to keep down the weeds. They hate competition early in life, you know."

"Don't we all!" John said, slipping his arm through hers. "Let's go in and talk with those two youngsters — and remember: I'm going to sell this place to you and buy Goonhusband. Watch their faces!"

Two hundred yards away, standing a little way back from the window of Will's room, Leah said to Ben, "There! See! D'you believe me now?"

"I suppose I have to," he replied. "Seeing's believing. D'you think she's playing tricks?"

Leah shrugged. "I honestly don't know. Pa thinks she is — and something more serious than tricks, maybe. At least, that's what he said when he came back. These last few days he's been more ambiguous."

"How did he come to tell you? I mean, how did the conversation come about?"

"After the first day — watching them together — I said I thought he was getting dangerously pally with her. And he just chuckled and said she'd soon find out just how pally he really was — the moment she tried anything on with him. But he forgets his own advice."

"Which is ...?"

"About doing business with a female."

"Oh, yes."

"And if she's still out to get the Old Glebe, house and land, by hook or by crook, then it *is* still business. Not ... what it looks like out there."

"It *looks* like the real thing," he said.

"Oh, yes?" She laughed. "How would *you* know?"

"Oh?" He bridled. "You think only a woman can tell the real from the fake?"

"*She* could." Leah nodded toward the field, where her father and Philomena were now gathering up their shovels and twine and strips of dirty hessian. "She knew about us. The moment she saw us going out to Goonhusband that day."

"Well?" he asked. "What of it? *I* knew about us then, too."

She butted him with her head. There was a brief tussle, which ended in a passionate kiss. Or two. Or three. Or ... until the sneck on the back door clicked.

"This will not do," she said, pulling away from him and straightening her dress, her hair, her collar, her hair, her dress, her hair ...

"D'you think he'll ask me about buying Goonhusband?" Ben said as they made their way down to the drawing room.

"I can't think why else he'd have sent for you."

"He might want to ask if my intentions are honourable."

"I hope he knows better than that," she replied menacingly.

"When you told him about Goonhusband ... I mean, did he say about getting in touch with me?"

"We didn't talk about it in much detail. He tried to seem surprised, which he obviously wasn't. It's funny. He's good at pretending in commercial situations but he's utterly hopeless in anything personal. I'm sure Philomena told him. The thing is — will he now try to play little jokes on us? Will he pretend that he thinks my original idea is still going strong? I mean, the idea that we should sell the whole of the Old Glebe to Philomena and all of us move to Goonhusband."

He chuckled. "Two can play at that. We'll just pretend to go along with it."

Philomena and John came through from the scullery; she still had a towel in her hands. "We made this rather dirty, I'm afraid," she said. "Where d'you want it?"

"Oh, just throw it at the bottom of the stairs," Leah told her — which, rather reluctantly, she did. When she returned, the line of her jaw said that in her house such things would be done very differently.

"Well, Ben," John said when they were all seated, "Leah has told me of your great kindness to us."

"Sir?" he replied warily.

"Letting us know about Goonhusband before the rest of the pack. We certainly appreciate it. It probably won't affect the price but it gives us longer to think about it." He chuckled. "I guess there won't be objections if I pull down that monstrosity of a barn at Goonhusband to make way for my hothouse!"

"No, sir!" Ben replied eagerly. "I know three of your new neighbours who will be only too delighted."

"Pa!" Leah cried excitedly. "D'you mean you've decided to sell to Miss Liddicoat and buy Goonhusband? How marvellous — and wasn't I clever to have thought of it!"

He glanced uncertainly at Philomena, who just laughed and said, "It's not going to work, John." To Leah she said, "Your father's going to stay on here, my dear."

"Stay *on?*" Leah echoed. This was not part of any little joke; it sounded ominous. Servants stay *on;* masters simply stay.

Philomena shrugged. "Hark at me! This is none of my business. I should just learn to hold my tongue. *You* tell them, John."

"I'm buying Goonhusband for you," he said to Leah. "That is, I'm using some of the money in your gran'maw's trust to buy it. The residue will be yours next August, anyway."

"What?" she asked, almost shouting the word. Her eyes were like saucers. You'd swear it was news to her.

She is good! thought Philomena, watching her closely.

"So there's little point in holding it back now." He turned to Ben. "Will you be farming it, young man, until after the wedding? I assume the idea is for Leah to take over once she's Mrs Coad?"

Ben scratched his head diffidently. "Well, that's something I hoped to talk to *you* about, sir."

His stress on the word caused Philomena to spring to her feet, muttering something about having things to do.

"No, stay," Leah urged. "Ben's only going to say that we want to get married in a month or two's time — as soon as the banns are called. Or as soon as we know the purchase will go through."

She looked from one to the other, slightly surprised. "Isn't anybody going to say anything?"

Her father just stared at his boots.

She tried again: "Like — 'Isn't that rather hasty, dear?' Or, 'Marry in haste, repent at leisure?' No? Nothing like that?"

Philomena rose again. "I will go, dears, if you don't mind. I do have rather a lot of things to see to." To John she added, "Don't worry, I'll be back tomorrow to look over my treasures."

He saw her to the door and returned, wiping his lips.

"I must say, I expected an explosion," Leah told him. "If any daughter of mine ever comes to me and announces her nuptials like that, she'll get a piece of my tongue."

Her father shook his head and said, "It's awkward."

Ben now rose to his feet again. "Perhaps it's my turn to go," he said diffidently.

"Stay!" Leah commanded. "This concerns you, too."

"I don't think it does," he told her. "Does it, sir?"

"You see, honey, I'm kind of in the same boat as you."

"Meaning?" she asked. Then, to Ben: "Do sit down, darling."

Ben obeyed, saying, "I think your dad's telling us he's asked Miss Philomena to marry him."

Leah laughed until she saw her father's face. Then she said, "No!"

He nodded miserably.

"But you hardly know her."

"Oh! Who's talking? Isn't that rather hasty, dear? Marry in haste, repent at leisure?"

"Well, at least I've known Ben for the best part of a year. Not two or three weeks."

"Some people you can know at once. I don't know how. It's just like that. And knowing them for *twenty* years more may add things but it won't change them."

"But you *don't* know her, Pa. She *seems* all sweetness and reason, but you don't know."

"I do now — if you'll hear me out."

"It's not a wedding ring she's after. It's the Old Glebe. Marriage is just a step for her. It gets her the title to this place without having to risk a penny."

He nodded. "That's what I thought, honey. So I set about testing her. I didn't exactly propose, I sort of ..."

"Why did you broach the subject at all?" she asked, still appalled, still taking it in.

"Because," he replied unhappily. "Because I felt myself ..." He glanced at Ben, then at the ceiling. "I was falling in love with her if you must know — and yet I needed to test her. To test someone you love! I felt awful."

"You weren't falling in love with *her*. I'll say it again — you don't know *her*. You were falling in love with the Philomena she wanted you to see. The Philomena she *wanted* you to fall in love with! Didn't I say as much when you came back from London, all full of it? Didn't I say at the time that *that* was the danger? And didn't you agree?"

"That's *why* I broached the subject — to answer your question, if you'll permit me? You seem much more interested in making your own points than in listening to mine."

She raised her hands. "Sorry. I won't say another word."

He gave a hollow laugh and said to Ben, "Just see how she keeps *that* promise!" To her he went on, "I didn't propose to her. I just raised the general idea of marrying. I asked her what she thought of it. And what d'you think she replied?"

"I'm sure she said what any sensible woman would have said, Pa — to a vague sort of question like that. She told you that she wasn't *implacably* against it — and then she waited for you to add something more substantive."

"Oh," he said.

"Why? Did you really expect her to leap about the room and smother you with hugs and kisses and say she could never thank you enough?"

Ben laughed and changed it into a cough.

Her father said in a wounded tone, "Nothing as exaggerated as that. But her lukewarm answer was a bit of a ..."

"And *did* you say something a little more specific then?" she interrupted. "I'll just bet you did!"

He stirred uneasily. "I might have. I think I said something about ... you know ... I made a joke about being mistress of the Old Glebe at last. But — and this is the point I keep trying to make — what d'you think she said to that?"

"Well, I don't know about her but I know what I would have said in her position. I'd say it was out of the question. I wouldn't even consider it."

"Exactly!" he crowed, breaking into a broad smile. "That's precisely what she did say, too. Now doesn't that *prove* she's not simply after the Old Glebe?"

"Not to me, it doesn't! At the risk of sounding brutal — which I don't intend — it shows only that she doesn't want *you,* even if the Old Glebe comes free with the gold ring."

"Ha!" He rubbed his hands as if she had fallen into his trap. "Well, that's just where you're wrong, Miss Cleverpuss! She's perfectly willing to live here as my housekeeper ... even" — he cleared his throat — "as my 'dearest housekeeper,' if you follow. But not as the second Mrs Carrington."

At last Leah was nonplussed. "Is it just the name?"

"That's what I asked her. I told her I'd change it to anything she liked — Liddicoat, even. But she said that wasn't it."

"What was it, then?"

"I don't know — and she won't say." He smiled thinly at her. "And it's obviously not some reason that 'any woman would give' — or you, daughter dear, would be reeling it off by now."

In a tone more like thinking aloud than actually speaking, Leah said, "Why would she be willing to live in sin with you — which is what it amounts to ..."

"Because she loves me," he responded awkwardly. "Or so she says."

"No." She shook her head. "I wasn't really asking *that* question. I meant why would she risk all the wagging tongues ... social ostracism ... all that ... when she could have the same life with honour? And the Old Glebe, which she admits to coveting all her life? It just doesn't make sense."

54 About two weeks after her father returned from London, Leah received a letter from America:

Weds., Oct 21, 1914
Dear Leah:

I hope this doesn't come as too much of a shock. I must have written you a hundred times, mostly in my head, of course, but this is the first I've mailed. The reason? I'm coming over to Europe! In fact, by the time you get this, I may already have arrived. Your brother wrote Willa Henderson to say he was now a mining magnate, set to make five fortunes out of some wolfram the miners of old left lying around for anyone to pick up, so that's how I got your address.

My boat is due in Southampton on Monday, November 2nd, and I will be spending some days in London. Then, at a date yet to be determined, I'll be going to Dublin via Liverpool, after which I will not be a free agent. I would be so much happier in my mind if I could see you some time after the 2nd. According to Bradshaw, it looks pretty easy to get from London to Cornwall and go from there via Bristol to Liverpool. So, if you are tied to the homestead and William to his wolfram, I could do that. I'll try to 'phone you from Southampton, otherwise from London, where I'll be staying with Father Cassidy, c/o the Night Refuge for Catholic Girls of Good Character at 9, Lower Seymour-street (I kid you never!).

Oh, there is so much to tell you. Not only the things in all those unmailed letters but the things that have been happening in my life this year. I'm bursting with them now. My heart runs over. But it would be impolitic to commit them to paper. So, till the day when we meet again — let it be soon!

Thine ever,
Tom

The arrival of this curious letter threw Leah into confusion and put her father's problems almost entirely from her mind.

'My heart runs over'? He had written a hundred letters? Then he was still in love with her. But, 'impolitic to commit them to paper'? They were rather the words of a lawyer than of a lover. And, 'Thine ever'! Could he have forgotten that those words came from a song sung by a blackface minstrel with a grating, adenoidal voice and that they had mocked him on campus all one summer? Or was Tom making a deliberate hint at something — at the childish amusements of gilded youth, for instance? She must have a clearer idea before she invited him down to Cornwall.

Lloyd's Register, which carried sailing details of neutral vessels only — to warn the belligerents not to go doing anything stupid — told her that the America Line's *Tallahassee,* which sailed from New York City on 25th October, was due in Southampton at midday on 2nd November — the only American liner scheduled for that day. There was no call from Southampton on that noon.

At three o'clock she telephoned the night refuge and spoke to a (presumably Catholic) Girl of Good Character, who volunteered the information that she had just changed the warming pan in the bed they were airing for Mr O'Leary; then she went off to find Father Cassidy. Her feet rang on a marble floor; the place sounded cold and echoey.

The priest agreed, reluctantly, to let Tom have her telephone number but he seemed to think it an impertinence that old friends from America should seek to get in touch with Tom, here in England. He didn't believe Tom would have much time for a social life from now on. When Leah asked why not, he said he had to go and rang off abruptly.

Leah was so perturbed by this that, although she hung up the earpiece, she forgot to ring off, and so the next call from London to Helston came straight through to her. It was from a woman in Hampstead who was giving a party the day after tomorrow and desperately wanted a barrel of live lobsters from a particular fisherman in Porthleven, who was to put it on the six-o'clock up train that evening. Leah turned the magneto handle desperately but could not get back to the knitting circle that ran the exchange. So she felt honour-bound to convey the message herself.

"And they say the telephone's a blessing!" she remarked to Pansy as she set off to find this man in Porthleven. And when she at last ran him down in the bar of the Commercial Inn, he merely said, "Well, my lover, you tell she to pay I for the last two barrels I sent 'er — and return they barrels to us — and I'll think about it. Maybe."

She fairly exhausted the pony in racing back by the direct, but hilly, road through Ventonvedna and St Elvan; but it was worth it. Five minutes after her return, the call from London came through and she heard Tom O'Leary's voice for the first time in ten months.

She said it was wonderful and he replied that it was pretty good. She asked what sort of crossing it had been and he said the first day had been awful but the rest had been fair for the time of year. Now the durned land wouldn't hold still beneath him. She laughed and said yes, she remembered that feeling. And, talking of feelings …

There was a pause before he said, cagily, "Yes?"

"Well, Tom …" She knew she had to get this in before her courage failed her and before the palpitations in her heart and the constriction in her breathing prevented it. "Things have changed, you know."

"They certainly have!" He almost crowed the words.

"I mean they haven't stood still."

"No, they've gone back! And I'm just *sick* about it all. I can't talk on the phone — obviously — but I could if I could just see you, even for a day, I'm sure I could tell you everything. So you'd understand the importance of it from my point of view."

Her heart fell. There was nothing for it but to tell him straight. "I'd love to see you again, Tom. And it's true — there is so much to talk about. I have a lot to tell you, too. I would have written and let you know about it anyway but it'll be so much … well, 'nicer' is hardly the right word! It'll be so much more honest and honourable to tell you in person."

"Tell me what?" he asked in a slightly bewildered tone. "I'm the one with news I'm bursting to tell you."

"Well …" She was more than a little miffed at this. "I have my own share of that commodity, you know. The thing is" — she swallowed heavily — "I'm unofficially engaged to a Helston man and it's about to become official any day now. And it won't be a long engagement, either."

"Oh!" he exclaimed, but more as if it were the change of topic, rather than the news itself, that surprised him.

Meanwhile Leah, hearing the echo of her last words, realized how they might be misconstrued and added, "Not that there's any particular *reason* to rush things — other than that Ben and I are buying a farm together and, well, Nature won't wait."

"Yeah … sure!" he said, still sounding quite bewildered.

And now Leah saw that she had dug herself even deeper into the mire. "I mean ploughing and sowing and reaping and mowing — *that* sort of Nature, Tom. Not … you know …"

"Well, that's just swell!" he exclaimed.

"Are you being ironic, Tom?"

"How d'you mean?"

"You know — swell … swelling … and me saying Nature can't wait. You're not by any chance making snide remarks along those lines?"

"In a home for young females of upright character — I should hope not!'"

She laughed. *"Now* I remember you, Tom! I was just beginning to wonder."

"Well, like I said, things *have* changed. So — you're going up the primrose path to the altar. Will I like him? Will I approve? Does William approve — that's the real question? He's a better judge of people than any of us. If he approves, then so do I. Shoot — I'm longing to see you all again! I just hope my schedule allows it."

"Father Cassidy didn't seem to think it would."

Tom laughed. "You know the Irish. They have to pop half a dozen corks and remember The Invincibles before anything gets going. I'll *make* time — never fear. Just tell me what days over the next two weeks you won't be free."

"Golly! In a way I'm already tied up *every* day. I mean I'm already running a farm here."

"Yeah — William said that to Willa — who sends her regards, by the way."

"Oh, thank you. But farming and free time don't exactly go hand in hand, you know. However, the chores can be rearranged and relief workers can be engaged. All it takes is a little notice. You let me know the day before you're coming down — two days would be even better, if you can manage it — and I'll make sure I'm free. Take the branch line from Gwinear Road to Helston. I'll meet you there. Did you get that?"

"It's already written down, honey."

"My! Things really have changed. You're getting organized! When did you last wear odd stockings?"

Silence.

"Well?" she prompted.

"I've just checked," he said. "And I'm going to plead the Fifth Amendment on that one. Listen — there's the Angelus. I have to go. But I *will* let you know."

"But, Tom — your folks are Baptists!" she objected — to an already silent line.

This time she remembered to ring off.

55 In the event, Tom gave the Carringtons two days' notice. On 10th November, a Tuesday, he phoned to say he would arrive at Helston early in the evening of that coming Thursday and would like to stay until the following Monday morning. He asked Leah to book him in at a good local hostelry. She told him not to be so stupid; he'd stay at the Old Glebe, of course. But at least he made the offer, she thought — which showed he understood the new situation.

The day after he phoned, Leah had a serious argument with Will. All that day she'd had the feeling that Pansy was avoiding her. When Pansy's sister Violet called by to collect an earring that Philomena had dropped into the lining of an armchair the previous week, she learned why. Violet could not be more different from her sister. Where Pansy was blonde and willowy, Violet was stocky and dark; and where Pansy was feather-heeled and carefree, Violet was intense and serious.

Leah told Violet she thought Pansy was avoiding her and asked if she could find out why. Violet had words with her sister (they had not had conversations for years) and, on her way out, told Leah that Ben Coad had given Will a lecture on the folly of dalliance with the household servants. Indeed, he had given him more than that, namely the addresses of certain houses in Constantine, Goldsithney, and Leedstown where those needs could be 'tooken care of' for a small outlay in silver. And — according to Pansy — Will was now 'so maggoty as a big ferret in a small sack.'

That evening, as usual, Leah hung around when Pansy brought the hot bathwater up to Will's room. And later that evening, *not* as usual, Will hit out at her for it. He said she must have a mind like a sewer to suspect him and the girl, and what tales she'd been carrying to Ben Coad he couldn't imagine, but he'd thank her to hold her tongue in future because he'd never been so humiliated and embarrassed in all his life.

It was much too long a speech, not only because he 'did protest too much' but also because it gave Leah time to recover from her shock at the onslaught and face her brother calmly — once he had finished speaking. Or, rather, once he paused to draw breath. "It doesn't wash, Will," she said calmly. "Pansy's with child and the game's up."

He sat down abruptly, his face drained of all colour. "She's not!" he said. "Oh, my God!" He closed his eyes and shook his head. "Why did she tell *you*, of all people? Why didn't she come to me?"

"She's done quite enough of *that*, don't you think?" she asked severely. "It was bad enough when you both went out to the old barn each night, but now …"

He rose again and made for the door. "I must go and see her," he said.

"Will!" she snapped.

He hesitated, poised on one foot. "What?"

"Let me give you *some* good …"

"I didn't need any advice, thanks, good or bad. Especially not from you or your precious Ben!"

".. good *news*, I was going to say. Very good news, in fact."

"What?" Now he was merely testy.

"She's not."

He just stared at her blankly.

"Pansy," she went on. "She's not with child."

"You …! You …" he spluttered.

"Careful!" She rose and came to him. "I might have been only rehearsing."

"Well, are you or aren't you?" he roared.

"Keep your voice down! The truth is I don't know whether or not she's in that interesting condition. And nor do you. And nor does she. A woman doesn't, you know, until it's almost two months too late. You've been going at it like rabbits for the past six weeks, so what I pretended was a certainty could well be a possibility. Are you going to sit down now and discuss it calmly?"

He just stared at her. She had never seen such anger in his eyes before. "I'll thank you not to meddle in my affairs in future …" he began icily.

But she behaved as if he were not speaking at all. "Have you promised to marry Pansy if anything like that should happen?" she asked. "Does she have some sort of understanding with you along those lines?"

"Whether any such understanding may exist between us or not is none of your …"

"Because, if not, then your affairs are not *her* affairs — and I shall certainly meddle in her affairs."

"She has come of age and she is a free woman who may make her own … oh, hell!" He was furious that she had seduced him into a discussion he had set his mind against entering at all. He turned on his heel and made for the front door. But there he found it was lashing with rain, so he had to come back and put up his oilskins. It ruined the grandeur of his intended gesture — flinging out into the night.

Leah stood at his elbow and said, "The title 'free woman' has a certain irony in this situation, don't you think? You'd be better off with the kind that charge for it."

"I'm not saying another word," he replied.

"Good! That gives me time to tell you more. I have been aware of your shenanigans — yours and hers — from the very beginning. And I warned her at the time that the one thing I would *not* tolerate would be if she tried to do the same thing with the old man. I also warned her against expecting any help or consideration if she broke her leg with you. So she's under no illusions about that."

He opened the front door again, still with several buttons undone and, at last, flung out into the night, leaving the door swinging behind him.

"Oh, Will, you are such a fool!" she called out into the dark.

She slammed the door and turned round to see Philomena coming up the passage from the kitchen end of the house. "I hope you don't mind, Leah, dear," she said. "It's such a filthy night I came directly from the yard in through the scullery. Was that Will?"

Leah nodded. "We've just had words, I'm afraid. Come into the sitting room."

Philomena did not move. "So I gathered. I suppose he's going down to Grankum to complain about you to Adelaide. Has he eaten anything?"

"No." Leah was hardly listening. She was wondering if she should go and play a variant of the same trick on Pansy, so as to drive the dangers home to her: 'My dear girl — from the way you've been behaving lately, you remind me of a friend of mine at around the time she conceived her first baby. And look at the texture of your skin! Are you *absolutely sure* you're not …'

Philomena said, "Nor have they, yet. So he won't go hungry — unless he's off to a certain house in Goldsithney! Or the other one in Leedstown!"

That got Leah's attention at last!

First the hostess resumed control. "Have *you* eaten, Miss Liddicoat?" she asked. "Do take pot luck with us."

"I haven't as a matter of fact, my dear. How kind of you — and all unprompted! But see here — hadn't we agreed you'd call me Philomena?"

"Yes. I'm sorry. I intended no ... I'm just rather *distrait* at the moment — what with Tom O'Leary coming tomorrow and now this quarrel with Will ..."

Had the woman hung back at the far end of the passage until Will had gone? Had she heard that bit about Pansy setting her cap at the old man? Leah groaned inwardly.

"Come into the drawing room," she said again, leading the way this time. "Put your shoes to dry out near the fire. We won't be dressing for dinner tonight — much to my father's delight. I try to keep up the old standards but it's hard to do that *and* run a farm as well."

"The colonel always dressed for dinner," Philomena said, but in such a neutral tone that Leah could not tell whether she approved or disapproved. In the beginning she had always spoken of her former employer with such admiration, but not nowadays. "Thank you for finding my earring," she added.

They sat down and reached their hands eagerly toward the flames. "It was easy once you were able to say where you had probably lost it," Leah replied. "I take it Violet told you about her discussions with Pansy, then? It's very *kind* of Ben to be so liberal with his directions to Will of houses of that sort. He seems to be a walking vade-mecum! I just wonder how he's able to reel them off so pat?"

Philomena chuckled. "Oh, my dear, everyone knows about them down here. It doesn't mean anything special in his case. I remember the time I passed the one in Leedstown and saw all the sheets hanging out in the garden to dry and I dropped some remark about it's being rather a grand house for a washerwoman — and everybody laughed. Nobody told me but I guessed. That's how one picks things up, of course." She smiled at Leah. "So don't go bending Ben's ear, eh?"

"Thank heavens I spoke to you first." Leah glanced at the clock. "Fifteen minutes. D'you want to go up and wash?"

She shook her head. "That won't take a moment. Actually, Leah, there's something I wish to speak to you about."

"My father."

"What else! I'm afraid I overheard what you said to Will just now, but I had intended asking you about it before — in fact, ever since the very first time I met him — met *them* — when he pretended to be John Hamden. Do you object to speaking bluntly about it with me? I take it there is nothing actually going on there?"

Leah shook her head. "Only with Will — which is bad enough. But there's no point in dismissing her because it would only continue between the pair of them. And then I'd have absolutely no control over her at all."

"Yes. I'd already worked that out for myself. I think you've done quite the right thing."

"Have I? Surely there was a time when shame and moral sense would have made such behaviour unthinkable? Among people like us, anyway."

"People like us!" Philomena gave a hollow laugh. "Perhaps there was, but it was before Adam delved and Eve span — I mean, before Adam *needed* to delve or Eve to spin. Ever since then we've each had to find our own accommodation. Tell me — is there any likelihood your father will overhear us?"

"None whatsoever. We'll hear him coming downstairs before he even reaches the landing. Why?"

"Because I think there are one or two things I ought to tell you — and one thing I ought to ask you, too. The main thing to tell you is ..." She sighed and, with a wave of her hands, sculpted something huge in the air between them. "It's as big as a whale. But what it comes down to is that the 'moral sense' you spoke of is a general prescription for the generality of people. It makes us promise never to tell lies even though we know we're going to tell Mrs so-and-so she's looking radiant and that colour suits her to a tee. Or that we'll never steal even though we know we'll reuse the next uncancelled stamp we find among our morning's post. Or that we'll never be slothful again — a resolution I found impossible to maintain in the bath at Earl's last month, even with people hammering on the door."

"Yes," Leah responded uncertainly. "But these are all trivial lapses …"

"Are they? We send Mrs so-and-so forth into the world, a laughing stock. We make the posting of letters more expensive for those who honestly pay for it. And so on. But if Pansy slips between Will's sheets at night — or I between the colonel's (which, I confess to *you*, I did) — who is harmed thereby? That's what it comes down to — who is *harmed* by it?"

Leah could only stare at her. Her heart dropped a beat and then raced. "How can you say that?" she murmured.

"Well — answer me? Who is harmed?"

"But … I mean, everybody *knows* …"

"Never mind what *everybody* knows. Tell me what *you* know. Tell me who is harmed?"

"Well — Pansy is for one. I mean, she could so easily become … did you hear what I said to Will earlier? The thing that started our argument?"

Philomena shook her head.

"I pretended that Pansy had told me she was expecting — just to shock him. To show him it *could* happen."

Again the woman shook her head, this time with a pitying smile. "Not if he's a gentleman — and she's cautious. There are ways to avoid it, you know. I don't want to go off on that track now. Just accept it from one who knows. It is a very small possibility when you go about it in the right way. And when you set it against the pleasure of the thing — a pleasure of which you cannot have the faintest …"

"Philomena!"

"What?" Her big, questioning eyes were all innocence.

"You know what! I mean, what you're advocating is against all common … I mean, what would become of society if we all …" Words failed her.

"I'm not advocating, dear. Nor seeking to promote some new and outlandish form of behaviour. I'm simply explaining the way things already are. As to what would become of society — look about you! The society in which you live is not one that would fall to bits if half its members engaged in clandestine encounters between the sheets, it is one that has already been shaped by such behaviour — all down the centuries. The pendulum has swung between periods of licence and periods of prudery, but that has merely led to greater or smaller discretion in the business."

Leah put her hands to her temples and pressed hard, as if to dislodge some obstruction. "Are you saying you wouldn't mind ... I mean, the question you asked earlier about my father and, you know, Pansy, and so forth — are you saying you wouldn't really mind if ..."

"Ah!" Philomena exclaimed, holding up a finger and smiling savagely. "Whether *I* would mind is a totally different matter. I was talking about whether society as a whole should mind particularly what we do in that sphere of life. But of course *I* should mind. I'd be beside myself with fury, let me tell you. I'd tear her eyes out. I'd dismiss her from this life, never mind from this house!" Her eyes glowed at the prospect, making Leah shiver. "And as for your father — oh, what torments would I *not* prepare for him?"

"But why? To quote you back at yourself — who would actually be harmed?"

"*I* would be harmed. My *amour propre* would be shattered. To know that he'd choose her when he could have me!"

"But he's asked you to marry him and you've said ..."

"I'm not talking about marriage. I'm talking about It. Doing It. I'll gladly come here as his housekeeper — and keep his bed warm — I've told him that."

"But you won't marry him! I don't understand."

Philomena smiled sympathetically. "You don't need to understand. Just accept that I have my reasons."

"Do you lose your inheritance from the colonel if you remarry — is that it?"

She laughed. "That proves you haven't sent for a copy of his will. It has gone through probate, you know. It's a public document. Anyone can purchase a copy. But I'll save you the money. That is not the reason. My inheritance was absolute and inalienable."

"Pa doesn't understand, either. He does love you, you know. It's driving him almost out of his mind."

"There's no need for him to torment himself a moment longer. He can have me at his side day and night. I'm growing to love him, too. It started in London. I never thought there would be another man for me — not after the colonel. But, against all the odds, your pa has crept in under my armour and ... well, 'nuff said. I'll move in tomorrow if he'll only say the word."

Leah sank her head between her hands. "But he never will, Philomena. He loves you too honourably simply to take you in as a housekeeper by day and a mistress by night."

"What a perfect description of a wife! Granted that the parties love each other, too, of course — which it seems we do."

"He'd never see it like that. He wants to take you round, show you off. He wants to swell with pride when he says, 'And this is my wife' — and people see how beautiful you are."

Just for a moment she thought she, too, had slipped a rapier-word beneath Philomena's armour. If so, the woman ignored the wound and riposted: "The great John Carrington, eh — who subdued the dragon in Philomena Liddicoat and put a band of gold on that finger! No, sirree — as he says! It might as well be a ring of gold through my nose, with an invisible chain to his key-ring! No, sirree again! One of us must yield and it won't be me."

"And *that's* the reason?" a shocked Leah asked.

"No," Philomena replied. "That's *not* the reason. Suffice it to say I have my pride. That's all. And I care for his reputation, also. You keep on telling him that — I have my pride and he must yield to it."

56 Tom's train was due at the Helston terminus at 6:02 that Thursday evening. Leah was there in good time but she need not have bothered; the main-line train had been delayed by troop movements at Exeter and, though it had made up for lost time since, the connecting train from Gwinear Road would be at least a quarter of an hour late. At six o'clock, just after Leah had found someone with sufficient authority to let her know these details, she was surprised to see Nicholas Liddicoat come sauntering onto the platform. And a curiously nervous kind of saunter it was, too. Perhaps it had something to do with the fact that he was still dressed in his working clothes. Claggy man-made clay hung like strips of cracked elephant hide around the bottoms of his trousers and his dark hair was grizzled with dust.

"Oh, it's you! Hallo," he said, making a half-hearted attempt at surprise. Meanwhile, his eyes roved up and down the ill-lit platform — the sun having set an hour earlier. "But where is your baggage?" he asked.

Something in his attitude made her decide to volunteer as little as possible. "I didn't bring any," she told him.

He nodded grimly, as if he had expected as much. "A bit of a rush decision, eh?" he said.

"At least I dressed for the occasion," she replied.

He looked down at his clothes, as if seeing them for the first time. "And to think I almost broke my neck coming down Sithney Common Hill."

"On your bicycle?"

He nodded. "All the way I kept praying it wasn't true, that Will was pulling my leg. I actually hoped he was, even though I'd smash his face in for it. I honestly didn't think I'd find you here. But I had to be sure."

This was such an absurd over-reaction to her present errand that, she realized, Will must have spun the poor Nark some quite different yarn. It was his revenge for her interference in his night-life, of course. That was why he had searched for her luggage. Will must have told him she was leaving by the next up-train, for some spurious reason.

So, how to break the truth to the Nark gently — but not so gently that he didn't go back and carry out some part of his threat to deal with the dear boy?

"I can't imagine why you should be so perturbed at a simple act of courtesy, Nark," she said. "It's terribly sweet of you to show such concern in my behalf but Tom is a civilized person, a graduate of Yale and a doctor of jurisprudence. I do not need a bodyguard just to meet him off the train."

"Tom?" He cleared his throat awkwardly.

"Tom O'Leary. Have I never mentioned him to you? Surely I have? Anyway, he's visiting us for the weekend, before going on to Dublin. And I'm meeting him here."

"Yes, well, I knew that, of course," Nicholas said, sticking his hands in his pockets and trying to seem nonchalant. Then, staring out into the dark across the tracks, he muttered, "I'll kill the fellow!"

Leah smiled. "Did he tell you I was going away, then?"

He nodded tersely. "Something like that. God, I could have killed myself coming down that hill without lights."

"But *why*, Nick?"

She so rarely used his name that he was astonished into silence; he just stared at her.

She went on: "Suppose I *had* been doing a moonlight flit — or whatever cock-and-bull nonsense Will gave you — what would you have done?"

He returned his gaze to the darkness that faced them. "Dunno," he said. "Waved goodbye, I suppose."

"Tell that to the horse-marines!"

"All right," he cried angrily. "I'd have somehow tried to talk you into staying."

"But why?"

"That's none of your business."

"Ah!" After a pause she began humming a little tune.

"I need someone to argue with," he said. "You're the best I know. All right?"

"Not that we have argued much lately," she remarked airily.

"Well, whose fault is that? You have been rather ... how shall I put it? Preoccupied?"

She could smell tigers in the country up ahead. "Before you say something you might regret ..." she began.

But he interrupted her. "Don't do it, Thistle."

"Do what?"

"That's what I came in here to say — don't do it. I meant don't run off, then, but I still mean it now. Don't ..."

"Will told you I was running away — and you *believed* him?"

"He made it sound very convincing. How you can't abide Aunt Philomena — it's not hard to make *that* sound convincing! How you ..."

"But I *like* Philomena. I didn't at first. None of us did. But we all do now. We can't understand why she refuses to marry my father though she seems perfectly willing to live in sin with him. D'you understand it?"

"Never mind that." He waved her question aside. "When I thought you were just running away from it all, I thought that included Ben Coad. So I came in here to tell you not to." He licked his lips nervously and drew a deep breath. "I still say it — don't! Not Ben Coad. You can do a lot better."

"Meaning?" she asked quietly.

"You're besotted with farming now. All right — it's new, it's exciting, it satisfies something deep within everyone. Lording it over land and livestock. Forcing Nature to our will. But it's not *you*, Thistle. You belong on a wider stage."

"All on my ownio?" she asked.

"That's a later question. Just think what's right for you now."

She sighed. "I don't seem to be very good at that. Whenever I try to imagine the future, it's always *with* someone."

"All right. Here's a picture for you. Imagine yourself twenty-five years from now. The children grown up and gone. Just you and Ben Coad. And he's still cracking the same feeble jokes in Helston market every Wednesday. And you're still looking out on the same fifty acres at Goonhusband, thinking we'll plough that field and put that one down to oats and cabbage in that one and return that one to pasture. And it'll hit you that you did exactly the same five years earlier, and six years before that, and four years before that for two years running ..." He gripped her arm fiercely and stared deep into her eyes. "And you'll remember this conversation then. And you'll say to yourself, 'The Nark was right. I *do* belong on a wider stage than this'! But it'll be too late. You think you're choosing to *do* something in marrying Coad. But I tell you now — you're really choosing *not* to do something." He smiled at her, rather desperately, and added, "Here endeth the first and only lesson."

She shook her head. "You have a much higher opinion of me and my capabilities than I do of myself," she said.

"Much higher than Coad's — if he really sees you as a happy farmer's wife till death do you part."

"Well, Nick, I'm afraid that's the way I see myself, too. That's why I think he's the man for me. Tell me why your aunt won't marry my father."

"Oh, go to hell!" he said quietly — and walked away, out of the station.

A moment later, however, he was back at the gate. "Pride!" he shouted at her. "It runs in *some* families, you know."

This encounter did nothing to dent her love for Ben nor her resolve to marry him and live the happy, contented life Nick had just sneered at. But it filled her with a great sadness for him. He had obviously felt much more for her than he had ever admitted to feeling. And now, with her apparently dramatic flight from home, he had seen his last chance to declare it to her. But the sadness did not soften her heart to the point where she might humour him, tell him she'd think it over, go along with him a little and hope to let him down gently over the coming weeks.

And that was fitting, in a way, because — as she suddenly realized — if Tom felt the same about her, she would be just as blunt and firm with him, too. People talk of being cruel to be kind; but there is also its counterpart, especially in matters of the heart — being kind to be cruel.

Also, his final taunt about the pride that ran in the Liddicoat family gave her something else to think about.

57 Outwardly Tom hadn't changed a bit. He stuck his head out of his compartment window as soon as the train had cleared the bridge, some hundred yards down the line. The light from within picked him out against the darkness — and he was still the golden-haired son of Yale with stars in his eyes. And he opened the door and leaped out onto the platform before the train pulled to a halt. "Leah!" he cried, throwing his arms around her and lifting her off the ground to swing her around in a great circle. But his quick, cheerful kiss on her cheek was in marked contrast to the long orgies of kissing that had attended her tearful departure at the beginning of that year in Connecticut.

"No husband-to-be?" he asked as he set her down again. "He trusts you with me?"

The bluntness of the question, even though he intended it jokingly, left her nonplussed. She could not think of a quick reply that did not belittle one or other of them. Then it came to her: "*I* trust me with you, Tom."

"Ah! There's that independent Yankee streak! How does it play in Helston?"

"Pretty well. Where are your bags?"

"Just the carpet bag." He paused to retrieve it from the luggage van. "I sent everything else on from London to Dublin. They have this wonderful system called 'luggage in advance' and they swear it's infallible."

SHADES OF THE FUTURE • 393

All the way down into Helston he enthused about aspects of England's novelties that she had forgotten by now. Most of all he had been impressed by the varieties of landscape he had passed through on the three hundred miles between London and Cornwall — the rolling beechwoods of the Thames valley, the picture-postcard farmlands of Berkshire (so unlike the mountainous 'Berkshires' of Massachusetts) and Somerset, the seascapes after Exeter, where the line is built on the tidal rocks and penetrates the cliff headlands in short tunnels ... the wild fringes of Dartmoor ... Brunel's magnificent bridge, soaring over the Tamar at Plymouth, and then the lush, damp, closed-in valleys of Cornwall itself. He had viewed them, appropriately, in the gathering dusk, as the train sped on into the dark, Celtic west. His final view, before night fell and the sparks and glow from the engine gave the line an infernal cast, was of the broad, treeless hills of the far west, like a school of black dolphins frozen against a burnished leaden sky.

"And all those familiar names!" he said. "Plymouth. Truro. Falmouth. Portland. Weymouth. Bideford — they have only one 'd' here, I noticed. And there are dozens more."

"You have to keep reminding yourself that they got them first. We borrowed the names from them."

"Yeah," he said. "Except that when we did it, we *were* them, too. The same people. We're not any more, thank God!"

She thought that a rather odd remark but she let it pass. "What's all this about going to Ireland?" she asked.

"Hey!" he exclaimed as they entered Coinagehall Street. "What a quaint little burg! What does it remind me of? If there was ocean down there at the bottom, instead of that green, it'd be like New Bedford in *Moby Dick*, don't you think? All these hunched houses leaning against one another as they march down the hill."

"Except they're built of granite, if you notice." She tried not to let his slightly patronizing admiration annoy her; but the fact that she had forgotten the time when her feelings were almost identical showed her how much she now belonged here.

"That's the Angel Hôtel." She pointed it out. "It was once the town house of the earls of Godolphin, who were ministers of state to Queen Elizabeth back in the days of the Virginia plantation. Doesn't it make you thrill to think of all that history?

I mean, it's our history, too — only back home it was just like the backdrop to the *Mayflower* settlement. It's as if a backdrop on the stage suddenly turned into real landscape. D'you know what I mean, Tom?"

After a pause he said, "Only too well, honey." He took her hand, briefly. "We'll always be friends, won't we?" he asked.

"Of course!" She laughed, slightly embarrassed by his intensity.

"No matter what I … I mean, what you may hear of me?"

"Good heavens, Tom!" Now her laugh was wholeheartedly embarrassed. "What are you intending to do in Dublin? Stage another Phoenix Park murder?"

"No," he replied vehemently. "That's the whole point. I'll tell you at dinner. I want your father to hear it, too."

"Ben will be there, too."

"Oh."

"Why d'you say it like that?"

"Well, I mean, he's English, isn't he?"

She chuckled. "He wouldn't thank you for the description. Practically his first words to us, when he met us on that same platform at the station, were to the effect that *he* was Cornish and *we* were Cornish — or that local people would consider us more Cornish than American."

"Good salesman!"

"No, it's true. Total strangers come up to us and say things like, 'My wife's aunt had a half-sister who got married to a nephew of your great-grandfather, William Carrington of Leedstown'! That actually happened to me — more or less those very words. We used to think the Irish were like that, over in America — always sorting out their genealogy before they can ask for a light. But the Cornish are just the same."

"Interesting," Tom said. "And your Mister Coad has no love for the English, either?"

"Oh, I wouldn't go as far as that. He sneers at a certain class of English tripper and insists that he's Cornish. But he wouldn't blow up the bridges and dig the Tamar clear through to the Bristol Channel."

Tom laughed at her imagery and said, "No. I guess God was kinder to the Irish in that respect."

At dinner that night he told them more. He had been offered a teaching post in jurisprudence at University College, Dublin;

there was a detour there while they sorted out that Trinity was for Protestants and UCD for Roman Catholics.

"But your people were always Protestants," John pointed out, repeating the objection Leah had tried to make on the telephone. "Weren't they?"

"We were Irish before we were either," Tom replied. Then, turning to Ben, he added, "I gather, sir, that you will understand the sentiment. We Celts are of our own nation before we sign up to any other."

"We are clannish," Ben agreed. "But I'm not sure the English don't favour us by posing as the common enemy. You Irish converted us Cornish to Christianity, you know — blithely ignoring the fact that we had been quietly practising the faith for three hundred years already. You came ashore from your little *curraghs,* with the wild fire of the new convert in your eyes, and with sword and dagger you did it. The carnage was appalling."

It was clearly not the message Tom wished to hear but, lawyer that he was, he found something in Ben's words on which he could build. "It is to help prevent such appalling carnage that I have accepted this post. You should have heard the murmurings in Boston, and other Irish communities over there, when the English suspended the Home Rule Act until the end of this war. Carnage isn't the word. And the same hotheads will take over the struggle in Ireland, too, unless we can have some movement on the legal front. If the English just dig in their heels and say no, no, no to all the peaceful, legal moves, then the blood will run through every street in Ireland."

Any worries Ben harboured — that Leah's former beau might still feel some lingering desire for her — evaporated during this speech. Looking into the man's eyes he saw the light of a new love shining there — the sort that leaves no room for others. He smiled and said, "I don't think you'd find echoes of such sentiments down here, old chap."

And so it continued the whole weekend. She proudly showed him a field of oats she had drilled herself; he remembered the Great Famine and the way groaning shiploads of cereals were exported from Ireland while millions starved to death. The stamps at Wheal Fortune were a metaphor for Anglo-Irish landlordism. The poisoned croft was the face of Irish nationalism, poisoned with ideas of physical force.

Tom O'Leary had turned into a zealot, consumed by one idea: that Ireland should be free and a nation once again. It left no room for any other. Leah could remember how his eyes, once upon a time, would follow any pretty girl who came into view, never realizing how much it pained her to see it. But now, when Pansy was around, even when she flirted with him in those ways she could not help, she might just as well have been a machine for all the notice he paid her. Indeed, if she had been a machine, he might have been more interested — wondering how cheaply she might be duplicated and put into the service of Erin the Brave.

Leah hated to admit it but, when he finally left them on the Monday morning, she had never been more glad to see the back of anyone. "It was the longest weekend of my life," she told Ben when she called by on her way back from the station.

"Poor you!" he said sympathetically, though he could hardly conceal his relief at the way things had turned out.

"Did my father give you a letter of authorization to retrieve the deeds to the Old Glebe from Frank Kernow?" she went on.

He made a guilty grimace and nodded.

"Which means you haven't done so yet?"

"'Fraid so. Things have just been so …"

"It doesn't matter, Ben. It's rather good that you haven't, because, if you do it this afternoon, it'll mean …"

"Not this afternoon!" he groaned.

"Please," she insisted. "It must be. You must bring them to the Old Glebe tonight. You're coming to dinner, by the way. And you'll call at the Angel and bring Philomena with you. Everything hinges on three conditions: the presence of my father, the presence of Philomena, and the presence of those deeds. So don't fail me! Eight o'clock."

"And if I tell you it will mean postponing yet again the final act of the Goonhusband purchase?"

"Then it just has to be postponed, Ben. I'm sorry. I cannot marry you until I'm sure my father is properly fixed up. And I think that means being *married* to Philomena, not just living under the same roof."

He sank his head between his hands. "Not all that again!" he begged. "I thought we'd agreed to give up trying. Let them stew in their own juice — isn't that what you said?"

"That was before the Nark let drop an amazing revelation about his dear aunt."

"What?"

Leah's eyes brimmed with merriment as she said, slowly and portentously, "Aunt Philomena has *pride!*"

He waited for more and then said, "And that's it?"

"That's it."

"Well, I'm blowed!" he exclaimed. "Who ever would have guessed it!"

"You think about it," Leah advised, unshaken by his sarcasm. "What particular point of pride would prevent her from marrying my father?"

And away she went to invite Philomena to join them for dinner that night — equally determined to take nothing but yes for an answer.

58 John Carrington had developed a taste for Rosewarne's export ale. Tom O'Leary had found that difficult to believe, even after — or, perhaps, especially after — he had tasted it, but John said it showed he had truly crossed the Atlantic and was now a Cornishman, through and through. There was a flagon of Rosewarne's export ale before him on the table that night. Philomena, by contrast, had confided once to Leah that a particular Saint Emilion claret called Château Clos des Jacobins was her favourite of favourites. When the merchant told Leah that it cost seven shillings a bottle she had turned pale. Nonetheless a decanter of the precious fluid, properly *chambré,* was at the woman's right hand that evening. Leah was leaving nothing to chance.

"I hear your American friend was a rather *intense* young man," Philomena said as soon as grace was over and they took their seats.

"You may say so," John responded. "He left me wondering why the British ever went into Ireland in the first place — and why they didn't march back out again singing hallelujahs the moment someone asked them nicely. No!" He put his hands over his ears. "I never even want to hear the country named again." He grinned at Philomena. "Please?"

"That's that, then," she said, a little miffed that she was to be told no more. "What shall we talk about instead?"

Will put up a finger, like a schoolboy.

"Behave!" Leah told him.

"May I introduce a topic, please?" he insisted.

"Has it any connection with the pan-Celtic nation?" his father asked warily.

Will shook his head. "Not as far as I know. It's to do with marriage ..."

"Whose?" Leah asked at once, trying to warn him with her eyes that he was trespassing and to back off.

"Mine," he said. "My engagement, anyway."

"Well now," his father said judiciously, "an engagement usually involves *two* parties. I realize that times are changing, but ..."

"It's your niece, Philomena," he said. "Adèle. I've asked her to marry me and she is thinking it over."

As soon as he spoke Adèle's name Leah looked up at Pansy, who was handing round the soup as she, Leah, filled each bowl. The girl grinned and winked back at her. The message behind that wink was much more than a 'see if I care!' it was more like 'don't imagine that's the end of what's going on between him and *me!*'

"When did this happen?" Philomena asked.

"About an hour ago. I asked her on my way home from Wheal Fortune this evening."

"And did it come as a complete shock to her? I'm sorry — perhaps 'surprise' would be a better word."

"Hardly. I've been dropping huge hints for weeks now."

"For instance?" Philomena leaned forward eagerly. "I long to know how you youngsters manage these things nowadays." She sipped her wine idly — then froze, made dainty connoisseur's smacks of her lips ... peered at the wine again, sniffed it, sipped it once more, and then — her question to Will forgotten — turned ecstatically to Leah and said, "You angel!"

Leah dipped her head modestly. "I was only testing you, actually, Philomena," she said. "Just to see if you could recognize it from a decanter, with no label to guide you."

"That was an expensive test, my dear. But you have my leave to conduct it as often as you wish!"

"We would talk, Adèle and I ..." Will began.

But another thought had crossed Philomena's mind, for she did not believe Leah would go to such trouble and expense for nothing. "Have you devised any other tests for me tonight, Leah?" she asked.

"Ah!" Leah held up a finger. "Now that would be telling, wouldn't it! There's no point in a test if you know it's coming."

"And am I left out of it?" her father asked.

"And me?" Ben put in.

"We are all being tested all the time," Leah replied in a pious tone. "Will — you were telling us how you littered the ground at Adèle's feet with hints as high as Olympus?"

Will glanced wearily at Ben, who told him, "I think marriage is the only way, old son."

Leah asked him what he meant by that.

"I mean," he explained, "that perhaps when Will is married, the rest of you will stop treating him as the baby of the family. You've all done it in the last five minutes — even Miss Liddicoat has caught the family habit."

Leah and her father were about to protest when Philomena said, "He's right. You're right, Mister Coad. We shall cease this cross-examination forthwith. Will — my humble apologies. There is no need to answer my question. I know very well how one drops such hints. One talks of one's taste in wallpapers, one's preferences among breakfast dishes ..." She hesitated a moment and then added, "... and how one would like this or that specimen placed in the garden."

John cleared his throat significantly and said, "Not in front of the children, my dear."

Philomena looked at Leah as if to say, 'Have I given you the opening you want?' And, had she actually spoken those words, she might have added, " — *before* your father's head is fuddled with ale and mine with the wine!' She clearly knew something was afoot and wanted to take over the agenda.

But Leah thought it much too early in the evening and so she demurely accepted her father's rebuke.

Will, seeing his chance, leaped in again. "It won't necessarily be a long engagement," he said. "If she accepts me, that is."

"*If* she accepts you?" Leah asked. "Don't you know she's had her heart set on you from the moment you met?" Glancing warily at Philomena she added, "And once a Liddicoat female has her heart set on one of you Carrington men, all the will-power and determination in the universe isn't going to help you! It's *pfft!*"

"I just wanted to say that, well, the fact that we're making so much money at Wheal Fortune has nothing whatsoever to do with her feelings," Will protested.

They all stared at him blankly. "Who said anything about that?" Leah asked him.

"I was about to," he explained. "That's why it won't necessarily be a long engagement. I just wondered if anybody here has any objections? If so, speak now or forever hold your peace." He looked at his father and Philomena in turn.

Leah stared again at Pansy, provoking her into asking: "Will that be all, miss?"

"For the moment, yes," Leah replied. "We'll ring if we need you. And just let me remind you — the bell rings quite loudly enough in the kitchen. You don't need to press your ear against this door to hear it."

Pansy flounced out. Leah noticed that Ben's eyes followed every wiggle and bounce — which annoyed her, just as Tom had annoyed her back in Connecticut with the same sort of behaviour. But then she saw that her father and brother did not so much as glance at the girl; indeed, their avoidance of her parade was studious. It made Ben's behaviour easier to tolerate.

"Are you asking me or your father?" Philomena said to Will.

"Either," he replied. "Or both, actually, since you each have some sort of interest."

His eyes, still darting between the pair of them, came to rest finally upon his father, who said, "I'm delighted enough to know you will no longer require an allowance, my boy. To learn that you may persuade someone to take control of all other aspects of your life is the cup that runneth over as far as I'm concerned." Then, glancing uneasily at Philomena, whose frown revealed that she considered his reply somewhat flippant, he added, "Of course, we'll have a serious sit-down before anything official is announced — going through your finances and prospects and so forth. And we must also address the question of your resumed education at the School of Mines when the war is over." He glanced again at Philomena to see if she approved.

She said, "I admit that I have — very occasionally — passed the odd critical remark about my niece Adelaide. This news, dear William, gives me the first vestige of a hope that she might buckle to and make something of her life after all. I, for my part, hope you and Adelaide will be very happy. Or" — this with a glance at Leah and Ben — "as happy as most people have any right to be."

The rest of the meal passed in light, inconsequential conversation — the sort of verbal grooming in which all well-knit families indulge. Leah did not return to her little scheme until they retired to the drawing room for coffee, by which time the claret and ale had done their mellowing work.

Her chance came when her father said, "Well, Ben, you've been rather quiet this evening. Does all this talk of marriage make you feel nervous?"

Ben shook his head. "I'd just like to be able to set the date, sir. That's all."

"Oh?" Philomena was suddenly alert. "Why so? Is the purchase of the property at Goonhusband not progressing as you had hoped, then?"

"On the contrary, Miss Liddicoat," he replied. "It has progressed with exemplary speed, In fact, apart from one small signature, it *is* completed." He smiled at Leah. "We could marry and move in tomorrow."

"So what in tarnation's name is stopping you?" John asked. "Certainly not any objection on *our* side."

Ben shrugged awkwardly and looked at Leah.

She could have hugged him there and then; he had obviously thought over their last conversation and was now improvising what assistance he could give her. "It's *deeds,* not words, that count," she replied vaguely.

He caught on at once. "Ah!" he cried, rapping his knuckles against his brow. "Is there anyone at home in here? Talking of deeds, I almost forgot. I've brought the ones you asked me to retrieve from Frank Kernow. They're in my briefcase." He rose as he spoke and went to the door. He popped out into the passage and returned a moment later with a large manila envelope, sealed and spattered with hard red wax. "I think you ought to cast an eye over them, sir, before they go to Jake Morvah. I'll put them on the bureau, shall I?"

John nodded and then, with a chuckle, said, "Neatly done, young fellow!"

Ben stared back in alarm, thinking he had given Leah's game away — whatever it was. "Sir?"

"You neatly avoided answering my question — why not set a date? And do it right now?"

"Pa!" Leah objected. Her tone suggested he was deliberately trying to embarrass them. "You know very well why."

"Do I?" he asked belligerently. "You may imagine I do, but I assure you …"

"Think!" She squirmed with embarrassment and looked apologetically at Philomena. 'Men!' said her eyes.

But Philomena took John's part. "It may be crystal clear to you, my dear," she said. "But let me say that I, too …"

"Well, it involves you, too, of course," Leah said, still embarrassed but now with a tinge of annoyance at their obtuseness. "It very much involves you — as I would have thought you, of all people …"

"Me?" she asked in a slightly wounded tone. "My dear young lady — I fail to see how your wedding and Ben's could have the remotest connection with …"

Leah interrupted her again, in the tones of one cornered and absolutely forced to speak out against her will. "How can I possibly leave the Old Glebe. Surely you can see my difficulty … things being as they are? "

"As they are? What d'you mean — 'as they are'?"

Leah gave a bitter little laugh. "Actually, I mean 'as they *aren't*'! And you know very well what I mean."

"Oh, well …" Philomena tossed her head. "*That* little matter is entirely up to your father."

"Now then, let's just everybody take it easy and calm down," John said. "This conversation has gone quite far enough. *Too* far, in fact. We'll talk of other things."

"He knows I won't budge — on a matter of principle," Philomena told Leah quietly. "But he refuses to draw the obvious conclusion from it."

"I said that's enough," John warned her.

Leah's eyes caught Ben's. He raised one eyebrow a fraction of an inch. They had rehearsed nothing, of course. Philomena would have seen through them at once if they had. She realized she had to trust him now — trust not only that he had divined her purpose but knew how to promote it, too. Fearing that Philomena might already have noticed this briefest of glances, she just sighed, and lowered her head, as if accepting her father's ordinance.

"Your pardon, sir," Ben said, "but I feel I should point out that I'm not quite as patient as my composure tonight may have led you to believe …"

"Young man," John warned him in an ominous tone. "I said 'enough' and I meant it."

But Leah, as if Ben's intervention had fired her own courage, now leaped back into the contest. "No, Pa," she said quietly. "You've been so caught up in your own difficulties that you haven't appreciated how the ripples of misery have spread. Nor have you, Philomena. This business has festered long enough. If we do not lance it tonight, we'll be throwing away the best opportunity that's ever likely to come our way."

"Talk your heads off! I shan't say a word," he replied curtly.

Leah turned her appeal toward Philomena.

The woman hesitated. She knew very well that Leah had been driving toward this point all evening — had even arranged the evening for that very purpose. But she had no idea what the girl might have in mind. So it came down to a question of trust. Could she trust Leah to further any interests but her own — and, to a lesser degree, her father's? Nothing within her leaped up and cried, 'Yes!' On the other hand, matters could not be allowed to drift much longer. Temporary stalemates had a pernicious tendency to set into permanence. Whatever Leah had in mind, it would almost certainly break the logjam. She would just have to stay astute enough to make sure the logs rolled the way she wished, that was all.

So, taking her courage in both hands, she said, in the same quiet tone as Leah's, "I think your daughter's right, John. We'll never have a better occasion than this."

He looked daggers at her. "In front of my own children?" he asked. "Are you mad?"

"When those same 'children' are talking of their own marriages, my dear, it's time to stop thinking like that."

"Talk away," he said again. "But don't expect me to take any part whatsoever."

Leah winked gratefully at Philomena and said, "Have you ever explained to him exactly why you refuse even to contemplate the idea of …"

"Him?" her father exploded. "Who's 'him'? *He* has a name, you know."

Leah repeated her question in exactly the same tone: "Have you ever explained to John Carrington why you refuse" — her father snorted angrily — "to marry him?"

"He does not require an explanation," Philomena said irritably.

"You mean because any person with just a bit of common sense could work it out himself?"

"Just so!"

Leah looked at her father, who folded his arms and stared intently at the fire, half turning his head away from his two female tormentors.

"It's a matter of pride, after all," Leah went on, as if she were now explaining Philomena to herself. "It may be a silly, distorted sort of pride but John Carrington, of all people, should understand that!"

"Yes …" Philomena agreed warily.

"I mean, one might think that nothing could be worse for a lady than to have everyone in the neighbourhood treat her as a scarlet woman. But there *is* something worse than that, isn't there! Much worse!"

Philomena did not respond. They were both watching John Carrington, who was now as tense as a steel spring and seemed hardly to be breathing. At last he became aware of their scrutiny and snapped, "Well?"

"Well, what?" Leah responded.

"Well, tell me — since you seem determined to bend my ear on this utterly distasteful subject — what could possibly be worse than to have every female tongue in Cornwall wagging away with talk of your moral turpitude?"

Leah and Philomena looked at each other. Leah said, "You tell him, then."

"Oh, no!" Philomena laughed. "You don't catch me so easily! If he *still* can't work it out, then …"

Leah cut across her and said to her father, "The thing that could be worse — and I can't honestly *believe* the thought has never once crossed your mind — would be to have those same tongues saying that she only married you to get the Old Glebe — the way the Liddicoats always wanted to get it."

John turned pale and stared at Philomena. "Tell me it isn't so," he said, barely above a whisper.

Her lips compressed to a thin, bloodless line.

"You mean you won't marry me because people would say a thing like that?"

"Yes!" she snapped.

"My God!" He stared at her, at his hands … the fire … the ceiling. "That does it, then," he said miserably.

"In what way?" Leah asked.

"Well, she'll never marry me as long as she's possessed by a crazy idea like that."

"I don't think it's crazy," Leah replied. "Nor would any woman with a streak of pride in herself — *and* more than a streak of love for the man in question."

John turned to Philomena. "This is turning into something completely unreal. I don't understand — *why* are you willing to live with me — in every sense of the word?"

"Because she *loves* you, you … you big palooka! Aargh!" Leah stood up and strode impatiently about the room. "Don't you understand anything?"

"When it comes to the ways of a woman, I've never staked the smallest claim to …"

"She loves you enough to sacrifice her honour in order to be at your side — because your own honour won't be touched by it. Men's honour never is besmirched in *that* situation, is it! In fact, the world would think you no end of a fellow. But it's *your* honour would be blackened if everyone thought she'd only married you to get her hands on this place. They'd say she hornswaggled you — or whatever the Cornish for 'hornswaggled' is. She'd be the smart skirt then, the wisenheimer of West Penwith, and you'd be the jackass. She didn't want to do that to you — don't you see? So tell her! Tell her she really ought to have explained all that to you!"

He questioned Philomena with his eyebrows.

She nodded.

He hung his head. "What a fool I am," he murmured. Then, glancing up at Philomena again, he added more robustly, "But you weren't much better — if I may speak quite frankly. D'you honestly mean to tell me that's really all that was holding you back? A little thing like ..."

"*All,* he says!" Philomena appealed to Leah.

Leah turned again to her father and said, "So?"

"So?" he responded. "What d'you expect me to do? Tell her she's been a fool as well?"

"No."

"What then?" he asked in exasperation.

"Do something that will make it completely impossible for people ever to say such a thing."

"Oh! Now why didn't I think of that?" he asked sarcastically. "I'll take a whole page in the *Helston Vindicator.* I'll tell the whole gossiping world that I am freely marrying ..."

"It wouldn't work," Leah interrupted. "Besides, there's a cheaper way."

He stared at her blankly.

"You could do it right now." She waved toward the bureau.

He followed her gesture, saw the deeds to the Old Glebe ... and turned even paler than before. "Oh, no ..." he whispered.

Slowly he turned his gaze on Philomena.

She knew exactly what he was thinking for it was what would be going through her own nasty, suspicious mind in his circumstances: Was this the culmination of a plan she had laid down in those days after their first brush with each other — when she realized that a frontal assault would never dislodge the Carringtons? And that marriage would bring her only half a loaf? And that for her, Philomena Liddicoat, half a loaf was *not* better than no bread, for she was an all-or-nothing woman. Would she now get the all and he get the nothing?

Her heart was racing so fast she was sure it could not actually be pumping any blood at all. Her whole body felt drained, weak, and shivery.

"Greater love hath no man than this ..." Leah murmured, fighting an urge to push her father ... guide his hand ...

He did not take his eyes off Philomena. "Greater love hath no man than I," he told her.

She nodded and tried not to blink, for fear that the tears in her eyes would roll. It was a futile struggle. Soon two juicy drops made tracks down her cheeks and gathered at her jawline, where she wiped them angrily away.

He rose and went across the room to the window, where he opened the curtain and peered out into the dark. A rather fitful moonlight gleamed on the fields and buildings — showing him all that he owned. Would he risk it all on what was no more than an intuition? The man of business flinched from the decision but the man in love continued to wonder. How great *was* his love? Did it measure up to this?

"By God, I'll do it!" he said, crossing the room again, this time to the bureau. "And I'll do it properly, too." He went to the door and bellowed, "Pansy!" just before he opened it.

She almost fell into the room, recovered her balance, and stood there looking sheepish.

"No need to explain it all to you, I guess," he said crisply. "I'm going to need your witness-signature. Yours, too, Ben." To Leah he added, "Honey, get pen and paper, I'm suddenly in a dictating mood."

He returned to the sofa, where he stooped and kissed Philomena on the brow. "My father is turning in his grave at this moment," he murmured.

"And so is old Honourable Carrington, too, I make no doubt," she replied.

"Tell me I won't regret it."

She shook her head. "I can't do that. It's your judgement, John. It has to be."

He sat beside her, placed the deeds symbolically in her lap, and took her hand. "I, John Carrington, being of sound mind and sober," he said to Leah, who was writing furiously at the bureau, "do hereby give in its entirety all those lands, dwellings, and outhouses known as the Old Glebe to Miss Philomena Liddicoat of Cheam. This gift I make with no consideration whatsoever in return." He drew a deep breath and closed his eyes as if in pain. And there was a hint of pain in his voice, too, as he added: "It is hers absolutely and inalienably, no matter what course she might hereafter pursue with regard to any other arrangements or understanding that may or may not presently obtain between us."

Philomena collapsed on his shoulder and whispered, "I do!" The deeds fell to the floor. Neither of them stooped to pick the envelope up.

"Wait till it's signed," he warned her.

"I don't need to …" she began but they were both startled by
a cry of anguish from Pansy: "Oh, sir! Oh, sir!" she repeated
again and again. She was panting as if she'd run a mile and the
tears were streaming down her cheeks.

"What is it, maid?" he asked in alarm.

"That was the most beautiful thing I ever heard. I can't bear
it! I can't bear it!" And, burying her face in her pinafore, she fled
from the room.

"We need you to witness!" Leah called after her, but she did
not return.

John Carrington signed the document with a flourish and
Ben witnessed it. "The mere fact that she saw it would stand up
in a court of law," he said.

"We'll still make sure," Leah told him.

She found Pansy out in the garden, holding on to the gate as if
wondering which way to run next. It was a mild night with a
waning moon holding its place among streets of high, swift-
moving clouds — though, curiously, there was hardly a breeze
at ground level. "Quick, before the nib dries," she said, handing
pen and jotting pad to the maid while she turned to 'make a
back' for her. Pansy had stopped crying by now and was sniffing
her salt-laden nostrils clear once more. "Why did the master do
that, miss?" she asked in a jerky, bewildered tone.

"Risk *everything*, you mean?"

"Yes, miss."

"It's called love, Pansy. And I think it made you cry because
you suddenly realized it's what you've been missing in your life.
Am I right?" She turned and took pen and jotter back from her.
"Am I?" she insisted.

Pansy nodded and stared at the ground.

"And as long as you persist in your present ways, you're not
likely to, either — eh?"

The girl sniffed and said she ''spected not.'

Ben came out at that moment and put his hands on Leah's
shoulders from behind. She handed the things back to Pansy.
"Take these indoors," she said. "And if my brother hasn't the
nous to leave the drawing room on some excuse, you find some
way to get him out."

Pansy started, none too willingly, back up the path. "An
excuse? Me? Like what?" she asked.

"Oh … I'm sure you'll think of *something*," Leah said heavily. Then she added, "And — remembering what we were just saying — take him anywhere except the tithe barn!"

Pansy turned round angrily and stuck her tongue out, thinking it would not be observed in the dark; but the moon and clouds betrayed her.

To avoid having to make a scene, Leah said, "And wipe that self-satisfied grin off your face!"

The offensive tongue was immediately replaced by a self-satisfied grin.

"That's better," Leah said.

When they were alone, Ben asked why she had been so specific about the tithe barn.

Leah looked at him sharply, wondering if he was being facetious. But when she saw he was not, she gave him a quick kiss on the nose and said, "Come along — I'll show you!"

Tamsin Harte

Malcolm Ross

PIATKUS

Here's to you

Mister Robertson

and at last

Mrs Robertson, too!

Contents

PART ONE
Shelter 1

PART TWO
The Facts of Life 113

PART THREE
Maiden Voyage 185

PART FOUR
An outing to France 281

Part One

The Morrab

Shelter

1 She saw them from quite a way off, strolling along the Esplanade toward her — the Father, the Mother, the Young Master hanging back a bit, trying to look as if he didn't belong, and the Dutiful Daughter, clinging to her father's arm. There were dozens of families like them in Penzance that summer but something about this particular group held Tamsin's eye. Step by step, as they drew nearer, she began to evaluate them, as she was learning to do with everybody nowadays.

Paterfamilias, as he doubtless called himself, ought not to wear those mutton-chop whiskers; they were far too straggly and thin. And too pale to count. The cream blazer with the broad red stripes was a mistake, too; it made his face look all bleached and it showed up the ancient straw of his boater. Still, he could be quite rich. Men so careless of their person and dress often were.

Matriarch was a little harder to pin down (as her maid probably said to herself each day). Any woman of mature years who could choose to go abroad by day in an outfit like that was either devoid of all taste and sense or she was so rich she could afford to do it for a lark. The skirt was borrowed from a hospital matron; the blouse from a French matelot, collar and all; and the hat from Ascot, 1899 — eight years out-of-date (and ten out-of-fashion even back then). She could at least have chosen *white* gloves; what was going through her mind when she selected the lavender instead?

Young Master was interesting, though — and only partly because he had just set eyes on her and now, seemingly, could not take them off again. He stood two inches taller at once and began to walk with a swagger. The Man who Broke the Bank at Monte Carlo. He may have been of their flesh but he was of a different mould. For a start, he had a keen sense of dress and fashion, with his tapering trousers and spotless kid spats over white leather shoes, and his white blazer with silk edges and thin stripes, both of a blue to make you notice his eyes, and his blue cotton square tied with nonchalant care to thrust aside the dazzling ramparts of his shirt, which had fashionably short,

rounded collars — the first she had seen in Penzance this
summer. And then there was his neat, military moustache with
its waxed points, pricked in perfect symmetry, and his merciless
but very kissable lips, and …

But that was enough, or he'd start leaping to all the wrong
conclusions. Tamsin would never be interested in him, except as
a means to an end. Everything and everyone was just that
nowadays — a means to an end.

The Dutiful Daughter was the most interesting of all. The
long, white, virginal dress, short enough to show schoolgirlish
ankles in patent white kid boots, told of one who had not as yet
come out. The red sash revealed a desire to complement, if not
compliment, the Paterfam. The sailor collar might have done
the same for the Matriarch if it had not been so obviously more
appropriate for the younger female herself. And the straw
boater, worn at the same insouciant angle as her elder brother's,
might indicate a touching desire not to leave him out of these
flattering sartorial quotations, either. In short — a girl so
incapable of making up her own mind that she borrowed willy
nilly from the little world around her.

Perfect!

Tamsin blessed the instinct that had led her to the Esplanade
this afternoon.

She gazed out to sea, wondering which of those lobstermen
were hauling cognac today — and which of those French barques
had dropped it — until the little family drew level. Then she
'noticed' Young Master's eyes upon her and gave an impatient
toss of her head. Pater and Mater, having already sailed by, saw
nothing, but Dutiful D, turning to smile at her big bro, caught
the gesture and giggled. Twenty paces farther on they both
turned and looked back at Tamsin again. She saw them reflected
in the glass of the shelter where she sat, for an obliging woman
in widow's weeds had seated herself in the other bay, on the far
side of that glass, turning it into a mirror.

"Some high-quarter folk, they!" said an old man at her other
side, a man she had barely noticed until now.

A seaman, perhaps, to judge by his blazer and roll-neck
pullover, both navy blue. Did he have 'Saucy Sal' stitched across
the chest?

No.

Still, the salt-tanned skin and yachtsman's cap said Old Man of the Sea.

"Do I know you?" she asked, meaning to cut him for his impertinence.

"Benny Peters," he said and touched the peak of his cap with the tip of his thumb.

She hesitated. Benny Peters? It rang a bell. One of the housemaids had mentioned the name only yesterday. A tragedy at sea ... a drowning ... the loss of two sons? Tamsin had listened with only half an ear. But her present hesitation lost her the indignant moral ground from which she could have spurned his advance.

"Miss Harte," she said. She even managed a smile.

"So what does Miss Tamsin Harte think to *they* folk, then?" He jerked his head after the family group, who were now half way toward the end of the constitutional mile.

"You know my name?" she replied.

"I've heard tell of 'ee — you and your mother. Plymouth folk, they do say."

"Do they!"

"High-quarter folk fallen on harder times, they do say."

"*They* do say an awful lot, it would seem."

"Not true, then, is it?"

"It's none of your business!"

"That's a fack and no mistake." He chuckled.

She could not feel as cross with him as his impudence demanded; he was so mild and jovial.

"I only thought as one high-quarter young lady might have a better eye for what you might call the niceties of the situation than what I got. That's all. Sorry I spoke, I'm sure."

"Oh, I didn't mean to be rude ..."

He bounded back at once: "So what do'ee reckon, then? High quarter or not?" Again he jerked his head toward the family group. "Hardly can't see 'em now."

"Hard to tell," Tamsin said. She still felt awkward at discussing people of quality with *hoi polloi* — though she did it perforce with the chambermaids, Bridget and Catherine, almost every day of the week.

" 'Tis the new sport in Cornwall," he said. "Tellin' apples from horseapples."

"So what d'you reckon to them?" She, too, nodded after the strolling family. She injected a little experimental tinge of Cornish into her voice — educated Cornish, of course, or else she would have said, 'to they.'

"They'm worth more'n they do show," he replied. "That's a fack, that is."

"You think so?" She made herself appear mildly surprised, though, of course, she had reached the same conclusion herself. Surprised and admiring.

Her condescension flattered him into an explanation he might not otherwise have bothered to give. "See they five there?" He inclined his head toward another family — a boy, a young man, a girl in-between, and their parents — walking up from the Newlyn end; the mother was glancing right and left with ferret eyes. All were in brand-new summer outfits. "That's new money, that is," the Old Salt added. "First generation."

"Parvenus!" She laughed. "You come down here to play the same game as me, Mister Peters!"

"How's that, then, Miss Harte?"

"Guessing which niche to put each Tom, Dick, and Mary into. How far d'you go?"

He winked. "All the way, maid — if I'm left."

Six months earlier, Miss Tamsin Harte of Elburton Villa, Plymouth, might well have slapped his face for such gross insolence; but that Miss Tamsin Harte had been in the market for an eligible husband — who would want his wife to be as unsullied by the vulgarity of the world as possible. *This* Miss Tamsin Harte, however, could no longer afford to hold herself so aloof; vulgarity had to be renamed — re-evaluated, in fact, as part of life's rich rough-and-tumble. Her livelihood now depended on it.

So all this new Miss Tamsin Harte did was dig him in the ribs with one finger and say, "Now, now! None of that. Don't you try to guess their trades and occupations? Take this *parvenu* family, now — what d'you think *he* does for a living?"

"Attorney's clerk? Floor walker? Highways surveyor? That sort o' caper. How about th'others — the high-quarter lot?"

"My guess is the father doesn't work at all. He's 'consoled up to the eyeballs,' as my father used to say, God rest him."

"Ay-men," Peters said automatically. "And the young 'un — the one as couldn't take his eyes off of 'ee?"

"Really? I wasn't looking too closely."

"'Course not. Still, you got some opinion, I speck?"

"He's still at school, I'm sure — not for the lessons but for the sake of the football. The 'Idle Rich,' eh — what a life!"

"'Twas yourn once, so I heard tell."

"What I meant was it's no sort of life at all, Mister Peters."

He chuckled. "So if some ol' piskey now was to jump out o' thin air and offer 'ee such a life back again, you'd say no thank'ee, Mister, would 'ee?"

"If it meant bringing my father back to life, then ..."

"That's not what I meant — and you do know it very well."

She insisted: "I was going to say that *even* if it meant bringing my father back, I'd say 'no thank'ee, Mister' if it also meant I had to go back to living in idleness." She looked him up and down. "I think you'd have said the same at my age. You may live in idleness now but I can see you've *earned* it. You deserve it. That's different."

"Now we're cutting closer to the bone!" He sat up straighter and rubbed his hands. "What would 'ee do, then, maid — with all the piskey's gold you could carry?"

"Oh, what *wouldn't* I do!"

"Such as?"

She wondered whether to tell him her secret. Then she thought why not? After all, it was nothing to be ashamed of — they were quite alone in this bay of the shelter and there was no one else within earshot.

Her eyes strayed beyond him, fixing on a point near the western end of the Esplanade. "I'd build an hôtel," she told him. "Just there — where there's a vacant lot. The best hôtel in Cornwall. Better than the Tregenna Castle. Better than the Falmouth Hôtel. Better even than the Queen's." She nodded toward it, for it stood directly opposite the shelter, on the landward side of the Esplanade. Then, feeling she had bared too much, she laughed and added, "I don't need your piskey gold, though. I'll have it all one day, you'll see. I've already started saving up." She opened her purse and showed him two sixpences. "There!"

He laughed, too, but she realized he wasn't entirely fooled into dismissing it as just one of those passing-cloud dreams.

"Two tanners!" he said. "I had two tanners once. 'Bout your age, I was, too. And I belonged to dream of a vessel of my own — just like you and your hôtel."

"And did you get it?"

He raised his walking stick and aimed it like a telescope at a fishing boat, about two miles out. "The *Merlin*. My son do sail 'er now. My son David, that is, my little Benjamin."

She knew then that her earlier half-memory had been correct. He was, indeed, the Benny Peters who had lost two sons at sea.

Meanwhile he reached out and gave her wrist a hesitant squeeze. "It can be done, maid."

"If you're a man," she said, "yes. A man can go off whaling, or drilling for oil in Texas, or hunting diamonds on the African coast … I know all the ways a *man* can fund his dreams."

"I went whaling, me," he said, not even pausing to offer token sympathy for her plight. "And there was a maid along of us — though none knew it. 'Course, she bound her chest and cut her hair … and chawed baccy and swore worse'n any man aboard."

The possibility intrigued Tamsin, though not in any practical sense. "But if none of the crew knew of it …" she began.

"Till we come ashore," he added.

"And then?"

He grinned and patted his breastbone.

"And then?" she insisted.

"Well," he replied, "let's just say that if I *hadn't* found her out, 'twould be some other son by some other woman out there now." He gestured vaguely toward his boat.

The Idle Rich, having reached the end of the Esplanade, by the pasture earmarked for Tamsin's dream-hôtel, had turned and were starting to stroll back again.

Benny Peters, seeing that her eyes rarely strayed from them for long, said, "I daresay *they* got 'nuff money for your hôtel, just in loose change round the house."

"People like that?" She laughed thinly. "They wouldn't even give me the time of day."

"Ah!" He raised a finger and grinned knowingly. "That would depend, now."

"On what?"

"On your nimbleness of wit — that's what." He glanced all about them, including through the glass behind, where two boys were crossing the road. One was carrying a bucket and the other had two spades, to dig for lugworm bait. He turned to her quickly and said, "Would it be worth one o' they tanners to become 'persona greater,' as they say — with the Idle Rich? Yes or no — quick?"

"Yes!" She swallowed heavily, for sixpence was a small fortune to her — a week's tip from a guest at their boarding house. "Yes," she said again, just in case she changed her mind.

"Give it us, then." He held out his hand and then, raising his voice: "Boy! Come 'ere!"

The boys were going to ignore him until they caught sight of the silver coin. "I was first," said the first to arrive.

"Mebbe you won't be so keen when you do hear what you must do to earn 'n," the old man said. "See these four fine-feathered folk coming up? When they do reach the steps 'ere, they'll go down to the beach. The boy who earns this tanner" — he wafted it under their noses like toasted cheese — "is to throw sand at the young maid's dress. And this maid 'ere" — he jerked a thumb at Tamsin — "she'll be right behind of 'ee, and she'll clip thee round the lug'ole and tell 'ee to be off. And she'll say she knows your mother and she's gwin to tell on 'ee. And all you do do is run off, baalin' like a calf on a dry cow. *Now* who do want the tanner?"

The first volunteer lost interest; his companion stepped into the breach and tried to claim his reward now.

But the old dog made it disappear with a magician's flourish. "Forehand pay is the worst pay of all," he said. "You shall have 'n once you've done your half o' the bargain. Step lively now — here they come!"

Tamsin held her breath. Half of her wanted to carry out this exciting plan; the other half longed to take back the sixpence and run all the way home.

The moment the family started down the steps, she asked old Peters how he knew they'd do that.

"They belong to do it every day 'bout this-here time," he replied simply. "Go on now, maid. Carpet dee-em!"

For a moment she thought he was going to place a hand behind her b-t-m and propel her out of the shelter (and, for a moment, he even considered it, too). All he did, however, was take her elbow delicately between finger and thumb and gently ease her on her way.

The world swam around her as she crossed to the edge of the Esplanade. She had to keep swallowing, because her heart seemed to be trying to climb up out of her throat. She also had to keep remembering to breathe out.

The bribed boy came down behind her; his companion wisely stayed by the railings at the top, guarding the bucket and spades. The lad wasted no time but picked up a handful of dripping wet sand as soon as he reached the bottom of the steps, where the last tide had scooped out a small pool. He was no fool, either, for he threw that first handful directly at her, Tamsin. *Thwack!* it went, right between her shoulderblades. She had no need to *act* her outraged cry.

But even as she turned, a second handful went whizzing by and hit the Dutiful Daughter square on her left thigh — and with enough impact to stick to her dress, her dazzling white dress, and leave a dark-grey streak all the way to the ground.

"You little devil!" Tamsin cried as she ran toward him, again without calling on her thespian reserves.

He was good, though. He stood, apparently aghast at his own miscalculation, until she was close enough to fetch him one good wallop. Then he fled like the wind.

"I know you!" she called after him. "I know where you live! I'll make you laugh on the other side of your face!"

She turned to the Idle Rich. "Sir! Madam! I am so sorry!" To the daughter she repeated the words: *"So* sorry! Here — let me see what can be done."

She ran to the girl and, without a by-your-leave, began brushing away the clinging sand.

The girl, embarrassed, kept trying to say it was not necessary, that the sand was clean and would surely leave no mark once it dried … and then she, in turn, started to brush the sand off Tamsin's back.

The sight was, apparently, comical enough to set the other three laughing — at which the two girls stopped their mutual grooming and joined in.

The Young Master's eyes were on the boy, still, who was running to the far end of the beach. He was the first to speak. "What is that little wretch's name, Miss … er?"

Tamsin bit her lip. "Did I call him a d-e-v-i-l?" she asked, spelling out the cuss-word. "Do forgive me, *je vous en prie!* I was just so *angry.*" To him she replied, "I don't actually know his name. I just said that to frighten him. But I have a fair notion where he lives, so he shan't escape chastisement, Mister … er?"

The mother smiled and relaxed somewhat. This young lady obviously had enough *savoir faire* not to introduce herself to a gentleman before he had done her the same courtesy. "Allow me to present my children," she said. "This is my son, Victor Thorne, and his sister, Charlotte."

"Tamsin Harte." She bowed her head in Victor's direction and offered her hand to Charlotte, who shook it eagerly.

This emboldened Tamsin to offer her hand to Mrs Thorne, too, though she responded with somewhat less enthusiasm. Her husband made up for it, though. She had an inkling that this was the most exciting thing that had happened to them for weeks.

"Would you care to walk a little with us, Miss Harte?" Victor asked. "The sea breeze is so pleasant today and it will help dry off your beautiful dress."

He spoke in jest, surely, for this vaunted sea breeze smelled of low tide and dead sea creatures.

"You have a companion?" Mrs Thorne asked as she scanned the esplanade. "A lady's maid, perhaps?"

This, Tamsin realized, was the moment when it might all come crashing down around her. There was nothing for it but to take the point head-on. "Ah, Mrs Thorne, those days are over for me, I fear."

The woman frowned. "How so?"

"Once I dwelt in marble halls," she replied gaily, stretching the truth a little. "My father was one of the most respected shipping merchants in Plymouth. Indeed, in the West Country." She waved a lordly hand eastwards. "False modesty aside — he *was* the most respected one in Plymouth. He employed sixty clerks and we had a villa on fifty acres at Elburton." She smiled, as if that were the end of the tale.

"And?" Mr Thorne prompted.

She shrugged and said, "Smash."

Then, seeing they did not understand (which was, in itself, understandable), she added, "My mother and I now own a guest house in Morrab Road." She waved a hand vaguely in the right direction. "A most superior guest house, to be sure, but undeniably a guest house nonetheless." She smiled at the mother. "I suppose you'd rather I didn't walk with you now? Believe me, I'd quite understand."

It was the simple truth but Mrs Thorne naturally felt obliged to deny that such a snobbish thought had so much as crossed her mind. Her husband and children chimed in with more genuine enthusiasm. Charlotte even took her arm to prove it.

Victor, who looked as if he'd like to join in on the other side, was still keeping an eye on the boy, Tamsin noticed. His lips looked even more kissable close-to. The lad had now run to the far end of the beach and was climbing the steps to the promenade (which, for some reason, did not become the Esplanade for another three or four hundred yards).

"To tell the truth …" Tamsin began, and then thought better of it.

"Yes?" Charlotte squeezed her arm encouragingly.

"Well, I was heartbroken when Papa died — naturally — especially when his death revealed that we were almost penniless. I thought there was surely nothing left to live for … everything gone …"

"But you have kept your faith?" Mrs Thorne tried putting the words into her mouth; that little hesitation had bothered her. "You believe that God is working in His own mysterious way."

"Of course," Tamsin agreed. "And that faith you mention has been richly rewarded, too. You may dismiss it as sour grapes but I assure you — I would not go back to our old way of life, now, not if …" She hunted for some image strong enough to convince. "Not if the celebrated Cornish piskey were to pass his bottomless purse into my keeping — there!"

She could feel her words had stirred Charlotte somewhat. The tension communicated itself directly. But Mrs Thorne was staring at her in disbelief. "You mean to say you actually *prefer* filling your house with inferior strangers and waiting on them hand and foot?" she asked.

"Well, Mrs Thorne, I don't exactly wait on them. We have servants for that — as many as we ever employed living-in at Elburton, I suppose. No, I supervise the running of the house while my mother looks after the books and the kitchen. I had no idea that the world is such an interesting place and is full of such interesting people, inferior or no! I would not go back to those endless garden parties and yacht-club balls and croquet afternoons and" — she shuddered at the word — *"cricket!"*

"Steady the Buffs!" Victor complained.

"Plays for Devon sometimes," Charlotte murmured, suppressing a giggle.

"Oh, I should love to *play* cricket," Tamsin protested. "It's the sitting on the boundary and watching it all happen a couple of hundred yards away that bores me."

"I think we should turn about now," Mrs Thorne said. "We are probably keeping Miss Harte from her, ah, exciting duties?"

"Not a bit, Mrs Thorne — though it is so kind of you to consider it. I work mornings and evenings. The afternoons are all my own. I am often down here on the beach or the Esplanade." She squeezed Charlotte's arm to make sure she understood why she was dropping this pearl of information.

Charlotte squeezed back.

They turned and began their return stroll to the steps. Victor was pleased at this, for now he could watch the boy without having to turn round.

Mrs Thorne monopolized the conversation most of the way, outlining the many planned excursions she and her brood would be making over the coming days, all, alas, to places that would not allow her, Tamsin, time enough to get back for her evening duties. So unfortunate! Tamsin suspected that the planning had all taken place within the past thirty seconds. She remembered how she herself had once been able to cut unwanted people from her life by assuring them that they must all meet for a good chinwag one day soon.

When they reached the steps, Charlotte looked down at her dress and said, "It's quite dry."

Tamsin brushed away all that had not already fallen of its own accord and said, "There! It's as if it had never happened."

She smiled at Mrs Thorne as she spoke. The woman seemed to take it as a promise not to presume upon their accidental acquaintance and too-hasty introductions; she smiled back happily. "I do hope we run across each other again, Miss Harte," she said, carefully not extending her hand.

"After you have completed all your adventurous excursions," Tamsin agreed. "We can have a good old chinwag about it."

She let go of Charlotte's arm, reassuring her with one last squeeze, and glanced toward Victor, who, she decided, might be quite fun, actually, for a brief summer fling. And if he were rich in his own right … no, best not to think *too* far ahead.

Victor was still watching that wretched boy. Her eyes followed his and she saw that Mr Peters had come forward and was now leaning on the rails — much too close to the stairhead for the youngster's comfort. He kept plucking at the old man's sleeve and glancing back over his shoulder to see if they were coming to get him.

When the promised sixpence changed hands, they had drawn close enough for anyone on the lookout to see it. Victor, who had been on the lookout ever since the incident itself, chuckled and glanced at Tamsin. Finding her eyes upon him, he gave her a reassuring wink.

Deception, she had just discovered — even a petty deception like this — is something of a two-edged sword.

2   When David Peters walked into the kitchen with a half-dozen fresh mackerel for their tea he called out to his father, "I saw *you* this afternoon."

"I seen 'ee, too," the old man replied as he came down the passage. "Out there. And I never needed no spyglass, neither." He sniffed at the fish, which were already gutted and scaled. "Call they wisht little things mackerel, do'ee?"

David ignored the taunt. "What's her name, then?" he asked as he picked off a few lingering scales around the gills of a couple of them.

" 'Oo?"

"You know who — the pretty maid in the white dress, that's who. Lucky I had the spyglass today and not the old woman!"

Benny started guiltily and put his finger to his lips.

"It's all right," David assured him. "I saw her next door with Mrs Oates." He laid the fish out head to tail to head to tail. "These would make a good starry-gazey pie."

"You wouldn't be interested in the likes of that young maid," he told his son. "Anyway, she'd not give 'ee a second look."

"She spent enough breath on you."

"That's as maybe. *You* wouldn't hardly be interested," Benny said again. "And no more would she." He refused to be drawn any further.

He had his reasons, too.

Victor Thorne, dressed for dinner, tapped lightly on his sister's boudoir door.

"Victor?" she called out.

He let himself in, closing the door silently behind him.

"You can do up my pearls," she said. Then, to her maid, "All right, Dobbs. Just make sure everything's in order for tomorrow and then, if Mrs Harper doesn't need you tonight, you may take the rest of the day off."

The 'day' in question had already lasted thirteen hours.

"Miss Harte has frightened dear Mama out of her wits," Victor said when they were alone. "D'you think there's any danger she might actually arrange for us to go on all those dismal excursions?"

"Well — what do *you* think of her?" Charlotte asked, smiling at him archly.

"That was going to be my first question to you," he replied.

"But I got in ahead of you." She waited while he pretended that the clasp to her brooch demanded all his attention. "Go on!" she had to say at last.

"I'm thinking," he said.

"I don't believe you. I'm sure you already know precisely what you think about the young lady. I know *I* do."

"Not thinking about that," he replied.

"About what, then?"

"About whether to discuss her with you at all. All right — I'll risk it. She rigged the whole thing, you know. And that old sea salt was in cahoots with her."

Charlotte, torn between wondering what he was talking about and why he would have reservations about speaking his mind to her, asked, "What does that mean?"

"In cahoots? It means they were in league with … they were in it together."

"No! I know very well what the *words* mean, but …"

"I'm telling you they bribed that urchin to pretend to throw stuff at her and to hit you instead. I could read it in his eyes. And later I saw the old man give him a threepenny bit — or it could even have been a sixpence. I wonder if he's some sort of relation of hers? Anyway, that whole scene was rigged."

"But why?"

"Why d'you think?" He tweaked the fine points of his rampant waxed moustachioes and surveyed himself in her looking glass.

"Are you asking me?" Charlotte said.

"Not really." He was plainly satisfied with his image.

"Well, I'll tell you, anyway. Contrary to *your* conceited opinion in the matter, I think she did it all in order to become acquainted with *me!* So there!"

"I suppose we all need our daydreams," he replied loftily, "but I always find that fantasies which lack even the faintest grounding in reality are just so unsatisfactory. That's my humble opinion, anyway. I could tell with half a glance that it is, in fact, *me* with whom she wishes to become acquainted. In fact, *more* than merely acquainted, I hope."

"Such airs, Maggie!" Charlotte told her favourite doll. "*You* know it's me she's interested in. And *I* know it's me. So that's all that matters. Let us leave him blinded by his own vanity."

"Well, there's one sure way to settle the business," Victor said. He had, of course, intended provoking some such argument from the outset.

"What's that?"

"Shall we take a little stroll along the Esplanade tomorrow afternoon, sister dear?"

*   *   *

Tamsin intended saying nothing to her mother of that afternoon's encounter with the Thornes. The trickery involved in engineering the meeting would give the poor woman a seizure. But Harriet Harte had already been told something of it by their neighbour, Mr Vissick, who ran Chynoweth, the guest house next door. She was now eager to hear more.

"Tell me about Mister Peters, dear," were her first words after they sat down to dine that evening. "Do the Peterses know anyone we know? Or knew?"

The thought that Mrs Peters, the woman who cut off her hair and bound her breasts to go whaling — and who drank and cussed worse than any man aboard — might have any friends in common with her mother was just too comical. Tamsin had to struggle not to laugh.

But she also needed time to discover how much her mother already knew, for she would have to tailor her own story to that.

Now it so happened that dinner was the one daily occasion on which Harriet Harte would not countenance the slightest mention of business; all such affairs, no matter how urgent, had to wait until the moment when, if there had been gentlemen present, she and her daughter would have retired to the drawing room. 'One may be poor,' she often said, 'but one still has to maintain one's standards wherever possible.'

So Tamsin replied, "Most of what I could tell you would have to wait until after we retire to the drawing room, Mama."

This fitted a common turn in their nightly talks with each other. Tamsin felt that her mother's restriction on commercial conversation belonged to their former life of leisure and frivolity; here, now, in their present straitened circumstances, it merely got in the way of all sensible dialogue. She often said as much, too, so her mother's hackles were well primed to rise at this first hint of tonight's instalment.

"Don't be absurd," she snapped. Then, curbing her annoyance and forcing herself to seem jocular once more, "Next you'll be telling me you engaged in *commercial* conversation with him — a total stranger!"

Tamsin smiled apologetically, "And if I did? We'd still have to wait until we reached the sanctity of the drawing room. Or — God send the day! — are you beginning to see sense at last? Are you now saying you *want* to hear about it? Commercial or not?"

Her mother, realizing she'd been led into a trap, said nothing. Her lips worked as if she were chewing vigorously — although she had not yet taken up a single spoonful of the fish soup before her.

Her daughter tasted a morsel. "No one can cook seafood half so well as Mrs Pascoe," she said.

Her mother did not know it but this was, in fact, the first shot of her daughter's latest campaign to improve their income. "One does not discuss such things either at table, dear," she replied. "You know that. And it's 'half *as* well,' anyway."

"One did not discuss them in the days when one's livelihood did not depend upon it. I know *that.*"

"We shall maintain our standards for as long as we are able."

"However inappropriate they may be?"

Harriet fell silent again, though the excellence of Mrs Pascoe's fish soup had almost tricked her into agreeing.

Tamsin persisted. "And even if it actually *harms* us?"

Still silence.

"I declare that if the house went on fire, you'd not let me run out of doors before putting on my gloves!"

"Who says a whale's a bird?" her mother responded lightly. It was a family saying — meaning 'you are no longer talking any sense so let's change the subject.'

After a further silence, Harriet said, "I merely wondered how you happened to engage in conversation with Mister Peters in the first place."

"You mean did I break the ice or did he?"

"'Break the ice'? Where do you pick up such lamentable expressions?"

"Which would be more dreadful in your eyes — me speaking to him first, or him speaking to me?"

"Tamsin, dear, I am trying my best to be pleasant and civil. Anyway, the correct English is *my* speaking first — not *me* speaking first."

"It's a wonder anyone can speak at all, sometimes," Tamsin said to no one in particular. "While you are merely trying to be civil, I, on the other hand, am trying my best to *make* something of our present situation."

"Oh? And do you suppose I am not?"

Tamsin adopted a conciliatory tone. "I'm sure that, by your own lights, Mama dear, you are. But your lights warn of rocks we have already left far behind us. We sail in new, uncharted waters now, and there is so much more we could be doing — *should* be doing."

"If your father were still alive ..." Harriet's lip trembled. But then she recalled that appeals to the dead father's memory had been proving less and less rewarding lately. Her lips compressed to a thin, bitter line. "... you wouldn't be talking to me like this," she concluded.

"If Papa were still alive," Tamsin said, "we should still have lost all our money. We should still have bought this place, or something very like it. And we should be doing our very best to recover our fortune."

"Then where's the difference? You still seem to be implying I'm *not* doing my best. I demean myself every single hour in this hateful business." Harriet shuddered at being forced to utter the dreaded word. "Your father would call you a most ungrateful child, I'm sure."

"Well, Mama, there we must agree to differ."

"You wouldn't be speaking like this — I know that."

"I quite agree with you — but not for the same reason. I think Papa would already be doing all the things that we are neglecting — things I'd like to see us doing."

"Oh! You keep trying to worm the conversation round to topics that you *know* are unseemly at a civilized dinner table — it is most vexatious!"

"This house, this *business,* is our ..."

"Tamsin! Stop it this instant! I will not tolerate commercial discourse at my dinner table. I never have done and I never shall. So please respect my wishes, young lady. *I* know you're far too old to be sent to bed without supper — so try to behave as if *you* knew it, too."

Tamsin wondered whether or not to develop a convenient headache. She decided against it, recalling that that particular tactic had been proving less and less rewarding lately. Instead she remarked, "I thought the Morrab Gardens looked especially lovely this morning."

"Yes, dear." Her mother agreed eagerly, glad to see her daughter was being sensible at last. "It must have been the overnight rain. The green — so bright!"

"And so *many* greens. That is their glory, of course — the infinite variety."

"The thought crossed my mind the very first time I saw them."

"Every green in the box."

"Just so."

"Viridian, emerald, leaf green ..."

"Yes, dear — we can agree that there are many greens to be found there."

"Chrome green, olive green, sage green ... even khaki, I shouldn't wonder ..."

"Tamsin!" Harriet rang the bell for Bridget, the maid, to collect their soup bowls and serve the main dish, which was cold cuts of yesterday's beef joint with sautéed mashed potatoes and new season's maincrop peas.

Several minutes later, after Bridget had withdrawn again, Tamsin said, "And then there are all the greens you can get by mixing. Chrome green and emerald, for instance, would give you the green of that cactus by the first terrace."

"Tamsin!"

"Yes, Mama?"

"I shall hurl something at your head in a moment."

"You mean not talk any more about greens?"

"Not another word."

"Very well."

They ate in silence — and with relish, for Mrs Pascoe was pretty good at roast beef, too. Then Tamsin said, "Of course, what shows them off so well is the rich *brown* of the soil and the multicoloured *greys* you get in the granite. One forgets how important grey is in any colour scheme."

Harriet recalled how, when Tamsin had cried as a little girl in the nursery, Nanny Pickford had cured it by cupping her ear and singing out, 'Loud-er! I can't he-ar you. More!' and, of course, poor bewildered little Tamsin had soon dried up. So now, in that same spirit, she said, "I know so little about the truly artistic mixing of colours, darling. Do tell me — it sounds absolutely fascinating, I must say."

"One thinks of grey as just the simple blending of lamp black and flake white," the girl replied. She knew very well what her mother was about but she was determined to win this one — eventually. "Yet in the right hands it can become the subtlest colour of all. Take the colour sold as 'Payne's Grey' ..."

It was the start of an impromptu verbal essay that lasted until, had there been gentlemen present, the ladies would have retired to the drawing room. Long before it was over, Harriet was listening in genuine fascination — not so much at the content but at her daughter's ability to keep it going. George, her late husband, had compared their daughter to the eternal drip that can wear away the strongest granite — which, of course, made it all the more important to keep her under control now.

As she'd said to Mr Vissick next door, when he told her of the encounter on the Esplanade that afternoon, "She's still a girl in a woman's outer form. She's young. She's headstrong. She's missing her father much more than she'll ever admit to. And, through some misguided form of bravado, she's actually embracing our decline in fortune as if it were the finest thing that could possibly have happened. She used to love balls and picnics and amateur theatricals and parties of every sort — as any young girl ought, indeed, to do. But now she'll pretend it used to weary her beyond all measure. She'll tell you she'd far rather be supervising the maids and dealing with guests — some of whom, as I'm sure you know very well, dear Mister Vissick, are dreadfully common persons — and indulging all sorts of commercial fantasies."

Mr Vissick tut-tutted sympathetically. Normally he would have glanced in horror at his watch by now and rushed off pleading the call of duty. But he was a widower — and not happy at it — and Mrs Harte was a handsome woman, alone in the world ... and the two houses, run together, would make an admirable private hôtel. So he fixed her with a large and sympathetic gaze and tut-tutted avidly.

"Of course, it will pass," Harriet went on. "The novelty of our new way of life will wear off while the drudgery remains. Then she'll meet a handsome young fellow with an income and prospects, who will sweep her off her feet and remind her where a woman's duty and best interests lie. And somehow" — she sighed — "we must contrive to keep the lid on things until that happy day."

The moment she heard herself say 'keep the lid on things' she regretted the phrase. More and more these days — and for reasons she could not divine — common and even slangy expressions were creeping into her speech. To say nothing of Tamsin's. While she struggled to think of a respectable alternative, words like 'assuage ... mollify ... propitiate ...' flitted through her mind but refused to settle. Vissick saw his chance. His parting words were: "If there's anything I might do ..." Later, Harriet wondered how he might have finished that sentence if he had stayed.

'It will pass,' she would say to herself whenever Tamsin's forceful personality threatened to sweep everyone else up in her enthusiasms. 'This is not the real Tamsin. She will calm down soon — O Lord, pray let it be soon! — and she will forget all this nonsense.'

She found herself rehearsing silent incantations to more or less that effect throughout the rest of their meal.

"Now!" she said magnanimously as they settled to a final cup of tea in the drawing room. "What have you been bursting to tell me all this while?"

"Oh, it hardly matters now," Tamsin replied curtly. "It's gone off the boil."

"Oh good!" Harriet took out a box of bonbons. "Just for that you may have *two* tonight."

Tamsin took one and said that, hot or cold, she'd better state the facts, just in case Mr Vissick's no-doubt third-hand account had got it all wrong.

"I was sitting in the shelter there — I didn't even notice this old sea dog beside me. But after a while — you know how one does — we got chatting and he ..."

"What about? Who started it?"

"Does it matter? There were several hundred people all around us, if that's what worries you. Oh, I remember now! There was this family — father, mother, daughter about my age, son a couple of years older — and they were obviously a cut above your average day tripper."

"Indeed?" Harriet's attention doubled suddenly.

"Yes. Old clothes — holiday clothes — nothing fashionable — except Victor, of course — the son. He's a real masher ..."

"Victor?" Harriet almost screamed. The horror of that vulgarism, 'masher,' was entirely swallowed up inside the larger horror of the Christian name. "You knew them? They were our friends once? But I don't remember a young Victor ..."

"*Calme-toi, chère Maman!* I didn't know them from Adam — not then, anyway."

"So when *did* you ...?"

"If you'll only listen, I'll tell you! The old sea dog, whose name is Benny Peters, by the way — a retired fisherman of Newlyn, but a man with a thousand tales of adventures on the seven seas, I feel sure — anyway, he made some remark about them."

"A remark? A low fisherman making *remarks* about his betters? Tamsin! Did you permit it? What were you thinking of? I hope you put a flea in his ear? I mean ... oh, botheration!"

"D'you wish to hear about this family or not?"

"Oh ... very well — go on. But I warn you — I don't warm to one single element in this tale so far."

"Captain Peters" — she decided to promote him, to ease her mother's mind — "likes to play this harmless but amusing little game. He sits in that shelter on the Esplanade and he tries to sum people up by their dress, their demeanour, the way they walk, and so on."

"And how does he know whether or not he's right?"

"He doesn't need to. It's only a game — and if you think about it, we're all playing it, all the time. Anyway, he said he was sure that the members of this unfashionably dressed family were 'high-quarter folk,' as he put it. So I followed them down the steps to the beach, hoping to overhear them — to see if he was right, you understand."

"Tamsin!"

"It was only a game, Mama. However, some wretched little urchin took exception to a remark I made — I told him not to splash about in the pool near the foot of the steps. So he threw a sandball at me — which missed and hit Charlotte instead. She's the daughter. Charlotte Thorne."

"Thorne?" Harriet's ears pricked up at the name. "Mrs Cunningham, who came from Dawlish Warren, she was a Thorne —

originally from Somerset. Yeomen farmers but they made their money out of quarrying that glorious honey-coloured limestone. I wonder if that's them? Go on." She suddenly remembered they had left Charlotte with a wet sandball on her dress. "Oh, good heavens! What did you do?"

"I apologized, of course, introduced myself ..."

"And, of course, they could hear at once that you are one of *us* and not one of *them!*"

"And we went for a little stroll along the beach — and that was all."

"All? Did Mister Thorne not give you a card for me? Will they call upon us?"

"I doubt it. I must say they seem to have planned a remarkably busy holiday."

"But you cannot possibly pursue a friendship with people who have not called upon your parents! Or parent, in our case. It's quite unthinkable."

"I said nothing about a friendship. It was a casual encounter on a holiday beach. It had an unfortunate beginning but a happy ending — I mean, we parted on good terms."

"But ...'Victor' and 'Charlotte' ... You seem familiar with their Christian names yet you call it a casual encounter? How can that be?"

"Oh dear, Mamma — you know how young people carry on these days."

"I don't, my dear. I don't know you. I don't understand you. And what is more — I'm afraid I never shall."

"Anyway," Tamsin decided to strike while not appearing to, "I was far more interested in Captain Peters."

"Oh?"

"As a source of the freshest possible fish — straight off the quayside, in fact."

"Oh dear!" Harriet slumped. "Business!"

"Yes. *New* business."

"Worse and worse!"

"But perhaps it had better keep for some other day."

The seed was planted, anyway, she told herself. Give it time to do what seeds usually do.

3   It drizzled most of the following morning, but come noon there were small patches of blue and by early afternoon there was enough to make a sailor's shirt. At half-past two, when Tamsin changed into a summer frock and white lawn gloves and set out on the short walk to the Esplanade, the cloud was thin and high, the breeze had stilled, and the evaporating rain raised the humidity to the point where nobody wanted to do anything at all strenuous.

Ladies with parasols drifted along the Esplanade like stately galleons of old, half becalmed; their attendant gentlemen were no more animated than the carved figureheads that would have graced such vessels then. Men and women who had 'seen the Great God Pan' — as the common euphemism had it — thought of lying naked and entwined in shady groves, lost in forests of spice trees, and making slow, soporific love together. Those who, like Tamsin, had not yet experienced that sublime vision wondered at the restless stirrings in their sinews and could not interpret the curious sensations of hunger that filled them, even after a good, sustaining luncheon.

The moment she moved into the shelter she understood why it was empty, despite the languid crowds all around. The glazed partitions shielded her from the slightest breeze while seeming also to magnify the rays of the sun, making them even more pitiless. She felt suffocated and moved out again without even sitting down. She raised her parasol and crossed the Esplanade to stand at the railings, looking out to sea. What little breeze there was came fitfully from that direction.

For a while she watched the horses on the Ladies' Bathing Beach as they backed the bathing machines out into waist-deep water, where the attendant uncoupled the horse and led him ashore again — after ensuring, of course, that each lady was safely secured to the machine by a rope buckled about her waist. Tamsin envied the women as they bravely launched themselves into the cool, slick-calm water and lay there, bobbing gently up and down in perfect safety until their time was up. She envied the gentlemen more, swimming off the rocks at Battery Point. No one told *them* that diving and vigorous swimming was injurious to their health. They could horse around for hours, 'bombing' one another, swimming to Chimney Rock and back, or even farther, to the mouth of the Larrigan River, almost half way to Newlyn.

If she were the last person in the world now, she'd take off everything and skip down to the water and swim as boisterously as any man, all the way to Newlyn and back. Even to imagine it made her shiver with pleasure. There was something so tawdry about the men skulking away over there on Battery Rocks and the women floating like tethered, dismasted hulks over here. A wave of anger passed over her. She wanted to pick up something and shake it. It soon passed, dissipated in the cloying heat, but it left behind a residue of frustration.

Thoughts of Newlyn led her back to practical affairs, to Benny Peters and the fresh fish he landed daily — or on any day when there was wind enough to put to sea. On this windless afternoon his son was probably tending lobsterpots, which could be done in a rowing boat from the shore. Not that any fisherman did much rowing hereabouts; they all seemed to prefer sculling with one oar over the stern. She wondered about his son, David. The old man was in his sixties, she guessed, so the son was probably in his forties. On the other hand, he'd been described to her as the youngest — the little Benjamin — when his brothers drowned, so he could be quite a bit younger.

Two friends in the fishing trade would be twice as good as one if her present plans came to anything.

And talk of the devil — or think of him, anyway — there was Captain Peters coming along the Esplanade now. Just when she was beginning to think that neither he nor the Thornes were venturing abroad today. He walked as if the heat had not yet reached him, striding out and swinging his cane. Tamsin compared him with other old men on the Esplanade, sour creatures hunched in bath chairs or walking on eggs and all looking as if they had never done a day's hard labour in their lives. It confirmed everything she had come to realize of late — that undeserved leisure was more of a disease than a blessing.

The day grew brighter at the mere sight of him. "I rather think your boat won't be out today, Captain Peters," she said as he drew near.

He accepted the title without complaint. He had trimmed and shaped his beard since yesterday; now it fringed his face like the rim of a white plate.

"Not so, maid," he replied, joining her at the rail. "See the lobster boat, the one nearest?" He pointed out a rowing boat with a single oarsman standing at the stern as he hauled up one of a line of pots.

"Your boy?" she guessed.

"The same." He drew out a spyglass and placed it to his eye.

"Is it lobsters or brandy today?" she asked.

He glanced at her sharply.

"I've heard tales," she told him.

"And tales is all they are, maid. The days of Harry Carter and brandy-smuggling in hogsheads by the dozens — they'm long gone. There's not a man left in the whole o' Newlyn could tell 'ee the first thing about smuggling now. How many bottles do'ee want, then?"

She laughed and said she'd have to consult with her mother about that. "So it couldn't possibly be brandy in those pots today?" she added.

He passed her the glass. "See for yourself."

The magnification was so great that she could not hold the image still. However, it was good enough to show the dancing silhouette of a youngish man hauling line but that was not good enough for her. She bent at the knees and rested the tube upon one of the knobs of the Esplanade railings. And then, with its restless hunting reduced to a mere tremor, she saw a slim, well-built young man, clean shaven and with dark if not jet black hair. The haze made colours hard to distinguish. All his movements were lithe and assured. She could imagine him being just as much at home in the roughest of seas. He did not look much over twenty-five.

There is a pleasure in watching anyone skilled at work — weaver, thatcher, juggler, trapeze artiste — their skills hold the attention long after they, as people, would have exhausted us. And that, Tamsin told herself, was why she continued to watch young David Peters at his toil. She kept it up so long that her unused eye protested and sent patches of blackness to overlay the view.

"Would I be able to come to Newlyn and buy fish from you direct?" she asked as she straightened up again. She collapsed the spyglass and passed it back.

"Miss Harte!" Before the Captain could answer, Victor's greeting, from no more than a dozen paces away, intervened.

She was about to turn and reply when the expression on the old man's face held her attention. It was a very particular expression and a perfect replica of one she had seen on someone else's face quite recently — just before they left Plymouth to come and settle here, she thought. Alas, the precise occasion eluded her, and she could delay no longer in greeting the Thornes; but it haunted her the rest of that afternoon.

"Miss Thorne! Mister Thorne!" She faced them with a smile though her heart was beating fast and she felt that strange, angry restlessness hovering near again. "What a pleasant surprise. I thought you would be lost amid the thousand-and-one antiquities of Land's End this afternoon. Are your parents cogging it all on their own?"

"I'll leave 'ee be," Peters said.

Tamsin turned back, intending to ask him to stay, but he was already moving off. "My question?" she called after him.

"You must ask your old woman, maid," he replied over his shoulder. "I must ask my young man. See 'ee 'gain."

"Strange man," she murmured. "I wonder why he came all this way, just to turn round and go back again?"

"That was the old sea dog you were with yesterday," Victor commented. "A friend of your family's?" Today he wore a cream blazer with a thin, dark-blue stripe and ice-blue binding, and he had a matching blue cane with a plain silver knob.

"I hope he soon will be — though I met him for the first time yesterday. Shall we walk a little?" She offered Charlotte her arm and they set off westwards, following the Captain by at least a hundred paces.

"You are swift in your alliances, Miss Harte," Victor said as he stepped to her side. He offered her his arm, too, but she tapped it with the butt of her parasol and said, "Not quite that swift, Mister Thorne."

He smiled, unabashed. "See!" Charlotte taunted. She was wearing another sailor-girl outfit, down to her ankles today.

"Not another word," he warned her. Then, to Tamsin, "What was the object of maritime interest?"

She was about to tell him the truth when something inside her refused. Instead, she told him a tale she had heard a few weeks ago. "D'you see the rocks that are just beginning to be exposed by the tide? There's an ancient mineshaft there, which goes down many fathoms. It's got an iron cover now and they say the sand is slowly infiltrating and filling it up. But in the days of Captain Peters's grandfather they extracted tin worth over seventy thousand guineas from it. There was a building over it, of course, to hold back the sea."

Charlotte tugged them to the railings and peered down at the sands and rocks. "It was only a century ago," she said, "and yet there's not a trace of it left. Vanity of vanities!"

Victor raked the heavens with his eyes and smiled apologetically at Tamsin. "Do tell us more about life among the *hoi polloi*, Miss Harte."

"Not if you simply wish to mock, Mister Thorne — and anyway, *hoi polloi* does not need 'the' before it. The Greek words already express the definite article." She stamped her foot. "And now you've made me sound like my mother! I warn you — I have never found it easy to forgive any man who causes me to sound like my mother. I shall not speak to you for five whole minutes."

He drew breath to protest but let it out unused when she added, "And if you attempt to address me, I shall make it ten. So tell me, dear Miss Thorne, how long shall you be staying here? And, indeed, *where* are you staying? I felt so sure yesterday that we were never to meet again that I neglected to ask."

Charlotte replied that they were staying at the Queen's Hôtel until the end of July. And would Miss Harte kindly consider calling her Charlotte? Tamsin thanked her for the compliment and asked her to reciprocate.

"And he's Victor," Charlotte added.

"No, he isn't, I'm afraid. He is *still* Mister Thorne. Tell me — I never had a brother, younger or older. It must be beastly?"

The girl caught her drift and fell in at once. "Pretty beastly," she agreed. "They think they are protecting one by frightening all their best-looking friends away."

"Perhaps they judge their friends' intentions by reference to their own — toward their friends' younger sisters and other females, I mean."

Charlotte giggled. "I think you must be right, my dear. He is a terrible masher."

"He? Oh! I assumed we were talking about brothers in general. Are we talking just about him?" Tamsin tilted her head in Victor's direction but paid him no heed. "Very well then. I hesitate to criticize people I barely know but I have to say I think it was imprudent of your parents to give him — to give any boy — the name Victor. The poor dear!"

The poor dear gazed skyward and whistled through his teeth.

Charlotte said, "I'm sure you're right, Tamsin, but I should adore to hear your reasons."

"Well, if they had named him ... oh, I don't know ... Admiral, say. Would they not have condemned him to a life before the mast, behind the mast, above the mast, toiling night and day until he had exchanged a snotty's spyglass for an admiral's gold epaulettes and fore-and-after? And just think what a laughing stock he'd be if he never rose above commodore! I feel sure that your brother — when we see fit to talk to him again — will break down and confess that all his life he's felt compelled to make conquests wherever he goes. His name compels it. How his friends would laugh if the Victor were more often the Van-quished! And oh, how he *longs* to climb off that treadmill of endless empty conquests and engage in warm, sincere friendships with all those young females whose hearts he feels driven to possess — driven by his slave-master of a name. Oh dear!" She stopped and bit her lip.

"What now, Tamsin dear?" Charlotte asked.

Victor sauntered on as if unaware they had halted.

"I hope he doesn't blub when he confesses it. I admire any man who's strong enough to admit he has a softer, weaker side to his nature — but not to the extent of blubbing. They always want to use my handkerchief. I draw the line at that."

Still Victor strolled on, head in air, hoping to compel them to call him back.

Tamsin put a finger to her lips, executed a full hundred-and-eighty degree wheel, and steered her friend back toward the shelter near where they had met — and also, as it happened, toward the Queen's, where they were staying.

They must, she reasoned, have taken several front-facing rooms — and, of course, several cheaper ones at the back for their servants. And therefore, even if Victor and Charlotte had been watching with only half an eye, one of them must have seen her out there with the Captain. Victor must have been the one, in fact, for Charlotte was so eager to meet her again that she would probably have rushed out hatless and gloveless. So why had Victor delayed?

It could be because of his enormous vanity over his wardrobe — she had to allow that. He would take longer to prepare himself, even for a simple stroll, than most women even. Or it could have been because he wanted to observe her at his leisure. Through binoculars, perhaps?

The idea both thrilled and angered her. What right had he? asked one half of her. On the other hand, she felt flattered. Simply by *being* — not doing anything special, just being — she had compelled him to notice her, to watch her, to think about her, to be intrigued enough to observe her.

So she was intriguing!

The sense of power it gave her was not exactly new; she had experienced it before at picnics and balls, ever since spotty boys had started eyeing her in that special, hangdog, hopeless way. But then she, too, had been trapped inside the gilded cage of social conventions. Now she was free. Or free-er. As far as her own behaviour was concerned, three-fourths of the pages in the etiquette books could be ripped out and discarded. And the sense of power was still there, as strong as ever — and as unfettered by rules as never before.

Tamsin did not reason it out in so many words, of course; but the feeling was all the stronger for that. Intuitions that remain unspoken cannot be tested (nor diminished) by mere logic.

In a curious way Charlotte now confirmed the general drift of those same intuitions. "We've shaken him off," she said, thinking that had been Tamsin's intention all along. "Now tell me about the freedom you spoke of yesterday — you know — the liberation you've felt since withdrawing from Society. I want to hear it all before he comes back."

"Really?" Tamsin's Society days were now so remote — in psychological if not in calendar weeks — that she did not immediately understand Charlotte's fears. "Why shouldn't he hear of it, too?"

"Oh, I'm sure he's *dying* to hear it all — and to ask a thousand questions beside — just like me. But he'd hate *me* to hear of it. Your words might unsettle me, you see." She glanced over her shoulder. "Damn! He's coming! Oops — sorry I said damn!"

"I say it ten times a day, don't worry. I say it even louder than that, too." A thought struck her. "You must have *some* sort of power over him. Why did he warn you — 'not another word' — back there?"

"Oh lordy! I couldn't tell you that! Not so soon, anyway."

"You don't need to tell *me*. Just remember what it was and threaten to use it if he starts getting uppity with you. Here he is!" Tamsin turned what she hoped was a dazzling smile upon him and, offering her arm, said, "Victor! Dear boy! You've decided to give up your sulks and join us at last. I'm *so* glad."

It unsettled him, as, of course, she had intended. Why should she be alone in this restlessness?

"What d'you mean — sulks!" he exclaimed in a wounded tone, though he was so eager to link arms with her that he could not complain too much.

"Now don't start all that again," she said, giving his hand a squeeze between her arm and ribs. "I was just about to explain those things I said to your mother yesterday afternoon. I fear she was rather shocked — though, of course, she's far too well bred and good natured to show it much. However, if I'd had time enough to explain myself more thoroughly, I'm sure I could have relieved her apprehensions entirely." She smiled at him again. "But perhaps you'd rather I didn't?"

Trapped between that smile and his own inner certainty that Charlotte could only be polluted by the no-doubt subversive sentiments this divine young woman would pour into their ears, he was paralyzed.

"I'm so grateful," Tamsin went on, "that when we were in Society my dear father encouraged me to study a wide variety of opinions — even those with which he violently disagreed."

"Did he by Jove! But why?" Victor asked in amazement.

"I remember asking him that same question once. He told me that he and Mama could not possibly hover at my elbow day and night until they passed me into the safe-keeping of a husband. The day would surely come when some engaging serpent would spring upon me some false idea — atheism, communism, socialism, suffragism, colonial freedom, love of Wagner ... the list was long ..."

"Can you talk like this at the drop of a hat?" Victor asked.

"You can go away again," Charlotte told him. "You don't *have* to stay, you know. Tamsin and I can perfectly well chaperon each other."

"Anyway," Tamsin insisted, "my father's point was that if I'd met the false ideology before, exposed in cold print rather than on the honeyed tongue of some beguiling wit, I would be armed against it. And indeed I am. Wild horses would not drag me to see *Lohengrin,* for instance."

Victor laughed hopelessly. "There must be some way of telling when you're being serious."

"You know very well the points I'm making, Victor," she replied evenly. "And what is more, you know it's right. Young ladies today cannot be shielded from the world as their mothers were. It is far too dangerous for them."

"You said 'points.' That's only one."

"You know the other one, too — it concerns you."

"I'd like to hear it!" He was rash enough to speak in that challenging tone which believes the other's words to be hollow.

"Then you shall," Tamsin said. "I know what went through your mind yesterday afternoon. You saw far more of what really happened than the other three members of your family ..."

"He thinks you conspired with the Captain and that urchin to make it all happen," Charlotte blurted out.

"And he was quite right."

The two of them halted in amazement. Indeed, Victor was so amazed that he quite forgot to crow over his sister at being proved so right so swiftly. "You admit it?" he asked.

"I'll do more — I'll even explain it. In fact, I could not honourably continue our new-found friendship without explaining it — d'you agree?"

"You are the strangest young woman," he said.

"I'm not at all what you had in mind, eh? The simple truth is that I saw two interesting-looking young people who seemed as if they would have made wonderful companions in the days when I, too, moved in Society. I was explaining my circumstances to the Captain, whom, as I say, I had only just met — sometimes one can unburden one's soul more easily to total strangers, don't you think? Anyway, I was pointing out that you were now so far above me in rank that even to think of striking up an acquaintance was impossible. And so, while you continued walking on down here and back, he persuaded me I was wrong. Or at least to give it a try. And so, between us — and the handy arrival of those urchins — we devised our little stratagem. It deceived you, Charlotte, for which I apologize deeply. But your sharp-eyed brother saw through it all at once."

Victor basked in this apparent praise until she added, "Not that it has benefited him much!"

"Oh?" He was stung.

"Be honest, now, Victor," she urged. "You thought I was simply flirting with you. Your aspirations did not rise above a brief 'fling,' as they call it — a seaside fling — and I'd be one more notch on your own private tallystick of conquests."

When she was only half way through, he jerked his arm out of her grasp. By the time she had finished his nostrils were flaring, the sinews of his neck looked about to snap, and he had trouble forcing his clenched teeth apart long enough to tell her he'd never heard so much rot in his life. He added, moreover, that she must be some kind of madwoman and that the rest of his holiday could not be more improved than by a decision, here and now, never to see her again. He was so angry that he strode off without commanding Charlotte to join him.

But Charlotte herself knew it was bound to come. "That's the end of that," she said bleakly, and very close to tears.

"D'you think so?" Tamsin replied evenly. "I think it's more like the real beginning." The truth was she did not greatly care which it might be, beginning or end. She was alive with pleasure now and that strange, unsatisfactory restlessness had been lifted from her.

4 There was a curious tailpiece to Tamsin's encounter with the young Thornes that afternoon. She suspected that Victor would go straight to his room and sulk until his self-esteem was restored. Doubtless he would gaze out of his window now and then and she wanted to be sure that every time he did so he he would see her out there, enjoying the day and never, *never* looking up to try to catch his eye. If nothing else it would show him that *she* had not been reduced to sulking at home.

But she needed something to underline the point. Or, better still, someone. To be seen as the the centre of a small, jolly group would be just the thing now; but even one conversational partner would do.

And that was when she remembered David Peters, who, she now saw, was still sculling round just beyond the Wherry Rocks. Surely he had lifted and rebaited all his lobsterpots long before now? Could it be that he was just drifting out there, trying to summon the courage to come ashore and introduce himself? Even if the Captain hadn't mentioned yesterday's encounter, his son must have been aware of their meeting today. And if his eyesight was any good at all, he must have noticed the pair of them watching him through the spyglass. She felt a slight rush of blood to her cheeks when she realized he must have seen how long she had remained glued to the eyepiece.

If he was just sculling around, waiting for courage, it was a further example of that strange power young women like her seemed to have over men. But this time her response was different. She would not welcome such power over this David Peters, whom she had not even met. Over Victor, yes. She was already fairly sure she wanted something more than a simple friendship with him — precisely what, she couldn't say, but whatever it might turn out to be, she wanted it on her terms, not his. Hence her little battle of wills with him today; if he wasn't willing to accept that … well, the sea was big and full of fish. And her choice out there was much wider than his.

But David Peters was not to be considered in that light at all. She already had a place earmarked for him in her scheme of things; he was part of quite a different battle of wills — the one against her mother. Young Mr Peters's part in it was to be commercial. Not *strictly* commercial, maybe. If they also became friends, it would do no harm. Indeed, it could help the commercial connection through difficult patches — and every commercial connection must certainly have such patches from time to time.

But that was all. She had no room for anything else. None of those games young ladies in Society might play — setting one suitor off against another … making half a dozen young men dance through the hoops. There was no time in her life for such idle games. She would decide from the very outset, even before they became acquainted, which young man should occupy *this* rôle in her life and which should occupy *that* one. And which should have no rôle at all.

She had already decided that Victor would do very nicely in the romantic part — for the moment, anyway. If he should turn out to be unsuitable after all, well, the Thornes would be leaving Penzance soon enough, and no doubt someone else would come along. On the other hand, if he proved suitable, she'd find ways to encourage him to return, on his own. He was probably over twenty-one and he must surely have private funds. All in all, then, he was, for the moment, by far the most suitable young man for that particular part.

So, if David Peters was milling around out there, trying to summon the courage to come ashore and make the first romantic overture, she really owed it to him to disabuse him of the notion as soon as possible.

She descended to the beach and walked straight down to the water's edge, at the nearest possible point to him. He noticed, of course. In fact, he stood stock still and watched her all the way. He was too far off for her to want to shout but she lowered her parasol behind her and used it as a mask behind which (or, from his viewpoint, in front of which) she waved.

She had to repeat the gesture several times before he dared pick up both oars (so they did carry two, she realized, even if they preferred to use only one) and row the boat in the conventional way. Around the rocks he steered and into the shallow, low-tide inlet between them and the beach. As he drew near he rowed even more vigorously — showing off to her, she suspected, until she realized that the extra speed would be carrying him farther into the shallows. In fact, so powerful were his strokes that the prow of his boat finally came to rest on dry sand — or undrowned sand, at least, for his feet, as he leaped ashore with the painter seemed to draw up the water and turn the dull sand into shimmering circles the size of dinner plates. He walked on circles of light.

"If there's one thing a fisherman hates," he said jovially, "it's getting his feet wet. There's nowhere on board for him to get them really dry again."

His educated speech, notwithstanding his marked Cornish accent, surprised her after his father's strong dialect. "Mister Peters?" she said. "I was talking with your father earlier."

She felt ashamed of herself. It seemed such a lame greeting, especially after his opening words.

"You have the advantage of me, Miss …?" he replied.

"Oh, I'm sorry. Miss Harte. Do forgive me."

"Forgiven," he replied lightly. "D'you want a lobster for your tea, Miss Harte? The sea has been generous today."

"Oh, how kind." She wondered how she'd carry it back.

"I'll tie his claws," he said. "And I can probably find an old bag under the seat."

"That's *very* kind."

He tilted his head toward the bay. "Care for a little trip? Round the Wherry and back?"

"Oh … well …"

She realized that a little competition — or the long-distance *suggestion* of it — would give Victor lots to think about. However, a half-hour trip alone in a boat with another young man would hardly do, especially coming right on the heels of their parting. She wanted to give Victor a chance to reflect, to return, to beg forgiveness, and to be more reasonable in future — not to give him an excuse to walk away entirely, muttering something about sour grapes.

He grinned. "My father was right. He said you wouldn't give me the time of day."

As he spoke his eyes quartered the Esplanade, looking, she realized, for the Thornes. From out in the bay he would not have been able to guess the nature of their parting; for all he knew they might have gone back to the hôtel for another pair of gloves or something equally trivial.

And suddenly — seeing a younger version of his father in the son's features — Tamsin remembered where she had previously seen that rather curious expression in the old man's eyes, the moment Victor Thorne had appeared. It was last year in Plymouth, on the Hoe, about a month before her father's death. There had been some kind of naval pageant there, part of which had involved a Græco-Roman wrestling contest between the crews of two ships. She had managed to get quite close to one of the teams before her mother hauled her away, saying it was not seemly for a young lady to stand so close to the wrestlers.

But just before that she had been watching the petty officer who coached one of the teams; he would massage the muscles of the young man who was about to go into the ring, and he'd talk to him all the while about his opponent. During that time, he, the coach, never took his eyes off that opponent. And the look in those eyes was identical to the one she had seen in the old Captain's as he surveyed young Victor from head to toe, or from straw boater to summer shoe.

This memory came back to her in a flash, so that the young man's words were still in her ears: 'He said you wouldn't give me the time of day.' Her memory and his words coalesced into a sudden understanding of what was really going on here. Then, too, she knew the answer to her own earlier question as to why the Captain had bothered to walk all the way round the seafront from Newlyn to the Esplanade, just to look at his son for half a minute through the spyglass.

"I'll bet he nags you about not settling down, eh?" she guessed, suggesting by her tone that she, too, was more than familiar with the experience.

"Often enough." David smiled ruefully but now his air was relaxed. His earlier, slightly amused wariness was gone. He half-sat, half-leaned against the gunwale of his boat, just to one side of the bow stem. "Parents!" he added. "What are we to do with them, Miss Harte?"

"What indeed, Mister Peters!" Her mind was still racing over the implications of this discovery.

"We could discuss it out on the water," he suggested hopefully.

"Ah, Mister Peters!" She shook her head sadly. "Agreeable though that would certainly be, I think we should postpone it to some other day."

"Tomorrow?" he suggested.

"Some other day," she insisted. "Meanwhile, I should tell you that I have put a certain question to *your* parent. A commercial question about the supply of fish directly off the quay. It will be interesting to know if he sees fit to pass it on."

"Perhaps he has other fish to fry!" He kept a straight face. "However, I shan't mention this conversation if he does. What sort of fish, may I ask? And in what quantities?"

"That's the thing." She shrugged. "I don't know yet. But let me explain. My mother and I operate the Morrab Guest House — in Morrab Road, of course."

"Bed and breakfast?"

"Yes — and that's my point. We have a kitchen that can turn out two dozen lavish breakfasts each morning and then, from mid-morning on, it reverts to being an ordinary domestic kitchen catering for Mama and me — and up to eight servants. It's absurd. It's as if a factory owner decided to operate his factory for an hour and a half each day. The cook who copes with twenty hot breakfasts could just as readily cope with forty dinners — and be glad of the extra wages. And the maids who serve ..."

"Twenty breakfasts?" he interrupted. "But *forty* dinners?"

"She can as easily cook forty as twenty — so why not open up to the public as well? I tell you — if we could somehow serve meals round the clock, I'd say *that's* using our facilities to the full. Even just serving breakfasts and dinners, we could be so much more successful than we are. Anyway — that is my challenge, to bring my mother to this point of view. And I've hardly started yet."

"But you will prevail?"

"What do you think?"

"I'm sure you will."

"Yes. So am I — it's so logical, isn't it. And when I do, I shall need a sure and steady supply of fish of the very highest quality. I have in mind an evening restaurant that serves only seafood. There isn't a single such place in the whole of Penzance ..."

"Nor yet in Newlyn, either. Even in Falmouth there's only one, from what I do know."

"Thank you — that's useful to know. But what a shame, eh? What a *shameful* shame! You fishermen risk your lives out there to catch some of the most succulent fish in English waters. And what happens? A few baskets of them end up as the third or fourth choice in the table d'hôte of our local restaurants. It's an utter scandal!"

It was an argument she had mulled over for use at some vaguely future date on the quayside at Newlyn, for the past several weeks. Delivered face-to-face in these more intimate circumstances it sounded rather bombastic. Even so, it caught his imagination; she could see a new excitement in his eyes.

So she fired the second barrel, also prepared earlier: "Such a restaurant could pay well above auction prices for reliable supplies of premier quality fish."

"I was just thinking that, myself," he replied.

"So then, Mister Peters, we both have something to think about between now and whenever we next meet."

"Which will be after you've beaten your mother?"

She jibbed at that. "I don't look upon it as beating her," she replied. "Dear Mama has both our interests at heart, you know. She's most eager to do what's best by us. It's just that she doesn't realize that this restaurant idea of mine *is* what's best."

"Yet," he said.

"Exactly."

He fished her out the fattest of his lobster haul, tied its claws, and then was surprised to discover a remarkably dainty linen bag, beautifully embroidered and wrapped in paper, beneath the helm thwart.

It did not deceive her, though. "I think we had better meet sooner rather than later, Mister Peters," she said as she took it and thanked him. "Before somebody misses this beautiful bag."

This time she did not bother to mask her farewell waves behind her parasol.

5 Cicely Thorne was outraged to learn that her children had disobeyed her and consorted with the Harte girl — so outraged, indeed, that she led herself into a foolish blunder. As soon as they had arrived back at the hôtel the previous day, she had sent telegrams to friends in Plymouth inquiring into the characters of Tamsin and Mrs Harte. It was the least precaution that a cautious mother could take. The replies, which had come that afternoon, had not been reassuring. To avoid stirring up a scandal in the locality she had sent the inquiries — in French, of course — from Penzance, directing the replies to a *poste restante* in Newlyn.

ELLES SONT NQOC, was one opinion; NQOC being Society code for 'not quite our class'.

ELLES SONT CREVEES D'ORGEUIL read another, with Saxon disregard for French niceties. DEFENSE DE REPAIRER — which may be accurately rendered: THEY ARE BUSTED WITH PRIDE. DON'T RE-COUPLE.

So, on strolling back from Newlyn, it had pleased her greatly to observe the Harte girl talking with a common fisherman down by the water's edge. Well, she noted with quiet satisfaction, *today* at least, the creature has found her true *niveau*. But her pleasure was short lived. On entering the hôtel she almost ran into Dobbs, Charlotte's maid.

"How dare you use the front entrance?" she demanded of the impertinent girl.

Dobbs was not even faintly abashed. "It's because of the ale and the fish, madam," she replied.

A typical Dobbs response, this. It was meaningless on the surface and yet, if you probed and probed, you'd find justification in it at last — except that by then you'd have played the inquisitor so fiercely that you *almost* felt obliged to apologize. Cicely had been burned that way too often even though the maid had been with them for less than two months; indeed, she'd have dismissed her within the first week if she hadn't been so good at her work that every lady in Cicely's circle would have snapped her up at once. Good servants of every grade were becoming as rare as hens' teeth nowadays; the last assistant cook she'd tried to engage had had the temerity to spend most of the interview questioning *her* — and then had said she, meaning Cicely herself, 'wouldn't suit'!

"Well, I suppose you know what you're talking about, Dobbs," was all Cicely said now. "I'm blessed if I do, that's all I can say. The real question …"

Dobbs cast a further small pearl: "Deliveries through the staff entrance, madam."

"The *real* question," Cicely insisted, "is why are you going out of the hôtel at all?"

"On a message, madam."

"I should hope so. That's not the issue, either."

By now they were blocking the entrance for other guests, one of them a craggy old gentleman with eyebrows like furze bushes. "May I go, then?" Dobbs asked.

"Not until I learn for whom this message is … er, for — you know very well what I mean. Intended. For whom is it intended?"

Harrumph! The bushy eyebrows throbbed with impatience. Indeed, the man's whole body probably did the same but the eyebrows were all Cicely noticed. Intimidated by them she plucked the maid aside and tried to soothe the fellow with a smile. Unsoothed, he forged his way across the lobby with his jaw set like the prow of an icebreaker.

The maid produced a letter from her bag. "I'm to deliver it in person, madam," she said.

It was addressed to Miss Tamsin Harte, The Morrab Guest House, Morrab Road — in Victor's hand.

"Just around the corner," Dobbs added.

Cicely was trying to contain her anger. One did so hate all public display of feelings of any kind — and the gentleman with the eyebrows still had half a malevolent eye upon her. "I know very well where *that* creature lives," she said grimly as she tore the envelope and its contents in two. "You may return this waste paper to my son this minute. At once."

Dobbs, who had remained quite calm throughout, turned to go back above.

Cicely immediately had second thoughts. "A moment, if you please," she said, following the maid to the foot of the stairs. "This way." She drew her into the ladies' lounge, where she took back the fragments of the letter and laid them out. They proved simple enough to piece together for the entire message comprised a mere couple of lines:

> Dear Miss Harte,
> You have impugned my honour as a gentleman. In the circumstances there can be no further intercourse between us.
>
> Yours (alas) sincerely,
> Victor Thorne.

Now Cicely cursed herself for her impetuous action in destroying a letter that could, at a stroke, have achieved her dearest present wish. However, it did raise the question: When was this impugning of Victor's honour supposed to have occurred? Not yesterday, certainly.

"Did they consort with Miss Harte while I was out this afternoon?" she asked the maid.

"Miss Harte?" Dobbs frowned. "That's a lady I do not know."

"Very diplomatic! Did they consort with anyone?"

"I believe they took a stroll along the promenade, madam. I was preoccupied with Miss Charlotte's gown for this evening."

So they must have met the Harte creature, Cicely mused. It was particularly annoying that she had been reading her telegrams and their solemn warnings at the very moment her two children had been cavorting upon the Esplanade with the NQOC girl herself. Still, all was not gloom, it now appeared. The little hoyden must have insulted Victor in some way, and it must have been serious enough to occasion this letter. It was vexing that they had disobeyed her, of course, but the outcome could not be grumbled at — except that she had, by her impulsive passion, nipped it in the bud. However, a scheme to undo that particular damage was beginning to form; after all, Miss Harte had no idea what Victor's handwriting looked like. "Wait," she commanded the maid.

She seated herself at the escritoire, took a fresh sheet of hôtel notepaper, and wrote out Victor's message once again. She sealed it in an envelope, as before, and dropped the fragments of the original in the waste-paper basket.

"You may take this instead," she said to Dobbs as she swept on out.

Dobbs, who knew that one *never* left drafts of letters in public waste-baskets, dutifully retrieved the original before setting off up Morrab Road.

They were a queer lot, the Thornes. Well, *all* masters and mistresses were a queer lot when you really got down to it. Jenny Saunders, whose mother had worked for the old queen at Osborne, said she was one of the very best. Any servant in her employ for more than ten years or thereabout became like one of the family. Of course, you still had to respect Her Majesty and mind your ps and qs, but even the lords and ladies of the court had to do that. But she'd tell you her thoughts and she'd expect you to share yours as well. And she knew all about your family and who was ill and needed asking after and such like. And she noticed if you were out of sorts and she'd give you little bottles from her own homeopathic cabinet. All the servants agreed that a real toff, a lord or a lady who was sure of their place in Society's ranks, was the best sort of master or mistress. Or 'employer,' as it was now more popular to call them — among servants themselves, anyway.

And they were all agreed that the worst employer of all was an ex-servant — someone who'd just moved up one rung of the ladder and wanted to make sure those on the old rung didn't forget it. They were the ones who paid in farthings, who never said 'Take the rest of the evening off,' and who'd 'never heard of such impertinence' when you asked for leave to attend a funeral.

Mrs Thorne came suspiciously close to the lower end of the spectrum that stretched between those two poles, Dobbs decided; she herself had only been with the family for six weeks and so had not had the chance to pry into her mistress's origins — yet. Whispers in the servants' hall tended to confirm her suspicions, but she was long enough in service to know that tittle-tattle was one thing and certain knowledge quite another.

She paused outside the Hartes', a large, imposing house that swept the eye around a bend in the road. It was built, or at least faced, in granite ashlars, with two semicircular bays that ran the full three floors — semi-basement, ground floor, and first floor — and ended in romantic, conical turrets such as you see on French chateaux. Small lights among the slates revealed that these turrets housed attic rooms, as well. She enjoyed a brief daydream of living in such a room, not as a servant but as one remote from the life of the world, content with the smallest portion. A woodman's cottage in a forest glade was another favourite of hers — and even less likely to find her in possession of it.

Tamsin opened the dining-room window. "Can I help you?" she asked.

Dobbs liked her at once, just from the sound of her voice, which was somehow warm and mellow. Inviting. "Miss Harte?" she asked, though she had no doubt of it.

"Yes."

The maid opened the gate and started up the short path to the front steps, speaking as she came: "I'm Miss Thorne's lady's maid, Miss Harte. I've been sent to deliver a message to you."

"Dear me!" Tamsin left the window and, moments later, reappeared at the door. "I hope it's one I shall want to hear."

"Read, Miss, not hear." She handed over the letter Mrs Thorne had given her.

"Who is it from? It's in a woman's hand, I see. Is an immediate reply expected?"

"It's from Mrs Thorne. She said nothing about a reply. Miss."

"Well, come in, anyway." Tamsin stepped aside. "I expect you could do with a cordial or something on such a warm afternoon." When the maid hesitated, she added, "No one is to know how long it took you to walk here ... much less how long it took the staff here to find *me*. We'll go into the lounge. There's no one about at the moment."

As they passed down the passage she rang a bell on the hatstand. A maid opened the servants' door and peered into the gloom of the hall. Tamsin said, "Two tall glasses and a jug of lemonade, Bridget, please."

She motioned her visitor toward a wicker chair and seated herself in one facing it.

"Well, that's short and sharp!" she said after scanning the two-line message. "Tell me, what's your name?"

"Dobbs, Miss."

"Just Dobbs?"

"Daisy Dobbs."

"And which d'you prefer?"

She smiled awkwardly. "Daisy, Miss."

"Good, Daisy Dobbs. In that case, I am Tamsin."

"Oh, Miss! I couldn't." But even as she said it she was thinking, *I jolly well could!*

"Suit yourself, Daisy, but I shouldn't mind in the least. You said this note was from *Mrs* Thorne?"

"I saw her write it — and seal it, Miss ... Tamsin." She contrived to make the name seem an alternative rather than an adjunct to the title.

Tamsin passed her the single sheet of notepaper, saying, "It's a lady's hand, as I said, but ..." She left the rest unspoken.

Daisy read it, frowned, and then, without thinking (except that later she suspected the not-thinking had been ever so slightly deliberate), pulled out the remains of the original. She extracted the torn contents, put the two halves together, and burst into laughter as she handed them over to Tamsin.

"I suppose," Tamsin said, "that, given time, I could imagine some circumstances in which a mother would intercept a note from her son to an unwelcome female, tear it up, and then copy it word for word in her own hand before sending it onward. But for the moment, I confess it quite baffles me."

Daisy explained what had happened, adding as a postscript: "I remember she quizzed me very particularly as to whether Mister Victor and Miss Charlotte had met with you upon the promenade this afternoon."

"And what did you tell her?"

"I said I had been busy with Miss Charlotte's evening gown — which was also the truth."

"Excellent."

Bridget brought their cordial and poured out two tumblers.

"Are you disappointed to read that?" Daisy nodded at the note in Tamsin's hand.

Tamsin relished her drink. "How serious d'you think he is?"

"He means everything at the moment he does it. Later he often regrets it, though."

"Well ... a man cannot expect to write a note like this" — she waved Victor's torn original — "with or without the support of his mother" — she waved the copy — "and expect to go *entirely* unpunished. Don't you agree, Daisy?"

Daisy giggled so much that a small quantity of lemonade went up into her nose, making her sniff and then cough. Tamsin rose and patted her on the back.

And somehow that small, even trivial act of intimacy sealed a bond of trust between them. Without the need for words or declarations, they were on the same side from that moment on.

"Tell me what you know of *Mister* Victor Thorne," Tamsin said. "Is he a plague to pretty young maids like you?"

"Nooo." Daisy drew the word out as if she suspected it might surprise her new friend. "Miss Charlotte says he's like the fox that'll never kill the rabbit that burrows beside its den. Did you ever notice that?"

"I can't say I have done."

"Well, it's true. There's a patch of woodland in the grounds of Peveril Hall — that's the Thornes' home, up Exeter way. It's a corner where they draw all the old treestumps after felling, and it's home to both rabbits and foxes, and the foxes never touch *those* rabbits. I don't know why."

"I can guess," Tamsin said. "It's so that when an angry farmer comes to confront the wily foxes with a couple of dozen dead chickens they can say, 'What, us? How could you suspect us when — as you see — we don't even kill the rabbits at our own front door!' At least, they could say it if they were in one of Æsop's fables. So!" She chuckled. "Young Mister Victor plays the virtuous innocent at home to hunt the more fiercely abroad, eh? I must say I had formed the same opinion of him as you. And Miss Charlotte is no dewy-eyed innocent, either — is she. I mean, she knows the ways of the world even if only as a spectator."

Daisy drank a deep draught of her lemonade this time. "Shall I carry a message back, then?"

Tamsin stared at the ample blank spaces around Cicely's copy, was tempted, but did not yield. "It would only get you into trouble, dear Daisy," she said. "I shall deliver it myself — and tip the porter there to be sure to get it to Mister Victor without his mother's knowledge or interference."

"What'll you say?" Daisy rubbed her hands eagerly. "May I tell Miss Charlotte? She won't let on."

"Oh … it'll be something vague, I'm sure. Something that sounds full of meaning but isn't. The main thing is to write it on the back of his mother's copy — that'll *really* put the cat in the dovecote!"

"Write it now," Daisy urged. "Miss Charlotte'll give me no rest if I can't tell her word for word."

"How did she respond to her brother's threat to cut me?"

"She knows nothing of it. Not yet, anyway. The fur will fly when she does!"

"Oh?" Tamsin leaned forward with abrupt interest.

"Oh, indeed. She couldn't stop talking about meeting you last evening when I was helping her dress. How you'd …" She hesistated, suddenly awkward.

Tamsin smiled. "How we'd come down in the world? I don't mind — except that I don't think of it as 'coming down' at all. It's been a most wonderful release from …"

"Yes! That was it. That's what she kept saying. How lucky you were. How you were no longer imprisoned by all the rules and conventions that *she* has to obey. You're a star to her."

"Goodness! Not a guiding star, I hope. I had to be pushed here, you know. I didn't jump of my own free will." Tamsin giggled again. "I say — I've just thought of what to write back."

She crossed the lounge to the bureau, taking her drink and Cicely's note with her. *The sea is unbreakable,* she wrote, *as any mariner will avow, yet it breaks eternally on every shore. Shall a woman's heart be otherwise? — T.*

Daisy read it three times — frowning, dubious, and finally laughing. "You keep thinking you know what it means," she said, "and then you realize you don't. It's like those drawings of faces that keep turning into other faces and every time you fix on one of them it turns into the other."

"And what two faces show here, d'you think?" Tamsin pointed at the page.

"One is heartbroken and the other is sneering."

"Good," Tamsin said. "Will you have some cordial?"

The nuances of this innocent-sounding query were not lost on Daisy. A well-brought-up person offering a second helping to a social equal would never use the word 'more' in such a question, for it would constitute the teeniest hint of criticism on the grounds of greed or gluttony. She held out her glass and said, "I thank you."

"I wish I knew just a wee bit more about the mother, though," Tamsin mused, leaning back in her chair and fixing her eyes upon the ceiling.

"You're not the only one," Daisy replied.

Still gazing upward, Tamsin continued, "We met so briefly and yet I felt a sense of … what's the word? Unease? Uneasiness? The minute I mentioned our transition from being *in* Society to being decidedly outside it, I felt it. Like a sudden change in temperature. Of course, we've had similar experiences with other worthy matrons in the district, even in this backwater they like to keep the barriers up. But this coldness from Mrs Thorne was something more than that. It was almost as if …" She fixed her eyes on Daisy at last but said no more.

"Almost as if what?" Daisy had to ask.

Tamsin laughed mildly. "Oh, I'm probably being much too fanciful. And I'm certainly being unfair in trying to engage you in a discussion of …"

"Pay no heed to that!" Daisy protested.

"Really? Are you sure?"

"Quite sure! A servant's loyalty has to be earned nowadays. Cicely Thorne hasn't even made a down-payment on mine."

"Cicely Thorne, eh? Do we know her maiden name?"

"Cunningham, I believe. Mrs Slocombe, our cook, says the family were ironmasters in Wales somewhere, or so she heard."

"The reason I'm asking — I want to be as frank with you as you are with me, Daisy — is that I had this fleeting suspicion that Mrs Thorne recognized something in me — or in my particular situation — something that other Society matrons have failed to see. It's very hard to pin down."

Her vagueness forced Daisy to express her own intuitions about her employer. "I've sometimes had the feeling she wasn't *always* as top-drawer as she'd like everyone to think."

"I say! Do you suppose that's it?" Tamsin behaved as if Daisy had suddenly cleared up the mystery for her.

"She's *such* a stickler for correct form …" Daisy began.

"You've absolutely hit the nail on the head!" Tamsin cut across. "My father used to collect ancient books on etiquette and how to write and speak good English and things like that — going right back to the middle ages. I remember an Elizabethan one that told men not to wipe grease off their fingers into their beards at table. And ladies shouldn't do the same in the fur of passing dogs or cats. He asked me why I thought such prohibitions had disappeared from modern books on good behaviour, and, of course, I said it was because you don't *need* to tell people such things nowadays because they wouldn't do it anyway. 'Just so!' he said. 'So what does that tell us about the behaviour of lords and ladies in Elizabethan days?'"

Daisy took it as a question intended for her and answered: "They were wiping greasy fingers in beards and dogs all the time!" She laughed.

"You see the point, though," Tamsin went on. "The *Don'ts* in all the etiquette books are an excellent guide to what people actually *Do!* So all those sad people who take them as gospel — the sticklers for 'Good Form' — merely betray their ignorance of actual behaviour in Society."

"That's Cicely Thorne to a tee," Daisy said. After a thoughtful pause she added, "How would one go about finding out things like that … people's backgrounds and things?"

"A birth certificate is a good place to start," Tamsin said. "There's that revealing column headed 'Occupation of Father.' Mine says, 'Ship's chandler'."

"Mine says 'Head Butler' which he was at the time."

"And now?"

"Now he's a civilian diver at the navy dockyards in Plymouth. I remember your father's firm there — Harte's the Chandlers."

"Really? How splendid! Do the Thornes give you much time off — while you're down here, I mean?"

She shrugged. "There wouldn't be much point … I mean, there's not a lot to do in Penzance, is there!"

"You could come here. And if I'm free, we could go for a stroll, and if I'm busy, you could sit and read or sew or whatever, knowing *they* couldn't interrupt with some annoying request. Think about it anyway."

There were noises in the hall. Guests were returning, scattering sand, bits of seaweed, tiny dead crabs, and clutching what they felt sure were semiprecious stones, half-polished by the sea.

"No rest for the wicked," Tamsin murmured as she rose to deal with them. She winked at her new friend — not to say ally.

6 Newlyn's postmistress was Oenone Peters, widow to Captain Peters's cousin. She often dropped by for 'a bit tay and chat' — especially when she knew that David had been lifting lobsters, for she almost always got invited back for supper. She was relishing her second slice of saffron bread when the young fellow arrived, and, even though he'd given the cream of his catch to the Harte maid, the best of the remainder was enough to make the mouth water all over again.

"What? No more'n thirteen?" Benny said. "I seen 'ee lift fourteen for sure. You haven't sold none?"

"If you saw me lift fourteen," David replied, "you'll also have seen me give one to Miss Harte."

"You admit it then!"

"Why should I deny it? She has the makings of a good customer, that one."

"Harte?" Oenone put in. "Is that a Miss Harriet Harte?"

"Tamsin," David said. "Harriet is Mrs Harte, the mother."

"They have a guest house in Morrab Road?"

"I believe so. Why?"

"Never you mind. How could she be a good customer, then?" David explained. "What d'you know of her?" he asked.

She gazed at the writhing heap of lobsters.

"You'll stay to supper, I 'speck?" Benny's wife, Peggy, put in. She spoke rarely but missed nothing.

"I'll come back," Oenone replied, already rising to go. "I shall have something for 'ee then, too, I daresay."

She hastened up the hill to her shop, hoping to catch the Penzance office before it closed; her aunt's husband's niece was married to Andrew Harvey, the postmaster there. In Cornwall such a relatively short hop across the family tree made her and him only slightly more distant than brother and sister; in fact, business and kinship conspired to keep them in closer touch than most siblings. So it was no surprise to David or his parents to be regaled with the contents of certain telegrams — a piquant sauce to their lobster supper that evening. Three of the exchanges were between Mrs Thorne and friends in Plymouth; the other two were between Mrs Harte and friends in Exeter.

Strictly speaking, these disclosures broke half a dozen of the strictest post office rules on confidentiality; but when family and business combine — to say nothing of a whiff of romance — what price rules made in London by men who may have high principles, and even higher collars, but who know nothing of the world and its ways?

"Here's a how-d'ee-do!" David said as he committed the brief messages to memory.

"This-here Victor Thorne," Benny said. "Is the Harte maid and him all hurrisome-like?"

"If they were, d'you suppose she'd tell me?" David replied. Then, when he guessed his father was trying to think of another approach to the same question, he added, "Can you imagine Miss Harte going all hurrisome over *anything?* Other than her own ambitions, of course."

His mother smiled at him approvingly. "That's right, my lover," she said. "Don't 'ee go courantin' with no maid like she. They'm nothin' but trouble."

David had not, in fact, meant to imply he found Tamsin's ambitions disagreeable, but he let it pass.

"I had a splendid bit of news today, darling," Harriet said as she and Tamsin sat down to dine that evening. "Can you guess?"

"There's been a new edition of your favourite book — *The Manners and Morals of Good Society* by 'A Titled Lady' — and it says a truly modern family may discuss its own business at ..."

"If you're going to be tedious at every single mealtime, dear," her mother said wearily, "we shall simply have to eat in silence. Guess again."

"You sent telegrams to friends in south Devon — inquiring discreetly about the Thornes, I imagine? And you have received satisfactory replies?"

Her mother's face fell throughout this response, passing from puzzlement through disbelief to anger. "Have you been rifling my bureau?" she asked.

"I have been emptying your waste-paper basket — a task I never entrust to the maids, as you know. Two envelopes torn from telegrams — taken together with the gleam in your eyes when I spoke of the Thornes last night — lead me to ..."

"Yes, yes, dear. All very clever, I'm sure. Take care not to become *too* sharp, though, or you'll cut yourself. What d'you think they said?"

"More guessing — this *is* fun! Well, since you called it 'splendid news,' I must assume that the Thornes have consols enough to paper their ample acres, that young Victor has somehow earned the distrust of the parents or guardians of every suitable spinster in the entire West Country, and that they are therefore reduced to seeking his bride among spinsters who would be suitable were it not for a blush or two at the bank."

Harriet supped her soup in stony silence.

"Am I warm?" Tamsin asked.

The news was too good to keep back, despite the girl's provocations. "He is promised to no one. It is quite certain. In fact, he has just concluded an acquaintance with one particular female, an acquaintance that might have led, in the fullness of time, to an engagement."

"Oh dear! Is the air now heavy with the stench of a costly breach-of-promise suit?"

"I'm sure Eleanor would have warned me if that were so."

"Good. We have an empty field, then."

"Quite. But that's only the beginning. At the age of twenty-two, it seems, he will inherit a substantial portion of his uncle's — I had this from Madge Cunningham, by the way, whose maiden name was Thorne, as I said — and, indeed, she is a cousin to Walter Thorne, your young man's father — and she says …"

"*My* young man?" Tamsin protested, though the news that Victor was to inherit a worthwhile fortune was interesting to her. "He is no such thing. In fact, he sent me a letter this very afternoon to inform me that there could be no further intercourse between us."

Harriet dropped her spoon into her bowl, which was fortunately empty. "He *what?* But what on earth have you done to provoke …"

"I merely told him that if he had come to Penzance looking for a brief, seaside fling, then …"

"*Seaside fling?* You used such a disgraceful vulgarism to him? Oh, Tamsin!"

"... then he would be wasting his own time in pursuing me. Was I wrong? Should I have encouraged him to look upon me as one of those discardable girls that men like him have no difficulty in finding? Even miles away from the shoreline?"

Her mother said nothing, being unable to say the honest no that would also condone her daughter's insulting brashness. "There are ways of saying these things, dear, without provoking letters like that." She rang the bell for Bridget to clear the soup and bring the entrée.

"Why are we so keen to discuss him?" Tamsin asked as they set about their second course. "With or without his inheritance, he is not the most interesting young man one could ever hope to meet. In fact ..." She hesitated. She had been about to say that David Peters was ten times more interesting but she realized it was a thought she did not wish to pursue, not even with herself.

"In fact what?" Harriet asked.

"In fact, he's pretty dull."

"No man with prospects of an inheritance is *dull,* dear."

"Ah! So it is wealth that makes him interesting?"

"Of course it is."

"Wealth? As in money? As in filthy lucre? Are you quite sure this is a fitting subject for the dinner table, Mama dear?"

She ignored this new provocation. "You must reply at once. Ask his forgiveness. Say that whatever insult he may have inferred, you certainly did not intend it. Put it down to your innocence and youth — and stress innocence and youth. It will do no harm to remind him that you possess both those qualities in abundance ..."

"You mean, allow him to understand I would make a docile and subordinate wife?"

"Not at all. I know you're trying to vex me again, so I shan't rise to it. You must allow him to understand you would not be a virago, a termagant ..."

"A shrew, a frump, a tigress, a scold ..."

"Tamsin!"

"Shall I write in blue ink? Or green?"

"What d'you mean?"

"Or I know — turquoise! Mix the two! The colour of my eyes — so daring!"

"What on earth are you talking about, girl?"

"Well, you seem to be laying down the law as to every dot and comma in this letter I am to write — why on earth should you balk at the choice of ink?"

"I'm only trying to suggest what's best for you, dear — for us both. And don't close your eyes and shake your head like that. You know it's true. Our best way out of our present difficulties is for one of us to marry, or marry again, and to marry jolly well. And so, since your prospects are a hundred times brighter than mine, you owe it to both of us to swallow your pride and write a letter that …"

"And grovel, you mean. Honestly, Mama! I know you think you're doing everything for the best, but times have changed. We've moved on. The sort of letter you're proposing would have been the bee's knees in eighteen-eighty, I'm sure. Today it's the spider's ankles."

"Bee's knees! Spider's ankles!" Harriet fanned herself with her napkin.

"In any case, I've already replied."

"You have?" The colour drained from her cheeks and the fanning stopped.

"I scribbled a few words it on the back of his letter and sent it back to him."

It was Harriet's turn to close her eyes and shake her head. "Dare I ask?" she murmured.

Tamsin told her what she had written.

Dread yielded to bewilderment. "But what does it mean?" she asked.

"It means whatever he cares to read into it. If he wishes to think of it as a 'docile and subordinate' reply, he's free to do so. Why should any girl go out of her way to feed a man with flatteries when his own gift of self-delusion will do it all for her?"

Harriet's mood swung yet again, this time to consternation. "Where did you learn such cynicism, child? Not from me, I'm sure. Nor from your poor, dear father."

But there she was wrong. Tamsin had, indeed, learned her views of the world and its ways in many a conversation with her late father — though he would have called it practical common sense rather than cynicism. It wasn't that he had had some foreboding of the impending crash in their fortunes — and was therefore giving his daughter a few hasty insights into the ways of the world. From the time she was ten he had always tried to provide her with a tactful counterweight to her mother's views, about which the very harshest words he'd ever used were 'sheltered' and 'rose-tinted.'

But then again, perhaps he had *always* feared for some catastrophe — in the way that any prudent businessman must keep the possibility of bankruptcy forever in mind. In which case he would have realized that to leave his wife and daughter with their heads stuffed with the naïve and gullible innocence that had seemed so desirable among well-bred young ladies of the 1880s would be a peculiar sort of cruelty.

He would also have realized that his wife was beyond persuasion. Naïveté was almost her second religion. It had secured her the husband of her parents' (and her own) choice at eighteen and it had delivered all its promises right up until the crash — which was, of course, an Act of God but of a different God. Little wonder, then, that he had concentrated his efforts on his daughter, instead.

For all these reasons, however, Tamsin could not directly enlighten her mother; she could do nothing to reveal that the father had been quite different from the husband. Not only would her mother simply refuse to believe it but she would also close her ears to any future discussion where her 'sheltered, rose-tinted' views clashed with her daughter's more pragmatic ones. All she could do was seek to chip away at the edges with a thousand tiny 'provocations,' as her mother called them.

So, when Harriet said that Tamsin could not possibly have obtained her views from her father, the girl let it go. "What I *did* get from both of you, though," she replied, "is a good pair of eyes. And I can see that two females in our circumstances do *not* get the same treatment from the world in general as the two ladies we once were. Shopkeepers do not come fawning to our carriage. Nor do they offer us credit. Nor do people call with cards …"

"Yes, dear," Harriet sighed wearily. "We know it all too well."

"Then let's behave as if we know it. Let's realize that we must now do things that those two ladies would have found distasteful.

And let's do them before even more distasteful things get done to us. Strike or be stricken, Mama — that's our choice now."

Bridget brought in the main course and set it before Tamsin to serve.

"Lobster thermidor!" Harriet exclaimed. "My dear!"

"What now?" Tamsin asked innocently. "It's one of your favourites, I thought."

"So it is — but the expense!"

"Really we ought to have a nice Bollinger with it," Tamsin said as she lifted the shell. "But I took the liberty of decanting some white *vin ordinaire* into the soda syphon and making it fizz — as we used to do for our servants' balls, remember?"

Harriet shuddered.

"And — once again — Mrs Pascoe has produced a culinary triumph. This is pure ambrosia. She is wasting her talent on kippers for breakfast."

Harriet ignored the by now familiar litany. "How much ... I mean, I hope you weren't too extravagant?"

"No, Mama, you mean 'what did it cost'? Well, it cost no more than a smile and the time of day."

An image of David Peters filled her mind's eye ... his strong arms, bronzed by sun and salt ... the muscles rippling as he pulled at the oars ... the lithe strength of all his movements ... his smile ...

No! Enough! She was not going to yield to silly, girlish daydreams of that nature.

"This fisherman-sea-captain who spoke to you so impertinently yesterday?" Harriet asked. "Did he ...?"

"His son David. His only surviving son, now."

"He has accosted you, too? Oh, Tamsin!"

"It was the other way round, if anything. I wanted to buy a lobster from him — they're not expensive directly out of the boat, you know. But he presented me with one instead."

"He'll want something in return, of course. People like that — they always do."

"Of course he does. And not just any old 'something'. I know exactly what he wants."

Harriet stared awkwardly at her plate; this conversation had taken an embarrassing turn.

"He wants me to persuade you that Mrs Pascoe's talents could be better employed than they are at present."

Harriet held her breath and counted slowly to ten. Unfortunately it gave time for the flavour of her latest mouthful of succulent lobster to bathe her senses. Tamsin's 'ambrosia' was an understatement, if anything. The steady drip of the girl's arguments must have eroded more ground from beneath her feet than she had realized; that and the ecstasy of her taste buds tipped her off balance enough to ask, "In what way?"

The tone was guarded, the eyes suspicious, but the question had been asked. The door was open. Even so, Tamsin had nous enough not to go rushing through it all at once. "Imagine!" she exclaimed. "Being able to dine on seafood of this quality any evening one wished! Think!"

Watching her daughter at that moment, Harriet felt an entirely novel emotion — at least, it was novel as far as her feelings toward her daughter were concerned. And it was not something she could easily name. To call it 'fear' was too crude; 'anxiety' was too feeble; 'alarm' too fleeting. Until this moment, Tamsin's persistence in arguing for her own point of view and badgering to get her own way had provoked little more than weariness in her mother; but now that she had been forced to concede, even in so slight a matter, she began to see it all in a different light.

She realized that Tamsin was going to win every such battle in which the two of them engaged. Her trivial concession on this particular occasion somehow confirmed it. Tamsin would see it as a reward for her persistence and it would make her doubly resolute in future. But even that was not the core of her mother's disquiet. Without admitting it to herself in so many words, Harriet realized that her concession was much more than a simple permission to break a firm rule of etiquette, just on this one occasion; it was, in effect, an admission that Tamsin might be right — that the rule itself was inappropriate — that the standards to which she had adhered since childhood might have to change. It was a moment as shattering as that other great watershed in her life — when Mr Samson, the family solicitor, had broken the news of their bankruptcy to her.

Perhaps, after all, 'fear' was not too strong a word.

7 Victor had been sitting out there in the shelter on the Esplanade, staring at the letter for a good quarter of an hour, when Charlotte came upon him. "What can ail thee, wretched wight?" she asked. "Shall we walk up an appetite before breakfast?"

He handed the sheet to her with a sigh. "I'm hemmed if I can make it out. See what you think."

"We are probably being watched," she warned, taking care to keep the paper below the solidly boarded part of the shelter.

"I know. The minute one of us passes out of sight they'll send a servant after us. I'm beginning to see what Miss Harte was talking about — freedom and all that. Turn it over. Read what's on the back."

Charlotte read Tamsin's response two or three times and said, "Extraordinary."

"Is that all you can say? I could have told you that. I send her a letter breaking off all intercourse and instead of returning it ..."

"*You* ...?" Charlotte began

But he continued: "Instead of returning it, she copies it out word for word and then scribbles that odd rigmarole on the back. What am I supposed to make of it?"

"*She* copied it out?" Charlotte's tone was filled with doubt. She turned the sheet over and read the letter again. "This is her hand? It looks very like Mama's, you know."

He snatched the letter back from her and examined it closely. "Oh, my God!"

"I'm right, aren't I?" she pressed him.

He nodded morosely. "But that only makes the whole business all the more mysterious. Why on earth should Mama ...?"

"Tell me from the beginning. You wrote her a letter ..."

"I've been sitting here trying to cudgel my brains as to why on earth Miss Harte should want to copy out my letter and then write her reply on the back. I could only think she wanted to preserve my original."

"Next to her heart, no doubt!" Charlotte sneered. "That would feed your vanity! Why, I daresay you might almost forgive her for that."

"What I wrote was identical … I mean, those are my exact words. It means Mama must have intercepted the letter …"

"After you posted it? Actually, come to think of it, she did go to the post office in Newlyn … no, that was before your little tiff with Miss Harte. Did you post it in the box in the lobby? That's not an official GPO box. She could get at it there."

"I didn't post it anywhere. I gave Dobbs sixpence to run round the corner with it."

"Then clearly Mama intercepted Dobbs."

"Yes, well, that's obvious now. But the wretched girl didn't say a word to me about it."

"Be fair. She's hardly had a chance. If we're not going for a walk, we could go in to breakfast now. I've already worked up my appetite."

He rose wearily and tucked the letter into his breast pocket.

"Who brought the reply back to you?" Charlotte asked as they crossed the road to the hôtel.

"The porter gave it me. He said Miss Harte called and left it with him. Yesterday evening."

"Called in person! She wanted to be sure you got it, then. Ah, there's Dobbs now."

Daisy, who had been hovering near the staff door, waiting for them to return, came forward in some agitation as they reentered the lobby. "Oh, Mister Victor!" she exclaimed. "Pardon me but I've been that eager to speak with you …"

"Never mind all that now," Charlotte told her. "We've pieced together most of the story. My mother must have intercepted you and …"

"Here, miss. On this very spot. And she took me to the ladies' lounge and got my message out of me … well, I couldn't tell an untruth, could I." She turned again to Victor. "I did warn you it was tempting fate to …"

"Yes, yes," he said. "What's done is done. But why did she send you onward with a *copy* of my letter? What happened to the original — the one I wrote?"

Daisy was now in a quandary. The last thing she wanted to do was admit she had retrieved the original from the waste paper basket — much less that she had shown it to Tamsin and had discovered the two letters to be identical.

"The way I saw it, sir," she replied, "is that the mistress tore up your letter, then sat down and wrote one of her own, and sent me on my way with it. She didn't tell me it was a copy of yours."

"And what happened to my original?"

Daisy shrugged. "I think she threw it in the waste-paper basket, sir."

"She tore it up *before* reading it," Charlotte guessed.

Daisy nodded.

"What difference does it make?" he asked glumly. "Tearing up is tearing up."

"Don't you see? She tore it up in a rage because she thought it was a *billet doux*. But when she calms down and actually reads it, she realizes what a mistake she's made. She wants us to have nothing to do with Miss Harte and now she's gone and torn up a letter from you that puts the identical sentiment in the strongest possible terms. So of course she copies it out again and sends it on, hoping Miss H won't notice it's in a woman's hand." She turned to Daisy. "Did she?"

"Beg pardon, miss?" Daisy was playing for time.

"Did Miss Harte notice the letter was in a lady's hand?"

"I believe she did say something to that effect, miss."

"And I asked you to hang around and try to study her face while she read it," Victor put in. "Did you manage that?"

"Yes sir. She read it and then she smiled."

"Smiled!" Victor was taken aback. "What, a putting-on-a-brave-face sort of smile?"

"No sir. More like *amused,* I'd call it."

"Devil take her!" He spun on his heel and would have left the building again if his sister's shocked cry had not halted him. "What now?" he asked truculently.

"I will not have you using language like that in front of my maid. Now come back here and apologize."

"Oh, miss ..." Daisy was embarrassed. "It's not necessary. Really and truly ..."

Charlotte ignored her. "Otherwise I shall have to ask Mama to deal with the matter."

He made a parade of his petty humiliation, rolling his shoulders and lifting his eyes to the ceiling to suggest that he'd humour her even though he thought she was over-reacting in a most childish way. "Sorry, Dobbs," he said in the least contrite tone he could manage. "Did she ... no, I don't suppose she did."

"Did what, sir?"

"Discuss ... you know ... the contents of this letter ... her response ... no, of course she didn't. Shouldn't have asked. Forgive me."

"Of course she didn't," Charlotte scolded.

"I already said that."

"And even if she'd tried it, Dobbs wouldn't have permitted it for an instant, would you, Dobbs."

"Not for an instant, miss," Daisy replied, glad her mistress had chosen 'an instant' rather than, say, 'half an hour.'

"She asked no questions about the letter? About us? Nothing?"

"Stop pestering the poor girl!" Charlotte cried.

"She gave me a glass of lemonade before I returned," Daisy volunteered. "There is just one thing, sir ... miss?"

"Yes?"

"Mrs Thorne didn't specifically order me not to tell you what happened, but she won't be too pleased to hear that I did."

"Mum's the word, Dobbs," Victor replied cheerfully. "I say — that's rather good, what? Mum's the word!"

"There's still the question of what Miss Harte's enigmatic reply actually means," Charlotte said as they went into the dining room.

Their parents were not about as yet. They helped themselves to porridge and chose a table as far as possible from the other diners, all of whom seemed to have chosen their tables on the same principle — such is the inordinate love of the bourgeois for their fellows.

"The sea is not breakable ..." Charlotte paraphrased from memory. "But it breaks every day on every shore. Shall my heart be any different? That was more or less the gist of it, wasn't it?" She chuckled.

"I see nothing funny in it," he grumbled.

"That's because she's won, Victor, dear."

"She most certainly has not!"

Charlotte darted her hand across the table and snatched the letter from his pocket. "Then we might as well tear this up and talk of other things. We'd save a lot of breath."

"Give it back," he said menacingly. "I'll throw it away, right enough — just try and stop me! But not before I've managed to work out what it means."

"Then she *has* won," she insisted. "Because the only way you'll ever learn what she meant is to ask her. You're going to have to seek her out and ask her." She grinned sweetly.

He stared into his porridge and said, "You could ask her for me instead."

"And disobey Mama?"

"Oh, of course, you've never done such a thing in your life before, have you!"

"I have. Of course I have. But only for my own benefit. Anyway, I don't need to ask her. I already understand completely what she meant."

"Am I permitted to …"

"But I already told you — she chose words so perfectly ambiguous that you'd be forced to break your own implied promise never to see her again and ask her."

He turned the letter over so that Tamsin's reply was face-up. Then he spun it side-on to him, as if some new meaning might then emerge from between the lines … the few, short lines. None did, of course.

"Is she trying to say I've broken her heart?" he asked.

"Or is she saying, 'I know you'd like to believe you've broken my heart and so, if it amuses you, think away to *your* heart's content. I am quite indifferent.'?"

"I'm asking the questions," he grumbled.

"Her questions — she's the one who put them into your mind. Don't you see?"

"I'm going for some more porridge. You?"

As they crossed the room to the buffet he said, "You might show a fellow a little sympathy?"

"I don't see why," she answered amiably. "This is a mess entirely of your own making."

The craggy gentleman with the bushy eyebrows entered the dining room and made straight for the buffet. Victor could not respond until they were on their way back to their table, where the waitress had, meanwhile, brought their toast and marmalade. They sent it back and asked her not to bring it until after they had finished the hot course from the buffet. They had asked for the same delay at every breakfast since the start of their visit.

"I don't see how it's a mess of my own making," Victor grumbled when they were relatively alone again. "Everything was perfectly straightforward until she weighed in with this ... this ... one can't even call it a reply."

"Riposte?" Charlotte suggested. "A flankonade. A hit! A palpable hit, egad!"

"I had no choice," he protested.

"Of course you did," she scoffed. "There was absolutely no need to climb up on your high horse like that. 'No further intercourse between us'! Faugh!" She mocked his tone. "You always regret it when you go all pompous like that."

"She made a quite scurrilous suggestion about me, to which I could hardly ..."

"All she said was that if you merely intended to trifle with her affections, you'd be wasting your time."

"And that's an insult. There you are!"

"You mean you *didn't* intend to trifle with her affections? Are we to believe that?"

"I don't care what you believe. It's the truth."

"What is the truth?"

"That I had no idea *what* I intended. For heaven's sake — we'd only just met. Why should I have any intentions at all?"

"Then, brother dear, why didn't you simply say so? You could have laughed it off and we'd have been spared all this confluffle. The very fact that your hackles rose at the merest suggestion that you might trifle with her affections suggested at once that there was something in it, after all."

"Suggested to whom?"

"To me, for one — and I'm sure to her, too. That's why I say you brought it on yourself."

"Well ... all I can say is I didn't mean it that way."

"Famous last words!'

He breathed deep and let it out in one long sigh. "I'm not really hungry," he said. "I wish we hadn't sent the toast and marmalade away now."

Charlotte smiled sympathetically. "Go and grovel to the waitress," she said. "It'll be good practice."

8 Walter Thorne threw up the sash window and breathed great draughts of what the town guide-book called healthy sea air, laden though it was with salt and marine decay. His intention was to gauge the weather for the coming day, to assist him in his choice between his club tie with a soft-collar shirt or a plain cotton square with an open-necked shirt. But the odour of decay started a different train of thought. "It's amazing, really," he said, "when you think of it, my dear. The sea is a vast liquid graveyard. Everything that lives in it also dies in it — to say nothing of all the activities they get up to while still alive …"

"Walter, dear," said his wife, "I think that is quite vivid enough. There is no need to pursue the thought. Meanwhile, we have a much more pressing …"

"Yes but my point is, you see — all these doctor johnnies keep going on about how healthy it is to bathe in the stuff and breathe the air that comes off it — it's a bit like advising people to haunt the cemeteries and sewage farms and to breathe the air that rises off the graves and … you know, those things that go round and round."

"Walter!"

"Is it red sky in the morning, shepherd's warning?" he asked.

Cicely glanced up from her dressing table, where Daisy was sorting out the curl-papers from her hair. "But the sky isn't red at all," she said.

"Just so. Therefore no shepherds are warned. Therefore it's going to be a fine day. So I'll wear my cotton square, I think. Until lunchtime at least."

"Luncheon," she corrected him automatically. "We have a much more pressing problem — *nos enfants et Mam'selle Coeur.*"

"Ker?" he asked as he crossed to the door of his dressing room. "Teacup Ker and her parents? Are they in Penzance?"

The Kers were friends from Devon; their daughter was called 'Teacup' because she had been born minus one ear. Her dowry was fabulous.

"*Coeur,* dear — as in *Coeur de Lion!*" She tapped her breast. "Think!"

"Heart? Oh! Ah! See what you mean. Say no more."

Cicely's eyes raked the ceiling — or, rather, they raked the image of the ceiling in the mirror before her. Unfortunately it was at such an angle that Daisy stood between her and it and so, naturally, assumed she was being invited to share her mistress's despair at the master's obtuseness; she, too, raised her eyes heavenward in sympathy. Mrs Thorne had never thought to ask her if she spoke or at least understood French, and she, for her part, had never felt the slightest need to volunteer the information that she could.

The mistress realized there was no way to make it clear to the servant that she had *not* invited a comment on the master's behaviour; she did not conduct that sort of household. Instead, she simply had to swallow her annoyance. "Dobbs," she said. "You may go and tell Greenhill that the master is ready to shave and dress."

Greenhill was Walter Thorne's valet.

The moment Daisy left the room, Cicely turned on her husband. "You could at least try to be a little more *au fait,* my dear," she said, laying a venomous stress on the word *dear.* "This sorry situation *vis-à-vis* Miss Harte and our own two youngsters is fraught with danger."

He stood with his hand to the doorhandle of his dressing room. "I'm not aware of any difficulty. I thought you said all was well. Didn't you tell me Victor had written …"

"That was last night. I've had ten hours to sleep on it — not that I did much sleeping — and not that *you'd* be aware of that. But you know yourself how impetuous Victor is. He'll explode like that one day and, come the next dawn, he's apologizing to all and sundry."

"I still don't understand why he exploded in the first place. Something about impugning his honour? What on earth was that all about?"

"I don't know — and I'm certainly not going to inquire. It's a hornet's nest."

"It must have been quite harsh. I mean, he wouldn't have flown off the handle unless she'd said something that cut him to the quick."

"More to the point, dear, he wouldn't have been upset at all if he was indifferent to her opinions. He obviously cares what she thinks — which means, equally obviously, that he cares about her. So when he recovers from his fit of pique ... well, it's quite clear what he's going to do."

"Bow and scrape."

"Quite."

"In other words," Walter added, "he'll concede the first round to her."

"Yes, well there's no need to sound quite so brusque. One would almost think you were cheerful. We mustn't let her win anything. We must stop the contest *now* — so that there isn't even a first round."

He let go of the handle and sat in the chair beside the door. "We could cancel the rest of our holiday here," he suggested. "Go to Torquay? Or" — he sought to conceal a note of rising hope in his voice — "to France? What was the name of that absolutely splendid hôtel at Deauville?"

Cicely shook her head vehemently. "Certainly not! Cut and run? Let the gold-digging intrigues of a scheming little hussy like her ruin all our plans? No! We shall do as I said in the very hour of our first encounter — fill our days with excursions and engagements that make any sort of meeting impossible. If it hadn't been for having to send those telegrams ..."

"And our evenings? And nights?"

"Miss Harte has to attend to their paying guests in the evenings. And as for the nights, well, we must simply exhaust the youngsters enough by day to ensure that they desire nothing but a firm mattress and a soft pillow at night."

To Walter it sounded a pretty forlorn sort of plan — like trying to prevent schoolboy vices with sports and cold showers. Also he had little doubt which generation of Thornes would be the first to succumb to the exhaustions of each such day.

Cicely, aware of his unspoken misgivings and having no adequate answer to give, tut-tutted with vexation. "Where *is* that girl?" She picked up the hairbrush and made a few incompetent stabs at her own coiffure where the curl papers had been removed. "I hate these miles of corridors. We should have taken rooms for the servants on this floor."

* * *

Tamsin was in the kitchen, preparing the breakfast pats of butter in a new way. When she had delivered her reply to the porter at the Queen's last night, she'd asked the fellow to let her out by the back way, just in case one of the Thornes spied her out front. On their way through the kitchens she had spotted the housekeeper in the still-room, using a machine that squeezed butter out in a sort of sunflower shape and simultaneously cut it into slices anything from one-to three-eighths of an inch thick. They fell into a large bowl filled with ice-cold water — indeed, there were fragments of ice floating in it. Stored in a chill cabinet overnight, they remained firm and crisp until sent to the breakfast table next morning. Seeing Tamsin's interest, the housekeeper had shown her how to make attractively curly butter-balls with an ordinary teaspoon; it was simply a matter of keeping the butter cold enough to stay firm yet not so cold that it broke into fragments.

"The advantage," the woman added, "is not just that it looks nice but you need only send out half the amount of butter to each table that you would if you sent it in blocks. A block as small as two of these star-shapes would look far too mean."

The Morrab Guest House had no chill cabinet (*yet,* Tamsin would have added); but a large earthenware jar, glazed only on the inside and kept moist under a slowly dripping tap, could get finger-numbingly chill inside, especially if stood in a draught and out of the sun. So the curly butter-balls she had made after returning home last night were as crisp now as they had been then. She doled them out carefully, so many per person, into little glass sorbet bowls for Bridget and Catherine to serve along with the toast. She put three per person in the smaller bowls, four in the larger ones; if none of the threes asked for more, or complained, it would be three per person from then on.

Mrs Pascoe, the cook, watched her out of the corner of her eye throughout the breakfast service. "You done that afore, have you, miss?" she asked when there was a lull in orders.

"Never. That's why I waited until no one was around last night before I tried to make them. You should have seen my first efforts!" She gauged the size of the butter block that remained, "Still, I think we can cut a pound or two off our weekly butter order at the Home and Colonial."

The arrival of another family in the dining room cut short their conversation. Tamsin went out to greet them and to see how much butter was being left at tables where guests had breakfasted and gone. It was gratifyingly little, and none of the threes complained.

"Very nice!" One young guest caught her eye. Briefly his fair hair turned to a cauliflower head and an equally imaginary pig's trotter was clamped between his jaws, like a gun-dog retriever holding a partridge.

This was her system — or her father's system, in fact — for remembering the dozens of names she had to hold in her head, so that she never called a guest Mr Er-um. The more absurd the pictorial association, the better it stuck in the memory.

The cauliflower was a veg, which rhymed with Reg; so this was Reginald Trotter, staying here with his mother. The generally expressed opinion among the staff was that he was convalescing after some quite serious illness — consumption, perhaps; the generally unexpressed opinion was that he was sweet on her. But Tamsin did not agree; in fact, she detected something rather cold — or at least indifferent — in the young man, though he was charming enough in every other way.

"The butter," he added. "Very elegant."

"Thank you, Mister Trotter." She paused just long enough to leave him feeling unsnubbed. "We learn as we go along and we try to improve a little each day. I hope your mother is well? Shall I send up to see?"

"No. I heard her thumping about before I came down."

She moved on to the new arrivals. In her mind's eye the man had a box made of thin cardboard on his head; on each of its sides was printed a single letter L; carton plus L equals ...

"Good morning, Mrs Carlton ... Doctor Carlton. I trust you slept well — your first night in new beds?"

They hadn't slept so well in years; it must be the sea air. The doctor had his practice in Gloucester. Always a great believer in sea air and salt-water bathing, he had seen remarkable cures. They usually went to south Wales for their holidays but this year they thought they'd try Cornwall, instead. Where was the best place to buy buckets and spades? And a canvas windbreak? And did the town council rent out deck-chairs by the day? What about a packed lunch? Could Miss Harte oblige? It was ten minutes before Tamsin escaped — miraculously without naming a price for the packed lunch, which she wouldn't have done without first discussing it with Mrs Pascoe. And her mother, too, possibly.

Five minutes later she was able to inform Mrs Carlton that she could do a packed lunch, consisting of an apple, a stick of celery, two full-round sandwiches (tongue and pickle, cheese and tomato), and a slice of rich fruit cake at sixpence each. She did not say it but she was prepared to knock twopence off the children's packs even though, at ten and twelve, they had appetites as large as their parents'.

Mrs Carlton said that Dr Carlton would have onion instead of tomato, which he believed was poisonous.

"And the same goes for you and the children, I suppose?" Tamsin asked.

"No, he doesn't mind us poisoning ourselves," she replied cheerily. "Would you consider charging less if we placed an order now for every lunchtime this week?"

Tamsin regretted that the price only just covered the actual cost of putting up the meals; however, as a gesture of goodwill, she would lend them a spirit stove on which they could brew a cup of tea whenever they liked. It might as well be gaining them goodwill, she thought, as gathering dust in the attic.

"What a very obliging young woman," Tamsin heard the ten-year-old daughter whisper as she returned to the kitchen.

"Lady, dear," her mother replied. "She's a lady. One can always tell."

Tamsin smiled to herself and wished her mother had been there to hear it. She drew a little notebook from her pocket and wrote, 'Find out prices of beach chalets on the eastern strand.'

If the Morrab Guest House could rent three or four of them throughout the season — at a good discount, of course — they could hire them out to their guests at a small profit and it would look good in their brochure and advertisements: *Exclusive beach chalets also available at nominal rates.*

"What are you grinning at?" her mother asked as she passed the office door.

"We may be poor," Tamsin replied, "but we do see life."

9 For two days Victor did nothing about Tamsin's ambiguous rejection of his over-hasty note — which is not to say that he mooned around the place doing nothing at all. Indeed, he and Charlotte, having a long experience of dealing with their mother's dictatorship, threw themselves body and soul into her plans to exhaust them by day and so leave them with no energy for evening mischiefs. For instance, on their tour of the Stone Age antiquities of the Land's End peninsula, if her guidebook spoke of some 'rock-embosomed tarn nestling in a nook upon a wild Atlantic headland, to which they simply must ascend,' they would race her and their father to its shore and there espy some noble, craggy eminence at an even greater altitude, from which the visitor simply must enjoy a commanding view of the mighty deep beyond.

"It's like in the Bible," Charlotte pointed out as they scaled the new height, leaving their exhausted parents trailing far behind. "If a man should compel you to go a mile, go with him twain ... that sort of thing."

On Sunday morning, after several days of this biblical retribution, Cicely fell asleep at matins — during a rousing hymn, no less — and it became clear that some less demanding way of occupying her children would have to be devised.

"Deauville it is, then," Walter suggested brightly as they returned to the Queen's along the promenade.

"Deauville it most certainly is not," she replied. "We stand upon this ground and fight."

Tamsin was meanwhile kept in touch with events by Daisy, who had time on her hands while the exhausting excursions were in progress. Chores that would normally have taken three hours were dispatched in one, leaving two to spend at the Morrab Guest House. If Tamsin were busy, she rolled up her sleeves and pitched in; otherwise they went marketing together or simply strolled around the town, criticizing houses, gardens, colour schemes, shop windows, and what passed for fashion among the ladies and gentlemen they encountered on their way.

They approved of fair hair in a woman as long as it was not silver or ash; gold was tolerable if slightly hackneyed; but pale auburn, strawberry, or honey was best of all. Brown hair was fine, too, as long as it was light enough to show off its chestnut richness — dark brown being just too dull to consider. Daisy was a rather pale auburn, Tamsin a rich, light chestnut, but they did not believe that swayed their taste in the matter.

As for dress material, stripes should enjoy a come-back, they decided. Especially the rich silks of the 1890s with their broad, boldly coloured verticals, which were so flattering to the figure. But, please, not the big bustles that went with them then, and all the frothy frills and tucks and gathers they, in their turn, required. The modern bustle, which you could almost believe was natural, was so much more becoming. And convenient.

On the other hand, there was something to be said for the plain homespun of the arts-and-crafts fashions, with no bustle at all and a sensible hang to the dress. It allowed a woman complete freedom of movement and didn't touch the ground, or, as Tamsin put it, 'didn't do half the crossing-sweeper's work for him.'

Daisy was less certain. "It would be a great nuisance, though. Think of all the attention we'd get from errand boys and street-corner loafers if we showed our ankles. Even now, if you lift your hem to step over a puddle …"

"Yes, but if we all did it, they'd soon tire of it. Like with the Greek dancing craze, remember? All the men flocked to join at the beginning — and we know why — but now the only ones left are those who actually enjoy the dancing itself. If all ankles were on display, you'd soon have to show a knee before the errand boys would whoop. If you suddenly came into a fortune, Daisy — if they found you were the only heir to some diamond king, say — so you could do anything you liked and no one could stop you, how would you dress?"

Daisy answered without hesitation: "I'd buy a little cottage in the middle of a wood — I'd buy the woods, too, of course — and I'd wear simple rustic clothes, which I'd make from cloth I'd weave myself from yarn I had spun myself … you know — that sort of thing."

"You, Daisy, are a simple-lifer!"

But now the dream was tapped, the flow of it was not to be stemmed with a single friendly-facetious comment.

"And I'd grow all my own food and I'd make up songs and poems and be friends with all the woodland creatures ..."

"And for company? You couldn't live entirely without ..."

"I'd have my cats and dogs, my pigs, my ducks and geese, my goats ..."

"And if you fell ill?"

"I'd find some berry or herb that'd cure it. There must be books that'd tell me such things."

"An herbal."

"If that's what they call it."

"And you wouldn't feel the lack of a husband? You wouldn't want a family of your own?"

Daisy shot her such a withering look that Tamsin almost felt she had committed a social trespass, though she knew it was a question most other women would not only understand but also feel obliged to answer. At the same time, the idyllic picture the maid had painted was seductive enough to make her wonder if her own ambitions had not been leading her down the wrong track entirely.

"More is less," Daisy said. "My mother was housekeeper to Lady Foster of Bledisloe Hall, up in Wiltshire. My father was head butler there, like I said."

"Yes, I meant to ask — how did he go from that to diver in the Royal Navy docks?"

"His elder brother, my uncle Joe, was head diver there. He trained him and got him the job. It's not *what* you know, it's *who* you know, he used to say. Anyway, Bledisloe Hall had one hundred and fifty-three rooms and each one was crammed to the cornice with pictures, china, silver, fans, butterfly cases, tapestries, stags' heads, suits of armour, old clocks, swords and shields ... and as for books! You could have lost the average town library among them."

"How does that make more equal to less?" Tamsin asked.

"Because when Lady Foster died none of her children wanted any of it. And I didn't blame them. They'd watched her collection grow. They knew it was what killed her in the end."

"From nervous exhaustion, I suppose?"

"From *physical* exhaustion — just walking round, supervising the cleaning, keeping everything in working order, repairing damage … fighting woodworm, bookworm, dry rot, wet rot, foxing …"

"So what happened to it all?"

"Sotheby's cleared the lot. The auction went on and on and on for three weeks."

"Oh, *that* was the place, was it? Bledisloe Hall — yes, I remember reading about it now."

"When it was all over I came upon the Honourable Gwendolen, one of the daughters, standing by one of the ballroom windows … a great, empty, echoing room by then, of course — I was only fifteen at the time — and she pointed out the woodland down one side of the lake, which her great-grandad had planted, and where her grandad had built ruined temples and things …"

"Follies," Tamsin said.

"That's what they called them, yes — including a rustic cottage — very ornate like in fairy tales — and she said to me, the Honourable Gwendolen, she said, 'You know, Daisy, if Mama had only been content to live in that little cottage, she'd still be alive today.' Tears running down her face there were. I've never forgotten it."

"No … obviously."

"So!" Daisy laughed. "That's enough of me. What'd you do if you won a four-horse accumulator and could tell the world to go and boil its head?"

"I'd build an hôtel."

It stopped Daisy dead in her tracks — they were strolling around Morrab Gardens at the time. "You'd *what?*"

"You heard." They flicked some raindrops off the slats of a bench and sat down. "I dream about it every night before I go to sleep. I can close my eyes and walk through every room — from the wine cellar and boiler room down in the basement all the way up to the water tanks under the roof."

"But why?" Daisy's tone was part intrigued, part appalled.

"Before we went smash I used to dream of being the owner of a vast Atlantic liner — the family connection with the sea, I suppose. What always intrigued me was the business of the public face and the private face. It's the same with the stage, even with amateur dramatics. Did you ever take part in anything like that, Daisy?"

"We did a play at school — *Tom and the Water Babies.*"

"Then you know what I mean — the secret backstage life and the public show out in the limelight. It's the same with a big luxury liner like the *Celtic* or the *Kaiser Wilhelm II* — a round-the-clock theatre for the benefit of the first-class passengers in which all the *real* workings of the ship are hidden away. Two worlds — that's what it is — two worlds that are joined together yet never truly mix. Even in our humble little guest house we've got a hint of it — but you must see it even more in the Queen's?"

Daisy gave a hollow laugh. "I don't think the guests would approve of everything that goes on in that other world."

Tamsin's eyes glowed. "Do *tell!*"

"Well …" Daisy rolled her eyes. "It's all little things. For instance, did you know you can serve cold cuts off yesterday's joint as if they were from today's fresh roast?"

"How?" She squirmed with pleasure.

"Say it's lamb — which is what the chef there did for dinner yesterday, Friday. All you need is good lamb stock — which he made last Tuesday when he roasted the joint. He cut thin slices off the leg, cold, of course, and put them on a hot plate with a teaspoon of the stock. Then into the bain marie and …"

"What's that — a bain marie?"

"It's like a steam cabinet. You stack the plates inside, with rings, and you cover them so's they don't get wet with condensation. Then you just heat them with steam. It keeps them piping hot without drying out, see? And after ten minutes the cold meat has softened and taken up the stock and you'd swear it was fresh-cut off a roast joint."

Tamsin laughed and clapped her hands, which surprised her friend somewhat. "That's what I mean, Daisy — the difference between the public show and the secret reality behind it all."

"And there's another thing. The barman told me that if they've got a guest who's already had enough to drink and he keeps on ordering brandy and soda or gin and tonic — stuff like that — he just wets the rim of the glass with the brandy or the gin and then fills it up with the soda or tonic."

"And they never notice?"

"Not according to him. He says they're more interested in pouring out their woes to a sympathetic ear. So as long as you're the most sympathetic listener in the universe, they're not going to suspect you of anything like that, much less accuse you."

"Oh, Daisy!" Tamsin rubbed her hands with glee. "I'm so glad we had this conversation. It makes me think I'll try for a place at the Queen's when we close over the winter — which we probably will have to. Even if I do it for next to no wages, like an apprentice. It'd be worth learning all these little tricks and things."

Daisy giggled. "Funny — you've almost got me thinking your daydream's a lot more tempting than mine."

Tamsin joined her. "What's really funny is that I thought the same about yours!"

After a short silence Daisy said, "You seemed a bit surprised I don't want a husband and brats hanging around — they don't seem necessary to your plans, either."

"No," Tamsin admitted, "except insofar as the men in this world seem to have most of the money. Your dream is cheap compared with mine. You could probably buy fifty acres of woodland for a thou' — with a cottage thrown in — and you could set yourself up with livestock et cetera for a couple of hundred more. So your daydream isn't impossibly out of reach. Mine would need thirty thou' at least. Fifty to do it properly."

Daisy drew a deep breath and said, "Thirty is about what Mister Victor is going to earn — if you can call it earning — it's going to be his annual income after next year, anyway."

There was quite a pause before Tamsin asked, "D'you think I'm being disgustingly mercenary?"

"It's not for me to say," Daisy replied awkwardly. "Me not feeling the slightest want of a man, anyway, I mean."

"Dear me, Daisy! Do you even *like* the creatures, I wonder?"

"I do not," was the emphatic response. "They're hairy, bony, knobbly, smelly things … weak and domineering and …"

"Weak?" Tamsin queried.

"Of course. Look how they moan and snivel when they get so much as a little cold — something that wouldn't keep a woman in bed a minute longer than usual. And they're weak in the head, too — they can only ever do one thing at a time. I've watched gardeners walk empty-handed past a wheelbarrow that needs bringing back to the yard — ten times in an hour I've seen them do it — and it's always because they're on some other errand each time. How soldiers can march *and* sing as they go is a complete mystery."

This concluding remark allowed them both to laugh off her earlier vehemence. Tamsin wanted to ask her where and how she'd suffered at the hands, or behest, of men; nothing else, she thought, could explain such passion. However, she felt that, for all the warmth of their new friendship, they had not yet developed sufficient intimacy to permit it.

Daisy continued: "I suppose, if you've got to have a man ... well, Mister Victor's not among the worst of them."

"He's very good looking — well, *quite* good looking."

Daisy shrugged and made a noncommittal noise.

"You don't agree?"

The maid sighed. "I've carried his shaving water away when Greenhill's been snivelling with the so-called 'flu. I don't see how any woman can have much opinion of a man once she's gazed into his shaving water." She shuddered.

Tamsin, who had often 'gazed deep' into her father's shaving bowl, loving the smell of his special soap and of the astringent cologne he had used for closing his pores again — to say nothing of the swirly patterns she could make with the razor among the little black hairs on the surface — did not challenge the opinion. Instead she said, "It doesn't necessarily have to come to marriage. I'd never marry for money and ambition if there wasn't also some degree of loving in it as well."

Daisy, who could think only of being wife or mistress, was glad she had not spoken when Tamsin continued: "There's partnership, too — business partnership, I mean. A man with lots of money and not much ambition could make an ideal partner for someone who has no money but lots of vision. And who's willing to work day and night to make it profitable. It could be even better than a love match, in fact."

"A lot better," Daisy said at once. "He'd only own the hôtel."

Tamsin saw a way to tease her — and possibly learn a little more about her into the bargain. "Suppose Mister Victor was to fall in love with you, Daisy ..."

"Ha!"

The sudden loud cry put up a flock of town pigeons on the terrace behind them.

"No, seriously — suppose he got to hear of your ambition to live the simple life, and offered you the chance as long as he could share it with you, would you take him up?"

But Daisy was cannier than she'd thought; the maid just grinned and asked if those herbal books had a chapter on deadly nightshade and death caps, and such like. "And what about yourself?" she dared to ask, now that Tamsin had opened the door to the next stage of intimacy between them. "Are you more inclined to marriage or to partnership at the moment?"

"Marriage, I think. Maybe that's just shades of my upbringing coming out, though."

"With Victor?"

"Well … there isn't anyone else, is there!" She thought fleetingly of David Peters and said more firmly, "No, there isn't anyone else."

10 That Sunday morning Tamsin woke at half-past four and was unable to get back to sleep. She turned this way and that, finding each new position comfortable for no more than five minutes … and throughout her stirring, yesterday's conversation with Daisy in Morrab Gardens, replayed itself over and over in her mind. The more she thought about it, the less certain she became of her own ambitions — or, at least, of her tactics for achieving them. With her background and upbringing it was understandable that she should think that the world of commerce was almost exclusively the preserve of men. The few women in that world became by that very fact remarkable, no matter how undistinguished they might be in every other way. So from there it had been a short and entirely logical step to assume that her dream's fulfilment would depend upon a man — financially at least, even if he took no active part in the day-to-day business.

Actually, as she now realized, she had not *thought* about it at all. Her thinking (if one could even dignify it with that name) had all been downstream of those basic assumptions. In effect, she had said to herself, 'Of course there must be a man, and of course he must be rich enough, and it would be almost impossible for him *not* to be my husband into the bargain — so let's take all that for granted and get down to planning the details.' And *bargain* was just about the most appropriate word for such a 'love,' when you put it in those stark terms.

In short, she had not even begun to think; she had merely toyed with pipedreams and assumptions. The trouble was, she suspected, that she was not very good at thinking. If only her father were still ...

Yes, well, that was a pretty profitless line to start down, too.

She remembered asking him once what philosophers did and he told her they sit in chairs and think.

"What about?" she asked.

"Life and non-life ... existence ... reality ... good and evil, some of them ... logic ..."

She had tried it — sitting in a chair and just thinking — about good and evil, as it happened. Her train of thought called at some pretty bizarre stations before she gave up: good, evil, last Sunday's sermon, Rev. Ransome, bad breath, the dentist, the taste of cloves, apple tart ...

That was *thinking* for you.

Really she needed someone to think with. To think aloud with. Because if there was someone else, she wouldn't dare go chasing all those butterflies. That was where Papa had been so good, because you could talk about anything with him and he not only listened, he seemed to know where your own thoughts were going next; so he was always ready with a new idea or a new question. And it didn't matter whether you took him up or rejected whatever he was suggesting, he went along with you — ahead of you, even — and was ready to cast the next little pearl. 'Playing devil's advocate' he called it.

She missed him more now than she had in the immediate aftermath of his death. There had been so much to do then. And the almost simultaneous blow of his bankruptcy had, in a curious way, helped them, bringing as it did the need to think quickly and act decisively to salvage what they could and get out with enough to start the guest house here in Penzance. So they had experienced grief in short, intense intervals between dealing with the most mundane and petty decisions about liquidating the business and settling with creditors.

That was when Mr Samson of Low, Beadle & Samson, their Plymouth solicitors, had complimented her and told her she could probably run a business better than most men he knew. She'd laughed it off, saying that her seemingly passionate involvement was just a way of coping with the grief — which was true enough. But his words had struck a chord within her and then, when she and Mama were planning the guest house, she began to realize that she was always the one who 'played Devil's advocate.' In fact, she played the part so well that Mama had more or less yielded the day-to-day management of the business to her, even before they first opened their doors. And at the end of this month, July, when she reached her majority and could open a bank account *with recourse,* she'd start pressing for some financial control, too.

But somehow she had leaped directly from that to the idea of owning a big hôtel. As she had confessed to Daisy, it had been a land-based version of her earlier pipedream about owning a luxury liner. What she hadn't admitted, though, was that Mr Samson's compliments had somehow made it seem achievable. And because *that* was the target out there in front of her, she had automatically assumed a Mr Moneybags to help make it real — preferably a husband, so he couldn't simply pull out and walk away.

Now, however, thinking about it for the first time — sweeping all those half-thoughts and assumptions aside — she began to glimpse a different route, one in which a rich husband played no part. Indeed, it was one in which no husband at all was needed, rich or poor. All she had to do was make the Morrab so successful that she and Mama could progress from there to one of the small private hôtels along the seafront, and then from there to … well, one step at a time; but you could easily see how an enterprising team of mother-and-daughter, hard working and with a good head for business, could end up with the controlling interest in a big luxury hôtel.

At least, you could if you were Tamsin Harte, *almost* twenty-one, and full of the confidence of youth.

All of which brought her back to her deepening grief for Papa, the only person in all the world with whom she could possibly have spoken such thoughts aloud. Mama was no good

— not for that purpose, anyway. You only needed to say a 'what if' to her and she immediately assumed you were going to rush out and spend a fortune on it that very day; and then, even if you did manage to get it into her head that 'if' meant IF and you might be talking about next year, or ten years from now, she'd relax and say something like 'let's cross that bridge when we come to it, darling.' With her, there was nothing between the immediate panic decision and the long-term complacency that things would sort themselves out, somehow.

By half-past six Tamsin realized there was no point in even trying to rest; and she had long since abandoned all hope of sleep. Besides, the mattress was growing harder by the minute. So she might as well earn a little merit mark by attending Holy Communion at St. Mary's, up near Battery Point. But after the service was over, she felt even more of a sinner than before, for she could not recall a single moment of it. Every minute had been filled with a churning and rechurning of the thoughts that had kept her awake since the small hours.

Outside she saw the young man with the cauliflower hair and the pig's foot in his mouth — Reginald Trotter. Her first instinct was to pretend she had not noticed him and to hasten home with her head in the *Book of Common Prayer*. But he had spotted her the moment she left the church porch so there was nothing for it but to call out, "Good morning, Mister Trotter," and wait for him to shamble across the road to join her.

"Not a very good morning, actually, Miss Harte," he replied as he drew near.

"It'll lift," she assured him as she set off at a brisk pace homeward. "This kind of early morning sea mist — 'wrack,' they call it down here — usually lifts before noon to reveal cloudless skies above. In fact, you can already see a tinge of blue if you look directly up."

"Ah, yes — oops!" He stumbled over a large pebble, probably brought up off the beach and then abandoned by some youngster.

"I'm not going too fast?" she asked. "I ought to be back supervising the breakfasts."

"Not at all," he panted. "I don't believe in all that stuff — Christianity and so on."

"It's a free country."

"I used to. I used to walk out of the house every morning of my life and feel the weight of God pressing down on me. It doesn't bother you?"

She laughed, more from mild embarrassment than from amusement. "No, I don't have that picture of Him — some sort of engineer-in-the-sky."

"Really?" He walked a cycle of three paces and two trots to keep up. Appropriate, really. "No picture at all? Long beard … flowing robes … nothing like that?"

"This is an extraordinary conversation for us to be having, Mister Trotter."

"D'you think so? Sunday morning — bells ringing all over town — swings chained and locked in the park — highly appropriate, I'd say."

"Between people who are already intimate, yes."

It was his turn to laugh, in between panting for breath. "I'll let you go," he said. "You obviously don't want to talk with me."

She stopped and turned back to face him. "You are most vexing," she said.

"I know." He grinned. "It's almost my profession."

"Come. I'll walk a little slower — as long as you don't talk about God and such like."

He drew level with her and offered his arm — which she pushed firmly away with her prayer book. Unabashed, he said, "You've not been in the guest-house business long, I'd imagine."

"Would you!"

"I would. I'm also a professional guest-house guest — me and my mater."

"Goodness! What a lot of professions!"

"They're all related."

It suddenly occurred to Tamsin that someone whose recent life had probably involved staying in a succession of guest houses would have useful tips and insights to pass on. "And how does our humble little establishment measure in your scales, may I ask?" Her tone was more cordial now.

"Oh, pretty good, don't you know. Near the top."

"Only near? What little extras would be required to place it *at* the top?"

"An evening meal — at a supplementary rate, of course."

"Mister Trotter!" She slipped her hand through the crook of his arm. "Do tell me more!"

He patted her hand and said, "That's better. You may not have been in the business long, but I see you learn fast."

She hesitated, considering how best to reply.

He continued. "Explain? Very well. I've been convalescing for the best part of two years now. In fact, I've long since recovered from the original consumption — which was never severe in any case. Now, the mater and I continue because we find it congenial. In the winter we travel from pension to pension around the Mediterranean and in summer we return to England. Migrants to our native haunts, you might say."

"You must enjoy it," Tamsin offered.

"Of course. Or we wouldn't be doing it. The mater likes novelty for its own sake — sightseeing, churches, museums, galleries, theatres, the opera … et cetera. And I? I enjoy meeting new people."

"And pestering them." Her tone was humorous now.

He took the challenge seriously. "It sometimes comes to that, but usually not. The thing about a limited stay in any one place — particularly when all involved know it is limited — is that people are much more forthcoming than they would be if I were a new permanent arrival in the neighbourhood. Let me ask — you're regular churchgoers, you and your mater?"

"Yes."

"And you've been living here five or six months?"

"Thereabout."

"And how many new friends have you made in that time?"

"Well now, running a guest house — especially when you're new to it, indeed, to any sort of business at all — leaves little time for …"

"None, in short. All these houses we're passing" — he waved a hand along the parade — "there isn't one of them of which you could say you know a little family secret that's hiding in there behind those curtains?"

"As I said …"

"And yet," he continued, "I'll bet you already know a secret or two about some of the guests you've had — things that amazed you at the time?"

"That's true!" Tamsin exclaimed. Each separate incident hadn't seemed very dramatic in itself but now that Mr Trotter drew her attention to them all — en masse, so to speak — it did begin to seem quite remarkable.

"For instance?" he asked. "I don't mean names and addresses but what sort of things did people tell you that you may be quite sure they would never tell a neighbour back home?"

"There was a girl who sobbed her heart out to me one evening when we were alone in the lounge, all about some unrequited love. I was pretty embarrassed. That was the first. I remember thinking that was quite amazing — opening her heart and soul to a stranger like that."

"And?"

"There was an ex-officer who told me all about why he resigned his commission — protesting against some terrible injustice he'd been forced to connive at. He was very upset. He obviously had to get it off his chest to someone."

"And who better than someone who didn't really know him from Adam and whom he's probably never meet again!"

"I suppose that's it." Mischievously she added an invented instance: "And there was another young man, too, who thought along very similar lines. He supposed that, since I 'didn't know him from Adam' and would probably never cross paths with him again, we could gaily indulge in a brief romance and no harm done."

It didn't fool him. "And, may I ask, what on earth did you tell the poor chap?"

They had reached the bottom of Morrab Road, so the conversation was inevitably drawing toward its conclusion.

"That's my secret, Mister Trotter," she replied.

"Well now, shall I tell you what you *should* say? Should have said, I mean."

"If you feel you have to."

"You should have said you'd think about it."

"And if he kept on pressing for an answer?"

"Just keep on saying you're thinking about it."

"Why?"

"Because you're in business, and he's part of it, and in business you should never shut a door until you absolutely have to."

Now more than ever she realized that this strangely cool — even cold — young man might have a great deal to tell her in the way of running the business.

"To be serious, Mister Trotter ..."

"Oh? Weren't we that already? I thought we were."

"All right. To be practical. You've stayed at a great many guest houses, in England and abroad. You must know a thousand little things ... little ways in which we could do better. Could you possibly ... I mean, would you be willing ..."

"How much would you knock off our bill?" he asked.

"I ... oh, well ..."

"Or would you do it for kisses? One good tip, one delicious kiss — fair exchange?"

For a moment she actually considered the proposal seriously! Then, with a hidden kind of internal shaking of herself, she looked him in the eyes. They were as cold as before. It wasn't that she couldn't imagine herself kissing him — she could, though with little feeling — quite the opposite: She couldn't imagine him kissing her.

"How much pleasure would that give *you?*" she asked.

She hadn't meant to lay so much stress on the word but what was done was done. His response was rather strange, even for such a strange young man. He lowered his gaze and she'd have sworn there was the hint of a blush about his ears and cheeks as he murmured, "No, you're right. Bought kisses are never worth the price, are they."

Bought kisses?

There was no time to ask what he meant, for they were at the front door by now and the air that sprang out to greet them was laden with the reek of burned toast.

11 Was Trotter on the lookout for her or she for him — or, Tamsin wondered, was her father still lingering in that twilight world between this and the next, nudging events, shaping them into a sort of learn-as-you go education for her? Whatever about that, Trotter was there on the seafront as she set out on her Sunday-afternoon stroll to Newlyn — a favourite summertime

walk for those who lived in the western end of the town. Newlyn's harbour was exclusively for fishing, and the sight of all those little boats tied up for the sabbath was most picturesque. Penzance, by contrast, was a commercial port as well, with all the *un*picturesque and scandalous sights that go along with such places; respectable persons avoided it — and the western end of the town was inhabited almost exclusively by respectable persons.

She strolled as slowly as possible past the Queen's, pausing twice to make unnecessary adjustments to her parasol (for her prediction about the lifting of the wrack had come true), hoping that Daisy would spot her and find some occasion to come out and join her when the coast was clear. She would surely have the afternoon off — and the evening, too, if the Thornes had any conscience at all.

A hundred paces farther on she saw Trotter by the Esplanade railings. He was easy enough to make out because everyone around him was gazing out to sea; he alone was leaning back against the top rail, watching the promenaders instead. Also, he was dressed with unusual elegance this afternoon, with a large hothouse carnation in his buttonhole.

He was probably wise, too, she thought, for, apart from half a dozen sightings of smoke or sail upon the horizon at any one time, the sea was dead calm and empty. People cried 'Ooh, look!' when cormorants dived or resurfaced.

He had not yet noticed her so she kept pace with those around her, not to stand out, and observed him. She soon realized he must be a very lonely young man; he clearly craved the company of other young men of his age. Groups of young women would saunter past, looking him over, as is the custom on those Sunday promenades, and he would barely give them a second glance; but any similar group of young men would hold his attention and keep it until another such group went by.

Just as Tamsin was about to attract his attention a young gentleman, also elegantly attired — and also, curiously enough, sporting a carnation — stopped to speak to him. From the way they looked each other up and down, she gathered they were strangers, and yet they were soon talking freely enough. She wondered if the flower were the emblem of some secret male society, like the Freemasons and their handshakes. Much of their conversation seemed to be secret, anyway, for they often leaned close together, almost as if whispering; also they looked about them every now and then, the way people do when they suspect others might be eavesdropping.

During one of those surveys Trotter's eyes happened to fall upon her. He broke into a broad grin, nudged his friend, pointed her out and said something, and then turned back to her with a welcoming smile.

"Mister Trotter!" she exclaimed as she went to join them. "I didn't wish to intrude."

"Not at all," he replied. "May I present a friend of mine, Mister ..." He turned to the fellow.

"Coverley." The man removed his glove and shook her hand. "Standish Coverley."

"Miss Tamsin Harte," Trotter said.

She knew all about Mr Coverley. He owned the Queen's Hôtel! Her heart began to beat double, for he was also quite a good-looking young man. Well, young-*ish*. Thirty, maybe.

While they engaged in the usual pleasantries, Tamsin studied their *habillement* more closely. Coverley was in white from head to foot except for his amethyst-blue gloves and the matching trim on his panama hat and blazer; even his silver-knobbed cane was lacquered white. His eyes were amethyst blue, too. And as for Trotter, it really was an extraordinary departure from the respectable but quite ordinary dress he wore about the house. He had shoes and spats of grey suède, and a grey cane with an ebony knob. His trousers, too, were of dove grey with the thinnest possible white stripe, and they tapered to hug his ankles; they must have elasticated gussets on the ankle seams, she thought, otherwise he'd never be able to thrust his feet through those openings. He wore a lavender-and-white striped blazer, edged in pale mauve silk — the same silk as trimmed his straw boater. The deep pink of that massive carnation was a bit of a clash, in her opinion, but, on the other hand, that was what made it stand out, too.

As the pleasantries flagged she told them she was thinking of strolling to Newlyn and back.

"Well now," Coverley said, "I was about to propose a drive out to Land's End. My motor is garaged at the Queen's. I'm sure

I speak for both of us when I say that Miss Harte's company would be an additional pleasure."

Trotter seemed slightly surprised at this but he agreed readily enough. What else could he do, Tamsin wondered, since his friend was so positive on the point? "A motor car!" she exclaimed. "I haven't so much as sat in one since last November."

Her father's beloved Wolseley had been one of the first items to go under the hammer.

"Shan't be a tick," Coverley said. "You may wait here. And don't worry — I have goggles and dusters and things for all and some to spare."

When he had gone, Tamsin said, "I'm quite willing to walk on alone to Newlyn, Mister Trotter — if you'd rather I didn't accompany you and your friend?"

"I'm sorry. Was it so obvious? I was just so happy to have met him that …"

"For the first time, I think?" she risked saying. "Is the carnation some kind of secret emblem."

He stared at her in a curious mixture of doubt and incredility, not quite knowing what to say.

Now she felt embarrassed; he was, after all, a guest. "Forgive me! None of my business — except that you're far too polite and good natured to tell me so. Now it's my turn to apologize."

"Not at all," he said. "As a matter of fact, the carnations *are* a sort of emblem, or signal. How clever of you to spot it! I can't name the sociey, of course, but our purpose in driving out to Land's End was to discuss certain matters …"

"Then I shall decline this invitation. And thank you for …"

"No no! I assure you it will not be necessary. You really are welcome. We should enjoy your company. But if at some moment you could be terribly-terribly tactful and … I don't know … ask for half an hour of solitude to commune with Nature … go collecting the local flora to press for your herbarium …?"

"I quite understand, Mister Trotter. How exciting!"

"It is, indeed." He grinned. "It's just that no one, absolutely no one, is supposed to know of it. However, I'd guess the secret is safe with you?"

Tamsin nodded reassuringly and tried to look as understanding as possible.

"Do I intrude by any chance?"

They turned to see Daisy, walking briskly along the Esplanade toward them.

"Oh dear!" Tamsin murmured. "This is a friend of mine. Look! I'll walk to Newlyn and back with her and you two go off on your motor-jaunt as originally ..."

"Not at all." He also spoke in a murmur. "Two young men ... two pretty girls ... Coverley's right. What could be better? Introduce me, please!"

The maid was too close now for any further discussion. "Daisy!" Tamsin cried. "How nice to see you again! Allow me to present a friend, Mister Reginald Trotter, who is presently staying with us. Miss Daisy Dobbs."

Daisy shook hands with him like a patrician lady; her gratitude to Tamsin for *not* introducing her like a servant overflowed. "Were you thinking of going for a stroll somewhere?" she asked, jumping to obvious conclusions and supposing they would welcome a chaperon.

"Actually, Miss Dobbs, we were just talking of going for a spin to Land's End. We shall be back in time for tea. Would you care to join us?"

Daisy's eyes gleamed but she took care to get the nod from Tamsin before she accepted.

"Here he comes now ..." Trotter's voice trailed off as the first glimpses of the car, turning out of Morrab Road, resolved themselves into ... "One of the new Rolls-Royces!" he murmured.

"Rolls-what?" Tamsin asked. "Is that a motor car?"

"Not *a* motor car," he replied. *"The* motor car."

"D'you like her?" Standish Coverley drew to a halt in the middle of the road, forcing the drivers of lesser motors and dogcarts to edge around him as best they could. "Another bonny lass!" he added when he realized Daisy had joined the party. "How ducky! Hop aboard — we'll drive slowly and put on our motoring rags at the edge of town."

By now the throng of admirers around the car was so thick that all other traffic was forced to wait until the two ladies had settled in the back seat and Trotter had taken his place beside Coverley, in front. It was an open tourer so they felt like royalties, sitting there, the centre of all attention, gazing over the hats of the crowds and trying to look as if this were a regular afternoon outing and a bit of a bore, frankly.

There was a metallic snick as Coverley slipped into bottom gear. He pressed the rubber bulb and the hooter, which resembled those trumpets or shawms you see in Ancient Egyptian murals, gave out a melodious toot, rather like the posthorn on the old mail coaches, which they still parade at county fairs from time to time. The crowds parted in awe and the vehicle glided forward as smoothly and silently as an electric boat on mirror-calm waters.

"Is it electrical?" Tamsin asked. "It's so effortless."

"Well bred," Coverley replied. "She's identical to the one they call the Silver Ghost. Surely you've read of it? They're testing her non-stop, back-and-forth between London and Glasgow. By the end of next month she'll have done fifteen thousand miles non-stop — except for Sundays, of course, when they garage her under RAC guard. I got the next chassis off the line from Manchester and asked Barker's to build the identical body for her — white lacquered aluminium with silver-plated brass fittings. Except for the gear and brake levers, of course ..."

He leaned back to show them how one could change gear with a fingertip touch.

"These are nickel close-plated — not electro-plated, mark you. D'you know, they actually beat out sheets of nickel until it's only six-thou' thick and then they solder it onto the alloy levers ..." His incomprehensible praise of the vehicle's wonders continued thus until they reached the cross-roads at Stable Hobba, well outside the town. There, since they had to slow down anyway, he drew to a halt — once again on the crown of the road — and made Trotter get out. Those wonderful close-plated levers and the spare outer tube barred any exit on his side. From a box slung beneath the running board, he drew out dusters, to hold down the ladies' hats and keep their upper garments clean, motoring caps, for himself and Trotter, and goggles, for all four of them.

"Now we can do some serious motoring," he said.

"Does the engine start up automatically when you move those lever-things?" Tamsin asked.

He laughed. "She's running now."

The others strained their ears but could hear nothing — except for the cooing of a some pigeons and a cow lowing for her calf out in one of the fields.

"I'll show you." Coverley undid the snaps and lifted the bonnet. "There's proof."

Now they could hear the hiss of the carburettors and — only just — the deep rumble of the 40/50 horsepower engine.

"Watch this!" He took out a gold sovereign and balanced it on its edge on the top of the engine. It did not fall, even when he picked up a twig and prodded the throttle lever to make the engine race, or 'rev up,' as he called it. "Even if you coax her up to sixty," he added, "they say the noise of the motor is no louder than you'd get from a typical eight-day clock. Come on — let's go!" He snatched up the coin, refastened the bonnet snaps, and opened the door to the ladies' seats in the back, all with a showman's flourish.

"We're not going to try to reach sixty miles an hour, I hope?" Daisy said.

He replied that they'd have to go to Hayle Sands if they wished to do that because the roads around Land's End were too crooked and bumpy. "Watch!" he said. "She'll start in top gear without a complaint."

She did, too.

"Why are cars and ships always 'she'?" Daisy asked. "Can anyone tell me that?"

Trotter turned and winked at her. "Because they'd go all over the place without a man to control them."

"If you ask me," Tamsin replied, "it's because they can carry any number of good strong men but even the strongest men can't carry them. So there!"

Daisy looked at her askance; the two men stared rigidly ahead; she had the feeling they were struggling desperately not to laugh.

"What did I say?" she murmured to Daisy, whose only answer was to put a finger to her lips.

She felt mortified, without knowing why.

To anyone used to the rumble of even the most elegant carriage, with its wooden wheels and iron tyres, this beautiful motor seemed to glide along like something in a dream. It made forty miles an hour, which Coverley swore they were doing, seem more like twenty.

"It's a curious thing," Trotter said. "This part of Cornwall has more prehistoric antiquities, just about, than anywhere else in England. Yet you hardly get a glimpse of one of them from this particular road.

"Where are they?" Tamsin asked, glad of the new subject. "Could we see some?"

"Another day," Coverley promised. "The summer's not half done yet. How long are you staying, old bean?"

"As long as I want," Trotter replied.

Tamsin made a note to tell him that if he wanted the last three weeks in August, he'd better book soon, because the places were going fast.

"Good egg! And you two ladies?"

Tamsin explained that she lived in Penzance; Daisy said she'd be leaving next Saturday — turning toward Tamsin with an expression that said 'so-now-you-know.'

It was only eight miles from Penzance to Land's End, and in all that way they had done nothing but sit and occasionally clutch at their hats, not trusting the security provided by their dusters. And yet, when they pulled off the road by the gate where a track led down to the first and last cliff-promontory in England, they felt out of breath. And when they took off their goggles they had to laugh because the pale white patches around their eyes made them look like Christy's Minstrels.

But Coverley was equal to all occasions, it seemed, for another delve into the box below the running board produced a handful of small facecloths scented with rosewater.

Daisy and Tamsin went a little way off to wipe inside the hems of their blouses, where the dust had penetrated.

They put back the cloths and Coverley took out a couple of picnic rugs, oilcloth on one side, woollen plaid on the other, one of which he passed to Daisy. Then the four of them went down to the headland, past the little hôtel and the abandoned shepherd's hut. Tufts of sea pinks and a lush, tough grass whose blades were almost indistinguishable from sea-pink leaves made a springy pad underfoot, turning an ordinary walking pace into something like skipping.

"It's like a hundred-acre feather bed," Tamsin remarked. "Wouldn't it be fun if we were children and could just roll down over it!"

Coverley passed his hat and gloves to her and did a couple of somersaults downhill — of the handspring kind so that his alabaster-white clothes did not touch the green. Although he reached toward Tamsin to recover his hat and gloves, it was to Trotter that he looked for admiration.

They stood on the coastguard path at the cliff's edge and found the promontory to be just one among half a dozen, all of them pretty nearly identical; had it not been for a little cast-iron plaque, they would not have been entirely certain which one was the actual Land's End. They stared down at some seals, basking on the rocks, and a few of the creatures stared back at them. The sea was oily slick, which is rare in those waters where the Atlantic meets the Channel; there was not a breath of a breeze, either.

"I'd give two years of my life to swim now," Tamsin murmured, envying the seals. "D'you think …?" Courage failed her.

"Go on," Coverley urged.

"Well … I'm surprised there aren't more people about," she said. "Any people at all, actually — on a day like this."

"That's the Cornish sabbath," he told her. "No omnibuses. No cherry-bangs. I wonder how many tourists must complain before Mammon wins over the Nonconformist soul? But what were you going to suggest?"

"Well — if Miss Dobbs and I could find our way down to this cove and you two gentlemen could get down one on either side, we could disrobe modestly and swim out to meet at that point where the seals are basking. I'm sure they pose no danger."

The men accepted the suggestion without demur and stayed only to help the two ladies down a not very difficult path to the rocks below. Then they scrambled back up and over to the next inlet. "First to evict the seals!" Coverley called down the challenge to them.

"Come on!" Daisy urged. "We mustn't let them win."

But Tamsin just stood there, shaking her head, staring at the water. "I must have been mad," she said.

12   There was a reassuring overhang of rocks on the northern side of the cove — massive and thick, and not at all friable, like most of the cliffs near Penzance. There the two girls could undress safely out of sight from all but about twenty yards of the coastguard path above.

"What d'you make of them?" Daisy asked. "Our two fine feathered friends."

"They certainly outdress every other man in Penzance. And that Rolling Royce machine must be the finest car in the West. I didn't know such beautiful machines could exist. I say — d'you think they're interested in us?" She longed to tell Daisy about the secret society but honour forbade it.

Daisy shrugged. "Dunno. Usually you get a sort of feeling. But with these two ... I don't know. We shan't offer them any encouragement, anyway. They certainly know how to dress well. There's a year's wages on their backs."

Tamsin turned her back to Daisy. "Can you just loosen the top lace? I didn't ask if you can swim — I'm sorry."

"Oh, I'd have sung out soon enough, don't worry." Daisy did as she was asked. "Anyway, there's a shallow bit there where a non-swimmer could stay in her depth."

She was naked now except for her shift and Tamsin noticed a silver locket hanging by a fine filigree chain around her neck.

"Hoo-hoo!" she challenged archly. "Is that a lover's portrait you carry next to your heart?"

Daisy removed it casually and hefted it in the palm of her hand. "Just a lock of hair," she answered casually. "For two pins I'd throw it out there as far as I could. And never go looking for it again, neither."

But she laid it delicately on top of her clothes and covered it with her shift. Then, suddenly, she seemed amused to notice how neatly Tamsin had piled her clothes. "Bet you weren't always so careful!" she teased. "Not when you had a maid to tidy up after you."

"That just shows how much you know!" Tamsin pouted playfully. "I always was neat and tidy." Then, more thoughtfully.

"Perhaps I never was intended to be a lady of leisure. D'you envy them, Daisy — people with all the leisure in the world? D'you envy Mrs Thorne all her wealth and freedom?"

Daisy pulled a face. "Not often. 'Specially not when you see how she uses it. Come on — we're about as ready as ever we will be. And they did challenge us."

Naked at last they peeped out from under the rocky overhang and, though no spectators were in sight, they crept along beneath its protection until they reached a point where they could slip into the water without racing over open rocks — a quick one-two and a mighty splash.

"Here we come, Mister and Mrs Seal!" Tamsin called out just before the sea swallowed her.

It was the first time she had bathed in Cornish waters. The shock almost killed her — at least, that was the thought uppermost in her mind as she surfaced again with a scream: *I'll die! I'll surely die! I'll never be able to stand this!* She was too shocked to speak a word.

Heedless of how Daisy was faring in the same arctic grip, she struck out in her strongest trudgen-stroke for the rock from which she had so blithely jumped not five seconds earlier. But when she reached it and shook the water from her eyes she saw that an elderly couple were sauntering along the clifftop path and watching them with interest.

So she was trapped in the water. She could already feel its icy fingers gripping tight around every part of her, intent on strangling her circulation completely. It was only a matter of time, measured surely in minutes, before the last bit of life-sustaining warmth was sucked out of her.

And only now did she look about her to see how Daisy was managing to survive.

The girl was calmly treading water a dozen yards away, and grinning broadly. "Give it a minute or two, love," she said, "and you'll swear it's boiling. You scared off all the seals, anyway. Keep moving — that's best."

"If those people weren't watching, I'd move fast enough! I'd get out and never come back in."

"Don't let them bother you. With the water being this calm and clear, there's not much they can't see, anyway."

"Oh, Daisy!" To stop all her muscles freezing stiff Tamsin began a sort of dog-paddle out to join her friend, and as she drew near, she saw that it was, indeed, true. She could see all of the girl's body, even though it was in flickering, shivering images that kept breaking up and joining together again. There were her bosoms, her belly with the dark, reddish delta beneath it, and the white limbs that walked an invisible underwater treadmill. "It's true! Oh, lawks — what about the men?"

"What about them? See if I care!" Daisy laughed. "If a cat can look at a king, then I suppose a king may look at a cat, as well!" She set off at an easy breast-stroke toward the rock at the mouth of the narrow inlet, where the seals had been basking earlier. She breathed out an explosive spray that gave her a brief rainbow halo.

"We must keep splashing — that's all," Tamsin decided. "I hope you don't think — I mean, when I suggested this swim, I never thought the water would be so calm and transparent."

"Well ... if we drive them mad, that's their funeral. It could be fun. Come on!"

When Daisy gained the rock she found a foothold and sprang from the water in another iridescent halo of spray, half-turning herself so that she landed sitting on its smooth edge, facing out to sea. "Beat you! Beat you!" she shouted toward the next cove northward, where, she presumed, the gentlemen were lurking still. Then she turned to Tamsin. "Are you coming out? This rock's lovely and warm from the sun."

She had a shapely figure and Tamsin, who had dabbled in art a little, admired the curvaceous pyramid of her hips as they tapered up into her slender waist. "But is it safe?" she asked, looking dubiously about them.

"Scared of sunburn?"

"No! You know very well what I mean." She trod water, glancing anxiously toward the next cove every so often. "Where did you learn to be so shameless, anyway?"

"A very good question!" Daisy said. She was suddenly quite serious. "My last lady, Mrs Ormesby, was a naturist. They had a tall yew hedge in the garden, all round a big square, where they could undress and lie in the sun or play tennis or they had a fountain where they could paddle and cool off. Brown as berries, they were, after every summer. She and the master used to go out there in winter, too, but the rest of the family wasn't so hardy. Or dedicated."

"You're right — it does feel quite warm after a while. And you mean to say they forced you servants to undress and go naked as well?" She prepared to offer sympathy.

"Not a bit. Only those who wanted to. Of course, it took me some time to see there was no shame in it. So when you called it shameless, you were móre ..."

"And then you lay in the sun and played tennis with them?" Tamsin was incredulous.

"Oh yes, very likely, I must say! No, we stood as per usual — the few servants who took to naturism, that is. We'd stand around waiting to fetch balls from the long grass or lemonade from the ... there was a sort of changing hut where the other servants would bring the tea or wait for errands. And we were the go-betweens, sort of."

"Is that where you formed your low opinion of men?"

Daisy hesitated. "Yes," she said. "But that was ... something else. Nothing to do with the naturism side of it. Maybe I'll tell you one day."

"Talking of men — here they are." Tamsin laughed at the sight. Two dark heads on the shimmering water, their beautiful hair plastered slick against their skulls. "They look like a brace of sealions. Come back in, quickly!"

"No, I shan't," Daisy said truculently. She turned and shouted, "Beat you!" at them again. Then she added, "I forgot to mention I'm a naturist. D'you mind?"

They looked at each other and Coverley answered, "No. I've dabbled a bit myself, in fact."

Trotter added, "But perhaps Miss Harte would object?"

"To what?" Tamsin asked, hoping against hope that they were all just teasing her.

"Tamsin!" Daisy said despairingly.

"Object to our sitting on the rock like so many solemn Scandinavians, enjoying the sunshine?" Coverley replied.

They were right beside the rock now.

When he put it like that, making it sound so dull and innocent, how could she possibly object? But it annoyed her all the same to be forced into a corner by them. She looked daggers at Daisy, who had started it all.

"It's like the cold of the water, love," the girl replied, unabashed. "You think you can't bear it at the beginning but later you wonder what all the fuss was about. Come on — I'll help you up. There's a ledge here. Careful, though. Don't kneel on it. There's millions of tiny barnacles."

"But none on the top." Trotter reached up and felt how smooth it was. "How odd."

"I expect the seals rubbed them all off," Coverley told him. "They bask here all year round."

While they sorted out the natural history, Tamsin took the first step into her own naturist history. She closed her eyes, put both feet on the barnacle-encrusted ledge, and let Daisy pull her out into the balmy sunshine.

She sat to Daisy's left, knees tight together, arms folded across her lap, and did not open her eyes again until the two men were seated as well; she was relieved to see they were a good yard beyond Daisy and on the farther side. She could not, however, resist a quick peep at Coverley, who, she discovered, had the body of a Greek athlete, as seen in all the best museums. She might have guessed it from the handspring somersaults he'd performed earlier; but guessing (and imagining) were one thing and seeing it with her own eyes was another.

She only took a quick peep, though.

"If one of those lonely men out there has a telescope" — Coverley pointed to the Longships lighthouse, just over a mile out to sea from where they were sitting — "he'll have a pretty eyeful this afternoon!"

They all laughed, a little nervously; now that the deed was done, the bullet bitten, they were all a little hesitant. And Tamsin discovered that Daisy was right, as always. There had been a few shocked moments as she died of shame — sitting there in a state of nature beside two handsome young fellows and a good-looking girl in the same scandalous state — and then the shame had withered even as the icy chill of the water had ceased to feel cold.

"No need to cringe and shrivel into a little ball like that," Daisy murmured to her.

Tamsin glanced at her and saw she was leaning back on rigid arms — so rigid, in fact, that they were bent a few degrees in the 'wrong' direction, as if she were double-jointed — and thrusting out her chest and lifting her chin to bare as much of herself to the sun as possible. "Some days can make up for months of misery," she said to no one in particular.

"Some days should go on for ever," Coverley murmured as he lay back upon the sun-warmed rock.

In fact, both men now stretched themselves full length and closed their eyes against the sun. Their feet were still in the water and every now and then they kicked idly, just to keep the circulation going.

Apart from paintings and statues, Tamsin had never before seen the undraped male body — and, since all the others had their eyes closed, she could not resist the temptation to make up for her ignorance now. Trotter was slightly podgy. Nothing that good tailoring couldn't hide but she could see each heartbeat make a tiny ripple down over his belly. He was also rather hairy, which was something you didn't see much of in marble statues.

Anyway, she wasted little time on him because his friend Coverley was quite the opposite — a flesh-coloured sculpture of Adonis, no less. She could not take her eyes off him.

Last year, before her father's death, she had enrolled part-time at Plymouth Art School, where her favourite pursuit had been clay modelling. She had done a quarter-size replica of the school's plaster cast of *Discobolo* — the famous Ancient Greek discus thrower with the tight, curly hair; the master said it was quite good. In art galleries she always wanted to touch the sculpture — to run her fingers over those marble hands and arms and shoulders and ribs and things; so it had been a great pleasure to have permission to do just that, even though it was only on a dusty old plaster cast that had seen better days.

But all that was as nothing compared with her present desire to touch that perfect body, stretched full out upon the rocks not a yard away from her. She did not think of it as having a name; it was not Standish Coverley; that would have made any sort of touching impossible — and even the *idea* of touching him, or, rather, it. *It* was not personal. It was a thing. An object of consummate beauty, as impersonal as Michelangelo's *David*.

David. The name stirred in her mind. Fisherman David. David Peters ... She pushed the thoughts away.

A thing of paramount beauty like this anonymous body at her side had something universal about it. Or did she mean immortal? Something that belonged to all the world, anyway. To all mankind, male and female alike.

Would she dare?

She could pretend. She reached out toward him, threading her arm between Daisy's double-jointed props. Daisy chose that moment to shake her wet hair, which incidentally moved her arms. In avoiding them, Tamsin touched Coverley on the shoulder. He opened his eyes and blinked in her direction.

"Sorry!" She laughed with embarrassment. "I was chasing away a fly and trying not to disturb you. You looked so ..."

But he did not wait to hear how he looked. He sprang to his feet and, all in the same movement, without a pause, did a pike into the water. His body arced through the seagreen fathoms in a streak of alabaster flesh and silver bubbles until he emerged again, a yard or so to her left and, still continuing the movement, burst from the sea, hands to the rock, shoulders rippling like the muscles on an Arab stallion, gymnast's spin on one hand ... and there he was, sitting beside her, knees bent, hugging them in his arms, head resting on them, looking at her with all the intensity those amazing, amethyst-blue eyes could muster. And not just looking at her, but looking her up and down, too.

She wanted to curl up with embarrassment but, to her utter astonishment, found that her body was doing quite the opposite — stretching out in the same way as Daisy, except that she kept her eyes open. She had no choice, in fact, for his now held hers in what seemed like a full-scale audit of her inner being.

"So, Miss Harte," he said, "tell me a little about yourself. Mister Trotter thinks you are one of the most admirable people he has ever met."

She swallowed hard. "Mister Trotter has no right to say such a thing." The answer was automatic but she could not think what else to say.

"A man has every right to speak the truth," Trotter drawled, sitting up and pulling his legs out of the water so as to adopt the same pose as his friend.

"I understand you went from wealth to relative poverty in the space of a few days and ..."

"It was a peculiar sort of poverty that allowed us to buy a substantial house in the most respectable part of Penzance and open it as ..."

"I did say *relative* poverty," he pointed out.

But she insisted. "It must happen to hundreds of people every day of the week. There's nothing very distinctive about it — especially if, like me, you discover you've landed on your feet and you actually enjoy the new life much better than the old. Setting aside my father's death, of course."

"Of course. But that's just what I find so interesting, you see: You enjoy managing the guest house more than ..."

"More than all those dreary balls and garden parties and playing tennis in long skirts and sitting in the butts admiring the men as they slaughter birds in their thousands? What d'you find so interesting in *that?*"

"Nothing. That was your former life. I'd much rather hear about what *you* find so interesting in your new situation. Unless, of course, you'd rather not talk about it?"

"Oh." Now she regretted her prickliness. "Well ... people, I suppose. The huge variety of people one meets. Actually, it's a combination of that and the discovery that we can meet all their different needs. Food ... advice ... all sorts of things. I mean, when people say goodbye and tell you they've just enjoyed their best holiday in years and they'll certainly be back next year ... well, I can't remember anything in our old way of life that was half so satisfying."

"Good," he said. "That is marvellous. Well done! And what d'you mean by advice?"

"Which is the best beach — we just want to sit on the sands all day? Can you arrange for us to meet a fisherman and to go on a fishing trip with him? We're rather high-church, so where's the best place to worship?"

Trotter laughed. "Like looking for a needle in a hay *field* down here, I should think!"

"Breage-and-Germoe's fairly high," she told him. "We can even arrange a taxi for them. That parish was very Royalist in the Civil War, you know."

"The Civil War, eh? You're developing a memory as long as any Celt's!" he chided.

"There's other advice we get asked for, too," Tamsin said, more hesitantly now.

"For example?" Coverley urged.

"One woman asked me what food she could give her husband back home to help him lose a few inches. And husbands have asked if they could accompany me on a marketing trip so that I can help them buy some trinket for their wives. I've even been asked how to get rid of those pale brown spots you get in old books …"

"Foxing," Daisy put in.

"That's it. People seem to think that because you've got a smattering of education *and* can manage a guest house without too many obvious disasters, you're the fount of all wisdom!"

"Ah me! Little do they know!" Daisy bared her teeth at her and winked.

Tamsin ignored the thrust. "Anyway, does that answer your question?" she asked Coverley.

"Admirably — and I'm grateful, Miss Harte." He rested his chin in the hollow between his knees and gazed out to sea. "Have you ever looked back through the very early volumes of *Punch?*" he asked.

"Who — me?" Tamsin said.

"Anybody. They're full of jokes about the *nouveaux riches* — not just the new-rich plutocrats but the new-rich middle class and, a bit later, the new-rich artisans and clerks — long before *The Diary of a Nobody* but people of that class. And you get the feeling that they're laughing at them because they think it's a temporary sort of fad and it'll go away in time. The basic thrust of *Punch's* humour, unlike almost all other satire, is that everything will get back to normal pretty soon and that nothing will ever, ever change. But, of course, it does …"

"Has this got anything to do with Miss Harte?" Daisy asked rather sharply.

"Everything — and with you, too, Miss Dobbs. Those old jokes tell us they were living through a revolution, a social revolution — a very English social revolution — but they were only half aware of it. They imagined they could laugh it out of existence. Well, *Punch* still has the odd joke against the new rich but for every one of them there are dozens against the New Woman — the feminist, the suffragist, the respectable single business lady ... even those vast-bosomed headmistresses who cannot see without the aid of lorgnettes. It is, I believe, a sign that we're living through yet another very English social revolution and that, whatever *Punch* may think, it, too, will not fade away. Even our servants are part of it."

Daisy felt sure he was speaking of her though he did not so much as glance her way. "Really?" she said nervously.

"Yes, indeed," he continued, still giving the impression he was talking about remote third parties. "Two generations ago a servant would have stayed with his master and mistress for life. And even if he left them, it would have been for a similar position in some other household. But now, I expect, not a week goes by but the minds of half the servants in the land turn over other prospects? Do we doubt it?"

Daisy just shrugged, since her direct opinion did not seem to be called for. Perhaps he hadn't, after all, twigged that she was one of that class?

Realizing her difficulty, Tamsin sought to divert the conversation. "But why does *Punch* laugh at feminists and so on?" she asked. "That's surely the question?"

"Fear," he replied. "Oxford undergraduates yell and throw bread rolls at women who try to sit for degrees. They fear to discover that the women might equal them in any subject, or even outshine them. Eminent doctors will give you two dozen reasons why women are physically and mentally unsuited to positions of power — all very scientific. But, quite simply, they, too, fear that women will prove no better and no worse than men when it comes to pulling the levers of power."

"But you're a man," Tamsin objected. "Why don't you fear this competition from women, too?"

Coverley reached out and patted her hand. "That's another social revolution," he told her. "But it is one whose time has not yet come, I fear."

Not understanding a word of it, Tamsin felt patronized. And annoyed.

13 Tamsin turned over a dozen ways of making her point to Daisy and, in the end, she just came straight out with it: "You recall what you said about men yesterday? Hairy, bony, knobbly, et cetera? You certainly can't say that about Standish Coverley, can you!"

They were dressing once again, having sun-dried themselves on a secluded rock near the point of the promontory, where the only prying eye would have been in that distant lighthouse. Even their hair was dry, though slightly claggy from the salt.

Daisy sniffed but said nothing.

"Can you," Tamsin insisted.

"Do I have to give an opinion?" Daisy asked wearily.

"Well, *I* think he's ... pretty ... tremendous, anyway."

"Looks aren't everything."

"But they are in this case. I mean, that's all I'm talking about," Tamsin protested. "Good heavens! You don't think I mean" — she swallowed heavily — "something soppy and romantic, do you? It never occurred to me. I only mean he's pretty tremendous to *look* at. If you could cast his torso in plaster ... I mean, it would knock most Græco-Roman sculpture into a cocked hat."

Briefly she wondered what her mother would make of that ghastly expression. It made her realize she'd been farther from her mother that afternoon, both in statute miles and in spirit, than at any time since her father's death.

Daisy made a small, noncommittal murmur through her nose.

Tamsin thought she must be pretending her indifference. No one could be *that* uncaring about such a man. "Also, he's a jolly agreeable person — don't you think?" she added.

"You sure you're not getting ideas about him?"

"Of course not!" she exclaimed, and almost immediately wished she had not been quite so emphatic. "Though I don't see why not," she added. "You can't say he's completely devoid of interest in me."

"I didn't notice it much."

"What about all those questions he asked ... he was really interested in my replies. And you didn't see his eyes when he was talking to me." She shivered with remembered pleasure. "He seemed to look right inside me." Then, fearing she was just sounding silly and romantic, she sought to add a harder edge to her enthusiasm: "Also he's rich. And rich people are always interesting. He owns the Queen's Hôtel. He's got that marvellous motor car. And, most important of all in my case, he's got no prejudices against the new-poor!"

Daisy shrugged. "There's just something ... remote about him. About the pair of them. That's all."

She was thinking of social class, Tamsin supposed. In which case — from her point of view as a servant — she was quite right. It would, however, be unkind to point that out. Best to drop the matter entirely.

"Don't you feel it?" Daisy asked. "Like monks. Or no, not monks but members of a club and not much interested in anything that doesn't concern it. Something like that."

Again, Tamsin almost blurted out what Trotter had told her. But how astute of Daisy to have spotted it anyway. She was certainly a bright, intelligent girl. It was a pity she'd be leaving Penzance so soon.

"Can you comb my hair out, there's a love?" Daisy asked. "I'll do yours after."

Tamsin took the offered comb and, sitting on the blanket behind Daisy, on a long, sloping shelf of rock, she began working away at the knotted ends all round, combing higher and higher up each tress as she went. "Anyway," she said, "whatever club you're thinking of, it's certainly not the usual kind. It's nice to meet men who aren't *men's* men. D'you know the sort I mean? Bluff, hearty creatures who live and breathe in yachting crews, rugby clubs, golf clubs ... those sorts of clubs. Men who go off and climb the Mountains of the Moon — all jolly chaps together. You have to allow that Messrs Trotter and Coverley aren't a bit like that — apart from his obsessive love of that Rolling-Royce. And even then, when you ride in it, you can quite understand him. If I had a car like that, I'd just drive and drive. Also, you couldn't talk music or art or things like that with *men's* men — not for more than two or three sentences. I've tried. I've probably got more experience of men's men than you have, actually. They try to turn the whole world into one vast boys' school where it's all 'Play up! Play up! And play the game!' You can't say Coverley and Trotter are like that." After a long pause she added, "Cat run off with your tongue, then?"

Daisy sighed. "I've said my say. We've both said our say. I can only repeat — they just seem a bit like … I don't know — people training to be vicars or something. Anyway!" In quite a different tone she added, "Did you get that — what I said about leaving next Saturday and going back to Devon with the Thornes?"

"Yes." Tamsin sighed. "That's sad-making. For me, anyway. I suppose it's inevitable."

Daisy stiffened and then turned round. "What do you mean? Are you suggesting it needn't be or something?"

There was such an intensity in her eyes that Tamsin had to think back to what she *had* meant. In fact, she hadn't meant anything in particular — just what a pity it was in general that life was full of such inevitabilities. Friendships and partings. "Mean?" she echoed.

"Yes. I mean … d'you think it's *not* inevitable?" She touched Tamsin's hand gingerly. "I'm not at all looking forward to saying goodbye, you know. I don't meet too many people I get on with so well, and so quickly."

"Nor me." Then the significance of Daisy's words struck her. "You mean you'd leave the Thornes — just like that?"

"Well, not 'just like that' — I mean, I'd give two weeks' proper notice. And then, by heavens, I'd give Madame Thorne a piece of my mind — though that's by the way. But it would depend on … oh! Stop beating about the bush, girl! It would depend on *you*. Tell me straight — would there be any chance of a place for me at your guest house? There!" She let out a great sigh of relief. "That's the long and short of it."

"Gosh!" Tamsin stared out to sea; her mind seemed to have gone numb. Why hadn't the same thought occurred to her? The impossibility of finding the money for her wages, that's why. Especially for a lady's maid!

"Well, I wasn't expecting you to get up and dance!" Daisy sighed and turned her face away.

"It's not that," Tamsin assured her. "I'd just love it if it were only possible. Is it possible? I'd move heaven and earth to … it's just that our particular bit of heaven-and-earth is so wretchedly small. And poor. How much ... I mean, what sort of wages ..."

"I'm getting thirty-five pounds a year at the moment."

"And 'the run of your teeth,' as Mrs Pascoe says."

"And one new uniform and shoes. What does Bridget get?"

"Thirty-five! I'm afraid ..."

"What does Bridget get?" Daisy asked again.

"Ten. Cornwall's a lot poorer than Devon, you know. We could never have afforded a house like ours around Exeter or Plymouth. And neither Mama nor I would have anything like thirty-five pounds to spend on ourselves in a year. Not even between us. Oh, I'm sorry, Daisy." She laughed with embarrassment. "We live in different worlds, obviously. You're rich. We're poor!" Desperate now to change the subject, she added, "Shall we go and see if the men are ready?"

"No!" Daisy grinned. "One thing I have learned is never make the running yourself. If *they* want something, make *them* sweat for it. If they don't, then running after them only panders to their vanity. Anyway you lose no face by sitting pretty. And apart from all that, don't you want me to comb your hair now? You've done a very good job on mine." She laughed. "Maybe *I* should take *you* on as my lady's maid!"

Their slightly forced laughter and the business of changing places allowed them to bury the topic.

But not for long. It was difficult to think of anything else to talk about.

"You're lucky your hair is so naturally oily," Daisy said as she ran the comb through Tamsin's locks in easy, graceful strokes. "The sea hardly touched it — and it's so glossy."

"It's murder on pillows, though. And it needs washing *every single* week."

The sun stole beneath the rock overhang, warm and kindly now that it had lost some of its noonday heat.

"Such a pity it burns one's skin brown and makes one look like a gipsy," Tamsin murmured, stretching her arms into its glow.

"My naturists said it's good for you. *Tanning*, they called it. It's all in the eye of the beholder."

"About what you said ..." Tamsin ventured.

"When?"

"You know — leaving the Thornes and coming to ..."

"Forget it. I shouldn't have asked."

"No. I shouldn't have said no like that."

Daisy popped her head over Tamsin's shoulder and grinned. "You didn't actually say no."

"I didn't exactly say yes, either!"

"Anyway, forget it." She returned to her combing.

"No, I shan't. I responded without thinking — or, at least, I only thought of the immediate situation. The way we manage things at this moment. But, if the business develops in the way I hope it will, well, I can't think of anyone I'd rather have — nor anyone more suited to be with us. I don't suppose you could stick it out another year with the Thornes?"

"What will change in a year's time, then?"

Tamsin described her plans for expanding the catering side of the business and for raising the general tone of their service so as to attract a higher class of guest.

"You see," she concluded, "just to give a specific example — Mrs Whyte brought me a pair of her husband's trousers last week. He'd sat in a spot of tar and she asked if we had anything to get it off. So Bridget said she always used butter to get tar off her skin, so we tried that, and …"

"Aaaargh" Daisy gripped her by the shoulders and said, "No! Tell me you didn't!"

"We did! It got the tar out all right. Then I was up half the night trying to remove the butter. And poor Bridget went into hiding all next day whenever I was around."

"A threepenny bottle of benzine, which you can get from the chemist, was all you needed."

"You make my point, Daisy. You see, we don't have enough rooms to accommodate servants, not like the Queen's, so if we're going to attract ladies who are used to being waited on hand and foot, we'll have to offer that sort of service. You could do it blindfold. So can we keep in touch? Can I write to you and offer you a place — *if* we've managed to attract people of that class by next season?"

But Daisy, having enjoyed her Pisgah sight of the Promised Land, was reluctant to abandon it, even temporarily. While she wondered how to keep the way open, Tamsin added, "Even then, I doubt we could offer anything like your present wages.

But, on the other hand, you could easily make thirty in tips. Even Bridget and Catherine look set to make ten apiece — equalling their wages — before the season ends. And all they do is make beds, empty chamber pots, dust ... that sort of thing. They're very happy about it, anyway. So what d'you say?"

"How much ..." Daisy began. "I mean ... put it this way. You say you and your mother don't have as much as thirty-five pounds each out of the business in a year. Or even together. Well, forgive me for asking this, but how much would the sum be, then? I'm not just prying."

"Gosh! I'm only guessing, anyway, because the season's only just getting into full swing."

"A guess is better than nothing at all."

"Well ... there are our clothes, of course ... we no longer buy perfume, nor any cosmetics except Mama uses some face-powder ..."

"I didn't ask for every little detail!"

"No, but I'm trying to work it out. It's not something I've thought of much — though I should have, I suppose. There's also an occasional bottle of ordinary table wine. And our library subscriptions. And the *Ladies' Home Companion* ..."

"All right, all right! It must easily come to one pound, seven shillings, and threepence three farthings! I take your point."

"Well, I wouldn't think it came to more than fifteen pounds, dear. Eighteen at the very most. We haven't been poor through one whole winter yet, not really. Should we count doctors' bills and medicines, perhaps? No, because if any of the staff fell ill, we'd certainly pay for the ..."

"I'd come for fourteen!" Daisy blurted out. "You think you manage on fifteen quid a year. I'll accept fourteen. There!"

Stunned by this, Tamsin pulled away from her and sprang to her feet, edging even farther away so that she did not tower above her. "But why?" she asked. She felt a constriction in her throat and a prickling behind her eyelids. Daisy was so intense again, so frightened, almost.

"I don't know." Daisy rose and slipped the comb back into her handbag. "It just feels right. Or nothing else would feel *as* right. I've got savings put by — and it's not for getting married, as you may well believe! So I won't really feel the pinch. It's just that I suspect that, five years from now, I'll be saying it's the best decision I ever made." She laughed awkwardly. "And I'd hope you'd be saying the same — from your point of view, I mean."

"Oh, Daisy! Even now I don't have the slightest doubt about that, but ..."

"I mean," she interrupted, "sometimes in life you have to make these decisions, don't we. Something tells you this or that is absolutely the right choice for one and we just have to go along with it."

"Yes," Tamsin agreed. "But we do have a whole week ahead of us. There's no need to make a hard-and-fast decision just yet, is there? And, anyway, I really ought to discuss it with Mama — even though I know she'll agree ... in the end. So let's just say it's something we're both eager to do and we'll make a final decision toward the end of the week. Agreed?"

"Agreed," Daisy echoed, even though she had privately decided to hand in her notice that very evening.

"And now shall we go and see if the men are ..."

"No! Just be patient. Everyone thinks the hounds hunt the fox. But any hunting man will tell you — nine times out of ten it's the fox that leads the hounds. And a good time is had by all."

They shook the sand off the blanket and folded it up. "My turn to carry it," Tamsin said.

Daisy let her have her way.

As they approached the coastguard path, Tamsin paused and said, "Just one thing ..."

"What?"

"Your decision to leave the Thornes and come to us ..."

"Yes?"

"It's not ... I mean, it hasn't anything to do with ... you know what I mean?"

"I do not know. Spit it out!"

Tamsin laughed. "Mama is going to love your turn of phrase! What I mean is, it hasn't got anything to do with ... today? Or has it?"

"Today? What in particular?"

"You see — you're being evasive about it!"

"I am not! Just to say 'today' is pretty vague. Lots of things have happened today."

"But there's one thing in particular."

Daisy gazed at the sky and whistled a few bars of *Up in a balloon, boys.*

"You know very well what I'm talking about, Daisy — the biggest thing that happened today was meeting Standish Coverley." Now that Tamsin had managed to 'spit it out' at last, she gabbled the rest: "You're not just deciding to stay because of *him,* I hope?"

Daisy just stared at the sky, fingered her locket, and said, "If only you knew!"

Part Two

Penzance from Newlyn
waiting for the fleet

The facts of life

14 Cicely Thorne noticed him the moment he entered the dining room at dinner that evening. By the time he was half way across the floor, everyone was aware that someone of importance was among them. The headwaiter practically bowed him in, all the way from the entrance to the alcove half way down the long side of the salon, where his table was set. It had had no occupant all that week, and Cicely had noted that, too. Now she studied him through her lorgnettes, which, though they were furnished with plain glass, nonetheless helped her to see the (largely inferior) world around her in true perspective. Tonight she could wish they were opera glasses instead. "He *looks* distinguished, anyway," she murmured. "Find out who he is, dear."

"Go over to her and look for laundry marks, you mean?" her husband asked.

"He's a Mister Standish Coverley," Victor said.

His parents turned to him in surprise. "How d'you know?"

"He was on the seafront this afternoon, just before we went out for our promenade. I saw him from my window."

"I don't understand," Cicely said. "How do you come to know his name — you couldn't see that from your window?"

"He has a Rolls-Royce motor — a beautiful, gleaming white beast ..."

"He's not eating," Walter said. "He's not even ordering."

"He's waiting for someone," Charlotte put in.

"You all seem to know a great deal about him," Cicely snapped.

"There are three other places laid," Charlotte pointed out.

"We only know what we observe, Mama," Victor assured her. He did not tell her that he had also observed Tamsin Harte and Dobbs climbing into that same beautiful, gleaming white beast — along with an elegant but unknown gentleman. It had rankled with him ever since.

"Coverley?" Cicely mused. "Could it be *de* Coverley, I wonder? Wasn't there an admiral of that name ... sometime in history?"

"An admirable dancer, certainly," Victor offered. "Sir Roger de Coverley. He may have been an admiral, too, of course."

"Don't be facetious, dear," his mother said — though she had, in fact, been thinking of that same Sir Roger.

"Good God!" Walter exclaimed. "Just see *who* our man has been waiting for!"

Trying in vain to disguise their movements as no more than the result of random interest in all parts of the dining room, the whole family turned in unison toward the door, where the headwaiter, once again, was treating new arrivals like royalty. And the new arrivals were …

"Miss Harte!" Cicely exploded in a barely contained whisper.

"And her mother, if I'm not very much mistaken," Charlotte added. "I wonder who the third party will be?"

They were certainly Coverley's expected guests for he had already risen from his place and was crossing the floor to welcome them.

Tamsin pretended to recognize the Thornes at that moment; she waggled her elegantly gloved fingers and called out, *"Bonsoir, mes chers amis!"* just loud enough for them to catch. She murmured something to her mother, who then glanced toward the Thornes and dipped her head gravely.

Walter automatically returned the bow but his wife pinched his thigh under the table and hissed, "Fool!"

She then rounded on Victor and said, "If you know so much about him, why did you not make his acquaintance when you saw him this afternoon?"

"Well, Mama," he began, *"if* I were allowed out of doors all on my ownio, then perhaps …"

But she had not finished. "Why isn't it Charlotte, your own poor sister, whom he is now helping into her seat instead of that … that …?" Polite words failed her. "You are the very epigraph of selfishness," she concluded.

"Epitome," Walter murmured.

"That's what I said — or meant to say. Does anybody know what Mister Standish Coverley *does?"*

"He owns this hôtel, madam," the waiter said. "Among other properties hereabouts."

Cicely looked daggers at him. "Who asked you to butt in?"

His face frosted over. He bowed stiffly and withdrew, lips tight shut against other choice tidbits he might have divulged.

"Is there anyone you are *not* prepared to offend this evening, my dear?" Walter asked quietly.

"I'm not hungry," she snapped, rising to her feet. "I have a headache. I shall go to my bed. Where is Dobbs? I've hardly seen her all day."

She kept her husband and son standing.

"Could that be because it's her day off?" Victor suggested.

"She has no right to a day off — not when I'm feeling like this." She swept from the room. Walter tried to follow her but she sent him back, in full view of everyone, even before they reached the door.

"She's definitely getting worse," Victor murmured to his sister before their father returned. "Dobbs will hand in her notice if she continues like this — and who could blame her?"

"I wish *I* could hand in my notice," Charlotte replied. "And despite what dear Mama just said, I do *not* need you to go scouting for suitors on my behalf."

"D'you think I would?"

"I'm just warning you."

Coverley and his two guests had a waiter each; the other tables had one for each three or four diners. People notice such things — people like that, anyway.

"He's very handsome," Charlotte said as their father rejoined them; he had gone out of his way to talk to their waiter — to make it seem to the other diners as if that were why he had left the table in the first place.

"A bit of a dandy," Walter said. "Did you see his cummerbund as he passed?"

"Moiré silk," Victor replied. "It's quite fashionable. He was all in white this afternoon, with blue trim. That and his motor created quite a stir — mostly the motor, of course. You should get one, Pater. Perhaps we'd be granted one waiter each, then."

A commis-waiter removed their soup bowls and their waiter brought the main course — fat, juicy sea-trout served cold with salad and mayonnaise. The sommelier poured their wine, a crystal-clear Piesporter Kabinett, and left the half-full bottle in the ice bucket.

These rituals over, Walter leaned toward his son and daughter, lowered his voice, and said, "Perhaps one shouldn't be talking

like this, but one is rather worried about your mother's present
state of health."

Victor glanced at his sister. "D'you think it's our fault? For
rebelling at the thought of yet another summer in a huntin'-
shootin'-fishin' lodge in bonnie Scotland?"

Walter sighed. "Well ... Cornwall has turned into a bit of a
disaster. It can't be denied."

"It's because she worries all the time about what people will
think of us," Charlotte put in. "She's always looking over her
shoulder. She can't ever relax."

"Listen," Walter said. "I think we all know the symptoms —
without needing to dwell on them like this. It's remedies that
seem scarce."

"Not Scotland again!" Victor said at once. "She wasn't
particularly happy there, either, if you recall."

"Where *is* she happy?" Charlotte asked.

"Visiting the big shops," her brother said.

"She enjoys her charity afternoons, especially the MA."

The MA was the Mendicity Alliance, a national charity that
gave its donors little printed cards that they could hand to street
beggars instead of money — 'which they'd only spend on
intoxicating liquor and horses.' On two afternoons a week the
local MA committee, of which Cicely was the chairwoman, met
at the parish-union workhouse and doled out cash in return for
the cards — but only in deserving cases. That was the beauty of
the scheme in its supporters' eyes. No one has time, when
importuned for money in the street, to make exhaustive inquiries
into the mendicant's circumstances, habits, attempts at self-
help, and so forth; but Mrs Thorne and her committee had all
the time in the world. Not until an applicant had bared every
secret recess of his or her soul, in an interrogation that often
reduced them to tears, would the MA part with a single brass
farthing of its charity.

"Yes," Walter agreed despondently. "I suppose she's happiest
of all there."

"Is there a local branch of the MA?" Charlotte wondered.
"You know — she could go along, introduce herself, and ask if
she might join their deliberations ... share information ...
experiences ... that sort of thing."

"It could keep her occupied for an entire afternoon," Victor said cheerily.

"One must make inquiries," their father said.

Further discussion was curtailed because Cicely herself returned at that moment. Looking radiant, too. "I can't find that Dobbs anywhere," she said brightly. "But my headache has quite evaporated, so it's of no consequence." As husband and son jointly thrust her chair back beneath her, she added, "I think we have misjudged poor Miss Harte — or, rather, were led to misjudge her by those spiteful telegrams from ... well, never mind whom. But I shall have strong words with them when we return, I don't mind telling you."

"Ah! Here's our third party now," Charlotte cried. "What a very elegant young man!"

15 Standish Coverley smiled at Reginald Trotter and said, "I'm so sorry your mother was unable to join us this evening."

"Bishops take precedence," his friend replied. "Even retired ones. At least I managed to get away before the pudding. They didn't seem to mind."

"It's funny to think of bishops *retiring,*" Tamsin put in. "It's supposed to be more of a calling than a profession, I thought. After all, artists don't retire. Nor poets, nor writers."

"But that's the great thing about the Anglican Church," Coverley said. "It's a profession like any other. And it really *is* just for Sundays — even for their clergy. On the other six days of the week they can ride to hounds, ply the fly, dig up ancient tombs, prove that the Cornish are the Twelfth Lost Tribe of Israel ... whatever secular pursuit may take their fancy. Some of the finest agnostic minds in the country wear their collars back-to-front, you know."

While they laughed at his witty perversity, Trotter noticed that one particular party in the dining room was eyeing them with more than casual curiosity: a handsome young man of around twenty, his slightly younger sister, and their parents. They had finished their dinner some time earlier but were lingering over their coffee. Every sign of jollity from Coverley's table seemed of particular interest to them — in the way that the Little Match Girl was so poignantly interested in the feast she could never join; the mother, in particular, was quite pained at each round of laughter. At last he had to ask if anyone knew who they were.

"Guests," Coverley said in a tone that implied it was really all anyone needed to know — as one might say 'ants' or 'seagulls.'

"They are Mister Walter Thorne, his wife Cicely, their son Victor, and their daughter Charlotte," Harriet said. "They live at Peverill Hall, Clyst Saint Mary, just outside Exeter. They are seeking a good match for the daughter." She smiled at the two men. "I don't know if that is a warning to either of you? Or would it be an encouragement?"

"You are well informed, Mrs Harte," Coverley said with genuine admiration. "Do you happen to know the daughter's opinion in the matter?"

"Charlotte will make up her own mind," Tamsin said firmly.

"It's a habit daughters have these days," her mother added.

"We had noticed," Trotter said.

"Miss Dobbs is — or perhaps was — Charlotte's lady's maid," Tamsin added.

Coverley stared at her; his expression was suddenly cold. "Really?" he said. "I assumed she was a friend of yours."

"She's that, too," Tamsin assured him. "Now you're annoyed. You think I tricked you into entertaining a social inferior."

"Tamsin!" Her mother, being aware of their host's sudden frostiness, was shocked to hear her daughter spell out its cause. "You didn't!"

But Tamsin had been annoyed at Daisy's repeated hints that Coverley was more Stand-*off*-ish than Standish; she was determined to provoke him into some display of emotion, if only to see where it might lead. For, if Daisy were right, what had she to lose? "Of course I didn't," she replied, not taking her eyes off the man.

His nostrils flared; he would have contradicted her flatly if he had not been such a gentleman.

She continued: "I introduced her without comment — just as she was — and I left them to draw their own conclusions about her." She glanced from one to the other, challenging them to deny it. "You'd hardly believe it now," she added, "but at the time they seemed rather eager to have us accompany them on their jaunt."

"True, old bean," Trotter said.

Coverley looked at him, then at her; though still stony-faced, he seemed on the point of breaking into a smile, however unwilling. Harriet, who had been about to put her oar in, sensed the change in him and kept silent. But Tamsin decided to push him a little further.

"If Mister Coverley can show me that I've done him or his reputation or his business some harm," she said, "I will, of course, apologize."

These words, which she had spoken almost without thought — merely to challenge him to speak frankly — had the accidental effect of setting her to think in earnest.

What was it that annoyed him so much in learning he had entertained a servant as a social equal? Daisy had not *tried* to deceive him; she was a well-brought-up lass, enough, at least, to claim a place somewhere in the middle class — and she had not pretended to anything grander. He hadn't spotted it, that was all. Was he annoyed with himself for that?

Coverley suddenly broke into a broad smile. "You did the right thing, Miss Harte," he said, reaching across the table and giving her hand a squeeze. "You let us size Miss Dobbs up without prejudice and we found her acceptable. Therefore she *is* acceptable. A salutary lesson!" He turned to Trotter and added, "To us both."

"My dear chap!" Trotter replied. "I've knocked about the world so much I long ago lost all trace of social snobbery. Sartorial snobbery, mind you, is quite another thing. I'd cut any man who wore brown shoes in Town — or blue shoes anywhere."

Tamsin would have thrilled at that gentle squeeze of the hand — and she would have given her mother a tiny, superior smile of triumph, too — if she had not seen the glacial light that lingered on in Coverley's eyes. Daisy was right. The man *was* a cold fish. Beneath his urbane exterior, behind the polished wit, there lived a passionless man; perhaps even his obvious friendship for Trotter had something chill and manipulative at its core.

Her infatuation with him, kindled that afternoon and fanned
to quite a fire by the time he issued his invitation to dine that
evening, was suddenly extinguished — a six-hour wonder. Which
was not to say she did not wish to continue their acquaintance;
indeed, she even hoped it might ripen into friendship. But the
special buzz of excitement that embellished her thoughts
whenever they turned to him was silent now.

For no reason she could think of, she suddenly remembered
David Peters — and, of course, the purchasing arrangements
she hoped to make with him. If young Mr Peters could be
furnished with a wardrobe as elegant as either of these two
gentlemen's, he'd cut an even more dashing figure than both of
them put together. Not that that was important — just rather
amusing to contemplate, really. The important thing was that
he enjoyed a universal reputation as one of the best fishermen
in Newlyn, and he would certainly prove a reliable source of
seafood of the finest quality. Yes, that was the important thing
about him.

She fancied that Standish Coverley knew much more about
the day-to-day running of his hôtel than he'd ever admit to.
He'd probably pretend to be way above all that sort of thing but
she had a shrewd idea that he'd know the thickness of each
butter 'star' to a thirty-second of an inch and what the deposits
on ginger-pop empties would return each week.

Daisy, who knew so much, might also know the secret of
getting beneath that suave exterior to the man beneath.

The following morning she was awakened not by Bridget's
gentle tap at her bedroom door but by the dainty clink of teacup
and saucer on her bedside table. And the sounds of a suppressed
giggling. And the rustle of a dress, as of someone sitting down.

She opened one bleary eye, for the day felt much too young
for her to be woken up yet, and tried to focus. A moment later
she opened both eyes and sat bolt upright in surprise. "Daisy!"
she exclaimed.

"Guess what?" The maid giggled.

Tamsin groaned. "You gave in your notice?"

Daisy pouted. "You needn't sound quite so pleased."

"It's not that, my dear. It's just that you are rather jumping the starter's gun. I haven't even mentioned it to my mother yet."

"Then book me in as a guest for a couple of weeks. I don't mind. I got a nice little *bonne bouche* from the old dragon — which was a bit of a surprise, I don't mind telling you."

"Of course I shan't book you in as a guest. Not a paying guest, anyway. So I take it you did hand in your notice?"

"A bit of both, actually — me saying goodbye and her ladyship gently letting me go. I was just about to give her a right old piece of my mind when she asked me what I thought I'd do without a character from her. So I didn't see any harm in letting her know what's what."

"You told her you were coming to work here?"

"I told her it was one of several possibilities. I thought she'd catch fire, but no! She suddenly turned all sweet and lovey-dovey. Gave me a good *bonne bouche,* as I said — and *this* for you." She produced an envelope and drew attention to its elaborate seal. "Be careful of that," she said. "Slip a hot knife under it to keep it intact."

"Why?" Tamsin took her seriously for a moment.

"Because — the way she goes on about it — it's probably worth a hundred guineas!"

Tamsin shattered the seal as they laughed. She read the note in silence, said, "Well, I'm jiggered!" and passed it over to Daisy, who read it aloud:

" 'Dear Miss Harte, We have absolutely fallen in love with Cornwall, and with dear little Penzance in particular. We only came down here to escape the smell of paint and the mess while the decorators carry out their annual business in our home. Now we hear that they will not be finished for at least a further week. But we are not *too* disappointed because, as I say, we are delighted with all we have experienced down here and long to discover more.

" 'One of my chief regrets is that we have not seen more of you this past week. From the moment of our amusing encounter on the beach last Monday, I confess I developed the warmest regard for you. And now it occurs to me to suggest that the remedy may be in our own hands. We must stay a further week and, though the Queen's Hôtel is all very congenial in its quaint, provincial way, we would much rather enjoy what I'm sure is the more genuine warmth of hospitality in your and your dear mother's establishment. (We had the pleasure of seeing her and you at Mr Coverley's table last night and took an immediate liking to her, as well.)

" 'Do please say you have three rooms vacant for us. I wait with eager ...' blah-blah." Daisy looked up. "What are you going to tell her?"

"Well done, Daisy!" Tamsin replied. "You managed to read it almost to the end without a single derogatory comment!"

"Have you got three rooms to spare?"

Tamsin nodded. "It so happens — if you don't mind sharing with Charlotte? I'll tell her it's the only way." She giggled. "We'll see how keen Madame Thorne is then!"

Daisy giggled, too, but she still pulled a face and said, "Definitely not the same bed."

"No, we've got two singles we can put in room eight."

Still the maid was unhappy. She pointed to Tamsin's fireplace. "We could put a single bed for me there," she suggested. "You won't be lighting a fire until November, I suppose."

Tamsin drained her cup of tea and kicked off the bedclothes. She shed her nightdress on the way to the washstand.

"Well?" Daisy asked.

"Don't rush me, dear," was the reply. "I'll still tell Madame that Charlotte will have to share. Just to see her response. Meanwhile, would you like to start singing for your supper — just a little?"

"How?" Daisy sprang to her feet and started symbolically rolling up her sleeves.

"No need for that," Tamsin assured her. "It's my turn to carry round the early-morning teas to all the bedrooms that ordered them. You could help by preparing the trays while I carry them round. That'll release Bridget to get on with blackleading the stove. And Catherine can whiten the front steps good and early. Oh, I do love Monday mornings, don't you!"

Daisy proved so efficient at preparing the trays that she quickly got ahead of Tamsin. So she decided to even things out by taking the double pot and two cups to room eleven herself. She knocked at the door and entered at the first sound, which was more like a groan than a 'come-in!'

The two young people, honeymooners by the look of them, were astonished to see her depositing the tray on their bedside table. But, quiet efficient servant that she was, she had gone before either of them could speak. Tamsin, coming toward her down the passage, said, "You didn't give him a pot?"

"Them," Daisy replied. "It was on your list — tea for Mister and Mrs Strong in room eleven."

"But they left yesterday. Tskoh! Bridget must have forgotten to put up the new list. It's supposed to be a Mister Wall in there — and his fiancée's in room twelve next door. Miss Roberts."

Daisy gasped and bit her lip, already more than half-guessing what had happened.

"I'll get it back," Tamsin said. And before Daisy could stop her she had opened the door to number eleven, stuck her head into the room, and said to the two frightened rabbits who sat up, clutching the sheets to them: "You didn't ask for early-morning tea, did you?"

"N-n-no," the man stammered.

"I'll take it away then," she said, removing the tray again.

Back in the passageway she found Daisy cramming her fingers into her mouth in a vain attempt to stifle her laughter.

"What now?" Tamsin asked.

Daisy just beckoned her down the passage, back down the stairs, all the way to the kitchen before she explained. And even then she closed the door first. "Just think what it must look like to them," she said. "I carry the tray in. You go in immediately after and pluck it out again. They must think we arranged it between us to find out if they were two or one in the bed."

Tamsin joined her laughter, but not wholeheartedly.

"You still don't get it, do you," Daisy said. "Do you have any idea what those two have been up to all night?"

Tamsin shrugged awkwardly. "Practising at being married?"

"Yes — hallelujah! You know what it means, then?"

Tamsin gave what could have been either a nod or a shake of her head.

"You don't!" Daisy said. "Well, if you're going to make a go of this guest-house business, I reckon it's about time you did!"

She had just finished explaining when there was a peremptory *ding!* from the entrance hall. Tamsin went out to find Mr Wall and Miss Roberts standing there, fully dressed for the street and with their luggage already piled up by the front door. After that first glance, neither would look her in the eye. They had decided, he said, to move on ... yes, without breakfast ... would Miss Harte kindly produce their bill? No thank you, they would find their own taxi.

Watching them walk down the path to the front gate, Tamsin tried to imagine them doing It — what Daisy had just explained. It was difficult, of course, being so new to her. And yet it was as if some very secret part of her had always known it.

16 From the way Daisy had described It, Tamsin had no difficulty in understanding why Mr Wall and Miss Roberts had been so ashamed that they felt they had to leave before breakfast. How could people behave in such a horrid way? Especially people like those two, who had seemed so decent and well behaved when they arrived. And even more especially, how could a thoroughly genteel young lady like Miss Roberts, so well spoken and reserved, permit Mr Wall to ... words yielded to a shiver of distaste. And then the sheer hypocrisy of paying for two rooms and using only one of them — for, although Miss Roberts's bed had been turned down, it had not been slept in, nor even sat upon.

"She couldn't wait, see," Daisy said contemptuously when she pointed out this fact during their subsequent inspection of the two rooms. "Little minx! They're like polecats!"

Tamsin could see no particular similarity but, not wishing to appear the complete ignoramus yet again, she said nothing. Or, rather, she changed the subject — as she thought. "She *was* engaged to him, though," she said. "She showed me the ring last night. A solitaire diamond. A beauty."

Daisy was shivering by now, caught up in the toils of an emotion too powerful to contain. So much so that Tamsin began to fear for her.

"You mean he *bought* her," Daisy sneered. "Like this ... was it this sort of thing?"

Her trembling fingers struggled with the fasteners at her neck and then they pulled out the silver locket Tamsin had noticed yesterday at Land's End.

"This!" she repeated as she opened it to reveal ... not the lock of hair she had mentioned then but a silver ring, also with a solitaire diamond. More interesting still, however, was the photograph that accompanied it. And, even though Daisy snapped the locket shut before Tamsin could see much detail, what she had spied in that briefest of glimpses was vivid enough to burn an image in her mind's eye.

It was a photograph of a young man, or, rather, just his head, carefully cut out of a photo and pasted on a black background. It had then been embellished with devil's horns and long pointy ears, minutely painted in white gouache and indian ink. Tongues of red and yellow flames licked all around his neck, or where his neck would have been before the scissors had guillotined him.

This picture lingered in her mind, too shocking to be spoken of, while she examined the ring. "Yes," she said. "Pretty much that sort of thing."

Miss Roberts's diamond had, in fact, been almost twice the size of this.

"Yes!" Daisy was slightly calmer now, though still breathing hard. "They give you these things and then they think they own you. They think they can treat you like those ... those ..."

To Tamsin she seemed to be hearing her words slightly *after* she spoke them, so that she could not censor them in advance but had to wait until they were uttered. Now she put a hand to her mouth as if she wanted them to stop their flow — in which case, she succeeded. "I'm sorry," she said in a small, dispirited voice. "They can't all be like that, of course. But there's more of them than you'd think out there — just waiting to pounce on us. So just you be warned, eh!"

She forced a smile and, stretching out her hand for her ring, said, "This will never break the back of the day, will it!" She held it up and eyed it sourly before popping it back inside the locket. "I was going to ram it down his throat and hope it'd choke him, but then I thought I could keep it as a warning — and sell it if ever I got in dire straits. Sell *it* rather than *me*!" She gave an awkward sort of laugh.

Tamsin laughed, too, though she did not really know why. "That young man …" she tried.

"Don't!" Daisy turned the incriminating bedclothes up again, ready to be turned down for the next guest that evening.

After breakfast Tamsin sent Bridget round to the Queen's with a note to say that the Thornes would be welcome on the usual terms, which they would find printed on the back. There was no mention of Charlotte's having to share with Daisy. That had been a pleasant fantasy but, really, they did not want to risk an angry refusal. As Tamsin said to her mother, they were too curious to see what Mrs Thorne was up to.

"Up to?" Harriet echoed in distaste. "Never end a sentence with a single preposition, dear — let alone two. You could have said '… to see what Mrs Thorne may have it in her mind to do.' That would have been quite acceptable."

Daisy winked at Tamsin, unseen by the mother. Later, as they set out to do the day's marketing, she said, "You know just how to deflect your mother off the big decisions and onto the little ones, don't you. I wonder if she realizes it's you that runs this place, really."

Tamsin, reared in a tradition where certain things happened but were never talked about, felt awkward at this exposure — and even more awkward at the praise. She did not know what to say. In fact, she began to wonder if she'd been altogether wise in her haste to take Daisy in. Not that she wouldn't be useful in so many ways, to say nothing of being good fun in herself; it was just that their basic approach to life and its myriad daily problems was utterly different.

She had never consciously thought of such things before, but the maid was forcing her into it.

Just then they stopped at the greengrocer's in Alverton Street. Daisy, sensing her reluctance, asked if she didn't agree.

"It's not whether or not I agree," Tamsin answered. "It's just that I was brought up to know that certain things are not always the way everyone pretends they are — but it isn't something to be spoken of."

"Like?"

"Like … not all the grief you see at a funeral is genuine. Not all mayors, aldermen, and town councillors are selflessly dedicated, body and soul, to serving the populace. Not all marriages are made in heaven ..."

"Ha!"

No further examples were necessary; Tamsin had hit the perfect one. "But it just makes life easier all around if everyone agrees to pretend that the exceptions are few. And trivial. Cauliflower or red cabbage? Oh look — broad beans! I love them, don't you?"

"Why does it make life easier?" Daisy asked.

"We could have cauliflower and beans, and we can see if Oliver's has some neat's tongue." She lowered her voice and added, "It's a pity there's no fishing on Sundays. I'd love some whiting — or a nice piece of fresh cod."

"Why?" Daisy insisted, still sticking to her line.

But Tamsin appeared lost for a moment in her thoughts. And they had nothing to do with vegetables, either, for Mr Trevaskis, the greengrocer, stood patiently waiting for her to speak — which, eventually, she did.

They paid and set the bag aside to collect on their return. Daisy did not feel she could press her question yet again. They strolled on in easy silence, past Sargeant's, the fishmonger, where Tamsin stooped to gaze into the almost empty window.

Suddenly her entire demeanour changed — from relaxed to alert, from bent to bolt upright. "Talk of the devil!" she said, turning to Daisy and grinning from ear to ear.

"What?" She was bewildered, even slightly alarmed — understandably, when one considered the picture she carried next to her heart. "Which devil?"

"Look!" Tamsin tilted her head toward the dark interior of the shop.

But David Peters was already leaving. "Miss Harte," he said as he stepped outside.

"Mister Peters!" She held out her hand, which he shook with some slight surprise. "Not fishing today?"

He licked a finger and held it up into the dead calm air. "No," he agreed. "Too stormy."

"Silly of me — of course not."

"We had a smallish catch on Saturday, which missed the London train when the wind dropped. We have it on ice, of course, but I'm trying to see if we can get a better price locally."

"I see. That was a wonderful lobster, by the way. I meant to come and thank you but I gather you were at sea most of last week?" She hoped it was true.

He neither confirmed nor denied it. She glanced at Daisy, who nodded. "Allow me to present you to a friend of mine," she went on. "Miss Daisy Dobbs. Mister David Peters." They shook hands, too, while Tamsin added, "Miss Dobbs is going to be my right-hand man at the guest house."

In fact, the pair shook hands for rather longer than was usual. And their eyes lingered in each other's for quite a while, too — as if each were waiting for the other to speak.

It irked Tamsin but she passed no comment. "If you're going to deliver fish here," she said in a slightly more snappish tone than she intended, "you could drop some off on us in passing?"

"Whiting or a nice piece of fresh cod," Daisy added, letting his hand go at last.

"I have both," he replied. "You can choose when you see them. Are you ladies going toward Causeway Head? That's my next port of call. We could walk together?"

They waited for a heavy dray from Rosewarne's brewery to pass, then skipped between it and a motor delivery van.

"You see?" David pointed to the name along its side. "Warring's, the furniture shop, they've sold the old horse and cart and gone in for a motor. That's what we're doing — except we'll keep the sails, too, of course."

Tamsin paused briefly at the foot of Clarence Street to gaze at the Western Hôtel, which was only a third the size of the Queen's; she looked it up and down, with her head on one side, much as any other woman might run a critical eye over a new hat. Then she trotted to catch up with the other two.

"A fishing boat with a motor?" she asked as she pushed herself between them. "Won't it frighten off the fishes?"

"Seemingly not," he answered. "We can set the trawl or the line a good way astern."

"You should get a Rolls-Royce engine," Daisy said. "They're quieter than a whisper."

"Yes, I heard all about your outing yesterday," he said. His tone hinted at scandal.

Tamsin was cross at Daisy for mentioning it anyway. And how dare he take that censorious attitude with her? What right had he to question her choice of companions? Or anything else, come to that?

Also she was worried, especially in the light of Daisy's revelations to her earlier that morning. She could not now believe that she had disported herself naked in front of Mr Coverley and Mr Trotter, two such gentlemen; never mind that they had not demurred. And how could Daisy have led her into doing such a thing — especially knowing all those horrid things about men and women and ... things? Could someone have spied on them? The lighthouse men ... a powerful telescope ... some semaphore to a passing coaster ... was it all over Newlyn by now? Tamsin cringed inwardly just to think of it, even though she had no choice now but to brave it out and pretend it never happened — just in case her fears were groundless.

As they turned into Causeway Head, she said, "Our guests sometimes ask us if we can arrange a fishing trip, Mister Peters. If you manage to outfit your boat with an engine, well, it would make such outings much safer and more reliable. In terms of getting back on time, I mean. Would you consider it, I wonder? And what sort of fee would be reasonable?"

"It's worth thinking about," he replied. "The *Saucy Sal* — trips to Saint Michael's Mount and back. First let me see what sort of motor we can get up at Smart's, the old blacksmith's. He was before your time, I suppose. But his son, George, has turned it into a motor shop. I'll get one as quiet and smooth as possible, then maybe you'll come out for a trip round the bay? Just to see what it's worth."

He was looking at Tamsin as he spoke but it was Daisy who answered: "Oh! Wouldn't that be fun!" A moment later she caught Tamsin's eye and added, hastily, "For *you,* I mean."

Tamsin was only partly mollified but at least it prevented an explosion. "Yes," she said to David. "That would be a good idea. Why not?"

"I'll bid 'ee good day, then." He touched his cap and left them, hastening away up the street.

Daisy fanned her face. "A narrow squeak!" she exclaimed. "Sorry, love — I didn't realize it was like that between you two."

Tamsin bristled. "Like what?"

"Like *that!*" She pounded her fist against her breast, hinting at a heart beating double.

"Don't be absurd!" Tamsin turned about and set off angrily for home, forgetting that Daisy had things to buy at the chemist's — toothbrush, dentifrice, soap ... that sort of thing.

"Come on!" Daisy ran after her and stood barring her way, staring into her face, trying to make her smile. "What did you mean back there when you said, 'Talk of the devil' — back there at that other shop?"

Tamsin shrugged impatiently. "What does anyone mean when they say that? I mean we'd just been talking about Mister Peters, hadn't we."

"But that's just the point — we hadn't. *You* had, I'm sure — up there." She touched Tamsin's forehead before she could draw back. "You said you wouldn't mind a bit of whiting or cod and then *pffft!* You vanished inside there." She grinned. "And now we know why."

Tamsin sighed and gazed over the rooftops opposite. "Go and get whatever you need," she said patiently. "I'll wait here."

Daisy, thinking it would be a good chance to let her simmer down, complied. But when she came back, Tamsin said, "You're a fine one to talk, anyway."

"I am?"

"Yes. All that ... that ... what's the opposite of misogyny? Where women hate men. Misandry? All that talk of yours, anyway, about how hateful men are — and then you go all dewy-eyed with the very first man I present to you, and ..."

"Is that what it looked like?" Daisy broke out laughing.

"You know very well. You could hardly bring yourself to let go of his hand."

"Dear God!" Daisy looked heavenward. "Strike me dead if I lie but I was waiting for him to ..."

"I don't wish to hear it." Tamsin turned homeward again and set off at a fair pace.

Daisy ran to catch up. Her words were oddly punctuated by her having to trot and skip at Tamsin's side. "I was waiting for him to *recognize* me, you ninny! I'm sure he did, too. I know I recognized him at once."

Yet again Tamsin stopped dead. "Recognized him? What d'you mean?" she snapped.

"Yes!" Daisy replied. "See what you miss when you jump to all the wrong conclusions, stop your ears against all the right ones, and flounce away like that!"

"I'm sorry!" She did not sound in the least contrite. "But what d'you mean — you *recognized* each other?"

"Just that. I had no idea you knew the man, or I'd have told you long before this. Honestly."

"So how d'you come to know him?" Tamsin was calmer now — and was beginning to feel ever so slightly ashamed of her earlier behaviour.

"Because ... what day did I bring you that note?"

"Last Tuesday."

"Well, the next morning, Wednesday, Miss Charlotte and Mister Victor, got me to accompany them on a stroll to Newlyn."

"No! What for? D'you mean to meet ..." She pointed vaguely in the direction David had taken. "But they didn't know him."

"Exactly! They had to go about the harbour side asking who the fisherman was who set his lobsterpots near the Wherry Rocks. No one would tell them, of course, because they're all tight as limpets down here. But finally they tried in the post office, where the woman said it could possibly be your friend Mister Peters. And ..."

"He's not particularly *my* friend."

"I believe you. Thousands wouldn't." Daisy winked. "Anyway, they caught up with him just as he was about to put to sea."

"And what did they talk about?"

"I don't know. Miss Charlotte took me away out of earshot. It was only Mister Victor who spoke with him. It could have been about arranging a fishing trip one day this week. Or — reading between the lines — maybe it was about nothing in particular. Just some errand that Victor made up so's he could ... how can I put it? Size up his ... *rival?*"

She grinned at Tamsin, who just tossed her head and said, "That's just ridiculous!"

"Yes — ridiculous. I quite agree."

"You can stop that at once, Daisy."

"Stop what? Didn't I say I agree with you?"

"I quite admit I'd like to know Mister Peters better. Even a great deal better — but only as a friend. He's one of the most honest, straightforward men you could ever …"

"Certainly. I mean, look how he came straight out with it that we met each other last Tuesday!"

"That was different. He was waiting for you to mention it. And when you said nothing, he decided you had your own reasons for not speaking out, so he didn't go against your wishes. He's a natural gentleman, that's all." After a pause she added, "I didn't have a brother but if I had, I'd have wished him to be like David Peters. There! That puts it in a nutshell. I'd like him as a sort of proxy brother. And you can just wipe that superior smile off your lips because I know what I feel like and you don't. There! Oh, bother! Now you've made me go and forget the cauliflower and beans. We'll have to go back."

17 When the two young women returned with their various messages they found Harriet beside herself with excitement. "My dear!" she exclaimed, whisking Tamsin off to their private drawing room. "You'll never guess what! You'll remember Mrs Lock — Miriam Lock?"

"Denzil's mother?"

"Yes. Well, it seems that her husband, poor old Harold, was in Germany last month …"

"The man we were never quite sure existed?"

"Well, that was your father's attempt at humour. Of course he existed. He was the life and soul of the golf club before … that unfortunate incident. Anyway, never mind all that. The point is that Harold Lock was in some spa in Germany last month — Baden-Baden, I think — and he became friends with the Count and Countess de Ath. It seems that the Count is dying — it's just a matter of time — and the Countess is quite … 'reconciled' isn't quite the word …"

"Resigned?"

"Of course — resigned. Oh dear me, I'm in such a fluster over this news!"

"You mean you *know* them both?"

"No, dear." Her mother's face screwed up as if in pain. "Just don't interrupt all the time. It's bad enough that we have to keep it all under our hats. We mustn't breathe word of it to a soul — did I say that?"

"No, you didn't, as it happens. But anyway, I'm sorry. Let's go back to where you said she was quite *reconciled* to his death — and pretend I didn't butt in."

"Oh, you are such a vexing creature! You know that's not what I mean. Anyway, the long and short of it is that she will be coming here — to Penzance — to stay with *us* for an indefinite period. There now!"

After a pause, to make it clear she was not interrupting, Tamsin said, "I hesitate to ask this but ... you are speaking of the Countess? Not Miriam Lock?"

"Of course I mean the Countess. Isn't that what I said?"

"And why has she chosen to come to *us* — out of all the thousands of hôtels and boarding houses in England? D'you mean you *do* know them both?"

"Miriam must have written to Harold, or perhaps she was visiting him in Baden-Baden. Anyway, she must also have told him all about our misfortune. And Harold, out of the goodness of his heart, I suppose, is doing us this enormous favour. He must have praised us to the heavens ..."

"He must indeed! What on earth is she going to think when she actually ..."

"She'll come to us when the Count dies — which could be at any time or he could drag it ... I mean he could linger on until the autumn. The Countess has been abroad for some years and has completely lost touch with her friends in London, or so Harold says. And the strain of renewing old friendships in the midst of her bereavement ... well, you can just imagine it, I'm sure. I know I can. Anyway, there it is — sometime soon, or maybe not so soon, we shall number a *countess* among our guests! It's exactly the sort of good fortune we've been praying for. Where one ventures, others will surely follow! We shall give her special terms, of course, and ..."

"We most certainly will not!"

Mother and daughter attempted to stare each other out. Eventually the daughter said: "Ask Mister Coverley if he gives

every unknown Lord and Lady Nonesuch 'special terms'! You'll
get a very dusty answer, I'm sure. Anyway, if she's at Baden-
Baden for an indefinite period, she's not short of shekels."

Harriet's nose curled in disgust at the phrase but Tamsin went
on: "The cheapest place there costs over two guineas a day."
She had no idea whether or not it was true, which is why she
spoke the words with such conviction. "But if she and the Count
are staying at a first-class hôtel and taking the waters and all the
other cures — to say nothing of concerts, the opera, *bals masqués,*
and all the other entertainments — not forgetting carriages and
the casino — why, it could easily top twenty-five guineas a day!
Do you think a reduction in our terms from twenty-one shillings
to seventeen and sixpence is going to mean the slightest thing to
a woman like that?"

"Not a woman, dear. A lady. A countess!"

But Tamsin, caught up in her own argument, was now having
further thoughts. "Exactly," she said.

"What does that mean?" Harriet prepared to become
exasperated all over again, even though she had been shaken by
the force of her daughter's words.

"It means we should be rather careful about this whole idea.
Before we hang out the bunting, let's make a few inquiries, eh?"

"I don't understand …"

"Ask yourself — why is a woman, a *countess,* who is used to
spending at the rate of twenty guineas a day … why is she so
keen to hide away here the moment her husband dies?"

"Hiding, dear? It's hardly that."

"Isn't it? She doesn't want us to tell a soul, and yet she's not
hiding? What do you call it? Anyway, why *can't* she look up old
friends in London? What better time could she possibly have
than immediately after a bereavement? Or does she owe them
money, perhaps? And does she owe money in Baden-Baden,
too? Is that the sudden attraction Penzance seems to offer —
the difficulties her creditors will have if they try to pursue her
over here?"

Harriet was on the verge of tears by now. Her splendid bit of
news, the answer to her nightly prayers, was shattered. Tamsin
slipped her arms about her and gave her a reassuring hug.
"Darling Mama!" she murmured. "I'm not saying it isn't

marvellous. But let's remember *why* 'poor old Harold' Lock was 'the life and soul of the golf club' — and why he was found half-dead on one of the greens that afternoon — which is also why he's been an invalid ever since. The leopard can't change his spots, they say — and nor can the born practical joker. We must ask Mister Coverley how one can find out about people like this Count and Countess de Ath. Especially her. Could you ask Mrs Lock if she knows anything more about her background?"

She took out her notebook and scribbled '*Almanac de Gotha* — de Ath family? — try the library.'

"By the way, Mama," she added, making herself all bright and cheerful, "you know the Trotters? It seeems they're aptly named. They're real globe-trotters. Or Europe-trotters, anyway. They live by moving constantly between hôtels and guest houses — all around England in the summer and Italy and southern France in the winter."

"How nice for them." Harriet tried to sound enthusiastic.

"Yes, well, that's not really the point. The thing is, we could hardly hope to meet a more experienced pair when it comes to judging our humble little establishment — its good points and its shortcomings. Why not let's ask them to give us their candid opinion, eh? We'd be letting a golden opportunity slip by if we didn't do it sometime before they leave ..."

"Oh — talking of their leaving — I meant to tell you about that," Harriet put in. "This other news sent it right out of my mind. Anyway, it's not definite yet, but Mrs Trotter came to me this morning, just after you and Dobbs went out ..."

"Miss Dobbs, please."

Her mother pulled a face. "Very well. Just after you went out, Mrs Trotter told me she might be going on a retreat. She's Anglican — very High Church. She was talking to the bishop about it last night. It lasts a month, apparently — on some holy island up in Scotland."

"Iona?"

"She didn't say. Anyway, if she goes, she'd like her son to stay on here. I said that would be in order. It looked all right according to the bookings book. And he won't be any trouble. He seems to spend all his time playing billiards at the Queen's."

18 When David Peters had chosen the engine for *Merlin*, their fishing boat, he brought his father back to George Smart's garage for a second opinion. It was a Thorneycroft, eight-cylinder, side-valve, marine engine with electrical ignition. Electrical ignition was almost unheard of in English motor cars at that time, not simply because it was an American gadget but mainly because, as motor manufacturers told the American company that tried to sell them, 'Our car owners are gentlemen. They employ drivers to swing the handle for them.' The engine for the *Merlin* also had seawater cooling and was capable of developing fifty horsepower. "Which works out at ten bob per horse." George Smart said in his finest salesman's style. "If you mind to look at 'n that way."

These facts meant nothing to the Captain. "What good is a hundred hosses when you'm out o' sight o' land?" he asked facetiously. "If you mind to look at 'n *that* way?"

Smart came back at once. "When they'm all bottled up inside that lump o' cast iron, boss, they could push the *Merlin*, full-laden, back home at six to eight knots."

"And in a contrairy gale?" the Captain asked.

"They'd at least keep her head-up to the wind and waves and stop her swamping."

The Captain saw the weight of that argument, at least. He said they'd think it over, which his son took as a sign that he was wavering. His strongest objection, however, he reserved for their journey home in the pony and trap: "How the hell are we goin' to pay for 'n, then?"

"By a combination of this and that," David suggested.

"Oh yes?" His father eyed him coldly.

"I reckon young Smart'd let us have 'n for half down and five pound a month …"

"That's still twenty-five down. And who's going to fit 'n?"

"I'll fit 'n, easy. It's no more than a bit of carpentry. The worst is to get the stuffing gland lined up true for the prop shaft. Harry would help us out with that."

"And the money?"

"I got fifteen now, to spare. And I needn't tell you where I could get the other ten. I could get double my fifteen in one moonless night."

"Our fifteen," the Captain said while he considered the suggestion. "New moon is the tenth — this Wednesday, so there's no moon tomorrow night, Tuesday. We could never make the arrangements in time."

"Oenone could send a telegram?"

The old man shook his head. "The Excise are now wise to that, so she says. They do get a copy of every cable to France from every port along the south coast. Betterfit you send a letter. The next moonless night'll be the eighth of August. That's a Thursday. You'll have to wait till then, boy."

"And miss half the summer season? Listen — if we had an engine, we could charge visitors four-and-six a go for a day's fishing along of us — and we could take half a dozen each time. Twenty-seven shilling a trip — come rain, come shine — come empty nets, come full! We shouldn't even notice five pound a month to George Smart."

"Thursday, August the eighth," the Captain repeated firmly. "Anything else is too risky."

But David did not give up that easily.

The very best brandy — superior old pale — retailed in England at around £8 a dozen. The same twelve bottles could be got in Brittany for £2 or less. The remaining £6 was, in the view of many a respectable Englishman (and just about *every* respectable Cornishman), a thoroughly iniquitous tax imposed by a grasping government through the Commissioners of Customs & Excise. Wherever there is an artificially raised price (and a tax is no more than that) there is room for enterprising men to make profits — £6 of room in the case of a case of superior old pale. Or 10s a bottle. Or 1s 8d to the Brittany fisherman who dropped them off on a regular fishing trip in English waters, 5s to his Cornish counterpart, who 'tidied up' after him and ran the risk with the Excise, and 3s 4d to the purchaser, who had the added satisfaction of spitting in the eye of a greedy and oppressive government. Small wonder, then, that the verb 'to smuggle' did not carry the opprobrium among the Cornish populace that governments could have wished for.

David had a plan. There was a particular Breton fisherman, Jean-Baptiste Clouet, who would supply the brandy. For £50 he'd bring over a cask, which could be bottled up and sold for £500. But first get your £50! For David's mere £15, however, he'd supply five dozen bottles of OSP; they had often cooperated along those lines in the past. He, David, would sell them for £30, thus doubling his outlay. Hence many jokes around the Newlyn taverns about 'double brandies' ... 'doubling up with laughter — or over in pain' — depending on how astute the Excisemen had been.

And there was David's problem: to do it all under the noses of the Excise. If they were going to poke those same noses into every telegram to northern France from every south-coast fishing port, he would have to turn that fact to his advantage rather than theirs.

When he handed in his telegram to Cousin Oenone, she looked at him as if he were mad. The message wasn't even in code; it read, simply: *'60 croissants pour Peters.'*

Croissants is French for 'moonfish,' which, in turn, is a euphemism common among fishermen for the sort of 'fish' one might catch in the wake of a Frenchman on a moonless night. "I do know what I'm doing," David assured her. "Just don't tell the old feller."

She agreed to hold her tongue but whether she'd stand by her word, he wasn't sure; if she just kept it until Thursday, all would be well.

He'd given Clouet little enough time to organize his end of the operation, so he had no way of knowing whether it could go ahead. He played his part, though, by placing fifteen sovereigns, securely sewn into a tube of sailcloth and tied inside one of his lobsterpots. But the night of the ninth was so perfectly moonless — and clouded over — that a hundred anxious scans of the inshore waters known as Gwavas Lake, chiefly between the Wherry and the Gear rocks, aided by a powerful telescope, had failed to reveal the smallest chink of light that might have been the Frenchman.

So far, so good. If he, knowing the time and place of the 'crime,' had failed to spot Clouet, the Excise couldn't possibly have managed it, either.

The following morning, Wednesday, he took a fine female cod over to the Morrab Guest House. When Tamsin saw his trap braked outside the tradesmen's entrance she ran downstairs to see him. "What progress on fitting out your boat with an engine?" she asked breathlessly, smiling far more broadly than the question itself warranted.

"How important is it to you?" he asked in return.

"Well ..." The question startled her. "It would be ... how can I put it? Useful? A feather in our cap if we could offer fishing trips — genuine fishing trips with a genuine Cornish fisherman — to our guests. No one else can, as far as I know. Not even the mighty Queen's. Why?"

"So ... fitting the engine to *Merlin* sooner rather than later would help?"

"It would be a great help, Mister Peters. Why are you asking all these questions?"

"Because you could greatly assist me in bringing that day forward, Miss Harte."

"We don't have any money to spare," she told him at once.

He laughed. "May I invite you to accompany me on the round of my lobsterpots this afternoon?" he said.

She shook her head. "Don't change the subject. Let's deal with this other matter first. How may I help you bring the day forward — if not with money?"

"By accepting my invitation."

Now she was bewildered. "That's all?"

"You'll understand soon enough," he promised her. "It'll be low tide at two. I'll pick you up off the beach inside the Wherry Rocks then."

After he had gone, Daisy kept a straight enough face while she said, "I was afraid you'd break your neck running pell-mell like that to see him."

Tamsin did not deign to reply.

When David arrived back at Newlyn, he heard an ancient cry that would normally have set him dancing all the way way around the harbour wall: 'Hevva! Hevva!' It was immediately taken up by all who heard it — 'Hevva! Hevva!' until the whole town rang with the excitement of it. The word itself is a latter-day corruption of the old Cornish word *hesva,* a school of fish.

The crying of it up and down the streets meant that anything up to a million fish had just taken up lodgings somewhere in Gwavas Lake, just outside the harbour piers.

"What is it?" he asked one of the criers. "Pilchard or mullet?"

If the answer were 'pilchards,' he was safe enough. Pilchards are not usually fished before August, when they are at their fattest and oiliest. They would not be fished today, in any case, and that would leave his plans intact. But mullet were best taken as and when they arrived, for they had a habit of moving on as swiftly as they had appeared. A shoal of mullet now would ruin everything, for every able-bodied man, woman, and child in town would be expected to drop his own work, no matter what, until the last individual fish was dispatched or banked — a process that could take days.

"Mullet," came the happy reply.

Happy for everyone but David.

He was already wondering how he'd tell his father he had squandered the fifteen pounds with absolutely nothing to show for it. His only hope was that the Frenchman had not had time enough to bring the bottles over. He sauntered up to the harbour wall, the only glum man in town, to inspect the cause of his impending ruin.

To prevent himself from giving way entirely to his despair, he began to run through the mullet-catching operation in his mind, looking for any small opportunities it might still offer him.

The technique was the same for both mullet and pilchard. George Croom, the huer, or director of operations, would soon be standing silhouetted on the cliff above the town. In Captain Benny's young days, Croom's father had held a branch of furze in each hand; nowadays his son preferred a pair of clubs, with which he'd be semaphoring directions to the fishermen below. He, of course, had an eagle's-eye view of the entire shoal, which, to him, would seem like a single giant creature, the size of twenty whales, in the bay at his feet. It would be shimmering silver if mullet, or blood-red if pilchard.

Following his directions the seine boatmen — six rowers, a helm, and a payer — would gently make their way out, with muffled oars, out into the bay, until they drew near one end of the shoal. Behind them they'd trail a line, all the way back to the shore. It was, of course, attached to the beginning of the net.

David stood on tiptoe and saw they were already manhandling the seine boat down the slipway toward the water. With every minute that passed, his chances of retrieving his brandy unobserved — and unarrested — dwindled away.

When the seine boat finally reached the edge of the shoal, Croom would drop his arms and Johnny Harvey, the payer, would begin to 'shoot' or pay out the seine itself — a giant net curtain, over half a mile long, with floats at its top end and lead sinkers at its bottom. It was four fathoms deep, which was more than enough to brush the shallow sandy bottom in that part of the bay between the South Pier and Carn Gwavas, some three-quarters of a mile south of the harbour. Any shoal in that part of Gwavas Lake was as good as dead once the hevva cry went up.

Within five minutes, if all conditions were right — and certainly within fifteen — they'd shoot the entire seine net in a semicircle on the seaward side of the shoal, completing the operation by coming ashore with a line attached to its other end. There they'd join the dozens-strong shore party and begin the long, careful process of winding the capstans that hauled in the seine. Meanwhile the follower boat would be stretching the much shorter 'stop net' across the open ends of the seine, which by now would have the form of a narrowing U with its open end pointing toward the beach. Until the mouth was closed, they'd beat the water with their oars so as to frighten the fish into the back of the seine and prevent their escape — though the juvenile fry would, of course, wriggle through the mesh to live, breed, and fatten for another day.

Ideally, if the shoal proved quiet and not too skittish, they'd try to shoot the seine at low water and bring it ashore on the rising tide — in short, working with the flow rather than against the ebb. When they had it close to land, in water deep enough to keep the fish alive and trapped but shallow enough to allow the men to extract them bit by bit, the whole of Newlyn — himself included — would have but one objective: to get as much ashore in as marketable a condition as possible.

By now David had run the whole process through his mind and had still found no point that he could exploit for his own purposes. What he had been hoping — before this heller of a

mullet shoal swam into the bay — was that the Excisemen,
having read his telegram to Clouet, would conclude that he'd be
out there tonight, lifting the brandy under cover of a darkness
that would still be moonless until just before dawn. They'd
never imagine he'd be rash enough to recover them and bring
them ashore by daylight. In fact, that had been his plan: to
retrieve the contraband while pretending to be taking a high-
quarter lady on a little rowing trip about the bay. So their guard
would have been down — and they might even have snatched a
few hours' sleep so as to be sure of remaining alert all night.
They had often done so in the past, and that was another thing
he had been gambling on, too.

Suddenly he saw a little gleam of hope. In concentrating on
the seine-netting side of the day's business, he'd overlooked
what would be happening among those not immediately
employed in shooting the net. Of course! Every man with
lobsterpots in Gwavas Lake would be out there this afternoon,
between low and three-fourths tide, lifting their pots while the
seine-boat and its follower were encircling the shoal. And they
wouldn't be resetting them, either, because the next few days
would all be given over to packing, or salting and banking the
mullet catch. So a couple of hundred lobsterpots would all be
converging on Newlyn harbour at roughly the same time.

Or at *exactly* the same time, if he could orchestrate it properly.
There were distinct possibilities here.

19 She was a fashion plate, standing there at the water's
edge, waiting for him to round the Wherry Rocks and
cross the low-tide pool to collect her. She wore a pale-blue dress
in glazed cotton, discharge-printed with tiny flowers in yellow
and red arrayed in bayadère stripes of an even paler blue. The
same fabric covered her parasol and provided the ribbon that
trimmed her straw hat. Her gloves were of white cotton lace,
tinted with liberal use of the blue bag. On any normal lobster
outing, such beautiful attire would have been ruined in the first
five minutes; but, if all went according to plan, today would be
very far from normal. He'd only be worrying about a couple of

pots — and neither of them would contain lobsters, unless Miss Harte wanted some for her table; nor would any pots be brought into the boat.

The keel grounded when David was still three or four paces from the edge. When he leaped into the shallow water, she floated again and he was able to get her a few feet closer — though still too far for Tamsin to jump.

He could have lifted the boat and dragged its prow right ashore. Instead he said, "I shall have to lift you," almost as if he were apologizing. He stooped to slip one outstretched arm behind her knees and to reach the other across her shoulder-blades. Before she could say a word, he had raised her as high as his chest. He made it seem no more strenuous than lifting an ostrich-feather boa.

She looked up at his face, considering it once again as a piece of artistic modelling. It was a good face, with strong lines and a firm contour. His straight, dark hair was rather long by current fashion, but it suited him well, framing his features and giving him the mien of a Celtic knight. Her romantic, artistic fancy could see such a man in his rightful place at King Arthur's Round Table.

He held her slightly away from him so that he could place his feet carefully among the rocks over the few paces between the shore and his boat. When he came to a halt, though, he let his arms relax a little, bringing the side of her chest tight against the front of his. He held her so awhile. It was a pleasant feeling and it made her realize how long it had been since anyone had given her even a mildly affectionate hug.

For a moment he stood there, gazing down into her face; his eyes had never seemed so intensely blue as now, catching as they did the light of the summer sky. For an awful part of that moment she imagined he was going to take the liberty of stealing a kiss. Her lips even prepared to receive it. And, when he set her upright, as light as thistledown, in the boat, she felt a surge of disappointment that he hadn't. But it was immediately followed by a more powerful wave of relief. That was *not* the sort of thing she wanted with David Peters. It was only some silly, schoolgirlish reflex, nurtured by Daisy's infantile teasing, that put such contrary ideas into her head at all.

"Take me to the horizon!" she said, stretching an imperious arm southward.

"You tell me how far it is and I'll take you there," he replied, putting a foot inboard, over the keel, and springing himself in. The boat grounded under their combined weight and he had to punt off with an oar.

"Oh!" She plucked a figure out of the air. "Twenty miles?"

He laughed. "How far is Saint Michael's Mount, then?" He took his seat and fitted the oars back in the rowlocks.

She turned her gaze eastward and exclaimed, "Goodness! It has sunk!"

"You're the one who has sunk, Miss Harte. Up there on the promenade you'd be what — fifteen ... twenty feet above sea level, counting in your own height? And then the horizon would be twice as far away — five or six miles. Down here it's only three, if that."

"You mean ..." She had a little difficulty with the idea. "The higher you go ... yes, I suppose that's logical. It just never struck me before."

"On Penlee headland, two hundred feet, you could see sixteen miles — across the bay to the Lizard. But you go up in a balloon — five or six thousand feet — and you could see a hundred miles or more — clear to Exeter!"

"My!" Her eyes gleamed at the very thought. "I'm going to do that one day. I'm going to do *everything* one day!"

"Beginning today?"

"Oh yes — today. Speaking of today, can you tell me now — how does my being here hasten the fitting of your engine?"

"Look beyond the rocks," he said. "What d'you see?"

They were moving swiftly over a calm sea by now, and just about to clear the eastern end of the Wherry group.

"Scores of other people tending their lobsterpots. How do you all know which ones are yours?"

"Look closer, just the far side of this nearest rock. What d'you see there?"

"Something floating — a bit of cork?"

"You'll notice something else when we get alongside."

"A coloured disc," she said as they closed the distance. "Red and white."

"That's mine, then. And there's nothing much wrong with your eyesight." He shipped oars and leaned out to grab the cork float as they passed.

He dropped it in the orlop and began hauling in the line attached to it.

"Clever," she said. "You all have different colours, I suppose."

"Here's the really clever bit," he told her as the pot loomed toward the surface. "See?"

"A lobster! Poor thing — I feel so sorry for them." Her mouth watered nonetheless and she wondered if she'd have to pay for it this time.

"Never mind him," he said. "What else?" He lifted it half out of the water. There was the muffled, submarine clinking of glass on glass.

She stared at what was rolling around in the bottom of the pot, then turned great, searching eyes on him and broke into a slow, accusing sort of grin. "No!" she said in a hushed voice, barely above a whisper. "That's against the law!"

"There's an old Cornish saying," he replied. " 'Mining's gone scat. Farming's gone scat. Fishing's going scat. So 'tis back to wrecking, boys!' Well — morally speaking — this is better than wrecking, anyday."

She was still staring at the half-dozen bottles. He, meanwhile, was tying the pot fast to the thwart that formed his seat, so that it was only just submerged, half way along the port side. "How much ...?" she asked.

"For the lobster? It's yours." He dropped the creature in the orlop, too, and set off for his next pot.

"No! Thanks, of course, but you know very well what I mean. Is it brandy? They have the shape of brandy bottles."

"Superior old pale — the best. Three-and-fourpence in France. Five shillings to me, there in the pot. Ten bob to you, on your table. Thirteen and fourpence in the merchant's shop."

"Whew!" She fanned her face. "And to think that Papa used to buy it by the case!"

"And I'll wager it was at thirteen-and-fourpence, too. Unless he got it from someone like me at ten bob."

She licked her lips and eyed him shrewdly. "So ... there's five shillings ... Lordy!"

"Say it!" He nodded.

"Five shillings profit to you in every single bottle!" She looked around and about at all the bobbing corks and the lobstermen plying among them. "Is that what *everyone's* doing? Out here in the full light of day?"

"No!" He laughed again, though he also admired the speed with which she grasped the essentials. "At least I hope not."

"So it's only us? Won't we get caught?"

"It's possible. Are you afraid of that? I'll put you ashore again, if you prefer?"

"No." She shook her head defiantly. The lobster was edging toward her; she pushed it back with her foot. "If you're not afraid, why should I be? You're the one who'd go to prison for it. I'd tell them you kidnapped me."

"How kind! That would just about quadruple my sentence, you realize?"

"I'd bring you soup," she promised, blowing him an ironic kiss. "Every day."

"I'll take the kiss, instead," he risked saying.

For the first time she was at a loss for words.

He pressed home his advantage: "Only I wouldn't want it blown across the empty air like that. It might catch cold on the way, see."

She found her voice at that. "Mister Peters. Before we proceed any further, there's one thing I'd like you to understand." She was glad he was hauling up the next pot by then, so that she did not have to look him in the eyes.

"And what's that, Miss Harte?" he asked calmly.

"I do so very much hope that we can be *friends.*" She swallowed heavily, aware that she was sounding like one of those prim heroines in the sort of paper novels the servants liked to read — girls who do a lot of flouncing and who toss their curls in defiance at every imaginable threat to their virtue, from the Young Master who wishes to steal a kiss right down to the wicked scullery maid who suggests they share a sixpenny piece found under the drawing-room carpet. *I do so very much hope we can be friends!* She heard the echo of her words in her mind and cringed with embarrassment. But she could not think of other ways to put it.

She needn't have bothered. Those ten words, it seemed, were enough to stir him to amazement: "But that's *extraordinary!*" He stopped hauling for a moment and stared at her.

"What?" she asked, slightly alarmed.

"That's *exactly* how I feel, too!"

"Oh ... you!" She kicked him lightly on the shin — or, at least, she did not intend to kick him quite as hard as, in fact, she did. It must have hurt him, for her toes were smarting, but he continued to clown — making his lips and eyelids tremble as if he were fighting back tears.

"I'm sorry," she blurted out. "All I meant to say was ..."

"I know," he interrupted her. And he was serious again — except, how could anyone be sure? "The very thought of any sort of romantic development between us is absolutely out of the question." He started hauling again.

"Well ..." She hesitated. "I wouldn't express it in quite those ... I mean, you put it very baldly. Lordy — more?"

"As well hang for a sheep as a lamb," he said as he tied this pot on the starboard side, balancing the first. "And there's another lobster going begging, too." He set it down beside the first.

"Six pounds!" she murmured, looking now left, now right.

"Only three — if you're talking about the profit."

"Still! Three quid! Just while rowing" — she stared back at the shore — "a couple of hundred yards!"

"About what you were saying ..." he began as he plied the oars again.

"The other lobstermen are all watching us," she replied, eager to get off that subject. "Do they know what you're really doing here?"

"Every man of them," he assured her. "But, er, about us being just friends, you and me — I completely agree."

"Yes, well, all right. I mean, we can take it as read ... and just drop the subject. All right?"

"Until you raised it, the thought never crossed my mind."

"Really? Well, in that case I'm sorry I ever mentioned it."

"I thought, you see ..."

"Look! There's nothing to discuss, Mister Peters. We both find ourselves in complete agreement. Full stop! Are we going back now?"

"No, there's a few more pots to lift. We're in agreement, as you say, on the negative side of things — about what *isn't* going to happen. But I wonder if we're equally of one mind on the positive side?"

"Ah. There's a red-and-white marker, by the way."

"Well, thanks!" He had genuinely missed seeing it. "You'll earn your keep yet." He backed one oar until they were on the right course.

She realized how clever he was at not making splashes; she had been the victim of many an incompetent oarsman before. "My keep?" she echoed.

"It's just a saying." In three strong pulls they reached the next pot. He started hauling, speaking as he worked. "When we met on the shore last week, and you put the idea to me of a commercial arrangement to supply your kitchens, I was very happy."

"Oh! But it was only the very *germ* of an idea ..." She started to explain.

"I know that. I fully realize it may all come to nothing. But I hoped it wouldn't — shall I tell you why? Ah — here's another thirty shillings!"

Six more superior old pale bottles gleamed dully in the bottom of the pot, which also contained three lobsters, one of them small enough to throw back.

"Talk of being hanged for a sheep!" she murmured. "You're going for the entire flock!"

He laughed as he transferred the half dozen to the pot that was slung to starboard. "Here — Joe!" he called out to the nearest lobsterman. "Take that home for I, will 'ee?"

Joe pulled across and took the empty pot — empty, that is, except for the surviving pair of lobsters. His only 'comment' was a nod and a wink — the nod to Tamsin and the wink to David.

The pattern was starting to become clear to her. They were going to transfer all the brandy, however many bottles there were, to these two captive pots, leaving his friends to carry all the others back to harbour. She still wondered how he was going to slip the two full pots past the eyes of the Excisemen — assuming they even knew the first thing about it. "There's your next-nearest," she said, pointing out a red-white marker just four pulls away.

She expected him to pick up his interrupted explanation. Instead he began singing a shanty, more to himself than to her, though she could make out something about 'Lord Franklin' and 'one night on the deep.' He stopped when he began hauling in the line beneath the fourth marker.

"You were saying?" she prompted him.

"What?"

She glanced heavenward. "About supplying fish to us ... and ... all that."

"Oh yes. I was saying hoped we would become very close friends as time went by. But certainly nothing of a romantic nature — verily, no!"

She was a little miffed to hear him being quite so positive. "Good heavens!" she exclaimed. "Do you mean to say I'm as off-putting as all that?"

"N-o-o," he replied judiciously, as if he had to think about it for a second or two first. "No, no — not in the least. But — oh dear — I thought you'd understand. I mean, you were just as emphatic on the point as me. So I just assumed you must have some gentleman friend ... the same as me with Sarah ... well, never mind. I was wrong." He began hauling in once more. "Let's drop it."

For a moment she was too stunned by this most unexpected turn in the conversation to respond. Then she said, "Sarah? Who is Sarah?"

"It's of no consequence," he replied mildly. "She's not interested in me, either. Ho-ho! And here comes another thirty bob! Harvey, boy — here's a pot for 'ee! And as fine a cocklobster as ever 'ee seen!" He transferred the half dozen to the port pot and gave everything else to another of his friends.

"As it happens," Tamsin said after pointing out their next 'pot-of-call,' as she named it, "there is no gentleman in my life at the moment, but ..."

"Ah, so I was wrong on all counts!" he cut in with cheerful self-reproach.

"My toe hurts where I kicked you," she said.

"Pull off your shoe and stick it in the water," he suggested.

She was on the point of following this advice when she realized it would mean showing him not just her ankles but quite a bit of her nether limbs, to say nothing of sprawling with those same limbs spread in front of him in a most unladylike manner. "Oh, it's not that bad," she lied.

A moment later it struck her as slightly unbalanced that she had sat naked as a babe on a rock with Messrs Coverley and Trotter, only three days ago, and yet now she shied away from exposing a few inches of one extremity, all of it well covered in a cotton stocking, to Mr Peters. It must indicate something but she could not imagine what.

"It's only temporary, anyway," he said soothingly.

"Mm-hmm," she agreed. She could bathe her toes in privacy when she got home again.

"An eyeable, doxy, high-quarter maid like you!"

"Pardon?"

"What you said — the lack of a gentleman in your life. It's only temporary. There'll be scats of them before long, surely? That Mister Thorne, for instance — he's more than a bit hurrisome for you, as they say." He started hauling in the fifth of his pots.

"I don't really wish to discuss him — or anyone else in that light," she announced, feeling once again like the sixpence-shocker heroine.

"Of course not," he agreed. "Even though that was … well, what I hoped for. Another thirty bob! How much is that now?"

"Seven and a half quid," she replied at once. "If you're thinking only of the profit."

"Who isn't!" His grin, and his wink of approval, made her feel absurdly pleased — especially coming on the heels of those obscure compliments (she assumed) about her being 'eyeable and doxy.'

"What d'you mean — it was 'what you'd hoped for'?" she asked. "Why should you hope I'd have 'scats' of men friends? There's our next pot, by the way."

He spun the boat on a sixpence to face it in that direction. "I feel like some edjack, now," he said ruefully, "but I'll tell no lie, maid. I've got no sister to talk to, nor no cousin of an age to discuss such matters with, either. None who'd understand. So I did sort of hope that — you being so high-quarter and me being, well, no more'n a fisherman, and any sort of couranting carry-ons between us being out of the question, like you said — I did hope that …" He ground to a halt, closed his eyes, and shook his head. "Never mind."

By now he was hauling in the next pot of gold.

"You hoped we'd become such good friends that we could talk about these matters with each other!" she exclaimed. "But that's extraordinary, Peter … I mean *Mister* Peters! Silly of me!"

He leaped at once through the gap she had inadvertently opened. "It's David, if you're seeking the name," he said lightly. "Miss Harte."

"Er … yes. I did know, actually. And your father is Benjamin."

"Benny, he prefers." He smiled expectantly.

"Oh … it's Tamsin," she said.

"A good Cornish name. And here's *another* thirty bob!"

"Nine quid! It's dizzy-making. How many to go?"

"We'll stop at fifteen quid," he replied, as if he had the choice of going a lot further.

"Yes," she agreed grandly. "It's always best to leave something for another day."

"Are your parents Cornish, then?" he asked as they set off for the seventh pot.

"My father's from Falmouth — *was* from Falmouth, originally. He was apprenticed to a ship's chandler down there, which was where he learned the business. If only he'd stayed there, and taken it over in time …" She shrugged. "Ah, well!" She had been about to say that he, David, wouldn't have considered the daughter of a small tradesman in Falmouth quite so far out of his reach; but then she realized it was not the sort of thought either of them wished to encourage. "Anyway," she went on, "I was about to say I have no brother, just like you with no sister. And I've often thought it would be so nice to have a man of around my own age, a man who was *just* a good friend. Nothing romantic. But someone I could share absolutely everything with — and who'd unburden all his cares and worries to me. I think that's what brothers and sisters can do … sometimes, anyway. Don't you … David?"

"Oh, Tamsin!" he exclaimed. "It's surely Fate that made me suggest this little outing this afternoon!"

"Don't get carried away now, David!" She laughed, partly out of embarrassment to admit, if only to herself, that to hear her

name like that, on his rich, deep voice, was ridiculously pleasing.
"We both know very well exactly what led you to suggest 'this
little outing' — it was to disguise its true nature from the eyes of
the Excisemen! D'you think they *are* watching us, by the way?"

He explained why he thought it not very likely — but why he
was taking precautions nonetheless. When she heard about the
excitement with the mullet shoal and the seine boat, she
absolutely insisted on going back to Newlyn with him to see how
they brought such a huge shoal ashore.

"And you can tell me all about your Sarah ... whatzername as
we go," she added.

20 When they had thirty bottles of superior old pale in the
port lobsterpot and thirty more to starboard, David
put the two live lobsters back into one of the pots and gave a nod
to Harry Peters, his second cousin, and 'Sonny' Sampson, a
cousin by marriage. Together the three lobsterboats set off for
the beach, making, it seemed to Tamsin, for the very spot where
he had picked her up. For the first time she began to wonder
about getting all five dozen bottles ashore — not in the sense of
hiding the activity from the eyes of the law but the far simpler
business of carrying them physically onto the land and then up
the beach to ... wherever.

For, even though they were submerged in the water now,
which helped reduce their weight by quite a bit, they were still a
considerable drag on the buoyancy of the boat; she lay lower in
the water by at least two strakes.

"Are you going to hide them somewhere?" she asked. "As
soon as we get ashore, I mean?"

"That's the general idea," David agreed.

"Where?"

"Best you didn't know," he replied with an apologetic tilt of
the head.

"We could hide them at the Morrab," she offered. "The
Excise would never suspect such a respectable house."

"Respectable house, eh?" For some reason he found that
highly amusing. "If you like, you can come with me when we

distribute this bounty all around the district. You'll see quite a few 'respectable houses' then, I can promise you!"

They landed several yards higher up the beach, for the tide had advanced while they had been working. He asked if she'd mind guarding the three boats while they stowed the brandy. He promised it would not take above fifteen minutes.

"Guard them?" she asked sullenly. "Fight marauders off with my parasol, perhaps?"

"The very sight of you — standing there and looking so fierce as that — would be enough to see any marauders off," he assured her as he took the centre position between his two kinsmen and set out. The lobsterpots creaked ominously; they were so heavy they barely swung between the bearers. Over his shoulder he shouted, "We'll drop the two lobsters off on your mother, as well."

She ran after him and said, "You're not going to leave any of these bottles with her, though?"

"Oh? Here's a change of tune!" he replied.

"Not unless I come with you — that's what I meant when I offered. She could never cope. She's a hopeless liar."

He laughed and assured her it was not their intention, anyway.

She returned to the boats, only to discover an urchin holding the three painters. It was a moment or two before she recognized him as the one she had paid to throw sand at Charlotte Thorne — a lifetime ago, it now seemed.

"You nearly lost these, missiz," he said, handing her the lines and holding out his other hand expectantly.

"Oh no I didn't!" She took the ropes from him and put them back under the stone that had been pinning them down before he arrived.

"Don't want your money anyway," he said, sticking out his tongue. As he set off westward, beachcombing along the tidal zone of the sand, he added, "I can get all the money I want kaybin' mullet over Newlyn, see. So there!"

She was moving the ropes to another stone, higher up the shore in the face of the advancing tide, when she saw Victor Thorne sauntering down the beach to join her. "That's no job for one of Penzance's most elegant young ladies," he called out. "Allow me."

She set her foot upon the stone in the pose of a big-game hunter with his kill. "I thought you were moving over from the Queen's this afternoon," she replied.

"Then we were both suffering under a misapprehension," he said airily.

"Oh?"

"Yes. You see, I thought you'd be there to greet us."

"Oh!" she responded airily. "If only I'd known you cared so much!" She wondered what *her* misapprehension might be, but not strongly enough to make her want to ask him. Instead she said, "Anyway, what made your mother change her mind about us — Mama and me?"

"About *you,"* he replied. "I don't imagine she had an opinion either way about your mater."

"From the moment she set eyes on me she took against me. And then, only a week later … what has she learned in the meanwhile to change her mind?"

He sat on one of the gunwales, took out a gold cigarette case, and offered her one. "You'll find they're Virginia this side and Turkish on that."

A reflex from an earlier life made her look to see if his name were printed on them — in other words, whether he had them specially made up for himself by Alfred Dunhill or one of those London specialists. He hadn't. Maybe he would when he inherited all that money next year.

Given a choice she always went for Turkish. They were oval, which looked more interesting between one's fingers. They were perfumed, too, which always seemed more feminine. She took one and hung it nonchalantly between her lips, catching a whiff of its perfume.

"I prefer the Virginia," he said as he struck a match for her. "They're more manly."

"I'll bet Messrs Coverley and Trotter smoke Turkish," she said, taking her first puff.

His Virginia made him cough.

"Have you met Mister Trotter yet?" she asked. "He's in the room next to you."

"Really?" he said, looking at her slightly askance. "Is that some kind of warning or what?"

"It's not a warning at all," she protested. "You complain I wasn't there to greet you and, I presume, to make the introductions all round, so these are the things I would have said had I been there in person."

"I was only teasing," he said.

She saw a chance to tease him back. "Well, I only mentioned Mister Trotter because you both dress with such elegance. My days of following fashion are, as you well know, all behind me, but I vividly recall the fun we girls had in talking about *la mode*. So I just thought that two such proud peacocks as yourself and Reginald …"

"Listen!" he shouted angrily, springing to his feet again. "I don't know what you've got into your pretty little head about me but I can assure you, I'm no peacock. I played in the first fifteen at school, you know. I'd have been captain, too, if it hadn't been for … well, never mind all that. Just because a fellow dresses carefully … one can't make you out at all," he grumbled.

"Obviously I've got the wrong end of the stick," she said. "The distinction between 'peacock' and careful dresser is evidently important to you though it escapes me entirely."

"You never spoke a truer word!" he said heavily. "For two pins I'd prove it, too."

"Well, I don't happen to have two pins about me," she replied, "but I could owe you."

He grinned. "I suppose I'll take that as an invitation," he said. "Come here."

"No. I'll get my feet wet. You come here."

"Now that *is* an invitation!" He leaned back on the boat and did a sort of gymnastic hand-vault forward, landing with his feet either side of hers. A split second later he was upright and they were touching each other from head to toe. And a split second after that his arms were about her and his lips were pressed hard against hers. She was too astonished to resist.

In fact, her first thought was that she mustn't burn his beautiful blazer with her cigarette — then that he mustn't accidentally burn her dress, either. And during those brief, fateful moments, the exquisite pleasure of being kissed by such a handsome, elegant young man of the world took control of her. A small, drowning voice within said it was her duty to resist … that all the world was looking on ... that one simply did not behave in this fashion in public in the broad light of day.

And anyway, David would be returning soon.

Curiously enough, it was that thought, more than any of the others, which made her break off their kiss at last — that and the sudden, urgent need to breathe freely again.

"Satisfied now?" he asked.

But she was looking up toward the Esplanade — where she saw that David and his friends were already returning. Actually, David himself was standing at the top of the steps, leaning against the railing, staring at her ... as far as she could tell at such a distance. His friends were already walking across the sand, so he had probably been standing there for a good half-minute. How much had he seen, she wondered?

"Eh?" Victor prompted.

"What?" She tore her eyes away from David.

"I asked if you're satisfied?"

She smiled and gave him another kiss, a brief one this time, to show the world — and David — that it was all very insignificant. "Compleeeetely!" she purred. "Listen! I'll see you this evening. I'm going over to Newlyn now to see how they catch these mullet. You've heard about this huge shoal that appeared in the bay this morning?"

"Are you going with your fisherfolk pals?" he asked.

"Don't be silly."

"Silly?" He relit her cigarette, which had gone out. "What's silly about it?"

"Childish talk like that. David Peters is a good friend, that's all. He's probably the best friend I have down here. But, honestly, that's all."

"Really?"

"Cross my heart."

"Then chuck this jaunt to Newlyn, Tamsin. Let's hire a gig and go for a jaunt of our own somewhere! There's so much I want to talk about — you ... me ... us! We could even find some place to kiss again — in private — properly."

She was tempted, for it really had been ... well, quite nice to be kissed by him and to feel his body tight against her. It was excitingly alien, and with a hint of danger, too, especially after the things she had learned so recently from Daisy. Perhaps it was that which tilted the balance at last — that and the sight of David striding down the beach toward them, easily overtaking his two companions.

"Hallo!" he called out as soon as he was within hailing distance. Then, when he was a little closer, he added, "I was afraid you'd be bored, but I see I needn't have worried. Mister Thorne — good to meet you again."

He held out his hand, which Victor accepted with some reluctance; perhaps only Tamsin's taunt of 'Silly!' persuaded him to it.

"Again?" Tamsin pretended to be surprised.

"It was nothing," Victor assured her. "We just went over to Newlyn to inquire about makng a fishing trip." To David he added, "That's all." He turned back to Tamsin. "Well … if you're sure?"

She darted forward and kissed him swiftly on the cheek. "À bientôt, chérie!" she murmured.

He nodded curtly at David and turned to make his way back up the beach.

"À toute à l'heure, monsieur!" David called after him.

He paused, briefly, but did not turn round.

"One in the eye for me!" Tamsin said as he punted them off again into the tideway.

"Yes, a great mistake — those education acts," David said. "Teaching the lower orders things they've no right to know."

"Tu parles français, mon frère, hein?" she asked.

"Naturellement, ma petite soeur."

His French accent was as provincial as his Cornish accent was when he spoke English. "You've lived and worked in France," she said accusingly.

"Did I say otherwise? They have fishermen over there in Brittany, too, you know — and, as you've seen today, we cooperate over many things."

In calling her his 'little sister' he had reminded her of their earlier conversation. "What did Victor Thorne really want when he came over to Newlyn?" she asked.

"You heard what he said."

"Yes. And I also saw your expression when he said it."

"Well, he pretended to pick me out at random to ask about a fishing trip. What he didn't realize was that, when he went into the post office to ask where he could find David Peters, he was actually asking my aunt. So he came looking for me. It wasn't a casual meeting. I didn't really know why, though, until five minutes ago. Did he think I might be some kind of rival?"

She shrugged awkwardly.

"Sorry," he went on. "Isn't this exactly the sort of thing you wanted us to talk about — to be able to talk about?"

"Ye-es," she admitted reluctantly. Now that it was actually happening, it didn't seem half as wonderful as it had in her imagination. In fact, for some reason, she would far rather be talking with Victor about David. "What about your Sarah?" she went on.

"Oh, her!" He drew a deep breath and launched himself. "She's the daughter of a Saint Ives fisherman. That's more than half the trouble. There's no love lost between Saint Ives boats and Newlyn boats. I don't know how to get near her even." He gazed at her hopefully. "In a romantic sense, I mean."

"How often do you meet? No — start at the beginning. How did you meet first? How long ago?"

He gazed out to sea. "Promise you won't laugh?"

"As if I would!"

"D'you believe in love at first sight? D'you think a man can look at a maid and, before he could blink an eye, *know* she was the one he was going to marry?"

The intensity of his tone held her in thrall. She could only nod and beg him with her eyes to go on.

"No matter that she won't even let herself *think* of me in that way. I mean, she's perfectly friendly with me. In fact, if she *hated* me, I think I'd stand more chance. But there it is. I shall wed her one day — I know it." He let go an oar and tapped his breastbone. "In here. I'm as sure of it as …" He gazed about them, at a loss for a comparison until, looking at her again, he said, "Well, as I'm sure of you sitting there now. And I knew all that the very moment I saw her. Thank you for not laughing, at least."

Laughing! Tamsin thought it the saddest, beautifullest, touchingest declaration she had ever heard — not that she had heard so many, mind. She thought this Sarah-maid must be one of the luckiest girls in Cornwall, to be the repository of such devotion. She must also be the stupidest, for spurning it aside. Or worse — for not even recognizing it.

"Does she have someone else?" she asked.

"That's what I suspected from the start," he replied, philosophical again. "And then lately I've had it confirmed. I've heard she's been seen couranting about with a young fellow from Carbis Bay."

"Next door to Saint Ives."

"Yes. A very *posh* little community. He's got money, of course."

"What does he do?"

"What do young men with money all do? Nothing!"

Tamsin felt his predicament so keenly now that she blurted out, "What a fool she must be! Is there anything *I* can do?"

He looked at her with new interest, hope even. "Like?"

"I don't know. You could take me somewhere where you're sure she's to be found … introduce me … leave us to talk? I'd be very discreet, I promise. I wouldn't say a word of your feelings unless I was utterly certain it'd do some good. But at the very least I could … you know, 'size her up,' as they say. Get the measure of her."

"I don't know, Tamsin." He bit his lip and shook his head dubiously. "It'd be a risk. What if she saw through us, despite all the care you took? In affairs of the heart, one usually gets no more than a single chance, you know."

"Oh, David!" Her lip was trembling and there was a horrid lump in her throat.

"Oh, come on!" He laughed. "It'll work itself out in time. I'm even more sure of it now, especially after this talk with you."

"Me? I don't see how I've been of the slightest help."

"Well, you have — just take it from me. Now it's your turn in the confessional. Do you always choose the most public place in town for your spooning?"

She pulled a face. "I didn't … I mean, that wasn't … Oh dear! I've got to be honest with you, haven't I?"

He nodded sympathetically. "Otherwise there'd be no point."

"Quite. Well, if you were any other person in the world, man or woman, I'd never be able to admit to you that what you saw back there was the first kiss of my *life*. The first real kiss, I mean

— not like at party games. Nor like those quick pecks one used to snatch at dances and balls."

"But you must have given him the nod — if not in so many words, then …"

"But I didn't. Or I didn't mean to. I don't know what I said but he took it as some kind of challenge that he had to prove he could kiss me. Anyway, it was very nice."

"For a first time."

"No. Just very nice." She giggled. "He didn't want me to come back to Newlyn with you. He wanted us to hire a gig and go off into the country somewhere."

"Why didn't you?"

"He's jealous of you, you know — until I told him you were just a friend."

"Ah! You told him that?"

"Probably the best friend I've got, I said."

"And he was happier then?"

She frowned. "I don't know, now that you mention it. Well, you saw the mood he was in when he left us — how would you describe it?"

He shook his head and smiled warily. "I never judge another man if there's a maid about to do it for me. You're so much better at it than us."

"That's true," she agreed. "Anyway, another reason I didn't go off with him is that no girl should ever fall in with all her young man's wishes all the time. What was it about Good Queen Bess — masterly procrastination? Something like that."

"Spin it out. A little goes a long way."

"Just so."

"No more kisses for a month."

"Oh no! That would be *really* spinning it out … oh, you were joking. Beast!" She looked about them suddenly. "I say! We're almost there."

He looked over his shoulder and said, "Yes — we made good progress, maid."

21 When Victor regained the Esplanade, he turned and leaned against the railings, not knowing what else to do now. The lobsterboats had formed into a flotilla, all headed home for Newlyn. Only one was not laden to the gunwales with lifted pots; but Tamsin would have been easy enough to distinguish, anyway — a dab of pale fabric in a cluster of sombre blacks, browns, and navy-blues. He waited for her to turn and wave. He waited until she was so far off that he probably wouldn't have been able to discern it if she had. He dropped his cigarette into the sand below and turned to face the town.

Life was not supposed to be like this for a rich young fellow without a care in the world. Jealousy was what you felt when some other chap picked the winner in the 2:30 at Sandown and your horse was so late it had to tiptoe back into the stables after dark; or when the chorus girl you were sure had winked at you walked off on the arm of your pal, who had been sitting at your side; or when that fellow you couldn't stand the sight of scored a century off the bowler who sent you back to the pavilion with a duck. Jealousy was for important, life-shaking events like that. It wasn't for thinking about a strange, wayward, strong-minded, infuriating, penniless girl, whom you hardly knew, anyway, sitting in a rowing boat with a common fisherman who probably couldn't shake more than a couple of tenners at the world.

He had intended going back to the Morrab and ... well, something would occur to him there. Perhaps Charlotte would like to join him in hiring a gig and going for a jaunt out into the country. Anything to escape from this dreary town for a while. She could dash off a water-colour and he could lie in the shade and engage in some serious thinking about his future. But he found himself unable to leave the seafront while that tiny pale spot still bobbed up and down out there on its slow progress toward Newlyn.

He lit another cigarette and sought the shade of the shelter. What was she, anyway, this Tamsin Harte, that she should so commandeer his thoughts? She was certainly NQOC. Her father, George Harte, had been no more than a chandler's apprentice

who had made a few astute commercial decisions and ended up
cock of the walk at Plymouth — until Nature balanced things
out again by causing him to make a few *un*astute commercial
decisions. No pedigree at all.

"Penny for them?" The mater's voice.

He sprang to his feet and turned toward her — or them, for he
discovered both his parents standing at the other end of the
shelter, staring at him with contrary expressions — his father's
bored, his mother's concerned.

"Pater, dear," she said in a voice that did not expect any
argument, "do go and see how late the Queen's serves those
delicious cream teas."

He went without a word.

She joined her son in the shelter and turned to stare out to
sea, following his gaze — or the gaze he had held while they
watched him unawares.

"I see!" she said with a smile. She looked him up and down,
the way a carter might gauge a draught horse to assess what
weight it might pull. "Little Miss Harte is revelling in it now, of
course. But, take it from me, darling — from one who knows,
that is — she'll tire of it soon enough." She seated herself as she
spoke. "She has bigger fish to fry." The metaphor was pleasing
enough to make her laugh.

"How do you know?" he asked, remaining standing. He had
meant the question to sound interested, conversational; but his
morose humour came through in his tone.

"I know you think I'm just being fickle, don't you, darling …"
she began.

"I think you're punishing us for not wanting to gambol among
the bonnie burns and braes this year. Have you seen my room?
It's a broom cupboard!"

"It's perfectly adequate, but never mind that. If you suppose
I'm just being wayward out of spite, then you understand nothing
— and that worries me."

He shrugged and turned away from her as far as he dared. She
always got him feeling like this — inadequate, incompetent,
unfit for the great big grown-up world. "I don't see there's much
to understand. You summed them up in one word — spelled
n, q, o, c."

"Which was true as far as it went," she replied calmly. "But mature reflection showed it didn't go far enough. That's all. Sit down and let me explain. And please extinguish that cigarette. I know we're in the open air but it does annoy me so."

He flicked the offending butt across the Esplanade; it soared over the railings and fell somewhere upon the sand below.

"Have a care! Someone might be sitting there," his mother reprimanded him.

"More fool they," he replied, sitting down.

"Oh dear, you are in a bate! Was she really beastly to you? Never mind. It's much more important, just at this minute, for me to explain certain things. You may know that I am from a cadet branch of ..."

"... of the Duke of Radnor's family." He spoke in unison with her. "I believe I have heard it mentioned a time or two."

"There's no need to be sarcastic, dear. The same noble blood flows in your veins, too, in case you forget it. What I may not have told you *quite* so frequently is that our particular branch was not just thin and straggly and almost leafless — it was severed entirely from its parent tree and, to continue the metaphor, in danger of being carried off to some peasant cottage. In short, when your father met me, we had nothing left but our ancient pride. I was like Tess of the d'Urbervilles. In my situation, I mean — not at all in character or behaviour, I do assure you!"

"You mean ...?" Light was beginning to dawn on Victor — and he did not like what he thought it illuminated. "You and Miss Harte ...?"

"Oh, but we were much worse off than the Hartes. They aren't *renting* the Morrab Guest House, you know. They own it. But let's not go wandering off into precise comparisons. The point I'm trying to make is that no one knows better than I that fortunes can wane as well as wax. For Miss Harte they have both waxed and waned during the course of her still-young life. For us Cunninghams the decline went through three generations. We once owned over four hundred thousand acres, putting all our family holdings together. Twice we saved the dukedom itself from ruin — once in seventeen forty-six and again in eighteen oh-two."

"Such is gratitude!" Victor said, becoming interested now for he had never heard those wretched Cunninghams portrayed in quite this way before.

"Indeed. But *I* was the salvation of our particular branch of the family. I met your father, won his affection, married him, and, though I say it myself, it was I and I alone who put *his* family's affairs in order."

"Eh?" Victor sat up, all ears, at this.

"Oh yes! We like to give the impression that money is something distasteful, something we don't really wish to talk about, something that's always just *there,* like a well, to be dipped whenever we feel the need. In fact, we think of it very like a well, don't we! We take great care not to pollute the source and never to extract more than it can replace naturally. That would be your general view of our family's financial affairs, I suppose? Tell me if I'm wrong."

Victor shook his head and said, "But … what?"

"Yes." She was pleased to see him following her line so closely. "It's a very big but, too. Because nothing in the world of finance is remotely equivalent to the rainfall that endlessly replenishes the groundwater and feeds the springs. So forget all thoughts of wells and concentrate instead on what really happens. Our income derives entirely from property, shares, and gilts — in other words, from rents and dividends — there's nothing God-given or automatic about any of it."

Victor stared at her in alarm. "You're not trying to work around to telling me … I mean, this move from the Queen's to that crabby little guest house isn't because …"

Her laughter cut him short. "Nothing of the kind. No. But it's all thanks to my constant vigilance, which means keeping a keen eye on the world, the way things are going … trends here, there, and everywhere. And the trends are not good. Let's start with property. How did Lady Bracknell put it in that wickedly witty play by that dreadful man whose name we've all agreed to forget — 'What with the duties expected of one during one's life and the duties exacted of one when one is dead, there's neither pleasure in owning it nor profit in passing it on'? Something along those lines, anyway. And it's even more true now than it was then."

"So it's stocks and bonds?" he guessed. "Perhaps I should look for a place on the Stock Exchange? Get us a ringside seat, eh?" He imagined that was where this homily was leading.

And his mother went along with it, for the moment, anyway, rather than let her argument be diverted. "It's certainly worth considering, dear," she said. "However — in the long run — they may prove even less reliable than property. You're too young to recall the dreadful depression at the end of the last century, following the wars and revolutions of the seventies. And even now we are merely living through a sort of truce. The old rivalries are still going strong. There'll be another war in Europe at some time within the next ten years. Some say within the next five. And when it's over, it will leave us all impoverished, except for the shipbuilders and armaments manufacturers."

"I hope we have shares in them!" He tried a laugh.

"Naturally, darling. But that's not my point, either. It's much bigger than that. What I'm saying is that at the moment we have all our eggs in just two baskets. And, while that's better than having them in one, it's not as safe as having them in three. Or four. D'you see?"

He shrugged. "I see that, of course, now you've explained it. But I don't see how it relates to Tamsin Harte."

She leaned forward and peered into his face. "It's a curious thing about you, Victor. You're an astute observer of *people* — more acute than most women, even. But the more abstract things like this pass you by. Most odd. However, I can't accuse you of being unobservant in this case because it passed even me by until last Sunday evening. When I saw Mister Coverley greeting the Hartes as his guests, well, it was as if a veil was suddenly lifted from my eyes. I realized I'd been thinking, or concentrating my thoughts, much too closely on the mother and daughter. In other words — forgetting the importance of the late father."

"Now that *is* odd," he said. "I, too, was thinking about him at the moment you arrived."

"Good! Excellent, in fact. What exactly were your thoughts?"

"The man had no class," he replied. "He learned a clever trick or two as an apprentice, made a fortune, but there was no 'bottom' to him. I mean no … *soundness.* No …"

" 'Bottom' will do, dear. We all know what it means. Go on."

"Well, anyway, he lost it all again, didn't he! What was so special about Coverley entertaining the Hartes?"

"He's a self-made man, too. I know he inherited quite a bit ... and went to Oundle and all that. But he's turned a small fortune into something very much larger — so he's self-made to that extent. And *that* is what's missing from our family's affairs. I can put them in order but I can't manage that sort of multiplication. I'm a housekeeper not a capitalist."

Victor sighed. "I still don't *quite* see, you know, why Coverley's entertaining the Hartes ..."

"But of course you do!" she snapped. "You're just not thinking. Miss Harte fascinates him. She has obviously inherited her father's commercial bent. If you could lift the lid and watch her brain-cogs working, I bet you'd be staggered at the vault of her ambitions. That girl is never going to remain a modest little guest-house keeper, or I'll eat all the wax fruits on this hat. And Coverley sees a kindred spirit in her. Apparently he took her and the Dobbs creature for a spin in his motor last Sunday ... which, incidentally, I'm surprised you didn't see fit to mention to your father and me when ..."

"You were hardly in the most receptive mood, Mater — if you'll forgive me for pointing it out."

"Water under the bridge, dear. The point is, he must have recognized her qualities at some time during that jaunt — otherwise he'd hardly have invited them to his table that evening."

"So ... are you suggesting he's going to invest money in her or something like that?"

"*Someone* is going to. You may be absolutely sure of that. She has the begging bowl out. Not crudely, of course, but in her own subtle way. I don't think her meeting with us — when that urchin threw the sand at poor Charlotte — I don't think that was quite as accidental as it seemed."

For a moment he considered confirming her suspicions but then he decided she was already self-satisfied enough with her own astuteness. It would hardly do to say he'd known it all along.

"However," she continued, "even if I'm wrong, she has inherited her father's nose for investable money, and she'll get it by hook or by crook."

"For what purpose?"

"Oh, who knows — with a girl like that? At the moment she's in the hôtel-guest-house line, so it's probably an establishment to rival the Queen's. But if she were to become more interested in the fishing trade" — she eyed her son shrewdly as she put forward the suggestion — "it could turn into quite another ambition. To own the largest fleet in Mount's Bay, for instance. And why stop there? Or it could be something entirely different. People with that sort of nose for commerce don't get a calling to one particular trade. They see them all as interchangeable opportunities." She glanced over her shoulder, through the glass screen toward the hôtel. "Your father's taking an age. Shall we go over and join him?"

They rose and made to cross the road, but were delayed by a pony and trap that was racing toward them from the direction of Newlyn. The driver was tooting a horn to clear the way, which people did smartly enough. Like them, Victor and his mother assumed he was desperate to get his *enceinte* wife to hospital on time, following some complication that made a home birth impossible. Only as they drew close did they realize it was David Peters and Tamsin Harte. They swept past, grim of face, looking neither right nor left, and almost took a spill in rounding the corner into Morrab Road.

"Well!" Mrs Thorne exclaimed. "Here's some excitement! I think we shall leave your pater to his own devices and hasten back to the guest house, instead."

As they crossed the road, Victor, who hoped to tie up one or two loose ends, said, "Surely Coverley would never invest in a rival establishment?"

"Why not? Penzance is nowhere near its full development as a holiday resort. There are bound to be more hôtels to compete with the Queen's. What better than to own one of them! Two eggs — two baskets. I wouldn't put it past him to marry her, either — just to make sure."

He cleared his throat, being uncertain about her intentions again. Finally he said, "So ... are you suggesting that I should get in first?"

She laughed. "Of course not, darling. A foot in the door will do. Charm her but keep her dangling — and don't tell me you haven't had plenty of practice! Meanwhile we'll have a close-to chance to find out just what she's made of."

Victor accepted the commission with a nod even though he knew that, as a gentleman, he ought to confess he had already begun to lose his heart to Tamsin. His conscience was eased by a conviction that his mother, in turn, was holding back something of equal importance. He could not imagine what it might be; he had, in any case, long ago given up trying to follow his mother's thoughts and schemes through the labyrinths of her mind. But she was up to something even more devious than anything she had so far revealed — he was never more sure of anything.

22 Poor David! Not only was he eaten with the fear of losing half his haul of brandy, which, in turn, would undo all his moneymaking efforts of the past two days, but he was also having to divide his attention between whipping the pony to a gallop (without goading it to bolt) and trying to contain Tamsin's anger.

"But you *promised,*" she cried. "As good as promised, anyway. You said you had no intention of leaving any bottles at our place. Those were your last words on the subject."

"What happened was that we …" was all he managed before she cut him short.

"Except you added you'd drop off the lobsters there. Only the lobsters. There was no mention of the bottles."

"The thing was …"

"And I *told* you — I explained. My mother would be no good at lying if the Excisemen came to search the place. I told you that, didn't I."

"We got as far as …"

"They've probably torn the house apart by now …"

"We didn't leave it in the house," he managed to deliver an entire sentence at last. "We didn't go near the house — except, as I said, to go round to the kitchen door and give your cook those lobsters."

"So where did you leave it — we're talking about one of those lobsterpots full, I presume?"

"Yes. Two and a half dozen. The thing is, what happened was, we got as far as ... the other place, and ..."

"One of the lock-up garages behind the Queen's, I presume?"

The jerk of his hands almost checked the pony to a grateful halt. "I never told you that." He cracked the whip above the creature's head again, which almost jolted her backward, out of her seat.

"God, one can't even trust you to drive properly! I'll tell you one thing, David — you are *not* going to carry any of our guests out to sea. I don't care if you fit Roll-Royce engines to your boat. If one can't even rely on your word in a simple case like this ... oh, I am so *mad!*"

He thought it best to say nothing more for the moment; just concentrate on his driving.

"Where did you leave it, anyway?" she asked after a while.

By now they were cantering up toward the Esplanade, which had the usual throng of holiday-makers and promenaders. He put his hand to the hooter and began a monotonously urgent parp-parp-parp!

"You know that holly bush inside your gate?" he said.

"You hid it under that?" She was scandalized.

"Well under it."

"Listen! That bush is so small, there's only under or not-under. There's no such thing as *well* under. What possessed you?" She saw Victor and his mater standing at the kerb but she had no choice other than to ignore them.

"When we got to the first hiding place ... how did you know it was a garage behind the Queen's, anyway?"

"Out of the three thousand other likely places within ten minutes' walk of the beach, you mean? Oh, it took a lot of guesswork! What happened there, anyway?"

"Standish Coverley, he was waiting to take it in, as usual. And that Trotter fellow with him. It was Trotter suggested putting half there and half somewhere else — split the risk, see? For him and me."

"So you thought at once of the Morrab — naturally!"

"Well, it's not but a hundred paces farther on. How was I to know that Exciseman back there, old Sterne, was going to take such an interest in you and where you live?"

They almost overturned when taking the corner into Morrab Road, at which point the guest house itself came immediately into view.

The street was apparently empty. No police vans. Not a sign of a blue uniform. The sun was baking the pavements and splitting the trees.

"Don't slow down!" she cried as he started doing just that.

He ignored her. "They could be lying in wait," he warned. "We don't want to appear agitated now."

"But they couldn't have got here ahead of us — we'd have seen them."

"They could telephone the Penzance police. 'Tis *they* could be hiding in wait to catch us here." The pony was down to a welcome walk by now, which gave David time to prepare Tamsin for the coming ordeal. "Just to find a few bottles in someone's front garden isn't ..."

"A few!"

"Listen — I didn't finish! Just to *find* them there isn't good enough evidence for a conviction. Enemies could have left them, hoping to get you convicted — and a clever lawyer could get you off on that argument alone. So, if the police *are* in hiding, they'll wait for us to go to that bush and then they'll pounce. They may not even know it's there, in which case they'd be just waiting for us to lead them to it. Mind you, even then we might be able to buy them off with a couple of bottles."

Somewhat calmer now she said, "I still don't know what possessed you to leave it there."

"Tradition!" He laughed.

"Be serious!" She was cross again.

"I am," he assured her. "I once had two boxes of brandy buried under rhododendron leaves in Squire Blewitt's garden out to Madron, there. He's the local chairman of the bench."

"*You* were taking a risk!"

"Hardly. A dozen of those bottles were for him! He knew it was there. The police knew it was there, somewhere. They watched us both for four days — because they'd have needed a warrant to go in and search, see? And who is it that gives out the warrants, eh?"

"The magistrates?"

"Right. So we beat them that time. And, with a bit of luck, we'll beat them this time, too. Here we are now." He braked the trap in front of her gate. "We'll go directly up to the front door, and the last place you'll let your glance stray upon, please, is that there old holly bush!"

Guiltily she tore her eyes away from it. In turning to descend from the vehicle she looked back down Morrab Road. "Oh dear," she said. "Victor and his mater."

"The more the merrier," he replied, handing her down.

But Tamsin was thinking of the shame of being unmasked as a criminal — and with Victor looking on.

She intended tapping gently at the front door, so as not to disturb her mother, who was probably taking a nap upstairs. But Daisy was there, already waiting for them to arrive. She opened the door before they even reached the steps. "What? No more lobsters?" she asked, pretending to be disappointed.

"Have the police been here?" Tamsin replied, stepping past her and going into the guests' lounge, which had a bay window to the front of the house. She stood well back and began a careful survey of the street.

Daisy followed her and, coming right up behind, rested her chin playfully on her shoulder. "See the Anglican Convent there? Saint Breaca's? The laburnum in their garden?"

"Got them!" Even as Tamsin found the house in question she saw two fern leaves moving just above the garden fence. "Someone should tell them that ferns do not grow horizontally," she murmured. "D'you see them, David?"

Now that there was a defined enemy and they were all in it together, her rage had quite evaporated.

Daisy stood upright again and glanced at him, surprised to hear Tamsin use his first name.

He winked at her and said, "They should also understand that ferns don't waggle about in the wind when there isn't any wind. There's two more behind the stone pillar at Morrab Gardens entrance. And I saw another three on this side of the road as we drew up."

Tamsin looked at him accusingly. "You didn't say."

"I didn't want to startle you."

"I don't know what they're waiting for," Daisy said.

"I'll give you one guess," Tamsin responded glumly. But then she saw that the maid's face was split with a grin from ear to ear. "Daisy!" she said with mock severity. "What have you been and gone and done?"

"Nothing much," she answered. "Three careless men left a lobsterpot full of old bottles out there under the hollybush."

"They've decided to move!" David had not taken his eyes off them since he had them all located. "Quick!" he said to Daisy. "What did you do with them?"

"Brought the lot in here and hid them."

"Where?"

"In a place Mrs Pascoe showed me. No one would ever find them, not unless they knew."

The bell clanged.

"It's the two Thornes and the police together." David chuckled. "I don't know which of them is more suspicious of the other."

Mrs Harte came downstairs from her nap. "What on earth is going on?" she asked. "The garden is filled with policemen. Have we been burgled?"

"They think we're smugglers, Mama," Tamsin told her. "Don't distress yourself about it. Go back and finish your nap. I'll deal with them."

"You will not! This is *my* house. I will not have them upsetting our guests with this nonsense." Harriet pushed past them and opened the door herself. "Smugglers, indeed!" she exclaimed.

"I *beg* your pardon?"

"Not you, Mrs Thorne," Harriet assured her. "These gentlemen from the constabulary. Do come in." She stood aside to let the Thornes pass but immediately barred the way to the police, who had assumed the invitation included them. "Now, what is this nonsense? Who are you?"

She addressed the nearest constable, who immediately looked toward his superior. "Sergeant Hocken, ma'am, of the county constabulary. We have reason to believe that certain contraband items have been concealed upon these premises ..."

"What nonsense! Reason, you say? I should like to hear it."

"Sarge!" A constable came up the path holding the lobsterpot. "Empty," he said — which they might have guessed already from the way he dangled it by just two fingers.

"Where did you get that?" Harriet asked.

"Under that hollybush, ma'am," the constable said.

"Well, take it away. We don't want it." She looked half over her shoulder. "Mister Peters? Is this anything to do with you?"

David pushed his way to the front and pretended to examine the pot minutely. "It could very well be, missiz. We left you a brace of lobsters earlier this afternoon. My assistant might have forgotten the pot when we left."

"Very clever, Peters," the sergeant said. "Listen now!" He beckoned David aside, took him half way down the garden path, and murmured, "A couple of bottles for me and my men and we'll see off the Excise for you."

Before they could come to any arrangement, however, the Excisemen themselves came thundering round the corner from the Esplanade in a van drawn by a pair of greys. The sergeant took off his helmet and mopped his brow. "We'll still do our best," he assured David as they rejoined the others.

Tamsin slipped her hand into Victor's and gave him a squeeze. "Exciting, eh?" she whispered before letting go again.

He took out his cigarette case and offered them around, but he himself was the only taker.

The two leading Excisemen hit the ground running. "Well?" the leader called out as they entered at the gate. He was Inspector Sterne, the one who had questioned Tamsin so closely — and so unexpectedly, according to David — when their boat tied up at Newlyn. He was well named, the fishermen all agreed.

Two further Excisemen descended from the van, of lowly rank, for they joined the two constables half way up the path.

In reply to Sterne's question the sergeant pointed to the empty lobsterpot.

"Then they've hidden them," Sterne said at once. "Have you searched the garden?" Without waiting for a reply he motioned his men to begin. "It wouldn't be the first time certain persons have concealed certain items under bushes," he added, staring balefully at David.

"Stop that this minute!" Harriet's cry brought a sudden, complete hush. The Excisemen froze half way across the little front lawn. "You will not search any part of these premises without a by-your-leave."

"We have a right to do it, ma'am," Sterne said. "And a duty, too. Mrs Harte, is it?" He bowed stiffly. "Inspector Sterne, ma'am. I hope we'll enjoy your complete cooperation, for I shouldn't think you had any hand in smuggling dutiable goods. Nor," he added heavily, "would you wish to be tried and sentenced along with them as did it, I imagine." He stared directly at David and Tamsin.

But involving Tamsin was his mistake. Harriet would have gone only so far to protect David Peters; to protect her own daughter she would have gone to the ends of the earth. "If you wish to search any part of these premises," she said, "you will have to apply for a warrant."

"We can certainly do that, madam," he replied frostily. "If that is your wish." He took out his watch and consulted it ponderously. "We may not manage it today," he added — untruthfully — so I shall have to place a night-and-day picquet on your gate with instructions to search all who enter or leave. I don't think your guests will take too kindly to that, but, if that is your wish, so be it."

"What a detestable little man!" Cicely Thorne exclaimed suddenly. "Sterne, did you say? I shall have a word about you and this disgraceful behaviour with Sir Napier Redmond, one of your masters."

Sterne did not flinch. "I know very well who Sir Napier is, ma'am," he replied. "I also know that 'disgraceful behaviour' would be his judgement on smuggling, not on actions aimed at combating it." He turned back to Harriet. "Well, it's your choice, Mrs Harte. A guard on the gate and a search warrant tomorrow, or a by-your-leave search now."

"What does a search involve?" Tamsin asked. "Ripping up floorboards? Taking out window casings?"

His smile was calculated to chill. "Ah, Miss Harte," he replied. "Again! Let me assure you — if you were to go indoors now and lift a single floorboard and then put it back again — just one in the entire house — I and my men would find it inside five minutes. I promise you — we will lift nothing nor remove nothing that does not show clear signs of suffering the same treatment — by other hands" — and here he looked at David again — "within the past few hours. Is it a bargain?"

He was actually conceding nothing for he had already decided that if a friend of Sir Napier's was in the house, this investigation, unlike so many others, was going to be conducted strictly by the rules. "Oh, and one other thing," he added. "When we have inspected any particular room to our satisfaction, it will be locked, and remain locked, with the key in my keeping, until the entire search is complete. Contraband has a strange habit of wandering upstairs and downstairs behind our backs in any house we search."

"You may not search my room unless I am present," Cicely said.

"I would absolutely insist on it, Madam," he replied cheerfully. "Mrs Harte? You or some member of your staff will have to stand proxy while we search the rooms of guests who are out."

"I would insist on it, sir," she replied coldly.

"Then let us begin." He was more than eager by now, for he had seen one of the party (Daisy, though he did not then know her by name) slip quietly indoors and he was sure she was even now concealing the brandy. Or making its earlier concealment doubly sure. He nodded at his own three men, who sprang into action at once, moving round the party and into the house. "Sergeant?" He now turned to the police.

"Our orders are not to enter private premises without a warrant," Hocken replied, adding a delayed, "sir."

"Even with the consent of the owner of said premises?"

"I have no instructions as to that, sir, but I could send one of my boys to inquire."

Sterne knew he was lying, of course, and that the 'boy' would take longer than any conceivable search of the guest house. In his heart-of-hearts, he could not blame Sergeant Hocken. A bottle of brandy shared out among them was preferable by far to the hatred of every fisherman in the bay and their sullen refusal to cooperate in future police inquiries. He himself knew all about that hatred.

"Sir!" One of his men was calling him indoors.

He thanked Hocken with elaborate sarcasm for his offer of cooperation and went inside. He found the man standing at the kitchen door, his way being barred by a fierce-looking Bridget, wielding a mop. The floor was covered with a mixture of tealeaves and wet sawdust.

"Now then, what seems to be the trouble?" he asked in rule-book fashion.

"She says if we trample that stuff underfoot and carry it all over the house, there'll be blue murder, sir."

"Quite right, too," he told his astonished subordinate. "I should feel strongly about that myself, wouldn't you?" Then, to Bridget, "Obviously you're going to sweep it up, maid. How long will that take?"

She wondered how long she could spin it out. "Twenty minutes, sir?" she suggested.

The Exciseman expected his chief to explode and to order it to be finished within five — which would be generous enough. But, sweet as pie, he just smiled and promised to return then.

The sweetness soured, though, as room after room yielded nothing. It had to be in the kitchen, then. And, from the attention that maid had been lavishing upon the floor, he guessed the hoard would lie in a cavity under one of those big flagstones. How boring! he thought. Some people had no imagination.

He called off the search of the attics, where the cobwebs had obviously not been disturbed for days, or even weeks, and brought all three men down to the kitchen. There, to his annoyance, he found that, although Bridget had swept the stones themselves clean enough, the cracks between them, where there would be telltale signs of any recent disturbance, were still full of the sawdust-tealeaf mixture. The girl was now blackleading the kitchen range, a great brass and cast-iron monster that also heated all the water for the house.

He crossed the room, taking care to step only on the middle parts of the stones, and went out into the scullery. He returned with two yard brooms and the brush Bridget had used. Handing them to his men he told them to sweep out all the cracks, starting at the inside edges of the room and working toward the back door. He, meanwhile, got down on his hands and knees behind them and produced a large magnifying glass, with which he started to examine the cracks minutely.

"Mister Sherlock Sterne!" Victor quipped. "Where's your meerschaum, man? And the deerstalker?"

There were a few nervous laughs. Daisy had not had time to tell them where the bottles had been hidden but, like the inspector, they had concluded it must be there in the kitchen somewhere and that its discovery was now only a matter of time.

Where? Tamsin mouthed the word at Daisy, who responded with a tight little shake of the head.

David realized that, by crowding around the door like this, in such an anxious knot, they were only strengthening Sterne's conviction that he was close to his goal. Agonizing though it would be, he suggested that they should all leave the men to their doomed quest and repair to the lounge.

"For a cup of tea and some fairy cakes!" Tamsin added. "Mrs Pascoe — would that be possible?"

Mrs Pascoe said it would be entirely possible and went to take the simmering kettle off the stove.

The mention of 'fairy cakes' in present circumstances seemed hilarious to all of them.

Sterne gritted his teeth at their laughter and silently promised they'd pay for it the moment he'd found which flagstone to lift. Meanwhile he kept a surreptitious eye upon that maid who was blackleading the range — or pretending to. It was quite clear to him that she was just wasting time over there, watching him like a hawk and, no doubt, planning a diversion of some kind when he got too close to the hidey-hole.

The reward for his covert vigilance came at last — when he arrived at a particularly large stone right underneath the kitchen table. The moment he put his hands to it and discovered that it rocked, he saw the maid look across the room at the cook. He followed her glance and was just in time to see the woman give a terse little nod in reply. When she became aware that the gesture had been observed, she fixed him with a nervous smile and said, "A dish o' tay and a slice o' fuggan, inspector?"

"Thank'ee, ma'am," he replied, "but I'd be more obliged if you'd direct my men as to where to move this table? I'm sure it doesn't usually stand here, for it's the most inconvenient place in the whole kitchen. And you, maid" — he turned to Bridget — "you may go call your mistress to attend. I fancy our search is about to be rewarded."

He rose and dusted his hands. These moments were always sweet, and they quite made up for the daily cold bath of hatred from the rest of mankind.

As soon as they had reached the relative sanctuary of the lounge, and closed the door firmly behind them, everyone turned on Daisy with Tamsin's unvoiced question: *Where was the brandy hiding?*

But she put a finger to her lips and whispered, "It's best I don't tell anyone. You wouldn't believe me, anyway — because I didn't believe it myself until I saw it — and you'd have a job not to look that way to see if it was true."

And that had to serve for an answer until Bridget came with Inspector Sterne's triumphant message. "I'll stay here," Daisy said as they all trooped back to the kitchen. "Just in case."

"Where is there any sign of recent disturbance?" Harriet asked as soon as it became clear that Sterne intended raising one of the flagstones.

"Why, everywhere, ma'am!" The inspector pointed at random about the entire kitchen floor. "Disturbance of evidence!" He stood on the flag and made it wobble. "This one was lifted, I'll dare swear, but all evidence of it was disturbed by the sweeping of sawdust and tealeaves."

David leaned close to Tamsin and murmured in her ear, "I see what you mean about your mother's inability to cope."

She reached out a foot and trod hard on his boot — having forgotten her already bruised toes in all the excitement. She remembered them again now and winced.

One of Sterne's men had meanwhile brought a heavy shovel from the coalshed; another had a raker from the range. The captain nodded and they put their levers to each side of the wobbliest corner.

"Inspector," Mrs Pascoe said. "You'm wrong if you believe there's anything to interest 'ee under there."

He just laughed.

Tamsin's heart was beating so hard she could hear it pounding inside her head. Her hands were starting to shake uncontrollably. Victor slipped an arm about her waist and she felt that he was shivering, too. They were all hardly daring to breathe. Only David seemed above it all. He stood there with folded arms, watching dispassionately; and when he became aware that Tamsin was looking at him, he just winked and returned his gaze to the flagstone, on which all eyes were now fastened.

The levers slipped several times until the third Exciseman took the poker from the range and used it to wedge the flag between each pry. As soon as it was elevated enough for a man to get a grip, all three of them thrust their hands beneath it and lifted it without difficulty.

Everyone craned forward, leaning over the barrier of Sterne's outstretched arms. The cavity beneath the stone contained half-a-dozen bottles of … ginger pop! They were instantly recognisable by the trapped marble in each bottle's neck.

"I don't believe it!" Sterne roared above the gales of laughter that suddenly filled the kitchen. "Rest that stone aside and pass us one."

It took two of them to 'walk' the stone to where it could be rested against a wall; the third reached into the cavity and withdrew one of the bottles, which he handed to his chief.

"It's some trick," Sterne mumbled. But when he put his thumb to the marble and pressed hard, it dropped from its rubber seat and there was a great eruption of ginger beer, which left his whole arm soused.

Mrs Pascoe passed him a dishcloth, saying, "Told 'ee!"

Tamsin was not alone in feeling almost sorry for the man. He was beaten and he knew it. As he did his best to dry his sleeve he looked about him wildly, " 'Tis here somewhere," he cried. "I know it."

"No you don't, Sterne," David said quietly.

The others stopped laughing and looked at him in surprise.

"You saw me and Harry and Sonny come ashore with lobsters for guest houses up and down Morrab Road — and a dozen for the Queen's — and you were so sure 'twas contraband that you never bothered to look in any of the other pots as were lifted in Gwavas Lake this afternoon."

They both knew that such an inspection would have been impossible — with forty men eager to get 'tucking' among the mullet and the whole of Newlyn depending on them, but it offered the inspector the smallest of fig-leaves, which he had little choice but to accept.

"You!" he cried, throwing the cloth into the sink and walking up to David with a single finger upraised, shaking with fury. He put it right below David's nose and growled, "You needn't think

I've done with you, boy! You may have the contraband put away somewhere — here or back home in Newlyn — but little good will it do you! The fine gentlemen of this district may nurse their thirst a while yet, for I'm your shadow, boy. From this day forth, I'll dog your steps until I catch you with it."

The threat was quite empty, of course. No one doubted that. Yet the man went up in the estimation of all for the dignity it allowed him to recover.

"My keys, if you please, Inspector!" Harriet held out her hand when it looked as if the man were about to depart without handing them over.

For a moment he seemed on the point of flinging them at her but then, perhaps remembering that friends of Sir Napier were present, he passed them over with a sickly smile.

When he had gone, taking his men with him, everyone crowded around Daisy, even though Mrs Pascoe or Bridget could have told them just as well; somehow the honour of revelation belonged to her.

She led them back to the kitchen and gave Bridget a nod. The maid opened a drawer, took out a small spanner, and went across to the range.

David's heart fell. "You never cooked it?" he cried.

For reply, Bridget undid the four nuts that secured a plate to one side of the range — the portion she had been blackleading while Sterne led himself up the garden path. The plate covered that part of the range where a buffer tank stored the hot water needed in the kitchen before passing on any excess to the tanks in the hot press upstairs.

But the bottles were not there, either — or not exactly. Daisy stood aside and gestured at a further cast-iron plate, deep within the cavity. It was beside the hot tank and in the wall of the cavity that was farthest from the range. "Mrs Pascoe can explain it best," she said.

The cook went over and patted the kitchen wall beside the open cavity. "There's an old bake-oven in there," she said. "The old range, the one as was there when they built the house, had an iron flue as went through 'n." She took off her pinafore and draped it over the hot-water tank. Then, kneeling down, she slipped an arm inside. "And if you slide this here old plate back

... so! You can ..." She grinned and pulled her arm out, clutching one of the brandy bottles, which she flourished so vigorously that David rushed forward to rescue it.

There was a loud, peremptory knock at the back door. Everyone stopped laughing and looked at the open hole in panic. With amazing speed, Mrs Pascoe popped the dismantled plate into the oven while Bridget placed the clothes-horse where it covered the open hole. David hid the bottle under his coat with a dexterity born of long practice. Daisy meanwhile opened the door.

It was Sergeant Hocken.

All he did was lick his lips and clear his throat.

David poked his head out of the door and glanced all about. Hocken smiled at him wearily, as if to say, 'D'you think I'd be standing here if there was any danger of being observed?'

David slipped him the bottle and he disappeared — and it all happened so fast that the others hardly believed their eyes.

"Well!" Cicely Thorne exclaimed. "Do you know — until this moment I've been feeling like the most wretched of criminals!"

Part Three

Kynance Cove

Maiden voyage

23 "We may all laugh about it now," Victor said the following day, "but I don't mind admitting my heart was in my mouth more than once."

He repeated the sentiment in different forms many times over the next few days. Tamsin, who could not disagree, nonetheless felt she had to stand up for David, who was, of course, the real, if unspecified, target of Victor's comments. "It was my fault — in a way," she would say (hoping the admission would never get back to David). "I did more or less suggest our house as a temporary hiding place."

She was more interested in the slight but unmistakable changes the episode had brought about among all who lived or worked at the Morrab. It would be too much to say that such a varied collection of people, brought together by chance and soon to disperse again, had been welded into a group of blood-brothers and -sisters, but there was a camaraderie, an informality that would not otherwise have existed. There were smiles when they passed one another on staircases where, before, there would have been formal nods and mumblings that might or might not have been actual words. Erstwhile 'Good-mornings' and grave 'Nice days' were replaced by cheery 'Hallos' and genuine inquiries after each other's health and untroubled sleep.

It caught on among the other holiday guests, too, even though all they were told of the incident was that the Excisemen had somehow got hold of the wrong end of the stick. They, too, caught the camaraderie infection. It was as if they had always wanted the chance to let their public faces show more of the private smile. Not too much, of course. The young man from Yorkshire who told another guest that he'd seen her 'hobnobbing' with one of the seafront photographers that morning was soon made to understand that such casual laxity of speech was not welcome — and it remained unwelcome even after the lady in question had had the actual meaning of the word explained to her. But, such unfortunate episodes aside, most of them said, as they paid their bills and left, that the Morrab Guest House was a real home-from-home.

Sterne's threat to dog David's shadow to the gates of Hell and back proved as empty as everyone had suspected it to be at the time he made it. Four skilled trackers, devoting their every waking hour to the job, could have kept one man under constant surveillance, given a large dose of luck. But what of his friends? And of all those people, spread throughout West Penwith, who had a financial or alcoholic interest in his success?

By the end of that second week in July every bottle had found a buyer. And David was working round the clock as a carpenter, building a sub-deck in the bowels of the *Merlin* to take the engine housing. Meanwhile his cousin Harry was reaming out a precise hole through the sternpost to take the stuffing gland for the propshaft. They were so eager to try her out they were even discussing ways of beaching her round in some remote cove beyond Mousehole and continuing to fit her during the sabbath, though they both knew it was the dreamiest of pipedreams.

Meanwhile Victor, having no rival, was more and more in Tamsin's company during her free afternoon hours. Strolling up and down the Esplanade soon palled. They could not swim together because mixed bathing over the age of thirteen was not permitted on the town's beaches; the women had the bathing machines at the western end of the Esplanade while the men had the secluded cove between Battery Rocks and Chimney Rocks beyond the extreme eastern end of the beach. The curious thing about such rules was that any female who suffered from ignorance or felt the slightest curiosity about a man's anatomy could stroll along the unpatrolled shingle between Larrigan Rocks and Newlyn's North Pier, where gangs of beardless youths sported in the waves as naked as the day they were born — and there was no lady warden from the Watch Committee to sting their bottoms with her cane.

Victor soon took to hiring a gig and, with Charlotte for chaperon, they would drive out into the countryside, ostensibly to have their mind improved by visiting yet more of the dozens of Iron Age sites for which the Land's End peninsula is famous. Actually, Charlotte was their chaperon for the first outing only. It began with a rather dull drive to a chapel near Hea, where John Wesley once preached. Then on to just beyond Madron, where a half-mile walk brought them to a ruined chapel with a dried-up baptising well. Then to Lanyon Quoit — three massive upright slabs and a capstone, which, their guidebook said, had once been high enough for a horseman to ride beneath it. Maybe too many horsemen did just that because it fell in 1815 and when they rebuilt it they cut the uprights down to just over five feet high. Then to a field with three standing stones, about four foot high, one with a two-foot hole carved in it. Significance not merely unknown but entirely unguessable. The book said that if you shook hands on a bargain through the hole and then broke your word, the piskeys would get you; that must have worried a lot of people. Then along an old packhorse trail, across some open moorland, to the stone circle called Nine Maidens. Here the book spoke of twenty-two original stones but Victor and the girls could find only six standing and five toppled, the largest being just over seven foot long — "So where the Nine comes from is a mystery," Charlotte remarked. "Or the twenty-two."

Victor, who had suggested this outing and who therefore had done some preliminary reading, explained that nine was probably a magical number, since pagan practices had survived hereabout long after the coming of Christianity. The Christians had retaliated by spreading the tale that nine maidens had gone a-dancing on the sabbath and, for their sin, had been turned to stone by an early Cornish saint. The remaining two (or thirteen, if the book was right) were fiddlers, harpists, and spectators.

"We've looked at an awful lot of stones today," Tamsin said plaintively. "Are there many more to go?"

"Well ..." He was reluctant to abandon what had seemed a splendid plan for an afternoon's jaunt. "We just walked straight past the remains of Ding Dong Mine, where they began digging for tin before Roman times ..." he offered.

There were no takers.

"I'll go back to the gig and start making the tea," Charlotte offered, knowing well that such was the chaperon's role. "You two could hunt for more stones or ... well, it'll be ready in about ten minutes, anyway."

Tamsin, unwilling to squander even ten seconds on coyness, ran to the lee of the nearest large stone and stood where none but choughs and hares could spy on them.

"Feeling cold?" Victor asked, thinking he'd tease her a little.

Her face soon disabused him of any such notion. He changed tack at once. "I thought this moment would nevermmm ..."

She had grabbed him by the sleeves and pulled him to her. Ever since he had kissed her on the beach that day, her heart had quickened and her lips had tingled as the memory of it returned to her, which was often. Now she was trembling all over and feeling decidedly weak at the knees; without the support of the stone she was sure she'd fall to the ground.

But would that be so awful? she wondered, half inclined to let it happen.

In the moment before their lips met once again, she opened her eyes wide and stared up into his. To her surprise he was gazing at her with a somewhat puzzled expression, as if he had not expected her to be so eager. But it didn't stop her. He could have looked at her with any expression he liked, or none at all, as long as he did not deny her the unbelievably sweet pressure of his lips and the crush of his arms about her and the dangerously exciting feel of his body straining against hers.

The pleasure was so exquisite it was almost beyond bearing. She seemed to have fallen deep into some dark void of passion — a well without walls — where everyday things and events, though still vaguely there around her, had become remote and hardly real. Far away she could both hear and feel that their breathing was shattered by the pounding of their hearts; indeed, several times when she tried to inhale, the turmoil within allowed no more than the briefest gasp, which was as likely to empty her lungs as fill them; vaguely she was aware that if she did not draw proper breath soon she would pass right out — but even that did not seem to matter. She was close to passing out from sheer ecstasy, anyway.

At last it was he who broke for breath. Yet, even as her breast snatched gratefully at the air, her lips were once again reaching for his, seeking more and yet more of that magical touch. "Oh, Victor!" she whispered desperately.

"Oh, Tamsin!" he moaned as he took her head between his hands, holding it like some priceless treasure as he closed the space between their mouths. Once again they strained to satisfy a hunger that seemed beyond all satisfying.

His fingernails began a gentle raking of her scalp, behind her ears and back around her neck, sending thrills and shivers through every part of her. Her fingers slipped up into his hair and did the same for him.

After that one brief kiss on the beach, she had thought that kissing alone must surely be the very pinnacle of courtship's joys; but this was as far beyond it as that had been beyond the sort of giggly, blushful kissing games she had experienced at adolescent birthday parties. What more could there be?

Strange things were happening in her stomach. It seemed to be hollowing out inside her. Or falling away, even deeper, into that same timeless void where the rest of her was floating in his arms. Or spinning slowly over and over. And, though she had never experienced such a sensation before, she knew at once what it must be — especially when it came all mixed up in the turmoil of those other delicious feelings: Love!

This was what love felt like. At last she knew it. This was that near-madness which drove poets to despair in their attempts to capture the precise nature of its … its … its *wonderfulnesses*. There — she was caught in the toils of that same creative inadequacy now! Why bother? Why try to speak the ineffable? Why not simply kiss and kiss and kiss her way across his cheek to the cavern of his ear and just whisper it: "Oh Victor, I do love you so!"

And, "Oh Tamsin!" he murmured into hers in return. "Oh Tamsin, Tamsin, Tamsin!"

Sweet though it was to hear her name murmnured so tenderly and across such an intimate distance, it had been sweeter still to hear those same three magic words from him.

"I love you and I love you and I love you …" she gasped, kissing the whorls of his ear and biting his lobe gently between the frantic outpouring of her words.

"I adore you, too," he whispered. "I worship every little stray hair of your head."

It was delightful to hear it, even when he left off his caresses for a moment to pull one or two of those worshipful strands out of his mouth; but it still wasn't the answer she desired to hear above all others from his lips. She wanted someone in this world to *love* her. And more than anyone else she wanted it to be

Victor — not just to love her as she now knew she loved him but to say so in what ought, surely, to be the three simplest words in all the world.

"The very thought of you when we're apart drives me to distraction," he said.

He tried to slip his hands down her back. She arched herself a little away from the stone and soon his fingernails were raking up and down her spine, bringing new and unexpected pleasures. He was obviously tiring of standing in the one position for he now moved his feet to a new position, to her right; then, finding that less of a relief than he expected, he moved them back again.

The resulting movement of his body against hers was yet another novel and delightful sensation.

Then, puzzlingly, he moved them back once more to the new position, only to return them to the former one yet again. When he repeated it twice more she realized he was not actually moving his feet at all — just the … well, the middle portion of his … of himself. Alarm bells began to ring — faint but clear. The pleasure it gave her put all the others into the shade; they had been located in lips, in fingers, cheeks, hair, neck, or spine — wherever the caress was also set; but this pleasure was everywhere within her, from the tingles in her scalp to the flutters in her feet. It threatened to take control of every nerve and fibre of her body, leaving her powerless in its grip. She had the first intimation that it was already starting to happen. Then, as someone standing at the edge of a crumbling scree and feeling it begin to slip and slide away beneath her will instinctively leap for the security of solid ground, so Tamsin now pushed him from her, held him at arm's length, and pleaded, "No! Please — no?"

His eyes could not hold her gaze. He hung his head and blushed. "I'm sorry," he murmured, taking her hands in his but still not looking at her. "Forgive me."

"No!" she cried, causing him at last to look at her — in surprise. "I mean, it's not something to forgive. I'm just thankful you are a gentleman, Victor."

The words puzzled him but he did not ask her to explain them. "And I'm just thankful that you are *you,* Tamsin. Utterly unique. I've never known a girl like you and I'm sure I'll never meet another."

"You're embarrassing me now." She held out her hand and, when he linked his fingers with hers, turned and tugged him toward the dead chimney of Ding Dong. "Charlotte will be regretting her ten minutes of generosity, I fear."

On their way back to the gig he said, "Thinking back to last week — that Excise raid, and what a close-run thing it was ..."

"Victor ..." she began.

"It makes one realize how easy it is at times to stumble into criminality. What a narrow ..."

"I really think we've exhausted that topic, darling."

"Well, I was only going to say what a narrow dividing line it is. It also made me realize that poor people live close to that line all the time, day in, day out. No wonder more of them end up in prison than people of our sort. I suppose one mustn't be too hard on young David Peters — for that reason. It's a timely warning to us, too, to stay well clear. That's all."

She said, "I've never been kissed before, you know — not like that. Are you shocked?"

"No!" He laughed in protest — and wondered if she'd listened to a single word.

"I mean — you don't think I'm just some silly *ingénue?*"

"Heavens, Tamsin! What is it you ..."

"What *do* you think of me, then?"

"I've told you — you're the most wonderful ..."

"Imagine you're in your club ... oh no, gentlemen don't discuss ladies in their clubs, do they. Or do they?"

"We try our best not to."

"Well then, imagine I'm a chum of yours and we're out here on a walking tour and you're trying to describe me to him, or what I mean to you — what do you say?"

"I say I've met this rather wonderful young girl. And then he sniggers and says, 'Oh yes?' because we chaps like to be manly about these things, don't-ye-know. And soft emotions tend to make us try to plait our toes. So he starts asking facetious and mildly indelicate questions. And I go all stiff and pompous and say, 'If you insist on discussing her in such terms, I would prefer not to speak at all.' And he says, 'Look! Isn't that a bog asphodel?' and for the rest of the afternoon we both indulge our botanical ignorance with enormous relief."

Behind his supercilious tone she detected something forlorn, a dirge for the prisoner trapped inside the cage of manly denial. She was still so emotionally overwrought that the perception brought a lump of pity to her throat. "Poor men!" she said, reaching up and brushing his cheek with her fingertips.

He caught it and carried it to his lips. "Oh, Tamsin," he said, kissing it fervently in the palm.

"Yes?"

"Nothing. Everything! Every moment alone with you is such joy, yet I fear it for it makes every minute apart such a torture."

"I was beginning to get worried," Charlotte called out from a hundred yards away.

Victor gave a start and tried to drop Tamsin's hand, but she held on tight to his and swung it demonstratively high as they walked, as children do when going along in crocodiles.

"Worried about what?" Victor asked his sister when they were nearer.

"That you might have been turned to stone, too, of course," she replied.

"Of all possible fates," he murmured to Tamsin, "that is the least likely, don't you think?"

She agreed; but her innermost thought at that moment — the one stirring in her heart-of-hearts — was that she was still pining to hear him say those three beautiful little words.

24 Despite the nonchalance that both Tamsin and Victor showed on their return to the gig, Charlotte sensed that more had passed between them than a bit of mild spooning behind one of those stones. She could not put it into so many words (and even if she could, she would probably not have wished to do so, anyway) but she insisted that the next time they went out on one of these afternoon jaunts, *she* should have a companion, too. Responsibility shared was responsibility halved. Obviously it could not be a man, for that sort of arrangement was considered worse than having no chaperon at all. Daisy was the obvious choice — indeed, the only one in their present circumstances, since the nearest friend of her own sort was over a hundred miles away.

Before that next outing took place, however, Harriet Harte made a surprise concession to her daughter's long-held wishes. Not that she put it quite like that. Indeed, to hear her talk, you'd have thought Tamsin had never spoken a word on the subject in all her life.

"I've had such an interesting conversation with young Mister Trotter," she said at dinner one evening. "While you were off counting stones the other afternoon, he invited me to tea at the Queen's. And no sooner had we sat down than that charming Mister Coverley joined us. Mister Trotter really is an extremely amiable man, too, mind. He'll make some lucky young gel an excellent husband one day — and so, I'm sure, will Mister Coverley, though, naturally, he is out of the running for you as long as Victor Thorne is around."

"Mama, dear!" Tamsin exclaimed. "What *are* you talking about? Is Mister Coverley now our wet-weather target, so to speak? Here you distract me with alternative quarry while I am dutifully shooting my arrows to pierce Victor Thorne through the heart — as directed by you!"

Charlotte was not alone in believing that a responsibility shared was thereby halved.

"Never mind all that!" Harriet waved the words away as if they were midges on the wing. "This is important. It is about the way we manage our ... oh, what was the word he used? Resources! Yes — how we manage our resources here at the guest house."

Tamsin was about to remind her that 'nice people like you and me' did not discuss money matters at the luncheon table either, but some instinct warned her that this was no time for such petty points-scoring. If her mother was about to break her strictest rule, then something important must be afoot. "Anything Mister Coverley might say on that subject would be well worth considering," she replied diplomatically.

"Just so, dear. He pointed out that a manufacturer who invested tens of thousands of pounds in factory machinery and then used it for only four hours a day would be wasting the other eighteen — which is a line of argument anyone of modest intellect can follow, I think."

"Especially if you said, 'the other *twenty*'."

"Yes, dear. But I was amazed when he went on to say that investment in a large hôtel or even a small guest house is no different in principle. The less use one makes of *any* investment, the more expensive it becomes when one does use it. I must confess that such a subtle argument had never even crossed my mind. And — correct me if I'm wrong — but I don't think it has occurred to you, either?"

Tamsin bit her tongue rather than follow the invitation to correct her; the last thing she wanted was to get into an I-said-you-said sort of exchange. "It sounds all too obvious when one puts it like that," she replied. She could have added that she had, indeed, put it *exactly* like that in the car on the way home from that swim at Land's End; but bless Messrs Coverley and Trotter for not saying as much!

"So," Harriet continued, "we need to decide if we intend to remain open all year round. We haven't experienced a complete winter down here yet, but it cannot be so very different from what we had in Plymouth."

"We were here in January — and that was fairly mild, though stormy. Perhaps we should look into the cost of advertising in the medical and nursing journals? We should have had a word with Doctor Carlton, you know — before they left for home this morning. We could have sounded him out on the possibility."

"Sounded him out, dear?" Her mother frowned at the expression. "What possibility?"

"Convalescents," said Tamsin, who had already churned over every conceivable winter use of the Morrab and its *resources*, including putting up some of the artistes from Galligano's Circus, which had its winter quarters not far from Penzance. "People who are advised by their doctors to take a long holiday abroad, but who cannot face a Channel crossing in winter, nor the thought of all that greasy, garlicky foreign food which awaits their palates on the other side. They'd put up with a bit of rain and a few gales for the sake of our fresh sea air and mild temperatures. And Mrs Pascoe is such an excellent cook, we could even offer them their own simple diets — individual diets, I mean, as long as they really were simple. Steamed fish, coddled eggs, spinach … that sort of thing. The point is — I don't think we could keep open through the winter if we just went in for holiday people. There aren't enough of them — and those who do come down here usually go in for hearty walking holidays from one guest house or inn to the next. We don't want to be laundering our sheets every day. But convalescents who stay three months would suit us very well."

Harriet was overwhelmed at the speed with which Tamsin had taken up *her* idea. But the girl had not nearly finished. "What's the name of that lady opposite — with the two adorable children? Didn't someone say she used to be a nurse?"

"Mrs Bosinney — Frances Bosinney. Why?"

Tamsin had known the name very well but she wanted her mother to be the one to say it first, so that later she might imagine the whole idea had been hers, too. "She had to give up nursing when she got married, of course, but I'll bet she misses it. In which case, she might be quite agreeable to put on starched cuffs and a wimple again for a couple of hours a day, just to take care of the medical needs of convalescents. A bit of pin-money for her. And it would be a wonderful addition to our advertisement: 'A State Registered Nurse is a member of our daily staff and is experienced in all nursing requirements' — something vague but impressive like that."

"Dear me, Tamsin!" her mother sighed. "I believe that if I were to set paper and pencil before you now, you could write out all the daily rosters without even stopping to think."

"The thinking is already done, Mama. But listen — decisions on closing or staying open for the winter are a long way ahead. Also, we don't know how long your precious Countess de Ath will be staying. Until her creditors give up, I suspect. But *meanwhile*" — she raised her voice over her mother's protests — "there are other ways in which we could ... how would your factory owner put it? — make the most economical use of our existing resources."

"Name one!" her mother challenged, as if she did not believe Tamsin could.

"The resources in question comprise the guests' dining room, the kitchen, and, above all, dear Mrs Pascoe. Also ..." She eyed her mother cautiously here. "Let us not forget a certain fisherman over in Newlyn who now owes us a prodigious favour!"

"Eh?"

"Fish, Mama! Direct from ocean to table — and of prime quality, too. The glorious thing about such fish is that one does not need to mess it around in the Continental fashion with a lot of fancy sauces and things — whose real purpose, as any true Englishman knows, is to disguise the fact that they're hundreds of miles from the nearest fish quay. Straight, clean cooking with a few herbs and a simple white sauce is all it will require. And I know Mrs Pascoe will welcome the chance to make a few extra pounds before the season ends — even if we do stay open as a convalescent home in the coming winter."

"Pounds?" The word frightened Harriet.

"Look! The dining room can seat twenty in comfort. We can charge three shillings and sixpence for a *table d'hôte* with a limited choice ... four and six with a good hock or chablis. If each seat were occupied twice over, we could be taking nine pounds a night — gross. Our outlay would be about two guineas. So our maximum profit will be the best part of seven pounds. And even if we have only twenty diners" — she avoided words like 'customer' out of deference to her mother's sensibilities — "we should still clear almost three pounds a night — which is the profit we presently make on six paying guests in an entire week."

Harriet sat down heavily. "Good heavens!" she exclaimed. "Goodness gracious me!"

"What now?"

"The speed with which you work these things out, dear! Scarcely have I broached the merest outlines of my idea and here you come with chapter and verse on every tiny detail! How do you do it? It was your father's gift, too, mind you — which is both comforting and frightening, remembering how it brought us down in the end!"

Tamsin walked past her to the window. Their conversation had suddenly entered tiger country. She must stalk her mother cautiously now or it would all come to nothing. "Forewarned is forearmed," she murmured, scratching idly at a tiny streak of dried paint beside one of the glazing bars.

"What does that mean?"

"Papa's gift for turning one guinea into two worked miracles when he confined the investment within the bounds of the expected return ..."

"And what does *that* mean?" her mother repeated herself more emphatically.

"Well, take this idea of ours for opening a fish restaurant. Even if only ten diners turn up, our investment would drop to one guinea or less — because we'd serve less fish, of course. And that would still be covered, just, by the profit on ten dinners. We start losing only if fewer then ten people turn up — which I'm sure will happen on one or two nights, but they will be more than balanced by nights when we'll have to turn people away." She crossed her fingers surreptitiously as she spoke those words. "In short, the investment is well within the bounds of the expected return. Papa's investments only began to fail when he forgot that golden rule — or so Mister Samson told me."

"He had no right to say such things to you!" her mother exclaimed crossly. "A well brought up young lady has no need to know ..." She faltered, realizing where her unthinkingly conventional response was leading. In the same moment she also realized she had just conceded Tamsin's main argument by chasing after such an irrelevance.

Somewhat to her relief they were interrupted at that moment by a tap at the door. "Who is it?" she called out.

"Only me." Charlotte stuck her head into the room. "I do hope I'm not intruding?"

"Not at all. Do come in."

"Such excitement!" the girl said as Tamsin left the window and came to join them. "Mama has persuaded Victor to be more pleasant to Mister Trotter and, as a result, we are invited on a picnic to the Lizard this afternoon — in Mister Coverley's Rolling-Royce. All five of us." She nodded at Tamsin to show she was included. "And we're to bring our bathing suits!"

"Oh, Mama!" Tamsin turned delightedly to her mother.

But she was not giving leave just yet. "And did your mother not insist on taking a maidservant along with you?" she asked.

Charlotte shrugged awkwardly; she might well have responded by asking, 'What maidservant?'

"Well, I shall certainly insist upon it," Harriet continued. "My daughter may only join you if Miss Dobbs is also included. I realize it will make for some awkward seating arrangements in the car but that is my final word."

25 The long spell of settled sunshine looked as if it might be drawing to a close. When the car had wound its way uphill through the contortions of Marazion's main street and reached the crest, they could see how the sky over the Lizard faded to a hazy colour that might have been washed-out blue or even pale mauve, and it would have taken more than an amateur painter to have captured the merest suggestion of mighty cumulus towers floating within it. Out to sea it was still a cloudless azure overhead, but wherever the sluggish onshore breeze hit the coast it tended to form fluffy white cloudlets that wandered inland like flocks of drugged sheep. Whenever Standish halted to let them admire the view, the breeze did little or nothing to alleviate the oppressive humidity that had been building up all that day. They were glad of the motion of the car when they resumed their erratic progress toward the Lizard, which was still some twenty miles away — though only thirteen or so as a crow might fly directly across Mount's Bay.

"What does Lizard mean?" Charlotte asked the world in general. "Not that the place is crawling with the beastly little things, I hope."

Standish replied, "It's from *lis,* meaning 'enclosure' and *ard,* meaning 'high-up' — there must have been an enclosed settlement on one of the cliffs there at some time."

"Does every place name actually mean something?" Tamsin asked. "What's Marazion, for instance?"

Victor got in before Standish this time. "It must be related to Market Jew Street in Penzance," he said.

It annoyed her that he seemed to think that any general remark of hers needed funnelling through him. Even the fact that she loved him to distraction did not give him the right to behave like that, she felt.

"How so?" Standish asked.

"Well ..." He explained it almost as one would to a child. *"Mara* must be 'market' and *zion* is quite obviously Jewish."

Standish offered an alternative: "The scholars claim that Market Jew is from *marghas yow* or 'market on Thursdays' —

which is what the old town charter allowed. Others say it's from *marghas byghan,* meaning 'little market'; still others hold it's from *marghas iou,* which translates as 'Joe's market' — take your pick." He glanced over his shoulder at Tamsin, who was sitting in the back between Charlotte and Daisy. "Four choices! Is that enough? One could think up a few more, I'm sure."

"Four is plenty!" she replied with feeling.

He continued, unabashed. "The advantage of a dead language, you see, is that nobody can prove that anyone else is wrong. This current attempt to revive Old Cornish is *carte blanche* for every crackpot scholar in the county. But let's not complain. While they're footling away with their glossaries they can't be out and about, doing actual harm to anyone."

Tamsin had no idea whether his etymologies for Marazion had been genuine or not; but the ease with which he produced them suggested a much greater familiarity with the Cornish revival than he seemed willing to admit. But why did he feel the need to mock it like that? Could it be that he was a far more serious person than he liked to pretend and so — as naval people put it — he 'made smoke' to disguise the fact?

He began to interest her more than ever. In the beginning, Daisy's confident assertion that he was a cold fish — with which she had, sometimes, to agree — made Standish more interesting, in the way that all forbidden, or unattainable, fruit has its own special fascination. Now, however, she was starting to realize that, if what Daisy said was true, then such a man would make an ideal surrogate brother of the kind she had hoped to find in David Peters. If Standish truly was incapable of developing a romantic interest in her as a woman — and yet was still interested in her as a person (which he showed every sign of being) ... well! He was ready-made for the part.

He stopped again at St Breaca's, the parish church of Breage, to show them some recently discovered frescoes, painted (quite obviously) in medieval times but covered over with limewash during the Civil War, to hide them from the Puritan iconoclasts, who went about England slighting all painted or graven images. There were a couple of bishops, or possibly saints, and a huge, twice-life-size painting of St. Christopher carrying a diminutive Christ on his shoulder.

They all thought Standish was going to make some further mock — and, indeed, perhaps he did. But if so, it was against them. For, as they stood there, ready to laugh and patronize these primitive daubs, he launched into paeans of praise for their vigour and strength. The boldness of the line ... the subtle strength of the colour ... the simple, direct expression of theme ... one would have thought that Michelangelo, Raphael, and Leonardo had all visited this little parish in some earlier, joint reincarnation and that God himself, recognizing creative competition when he saw it, had divided and diluted that single unknown artist into those three giants for their next cycle of life on earth.

"Every artist in England," Standish said, "should be brought here in fetters and locked inside this church on bread and water until he or she can see what they've been missing in their own feeble efforts."

On their way back to the car, Victor murmured to Tamsin, "If he starts foaming at the mouth, just get behind me, eh!"

"I think he makes a lot of sense," she replied.

His lips compressed to a thin, bloodless line and he stared rigidly ahead. How to make her understand that girls who did not agree with him soon fell into disfavour? If it wasn't for keeping his mother sweet, he'd start disentangling himself now.

She saw she had upset him and, fearing that reconciliations would eat up precious kissing time later, gave his arm a squeeze and said, "Sorry."

He smiled at her — not *too* affably, in case she should believe it was always going to be so easy — and said, "That's better."

She risked a tiny whisper: "I love you!"

"Me, too," he replied.

At the bottom of Breage Hill, where they could have gone directly onward to the top of Sithney Common Hill and so down into Helston, they turned instead toward the picturesque little fishing village of Porthleven. There they parked the car on the quay — well away from the coalyard, where a coal tramp was being unloaded, making enough dust to empty every washing line in sight — and strolled out to the end of the long stone jetty, which protected the harbour from the worst of any storm. Standish and Victor both brought their binoculars along, for the seabird life on the cliffs to the west of the harbour mouth was famous — being sustained by one of the busiest fishing quays in the entire bay.

"When the fleet returns," Standish said, training his glasses on the cliffs, "the sky is black with gulls of every kind."

Tamsin was watching Victor at the time. He was scanning the sea through his glasses; it seemed that, whatever Standish was doing, he would have to do something else. She was just about to make some quiet remark, to show him how petty she thought he was being, when she saw him give a little start and then peer intently, still looking directly out to sea.

Eventually he became aware that she was watching him. At once he offered her the glasses, saying, "Porpoises." But he pointed well to the west of the point on which his own gaze had been trained. "Leaping like athletes."

She searched the sea where he had indicated but, finding nothing, swivelled round to look at the cliff instead. "Golly!" she exclaimed. "If one had a sardine, one could pop it right down their throats!"

She passed the glasses on to Daisy, since Standish had already passed his to Charlotte. Later, when Charlotte had finished looking, he offered them to Tamsin, saying, "See if they look as big with these."

"Every bit," she said after focusing. "Let's see if we can spot those porpoises!"

And now she swung back to where Victor had really been looking when he gave that little start — and almost at once she discovered why. For there, less than a mile out in the bay, was the *Merlin,* with David Peters at the tiller and his cousin Harry at his side. The sails were up but were flapping in such a way that she could not believe they were urging the boat forward at such speed. So they must have fitted the new engine already — in which case, this outing was part of their trials. They were heading eastward, away from Newlyn.

A sudden, intense pang of disappointment made her realize how much she had wanted to be with him — with *them,* rather — on that great day. If only she'd realized how quickly they'd manage it, she'd have kept in better touch.

"Found them yet?" Victor asked anxiously.

"No," she replied calmly, passing the glasses back to Standish. She was determined not to show her disappointment to any of them. "Which way were they going? Toward Penzance?"

"That's right," he answered.

They stopped at the bottom of Helston to fill up with ethyl and to buy a couple of spare cans. The blacksmith was proud of his new pump, which had two large glass 'optics,' each of which held one gallon. He cranked the pump to fill the left-hand one with the pale, straw-coloured fuel, then flipped a valve to let it empty into the car's tank by gravity — during which time he continued to crank the pump to fill the right-hand optic. It drained out so quickly that the flow of ethyl into the car tank was almost continuous.

"You can see you'm getting the full gallon, boss, and I'm not obliged to store a couple o' hundred gallon cans so close to the forge, see?"

He spoke to Reg, for Standish had taken Tamsin a little way back down the hill to point out the town's electricity works. "See that?" he said. "That was opened seven years ago by a remarkable woman — someone you ought to meet, I think. I'll try to arrange it, if you like."

"A woman?" Tamsin felt a little surge of excitement.

"Jessica Trelawney — Mrs Cornwallis Trelawney, that is — though back in those days she was Miss Jessica Kernow and barely twenty-one years of age, too. Indeed!" he added, seeing her eyes go wide. "A young woman of around your age did that — and in the teeth of local prejudice and her father's direct opposition. First they laughed at her, then, too late, they realized their mistake and tried to organize their own scheme to rival hers, but she licked the lot of them."

"Why are you telling me this, Mister Coverley?" she asked. "No, I mean why are you telling *me* this?"

"Because you're like a jumping squib in a barrel, Tamsin. D'you think we can dispense with the formalities, by the way? I'm Standish. And I think Mrs Trelawney could be the one to help you take the lid off your barrel and jump right out."

"Well, Standish, you flatter me much too much, I think. But I should certainly like to meet someone who can achieve anything half as grand as that!"

They returned to the blacksmith, where Standish paid for the ethyl and then started the car by running her off backwards, down the hill.

"What was the attraction?" Victor asked.

"The electrical generating station," she told him — not that he believed her.

As they left the town behind them, purring over Culdrose Downs, Standish said, "I've just realized that I'm driving through a completely different landscape from the rest of you. What you see is a smiling, fertile countryside complete with the customary farms and grand or grand*ish* houses. But I know that the man who farms there" — he pointed out one of the farms — "was the childhood sweetheart of the woman who lives in that house back there — with her husband and half-dozen children, I hasten to add. And that that same husband once erred and strayed like a lost sheep with a young widow who lived in that house there and who, in turn, was the wife's closest friend."

"I say, old chap," Victor protested. "D'you think this story is entirely suitable for ladies' ears?"

"Let's ask the ladies themselves, *old chap,*" Standish responded easily. "What's the vote?"

"Yes!" the three ladies chorused gleefully.

Victor said to Tamsin, "Well, I don't much care for *you* to hear such things, my dear."

"Now that *is* interesting," Standish said. "What does your solicitude imply, old chap?"

"I should have thought it quite obvious," Victor replied.

"On the face of it, yes. But look below the surface and nothing is clear. You obviously do not wish Tamsin to hear how husbands and wives and ex-sweethearts behave in real life. Yet ..."

"How *some* husbands and wives and ex-sweethearts behave — and very few, I should think."

"My dear old chap — you're talking to one who owns an hôtel, and at the posh end of the market, too. One week behind its genteel façade and you'd have to concede I'm talking about many if not *most* husbands, wives, and ex-sweethearts."

"What happened?" Tamsin cut across this sterile debate. "The farmer who was her childhood sweetheart — did he run off with her in the end?"

Standish laughed. "That would have been a true romance, wouldn't it! They would have lived in exile in France and the author would have made sure she soon died of consumption and he'd have gone off and become a lay missionary, teaching farming to the fuzzy-wuzzies. But no, alas. This is real life. He ended up marrying his housekeeper — a very pretty and determined young woman who had her sights on him from the moment they met. The widow married someone else — I don't remember who. And the husband and wife are reconciled and happy enough, I gather. It was just a storm that passed them by, you see. But that's *my* view of this landscape. Has it changed for you, too?"

They all agreed that it had.

All except Victor, who said, "There are *some* sorts of behaviour in real life that I should not like *anyone* to hear of."

"I quite agree, old boy," Standish drawled. "So let's all agree not to talk about them, eh!"

26   They did not actually reach Lizard Point that day — the southernmost cape on the British mainland. Standish said he had never swum there and could not recall if any of the nearby coves was even accessible, much less suitable. He did, however, know that Kynance Cove, a couple of miles short of it on the Mount's Bay shore, offered excellent possibilities at low tide, including a sandy beach and several caves, in any of which they could change in perfect seclusion. Also, many of the rocks had huge veins of pure serpentine and steatite, whose colours glowed quite magically, especially when wet. And to crown it all, there were two cottages where delicious cream teas could be obtained for very little money.

They parked on the verge at the beginning of a track that led half a mile, past the remains of yet another ancient settlement, to the edge of the cliff. The view from there was easily the most spectacular that Tamsin had seen since her arrival in Cornwall six months ago.

"*I* know why it's called the Lizard," she said. "See? Those rocks are just like a huge dragon's tail going out to sea. Which means we're standing on its body. Dragons are sort-of lizards, aren't they?"

"It's the most convincing explanation I've yet heard," Standish agreed solemnly. Then, in a different tone, "Oh dear! I see two people have already beaten us down to the sands. Cornwall is getting *so* crowded."

"Blame those hôteliers and guest-house keepers," Reg told him. "They make the place sound so attractive."

"Yes," Victor added. "And by the time the poor gullibles get here and discover the truth, they realize they're so far from home they might as well stay!"

The others conspired to take this as a joke and so, laughing, they wended their way down the path to the cove; around the half-way mark they reached a position where Rill Point, the headland to the northwest of Kynance, became visible — and, of course, all that part of Mount's Bay beyond it. And there, not quite a mile away, Tamsin once again spied the *Merlin* — she was sure it was the *Merlin* — apparently putting about and heading for home once more.

It was all she could do not to scream out at the top of her voice, and jump up and down, and wave, and do anything else she could think of to attract their attention — though nothing would actually have carried over so great a distance. Then she saw it put about again; and, a short while later, yet again. She realized then that they were conducting some sort of trial that involved going in tight circles and zigzags.

The others had continued on down to the beach, all except Victor, who said, "Did you tell him about this trip?"

Tamsin looked at him, then at the *Merlin,* then back at him. If ever there was a single moment when she decided to return to her original notion — that Victor Thorne was *just* a young man for kissing, in the same way that David Peters was *just* for serious and intimate conversation — that was it. "I can understand *why* you ask the question, Victor — though I must also say that I don't find it very admirable — but I can't for the life of me see *how* you can ask it. Just think — if you're any longer capable of it. *How* could I have told him? And *how* could I have guessed we'd be here at Kynance Cove, when it's clear that Standish himself only stopped here on a whim?"

"I don't believe you should talk to me like that," he replied stiffly. "I am, after all, a paying guest of yours. Are you equally offensive to …"

"Good!" she shouted as she turned to go. "If that's all you wish me to be, you'll soon discover I can play the part to …"

"Oh, Tamsin!" He reached out and grabbed her hand. While she struggled to free it, he continued: "Darling! I'm so sorry! I didn't mean it, honestly. I don't know why I said it. Well, I do, actually. You've got me in such a lather. I've never met a girl like you. I'm in hell, I'm in heaven — a hundred times a day — all because of you."

She stopped struggling and let him keep her hand.

"I know I have no formal claim to your heart," he went on, "and yet, when I see you even looking at someone else, some other fellow, or laughing at his wit, I just get so insanely jealous."

His grip had relaxed enough to free her hand. She slipped that arm around him and, leaning her head against his shoulder, impelled him onward, down the path to join the others. "It's just so silly, darling," she began.

"There! You see! When you speak to me tenderly like that, my heart leaps up into the seventh heaven. And yet I know that the minute Coverley or Trotter says something to make you laugh, I'll see red again."

She realized that, since he was in somewhat of a confessional mood, she might as well press him a little. "Has it been the same with every other girl to whom you've taken a liking?" she asked. In fact, she already knew it had not been so, having been warned more than once by Daisy about his habit of 'toying with a girl's affections,' 'dangling her on a string,' 'taking his pleasure, his hat, and his leave' — and several other graphic descriptions of this young man and his ways.

He made several awkward noises and pretended that the steepness and unevenness of the path demanded all his attention.

"If so," she added, "one can understand your arrival in Penzance, unattached."

That goaded him into blurting out, "No! The very opposite. I deserve every moment of this torment for the way I've treated the girls who fell in love with me."

"But I fell in love with you," she objected.

If he noticed her use of the past-historic tense, he made no comment on it. "But you don't behave as they did," he replied.

"In what way am I so different, then?"

But that, apparently, was one question he was not willing to answer. "The others are too close," he mumbled. "We must talk about this later."

As if she were not already wary enough, an alleged agony that could be turned on and off so speedily made her doubly so. It made her wonder, too, about the words with which he had begun this latest exchange, drawing attention to the *Merlin* and its occupants.

What would *she* have done if their positions had been reversed? What if she had seen him gazing after another girl, and not just any other girl but one for whom she suspected he already nursed some tenderness? She would surely have pointed in a different direction and murmured, 'Just look at that view!' Or, more subtly, she would have grabbed his arm and pressed it to her, saying, 'Let's slip away from the others once we're in the water — there are so many little secret inlets down there among all those rocks!' The very last thing she'd have done would have been to draw his attention to that other girl — much less start talking about her.

So was it just that Victor had not the first idea how to handle his own emotions — much less hers? Or was everything he did quite calculated — including his pretty convincing display of ecstasy and torment?

Behind these doubts lay one basic question: What had he to gain back there by behaving in such an apparently stupid and self-defeating way? To answer that — or even to think about it — she would have to put herself back into that frame of mind she had cast off so readily when Papa's death and bankruptcy had removed all the old protective wrapping and left her pleasantly exposed to the challenges of the real world. In short, how did an upper-middle-class young man, torn between head and heart — or, more accurately, between desire and purse — weigh up the pros and cons of a romance? David Peters, dear obliging man though he was, would not have the first idea when it came to navigating those treacherous waters. But Standish Coverley, who had a foot in both worlds and bestrode them with such elegance, would surely know all the answers. More than ever she needed some time alone to talk with him.

By now the sun was half hidden in its own heat haze, for which they were all grateful. It cast a rare silvery light upon the scene, giving it a strange, almost mythic quality that held them spellbound — even Victor. Tamsin's earlier remarks about dragons seemed even more apposite now. The nearest rocks were two ragged cones, thrusting upward out of the sand; even the smaller one dwarfed any human standing nearby. They were like shrouded giants, frozen in some ancient, pagan act — a vassal kneeling before his king, say, or an acolyte before an old arch-druid. Beyond them, as a dramatic backdrop, were three huge triangular rocks, their feet just in the water. In this eldritch light, they seemed part of some Arthurian legend — magic islands afloat in the mists of Time, all on a silvered sea that had no discernible horizon.

"Merlin ahoy!" Victor broke the spell, pointing toward the boat, which was just then rounding the islands and threading a careful way among the reefs at the other end of the little cove.

There he goes again! Tamsin thought.

"Engines and all," Standish added. "Courtesy of His Majesty's Customs and Excise! Just think how much the government could save in money *and* lives if it dished out subsidies directly to the fishermen! To buy engines, I mean."

"If they'd throw a line overboard," Reg said, "we could take turns to be towed through the water. Wouldn't that be joll!"

They hastened into the caves to change, so as to be in the water by the time the *Merlin* had worked its way into the middle of the cove, which seemed to be David's intention.

"Do you think your brother wants to go back to Penzance in the *Merlin?"* Tamsin asked Charlotte as they slipped out of their dresses.

"Good heavens!" she exclaimed. "Why?"

"It seems to fascinate him. He drew my attention to her when we were on the cliff path. And he was obviously just waiting for her to make an appearance round the point — the way he spotted her the moment she did."

Charlotte said she thought that a trip in the *Merlin* back across Mount's Bay was the last thing Victor would ever want.

Their costumes were, in effect, black trousers with black frilly legs beneath a black frilly knee-length skirt, and topped by a black blouse with black frilly epaulettes and more frills to disguise the contour of the bosom, and sleeves that finished below the elbow in yet more frills. And, of course, black frilly bonnets with a thin ribbon to tie them.

"D'you think this colour is *me?*" Tamsin wound the blue, one-eighth-inch-wide ribbon round her index finger and displayed it for the other two to judge.

Charlotte blushed and put a hand to her mouth, gazing from Tamsin to Daisy and back in a kind of amazement.

"What?" Tamsin asked. "It's just a bit of ribbon."

"No. Not that." She pointed to a hole through the cave wall. "That!"

"What about it?"

"I just saw someone's ... you know ... b-t-m through it. Mister Coverley's, I think!" She giggled.

Tamsin picked up a stalk of kelp and drew a serpentine line in the sand. "Was it like this?" she asked, hinting that it would be no novelty to her.

"You're *awful!*" Charlotte stamped on it and rubbed it out with her foot.

Then, laughing wildly, they ran out of their cave, down the beach, and, shedding their towels just below the high-tide mark, continued hand-in-hand into the sea. Though still cold, it was several degrees warmer than the oceanic waters at Land's End. Tamsin, now feeling quite the veteran, made no fuss, though it cost her all her will-power to stay silent. This time it was Charlotte who shrieked and just *knew* she was about to die, even as she started to wade ashore again. The other two grabbed her arms and dragged her without mercy into deeper waters until, at last, she had to agree it wasn't anything like as bad as it had seemed at first.

By then the men had joined them, manfully withholding their cries as their white flesh turned swiftly blue. Reg dived into a bed of kelp, visible on the surface at low tide, and sprang out upon a rock, clutching a handful, which he draped all around him, claiming to be the Old Man of the Sea.

The *Merlin* idled in among them, her engine shut down.

"Trouble?" Victor asked.

"In a way." David looked at them in turn, settling finally on Tamsin. "She drinks more petrol than we bargained for. Is there anywhere nearby that sells the stuff ashore?"

She grounded in the sand and he picked up two empty cans, ready to jump and wade the last few yards ashore.

Standish offered the two full cans of ethyl strapped to the running board of his car; he could refill the *Merlin's* two at Furber's in Mullion on the way home, he said. "And you can repay me in crab or lobster if you wish," he shouted after David as he went up the beach.

"Why don't you join us for a swim while you wait?" Tamsin asked Cousin Harry. "The water's lovely."

But he shook his head and said that wise fishermen forget how to swim when they turn fourteen. "Swimmin' for the likes o' we," he told her, "is just a longer form o' drownin'."

The bleak realism of his reply made her shiver.

"Last one to Gull Rock's a cad!" Reg challenged the other two men as he dived back in, giving himself a head start.

"Or a cadess!" Charlotte struck out after him, though doomed to failure by all those frills.

Tamsin tried to follow Reg's lead and cheat her way to the front by climbing out and running along the rocks at the foot of Asparagus Island, the first of the three that formed her fanciful 'dragon's tail.' But it was so deeply fissured, and so encrusted with tiny, razor-sharp limpets, that she even lost what advantage she'd had.

In the end the race was abandoned because Gull Rock proved to be farther out than the haze had made it seem and because the inlet between it and little Asparagus Island looked so inviting. To Tamsin, who had almost burst her heart and lungs in making up the lost ground — or water — a smooth, flat slab at the foot of Gull Rock looked more inviting still. But it was a little too high out of the water and there was no obliging ledge to give her a springboard onto it.

She was still struggling for some smaller foothold when she felt what she took to be a seal beneath her feet. Before she could even scream or kick out, it stood up, turned into Standish Coverley's shoulders, and raised her smoothly to her desired perch. He disappeared at once, below the surface again, only to re-emerge a moment later in a great eruption of spray and, with an athletic twist, land on the slab beside her.

"Pity those Thornes are here," he murmured as he wiped the water from his face and hair. "It was so much more pleasant to swim *au naturel,* don't you think, Tamsin?"

She agreed it had been pleasant — after the first shock.

"I do think young David Peters might have postponed the maiden voyage of the *Merlin* until you were free to join in," he went on.

"It would have been more thoughtful," she agreed.

"Especially after you saved his bacon — or, rather, his brandy — like that."

"Maybe he wanted to be sure she wouldn't leak after the refitting," she offered. "Or the engine wouldn't die suddenly out in the middle of the bay."

"Well, he must by now be pretty confident that neither of those things is going to happen. So, if you want to go back with him — as far as Porthleven, say — we can pick you up there on our way back."

The sudden gleam in her eyes was answer enough.

"Daisy!" he said — not needing to raise his voice too high, for she was swimming close by, eyeing them warily. "You're such a powerful swimmer, my darling — would you be an absolute angel and go and fetch Tamsin's clothes? Bundle them up well and pass them to Harry Peters there."

"Why?" Victor asked, for he was also treading water not too far away.

"Because I want to say I was on her maiden voyage," Tamsin told him. "As a motor trawler, anyway." As a sweetener she added, "Just as far as Porthleven."

"But that must be miles!"

"Nine, to be precise," Standish told him. "But there's a strong tide in their favour. They'll do it in an hour and we'll be there ourselves by then."

After that the only way Victor dared exhibit his displeasure was to swim away across the cove, as if to say he did not give a fig what she chose to do.

"He's a hard man to make out," Tamsin murmured.

"Really?" Standish seemed surprised.

"So hot one minute, so cold the next. Apologetic ... arrogant. Begging ... demanding. He keeps leaping between opposites."

"He's trying to protect you from me," he replied mildly. "But he'd hardly want to do that by putting you on a boat with young David Peters!"

"It's so silly!" Tamsin exclaimed.

"Are you in love with him?"

She was astonished. "That's not the sort of question a gentleman should ask a lady about another gentleman!"

"Well said!" He grinned. "I'd still like an answer, though."

She sighed. "I thought I was — until this afternoon. He's being so stupid."

"I'm still wondering why his mother moved the whole family out of the Queen's and into your place. It's certainly not the money. It's as if she suspects there's something afoot between you and me ... D'you mind my being so candid?"

She swallowed heavily. "No! Please go on."

"It's much harder for a guest at the Queen's to keep an eye on me than it would be for a guest at the Morrab to keep an eye on you. But *why* would she be so interested? Has she said anything to you? Hinted anything, even?"

Tamsin shook her head. "Nothing comes to mind."

"Well, maybe I'm completely barking up the wrong tree. But I can't think of anything else. Shall we try to force her hand? Force her out into the open?"

"How?" The very thought excited her for she, too, had felt that Mrs Thorne was hatching some plan; indeed, she seemed the sort of woman who couldn't watch two raindrops sliding down a windowpane without plotting to hinder one and help the other.

"Victor's going to go home a pretty disgruntled fellow today. At least, he will if I have anything to do with it! Which, incidentally, is why I had to know if you were in love with him. Perhaps that will be enough to goad his mama. If not, we shall just have to pour on a little more ethyl."

"He's changed his mind. He's coming back."

"While we're in the confessional, may I ask how you feel toward David Peters?"

She laughed. "While *we* are in the confessional," she echoed, "are you going to ask me how I feel about *you?*"

He dipped his head, conceding her point. "All right. How *do* you feel about me?"

She thought rapidly. She wanted to leave as many possibilities open as she could, but without seeming too forward just at the moment — or no more forward than she must already seem. Though he started it, so he could hardly complain now. "Feelings change," she replied. "So I'm only talking about now, this minute. Or this day. And just at the moment, I'd like to think of you as a friend to whom I could talk — as freely as we are talking now ... who would listen — as, indeed, you do ... who understands all the ins and outs of human behaviour much better than I do — which you've just proved."

"In short, you like things just the way they are?"

She grinned cheekily and stroked his forearm with the tip of one finger, lazily up and down, twice. "For the moment, yes."

27 David took one look at Tamsin's elegant dress and said, "You'd best put up a pair of dungarees, maid, and save those glad rags till we put in at Portlemm," by which he meant Porthleven. He found a cleanish pair and an oilskin jacket, which she put on (or put *up,* in the local dialect) in the lee of the wheelhouse — a glazed sort of sentry box just forward of the engine compartment. She changed in semidarkness for he had draped a sail over the housing for her privacy. When she had finished she could only half pull it off. Harry took it down completely and folded it away. "You might make a sailor, Miss Harte," he said, running an admiring eye over her figure in the dungarees, "but never a boy."

"Of all possible ambitions, Mister Peters," she replied, "you have chosen one that has never crossed my mind."

She waved at her companions in the water. Standish blew her a kiss. Daisy called out, "Bring us back a parrot and some coconuts, love!" Victor, sitting on a rock, hugging his knees, made no response.

The only furnishings in the wheelhouse were the helm itself, a compass, and a handle by which one could swivel a rubber squeegee against the outside of the glass windshield, to clear it in stormy weather.

She tapped the compass, which did not change its direction; she swivelled the squeegee, which dislodged nothing but a daddy-longlegs — or a 'tom taylor,' as Mrs Pascoe called it; and she spun the helm hard to both port and starboard. This produced a gurgling sound beneath the stern and sent two rings of slightly overlapping ripples outward.

"That's what I like to see," David told her as he screwed the cap back on the second spare can, which he had just emptied. "A volunteer. The place is yours, maid."

"No!" Tamsin cried, even as her hands sought the spokes of the wheel. "D'you think I dare?"

But he was already busy cranking up the flywheel. When he considered it had enough momentum he gave a nod and Harry released the exhaust lift. For a couple of revs she fired on one cylinder only, then two, then all four. With a sigh of relief he removed the starting handle and pushed it into its clips; everything was gleaming — the brass bright and the cast iron black and matt. The roar of the engine fell to a background hum when they closed the cowling.

"Is the propellor turning?" she asked. "Because we don't seem to be moving much."

"It has a variable pitch," he explained. "She's set to feather at the moment. Now see that compass needle? As soon as we get under way, you steer until the needle's on two-two-five, and hold that course until I tell you otherwise."

"Due southwest abaft the lee quarter it is, sir," she replied, reading the verbal bearing off the compass circle as she took a firm grip on the wheel. "Brace the t'gallants and royals, Mister Midshipman Easy, let go fore and aft, and port the helm — or something like that!"

David and Harry stared at each other; David shrugged and pulled a humour-her-at-all-costs face as he increased both the throttle and the pitch on the propellor.

The deck vibrated under the sudden strain. As the *Merlin* lurched forward her exhaust came clear of the water for a moment and there was a satisfyingly deep throaty roar to send her off. Then the bows lifted a few degrees, enough to suggest an eager leap toward the open water. Amid a chorus of farewells which would have done a liner proud — from all but Victor — they motored out of the cove and into Mount's Bay.

Half a mile out, David shouted, "Starboard the helm to three-twenty, bosun!"

"Starboard to northwest and five, sir," she replied. But when the needle settled on the figure she peered dead ahead and added, "Why didn't you just tell me to steer toward Porthleven? I can see the Institute tower quite clearly."

He came into the deckhouse and, standing just behind her, leaned across and blocked out the glass with his jacket. "Now it's night time," he said. "Worse — there's a storm brewing and this is the first time you've ever done this line, Kynance to Portlemm, after dark. And every time you've done it by day, you just said 'point at the Institute tower.' So how are you going to know the compass course to steer, eh?"

"I see, yes. That's very good."

"And none of your 'north by west-north-west' navy talk, either. Leave that to Captain Marryat. Always take a compass bearing in full-circle degrees and learn it by heart." He took his jacket back and tousled her hair. "We'll make a full-ticket bosun of you yet, maid."

"What if I get seasick? We never thought of that."

He patted the wheel, as if that were the sovereign remedy. She soon saw why he had accepted her aboard without a murmur. For most of the trip he and Harry performed a repeated series of dead-reckoning tests. They would first make a note of the throttle position and the propellor pitch and then they'd throw a glass float attached to a line into the water. As the float held its position among the waves, they would pay out the line, keeping it slack so as not to tug at the float. The line had much thinner bits of line tied around it in knots at regular intervals and they would count how many knots were payed out in a given time. Harry was the timekeeper, David the knot-counter. Then they hauled the float inboard, changed the throttle position, or the propellor pitch, and repeated the cycle.

"Now we know why we guzzled so much petrol on the way out," he said to Tamsin when they had finished. "At full throttle we only get one more knot out of her than we do at just under three-quarter throttle. The extra speed's not worth the extra petrol, see?"

Porthleven was now just over a mile off, still dead ahead. And he was right — her concentration on steering properly had kept her mind busy with other things than seasickness.

"So I have been of some use?" she said.

"Couldn't have done it without you. You want to put up your glad rags now, do you? Harry! Come and hide your eyes until the maid is changed up."

David hung his jacket over the window again and steered by compass until Tamsin was back in her finery. She felt something of a wrench as she discarded the old dungarees, even though they smelled of fish and their coarseness had grated on her skin. On a day like this, she thought, a fisherman's life must be one of the best. Of course, one must not forget those other times, and the boats that never came back, and the young widows who went to the cliffs at sunset and scanned every aching, empty inch of ocean until they were sure that today was not that miracle day — again.

And yet, she suddenly realized, she could not think of David in that same category, the cast of the vulnerable. If the *Merlin* sank under him, far out to sea, he would somehow make it ashore and live to fish again. It was hard even to think of him ageing slowly and losing his faculties one by one.

This struck her as something so singular that she felt she had to tell him at once. She went back to the wheelhouse and took down his jacket.

"My!" he cried, looking her up and down. "You'm so pretty as a mabyer, maid!"

"Well!" She preened herself. "I hope a 'mabyer' is pretty, too — whatever it may be?"

" 'Tis a pullet. And I'd say you're prettier still than any pullet as ever I saw."

She bobbed a curtsy. "What would 'ugly' be in Cornwall? As ugly as a … what?"

The two men looked at each other in a way that suggested the obvious word would also be indelicate. "How about paddypaw?" Harry suggested.

David nodded. "So ugly as a paddypaw."

"What's that?"

"A toad." He offered her another one: "So quick as a witnick — that's a stoat, or a ferret, see."

"What would slow be, then?"

"So slow as a bulljink. That's a slug. Or as a bullgrannick. That's a snail."

" 'Course," Harry said, "you do know the famous one: So cold as a quilkin in a cundard. You heard that, surely?"

She shook her head.

David translated. "So cold as a frog in a drain." He laughed. "Us'll make a Cornishwoman of 'ee yet, maid."

"Can I go and stand right in the bows?" she asked.

He passed the wheel to Harry and accompanied her, standing immediately behind, one hand on each gunwale.

She leaned far out over the prow, lifting her head so that she could not see any part of the boat except the jib. "Whee!" she cried. "I'm a seagull, soaring over the briny, free as the wind!" Then she became aware how close he was; she looked over her shoulder and saw the protective semicircle of his arms. "What's that for?" she asked.

"To steady you if the pitching should throw you backward."

"Oh. And if it threw me forward? Would you jump in and save me from drowning?"

"A man who can't swim a yard to save his own life jumping overboard to save a maid who can swim a mile? That'd make a lot of sense! Who'd save who?"

"What *would* you do, then?"

"Put about and throw you a line."

"And what if I was your Sandra?" She deliberately misnamed the alleged love of his life because, thinking about it later, certain bits in his story, coupled with evasions in his telling of it, had led her to doubt the woman's existence entirely.

"My Sandra?" There was bewilderment in his voice but also, she thought, a tinge of panic; she guessed he was nine-tenths certain he had not named this (nonexistent?) young female Sandra but could not, on the spur of the moment, remember what name he had given her.

"I never told you about Sandra *as well*, did I?" he asked at long last.

Was he cleverly kicking for touch or had she, quite by chance, picked the name of some other *amour* of his?

"The daughter of the Saint Ives fisherman."

"Oh!" He laughed, but was it in relief that the name had just come back to him, or had she mistaken his genuine bewilderment for panic? "You mean Sarah! Sarah Rowe."

"So who is Sandra?" she asked quickly, not to give him time.

"She's the opposite case." He sighed. "She ... I don't want to sound vain, now, but she set her cap at me when we were in the national school still, and she's never stopped since. Whenever we put to sea, she's there with a pasty for me. When we come home to Newlyn, she's there again, ready to unload. She won't take her eyes off me in chapel ... knits me stockings and rollnecks in oiled wool ... cooks niceys for me ..."

"Poor man!" She laughed. "It must make your life a misery."

He ignored her sarcasm. "It does. I fear she'll get me in the end. One moment of human weakness and *snap!* She'll have me alongside of her at the altar."

"Still," Tamsin said, "since you cherish the same hopeless feelings for Miss Sarah Rowe, you must know exactly how wretched she feels."

"That's it," he agreed. "You hit 'n squarely. I can't turn her away, though I know 'twould be kindest in the long run. There's many a man would go down on his knees to her and make her a good husband, but she spurns them all."

"Perhaps you're the one who's being too choosy," she suggested. "Mooning after the unattainable Sarah. Shouldn't you cut your coat according to your cloth?"

"There's truth in that," he replied. "But 'Love is to all things blind, / Except to this — the wayward mind. / What it can have it will not see. / What it *must* have won't let it be.' So there!"

"That's neat," she said. "Who wrote it?" He did not reply. She turned at looked into his eyes. "You?"

He shrugged awkwardly. "I never wrote it down." Then, as if he thought he needed some kind of excuse: "There's not much to do, keeping the compass on just the one bearing — and no maid to talk to, only Harry and Sonny and some dead fish."

Harry cut the revs to half-throttle and came about to northeast as they lined up with Porthleven's outer harbour.

"No sign of our shore party yet," David remarked, scanning up and down the quayside. Then, seeing that his cousin was making for the iron ladder below the Institute, which Tamsin could never have scaled in her dress, he pointed instead to the steps in the middle harbour, on the eastern or Sithney side.

Harry nodded and altered course slightly.

"They probably delayed over their cream tea," Tamsin said.

He caught a note of wistfulness in her voice and offered a slice of fuggan cake or of saffron bread — all he had left.

"And which of them was baked by the poor, lovelorn Sandra?" she asked.

"Neither," he admitted.

"Listen!" She flapped her hands at him. "If there are two more hapless females who cherish an unrequited love for you — and who foolishly believe the way to your heart is through your belly — I simply don't want to hear of it. I'm sure I can get a cream tea in one of those cottages on the harbour front — if you'll just drop me off here and go your ways."

But he wouldn't dream of it. As the *Merlin* nosed into the alcove that held the broad granite steps, he leaped off ahead of her and held out his hands to help her make the small leap after him. The narrowing of the harbour had the effect of turning a barely perceptible two-foot ocean swell into six-foot waves, which could drop the boat right out from under you if, like Tamsin, you had only one foot ashore at the time. David grabbed both her arms and pulled her hard, making no allowance for her own efforts in the same direction. The impact of her body thrust him a couple of paces back against the inner wall of the recess — and impelled her from his arm's-length grip into his embrace.

She struggled for all of half a second and then surrendered. Or, rather, it was not she who surrendered but her unthinking body, which found the crush of his arms and the hard contact of his strong, lean frame impossible to resist. His earlier words — 'one moment of human weakness' — echoed vaguely somewhere in her mind but they were distant and she was no longer there to heed them. She was in her bones, her sinews, her nerves — in every living part of her flesh — rejoicing.

But her self-control did not entirely desert her — only to the extent that she did nothing to break off this rapturous, if accidental, embrace. She pressed her head against his chest, knowing that if she looked up at him, he would kiss her. And though at that particular moment she could not think of anything more pleasant in all the world, she knew it would change everything between them utterly. It would upset the delicate relationships of her world and play havoc with their carefully chosen purpose in her life.

It lasted no more than ten seconds — but for seven of them they were perfectly stable on the granite steps and in no need of mutual propping up. In the end it was David who pushed her away — he being unable to move, with his back to the massive stone wall. His hands shivered, his arms shook, as if the muscles were at war throughout his body. "Let's see about that cream tea," he said. Over her shoulder he pointed at Harry, who was grinning and making crudely encouraging gestures, and then toward the inner harbour.

Harry grasped his meaning and, pausing only to throw the bundle containing her towel and bathing things up the steps ahead of them, set off for the narrow mouth that helped protect Porthleven's fleet from storms and their mountainous seas.

"Mister Victor Thorne did not seem too pleased when you came along of us." David picked up the bundle and moved to her seaward side — there being no handrail to the steps. He took her gently by the elbow.

"Mister Victor Thorne is not too pleased with most aspects of his life at the moment," she replied, taking his hand and wrapping it firmly around the crook of her arm.

Now that he was no longer holding her, the intensity of her feelings only a moment or two earlier seemed inexplicable. But they had left her shaken — and not just as a figure of speech but quite literally, too. There was a sort of shivery weakness running right through her — the same as she could feel in him.

She went on: "Mister Victor Thorne has too much money, too much time on his hands, and not enough to occupy him — that's my opinion. He has no inner resources."

"And would you say the same of Standish Coverley?" he asked as they reached the top of the steps.

She noticed he did not accord Standish an ironic 'Mister.'

"Would you?" she responded.

"There's something of the same lack about that man," he said. "Not that he's idle. But he plays with things. He's a bit like a monkey — picks things up, plays with them a bit, then puts them down and picks up something else."

She grinned at him. "Is that a warning for me?"

"No, no. Not people. Things. When he bought the Queen's and turned it into the first-class hôtel it is, why, he hardly slept o'nights and …"

"Really? I thought it was a family inheritance. How long ago was this?"

"Half a dozen years. Round the turn of the century. He bought it off of his uncle, so it was in the family before. But then, like I said, he was heart-and-soul into it. Now he's hardly there but two days a week. He'll be looking for something new afore too long — you'll see."

"Maybe a coachbuilding works for posh motors?" she suggested, thinking of his obsession with his car.

"Or mebbe he needs a good woman to keep him steady."

"Not this woman — if that's what you're thinking," she said. A moment later she wondered why. Then, to make her comment seem more general, she added, "I don't think he wants that sort of complication in his life — just at the moment, anyway."

"What a person *wants* and what that person *needs* are rarely the same thing." He pointed along the harbourside road, where the white Rolls-Royce was inching and bouncing along. "He's now coming. We shall have to have that cream tea another day."

The coal tramp had discharged her cargo and was now waiting for the evening tide to float her.

"Tomorrow?" Tamsin suggested eagerly.

He shook his head. "I shall be at sea these next few days. If this slack breeze holds, I can fish where others can't."

"Good luck, then," she said. "And oh, by the way, what's the Cornish saying for 'warm'? I know 'so cold as a quilkin in a cundard' but it'd be 'so warm as …' what?"

"So warm as a peach," he replied.

"That doesn't make sense."

He laughed as he walked away. "It would if you knew what 'peach' can also mean. See'ee again, maid. I'm glad you were on the maiden trip after all. It felt incomplete without you."

28 Ten days after the jaunt to Kynance, Tamsin came of age. She awoke early, wished herself a *Happy Birthday!* (silently, to avoid waking Daisy in her bed by the fireplace) and began a thorough inventory of body, mind, and spirit to see if she could detect any difference. It ought to be possible, she felt. The wise lawmakers who decreed that yesterday she was unfit to own a bank account, run up debts, or marry without parental consent, whereas today she was fully capable of all three, must have had their reasons. Mind you, those same wise lawmakers also decreed that she was unfit to vote, to sit on a jury, to fight for her country, or to work above the most menial levels of the Civil Service, so perhaps 'reason' was not their strongest suit. All the same, a twenty-first birthday was one of life's big gateways — the portal where one shed all childish things and put on the mantle of maturity.

And what mature decisions now awaited her?

Well, for a start, she told herself, she must try to distinguish ambitions from pipedreams and desires from real needs. She really must. It was urgent. And she must go beyond that, too. She must start taking account of the way ambitions and real needs interact. For example, if it truly was her ambition to turn the guest house into a small hôtel by ploughing back every penny of profit, it would mean years of skimping and saving and very little money for spending on fun.

Could she tolerate that, especially since fun had started coming back into her life lately?

Don't answer yet, she advised. Continue the line of thought to its logical end. That would be the mature, responsible way of doing things. Take plenty of time about it. Be thorough. Think everything through.

Because even the small hôtel was only a way-station in the unfolding of her full ambition. The idea would be to trade it at some time for a medium-size hôtel. And then — how many years later? — to graduate to something as grand as the Queen's. Or even grander! Why not? Ambitions are but guiding stars, and even the Three Kings never actually reached theirs. They just let it guide them to their real goal.

It would mean not marrying, of course. No husband, no children, no ordinary domestic life. And no love — except that hopeless kind which never got closer than three pews away. There would be no one in all the world who thought you were the most wonderful, most special person ever — and no one of whom you could say the same in return. None of that. She'd be a spinster … an old maid. A *sour* old maid. One of those quavering voices that filled a third of the church each Sunday. Those whiskered women in black and clerical grey, with their creaking bones in their withered shanks. Would the wealth and power that went with the ownership of a place like the Queen's be compensation enough for that?

Oh dear — choices! They were wonderful things when you had them all set out before you, like so many birthday presents all wrapped in gaudy paper. The trouble was, the moment you opened one of them and said, 'Mine!' the others just shrivelled and blew away. Perhaps that was what maturity meant — making your one true choice and kissing the others goodbye. 'Forsaking all others, keep thee only unto him or her' … it was the same thing.

The trouble was, she really did *desire* Victor and it clouded her every attempt to think calmly and rationally about all the other choices in her present life. She knew very well that he was a spoiled and selfish … well, *child* was not too harsh a word. It made no difference to her wanting him. That he adored her — if only for the present — was obvious. And his talk of being alternately in heaven and hell, all because of her, was nothing more than his vanity fighting against that feeling of being trapped by his love; he loved her insanely and he hated her for having that enslaving effect on him.

For her part, she now doubted she loved him in the smallest degree; but that made her desire to be kissed and held by him all the more naked, since she could not cloak it in the gentle blush of romance. Now that she knew all about It — the thing that adult men and women did together — thanks to Daisy's disgusted but vivid description, she realized only too well that kissing and hugging were not ends in themselves but mere overtures to something dark and hot, powerful and dangerous, repellent and yet enticing.

As a child she had loved to be frightened — when Papa got into a dark cupboard with her and did *Fee-fi-fo-fum* or stuck his finger in a mousehole and shouted and roared, pretending it was being bitten to the bone by rats. Was her obsession for Victor just a subtler, older version of that same basic need for fear? Put it another way — was she ever going to change, or would she just find more and more adult ways of satisfying the same endless, elemental urges?

She sat up and looked over toward Daisy's bed, to see if she was awake yet. To her surprise it was empty. Daisy was not an eager riser in the mornings; and on this particular Tuesday, the last day in July, she would have been even more loath than usual, since no guests were due to arrive or depart. It was, by the standards of the high season, a slack day.

Tamsin's bewilderment did not last long. She was just sitting up and struggling into her dressing gown — for it was now seven o'clock and past her own usual time for rising — when Daisy pushed open the door with her foot and advanced to the bedside carrying a breakfast tray and singing, *Rah, rah, rah for the birthday girl!*

Tamsin's surprise was doubled when she saw her mother, right behind Daisy and carrying a vase of deep-red roses. "Has my clock stopped?" she asked as she smoothed out the bedlinen to accept the tray.

"Don't be rude, dear," Harriet answered with a smile. "I'm quite capable of rising early if the circumstances warrant it. Guess who these are from!"

"You mean 'from whom these are,' don't you? I was going to guess *you?*"

Her mother set the vase down upon the tray and tweaked a miniature envelope out from among the stems. "Read it," she said, stooping to exchange a kiss.

The envelope was mauve with scalloped edges embossed in glossy purple ink. So was the card inside. Both smelled of attar of roses.

"No *two* guesses, now!" Daisy warned.

"As if!" Tamsin replied.

The card read: 'Many happy returns and congrats — let the motley begin! Warmest regards, Standish.'

"You must keep this for your album," Harriet said, plucking it from between her daughter's fingers and tucking it back inside its envelope. "It's a pity the perfume will fade." As she left she added, "I have a little present for you downstairs, darling. D'you feel any different?"

"Heaps," Tamsin replied.

"I've got one for you, too," Daisy said, producing a plain envelope from her pocket. "No scents, just good sense."

Inside was a simple white card on which Daisy had written in three different coloured inks:

A WISE WORD FROM THE WISE TO THE WISE
    16 nods = 1 smile
    16 smiles = 1 word
    28 words = 1 tryst
    4 trysts = 1 kiss
    20 kisses = 1 proposal
    2 proposals = 1 engagement
    1 engagement = 3 times cried in chapel
    3 times cried in chapel = 1 marriage
    1 marriage = 50 years' misery
    50 years misery = 1 funeral
    1 funeral = the happiest day in a woman's life

To Tamsin Harte from her sincere friend Daisy Dobbs.

"Oh, Daisy!" Tamsin's laugh was half humorous, half despairing. "There's something amiss with your arithmetic, anyway. I'm far beyond twenty kisses … and still no proposal in sight."

"The currency is debased, then," Daisy answered primly.

"Nothing from Victor? What has my mother gone and got for me, I wonder?"

"Eat your toast while it's still warm."

"Tell me, then."

"No. I'm not going to spoil the surprise."

"Why not?" Tamsin buttered a slice and spread it with marmalade. "You've already ruined the surprise of marriage for me. What's the spoiling of one little birthday treat! Is it something I ought to know about?"

"I don't know about *ought,*" Daisy replied warily.

"Mmmm! You're an angel for this." Tamsin ate with relish.
"Is it something I should be prepared to grin my head off at —
but which might make my face fall if I wasn't forewarned?"

"I don't know, I'm sure." Daisy was growing more uncomfortable by the minute, which did nothing for Tamsin's confidence.

"But you do know what it is?"

"I saw it before she covered it with a cloth, yes."

"Is it something you'd want for yourself?"

"It would be too expensive for me," Daisy assured her. "It's
more what you'd call an heirloom."

"Oh no!" Half way through buttering a second slice she
dropped the knife and covered her face with her hands.

"What?" Daisy asked.

"I have a horrible feeling, that's all. Is it made of wood, with
four ugly, ornate legs, about so high, and plastered all over with
brass and ivory inlay?" She could tell from Daisy's face that the
shot was a bullseye.

"How did you know?" the girl asked. "She went to such pains
to keep it secret. It's been hidden in five rooms in this house
over the past two weeks to my certain knowledge. Inspector
Sterne himself would never have found it."

"It was my Great-aunt Biddy's sewing box …"

"There's enough in it to make a tapestry fit for a royal palace."

"You don't need to tell me! When we put it in the auction,
Mama wept and I had to pretend to be sad, too. In fact, I had to
get up at midnight and dance three times round the tennis court
to work off my glee. But when I tried to find out which unfortunate
soul had bought it, the auctioneer's list just said 'A .N. OTHER —
cash paid.' I had a certain foreboding then, but, when it didn't
turn up here, I thought we were spared. Oh dear! This is going
to call for all my thespian skills — and you, Daisy, did absolutely
the right thing to blurt it out like that."

Daisy drew back her fist and then laughed. "You're absolutely
incorrigible, you know."

"I'm twenty-one! What did you do on your twenty-first?"

"Went through all Mrs Ormesby's furs looking for signs of
moth and then replaced the camphor balls. Shall I go on?
There's more."

"My father used to make little paper boats that were driven by camphor balls. It's true! You put a camphor ball at the stern and it'll go forward by magic. What d'you make of Standish, eh? A dozen red roses and a rose-scented note!"

Daisy shrugged. "I can't make him out. Hot one minute, cold the next. Turn your teacup upside down and I'll tell your fortune in the leaves."

Tamsin did as she was told, saying, "That never works for me. All I ever get is dogs — blobs of leaves that couldn't be anything other than dogs. See — it's done it again! Oh, and look — now there's a cat as well!"

Daisy took the cup from her. "Dogs and cats!" she said scornfully. "Look at that! What d'you see there?"

"A letter U? Victor's going to give me an umbrella? I'm going to go *Up* in the world? I know — you're about to Utter nonsense! And it will be Utter nonsense."

"And if we turn it this way up?" Daisy asked patiently.

"Oh, how clever! It's turned into an upside-down U."

"Nonsense. It's a crown — a royal crown."

"Oh yes!" Tamsin laughed in fascination. "You didn't twiddle the leaves about a bit, did you?"

"Certainly not! Who wears a crown like that? Not a king. Theirs have those bulgy bits."

"A queen!" Tamsin giggled. "It's saying I'm to be the queen of someone's heart!"

Daisy clenched her eyes tight and gritted her teeth. "I obviously have to lead you every step of the way. *You're* supposed to see these things, not me! If it's not the king's crown then it's …? Fill in the missing word."

"The queen's!"

"Allelulia! Perhaps the name rings a bell?"

"The Queen's! Oh, my!" Tamsin stuffed her fingers into her mouth and stared at Daisy wide-eyed. "D'you think …?"

"Destiny!"

"It can't be. How can it be? It can't — we both know that."

"Well …" Daisy pulled a reluctant face. "I *thought* I did. But the tealeaves never lie — as long as you know how to read them." She stared critically at the pattern in the cup. "Yep! It's a crown all right. And it's the Queen's for you."

29 Harriet eyed her newly adult daughter nervously as the girl ran exploring fingers over the dustsheet. "I do hope it's the right thing, dear," she said.

Tamsin, postponing the moment when, as she had said, all her thespian skills would be needed, stared in apparent fascination at the cloth, which came down all the way to the ground on all four sides. "You've probably disguised it," she mused. "So this isn't its true shape. But what could it be? A bicycle? You've bought me a bicycle so that I can get through the marketing in half the time!"

"Oh dear!" Harriet said. "Is that what you'd have preferred?"

"So it's not a bicycle. Is it a badminton set for the beach?"

"Unveil it, darling. Just tug the cloth away. There's no need for all this guessing. I'm quite sure you're going to love it. I remember how … well, never mind. I'll tell you when you've … oh, go on, do!"

Unable to postpone the dreaded moment any longer, Tamsin gripped the cloth and swirled it away with a magician's flourish. Later she rather thought she overdid the delighted surprise but her mother accepted every squeal and sigh as genuine. "Great-aunt Biddy's sewing box!" she cried. "Oh, Mama — you utter utter *angel!*"

"I remember how you wept when it had to go into the auction, so I secretly bought it out again and kept it for this day. You are pleased, aren't you?"

"Pleased? *Pleased?* The word just isn't strong enough." She opened the lid and ran her eye over a good half-acre of bobbins displaying every known colour in the universe; silk, art silk, cellulose acetate, wool, cotton, twist, button thread, cobbler's thread, sailmaker's twine … if someone made it and dyed it, anywhere in the civilized world, Great-aunt Biddy had sent for a mile of it and found room for it here. The thing was a portable museum of the seamstress's art — and that was only the top shelf. On the one below were needles of every shape and size — for milliners, embroiderers, tapestry weavers, boot makers, upholsterers … name the trade and its practitioners would find their tools here. There were semicircular needles, ribbon-threading bodkins, gold-eyed stitchers, blunt-nosed darners, and triangular-sided things that looked like sabres for Tom Thumb — or so they had seemed to Tamsin as a little girl. And, of course, thimbles; thimbles from Dresden and Sèvres for looking at; thimbles from Sheffield for use. On mining even deeper into this chest of treasures one came upon shears and scissors of every kind, hole punches, hammers and anvils for eyelets, balls of wax, liners of soap and chalk, darning frames, embroidery harnesses, and two whole compartments for knitting needles and crochet hooks. Finally, there was an ornamented box-within-a-box full of bobbins, pins, hooks, and a well-stabbed cushion for lace-making.

It was, indeed, an heirloom. Daisy could not have picked a word more apt. Objectively, Tamsin knew she was being given something her grandchildren (if she ever took the first step toward begetting them) would probably drool over; but oh! the weariness that weighed her soul at the very sight of it now. Some Biddys are made to ply the needle like wizards, and some Tamsins are not. She would rather pull a cartload of weeds from a virgin garden than crochet a single doily for a cream jug — though, given the choice, she'd rather go for a ride in a Rolling-Royce than either. Or a sea trip in the *Merlin* even.

So it was no mean theatrical feat to sustain her outward joy in the face of her mother's anxious scrutiny.

Harriet, satisfied at last that her kindness was well received, relaxed and said, *"Now* let anyone who dares try to say you are not suitable!"

This was such a gnomic utterance that Tamsin, half against her better instincts, had to ask for an explanation.

"Well, dear," her mother replied. "Try to see yourself as others must see you — a well brought up girl without a dowry. You are familiar with Good Society. You are *au fait* with all its rules. You are at ease in the highest sort of company. And, in helping to manage this guest house, you demonstrate that no household, however large, will ever get the better of you. Why else d'you think I have allowed you such a free hand here, if not to make that plain? These assets half make up for your lack of a dowry. There is no household in the kingdom you could not manage. You could hold your own with duchesses and American heiresses and ..."

"Mama!"

"No. Hear me out. This is important. I have much to tell you on this important day — indeed, it could well prove to be the most important day in your entire life. Come and sit down here by the window. I have given orders we shall not be disturbed."

With sinking heart Tamsin followed her to the settee in the bay window; at least there would be the whole fascinating panorama of Morrab Road to distract her.

Her mother resumed the homily. "Your character and capabilities, as I said, amount to half your assets — and a very considerable half they are, too. And this sewing chest of Great-aunt Biddy's will, if properly used, add a further quarter."

"I have to *use* it?" Tamsin could not help blurting out.

But, if her mother noticed this sudden change in tone, she did not react to it. She was too eager to press her own argument home. "I know you have not inherited Great-aunt Biddy's skill with the needle along with her chest, dear, but you might have a little embroidery on the go — something you can pick up and stab away at when you are entertaining gentleman callers."

Gentleman callers? Tamsin felt the rational world beginning to dissolve around her. Was her mother going ever so slightly dottissima? "D'you mean Victor Thorne?" she asked.

"For one," her mother conceded.

"A rather lonely one at the moment — and I can't think of anything more calculated to make him come all unglued than to see me stabbing furiously, not at the embroidery but more likely at my own fingertips and bleeding all over his ..."

"Yes-yes, dear. Very vivid. But not at all helpful. The point is, Mister Thorne is no longer your sole gentleman caller. How can you have forgotten that lovely bunch of roses already!"

"Standish Coverley?"

"Oh, good — you haven't forgotten! Yes, Mister Standish Coverley. I know he's in trade, but then so are we — for the moment. And anyway, he hardly bothers himself with the sordid details of the hôtel and his other commercial properties and interests. So it's almost like owning land and stocks and things. You would make a very suitable young wife for such a wealthy man. An ornament. A jewel in his crown. And, since he seems interested in you — to put it no higher — well ... now you have *two* eager suitors, which is not just twice as good as one, it is two *thousand* times better. Besides, you needn't worry about producing an impressive bit of embroidery. I can do that for you after the whole house has gone to bed." Harriet smiled magnanimously, already forgiving her daughter for her lack of needlework skills — as long as she could use the ammo provided by this family heirloom to conquer her man.

Tamsin decided that, whether or not her mother's mind was 'coming unglued,' she had better assume it so. How on earth did Great-aunt Biddy's sewing chest provide a further quarter of her 'assets' in the marriage stakes? (And what constituted the other quarter? Though she would not pursue that question until this sewing-chest business was sorted out.)

Harriet, seeing her daughter's perplexity, smiled graciously and said, "I can see you have not entirely grasped my purpose in giving you this sewing chest, darling. Let me explain. The way you manage the day-to-day affairs of the Morrab Guest House ... your quiet, calm proficiency ..."

"You don't hear me in the kitchen every now and then!"

"I do, dear, but the others don't. So, as far as the world is concerned, it doesn't happen. But, as I was saying, your proficiency might suggest to a gentleman caller that you are a domineering sort of female who must have her way at all costs."

"Well, to be quite honest ..."

"Do stop interrupting, dear. We are not talking about honesty here. Honesty doesn't come into it. We're discussing appearances. And you might *appear* to be a sort of termagant once you get inside your own front door. So — don't you see? — the sight of you with your sweet, pretty head bent over an embroidery frame will help redress the balance. A flawless mistress of the domestic staff but a submissive and happy little embroiderer in her leisure hours — with no wider ambitions that might challenge a gentleman in his own manly world. Why, soon you will have not two suitors but *twenty*-two!"

"Steady the Buffs, Mama dear!" Tamsin forced a laugh. Her mother clearly *was* losing a hinge. However, there was no point in arguing, so all she said was, "But I do see what you mean."

"Twenty-two is a bit of an exaggeration, I know. But if you can manage to project such a rounded picture of the perfect wife for a gentleman, well … it is certain to attract more to your side than the current two!"

"It's certainly worth a try." Tamsin was already thinking in terms of scalded fingers, sprained wrists … anything to avoid picking up a needle. And did Penzance have a choral society, a debating club, a philately group — anything to occupy time that might otherwise be spent in bending her pretty little head over an embroidery frame. At least in a group of stamp collectors she'd be mingling with people who were only *half* mad.

"Of course it is," her mother agreed. "I know that needlework is not your most congenial hobby. I did think of other feminine accomplishments. Water-colours, for instance. But down here in Cornwall, painting is such a *professional* business. Last Saturday one could hardly walk through Newlyn without tripping over sketching easels — and female artists showing much too much ankle to be ladies. So, all in all, a little light embroidery will be best, I think."

"So that takes care of three-fourths of my … *assets* in the marital stakes. Whence cometh the fourth fourth?"

To Tamsin's surprise her mother blushed slightly and looked away, out into the street. Unfortunately for her, just at that moment, three dogs and a bitch were preparing to do what they so often do in the street — and three impudent boys were gathered to watch them, waiting to laugh.

To Tamsin's further surprise, her mother did not twitch the curtain to hide the distressing incident from view. "Perhaps it is a blessing in diguise," she murmured, still uncomfortable but now with the slightly martyred air of one who cannot escape a distasteful duty. Pointing toward the dogs but keeping her eyes fixed on her daughter, she said, "You know all about *that* sort of thing, I suppose?"

Tamsin swallowed hard and tried to seem nonchalant, though her heart stopped a moment and then came back with a thump. "A little, I think," she said. "The dogs are *serving* the bitch and in due course she'll produce a litter of puppies."

"Good." Her mother was shaking a bit, too. "And humans … men and women …"

"Engage in something a little more civilized but essentially the same. Didn't girls at school talk about such things in your day?" She took charge of this conversation, although it made her want to knit her toes, because she didn't want her mother to get anywhere near discovering Daisy's role in her enlightenment. In fact, older girls at her school *had* whispered furtively (and grossly inaccurately) about such things, but it had passed right over Tamsin's head at the time.

"I was educated at home," Harriet replied. "D'you mean they *did* at Bishops Cheriton?"

Tamsin nodded and smiled apologetically. "Not that I understood much of it, mind."

"Well, I'm overjoyed to hear it. But ..."

"So you see — if you find it difficult to talk about, there's no need!" She smiled, happy that it was over.

Her mother did not smile back; it was not over. "It *is* difficult, precious," she admitted, "but not half as difficult as the things I really have to tell you now. Merely to understand the ... the *biology*" — she produced the word with elegant distaste — "does not get one to the heart of the matter. Not even close. The thing is ... um ... how can I put it? Perhaps an analogy will serve. We all know it is wicked and wrong to use cosmetics — and yet we all do it when the occasion demands. Whenever you hear a grand matron bleating about 'painted Jezebels' and the like, you may be sure she has discreetly reddened her own cheeks and lips or darkened her eyelashes or put laudanum drops into her eyes to make the pupils go big and dark and mysterious. We've all done it."

"Discreetly," Tamsin added, hoping to hurry her mother away from the analogy and toward the point.

"Quite so, dear — discreetly. You take the very word out of my mouth. Now the purpose of marriage — one of its purposes, anyway — is to take, er, *that* sort of thing" — again she waved a hand toward the dogs without so much as a glance in their direction — "and regularize it. Confine it to hearth and home ... well, not even the hearth, actually. To the bedroom."

By now, Tamsin was starting to wonder where the analogy with cosmetics fitted in. "Is it nice?" she asked. "You know what I mean — is it a pleasure?"

Her mother gazed at the ceiling ... into the empty grate ... at the hand-coloured photograph of St. Michael's Mount ... at a cinder burn in the hearthrug. "Perhaps not all that smutty schoolgirl talk passed over your head, eh?" she murmured.

"But is it?"

"Yes, dear." She spoke as if defeated in some way. "With the right person it is. With the man you love it is a pleasure almost too sweet to bear. I hope I'm doing right to tell you this. I hope I don't need to add that it should not be attempted, not even with the man you love — and no matter how desperate that love may be — unless that man has put both a diamond and a golden ring upon your hand. Anything else is wrong, wrong, wrong." Then she closed her eyes and added, "However ..."

Tamsin sat up, all ears suddenly. Here at last was the real nub of her mother's homily on this, the most significant day of her life so far. "Yes?" she said encouragingly.

"You remember what I said about painting and powdering one's features? How, even though we all agree it is wrong, we all do it discreetly? Just a little bit. We don't paint ourselves up like clowns or Jezebels. We don't 'go the whole hog,' as the saying has it. Just a little bit, you see — a discreet little bit."

"Like kissing?"

"A little bit more than that, dear." Her mother's hand strayed toward her bosom and then lost courage.

But Tamsin nodded to show she understood.

Harriet, glad at last to be over the summit of this particular talk, continued: "One can't lay down hard and fast rules — thus far but no further. But the principle is that you must always remain in control of the situation."

"Was this so in your day?" Tamsin asked. "Or is it something new, for nowadays?"

"I suspect it has always been so, darling. We think of some ages as being notoriously licentious and others as being impossibly puritanical, but I suspect that what I'm talking about has always gone on, regardless of the tides of public opinion on the matter. Perhaps it is a little more necessary these days. There are so many seemingly confirmed bachelors around — all of them rich and quite contented to remain idle and free of domestic hindrance in their selfish pursuit of pleasure. And, I'm afraid I have to say, there are also too many women of the wrong sort to assist them in that purpose!"

"The ones we don't look at down around the harbour?"

Tamsin had never come within miles of such a frank, grown-up discussion with her mother before; now at last she felt that the unnoticed stroke of midnight last night had truly marked a great divide in her life.

"Not quite so degraded as those creatures, darling — or not so conspicuously degraded, anyway. In fact, you could pass them in the street and not be able to tell them from rich and respectable misses. So you see — with such competition out there — we have to break the rules a little, both in the business of cosmetics and, er, the seemly rituals of respectable courtship. But never lose control, as I say, and never permit anything that involves lifting the hem of your skirt."

Tamsin wondered where swimming and sunbathing in a state of nature came in her mother's scale of things, but she was not so foolish as to ask. Instead she said, "Do you miss it, Mama? D'you miss Papa in that way, too?"

Harriet was surprised almost out of her skin to think that this conversation had reached a point where the girl could ask such a question. She was even more shocked to hear herself answer it: "More than I can tell you, dear. After twenty-odd years you think it's just a habit. Then it goes away and you realize how much it really meant. Still ..." She forced herself to be bright. "Let's get you settled first. Then I'll do something about me."

30 It was as well that no party had been planned for Tamsin's twenty-first; just a bit of a spread at teatime, including a birthday cake with twenty-one candles. That very afternoon a telegram arrived from Baden-Baden to say that Count de Ath had died in his sleep the previous night and that the Countess would be returning to England immediately after the funeral, which was to take place quietly on the first of August; she expected to arrive on the third, which was the coming Saturday. That left only three whole days (plus two half days) in which to prepare to receive this grand old lady; if Harriet had had to cope with a coming-of-age party as well, and on the day this news arrived, she was sure her mind would have snapped. Especially as every room in the house was already fully booked for the entire fortnight.

Tamsin tried pointing out that Saturday was their regular change-over day, when around half their PGs left and a new half arrived to take their places. "And since 'half,' in our case, amounts to no more than six families," she added, "fitting in an extra one person is hardly going to break our backs."

"But that's the whole point!" Harriet shrieked, pointing at the bookings ledger.

"Shush!"

"I will not shush! Don't you understand — *we have no room available!* Unless someone cancels …" Her voice trailed away and a crafty look stole into her eyes. "Or unless *we* cancel *someone!* Who's farthest away?" She turned the ledger toward her. "Mister and Mrs Macrae, Edinburgh. They'll do. If we say we've got scarlet fever or something here — the truth will never reach them. Anyway, it may even be true. It must be. There must be a case of scarlet fever somewhere in Penzance, surely? And I'm certain there are *lovely* seaside places in Scotland where they'd be much happier …"

"Mo-ther!" Tamsin only called her *mo-ther* — in two admonitory syllables like that — when she was about to lose all patience with her.

"What now? We must send a telegram at once."

"No telegrams will be sent to the Macraes." She rotated the ledger back toward her so that her mother could not read the address. "We shall not turn away any of our custom — especially if it is merely to oblige a highly dubious lady, with a foreign title, who may end up doing a midnight flit on us."

"We're not turning her down!"

"No, we're not turning her down, either. She may have your room. You can have my bed and I'll play sardines with Daisy." Her mother did at least appear to consider the proposal. "Or," Tamsin went on, "perhaps Chynoweth next door has a vacancy. Or a cancellation. If so, you could take a room with Mister Vissick and compare notes."

"Darling! I hardly know the man," Harriet objected.

Such mild reluctance meant the idea appealed to her.

"Hardly know him? Why, you only spend ten minutes hobnobbing with him every time your paths happen to cross — which is just about every day."

"Hobnobbing!" she sneered. "I do no such thing. What a disgraceful expression. Mister Vissick and I engage in civilized conversation, that is all."

"Pop next door and ask him now. I'll give you ten to one he says yes. He's got his eye on you — you know he has."

She had wanted to say as much earlier, at the end of that morning's embarrassing conversation in the bay window; but it had not seemed quite the right moment for a little gentle teasing. In fact, it was so gentle that she was surprised to see the tips of her mother's ears, which she always prided for their delicate, alabaster quality, turn a decided shade of pink.

"Such nonsense!" she exclaimed, though she was already reaching for a notepad to draft a reply to the Countess.

Tamsin pressed it further. "He *has* got his eye on you — and you know it. Anyone can see that. He has dynastic ambitions to amalgamate the two properties and, perhaps, run them as a small temperance hôtel."

She did not add that Bill Vissick was quite a handsome eyeful in himself. A tall, wiry man with a mane of wavy hair, beetling brows, dark and deepset eyes, chiselled lips, and a rugged chin … always in command of himself and the situation … never sly, never flustered … he was the cause of many a hopeful sigh among the spinsters and widows of the town.

But none of them owned a successful boarding house right next door! *Owned,* mark you. That was her mother's trump card and maybe this was the moment to play it — from every point of view. For the girl could not help thinking that a mother who was caught up in affairs of her own heart would have less time to worry about those in which her daughter might be engaged — and would, in any case, be on lower moral ground than otherwise when it came to dishing out the crits.

"Do it now before you think better of it," she advised her mother. "Because there isn't actually any 'better' for you to think — is there!"

It required half an hour's preparation and a complete change of clothes before Harriet felt able to walk the dozen yards that separated the Morrab from Chynoweth. And, notwithstanding the extreme urgency of the situation — considering that they only had about ninety-five hours left in which to make up a bed for the Countess and, er, well, make up her bed — it seemingly required a further thirty-five minutes to ascertain whether Mr Vissick had a room free.

He had — and it would, indeed, be *free* to Mrs Harte. And why wait till Saturday when the room was empty now? Mrs Harte said she'd think about it, thought about it, and accepted.

And so the Countess's room was ready and waiting before they even sat down to Tamsin's slightly delayed birthday tea. Charlotte came, with an invitation from her brother for Tamsin to dine with him that night at the Queen's. Her parents, she announced, had taken the early-morning train home to Exeter to inspect the recent progress on the refurbishment of Peveril Hall; they were not expected to return until tomorrow.

"What is Victor doing at the moment?" Tamsin asked.

"Playing billiards with Reg Trotter and Standish Coverley at the Queen's, I think. And smoking like a chimney, I know."

"He seems to be spending more and more time with them lately," Harriet commented as she carried the taper from candle to candle on her daughter's cake.

"I know!" Charlotte pulled a glum face.

Harriet missed the expression but caught the tone of voice. "You sound as if you don't approve?"

"No. I think it's just so silly, Mrs Harte. I know I should be grateful and all that rot. And I know that all mothers have their daughters' best interests at heart always and for ever. But I still think it's silly."

"There! All with one match — thanks to a little cheating." Harriet blew out the taper and surveyed the cake with pride, though she had done nothing beyond sticking it with twenty-one candles. "What d'you think is silly, dear?"

"Oh! The only reason Victor's spending so much time with those two is to humour this whim of our mother's." She went on to explain Cicely Thorne's quaint ideas about the effeteness of rich families and how they need to renew their capitalist spirit every so often by marrying outside the narrow caste of people with inherited wealth.

Harriet, whose nimble mind raced ahead of the girl's diffident rehash of her mother's ideas, thought she now understood why the Thornes had left the Queen's and come to the Morrab. If anyone had possessed the capitalist spirit, and in goodly measure, too, it was Tamsin's father. So Victor was under maternal pressure to propose to the sprig of that worthy stock!

This happy thought rang so loud in her mind that she almost missed Charlotte's conclusion: "So poor Victor is having to ingratiate himself with Mister Coverley in the hopes that it might bring him closer to *me!*"

"No!" Daisy, Tamsin, and Harriet all cried out simultaneously — and then stared at each other, abashed at their sudden unanimity.

It surprised Charlotte, too. She turned to Tamsin and asked why her denial was so vehement.

"I just ... well, he strikes me as the sort of bachelor who's having much too much fun *being* a bachelor to even think of marriage." She waited for her mother to say something about splitting infinitives but no word came.

Instead, Harriet asked Charlotte what her feelings in the matter might be.

The girl leaned forward and lowered her voice. "I don't really want to marry anyone just yet. Mister Coverley's very nice but there are lots more fish in the sea."

"Good for you!" Harriet cried — to Tamsin's astonishment.

Meanwhile, Tamsin realized, she now had part of the answer to Standish's question: why had the Thornes moved from the Queen's to the Morrab?

Charlotte continued: "I don't see why bachelors should have all the fun of being single. I want to go to art school and have some fun myself."

"Be a bachelor-*girl!*" Tamsin suggested.

"Spinster, dear," her mother said abstractedly.

The three young women exchanged smiles: 'spinster' and 'bachelor-girl' were not synonyms.

Harriet, meanwhile, was busy putting the best possible construction on this revelation: Victor's true purpose — *and* Mrs Thorne's true purpose, since Victor was partly her agent — was to distract young Coverley with thoughts of Charlotte, leaving the way to Tamsin's heart clear for himself. After all, why should the Thornes wish to import this so-called 'capitalist blood' into the *female* line? The offspring of any union with Charlotte would be Coverleys, not Thornes. No! Preposterous though that woman's fanciful notions might be, the 'capitalist blood' was in Tamsin, just as she, Harriet, had assumed on first hearing of it. And the offspring of her marriage with Victor would be Thornes.

"Just think how different all our social arrangements and calculations would be if surnames followed down the female line instead of the male!" she said brightly.

This apparent non-sequitur silenced them for a moment and then there seemed no point in picking the subject up again. In any case, Bridget came in at that moment to say that David Peters was at the kitchen door with 'something for Miss Tamsin.'

In rushing to her feet Tamsin almost bowled her chair over; and the speed with which she raced out back made Charlotte and Daisy giggle — until Mrs Harte told them she saw nothing amusing in such unpolished behaviour.

"David!" Tamsin cried, throwing her arms about his neck and giving him a hasty kiss on the cheek. "The only man who cared to turn up to my birthday tea in person! Come on in."

"'Twas only to bring these," he replied, waving a bottle of champagne from which the sea had washed the label, and as fine a brace of sea-trout as ever came ashore at Newlyn. "I can't stay, no more'n a minute."

"Nonsense! Of course you can. You must." She gave him another peck and let him go. "Come on in and have some of my cake. No one will mind how you're dressed. We're just four old maids longing for some manly company."

Even then she had to drag him up the passage and into the dining room. "A chair, Daisy," she cried, "for the guest of honour. I'll get some glasses."

He had left the fish with Mrs Pascoe but he still had the champagne in his hand. "Bollinger," he said, putting it down beside the cake, where the candles had almost burned down to the sugar roses that held them.

"Leave the glasses, darling," her mother cried urgently. "The candles are nearly dead. It's time to make your wish."

"My wish! Golly!" She hadn't thought. There were so many possibilities. Wishes for herself. For her mother. For their joint prosperity. For …

She bent over the table, bringing her lips as near the cake as she dared, and drew the deepest breath she could manage. At the last moment she looked up and saw David's eyes upon her. Then, with all the world to wish for, all she could think of was: *I wish David and I will always be … will be …* Her mind hovered over the word. She knew it so well, and yet it stubbornly refused to be thought.

She could hold her breath no longer, so she blew and blew, this way and that. *Friends!* That was the word. *Just* friends. How stupid! Twenty candles smoked; one guttered and sprang back to life — after she was sure she'd blown it out. And she had no breath left. So the wish wasn't going to come true, anyway. Despondently she drew a second breath, but David reached out his great, work-toughened hand and pinched the flame out. "No one saw that, did they?" he asked innocently.

"I'm not sure, Mister Peters …" Harriet began.

"Act of friendship," he said.

An uncommon sympathy of minds? she wondered. Or could it be pure coincidence?

Everyone agreed that the cake was another of Mrs Pascoe's minor miracles; they had two slices each. And that made it necessary to have two glasses of champagne each, as well. And so they all became a little giggly — except for Harriet, who, even then, was racking her brains for ways of keeping David Peters away from the house while the Countess was under their roof.

After tea, David said he really did have to leave now. He was due to go on a three-day trip to the mid-Channel, where there were rumours of a mighty cod shoal and he could earn enough to buy the *Merlin's* engine outright.

Tamsin remarked that she could do with a breath of fresh air and suggested accompanying him — with Daisy and Charlotte along for company, if they wished.

Harriet said it didn't matter what *they* wished, she, Tamsin, wasn't going unless they went along, too.

Out in the hall, while the girls were changing into outdoor boots, she managed to murmur a few more instructions in her daughter's ear — namely that she was not to dine at the Queen's that night without having first listened to a few more words of advice and wisdom. "And dear little Charlotte," she whispered, "charming gel though she is ... we have to kill any idea of a liaison between her and Mister Coverley stone dead. I'm sure it's nothing serious — that is, I'm sure it's a feint on the part of Mrs Thorne, but these tricks have a way of going horribly wrong, so ..."

"May I go, please?" Tamsin asked.

There were dust devils in the road outside, scurrying along at random like upside-down monks, spinning on their pointed cowls. A hot, dry, fitful wind stirred through the gardens, making a clatter among the palm trees and rattling the gates.

"There's a change on the way," David told Tamsin.

Charlotte and Daisy were walking a discreet four or five paces behind them.

"A storm?" she asked anxiously.

"Heavy weather, anyway."

"And you'll still go to sea? Is it safe? You won't wait for it to blow over?"

"It's a question of whether the cod will wait. Anyway, we've fitted double tanks for this voyage. Also, mid-Channel's the best place to be when the weather closes in. You're out of the shipping lanes and the waves are longer and not so high."

"Well, just be careful," she said, feeling helpless.

"I'm always that. But if I'm numbered to go, then I'm numbered to go. And that's all about it."

She shivered and grabbed his arm. "Just don't talk about it." Then a new thought struck her. "Perhaps you'd better give me Sarah's Rowe's exact address — so that if anything does happen, I could let her know?"

"Her!" He gave a sardonic laugh. "She wouldn't want to know, anyway."

"Or Sandra whatzername's, then?"

"She'll know soon enough — before you do, in fact."

"Oh, I just hate it when people are so fatalistic! If I offered you money not to go to sea tonight, would you accept? I can't, mind, because I haven't got any, but would you?"

"Why is it so important, Tamsin?"

His words had the form of a question but they sounded more like a challenge to her. She became more cautious at once. "I don't know," she answered. "Maybe it's not important at all — except …"

"Yes?"

"Well, I'd just feel … I mean, this place just wouldn't be the same if you weren't there any more. That's all I'm saying."

He gave a baffled laugh. "We don't hardly meet more than once a week — if that. So I can't see as *I* make much difference."

"It's just nice to know you're *there*, that's all. Look — don't force me to make a big song and dance about it. Let's just drop the subject."

"That's all right by me."

After twenty or so paces in silence she said, "That was superb champagne. I can still feel the tickle. Have you been sending more messages to Brittany lately?"

"No." He sighed. "I've had that bottle nearly two years now. I thought I might as well dedicate it to a happy occasion as see it there, under the slates, mouldering away."

"Champagne doesn't moulder away. It gets better with age."

"So they say."

"Well then! You could have left it to improve — still, I'm glad you didn't."

She suspected he had put it aside against his eventual wedding day with Sarah Rowe — *if* she existed at all. Either way, he was trying to fix that thought in her mind without so much as a single direct word about it.

"Have you got any more?" she asked. "Or was that the last?"

"There's naught but one bottle to go," he said with a smile. "Such is hope, eh?"

31 Victor fretted in the lounge at the Morrab, waiting for Tamsin to be ready. Eventually Harriet sent Daisy to tell him to go on ahead and make sure of the table as the dear gel would be some time yet.

"He'll get his own back for that," Tamsin warned. "He'll sit near the entrance and then pretend not to notice me when I arrive. He's so childish, you know — I can read his every move."

"Then you'll not only be ready for him, you'll also astound him with your beauty." She eyed her daughter critically, head on one side. "Try pinching your cheeks."

When that didn't work, she locked the door, opened the secret drawer in her dressing table, and took out a pot of terracotta dust and a hare's foot. Also an eyebrow pencil. Also a box of powder and a puff.

"You'll make me look like an old woman of forty," Tamsin complained. Then, remembering that her mother was exactly that age, added, "I mean forty-five."

"Neither age could be called old these days," Harriet replied grimly. "Besides, we shall use these aids to beauty *very* discreetly."

"Discreet! That's the watchword for today."

"And so it should be. Why d'you think it's called 'reaching the age of discretion'?"

Tamsin surveyed the result of using the hare's foot *very* discreetly and was actually quite pleased. But she still kept up her complaint. "Victor sees me every single day with my face shining like a pearl and my lips as pale as raw mackerel. *This* won't deceive him one bit."

"Our purpose is not to deceive, darling. It is to show him — and, incidentally Mister Coverley, if he's there — it's to show each gentleman the sort of lady who might be standing by his side, greeting their guests at the entrance to some grand soirée. A wife is not merely a support, a helpmeet, a mother, a nurse in times of sickness, and … the other thing, you know. She is also an ornament for her husband to show off with pride. That's what this is all about. Of course he knows what you look like every day. This is to show him how you could look on a *special* day — and how he could be getting so much more for just a teeny little extra effort. Sit still or it'll smudge."

Tamsin surveyed the latest stage in her transformation and could not deny that her mother's subtle use of terracotta on her cheeks, pencil on her eyebrows, and *Bois de rose* cream on her lips had achieved a startling effect. "If only I could be sure of looking like this first thing every morning," she said, "I think I'd rise an hour earlier."

There was a further tussle between them when it came to deciding the degree of her décolletage. Harriet kept pulling it down an inch and Tamsin would hitch it up again. In the end, since Harriet realized that the girl could place it wherever she wanted the moment she left the house, she settled for an artistic solution, instead. She drew an eyebrow-pencil down the midline of her daughter's cleavage and feathered it outward on both sides with her thumb to accentuate the shadow; then a little pale powder on the most prominent parts of each bosom — and the effect was as good as the one she had wished for with a lower line to the bodice. The ultimate touch was an oriental jacket of the finest, most transparent gauze, embroidered with gold thread in Arabic sort of patterns, and all so feather-light that Tamsin hardly knew she was wearing it.

Harriet looked her up and down and saw that she had achieved precisely what she had set out to achieve: the dignity of the grand actress combined with the seductiveness of the ingénue chorus girl.

"We should have your likeness taken in this," she said. "it would be something to show your grandchildren."

"Yes, I could say, 'But for this gown, my darlings, you might not even exist, for this is the one that brought your grandad to his knees'!"

"You young gels don't know how lucky you are — the *freedom* you enjoy nowadays. When I was your age it would have been absolutely unthinkable for a single girl to dine out alone with a man — except, perhaps, in the very final weeks of a long engagement. Heaven alone knows where all this freedom is going to end."

On the way out Tamsin's last words to her mother were, "You know — the more I contemplate remaining a spinster, the more desperately do I feel I must find someone to marry. And yet the more I contemplate marriage, the more attractive it seems to remain single!"

"Go on with you!" Harriet said. "You're not the first young girl to have had such thoughts. They evaporate almost entirely once there's the sparkle of gold on that particular finger."

"*Almost* entirely?"

Her mother made sure the carriage was waiting before giving her a final push. "The few misgivings which remain after that are best dismissed as the *mystery* of marriage."

Tamsin had forgotten the discomforts of travelling inside a carriage — the rumble of the iron tyres and the excessive bounciness of the springs on seemingly level ground, contrasted with their obstinate stiffness when lurching over potholes. How different it was when those same springs were applied to a couple of tons of wrought steel, driven by an engine as silent as a ghost! It was such a pity that Standish Coverley, so warm in friendship, was so cool on romance; if she had to find some husband for sound commercial reasons, he was worth ten of Victor Thorne. If he were in the hôtel tonight — and saw her looking like this — perhaps he'd change his mind. The image that had faced her in the looking glass came back to her now: herself transformed. Herself and yet not herself. Herself almost as a third person. A property up for bids. That was it, really. Tonight she was a desirable property, launched into the oldest market on earth.

The idea that she was *desirable* sent a strange, thrilling kind of tremble all through her. That image of oneself as a third person, a semi-stranger staring back at one … there must be something in every mature woman that allows her to inspect herself in that way, to see herself as a man might see her. To see desirable features as a man might see them — the blush on the cheeks, the gleam in the hair, the rose-red lips, the swanlike neck, the swelling bosom.

She shivered with a curious mixture of excitement and fear. Half of her wanted to turn about and scuttle home and wipe all these powders and pigments away and curl up with a good book; the other half could not wait to cry 'On with the motley!'

There were a few spots of rain on the wind — and quite a boisterous wind it was, too, out there on the exposed Esplanade — as she huddled into herself beneath the doorman's umbrella and trotted across the pavement to the hôtel entrance. She thought briefly of David, somewhere out there, and then pushed him from her mind. David was this afternoon; the evening was Victor's. And, who knows, Standish's, too?

Victor was waiting for her in the lobby — waiting in the sense that she had predicted. He was lying almost to attention in a chesterfield armchair, pretending to be engrossed in one of the Plymouth evening papers. Colonel Hill, the craggy old gentleman with eyebrows like furze bushes, who had lately become a permanent resident and who now considered that particular chair to be his by right of custom, sat erect in an identical chair a little way off and trained upon the oblivious young man a glare that had reduced new subalterns to a month's voluntary silence in the mess. But that was in better days — far, far better days than these.

Tamsin fixed him with something that could almost have been a smile and started to walk across the lobby toward him. At first he surveyed her with manly interest, admiring just about everything he saw, except for that ridiculous hat, which looked like a hussar's shako after an accident with a cock pheasant. But his interest swiftly turned to alarm when it seemed she was intent on forcing him to offer up his seat. Him! Colonel of the 52nd of Foot — the Oxfordshires! Hero of the relief of Kimberley and the battle of Paardeburg in the late war! The man who had risked his life in far-flung lands for whippersnappers like this insolent young lounge lizard basking in *his* chair! He had just begun a plaintively awkward rise from his present, temporary seat when the tottie in the gauze jacket breezed past him with a smile and kicked the lizard on the shin, saying, "If you haven't smoked yourself to exhaustion, Victor, you could propel me vaguely in the direction of some grub. I could eat a horse, I ought to warn you."

The person she called Victor looked up over his paper, said "Righty-oh" and rolled lazily upright, half supporting himself on her outstretched arm, adding, "You look pretty edible yourself, you know."

And she, the minx, appeared to take it as a compliment!

This caused the colonel an even greater apoplexy than had the thought of vacating his seat. If he had ever been so remiss in his social duty at the age of this Victor person, he would have locked himself in his room with a loaded revolver and done the decent thing. And to crown it all, he raced out of that temporary chair and into his rightful one with such force that he cricked his neck — the neck that had gone through the Indian Mutiny without a murmur.

"Happy birthday, by the way," Victor said. "D'you feel any different now?"

"Curiously enough — yes," Tamsin replied as they glided across the dining-room carpet. "When I woke up this morning I realized at once that some enormous change had occurred during the night."

"Goodness!" He let the waiter deal with her chair. "Does it hurt? Is it curable?"

"I realized that my standards had just about doubled in height. You will find me much more demanding now that I have put away childish things."

"Well, I'm more than aware that you've put away your childish *dresses*. Am I allowed to say that that is quite a spiffing gown?"

"No, but I'll permit it on this occasion — on condition that you do not imspect it quite so blatantly for more than a few seconds each minute. Otherwise you will make me so self-conscious that I shall feel obliged to retire."

By now he could not have withdrawn his gaze from her face even if he had wanted to. This was a Tamsin he had never seen before — in fact, a Tamsin he had never even *met* before. So poised, so ready with her repartee ... and so subtly and inexpressibly beautiful. Some of it must be artificial, of course, but by candlelight he was damned if he could tell where Nature stopped and the apothecary took over.

He held the menu well up into his field of view to prevent his gaze from slipping down to that astonishing revelation of a bosom which, like her standards, seemed to have doubled in size overnight.

Had Dobbs achieved this transformation of face and torso? If so, his mother had let a jewel pass out of her hands. This was precisely the transformation Charlotte needed if she was to raise her sights beyond the few rural boors who were currently on the *qui-vive* around Peveril Hall. That and a few lessons in repartee from this extraordinary young lady.

It occurred to him that, since she seemed to be in such a worldly mood tonight, he might try nudging his luck a little further out along the scales of licence. "I'm interested to hear you say you'll permit such-and-such *on this occasion,* Tamsin. Do you believe that *all* permissions are nowadays conditional upon their occasion, then? Have we left the age of inflexible and unvarying rules behind?"

"Mock turtle soup and cold tongue with the vegetable compôte, please," she said. "You only need inflexible rules if you think that most people are determined to break them, and will do so at every opportunity. The more you can *trust* people to behave sensibly, the more flexible you can afford to be."

He ordered a dozen oysters and steak and kidney pudding with mashed potatoes and peas.

"And champagne," he added, raising a finger to the sommelier.

"It had better outshine a Bollinger," she said airily. "If that's at all possible."

"The old widow — a Veuve-Clicquot — is just as good, I think," he replied. "Why?"

"David Peters brought a bottle of Bollinger to my tea party this afternoon. It was wonderful. So you see — even my standards in champagne have leapt up overnight."

"The devil he did," Victor muttered. "Bollinger, eh? We'll go for a vintage, then."

"Look who's here!" she exclaimed. And when he did not follow her gaze she added, "Standish Coverley and Reg Trotter — but who's that lady with them?"

He still did not turn around. "Shortish woman?" he asked. "Dark? Rather bonny?"

She was gratified to see that Standish did not (could not?) take his eyes off her all the way across the floor. "Yes. You know her? Shh! They're coming here."

Victor sprang to his feet.

The woman said, "Oh, please don't get up." But he was already up so he didn't sit down again.

Reg gave Tamsin a passing nod and a smile and continued on to their regular table in the alcove, where he stood waiting for the other two.

"We shan't disturb you," Standish said. He turned to Tamsin, who at once thanked him for the roses.

"'Not so much honouring thee,'" he replied. "'As in the hope that in thy house, they might not withered be.'" He gave a little bow. "But now — allow me to present you to Mrs Cornwallis Trelawney. You may remember my mentioning her when we were looking at the Helston generating station. This is Miss Tamsin Harte."

"Oh yes — magnificent!" Tamsin said as they shook hands. "I do admire you."

She shook hands with Victor, too, apparently with no need for introductions. Meanwhile Standish continued: "She and her husband are singing in the Penzance Operatic Society's production of — what else? — *The Pirates* of that ilk. And most beautifully they do it, too."

Mrs Trelawney bobbed him an ironic curtsy. "Perhaps we can all meet up over coffee in the lounge later?" she suggested.

And so it was arranged.

"You and she have already met?" Tamsin asked.

"This afternoon," Victor said as he resumed his seat. "She popped in to pow-wow with Coverley between rehearsals. I think they're in quite a few enterprises together. From what he told me this afternoon, she had a Gog-and-Magog of all battles with her father when she was struggling to set up the generating company. He accepted her in the end — in fact, they now trade rather endearingly as 'Kernow and Daughter.' Kernow's her maiden name. But she's never trusted him fully, so she and her husband have formed business alliances elsewhere, including some with Standish, I gather. She may even be a partner here in the Queen's Hôtel."

On hearing this Tamsin clenched her fists and uttered a strangled, "Aaargh!"

"What now?" he asked in surprise.

"To have part-ownership of a hotel and just turn up for the occasional eats! If it were me, I'd want to spend every waking hour here."

"Well — that's enough about them," he said. "We'll get more of it over coffee, I'm sure." He preferred the nonchalant, sardonic young lady to this zealous fantasist.

She sensed it and, for the rest of the dinner, obliged him — this was, after all, *his* dinner in *her* honour. Throughout the meal his own attempts at nonchalance grew thinner and thinner, revealing a deeper excitement. At first it pricked her curiosity but that soon gave way to unease and, finally, to alarm. For it suddenly struck her that he was showing every sign of a man trying to work his way round to a proposal. Not that she had ever faced a man in that condition before, but the same instinct which tells a gazelle she is being stalked now warned Tamsin that a proposal was in the offing.

She tried not to panic. She would say no, of course, but the question was, how? She dismissed at once the first and most childish response, which would be to plead a call of nature the moment his intention became clear. Not only was that infantile, it merely prolonged the dilemma by five or ten minutes. But the etiquette-book response — that she was sensible of the honour, blah-blah, and would think it over most seriously — was no different in essence; indeed, it was worse, for it prolonged the dilemma by five or ten *days*. What she needed was some kindly way of saying a very cruel thing.

Here was a man — a fellow member of the human race, a decent, kindly, well-meaning fellow, even if he had not yet quite grown up — who was about to bare his innermost feelings, to pledge himself like a knight of old to serve and honour her unto death, and she had to find some amiable way of saying, 'No thanks, Victor. I'm waiting for something better to come along'!

It was impossible.

And ohmigod — he was about to begin!

She felt the blood drain from her face — indeed, from her entire head, for the room began to sway uneasily, like the deck of a boat on a mild sea. Paralyzed with panic she could only sit and watch as Victor gave their waiter a conspiratorial nod. Then he leaned forward and smiled at her — rather as her mother had smiled that morning when leading her to the unveiling of that dreaded sewing chest. Until this moment, though, she had not imagined that any birthday present could be less welcome than that monstrosity.

The waiter brought a box, a cube of about three inches, all wrapped in gaudy paper and tied with a gold thread.

"For you, my dearest," Victor murmured, taking it from the man and passing it immediately to her.

"For me?" She was amazed at how excited she managed to sound, considering how miserable she actually was. "Oh, Victor, I don't know that I'm …"

"Just open it!" He was quite literally sitting on the edge of his seat, performing what was indelicately called a buttock-jig and breathing like a runner after a hard sprint.

Her fingers, allies to her fear, fumbled with the knot. "I don't know why you should think I'm ...."

"Open it!" The words were loud enough to attract amused attention from several nearby tables.

Only when he reached across and threatened to open it for her did her fingers stop tripping each other up and do what they could have done in half a second at any other time. She slipped a nail under the edge of the paper and tore the glue spots apart. The wrapping fell open to reveal a distinguished-looking box, flocked in black to resemble velvet and embossed in gold with the copperplate legend: *F. Wearne, Goldsmith, Silversmith, and Jeweler — Causeway Head, Penzance.*

"I popped out and snapped it up today," Victor said, back in nonchalant mode now that it only remained for her to lift the lid.

Tamsin's heart fell yet further, which was another thing she would have said was impossible until that moment came. If this was the modern sort of engagement ring — that is, with a diamond setting rather than the simple gold band of their parents' generation — then he must have bought something the size of the Koh-i-Noor, the 'Mountain of Light.'

Her trembling fingers closed around the lid. She looked up, into his eyes, and whispered, "I'm scared!"

"No need, old thing." He laughed, now as overnonchalant as he had, moments earlier, been undernonchalant. "It's just an antique bauble."

Again it was his reaching across to perform the opening ceremony that galvanized her to act. She lifted the lid and, just for a moment, had no idea what she was looking at. She had been so direfully certain of finding an engagement ring inside that the gigantic blue-green blur meant nothing to her.

"Like it?" he asked eagerly, buttock-jigging once again.

Like it? What *was* it? Slowly, as she emerged from her daze, the gigantic blue-green blur resolved itself into the largest turquoise she had ever seen. "Oh, Victor!" The delight with which she now gazed at him was entirely due to the fact that here was no engagement ring, but he was not to know that.

"You do like it!" he exclaimed. "I knew you would. It's exactly the colour of your eyes — that's why I chose it. Here, let me put it on." He rose and came round the table.

"Oh, but ..." A sense of reality came flooding back. She clapped her hand over the open box. "I couldn't possibly ..." She was going to say, 'accept this,' but then realized it would be almost as cruel as the kindly kiss of death that had eluded her earlier. "... wear it with, er, this jacket. It would clash."

"Nonsense!" he replied. "You're just being modest. You'd never pick anything that clashed with the colour of your eyes."

It was too persuasive a point for her to be able to resist his fingers as they removed her hand and lifted out the gem.

There were gasps of admiration and envy from those same nearby tables. Tamsin surrendered to the inevitable. There was now no form of kindly rejection that would not also be a public humiliation for him.

"It was a brooch when I spotted it," he said, "but I had them remake it as a gold necklace."

As he leaned over her, lowering it slowly before her eyes, she became aware that he must be staring down into her cleavage. To her amazement, instead of doing the girlish thing and trying surreptitiously to shrink into herself, she breathed in deeply and leaned an almost imperceptible degree or two backward. In some obscure way, which she did not even want to think about, she knew she was instinctively rewarding him for this costly and quite unexpected gift. And the instinct was somewhere 'down there' in her sinews, not at all in her mind; indeed, if she had contemplated it for a moment, she would have remained as paralyzed as before.

This was a continuation of her thoughts on the way here; in fact, they had prepared her for this revelation. There was something in her veins that wanted, quite automatically, to gratify the male fascination and something in her mind that would equally robustly deny it and take refuge in her feminine modesty. Both felt quite natural, and both were at war inside her, but she had never felt the clash of them so strongly before. With some sense of irony, she also realized that, even without the embarrassing little homily that morning, she would instinctively have discovered that *discreet* relaxation of the moral code which her mother had urged upon her.

Victor clicked the two halves of the clasp together, checked that they held, and then gave their waiter another little nod.

Like a magician, the man produced a mock-tortoiseshell hand mirror from somewhere on his trolley.

"Oh, but I couldn't *possibly* look at myself in public!" Tamsin exclaimed. "It just isn't done."

"Of course it is!" He lifted the wing of his tail coat and made a symbolic protective curtain, smiling jocularly all around. The nearby diners, amused at the antics of Young Love, pretended to look away — that is, they *did* look away but only until Tamsin yielded and glanced at herself in the glass.

Glanced?

Gazed!

If her mother's discreet modifications had earlier amazed her, the addition of this magnificent gemstone — which was, indeed, precisely the colour of her eyes — was something quite transcendent. The mirror revealed a beautiful, refined, mature young lady who seemed to be offering an Alice-Through-the-Looking-Glass invitation to leave the stale old world behind and join her in there, in that exciting new order.

She had at last been transformed into that object of desire which can make men hollow-eyed and sleepless. More — she could feel that desire within her, too, fluttering, palpitating ... a lust for herself. In future, whenever she saw that hooded, enigmatic plea in a man's eye, she would know it for what it was, not as something alien, but as an echo in herself. She would become a fellow conspirator in his enhungered craving, too.

She turned from herself with a shiver. She closed her eyes and breathed deeply until it passed over.

She relinquished the glass at last and looked around. Mrs Trelawney was talking to Standish but he was gazing at her, Tamsin. He smiled at her and only then returned his attention to Mrs T. For some reason she now felt much more comfortable about accepting this gift from Victor.

He, meanwhile, had let his coat resume its natural, figure-hugging shape and the nearby diners were once more watching with amused, tender, undisguised interest. The women smiled encouragingly at her while the men divided their admiration between her and Victor. She knew well enough — now — what they were thinking: *Well done, you lucky beggar! You're on your way to the Great Reward.*

"I'm overwhelmed, Victor," she said as he resumed his seat. "And also a little ashamed."

"Ashamed? For heaven's sake — why?"

"Because I feel I've given you so little — certainly nothing that deserves this."

"But you have!" he insisted. "You've given me the most precious thing a girl can give a chap."

"What?"

"Hope, of course."

"Oh," she answered bleakly. "In a way, that's what I meant."

32 Mrs Trelawney and the two gentlemen were already in the lounge by the time Victor and Tamsin joined them. They had all witnessed the drama of the turquoise necklet and Mrs Trelawney mentioned it at once, begging to be allowed to see and touch it. Observing her now in a rather stronger light, Tamsin thought she looked rather young for a woman who had already achieved so much — under thirty, even. She held up the stone and at once noticed its perfect match with Tamsin's eyes. "You are so lucky, Miss Harte," she said. "The only thing that matches *my* eyes is amber — and I won't wear it because I can't bear the thought of all those teeny prehistoric insects being trapped like that."

Laughing, they all sat down again, and the woman went on: "We were playing a little parlour game just before you arrived — something like that one where you look at a tray full of random objects for ten seconds and then hide your eyes and see how many you can remember. Only we were playing it with real live people."

"The people in the dining room," Standish added. "I made a list of them all, so I'm referee. These two have to see how many of them they can remember."

"How *few!*" Reg corrected him.

"Quite," Mrs Trelawney concluded. "We are thoroughly ashamed of ourselves."

"Care to play?" Standish invited the newcomers.

"I'm afraid Tamsin and I only had eyes for each other," Victor announced grandly.

"Speak for yourself, sir!" Tamsin rejoined. "I think I could tell you most of them."

"Easily said," Standish challenged.

She took up the gauntlet. "All right! Fire away — where d'you want me to begin?"

"Clockwise from the alcove where we were sitting." He consulted his list. "The fat jolly couple at table thirteen."

She eyed him suspiciously. "Have you changed all the table numbers, then?"

He grinned as if she had caught him out — which, indeed, she had. "Why d'you ask?"

"Because you don't even have a table thirteen. The table you mentioned is table six, I'm almost sure."

His grin broadened to a laugh. "That's amazing. How d'you happen to know that? You've only been in the dining room once before tonight, and that was when you and your mother dined with me and Reginald. I didn't see you going round all the tables on that occasion."

He glanced inquiringly at Victor, who said, "Nor tonight, either, old chap."

They all turned again to Tamsin, wondering how she would explain it. She gave a guilty smile and admitted she had actually visited the dining room before either occasion. "It was immediately after we moved to Penzance," she said. "The week before we opened at the Morrab. I wanted to see how the premier hôtel in town laid their tables — because I was determined we'd be equal to them at least. So I sneaked in before the dinner service began and took notes."

Mrs Trelawney clapped her hands and cried, "Capital! And you remembered all the table numbers from that one visit?"

"It's not too difficult," Tamsin assured her. "It starts at table one in the corner farthest from the big window and goes round clockwise in a sort of spiral, except for number thirteen. Our table tonight, by the way, was twenty-one — appropriately enough!" She turned again to Standish. "And there was no fat couple at table six, only a pair of middle-aged gentlemen as thin as rakes. My guess is that they're on a walking holiday around the coast — from the way they both limped and tried to disguise it from each other. I hope you offered them a mustard bath?"

Mrs Trelawney was even more delighted at this and encouraged her to continue.

After she had described the occupants of the next three tables in equally sharp detail, it became clear that she could have gone on to dispatch all twenty-four. Then Standish challenged her to a few more tables chosen at random, by number. And when she managed that, he tore the list in two and said, "You're the outright champion, Tamsin. The rest of the field may retire."

"Then I claim a reward," she replied swiftly, before he could suggest something boring of his own. "A kiss from the umpire, if you please." And she pointed her left cheek at him.

Standish did the thing properly, going down on his knees and making such a production that even Victor was amused. And he kissed her in that ambiguous area between the corner of her lips and her cheek proper. In the circumstances, and with all that melodramatic build-up, she found it not nearly as exciting as she might have done; indeed, it was not exciting at all. He must have had the steak au poivre, she decided.

Still, it was an ice-breaker of sorts. Next time would be easier. And different.

"Tell them how you remember my name," Reg said when Standish was seated again. "She's the Memory Lady!"

Two waiters poured their coffees in demitasses and left a full carafe to keep hot over a low candle.

"Oh, Reg!" She gave an embarrassed laugh. "I don't need to do that any more, not in your case."

"I know that. But you still do it with the names of all the new guests. Tell them how you did it with mine when Mama and I first came."

"I've even forgotten," she said. "Did I imagine you mashing a plate of cabbage with a pig's foot?"

"What?" cried a fascinated Mrs Trelawney.

"No!" Reg replied. "The principle's the same but it was much funnier." He turned to the other two. "She imagined my frizzy hair was a cauliflower head ..."

"No need to *imagine* it," Victor put in.

Reg made a fist at him and warned him that he didn't yet know how she remembered 'Victor Thorne.' "Anyway," he went on, "she imagined me holding a pig's foot in my mouth and my hair turned into a cauliflower head."

Mrs Trelawney frowned in bewilderment at Tamsin, who explained: "Cauliflower gives me veg. Veg — Reg. And pig's foot — Trotter."

"She never gets them wrong, either," Reg added.

"I do," Tamsin admitted. "There was a dreadful moment when I called a Mrs Hastings, 'Mrs Battle'."

"What about Trelawney, then?" the woman challenged.

"Easy," Tamsin told her. "The moment we were introduced — that's always the best moment for this memory trick — I made myself picture you up a ladder, in the branches of a dead tree, sticking patches of green turf all over it. Making the *tree* *'lawny,'* you see? When I started with this trick I would just have thought of a tree, a lawn, and a knee — in your case. But it doesn't work. I don't know why. The image will only stick in your mind if it's utterly ludicrous."

"Now Coverley," Standish challenged.

"I pictured you lying in a meadow — a lea — and I mean *in* it, so that it covered you. Like a tumulus."

"Gruesome!" Reg exclaimed.

"Don't leave me out, please," Victor begged.

She'd been waiting for it ever since Reg had returned the sneer. "I needed no assistance to remember your name, my dear," she replied. "From the moment our eyes met, you were the *victor* over my heart."

"Oooaah!" the others chorused, slightly embarrassed because she actually seemed to mean it.

"And the Thorne part?" he persisted.

"Where would love be without its thorns? — one of which, I must warn everybody, is about to begin, this very minute, unless you can manage to change the subject! In my opinion, little twenty-one-year-old girls should be seen and not heard!"

Victor turned to Mrs Trelawney. "Do tell us about this Gilbert and Sullivan production. Where is it to be? Can we take a box and bring all our friends?"

And so, for the rest of the hour they passed in each other's company, the conversation moved from one generality to the next. Toward the end Tamsin went to the ladies' room, where she was joined a moment later by Mrs Trelawney. As they stood in front of the looking glasses, scrutinizing their appearances before rejoining the men, the woman said, "Forgive me if I trespass, Miss Harte, but from the moment Mister Thorne produced that jeweler's box in the dining room, I could not take my eyes off you. It's none of my business, of course, but I assure you I do not ask out of idle curiosity. I had the impression you were expecting it to contain something quite different — an engagement ring, perhaps?"

The woman was so pleasant, her whole attitude so unthreatening, that Tamsin found it impossible to take offence at this intrusion; in fact, it hardly seemed like intrusion, at all.

"Bullseye!" She pulled a face. "I assure you things have not progressed so far between Mister Thorne and me, but he is so ... well ... what can I call it?"

"Mercurial? Impetuous?"

"To put it kindly. In fact, he has no right, really, even to give me this pendant. I don't know how I'm going to be able to accept it. But I couldn't turn it down on the spot — it would have been so humiliating for him. I just wish he hadn't done it, that's all. Have you any suggestions?"

Mrs Trelawney smiled. "If it should ever come to a clash of wills between the two of you ..."

"Oh, it will!" Tamsin assured her.

"Then, if it's of any comfort to you, I don't think *your* will is ever going to experience the slightest difficulty in prevailing over his. And in the meantime I shouldn't worry too much about that turquoise. After all, the decision to buy it was his alone — and it was obviously *made* for you, with those eyes!" She touched Tamsin's cheek gently, taking care to avoid the terracotta portion. "Do forgive my impertinence but I did just wonder if wedding bells were in the offing."

"Not with Mister Thorne, rest assured!"

Mrs Trelawney caught the hint of an unspoken 'but ...' behind her reply. "Then with someone else?" she dared to ask.

Tamsin blushed. "I'd rather not say."

The moment she spoke the words she regretted it — especially when she saw the look of intense disappointment that passed across Mrs Trelawney's face.

"I mean," she added, "*he* hasn't the faintest idea of my feelings about him. And — to be honest — I'm still in two minds about the man myself."

"Enough said!"

On their way back up the corridor Tamsin said, "I wonder if Standish will ever tie the knot?"

Mrs Trelawney halted and stared at her. "Is that idle curiosity, or …?" She did not name an alternative.

"Idle curiosity," Tamsin assured her. "I probably won't get the chance tonight, but you will. You could let him know I have at least part of the answer to a question he once asked me — if you'd be so kind?"

"Gladly!" Her eyes danced with amusement. "Perhaps he'll explain it to me, too?"

Tamsin nodded, ignoring the blatant invitation. "That would be his prerogative, not mine."

Just before they re-entered the lounge, Mrs Trelawney said, "There's something my husband once said to me before we were married, and I've never forgotten it. Perhaps you won't mind if I pass it on now?"

"Please do." Tamsin waited eagerly.

"It was when I was working day and night to beat my father at his own game. Just because he wouldn't take me seriously and tried to freeze me out. And Cornwallis — he's my husband now, but at that time he was my appallingly neglected fiancé — he advised me to be very careful when I compiled my list of wishes. 'Because,' he said, 'strong-minded people like you have a way of persuading Fate to grant them all.' "

"And you think the same applies to me?" Tamsin asked.

"What I think is neither here nor there. It's what you think that matters. If you think the advice might apply to you, there's no harm in heeding it."

It was by then close to midnight and Tamsin said she had to go home, otherwise she'd be turned back into a pumpkin. Standish insisted on accompanying them to the cloakroom, then to the door. There he kissed Tamsin's hand, rather theatrically, and, referring back to her spying mission in his dining room, asked her casually if the Queen's had any other department she would care to investigate.

She was on the point of telling him what Charlotte had blurted out that afternoon; but she realized it would take far too long — and Victor was already chafing, probably. Besides, Mrs Trelawney would tell him, and that would make him very keen to see her again — unencumbered by other social obligations. So, although she realized he was just being facetious with his offer to inspect other departments of the Queen's, she also saw it was too good a chance to pass by. *"Every* department," she replied firmly.

It took him by surprise, of course, but he was too good a hôtelier to let it show; in fact, he even pretended to be pleased. "Shall we say this Friday, then?" he suggested. "Come to luncheon and I'll show you around afterwards." He bowed and was gone.

A full gale was blowing outside. Tamsin felt guilty that she had not given a moment's thought to poor David, somewhere out there, since the moment they had entered the hôtel, about four hours earlier. She asked the driver of their carriage if he thought any of the fleet had put out from Newlyn and he replied that Newlyn men were all mad but none was mad enough to do that. She wondered if common sense had kept David in port after all, even though he had seemed so determined to test the *Merlin's* new engines to the limit against this deterioration in the weather. If Victor had not been there, she would have directed the coach to Newlyn first, just to set her mind at rest.

In the carriage on their brief journey home, Victor took her in his arms and kissed her with a barely controlled passion. Physically she found it as pleasing as ever but her worries about David made it impossible for her to yield as completely as she usually did — indeed, as she would have liked to do.

His left arm crushed her to him, leaving his right hand free to caress her face, her cheek, her neck ... So much was by now part of their established ritual. But tonight he added something new. The thumb and three fingers of his right hand stayed above her collarbone, but the little finger began straying just below, into territory that was usually well covered up and scarcely available to fingers, big or little.

When the incursion met with no immediate protest a second finger slipped down into that hitherto inviolable space. She held her breath. It wasn't unpleasant — quite the opposite. And this

was, after all, something along the lines her mother had exhorted
her to encourage …

But no! That was to help a man decide that you were the only
girl in the world — and she was pretty sure that Victor was there
already. So if she continued to permit his fingers to stray, it was
merely to satisfy her own curiosity. That was all right as long as it
was clearly understood. By her, anyway.

It wasn't many seconds before a third finger joined the two
already there — then a fourth and finally the thumb

By now the space between her collarbone and the hem of her
bodice was tingling with stray fingers. She felt an answering
tingle in her nipples, even though his fingertips were still inches
away from them; all the same, she knew they wanted to feel his
touch there, too.

And yet the moment his little finger, the smallest and boldest
pioneer of the five, touched her there (and, to be fair, it could
have been an accident, caused by the sudden jolt of the carriage
as it drew up outside the Morrab) something inside her head
cried *Stop!* so loudly that she felt sure he must have heard it, too.
She had not the heart to push his hand roughly away, so,
instead, she folded her entire body inward, toward his, and
pressed herself tight against him until only an oyster knife could
have parted them again. She made it seem like a sudden rush of
overpowering passion, so that he wouldn't feel rejected. Tonight
of all nights she owed him that.

And tomorrow could take care of itself.

33   When Cicely and Walter Thorne returned from Peveril
Hall the following day, and heard what Victor had
done, they were furious. Cicely, seeking a private place for her
inquisition, made him accompany her out onto the Esplanade,
where it was still blowing a full sou'-westerly gale. Unable to
converse above its roar, they walked toward town and, near
Battery Point, found a deserted café where they were welcomed
like rescuers. Cicely chose a seat by the window, where the
moaning of the wind would mask from other ears what she knew
would be a frank and painful conversation.

"What did I tell you?" she demanded as soon as the waitress had taken their order. "What did I say was our purpose in moving out of the Queen's and into that poky little boarding house of theirs?"

"Block Tamsin. Spotlight Charlotte," he replied laconically.

"That is a crude pastiche of what I actually said. I told you to steer the narrowest path between the courtship of Miss Harte on the one hand and mere friendly association with her on the other. I said you were to remain cooler than the first but warmer than the second. The whole idea, as I'm sure I made quite clear at the time, was to place a temporary obstacle — a *very* temporary obstacle — between dear Mister Coverley and the Harte girl while simultaneously opening the way for the man to see what a catch Charlotte would be, especially as she was no longer a guest under his roof. I'm sure you recall it all now?"

"Just so," Victor agreed. "Block one, spotlight t'other. Isn't that what I said?"

The waitress brought their tea and Bath buns.

And the mater was waiting for a proper answer. He could hardly tell her the truth — that he had adopted her absurd 'plan' in the first place because he was bored with Penzance and Tamsin was the only interesting feature in the entire county — that he knew Charlotte had her mind set on other things, anyway — that, from being merely fascinated with Tamsin, he had become obsessed with her — that he was now fighting to cure himself of that obsession as fiercely as any dope fiend might fight to abstain from the fatal poppy — and that last night's *tête-à-tête* with the darling girl had been as irresistible as an opium pipe to the same poor slave.

"How much did this turquoise cost, anyway?" his mother asked — still waiting for her son's defence.

"It was a brooch in the shilling tray in a rag-and-bone man's shop," he lied. "The fellow thought it was a piece of coloured glass. It cost me more to get it changed to a pendant with a gold chain and patent clasp."

"How much more?"

"Ten bob — and you're the only person who knows it. So if word should reach Tamsin's ear, I'll know how. And, more important, by whom."

She bristled. "How dare you threaten me! I shall, of course, consider what you have told me and, *if I so decide,* I shall tell Miss Harte everything. You speak of confidence? Let me tell you — your father and I have lost all confidence in you and your sense of judgement. You were entrusted with the simplest of tasks — *two* simple tasks — and, as far as anyone can tell, you have failed at both. The fact that *you* paid a mere song for this expensive turquoise is really neither here nor there. You have obviously allowed Miss Harte to believe you gave full value for it — and it *is* a valuable stone, am I not right?"

He just managed to stop himself from replying that its value was not one millionth part of a millionth part of the preciousness of her who received it. "It's just a lump of cupro-aluminium phosphate," he replied. "But I suppose they'd ask a fair bit for it in Bond Street."

Neither his sarcasm nor his admission that the stone was valuable pleased her. " You're so impetuous," she said. "You just don't think ahead at all. When a man gives a lady jewelry of any kind, she is bound to see a link between its value in the world and her value in his esteem. A gem of any kind would have misled Miss Harte into supposing you are in love with her. To give her such a large and costly stone is as good as saying that she, too, is most precious and your love is equally large. Well, the harm's done now — though no actual promises were made, I hope?"

"What sort of promises? I say, these are good buns, what?"

"Don't be deliberately obtuse, dear. I know you too well. You have not made a proposal of marriage?"

"No."

"And I trust you have not spoken those three fatal words, 'I love you' yet?"

He shrugged awkwardly. "Not just those three, no."

"What *have* you said, then?"

"Well, she's spoken them to me ..."

"That's neither here nor there. Nobody's going to sue *her* for breach of promise!" Cicely laughed.

He saw a way of nudging her onto a related but less awkward topic — from his point of view. "Ah, yes — but what about *her* feelings, though?"

"What about them? They're her business, not ours. If you had only acted throughout in the way I directed, you would have captured her affections on nothing more than the promise of a light-hearted summer romance at the seaside. If she had chosen to take your playful advances seriously, then that would have been her bad luck. One could have told her not to be so trusting the next time some handsome young *flâneur* winks at her along the Esplanade. But this costly gift makes *that* escape a little difficult." She vanished into her own thoughts for a moment and then added, "I wonder if there's not some way of getting it back from her?"

"Absolutely not!" he exclaimed.

"I'm not talking about your attempting it," she said. "Obviously *I* would have to arrange it all."

"Steal into her room at night?" he sneered.

"No," she replied calmly. "Just explain what sort of a romantic, hot-headed idiot you are and tell her to expect nothing to come of it in the end. She might even accept money for it, then. Yes! She wouldn't dare sue for breach of promise if it could be shown she was as mercenary as all that!"

He peered out of the window, watching huge breakers smash against the sea wall of the Esplanade — sudden vertical sheets of white, and whiter than any laundry would dare to promise. If David Peters had been fool enough to put to sea in the teeth of this gale, he thought, the man deserved everything Old Father Neptune threw at him.

"As for Mister Coverley," his mother went on, "I begin to fear that he is a broken reed."

"It would be news to him, I'm sure."

"I wonder ...?" she mused.

Victor caught a certain sharp edge to her tone and became alert at once. "You know something," he said.

"I heard a whisper or two. Well-connected friends in Exeter — never mind who. I think there may be trouble brewing for Mister Coverley."

"What? Do tell?" This was the best news of the season.

She eyed him coldly a long while, making him shiver. At length she said, "I think we'll leave it at that for the moment. I only tell you this much in order to explain why I've changed my mind about him. It may all blow over — or he may be the innocent dupe of ... of an extremely cunning plot. It's really no concern of ours. But for the moment, all attempts to — how did you express it — *spotlight* Charlotte are to cease. We shall cut our losses and return home as soon as possible."

"Today?" he asked in dismay.

"Of course not. Such haste would arouse suspicions if this expected trouble does befall Mister Coverley — suspicions that we were implicated in some way. No. We shall give due notice and leave at the agreed time."

"Well, if I'm to have no more to do with Miss Harte," Victor said, "we can't leave soon enough for me!" He was thinking that, with his parents and sister out of the way, he could return to Penzance and enjoy a clear field. True, he hadn't the income as yet to support himself independently — and almost all his savings had gone on that turquoise for Tamsin — but the moneylenders would fall over themselves to let him have whatever he wanted against next year's inheritance.

She was at once suspicious of his eagerness, but all she said was, "I'm glad you agree. In fact, but for one thing, I'd tell Mrs Harte we'll be leaving this Saturday."

"What's that?"

"This Countess de Ath. I'm intrigued. What do we know about her? And why should she pick an obscure little boarding house at the tail end of England for her bereavement? Our library shelves were still under the dust sheets or I should have hunted for the *Almanac de Gotha* yesterday."

"No need for any of that," he assured her. "Tamsin has already looked her up — in the public library at the top of Morrab Road."

"Well!" His mother was obviously impressed but — equally obviously — unwilling to say so. "The *public* library!" she said. "It would never have crossed my mind. What does 'Mrs Lock the turnkey's wife' or 'Tom Tallow the candlestick maker' want with a reference book on the aristocracy of Europe? Never mind, though — what did she learn?"

"That the said Countess must be well into her eighties, for she married the Count in the eighteen-forties ..."

"What was her maiden name?"

"The Count turned ninety-two last month. Her maiden name was Esterhazy."

"One of the grand families of Europe! Curiouser and curiouser! Any issue?"

"None listed. Of course, there could be a few on the wrong side of the blanket. But the title will have died with him."

"So — barring a few no doubt trivial bequests to illegitimates — she will inherit the lot. How many addresses were given, did Miss Harte say?"

"Not to me. But you can go to the library yourself and …"

"Me? Go into one of those places? How *could* you! They're full of smelly tramps secretly drinking methylated spirits while they pretend to be reading leaders in the *Morning Post*. I've heard all about them at Mendicity Alliance meetings. But you could do it for me, dear … please?"

"If it means I'm forgiven?"

"It would mean you've taken the first *teeny* step toward forgiveness." She became thoughtful again. "There's still the mystery of why an octogenarian countess from one of the noblest families in Europe should arrange to spend her period of mourning in a modest boarding house as far from Europe as you can possibly get — without going to Ireland, of course."

"Tamsin says some friends of theirs called Lock — Harold and Miriam Lock, I think — met her in Baden and puffed the place up no end."

"Even so … it's pretty odd. Especially as she made the preliminary arrangements even before he died — or so I hear."

"Oh, that's true. She did. Tamsin thinks they may have spent themselves out. They may have run up substantial debts and so the Countess is coming here to hide from her creditors. She says they're going to ask her for some payment in advance."

When his mother made no response to this he said, "What are you thinking now?"

"Miss Harte," she said. "That girl is too shrewd for her own good. At twenty-one a girl should be innocent, trusting, naïve, ingenuous, and charming … unsullied by the world and its ways — like your dear sister. But Miss Harte at twenty-one is already what she should not become until she has been thirty-nine for some years at least. What will she be like then!"

Still your daughter-in-law, I hope! he replied in the silence of his thoughts.

"However," his mother continued, "if her speculation is correct, then I do not see how we can possibly leave Penzance without witnessing the Countess's arrival and her settling in. If she should turn out to be a lively sort of eighty-year-old — and I have met many who become so in the months after widowhood turns their hair gold with grief — without children of her own — and with or without a goodly fortune ... who knows? She might quite like to take Charlotte under her wing and help bring her out in the world. Such patronage can lead to an extremely advantageous marriage. In fact, if she were broke, she might be glad of a little honorarium in return."

The furious mother who had entered the café not half an hour earlier had completely gone; in her place was a smiling, dedicated woman with a new sense of purpose. Indeed, she was so ecstatic at the prospects for the week ahead that she mistook a silver sixpence in her purse for the fractionally smaller silver threepenny bit and so tipped the waitress twice what she considered the girl to be worth.

But what unquestionably revealed her excitement was that fact that, once she discovered her error, she did not return to the café and ask the girl for threepence back.

34   Tamsin fretted through her work on the morning after her coming-of-age celebration at the Queen's. She did not even dare look at the turquoise Victor had given her; heavy though it was as a gem, it lay heavier still on her conscience. She thought of a thousand ways of returning it to him, but none that would not also hurt him where he was most vulnerable — in his pride. However, if the best antidote to worry is an even greater worry, she had that, too — the worry of not knowing whether David had put out from Newlyn the previous night.

She lingered over her marketing in the town that morning, calling at every fishmonger and asking if they had news of any boat sailing from the port last night. The answer was a double no — no one in his right mind would have done so, but no, they had no personal knowledge of the matter, one way or the other.

So, having forced herself to eat a hearty lunch — for she did not know what sort of afternoon now faced her and she did not want the distractions of hunger on top of everything else — she set off to walk around the shore to Newlyn. Never had one statute English mile seemed so long. Bent almost double against the gale, she had to thrust herself step by step into its steady blast. Running was impossible. Even walking over the level ground seemed more like climbing a steep slope. Time and again she had to stop and fight for breath; and the muscles down the front of her legs, beside her shinbones, seemed perpetually on the verge of cramp. Thank heavens the rain had at least passed over.

In fact, the sun put in a fitful appearance when she was half way there — or, rather, half a dozen fitful appearances as gaps in the cloud opened up. It showed itself in searchlight beams that played fitfully across the bay, highlighting at random the white horses that stretched as far as the eye could see — which, as she knew from David's little talk on the subject, on a much happier day than this, was not actually very far.

Curiously enough, that knowledge was a comfort to her now. To know that 'the far-distant horizon' of the poet's imagination was, in fact, no more than eight miles away from her present elevation meant that David could, even now, be a mere nine miles from port and yet be out of sight. And nine miles was the distance she had steered between Kynance and 'Portlemm.' He might even have put to sea, realized how foolhardy he had been, and run before the gale into that very harbour. If so, a telegram from Porthleven would surely be waiting to set her mind at rest the moment she arrived at the Peterses' little cottage on the harbour front.

'No fishing' does not mean a day of rest for fishermen. At every loft the doors were open and men sat or squatted about, mending nets, repairing sails, inspecting long lines of vicious-looking fishhooks, or making good the ravages of time and tide — and brandy — upon their lobsterpots. Most were one floor up. She stopped by the first one she found at ground level and peered inside. It reeked of tar, chewing tobacco, and fish. At first she could see nothing, for they worked without candlelight, making do with whatever daylight filtered in through the open door — half of which was now occupied by her. Soon, however, she made out one dim figure, nearest her, sitting cross-legged to splice a rope around a metal eye. She asked him if anyone had put to sea the previous evening.

"He did, Miss Harte," the man replied — for, of course, the whole village knew of her and of David's interest. "Step inside if you mind." He rose and came to join her at the door — a short, muscular man with the rolling gait of a sailor. "Stop out the wind a bit."

"And has he …"

But his face answered her before she could finish the question.

"Could he have put in at Portlemm?" she asked. "And if so, would he have sent a telegram or something?"

The man poked his head out into the wind and then caught hold of her arm, propelling her half out again. "See that there woman — with the dark-brown skirt and the black shawl — goin' 'long by th'old quay there?"

'Drab skirt and drab shawl' described just about every woman in Newlyn, but, fortunately, only one of them was passing the stub of the old quay at that moment. "Yes," she said.

"Well, that's Oenone Peters, the postmistress. David's aunty. Her could tell 'ee more'n anyone else here. 'Specially if there's been a telegram."

She turned to thank him but he pushed her onward, saying, "Run, maid, and you'll catch she up. Her's now gwin up with that basket to Penlee Point, to old Benny Peters, see."

Tamsin caught up with the woman at the edge of town, where the coastal lane leads on to Mousehole, the next fishing village, a mile or so to the south. "Mrs Peters!" she called out with her last gasp of breath.

The woman turned round. "Miss Harte?"

She nodded, being too busy getting her breath back to speak.

"I said you'd come. Old Benny said you wouldn't. He said you'd just send to find out."

"Has there been any word?" she managed to ask at last.

"No, my lover. The old man's been there since sunrise. I'm now taking a bit croust and tay for 'n." She lifted a corner of the cloth that covered her basket and Tamsin caught the whiff of hot pasty.

"Can I take it up to him for you?" she asked. "Or were you going there anyway?"

The woman hesitated. "Well," she said. "Tell 'ee what — I'll take 'ee so far as the path that do go up Penlee Head. That's some climb for these old bones."

Tamsin took this as a hint to relieve her of the basket. She wondered if, when she reached her early forties, she, too, might be talking of 'old bones' to youngsters half her age.

Talk was desultory even though they were now in the lee of the hill, which reduced the force of the gale considerably. But she did manage to establish that the entire Peters family — indeed, the whole of Newlyn — was angry at David and Harry for tempting fate by putting to sea last night. The so-called engine test over calm seas, in full sunlight, inside the bay had proved nothing. It only needed the spark to fail once and the gale would drive them bare-masted onto the rocks.

"Why did they do it, then?" Tamsin asked. "Surely they understand that as well as anyone?"

"Well now ..." Oenone stopped to catch her breath. Selling stamps and writing out telegrams did little for a person's fitness. "That's a question, see. You do know, I s'pose, he lost two brothers — Harvey and Jacko — backalong a while. Nineteen-oh-three it was. In the Fall. November time. The eighth as I recall — the sabbath. They should ought to of been back the day before, by rights." They set off again. "David wasn't but twenty then but he always said as if he'd been aboard, they wouldn't never of foundered. He's always been the last to put back to port in bad weather — like he's got to prove it, see?"

They were nearing the headland now, which reduced their shelter from the wind. About a hundred paces short of it they came to a stile beside the road and, beyond it, a path that wound in a zigzag up the slope.

"Now, my lover," Oenone said. "That's the path as many a widow has trod! When you do get up top there, you'll see a coastguard shelter and the old man leaning fore'nenst it to steady his spyglass, I'm sure — if he's not inside."

Tamsin thanked her and set off up the path. There were places where the strong and fit had shunned the zigzag and gone directly up the slope. She tried the first few and then settled for the longer but gentler path for the rest of the way. It was a climb of two hundred and fifty feet in only a quarter of a mile. And, as David himself had told her on the day they had lifted the brandy, the view from the top was over eighteen miles.

The Captain, as she still liked to call him, saw her when she was just a head and shoulders, cut off by the edge of the hill. "You come when you could then, maid," he called out, his voice carrying to her downwind. "I said 'ee would."

She was too puffed to reply. She had to push hard down on her thighs with her free hand, like a pistons, to make the last few yards. He came back along the path to meet her and relieve her of the basket.

"Meet Oenone, did 'ee?" he asked. "Her'll be some glad she never had to make that climb!"

"Believe … you …" she panted.

He put an arm around her shoulders and pressed her forward into the shelter of the lookout. "Coastguard'll be here four o'clock," he said. "Us'll have to get out then." He laughed. "We met first in one shelter and now we meet in another!"

With eager hands he disinterred the pasty from the cloth, broke it in two, and offered half to her. "Eat 'n fitty-like," he said. "There's no knives nor forks."

She thanked him and explained that she had already had a good lunch — for this very purpose. The pasty did smell delicious, though. Perhaps she and Mrs Pascoe should look out some old Cornish recipes and offer them alongside a purely fish menu? "No sign of the *Merlin,* I suppose?" she asked.

"She'll come back when her hold is full," he replied.

So he wasn't going to admit to her that David was in any danger; the good news he was so anxiously waiting for up here was merely of a full hold, not of the safe return of his last remaining son from the storm.

She had to admit that, from this height, the sea did not look nearly as ominous as it did from the shore. The white horses that dotted its surface were fathered by the wind, acting on ripples. The waves that made up the underlying swell were much farther apart — several boat lengths, in fact. They did not seem menacing until they reached the shallows, inshore, where they reared up suddenly and fell upon the beaches and rocks with a thunderous roar. All around this end of Mount's Bay, as far as Cudden Point, six miles away to the east, she could see the sudden stabs or streaks of white as the waves boiled and foamed in their death throes against the land.

Porthleven was hidden behind Trewarvas Head. In fact, the next part of the coast she could see from there was the blue-grey streak of the Lizard Peninsula, lost in the haze that hid the entire horizon.

"We can see what? Eighteen miles?" she asked.

He could only nod, his mouth being full of beef, potato, and turnip. "You'll share a dish o' tay, maid?" he asked when he had swallowed it. He took a pint lemonade bottle, full of sweet, milky tea, from the basket and filled a black enamel mug. "This'll be my side, that's yours," he said, offering it to her first.

She sipped and then drank gratefully. Normally she'd rather drink ice-cold seawater than sweet tea but somehow her exertions and the buffeting she had endured turned it into an elixir. He topped up the mug and drank from it in turns with bites of pasty — 'cement mixing' as her father had called it. But, she supposed, it was something one simply had to do if one had lost a lot of back teeth.

Since he was pretending that nothing was really amiss, she decided to challenge him head-on. "Your sister-in-law says it's a stubborn streak in David that drives him to do reckless things like this," she said as soon as the last of the pasty had been washed down with the last of the tea.

"Stubborn?" He nodded. "'Es, stubborn." His tone was ambiguous; she could not tell whether he was proud or critical.

He put a spyglass to his eye, resting its other end against the stone that fringed the open doorway, and scanned the sea from west to east; she said nothing to distract him, though she longed to know what he really thought of David's chances against last night's storm. After three sweeps he handed the glass to her, saying, "See if they young eyes of yourn can do better."

She took it from him with trembling fingers. The wind had filled her eyes with water and she had to wipe them, too. *Please, please, please let him be there!* she prayed silently, though whether it was to God or to some more primitive arbiter of human destiny she was unclear. She raised the glass to her eye.

She copied the Captain, sweeping from west to east, beginning at the horizon and working closer with each successive sweep. There were plenty of steamboats and tall-masted sailing ships out there — well out, for the Cornish coast is a notorious graveyard of the hundreds that have sought its shelter. But she saw no sign of a small mast and a trapezoid sail. Or ought she to be looking for the flotsam of a wreck? She did not ask it aloud.

For the next hour they took turn and turn about to scan the bay. Often, in the act of handing over the glasses, he would pause and start a conversation. One time he admitted that when he'd agreed to buy the engine for the *Merlin,* he'd intended it to make normal fishing trips safer, not to encourage his son to put to sea when no sane man without an engine would set his nose beyond the harbour wall. But he spoke in such an offhand way — as if to say, 'Just my luck!' — that she could not give *her* true opinion of his folly.

However, if he was trying to buck Fate, or whistle down the wind, with all this seeming nonchalance, it was a bad decision, for he could not keep his true feelings back forever. She, for her part, had simply tried to match his mood and seem equally unconcerned. So, she wondered, was either of them deceiving the other any longer?

" 'Twas good of 'ee to come all this way, maid," he said on another of those occasions.

And she pooh-poohed any claim to goodness ... she had been going for a walk anyway ... happened to meet his sister-in-law ... volunteered to carry his basket of croust. That was all.

"Shall I tell the boy you did come all the way out here to see was he safe or no?" he asked another time.

"If you don't," she replied lightly, "I'm sure Mrs Oenone will, so where's the harm?"

At other times he tried to disguise his fears by telling the sort of tales any Cornishman will tell another at any sort of meeting at all — at a bus stop, by the hearth, sharing a mile ... anywhere at all. He told her, for instance, of a farmer who had the land on the far side of the valley from where they were standing — over toward the hamlet of Sheffield, above Mousehole. "Stanley Roseveare, he'm called. And when he's out ploughing or harving he won't stop for man nor beast, see. His missiz can stand by the headland and baal her head off and he won't pay she no more heed than he'd pay a mother-marget on his coat ..."

"What's that?"

He thought a moment and said, "A bluebottle. So then one day when she had her mind set to stop 'n, out she goes to the field with a basket on her arm and a cloth over the basket. Nothin' in the basket, o' course, but he don't know that, see? And ole Roseveare, he dropped the hames, left the horse stood where 'twas, an come running like ... like ..."

"So quick as a witnick?" she offered.

"'Es!" He laughed delightedly. "You got 'n — so quick as a witnick! My soul! Us'll have 'ee Cornished yet, maid!"

But all the stories and all the good-humoured banter in the world did nothing to disguise his anxiety for his son.

She wished there was something she could say, some sign she could make, to let him know that she, too, cared more than she was admitting.

She tried an oblique approach in the end. "I wonder if Sarah Rowe would be here if she knew he'd put out to sea last night."

"Sarah *Rowe!*" he exclaimed. "Why she's dead these thirty years. He never told 'ee about she?"

Tamsin was on the point of explaining that it must be a different Sarah Rowe when the old man added, "Why, I courted she for years — or tried to — afore I settled for th'old woman I got. Saint Ives people they were. Lot of actions, they had."

"Actions?"

"Lawdydaw folk. Her wouldn't so much as look at I. A Newlyn boy!" He spat down the wind and laughed.

"Was she the one who married some fine fellow up Carbis Bay?" she asked.

"That's the one! Henry Noy — son of Cap'n Noy, who retired from the East India trade and ran the ferry between Lelant and Hayle. Much good it did her, too. He never could fix no babby in her. And then she died of a malignancy. Weel!" He looked at her with new interest. "So David has told 'ee all about that, then, has he? He must be some hurrisome for *thee,* maid — that's all I can say."

She wanted to explain that David had, in fact, merely purloined the story in order to ... well, what? To put her off, she supposed.

Well, she didn't need any putting off, thank you! All she ever wanted to be with him was friends. However, it was getting too complicated to explain, so she just let it go and went back to scanning the bay, with or without his spyglass. And always, before each sweep, she repeated that same silent prayer — *Please let him be there this time!*

She tried to picture the map of Mount's Bay and let her mind's eye roam this way and that, north to south, east to west, until something inside her cried, *There!* — a sort of mystical, mental dowsing. Then she would sweep that area minutely through the glass, feeling sure that this time her intuition had borne fruit.

It was all to no avail. By four o'clock, when the coastguard ought to have arrived and kicked them out, she felt she could draw from memory every rock on every cliff from Marazion to Cudden Point, to say nothing of the dozens of reefs and shoals that ringed the shore, each one a hazard for the unwary.

She was just about to tell the Captain that she had to be getting back to Penzance when he nudged her with his elbow and, passing over the glass, murmured, "I hope these eyes do not deceive me now."

She followed his pointing finger, almost due south, and at once saw … no, that could not be it — a two-masted sailing ship right on the horizon. A sloop? A brig? A barquentine? She almost laughed — here was a matter of life and death and she was worrying about naval correctitude! "That two-masted ship," she said, "which way from that? If you imagine that's the centre of a clock face?"

He took the glass back from her, hunted around, and handed it back, saying, "Seven o'clock." His attitude was subtly different this time — much more sure of himself and thus much less dependent on her confirmation.

This time! she prayed yet again.

And this time she found him. It was the *Merlin,* all right, running with a reefed sail before the wind. The glass shivered and clouded over. She did not realize, until the Captain took it from her and wiped it, that she was weeping. She turned from him and tried to bury her face between two stones in the rough wall of the shelter.

He touched her gingerly on one shoulder. "Shall I tell 'n you come looking out for 'n, then, maid?" he asked, repeating one of his earlier questions.

"Tell him anything you like," she cried. "Tell him I'll kill him next time I see him!" She wrenched herself away and stumbled, half blind, outside. "You tell him that," she added as she strode away, wiping her cheeks on her sleeves. "Tell him to keep away from me if he knows what's good for him."

Part Four

'Portlemm'

An outing to France

35 By Friday morning Tamsin was doing her best to forget the entire episode. Shame at her sudden and unexpected weakness had made her shout out those ridiculous threats to the Captain on Penlee lookout; and now she felt doubly ashamed that she had allowed her emotions to boil over like that. If anyone deserved punishment, it was herself. It wasn't as if David meant anything to her. He was just a friend. There was absolutely no reason why her happiness at his safe homecoming should not have turned to tears like that. And if she had simply laughed at her own weakness and dried her eyes, no one would have thought any more about it. All her outburst had achieved was to give everyone the wrong impression and make things awkward for the future.

She resolved then to stay away from David, have nothing to do with him, make no inquiries about his ordeal at sea — if, indeed, it had been an ordeal at all ... in short, to cut him out of her life as far as the world was concerned. For how long? Well, there was no need to decide that now. For a good long time, anyway — at least until people could see for themselves that she had no feelings for him beyond plain and simple friendship.

She would miss him of course ...

She shook her head angrily. There was no point in thinking about that now. The damage was done and it had to be repaired first. Friendship could wait.

Whenever anyone asked her — Daisy, Charlotte, her mother ... everyone except Victor — how David had fared, she replied offhandedly that she knew very little more than they did. She had gone for a simple afternoon stroll (to Newlyn, as it happened) and she had heard that someone had spied him from some lookout or other. Near Mousehole, they said. And the *Merlin* appeared to be sound — which was good news, wasn't it, but excuse her please as she had work to do before taking luncheon with Mr Coverley at the Queen's. Also the Countess would be arriving by the afternoon train tomorrow — in case they'd all forgotten it.

Busy or not, Cicely Thorne found occasion that Friday morning to beg a moment of her time. Tamsin suggested the guests' lounge. Cicely said she didn't wish to take up precious minutes and offered instead to accompany her on her regular outing to the shops.

"Presumably you'd rather Daisy did not accompany us?" Tamsin said.

"Quite so," Cicely agreed.

"Only she usually helps me carry things, you see."

Tamsin thought that would put a stop to this unwelcome suggestion, for she was quite sure the woman would rather be seen dead than walk abroad carrying bags or parcels. And, indeed, it looked that way for a moment; but then Cicely brightened. "I know," she said. "Let us do it in proper style. We'll take a motor cab from the rank on the Esplanade and make the shopkeepers come out to serve us."

Tamsin, whose limbs were still weary from a walk that had seemed more like a climb, and a climb that had seemed more like a vertical ascent, accepted the first part of this offer but insisted that she would have to alight from the cab herself and choose the produce, as the shopkeepers of Penzance were not used to the *grande dame* style of marketing and would certainly palm off inferior goods on anyone who tried it.

There was a slight altercation at the cab rank when Cicely passed by the first three cabs and picked the fourth. The man refused to accept them until she explained that his was the first cab in the line that had a glass partition between passengers and chauffeur, and she wished to have a private conversation with her young friend.

Tamsin directed him to Oliver's, the butcher, first.

"Now," Cicely said as soon as they set off, "I've just heard that my silly little boy gave you a rather splendid coming-of-age present last Tuesday?"

Had it not been for her upset over David, Tamsin might have taken a completely different line in answer to this opening sally. She really did not want to keep the turquoise, notwithstanding Jessica Trelawney's advice; she did not wish to feel under any obligation to Victor nor do anything which might seem to acknowledge that his undoubted love for her gave him any rights. And, she realized, that was still much the most sensible attitude for her to take. Unfortunately, something deep inside her, not amenable to logical calculations of best and worst interests, refused to adopt it. Instead she would punish herself by doing the opposite — and, in some obscure way, which she would have been ashamed to explain in so many words, it would also show David where he stood.

So she replied, "Yes! 'Silly little boy' is just right! But he's utterly adorable, too."

"If you say so." His mother's tone was distant. "Of course, I have not actually seen it yet — a turquoise, was it?" She was colder now that she suspected she was in for a long haul.

"Yes, the biggest one I ever saw. And beautifully polished and set, too. Flawless. I was brought up never to wear jewelry before evening." Here Tamsin glanced for the merest fraction of a reluctant second at the pearl brooch and ruby ring the woman was wearing. "Otherwise I could show it to you now."

"Well, I'm looking forward to seeing it — whenever you can find time. He told me of his extraordinary luck in finding it in the … well, in the place where it was. I suppose he told you, too?"

"He told me so many things that evening, Mrs Thorne. We got on famously. Actually" — she glanced all about and lowered her voice dramatically — "I don't mind admitting it to *you*, but I was in a blue funk when he produced the box and I saw the jeweler's name upon it. For one awful moment, I thought it would turn out to hold an engagement ring!"

Surprise at this unexpectedly frank admission caused the woman's mask to slip. Tamsin saw that she had achieved her purpose — to put Cicely Thorne in a blue funk, as a punishment for daring to interfere with *her* decisions about *her* life.

"My dear Miss Harte," she replied. "I confess I'm glad to hear you speak of a possible betrothal in such terms. It would, of course, be absurd and out of the question. But tell me — have things progressed so far between you that such fears could …"

"Time!" Tamsin interrupted airily. "What is time to those in love! They say love laughs at locksmiths. I believe clockmakers and calendar printers should be added to the list."

"Well, dear, I regret to say that you force me to speak quite bluntly. I hope you understand that time is not of the essence here — in any case. No matter how long the friendship between you and my son may endure — and, of course, one hopes it will endure a lifetime — there can *never* be any question of a betrothal between you. Much less of a permanent union."

"Really?" Tamsin said icily. "Since we are both of age, I don't quite see how …"

"Oliver's, ladies!" the driver called through the glass partition.

"Shall I come with you?" Cicely asked, knowing not only that Tamsin would refuse the offer but also that it would give her a few precious minutes alone in which to think.

Tamsin did, naturally, refuse the offer, adding that she'd be as quick as she could.

Cicely knew very well that the girl was trying to hurt her. She knew Victor was an unreliable mixture of the sentimental, the bull-headed, and the impetuous, but she doubted that even he would go so far as to engage himself after so short an acquaintance. However, Victor was not the problem here. Tamsin was. And it would be useless to lay down the law or to appeal to the conventions to *that* young miss. Cicely would have to show her that marriage to Victor would threaten her *own* ambitions.

It would, of course, be helpful if she knew what Tamsin's ambitions were. She did not doubt that the girl was consumed with them. You only needed to watch her make her selections, in there with the butcher, poor man. She made him turn every piece over; she looked into every corner to see whether a better cut had not been set aside for a more favoured customer … and when it came to price, no doubt she'd shave every halfpenny to a farthing. Here was a young woman determined to beat all challengers and emerge on top. What was that, if not ambition?

On her return Tamsin left the wrapped meat in the taxi's luggage space beside the driver and directed him next to Trevaskis, the greengrocer. Normally she'd have got the butcher to deliver but she remembered saying that Daisy usually helped her carry things.

"About what you were saying," she began as she climbed back into the cab.

Cicely laid a soothing hand on her arm. "Let me first explain my point a little more fully — to save us both from pursuing the wrong hare. I know what you're thinking — and also, I suspect, what you're *not* thinking. You probably imagine that when I say marriage is out of the question, I'm referring to the reduced circumstances in which you and your dear mama find yourselves. Nothing could be further from the truth. It would be ridiculous to think of you as fortune hunters. And in any case, I trust Mister Thorne and I are above such snobbery."

"If that is true, Mrs Thorne, I'm sure you won't mind my asking what else could induce you to lay down such ..."

"You may certainly *ask*, my dear, but I should think that, of all the people in the world, the one most qualified to answer the question is *yourself!*"

"Me?"

"Indeed. Who knows you better than yourself? Who knows your dreams and ambitions down to the last detail — and I'm sure you have both in abundance! Believe me, I am not 'fishing,' as they say, to discover what they may be. But I'm sure that marriage to a wealthy husband would go a great way toward achieving them. However, I wonder if you have pictured yourself trying to achieve them if *Victor* were that husband? He is very fond of having his own way, you know. He will never tolerate a dilettante mother. No hobbyist home-maker for him! And he will expect a family — a large one, if I know him. And families do have a way of interfering with one's own grand schemes! So let me rephrase the question you were about to ask: How closely do his expectations connect with yours?"

When Tamsin did not reply, she added: "And so was I not right to say that any betrothal between you and Victor would be impossible — by which I meant that it would be a cruel deception of a man whose heart has temporarily outpaced his brain?"

The girl's thoughtful silence implied that she did, indeed, have ambitions as big as a barn — and that Victor's expectations would do as much to frustrate them as his money would do to foster them. An irresistible force had met an immovable object.

"Am I not right, dear?" Cicely prompted.

Still the girl did not reply.

"I hope I am," Cicely continued. "Because in so many ways you would make him an excellent wife. But I have watched you about the Morrab and I could almost think some guardian angel arranged for your straitened circumstances. *Not,* I hasten to add, for your father's death! That would be too crass. But for the chances that brought you to that guest house. I could almost

think you had managed a much grander place in a past existence.
Am I getting warm?"

Tamsin nodded — and even managed a tight little smile.
Trevaskis opened the door at that moment, giving her time to
consider how to continue this discussion now that the woman
had so completely turned the tables on her.

As if to emphasize her victory, Cicely added as Tamsin got
out: "And I'm sure your hopes are not something you'd relinquish
in order to conform to my son's expectations of a good little wife
— not for all the wealth in Lombardy."

When her business with the greengrocer was done, Tamsin
put the vegetables she had bought directly into his messenger
boy's basket, together with the meat from Oliver's, and saw him
on his way.

"You could have done the same at the butcher's," Cicely
commented. "I've seen his messenger boy about the town."

"Except that he switched cuts on me once when I let him do
that, so now I always carry it," Tamsin explained — wishing she
could find as easy an escape from Mrs Thorne's other arguments.
She directed the cab back to the Morrab.

"Shall we lay all our cards on the table now?" Cicely proposed.
"It's less exciting to play with open hands, I know, but in this
case it might prove more profitable to both of us. Shall I begin?"
She smiled. "I'm probably more used to it than you are!"

"I don't know." Tamsin shrugged. "Everything's happening
at once. It's like cramming spring, summer, autumn, and winter
all into one day."

"When I saw that Victor was taking an interest in you, I knew
he must be making secret plans to return to Penzance after we
had left — assuming we had left when we originally intended. So
I wrote to our steward, Mister Merrick, and asked him to carry
out certain refurbishments to Peveril Hall — which I knew he'd
been eager to do for some time. Then we moved into the
Morrab. One way or another, I knew that would bring matters
to a head — as, indeed, it has."

"I must admit," Tamsin put in, "the same thought had occurred
to me — that Victor might return, I mean."

"And you were looking forward to it?"

She shrugged.

"Well, I shall not press you for a decision now, my dear. You are a mature and sensible young woman, I know. But you will require a little time to think these matters over. You are taking luncheon with Mister Coverley, I hear?"

"At the Queen's, yes. He is going to show me how a great establishment like that is run."

"Is he, indeed!"

Her knowing tone surprised Tamsin. "D'you think that's extraordinary? The Morrab is hardly any competition to him."

The woman smiled. "Perhaps that's the last thing on his mind — just at the moment." She looked Tamsin up and down. "Do you think you could manage a big place like that?"

"What an extraordinary question!" she exclaimed. "If we're talking about 'the last thing on his mind,' I'm sure that is it."

"You're probably right, dear. We shall see what we shall see."

36 The luncheon was to be served in a private room. Tamsin was wary of this arrangement until she heard that she was not to enjoy the *tête-à-tête* she had expected; both Reg Trotter and Mrs Trelawney were to be there, too. Wariness then gave way to disappointment. It crossed her mind that one very good way of getting all the girls in town interested in you would be to behave as if you were interested in none of them!

Mrs Trelawney was so relaxed and so poised. Tamsin saw what wealth could do for a woman, especially wealth she had created for herself. True, Mr Trelawney had not exactly been poor, but — or so it was said — she had been able to match him pound for pound on the day they were wed. And his was family wealth whereas she'd made hers all by herself.

The conversation ranged over many topics — the meaning-behind-the-meaning of *The Pirates of Penzance* ... Mata Hari, the new Hindoo dance sensation in Paris ... what the accidental drowning of the bishop of Hong Kong had revealed of God's will ... the anti-infidel riots in Casablanca ... Galsworthy's latest novel of the Forsytes, *A Man of Property* ... and whether Penzance should build an open-air salt-water swimming pool at Battery Point. Tamsin soon realized that the other three expected her to have an opinion on each and every topic, no matter how little it related to her life or theirs. In the circumstances she thought she did well enough not to have annoyed any of them by making a point that, quite accidentally, ran contrary to one or other's strongly held beliefs.

Why people should concern themselves with such things when there was so much work to be done and money to be made was a mystery to her, but she supposed it was the sort of thing they could indulge in once they were secure and could afford to enjoy their leisure. As far as she was concerned, though, it was a bit of a bore and she had to call on all her self-discipline not to let it show. Still, the wine flowed freely — a Montrachet followed by a deliciously sweet Barsac — so she could not really complain.

Toward the end of their meal, when she felt she'd had enough of world gossip, she asked Standish how he was finding the season so far. There was a little frisson of embarrassment around the table. Clearly one did not talk shop on such an occasion; but she was past caring by then. She had a clock ticking in her head, even if the others couldn't hear it.

"Not bad," he said. "We've had better. Middling, I'd say. How about you?"

"Well, we've no previous years to compare it with but I'll say that future years will find it hard to beat this one. We're fully booked right through to the first week in September. Mama has even had to take a room at Chynoweth, next door, where they still have vacancies — to make room for this Countess de Ath, who's arriving tomorrow and leaving God knows when."

When that had been explained, and the excitement had died down, Standish said, "That's a marvellous achievement for your opening season, you know."

"Well," she gushed, "we thought at first it was going to be a disaster. We opened the doors at Easter and for weeks we couldn't get beyond half full."

"Half full!" Standish chuckled. "Most of us would give our eye teeth to be as busy as that in spring! Anyway, what brought about the change?"

"I think it was word of mouth. Most of the guests we're getting now say something like, 'We're so looking forward to this holiday — we've heard all about you from our friends the

Snoddys'... or some such name. And, it turns out, the Snoddys, or whoever, were guests of ours earlier in the season. Also about half of them are already booking to come back next summer — which is very gratifying."

After that, Standish took her on the promised guided tour of the Queen's, which was as fascinating to her as a tour of a railway works would be to most little boys. He covered everything, from the servants' quarters, where the live-in maids slept four to a room in bunks, to the cellar-within-a-cellar, where the rarest wines and finest brandies were kept. Half a dozen of the latter looked rather familiar.

"Where are the other six?" she asked.

He laid a finger against the side of his nose and winked.

Suddenly she realized they were all alone, here, in what was probably the most private place in the whole of Penzance. If there was a better moment to test his interest in her, she could not imagine it. *Now!* she told herself. *Before you get cold feet.*

"Just a mo ..." She peered at his face in the flatteringly golden light of the single candle he was carrying — one of the most rugged, attractive, manly faces she had ever seen. Especially as close as this.

"Eh?" he responded.

Her heart began to race; it hammered in the back of her neck, near the base of her skull. Surely he could hear it, too? "You've collected a cobweb," she said. He had, too — a rolled-up skein of silk, heavy with dust. She reached out and peeled it off his collar, lifting it where he could see she wasn't playing games.

"Don't move yet!"

"More?" he asked.

"It's left a mark." She had to go very close to him to brush off the smear. Even though they were not touching — except where her hand brushed his collar — she could feel the whole of her body glowing at the nearness of him.

"You hate disorder," he murmured.

Oh, if he could only sense the disorder inside her!

"I admire order," she agreed. "I admire the people who bring it about, too." She looked up into his eyes. "I admire you, Standish, for what you've achieved here. In fact, I think you're a pretty wonderful person all round."

He swallowed heavily but, for once, seemed tonguetied.

Committed now, she sprang on tiptoes and kissed him quickly on the corner of his mouth.

His whole body went rigid — surely not with distaste? Please let it be anything but that!

"You don't mind?" she asked, rocking back on her heels.

"Mind? Of course not!"

"Kiss me, then."

He set the candle down behind her and, for one delirious moment, he took her head between his hands. And then he kissed her on the forehead. Her throat tightened. Tears sprang to her eyes. She would have shed them, too, if he had not added, "You are in such a hurry, Tamsin — my dear girl. But there's no need. Just slow down, eh?"

The tears turned to laughter, equally hysterical but much easier to bear. She blew out the candle, grabbed his arm, and said, "Lead me back to the light!"

She had meant it as a challenge, to see how well he knew his way around his own hôtel. But what had been pitch dark when the candle went out was already turning to a paler shade of black and, by the time they reached the end of the bins, the exit door was easy to discern.

Before they went back upstairs, however, he caught her by the arm and said, "I had a particular reason for bringing you down here. *Not*, I regret to say, the one you may have suspected."

"You mean you don't find me attractive?" she blurted out — determined to make him come down off the fence for once and for all.

"On the contrary!" he exclaimed fervently. "I've been well aware of a growing mutual interest between us. But there are things you do not know."

"Obstacles?"

"Yes. You see …"

"You're married already!"

"No. Just listen, and you'll understand why I've seemed so lukewarm. I've brought you down here because it's the one place I can be sure of not being overheard. Some years ago I entered into a very foolish partnership — not a marriage — a commercial partnership, with a man who … well, he seemed to have the Midas touch. Without going into all the gory details, I'll just say I lost a lot of money. Not everything — obviously — but a fair few shekels. I put it down to experience and dissolved the partnership. I can warn you now that, if ever anyone should offer you the chance to buy into a hundred-percent, copper-bottomed, sure-fire money-making scheme that will return your investment many times over, and hustles you into a quick decision before the shutters come down — just thank him for thinking of you and walk away. It's what I should have done. The only reason I'm telling you this, Tamsin, is that my erstwhile partner, a man called Marcus Mitchell, has continued with his swindling ways — of course — but, in an attempt to cover his tracks, he has fabricated a number of documents, dating them back to the time of our partnership, and he has forged my signature upon them. So, you see …"

"Oh, Standish!" More than ever now she wanted to hug him, to comfort him, to ask how she could help, no matter how small or trivial the way. "How long has this been going on?"

"You mean when did I first hear of it? About this time last year. I just laughed at first, because I thought nothing would be easier than to prove they were forgeries. But Mitchell's a lot cleverer than I bargained for and, though the wheels of the law grind exceeding slow, they are relentless. Just lately it has become a great deal more serious. So you will surely understand that any sort of romantic entanglement at this time would be the height of dishonour on my part."

"If I can help in any way …?" she stammered.

"You can!" He rubbed his hands briskly. "I'm not beaten yet — not by any means. And meanwhile I have this hôtel to run. So, if you wish to help me right now" — he took her arm and started back upstairs — "you could tell me why you're so interested in our operations here. So few people take any interest in what goes on behind the scenes — though they soon let you know if anything goes wrong out in front!"

She confessed then, that it had been her passion from the moment the Morrab was just a gleam in the eye — and she went on to tell him about her fantasies of managing a great liner.

"Well," he replied, "if it's confession time, I must admit that I feel I've run into a brick wall here. The place is a success. It has developed its own set ways — and because they work, no one wants to change them, including me. But I know that can be fatal. Traditions will kill you unless you continually adapt them to the ever-changing situation. You remember what you said at lunch when Mrs Trelawney told us she'd just bought the piano transcription to Elgar's new 'Pomp and Circumstance March'?"

"No. I was completely out of my depth during most of those conversations, I hope you realize."

"Go on with you! You said, 'The trouble with England is too much pomp and not enough circumstance.' I thought it was the best comment anyone made throughout the entire meal."

"Really? It's just the way I feel."

"Anyway — it shows you understand the need to keep old traditions on their toes. So come on — put your penny on the drum: What changes would you make if you were me?"

"I wouldn't wear a white blazer down into the cellars," she replied. "Look at you!"

He laughed.

They had reached the cloakroom by now, where he helped her back into her cape and retrieved her parasol. Then he saw her to the door — and beyond. Another place beyond the reach of eavesdroppers.

"I'm serious," he said, leading her across the Esplanade to the railings overlooking the beach. "If you owned the Queen's, what changes would you make?"

"I'd have a different menu every day for fourteen days," she replied at once.

"Why?"

"You have a seven-day rotation at the moment, right?"

"Yes."

"Which is probably all right in the winter, when most of your custom must be from travelling salesmen and people on blustery walking holidays. But for people who stay a full fortnight in the summer it means they get the same menu again each Monday, Tuesday … and so on. It was one of the first things Mrs Thorne commented on when she moved in when she moved in at the Morrab — not a single breakfast menu has been repeated." She laughed. "She'll get a shock next week, mind. It will be day after day of 'dayja vu'!"

"Any other changes?" he asked.

"I'd offer special cheap Saturday luncheons for boarding-house landladies — and gentlemen. There are dozens of them all around you — as you surely know. I'd do it even at no profit. Let me tell you — Saturday mornings are hell in boarding-house land. It's when half your house empties first thing in the morning so that they can catch the early trains back up country. Then you have all the rooms to turn out and get ready. Then there's this ghastly pause when you're too exhausted to make a meal ..."

"Wait! What about the cook?"

"It's the best day for her to take off — because most of the breakfasts are early and she can go for an early start. Anyway, then there's a new rush when the up-country trains start arriving around three o'clock in the afternoon. And it goes on until quite late in the evening. So if someone said, come and have a cheap lunch at the Queen's ... we'd all leap at it."

"I'm sure you would — but what's in it for us?"

"Us? We wouldn't rest. We'd go from table to table, showing them our menus, asking their opinions ... flattering them ... making them feel we're all in it together — this wonderful business of catering for visitors. So when their bed-and-breakfast guests ask where to go for lunch or dinner — as ours do all the time — what will they tell them? We could even send them away with little cards saying, 'For first-class cuisine, including many local Cornish specialities, all at prices that won't give you indigestion ...' you know — something like that. However, d'you know what I think you *really* ought to do?"

He eyed her warily. She laughed and said, "If you can afford it, I think you should buy the Mount's Bay next door, knock it down, and extend the Queen's in the same grand style ... double the size of your ballroom, and ..."

"Stop!" He put his fingers demonstratively in his ears. Then, "You haven't just thought of all this on the spur of the moment, have you! You've been mulling it over for some time."

"Not just about the Queen's," she replied.

"Oh?" He was wary again. "Where else, then?"

"It doesn't matter. It's just a pipe-dream." All the same, she could not help glancing down the Esplanade at the empty space opposite the bath house.

He saw it, followed her gaze, then turned slowly back to her. "Dear God!" he murmured.

"Of course," she said jovially. "If you'd rather spend the money on *that* ..."

"Get thee behind me!" he cried.

She told him she really had to go — if only to stop her mother from having a fit over the arrival of the Countess tomorrow.

On her way home she remembered she still hadn't told him about Charlotte's outburst on the afternoon of her birthday party. However, in view of what he had just revealed, none of that seemed to matter any more.

37 When Bridget discovered that carnauba-wax polish does not lie down very well over freshly shone beeswax, Harriet Harte threw her fifteenth panic-tantrum of the morning. Tamsin bore it as long as she could before remembering an urgent errand, which allowed her to escape.

"Don't go in there," she warned Daisy, just outside the door. "Honestly! If there is ever to be another morning in my life quite like this, then please someone give me enough warning so I can lay in a stock of ether, laudanum, cask-strength whisky ... *anything* to keep me mercifully oblivious to it!"

Daisy pulled a sympathetic face.

Tamsin, finding it a great relief to let off steam, took her arm and led her away to safety. "She's being *utterly* insufferable," she said. "As if we didn't have enough to do already, what with half our regular rooms turning over this morning. She knows very well how much extra work that means, but, no, everything must yield to making the wretched old Countess de Ath feel as if she were coming home to her palace — or whatever grand *loge* might be her habitual residence."

"I was totting up the bills for the departing guests," Daisy said, almost apologizing for not taking her share of the agony.

"Yes, bless you! I'd stay out of the way among the ledgers, if I were you. Tot them all up again. *Someone* here has to maintain her sanity."

"What's this smell?"

"Perfume, please! It's quadruple strength lavender beeswax. Poor Bridget and Catherine have polished every surface in the Countess's room *three times* already this morning. Then dear Mama remembered that carnauba wax is more durable and gives a deeper shine. So Bridget must go out into the town to wake up the nearest colourman and get some from him. Oh! I know what the *rest* of the stench is — turpentine. Bridget had to boil some up to dissolve the carnauba wax — plus, of course, gallons more oil of lavender."

"And doesn't it work?"

They were passing through the kitchen by now. Mrs Pascoe raised her eyes but made no spoken comment.

"We're just going out for a bit of fresh air," Tamsin told her. Safely in the back garden she answered Daisy's question. "It works perfectly well — provided you haven't already put down three layers of soft beeswax first. Then the carnauba wax just pushes it into streaks. And what d'you think will bring back the shine then? Apart from elbow grease? Silk? No, not silk. Cotton, then? No, not cotton, either. Linen? No — positively not. We've tried all of these. And if the wax won't wash out, we have a heap of what was once good clothing and is now only fit for the rag-and-bone man."

"Didn't you try wool?"

"Oh, Daisy — we should have asked you first. Yes — lambswool works a treat." She sighed. "I just hope the Countess has always wanted to die of lavender poisoning — if there is such a thing. Otherwise, she is not going to appreciate the gallons of the stuff that we've poured into every crevice in her room."

A window above shrieked open. *"There* you are!" Harriet cried. "How dare you skulk out there while there's so much to do?"

"We're trying to organize the day calmly," Tamsin replied. "Daisy has the bills all ready to present." Then — foolishly, but in the hope of deflecting her mother's thoughts — she added, "I was just saying that I hope the Countess *likes* the smell of lavender. We haven't given her much choice in the matter."

"Mis-ta-ake!" Daisy murmured.

And a moment later, Tamsin could only agree, for her mother immediately flew into a fresh panic over how to get rid of the smell of lavender.

Tamsin, kicking herself, ran back indoors and up the stairs. "Mo-ther!" she cried breathlessly. "I wasn't serious. The woman must be in her eighties. She's probably blind, and she'll have as much sense of smell as a tailor's mannequin."

It was to no avail. Bridget was already putting up her bonnet for her second errand of the morning, this time to buy as many carnations as her arms could carry.

Tamsin gave up and turned instead to the normal business of a Saturday morning — serving the early breakfasts for those with trains to catch and making sure the bills were paid.

Daisy took her turn at keeping Harriet as calm as possible.

When the Countess's room was filled with all the carnations Bridget brought home, the combination of the two perfumes was so overpowering that even a tailor's mannequin would have turned pale.

"What do you think?" Harriet asked Daisy.

"Perhaps four bunches would be enough?" she suggested. "And if both windows were left wide open ...? After all, she isn't due for another six hours. It might clear by then."

So all but four bunches of carnations were removed and distributed through the house.

Down in the dining room an elderly lady who had spent the entire past week on the clifftops, potting seagulls with an air gun, asked if a dog had been sick.

Tamsin assured her there was no dog in the house and that the smell was, in fact, carnations.

"I know that perfectly well, you stupid girl!" she replied. "Carnations mask the smell of dog vomit — didn't you know?"

Tamsin thought it was not a helpful comment to be made out loud in the breakfast room, but she said nothing.

As the morning lurched on from one panic to the next, Tamsin had to assure herself, several times, that this was not a nightmare — it was all actually happening *sub specie æternitatis*. Even more frequently she had to pacify poor Bridget and Catherine and assure them that the day would end, as all days must, and that everything would be different once the Countess was settled in. "After all," ran her trump card, "her ladyship would not have chosen to stay at a small guest house if she was expecting the sort of service she'd get in a first-class hôtel." Like lick and brown paper when the glue has run out, it just about held them together.

The high point of fantasy came when, around two o'clock, she found herself taking part in a curtsying class for the two maids and Daisy, and, of course, herself. By then she had realized that any objection she made only served to screw her mother's panic to a new pitch — besides inducing rebellion among the maids. By two-fifteen, no ballerina ever curtsied more elegantly than those four young females; unfortunately, Harriet herself was in such an excitable state that she went down as if her limbs were broken in several places.

At two-twenty, dressed as if for a state wedding, mother and daughter were about to climb into a taxi (ordered four days ago and confirmed twice a day since then) for the five-minute drive to the station when there was a shawm-like hoot from down Morrab Road and they saw Standish Coverley milking the steering wheel of his Rolls-Royce as it glided out of the mews behind the Queen's. Reg Trotter was at his side.

"Thought you'd like to greet the old dowager in style," Standish said as they both leaped nimbly out — Reg to help the two ladies climb in, Standish to settle some minor compensation with the cabbie before setting off. "Knew you'd want to be good and early," he added.

Harriet was too overawed to speak until they reached the Esplanade. Then the thanks simply poured out of her in a stream of consciousness that slowly turned dark, revealing all her old fears about this momentous occasion.

"Where will her ladyship sit?" she asked, looking about her and finding no extra room. Ladies' dresses were so ample.

"Trotter can take a cab back and supervise her luggage," Standish assured her. "Then Tamsin can sit in front by me and you can take care of the Countess in the back."

"Is it 'Your Grace' for a Countess? No — stupid! Your *Ladyship!* These foreign titles are so confusing. Would she sit above or below an English countess?"

"I doubt that'll be much of a problem, Mo-ther," Tamsin said heavily. "But if you really want to know, the Congress of Vienna decided that a count and countess will rank as a duke in those countries that ..."

"A duke?" Harriet almost shrieked. "She ranks as a *duchess?* Heavens, child! Why did you not tell me before?"

"Because the way you are behaving now is sufficient answer to that! Listen! They will rank as a duke and duchess *in those countries whose peerages have no dukes or marquises.* The English court has never accepted the ruling and in England they rank with the eldest son of the equivalent English rank — in the Countess's case she would rank as the *daughter* of an earl and countess rather than as a countess in her own right."

"I say!" Standish glanced briefly over his shoulder at her as they took the corner into the commercial harbour. "How d'you know all that?"

"Because I went to the library and mugged it up the moment she confirmed her booking."

"Mugged it up!" Harriet muttered distastefully. "Please avoid such locutions when her ladyship is present." Then, looking all about her with horror, she added, "We must not bring her back *this* way!"

"No, certainly not. I thought we'd go out through Market Jew Street, past the statue of Sir Humphry Davy, which is quite imposing, and the Old Town Hall, out to Stable Hobba, then back by way of the Esplanade …"

"That would give time," Tamsin cut in, "for Reg to get back to the Morrab with her bags — which would impress her."

"Two minds with but a single thought!" Standish remarked as he drew up on the station forecourt — or, rather, sidecourt.

The usual crowd of fishporters, urchins, and idlers gathered around to admire the car. Standish went over to the kiosk where the beach photographers, Collett & Trevarton, displayed and sold prints to departing holidaymakers; the salesman there agreed to keep an eye on the car.

"Can you trust him?" Harriet asked.

"They use one of our old stables behind the Queen's as a darkroom every summer," he replied as they entered the station. Then, turning to Tamsin, "Which reminds me — seeing you in all your finery the other night, I thought it deserved a photo."

"Photo*graph,*" Harriet said.

"I can thoroughly recommend Jim Collett — a real artist with the camera."

"Please!" Harriet said anxiously. "We have no time to think of such things now."

It wasn't true. They had nearly half an hour, for, as one of the station officials told them, the train was just leaving Camborne, about fifteen miles up the line, with further stops at Gwinear Road, for Helston, and St. Erth, for St. Ives.

Reg suggested a cup of tea at the buffet.

Harriet said, "How could you!"

So, after buying platform tickets they drifted back outside. Harriet objected until Tamsin pointed out that the station, a vast, arched barn open to the sky only at its eastern end, was full of smuts and they didn't want to look like colliers when her ladyship arrived, did they.

They went down to the harbour wall, where most of the fishing fleet was already tied up, ready for the sabbath tomorrow — a third of a square mile, filled with bare masts, nodding on the gentle swell. A couple of smacks were still unloading their catches at the fish quay, beside the ice house. The system was quite different from Newlyn, where the fishwives waded out to the boats and carried great creels of fish ashore. Here the creels were loaded in the holds by the crew and winched ashore by derricks, directly into the open-sided sheds, where men and fishwives gutted the fish as fast as the eye could follow them. Then, sorted into boxes and packed in ice, they were hauled on trolleys to the railway goods yard. There a marshalled line of wagons stood, dripping meltwater that reeked of dead fish, ready to depart within the hour.

"Swimming free in Mount's Bay this morning," Standish mused. "Dead on a marble slab in Billingsgate by two o'clock tonight! What a fabulous civilization!"

"What a dreadful smell to greet our visitors!" Harriet responded. "Why couldn't they have moved the harbour a little way up the line?"

Reg drew breath to explain but Tamsin silenced him with a shake of her head; economic geography and stark social terror did not mix.

They remained outside the station until five minutes before the train was due, when, smuts or no smuts, Harriet could tarry no longer. On re-entering the station they were surprised to see

Cicely Thorne at the newsagent's stall — and even more surprised to discover her concealed behind a display of picture postcards, apparently trying to make her choice in the darkest area.

"It does rotate, Mrs Thorne," an amused Standish pointed out, demonstrating the facility with the flick of a finger.

The woman froze. Her eyes looked straight through him and she said, "Dear Mrs Harte — and Tamsin! No need to ask why you're here, though I doubt you fête *all* your PGs thus."

"I say, are you cutting me?" Standish asked.

She ignored him and returned to her choice of postcards, now from the well-lighted side.

"You are!" Standish laughed. "I say, Reginald, old boy. We are being cut."

"Oh dear, oh dear, oh dear ..." Harriet wrung her hands in misery. "At a time like this ... such a thing to ... I can't ..." Her voice broke, her lips trembled.

"Mo-ther!" Tamsin put an arm around her and looked daggers at Cicely Thorne. "How *could* you!" she spat. "Come away, Mama. Pay her no heed. She's obviously got some new bee in her bonnet — silly woman!"

A shocked silence followed this denunciation; even the pigeons ceased their cooing, though that was no doubt coincidental.

"Mister Coverley!" Cicely rapped out as they moved toward the arrivals platform.

He stopped but did not turn to face her.

"You have less friends than you may think."

"Fewer," Harriet said.

He turned to her then. "It's a brave woman who dares count *her* friends aloud and in public, ma'am," he replied.

Tamsin alone saw the smile on Cicely's face as the others turned away. So she must have discovered something more concrete than the vague rumours she had hinted at yesterday — God, was it only yesterday! She must warn Standish that his troubles with that Mitchell man were more widely known than he believed. All the same, she thought it rash for a woman who was sixty miles away from all her influential friends — and all of them in another county, at that — to threaten a man as well established and popular as Standish Coverley, here in his own back yard.

However, the ticket collector, whose ears could detect sounds that were meaningless to others, told them that the London train was now steaming through Longrock, a couple of miles out from the terminus, so they gave him their platform tickets and went through. The first-class compartments would be at the rear of the train, he added, between the dining carriage and the guard's van.

"I love the guard's van, don't you?" Tamsin said to the two men as they made their way up the platform, out into the sunlight once again, for the platforms were twice as long as the covered portion. "A dear little caravan on wheels, with its own stove where you can fry eggs and bacon and brew tea, and the observation platform at the back. If I were a man, that's what I'd be — a train guard."

Standish was not as amused or relaxed as she expected. He, too, must have worked out the implications of Cicely Thorne's absurd insults.

"How can your head be full of such scribble at a time like this?" Harriet asked crossly.

"How can it *not!*" Tamsin replied robustly. The train was in sight by now, less than half a mile up the track. "Is the world going mad? What with Mrs Thorne off on some lunatic tack of her own, and you going completely overboard about ..."

"About the honour of entertaining Ivy, the Dowager Countess de Ath beneath our roof. You don't seem to understand ..."

"Ladies!" Standish intervened. The train was approaching so fast that he feared it would run into the buffers.

But Tamsin was not going to let her mother have the last word. "What *you* don't seem to understand is that an old woman of eighty is no asset to a boarding house like ours, dowager or not. She belongs in a nursing home. What if she kicks the bucket *beneath our roof?*"

"Oh! Aah! I can't breathe!" Harriet gasped and fumbled with the hooks and eyes at her throat.

"Now then, Mrs Harte!" Standish put an arm about her and hugged her tight — which seemed to rally her remarkably. It was his turn to look daggers, now at Tamsin. "Your daughter has very little sense of occasion, I fear. We must all do our best to educate her. Now here's the train, so take long, deep breaths —

long and deep, long and deep. That's it. Can I let you go now — before the Countess gets the wrong impression?"

"Oh God! Is she here?" Harriet opened her eyes and blinked at the watery blur before them.

"She soon will be. I think we're in the perfect position."

He let go and turned to frown once more at Tamsin, who was stuffing a handkerchief into her mouth to avoid hysterics. He turned his fist into a symbolic pistol and shot her dead between the eyes.

"Perfect!" Reg said as the first of the three doors on the first-class carriage came to a screeching halt directly in front of them.

Harriet had passed from deep breathing to hyperventilation. Her head swam. She felt herself going. It was all too much. Only a curtsy would save her … get her close to the ground.

With a creaking and cracking in her knees she sank, her body leaned forward … one set of knuckles casually but oh so necessarily touched the tarmacadam … and …

"Cor lumme!" cried a cultivated voice — cultivated well within the sound of Bow Bells, that is — "Here's a welcome party then!"

The other three stood with their jaws agape. If Ivy, the Dowager Countess de Ath, could be considered so much as twenty-three years old, it would be more thanks to cosmetics than to the calendar. She was in black from head to foot, of course — but what a silken, glossy, figure-hugging black it was. And what a head! What a foot! What an everything-in-between!

She writhed wickedly, like a knowing snake, as she descended to the platform. From her shoulders to her hobbled knees her dress clung to every subtle nuance of all her ample curves; from her hobbled knees down to her ankles it burst into a froth of black tulle at the front, through which the high-booted outlines of her shins, calves, and ankles could easily be glimpsed. Even the extremities of her boots looked more like dainty black feet than anything a cobbler might have made.

"You must be Miss Tamsin Harte." She offered her hand.

Standish became aware that Harriet was about to tumble. He and Reg took an arm each and raised her again.

"Yes, your ladyship," Tamsin said meanwhile. "Are you …" She could not think how to phrase it.

"You were expecting a *real* dowager, eh?" She laughed. "That was poor old Josie, God rest her. Lovely lady. She passed away, very sadly, just the week before Christmas last — and now the dear old Count has gone to join her."

"But you *are* ..." Again she fought shy of the actual words.

"Oh yes, pet — I most certainly am! We got married Christmas Day!" And she stretched forth a right hand on which every finger was crusted with jewels — among them, by inference, rings that symbolized betrothal and matrimony in the Continental manner. "And Mrs Harte!" She swivelled the hand round and offered it, not for a kiss but to be shaken. "It's so kind of you to meet me. I wasn't expecting such a thing."

Harriet made a few noises in her throat, shook the hand, told herself to stop staring — and found that she was quite unable to obey the command.

"And who may these fine gentlemen be?" Ivy turned her huge, blue, limpid eyes upon Standish and Reg. "Do please present them to me!"

Standish, more accustomed to an all-sorts world than the others, was the first to recover. "Standish Coverley, Countess," he said, kissing that same hand. "Penzance is suddenly brighter."

"Ooooh!" she said on a rising-falling tone. "I think I have to agree, Mister Coverley."

"And may I present my very good friend, Reginald Trotter."

Reg, too, kissed her hand and told her they were fellow guests at the Morrab, where he was looking forward to her company.

"Oh, really?" she replied, looking again at Standish with a raised eyebrow.

He shook his head. "I, too, shall look forward to your company, Countess, but not at the Morrab. I'm connected to a rival Penzance establishment."

"Mister Coverley owns the Queen's Hôtel," Tamsin put in. "The biggest and best in Cornwall."

"Hardly!" Standish murmured, pleased, all the same.

"I see." The Countess's eyes scanned rapidly between the two of them. Her brain was obviously working double-tides, for why else would a handsome young man turn out to greet a rival's honoured guest — unless said rival was a remarkably good-looking young woman?

"Where is your ladyship's lady's maid?" Harriet asked, anxious again and peering up and down the platform. Two porters were unloading what eventually amounted to a dozen portmanteaux and travelling wardrobes from the luggage van, but there was no sign of the valet, groom, or lady's maid who would normally be keeping a tally.

"I dismissed the lot," Ivy sneered. "Snooty Continentals — I can't abide them. Quack-quack — all that French. I thought I might pick up a good old English one down here."

"We can offer all the services of a lady's maid at the Morrab," Tamsin said.

Her mother plucked her sleeve. "Say 'your ladyship'!" she tried to whisper.

"Oh, forget all that!" The Countess dismissed the injunction with a wave of her hand. "'Countess' will do till we get on better terms. Or nothing at all."

"Are those all your boxes, Countess?" Reg asked.

"I only need the two purple ones," she replied. "They've got my weeds. The rest they can stop here till we find a repository."

Reg went to instruct the porters. The others started to walk down the platform. Tamsin asked if she had been to Penzance before. She said no, and that was one reason why she chose it.

"Well," Tamsin went on, "talking of *choosing* places, we know you met our friends the Locks at Baden-Baden, but … I hope you realize — the Morrab is a very modest establishment."

"Can't you guess why I'm here? Now you've met me and seen what a common little Cockney blowsabella I am — you still can't make a guess?"

Tamsin shook her head. "And anyway," she said, "I don't think you do yourself justice."

"If yoo cahn't even guess," she said in a parody of upper-class speech, "then ay shall just hev too tell yooo."

The inspector accepted her ticket without looking at it, because he was unable to take his eyes off her — even after she had passed beyond him into the concourse.

Standish saw Cicely Thorne, still rooted near the newsagent's stall. He turned to the Countess and asked if he might buy her a guide book to the town and locality. She accepted, slightly baffled — as, indeed, were the others.

"Come and choose," he said.

Cicely made those small, flustered movements people make when they are about to meet royalty or anyone of social prominence, but Standish led the Countess straight past her, bought a shilling copy of the official guide (published under the direction of the mayor and corporation), presented it to her, and led her back to join the others, who were outside by then. He did not so much as glance at Cicely, though he passed within inches of her.

"Who was that woman staring at us," the Countess asked. "She seemed to know you."

"Mrs Thorne — Cicely Thorne of Peveril Hall, near Exeter. She knows me very well but she cut me dead on our way into the station, about ten minutes ago."

"I see," the Countess said coldly. "You just used me, then!"

"Her only purpose here was to inspect you — and, if possible, carry back some scandal or gossip."

"Yet she cut *you* — even knowing you were going to meet me off of the train. That sounds serious. D'you know what you've done to offend her?"

"I suspect she has heard certain rumours about me — quite untrue, I assure you, but they have alarmed her."

The Countess's eyes raked the skies — or the dirty glass overhead. "And all I wanted was some peace and quiet!"

38 Even the two purple portmanteaux were so heavy that they would need the Great Western delivery dray, and the company's burly delivery men, rather than Reg and a taxi, to get them to the Morrab. So Standish's plan for their seating was abandoned. Besides, the Countess took charge at once.

She went into raptures the moment she saw the car — and forgave, or forgot, his use of her to revenge himself on that woman in there. "Crikey!" she shouted, running at the hobble ahead of them, and with such sinuous movements that none could take their eyes off her, especially not the fishporters and idlers. "You've got one of *these!*" She turned excitedly back to Standish. "I've seen one in Baden. The archduke of whatsizname

has one … what's the place called? That little country. Sneeze
and you miss it. Anyway, he's got one, only it's nothing like so
good as what this one is."

She ran admiring hands over the white lacquer and touched
the polished metal with delicate, black-gloved fingertips, as if
she could not believe anything could be so smooth and shiny.

"I'll stand on the running board," Reg offered.

"You will not!" she insisted. "Come on, Mrs Harte, dear —
you in the front. Then you, pet." She nodded at Tamsin. "In the
back with you. And Mister T between us. No fighting, eh!"

And so the day's honoured guest ended up being the last to
enter the car, but all at her own behest. She did not seem to
notice that Harriet Harte was being rather cool and withdrawn.
In fact, none of the others *seemed* to notice it, either — though,
of course, all of them did. And then, in that way people have
when one of the company has made an embarrassing fool of
him-or-her-self, they became extra-jolly in the hope that their
heartiness would cover up the silent one's embarrassment and
encourage it to vanish.

Standish tossed a coin to the man who had swung the starting
handle and, with a wave of thanks to the attendant in the
photographer's kiosk, pulled out into Station Road.

"So this is Penzance, eh," the Countess went on as they left
the station yard. Her eye scanned the hundred and more fishing
smacks at anchor in the harbour. "Just count those boats! I'm
surprised there's a fish left within a hundred miles. Though my
nose tells me there is!" She laughed.

"You were going to explain why you chose the Morrab,"
Tamsin said as they turned away from the quayside, up Albert
Street toward the bottom of Market Jew.

"Come on!" the Countess chided. "Surely a bright girl like
you can work it out?" She adopted an exaggerated Cockney —
or perhaps it was her original speech. " 'Ere's me, common as
could be but with oodles of oof, and you and your mum, down
on your uppers but with class coming out of your ears." Then,
back in her more refined speech, though still with an unmistakable
East End overtone: "Market Jew Street! That's a funny name!
Anyway, do you get it now, pet?"

"Sort of, I suppose," Tamsin replied.

"Toot court — can you make a silk purse out of this sow's ear? That's what it boils down to. I got along all right on 'Le Continong,' see, because they don't know Mile End from Mayfair. And table manners and visiting cards don't trouble me no more — *any* more. But here in England — where I'd much rather be living — it's a different story. One word out of my mouth and I can hear sniggers all around. So — before I resume my noble career — I want to buy a touch of class, see? On the outside, anyway. And the moment the Locks told me your sad tale, I thought we could each do the other some good. Of course, if you'd rather not …"

"No, no!" Tamsin cried, for she had already taken a great liking to this strange and strangely endearing young woman. "Given five years, I think we might manage something."

"Tamsin!" Harriet exclaimed.

The Countess reached behind Reg, who obligingly leaned forward to let her give Tamsin a gentle pinch on the arm. "It's six months or my money back," she said. Then, to Harriet, "I hope your daughter speaks for you, too, Mrs Harte?"

"I'm not sure, Countess." She only half turned as she replied, so that she avoided looking the woman in the eye without seeming to do so deliberately. "It's not something one can decide within five minutes of first meeting, I think."

"Good," the Countess said in a disappointed tone. "As long as it's not out of the question from the start." Half to herself she added, "The Locks seemed to think you'd leap at it. *They* didn't think me unsuitable."

Tamsin tapped her on the shoulder and made a soothing gesture. Meanwhile her mother was saying, "It's not a question of being unsuitable … oh, dear!"

But, of course, it was precisely that.

"You mentioned a 'noble career' just now, Countess," Standish said. "What would that be?"

"Who's that noble-looking fellow? And what's he holding?"

"That's Sir Humphry Davy, Penzance's most famous son. He invented the miner's safety lamp — which is what he's holding. And this is our old town hall."

"Blocks the traffic a bit, what? Anyway — my noble career. My career … I suppose if I've got to *prove* my suitability, I shall have to tell you the lot." She rolled her eyes upward, pulled a face, and then looked all about her, especially at Tamsin. "We're all grown up here, I hope? We all know how one and one can make three?"

"I really think …" Harriet began in alarm. "I mean I hope …"

But there was no stopping the Countess now. "Cards on the table," she said. "Penny on the drum. My noble career, you might say, began at the age of sixteen when I had the honour to become Lady Summers, the second wife of Sir Morgan Summers of South Audley Street, Mayfair — which I remained until I reached the age of twenty, when Sir Morgan passed over. Then, last Christmas, at the age of twenty-two, I married Hugo de Ath, Comte d'Aumer, and, of course, became his countess. That was in Paris. He, too passed away — as you know — last week. No — this week. Aiee! Is it still only this week?"

She knew what they were all thinking: *These statements are verifiable in the public record. Would she make them if it were all a pack of lies?*

"Hard to credit, eh?" she went on. "But I'm not ashamed of marrying two rich men in their declining years. I'd do it again … because I don't think a woman all alone in the world can have too many friends at the bank, do you? What's that?"

"The hospital," Standish told her. "And the new town hall."

"Lovely. Anyway. Like I was saying, both gentlemen said I gave them the happiest years of their lives, and …"

"Years?" Harriet queried. In her innocence she supposed that she had caught the woman out. "Pardon me, but didn't you say you married the Count only last Christmas?"

"Yes, but it wasn't no whirlwind romance, Mrs Harte. The then Countess had been ailing for many years. It was she who introduced me to her husband — not long after I was widowed. And she encouraged our friendship until the day she died, which was only four days before the Count married me. She gave us her blessing. She was a saint. Almost her last act on earth was to wrap her grandmother's lace shawl as a wedding gift to me …" Her voice broke on these last words.

"Well … well …" Harriet was mortified that she had unintentionally pushed the poor woman to this.

The Countess sniffed deeply and said, "There now — no bones broken. So now you know — that's my noble career in a nutshell. Here! Where are we off to? I thought the Morrab Guest House was *in* Penzance?"

"So it is," Standish assured her, swinging the car around toward the bay. "This is Stable Hobba. We'll be going back along the seafront."

"Oh good. Anyway, like I said, I'm not ashamed of ..."

"*As* I said." Harriet just had to correct her. "Not 'like I said'."

"Bless you!" she replied, taking it as some kind of acceptance of her tale. "You've started work already and we haven't even agreed a rate for the job!"

"Sir Morgan's first wife," Tamsin said. "Did he and she ... forgive me for asking, but ..."

The Countess laughed. "You're quick, pet! Yes — they had two sons. Harry and John. Harry inherited the baronetcy but nothing else. They were a very fiery family — always quarrelling, always making it up again. But then there was one quarrel they couldn't make up. No prizes for guessing what about. Or *who* it was about."

Harriet's lips mimed *whom* but she held her tongue this time.

"And, to save you asking, the Count had no issue — or none as he'd own up to."

"Up to which he'd own," Tamsin said, watching to see if her mother reacted.

"Eh?" the Countess exclaimed.

"Only joking," the girl assured her.

"Only teasing me!" her mother added.

"So!" the Countess concluded. "Though I know it's bad form to speak of one's money, I am the heiress to two fortunes. But I'm sure you'll forgive me for mentioning it — especially seeing as it was the whole purpose of your question!"

"Never mind that," Reg said. "It's a fascinating story."

"I'll tell you something more — I kept both of those fine gentlemen happier than that Consuela Vanderbilt managed with her duke. What d'you think of her, anyway? If the daughter of a Yankee millionaire marries into a near-bankrupt English dukedom — her for the sake of his title, him for the sake of her dollars — is that better or worse than my own noble career? Much worse, I'd say, because instead of keeping her duke happy, she went and divorced him."

"Perhaps the dollars were all he needed to keep him happy," Tamsin suggested.

She laughed. "Yes, well, you may have a point there. No flies on *you!* But listen — one thing I want to make clear. The way it was between me and the Count, while his first wife was still alive … I mean, I *was* a widow then. It's different for a widow, don't you think? Anyway, it *wasn't* like that between me and Sir Morgan, despite all his tricks. None of that while *his* first wife still lived — nor for a good while after, neither. Not till he put that ring on my finger. Ah, here we are, back at the sea."

"And that's the Queen's Hôtel," Reg told her. "The big building up ahead. Mister Coverley's place, you remember."

She looked admiringly at the hôtel, but all she said was, "Can we get out and go for a stroll? I've been cooped up all day and I'm sure they can't have delivered my bags yet."

"Spiffing!" Reg said.

"I'll go home," Harriet said. "They'll be along with those portmanteaux and someone must be there to receive them."

"I'll take you there," Standish said. "Then, Countess, I'm afraid I have some urgent affairs to attend to — so have you, Reginald, in case you've forgotten."

"Eh? What?"

Standish glanced at him briefly, over his shoulder — after which he said a not-very-convincing, "Oh yes, of course! Silly me! I did forget."

Standish set them down opposite the entrance to the Queen's.

"There's a man in some sort of trouble," the Countess murmured as she and Tamsin stood on the Esplanade, watching the car take the corner into Morrab Road.

Well! Tamsin thought. *No flies on this Countess, either!*

She led the woman a few paces more, until she could point out the guest house.

"All I've got is cash and jewels and clothes," the Countess said. "It must be funny to have very little cash and yet to own a *house,* Tamsin. May I call you Tamsin? I'm Ivy, by the way." She chuckled. "Not the most aristocratic name in the world!"

"Surely you owned that house in South Audley Street?" Tamsin replied. "After Sir Morgan died, I mean. Or didn't you inherit that as well?"

"Oh, I inherited, all right. But I turned it into cash as soon as I could, before the sons, Harry and John, could come down on me with a ton of writs — which they did. But that money's all in Monaco where they can't touch it." She took Tamsin's arm. "I'll tell you one good thing about cash, love. Gold, that is. It's portable. An English judge, faced with a choice between Sir Harry Summers, Baronet, deprived of his inheritance, and little Ivy, the servant girl from Mile End who twisted the master into marrying her, is going to make his mind up before she even opens her common mouth — isn't he. But put everything into cash and send it all abroad, beyond the reach of English so-called justice, and it's only amazing how the best legal minds in London lose all interest in the case! Still — enough about me. Tell me all about you and Penzance — the exciting bits. Where's all the fun when the sun's gone down?"

"Oh, there's so much!" Tamsin replied. "Where shall I begin? D'you like embroidery? Amateur piano playing? Would you swoon at the prospect of a lantern lecture from an explorer who climbed two-thirds of the way up Mount Everest before throwing in the towel? Or how about a returned missionary with several amusing fuzzy-wuzzy anecdotes including how he nearly got cooked for their supper, and how he came across a ruined hut where Doctor Livingstone once spent the night?"

"Ohmigawd!" Ivy groaned. "As bad as that?"

"I won't tell you my best fun lately."

"That means you're going to — sooner or later, so why not get it over with now?"

"D'you want to go down on the sands?"

Ivy shook her head and waited.

"You won't laugh? Most people think I'm a bit cracked."

"Go on!"

"My best fun lately was being shown over the Queen's by Standish Coverley himself. In person! He showed me everything."

"And?"

"That's it."

"And that's fun?"

"Oh yes! I'd just love to own a big hôtel. I think they're the most fascinating places in all the world."

Ivy, watching her face light up, did not doubt a word of it.

"Does his nibs know?" she asked, tilting her head in the direction of the Queen's.

"Of course. I can't seem to keep it a secret." Tamsin smiled ruefully. "As you have just discovered."

"Hmm!" Ivy was thoughtful. "I'm just beginning to wonder if he has the same problem? Secrets, I mean — leaking out?" She peered intently into Tamsin's eyes. "D'you know what I'm talking about, pet?"

Tamsin shook her head.

Ivy shrugged. "No business of mine, I suppose. He uses me — me, who he's only just met — to score points off of that Mrs Thorne, but no, it's no business of mine!"

She glanced at Tamsin and saw her weakening.

She went on, "He told me certain ugly rumours were circulating about him but they're all lies."

"They are!"

"They are circulating or they are lies?"

"Both."

"About him and Mister Trotter?"

"No! A man called Mitchell. Marcus Mitchell."

"That name rings a bell. Was he in the papers lately?"

"I shouldn't be surprised. He's a professional swindler. I might as well tell you all I know — which isn't much — seeing that Mister Coverley told you the gist of it anyway. Mitchell has forged some papers that incriminate Mister Coverley in something illegal. Mister Coverley's been fighting the accusations on and off for the past year but ... I don't know. All I do know is that it seems to be getting very serious."

The Countess stretched and yawned. "'Scuse me! It's all this sea air after beeing cooped up in that compartment all day. Shall we go home? I wouldn't worry too much about Mister Coverley if I was you. He strikes me as a man who can take very good care of number one."

39 On their way back to the Morrab, Tamsin and Ivy saw Victor coming toward them, or, rather, coming in their direction, for he clearly did not notice them — nor anyone else for that matter.

"Here's a young fellow with the cares of the world about him," Ivy said. "Not a bad looker, either!"

"He's Victor Thorne, son of that Mrs Thorne at the station," Tamsin replied. "One of your fellow guests under our roof."

Ivy, aware that Tamsin was being just a shade too nonchalant, said, "You get the pick of them, don't you!" and was rewarded with a blush. "Is he rich?"

"He will be next year. Or soon. I don't know exactly."

When he was still a dozen paces away, Ivy stepped into his path — a movement that caught his attention for the first time. He halted, still a few yards off, and stared in confusion, seeing an elegant young lady in deep mourning and, yes, Tamsin, his own beloved. Understanding followed a fraction of a second later for, until that moment, he had been a hundred miles away.

"Countess," Tamsin said. "Allow me to present Mister Victor Thorne of Peveril Hall, near Exeter. Ivy, Countess de Ath."

She offered her hand for a kiss. While Victor lowered his head Tamsin saw his eyes conduct a lightning audit of her person, from the neck down; again, as far as she could tell, he, too, liked what he saw — as who would not? "Allow me to express my sincere condolences, Countess."

"Ah well," she replied. "These things happen. He had eighty good years and four *very* good ones."

He started in surprise at her accent, though he still lingered over releasing her hand.

She winked at Tamsin and said, "See!"

"Forgive me for not noticing you." He released her hand at last and turned to Tamsin. "I've had a bit of a blow, to tell the truth. The mater and pater are determined to leave tonight."

"Oh!" Tamsin glanced toward the Morrab, almost as if she expected to see them coming down the path. She relaxed a little when she recalled that her mother and Daisy were at home; neither would let the Thornes go without settling.

"It's all right," he said. "The train's not until half-past eight — though how we'll manage the fifteen miles from Exeter to the Hall is anybody's guess."

"Do *you* have to go, too?" Tamsin asked.

"I'm sorry, Countess," he said. "This must be very tedious to you, especially after such a long train journey."

"Don't stand bareheaded in this sun, please," she replied.

"Walk back with us," Tamsin suggested. "Unless you were on some particular errand?"

"No, no," he replied lugubriously. "I was just going to drown myself or something. I'll come part-way." He turned and took the gentlemanly position nearest the kerb but Tamsin stepped beyond him and sandwiched him between them.

"If you insist," he said. "The thing is, you see, I do, more or less, have to go back with them — finding myself a little short of steam at the moment. I was actually on my way to touch old Coverley for a few quid, if you really want to know — because the last place on earth *I* want to be at the moment ..."

"Gambling?" Tamsin guessed.

He gave her a wry smile. "In a way. You could call it that."

She realized he was talking about the turquoise necklace. "Would you borrow from me instead?" she suggested.

"From a *lady?*" He was horrified, or made it seem so. They halted and formed a triangular group again.

"Fair exchange is no robbery," she said. "And the pawnbroker in Jennings Street is very discreet, I'm told. Ladies can approach him through the milliner's next door."

"Well ... at the risk of sounding churlish, may I just say I'll keep your kind offer in mind, but I'll first see if Coverley's in a generous mood. That's where I'm actually heading — because, as it happens, I'm in a position to do him a big favour, too."

He tipped his hat and was about to continue on his way to the Queen's when Tamsin said, "Just a mo! Why are your parents in such a rush? Is it something *we've* said? Or done?"

"No." The reply was awkward. "They just don't want to be in Penzance tomorrow morning."

"For any particular reason?"

"Nothing you've done, anyway — you and your mother. But it's why I have to see Coverley now — rather urgently. So, if you'll excuse me ...?"

"You didn't tell me about *these* excitements," Ivy said as they resumed their homeward stroll. "Is Penzance always like this?"

"Not at all. But rather a lot seems to be happening lately. David Peters being almost drowned at sea ... the brandy smuggling ... there's a lot to tell you, Ivy."

"David Peters?"

"Oh ... just a fisherman I know. He works from Newlyn, which is ... no, you can't see it from here. But it's a mile or so that way. You can see it from my bedroom window."

"Ah!" Ivy said knowingly. "Just a fisherman you ... *know?*"

"It's nothing like that," Tamsin assured her. And she went on to explain about the seafood restaurant and David's role.

Ivy paid less attention to the words than to the animation that showed in the face of her new-found friend.

"Mmm-hmm," was her only comment. Then: "I like the look of your Mister Victor Thorne, though. Did I gather just now that he's cleaned himself out in buying some present for you?"

Tamsin explained about the turquoise, and then all the reasons Cicely Thorne had given for not marrying him — which were utter common sense, really. "So," she concluded, "I think I'll ask Daisy to slip out tonight and pawn it — and give him the money and the pledge. I've been racking my brains for days how to return the present without hurting him. This is ideal, and it'll be one less weight on my mind. What d'you think?"

After a silence, during which they arrived at the front gate, Ivy said, "If it's a good turquoise ..."

"Oh, it is. The best I ever saw."

"The colour of your eyes?"

"That's why he bought it — so he said."

"Well, if it's as good as all that, you could pawn it with me, instead — only don't let him know."

"Really? You're not just being kind?"

"Kind to myself, if anything. I don't imagine this town is bristling with handsome, rich young *boolevardiers* like him?"

"Certainly not! Standish and Reg are the only other two I know of."

"Point taken! So it would be a kindness to me, above all, if he was free to remain here — at least until I've had a chance to size him up."

Tamsin paused inside the gate. There was one question she just had to ask this woman of the world and it would be impossible if others were around. "D'you think it's wrong for a woman to be mercenary, Ivy?" she asked.

"Like me?" She laughed.

"I'm thinking more of myself. I mean, if a rich man asked me to marry him — and I don't mean one who's young and handsome, like Victor, though of course that would be ideal — but any rich man — fat, old, ugly ... anyone — and if he said I could have as much of his money as I wanted so I could build my hôtel, well ... I don't think I'd hesitate too long. Is that awful?"

"How would you treat him?" Ivy asked. "Would you keep your side of the bargain — spoken or unspoken? Make sure he dies with that certain smile on his lips? Know what I mean?"

"No, I think I might be more like Consuela Vanderbilt," Tamsin admitted.

"Then it would be wrong, pet. Very wrong."

40 It is curious how life can bubble along quite merrily for years and then suddenly, in the space of half an hour, everything can change. It happened to Tamsin the following morning, the first Sunday in August, and it came without warning out of a clear blue sky — or, more precisely, a grey and threatening sky. On Sundays, breakfasts were served an hour later than usual, so Tamsin had the chance of a well-deserved lie-in. She would have indulged herself, too, if her restless spirit had not woken her even earlier than her usual time.

She rose and dressed without disturbing Daisy and went downstairs, thinking she might as well go to early Communion — and would God mind if she had a ginger faring and a glass of milk first? She was surprised to find Victor and Ivy already in the kitchen, rather sheepishly helping themselves to bread and marmalade. They, too, had the Communion service in mind, mainly because, duty done, they'd have the rest of the day free.

"Your parents left some books behind," Tamsin told him. "A Wilkie Collins and a couple of Sherlock Holmes yarns."

"Put them in your bookshelf," he said. "They bought them down here and, somehow, I don't think they'll be wanting too many souvenirs of Penzance!"

They left together and walked down Morrab Road to the seafront. It had been a fine, warm night but they could now see the last of the blue sky vanishing over the Lizard. Overhead was a mass of pale grey cloud that seemed curiously upside-down. Usually the lowest part of a cloud is flat bottomed and dark; here it hung down in bulbous clumps, each one of which seemed to be lit powerfully from within by flares of sulphur. Victor remarked that it was like a giant cauliflower, daubed grey and yellow, and hung upside-down overhead. They all hoped it did not mean that the fine weather of the past two days was breaking up yet again.

Then, just after they had crossed the road to walk along the seaward side of the Esplanade, the doorman from the Queen's came hurrying after them.

"Miss Harte!" he called out when he was still some way off. They stopped and turned to face him.

"Sorry!" he panted as he drew near. "It's just Miss Harte, really. The boss sends his compliments and asks would you join him for breakfast, miss?"

"Really?" She was astounded. "But why?"

"It's urgent, miss. That's all I know."

She glanced at Ivy, who said, "I think you should ought to go, pet. We'll make your apologies for you!" She raised her eyes toward that huge upside-down cauliflower above.

Mystified, Tamsin followed the man back to the hôtel. There a waiter took over and guided her upstairs. Her bewilderment turned to mild alarm when she saw she was expected to dine alone in one of the bedrooms with Standish; and the bed wasn't even made.

"Where's Reg?" she asked.

"He's gone ahead of me to France," he replied. She had never seen him so agitated.

"To France?"

"Sit down, Tamsin — please. And loosen anything that might impede the flow of blood to your brain, because you're going to have to think as you've never thought before in all your life." To the waiter he said, "That's all, George, thank you."

He followed the man to the door and locked it behind him. "Don't be alarmed," he said, pocketing the key. "It's just a pre-caution. What can we offer you?" He went over to the dressing table, which had been turned into a makeshift buffet. "Kipper, haddock, fish kedgeree, devilled kidneys, scramblers, bacon ..."

"What are you having?"

"I couldn't touch a thing, love."

"Standish!" She touched his arm gently. "What's happening?"

"What's happening is that that devil Mitchell has won. This round, anyway. I have to get out of the country, if I'm to stand a chance of continuing the fight to prove my innocence. And I have to get out toot sweet! I may already have left it too late. Unless ..." He eyed her uncertainly.

"Unless what?"

"Unless you help me. Sure you don't want to eat anything?"

"Not until I know what's what. How on earth can I help you?"

"Do sit down — please." He held a chair expectantly, more or less forcing her to obey.

He seated himself opposite her and spoke to a point somewhere just in front of her empty plate. "Please consider what I'm about to ask you very carefully," he said. He spoke slowly, as if he had rehearsed his words many times — which, she soon suspected, was indeed the case.

"I'm going to ask you to commit an illegal act ..."

She missed the next few words — perhaps even a sentence or two — because her mind was reeling and her fingers were automatically loosening the hooks in her bodice, at her throat.

"... assured me I would have time," he was saying when the dizziness passed.

"I'm sorry," she blurted out.

"Don't say no yet," he pleaded. "Just hear ..."

"No, no — it's not that. I didn't catch everything you said ... something about not being pursued."

"Oh. I was just explaining that the chief constable is an old family friend and he says he can hold the hounds at bay but only until this evening."

"Standish, have you ..." She paused and then thought better of it. "No. You go on. I won't interrupt."

"I'm actually going to ask you *two* huge favours. One of them is going to sound like a bribe to induce you to ... to carry out the other. But here goes. I would like you to consider taking over the management of this hôtel in my absence."

She gasped. In her confusion, the only thing she could think of asking was, "Is that an illegal act?"

He laughed, with little humour. "No. It's the bribe — though the offer stands even if you do not wish to do me the other favour, the illegal one. You undertand that? You'll be manageress here, come what may — whether I'm in gaol or France."

"France! You're going to France as well?"

"That's the idea. Reginald is being absolutely marvellous. He knows a hundred pensions and so on where I'll be safe — and meanwhile he'll be free to pop back and forth across the Channel, tend to his mama, collect papers, brief lawyers and private inquiry agents ... all that sort of thing. I do not deserve such friends. Even young Victor ..." He seemed lost in thought.

"We met him last night, the Countess and I. He talked of doing you a favour, too."

"And so he did — an enormous one." Standish smiled ruefully. "I wish we'd worked out earlier what his mother's intentions were when she moved from here to your place. I wouldn't have made such an enemy of her — and then I might have had another month or so to order my affairs here."

Guilty that she had said nothing when she had known everything, Tamsin asked, "How has she brought it all about, then?"

"It's more a question of *why,*" he replied. "I had a long, enjoyable chat with Charlotte, who told me all about her ambitions to become a professional artist. And I rather encouraged her, I'm afraid. I should have realized that if a mother like Mrs Thorne allows her daughter an hour of unchaperoned intercourse with a gentleman, she has hopes of a certain outcome. And if that gentleman then encourages the daughter to strike out on her own" — he smiled wanly — "he's asking for trouble. And I certainly got it!"

Tamsin frowned. "Even so, how could she ..."

"Don't ask me! I can only assume that Devon is crammed with retired legal bigwigs who can still bend an ear and twist an arm up in London — and that many of them are friends of the Thornes. Anyway, that's what Victor came to warn me of last night. So — can we come back to my offer of the management of the Queen's? You would have complete day-to-day control of the entire business."

He went to the window and peeped out at the street through a crack between the curtains.

"Oh!" She felt that swimming feeling come over her again. "But I'm not ..."

He interrupted her as he returned to the table. "Time's short, Tamsin. If I'm wrong about you, then it's my responsibility. But I'm sure I'm not wrong. Indeed, I've never been so sure of anything in my life. Also, Jessica Trelawney agrees — and she's nobody's fool when it comes to judging character and ability. Listen! The farmers hereabout have a saying — 'The best dung is the master's boot,' meaning that you can spread all the artificial fertilizer you like on the land but if the master takes no interest, it's not going to do much good."

"But Standish! To expect me to run an hôtel the size of the Queen's! *You* may have confidence in me, but I don't."

"I'm only talking about day-to-day running. Jessica will retain control of all financial affairs and will remain the ultimate authority. Think of yourself as the public face of the Queen's — the hostess who stamps her personality upon the place — and heaven knows it needs such a person. And that person is you, is you, is you! Especially with Jessica standing discreetly in the wings to support you. She's full of admiration for you, you know. So am I, of course. And, believe me, *I'm* not likely to interfere with your management from somewhere deep in the Gironde or the Dordogne!"

She could feel her doubts crumbling inside her. She decided to gamble everything. "What if we got married, Standish?" she asked. "That would make it ..."

"Married!" he exclaimed.

"Is it such an outlandish idea? I could so easily love you — I think. The difference between love and what I feel for you already is so fine ..."

"Oh no it isn't, Tamsin. If you think that, then you're not even close to loving anyone — yet. Believe me, I'm not insensible of the honour you do me, but an hôtelier sees enough of loveless marriages to know what hell-on-earth they are."

"But it could so easily *become* love," she insisted.

"How can I make you understand?" He closed his eyes a moment and then began again. "When your father died — forgive me if it's still painful — but didn't something deep inside you simply refuse to believe it?"

She nodded. She had been close enough to tears before he spoke his latest words; now she was afraid he'd drive her over the edge.

"And didn't you go around for days, looking for him, almost expecting the very intensity of your grief to bring him back?"

"Yes," she whispered.

"And ... I don't know — was he a sailing man?"

She shook her head. "He said he had enough of the sea at his work. He liked walking."

"Well then, suppose he'd gone walking up on Dartmoor and didn't come back when you expected. Got lost in the mist or a storm or something. Wouldn't you have gone racing up, on foot, on pony, any way you could, and stood on some tor up there, scanning every acre of bog and heath for some sign of him?"

"Yes." She laughed.

Surprised, he said, "It wouldn't be so funny at the time."

"No ... I was just thinking ... it doesn't matter."

"What?"

"Well, only last Wednesday I was standing at the lookout above Penlee Point, alongside old Benny Peters, scanning every part of Mount's Bay and the Channel for some sign of David, who had gone out in that tropical storm or whatever it was — the idiot!"

"And he came back, surely? The whole town would have ..."

"Yes. Calm as you like — I could have hit him! I would have, too, if I'd stayed until he made landfall. Sorry, but it doesn't exactly support *your* point, does it!"

"You did all *that*? As soon as you heard he was missing?"

"No, I waited until the afternoon. It was stupid of me."

He hesitated, as if he would say more, but then he just shrugged and said, "If you say so. My main point, however, is that what I was describing ... what I was trying to evoke in recalling your own love for your father ..."

"Oh, but you were right there. That *does* support what you were saying."

"Well," he said simply. "Until you feel with that sort of intensity ..." He let a shrug complete the thought. "Now let's talk about your salary — a proper salary. A thousand pounds a year, I'd suggest — if that's acceptable to you?"

He misinterpreted her shock as some kind of doubt. "Plus ... what shall we say? Ten percent of any increase in profits at the end of each year? No, ten is niggardly — because we're only talking about the *increase*. Say, twenty-five? A quarter of any increase in profits? You'd deserve it. Anyway, you're quite right not to say yes and not to say no just at the moment. We can come to some arrangement later. The main thing is for me to get to France as soon as maybe and without getting myself arrested." He glanced nervously toward the window again.

"Was that the other favour?" she asked, already having a good idea of the details.

He nodded and gave a nervous smile. "And, as I said, it's not conditional on your becoming manageress. The other way round, I mean."

She smiled and said, "Would you mind terribly if you arrived in Brittany smelling of fish?"

41   If Tamsin hadn't known Cornwall so well by now, she'd have assumed that someone of importance to the whole community of Newlyn had died. Black was the sabbath colour there. So black was the colour of most people's only good clothes. So black was the keynote of galas, fêtes, festivals, and holidays, too — not that today was any of those. The entire harbour was ringed with black-clad men and black-garbed women, ostentatiously honouring the day of rest. Finding David was going to be like looking for one redcoat in an entire army.

The skies were sombre as well, as if to match their mood. People were predicting rain — and maybe winds to go with it, but certainly rain in abundance.

Offhand, too, one would have said that Ivy, in widow's weeds from head to toe, would not have looked out of place in such a throng. But no woman of that village, who from a distance and collectively resembled so many black beehives, could ever have been mistaken for her. Today, in yet another figure-clinging outfit of shimmering black silk, she had all the sinuous grace of a wet otter at play. Men gazed after her with hooded eyes as she passed and they thought of the hour, that afternoon, when the children would all be safely out of the house at Sunday School.

She, for her part, seemed oblivious to it all, being much more interested in hearing about Tamsin's interview with Standish that morning; she spent most of their walk to Newlyn talking about it, picking it to pieces, analyzing it, and putting it back in every possible way. "I still think you should hold out for marriage, pet," she finally concluded.

"Possibly. But the important thing, just at the moment, is to get the poor man safely away to France."

"Right, I can see that. But *then* you can ... aren't you going to ask any of these people where your friend is?"

"I don't think so." Tamsin spoke softly in case her words carried. "I'm going to ask him to put to sea on the sabbath — which is like social death here."

"I can imagine!" She gazed around at a sea of dour, suspicious faces. "Anyway, once he's safely in France — assuming you get him there — I think you shouldn't waste much time in making it clear that this manageress idea is just for the time being."

"I don't really think it's *that* important, do you?"

"Not important? Listen! What if he meets and marries some other bit of skirt over there, some French mott. And then suppose that something nasty should happen to him, which God forbid, but she'd become the owner and you could be out on your ear. Take it from one who knows — nothing beats that little gold band just *there!*" She stretched out her right hand and admired it. "Well, of course, it's on the other hand in England but you know what I mean."

"It certainly is a point," Tamsin had to agree. She kept on scanning the crowds, looking either for Cousin Harry or for David himself.

"It's not *a* point, pet. It's *the* point — the only one. The Married Women's Property Act beats any contract of employment into a cocked hat — especially a verbal one. It's as good as any title deed."

"There he is." Tamsin nodded toward the end of the South Pier, where David was standing alone, staring out to sea.

A moment later they met Harry. After introductions and a few solemn pleasantries, Tamsin asked him what he thought the chances were that David might put to sea in the *Merlin,* either that afternoon or early that evening.

"As close to nothing as do make no odds," he replied. "You heard, then?"

"Heard what?"

He became suspicious. "How are you asking about me putting to sea if you haven't heard?"

"I've got my own reasons. Heard what?"

He refused to say more. Her eyes took in the situation — David standing alone at the pier's end ... the rest of the village gathered around the inner-harbour wall. She made a leap: "You mean he *wants* to go out — himself — anyway?" She turned to Ivy. "That's good news!"

"I doubt it is," Harry said. "If he goes, he'll go alone — which even he's not edjack enough to risk. I shan't go with 'n. Nor will any other man — or none he'd trust. So I reckon as he's stuck here till tomorrow, anyway."

"Come on," Tamsin said to Ivy when Harry had moved away. "Let's hear what the man himself has to say.

There was an exciting tingle in her spine as they set off along the stone road of the pier. Like a child, suddenly, she walked along the shiny rails of the narrow-gauge line used by the fish drams that unloaded catches from the larger trawlers, the ones that could not come to the fishwives inshore. Judging by what Harry had said, it would seem that David had some urgent reason to put to sea quite soon — before midnight, anyway — and that no other fisherman was willing to breach the sabbath and go with him. Or maybe they had some other reason — like not wanting to put to sea in a small boat skippered by a lunatic?

Ivy was silent, too, for once. All she did was keep a close eye on Tamsin, all the way.

"And the same to you!" David called out the moment he spied them approaching.

"I was about to say you look as miserable as that fisherman who lifted a lobsterpot and found nothing inside it apart from only a dozen huge lobsters."

He laughed, almost against his will, it seemed. And he soon became morose again. "You hit the nail on the head, fair and square," he sighed.

They were close enough now for introductions. He was not greatly awed by Ivy's title.

"Is that the *Merlin?*" she asked with a nod toward the boat Tamsin had pointed out to her as soon as they came in sight of the harbour.

"Yes," he agreed. "For all the use she is to me!"

"We met Harry," Tamsin said. "He seemed to think you wanted to go fishing on the sabbath."

"The sabbath!" he said wearily. "It'll be over, well over, by the time I reach the grounds I'd want to be fishing tonight." He stretched an impressive arm southward. "Over the harrizen, as Edward John used to call it."

"It must be some fine shoal of fish to make you want to risk it."

"Fish be damned," he replied. "Pardon my French, Countess. It's a shoal of a different order. A shoal worth ..." He hesitated.

"You can trust the Countess," Tamsin assured him.

He looked all around and, lowering his voice to a purr, said, "One hundred and twenty-five pound!"

Ivy whistled and looked at him with a new respect.

"Two hundred and fifty bottles?" Tamsin asked, almost in a whisper. "Where will you fit them all?" She gazed again at the *Merlin.* "And how will you bring them back past old Sterne?"

She had told Ivy all about her encounter with the Excise during their walk to Newlyn.

"How many gallons in that many bottles?" David asked. "I'll save you the bother — forty-two."

"Ah — it's a barrel, then! Or a firkin?" As the future manageress of the Queen's, she thought it best to get such things right.

"One barrel," he agreed. "The French equivalent."

"Even so," she went on, "how are you going to ... oh, never mind. That's your problem. Mine is that I want to help Standish Coverley get to France tonight without anyone knowing. D'you think our two problems might have something in common?"

"What's it worth to him?" David said at once.

"No, David." She shook her head firmly. "What's it worth to you? What will you pay him to crew for you?"

Ivy laughed but he was not amused. "And what about coming back?" he asked. "Never thought about that, did you!"

"No, it completely slipped my mind," she said, unruffled. "Well, I thought I'd just be coming along to enjoy the ride, but I can see I shall have to roll up my sleeves and get stuck in, too."

This time Ivy not only laughed, she spun a full circle and slapped Tamsin on the back, saying, "My! Ain't you the gel!"

Tamsin knew at once that David was going to agree, just as she knew he was going to hold out against the suggestion until the last possible moment. Then, suddenly, the hair bristled on her neck and she knew why he had risked putting to sea in that storm three days ago — it would have been worth five hundred pounds. Somehow he had missed the rendezvous when the Frenchman was on the way out to ... wherever. Biscay or the South Irish Sea. Tonight was his only chance to pick them up during their return up the Channel. If he didn't make a meeting tonight, a hundred and twenty-five pounds' worth of brandy would go all the way home again to Brittany!

Then she knew not only that she had him but also the why of it — which made her position impregnable.

42   The chief constable had given Standish twenty-four hours to settle his affairs. He could explain it away as a ruse to net any accomplices Standish might have in this sorry business. Standish would not be arrested if he left the hôtel during that time but he would be followed — with all the resulting scandal. He was more sorry than he could say but that was the best he could promise.

The first plan to thwart these arrangements was for Victor to dress in some of Standish's clothes and, wrapping himself in mufflers and goggles, drive the Rolls-Royce out toward Longrock — drawing the police away while Standish and Tamsin went off in a gig in the opposite direction, toward Mousehole, where they were to rendezvous with David at five that evening. But when they found that an extra constable had been stationed in the mews, as well as the one they already knew about on the Esplanade, they had to abandon that arrangement.

"What about the car, anyway?" Victor asked.

"You can drive it up to Plymouth and bring it over to me anytime you like," Standish told him. "Only for God's sake choose dry days. The hide stinks after rain. Otherwise," he added, "Reginald can collect it on one of his visits."

After that setback, their actual escape owed more to the appalling weather than to any cunning plan on their part. The curiously bulbous, sulphur-yellow clouds continued to hang overhead throughout the day. Around four o'clock that afternoon, half an hour before their deadline for leaving the hôtel, sheet lightning began to play somewhere above them, giving the effect of arc lights, flickering in a pale yellow jelly; there was no accompanying thunder, which somehow made the effect even more uncanny. Everyone was jittery — including, they hoped, the man on watch along the Esplanade.

At half-past four, when their timing was getting pretty critical, the heavens opened at last — and not just in ordinary summer rain but in a flood such as Tamsin could not remember at any time in her life. The man on the Esplanade ran for the shelter, where he could continue to watch the entrance through the glass, though how much he could actually make out through that cascade of stair-rods was anybody's guess. It was still more than three hours to sunset but the eerily bright daylight, combined with the rain, did more to hinder visibility than to help it.

A motor cab drew up to let a couple alight. The commissionaire shielded them as best he could with his umbrella and asked the driver to wait.

"Now or never," Tamsin said, peering out of the front lobby.

A chain of signals brought Standish running from the manager's office, out onto the pavement, where, again sheltered (and hidden) by that capacious umbrella, they made it safely into the cab. The commissionaire thrust the umbrella in after them.

"Where to, Mister Coverley, sir?" the man asked, adding that he was surprised anyone wanted to go out on such a night.

They directed him to Mousehole.

"When are you going to change?" Standish asked Tamsin as soon as they were off.

"Why not now?" she replied. "Good idea."

They were both already wearing fishermen's oilskin jackets and hoods. Now she pulled on a pair of Victor's cricket flannels, loaned for the occasion, before unhooking her skirt, which she folded up neatly and placed in the carpet bag. Fortunately, the cabbie only had eyes for the road ahead, or what he could see of it through the vertical river from above.

"You've got your passport?" she asked.

Standish patted his pocket. "Plus enough francs to bribe my way out of any little difficulty. Also I *am* going to pay David Peters. I wouldn't dream of not doing so — whatever you say."

When they arrived at the tiny fishing village, no one was abroad, for the rain was as heavy as ever; they could not even see to the end of the harbour wall. Though David had selected this cove for no better reason than that it lay nearest his route between Newlyn and his meeting with Jean-Baptiste Clouet, his Breton fisherman-accomplice, the choice was nonetheless perfect for such a venture. The long, narrow, crooked valley, studded with houses that seemed more to hang in space than to perch on those impossibly steep sides, closed around them in a protective scrum; and the tiny, oval harbour — a sea puddle, really — between the towering bastions of Penlee and Halwyn was invisible from Newlyn, Penzance, Marazion ... from any place, in fact, where authority might lurk. To see *into* it from outside, even on a good day with the rising sun behind you, you'd need to be on a clifftop miles across the bay with a good pair of glasses — and even then it would be little more than a grey blur on the wide green sprawl of the Land's End peninsula. The two runaways felt safe the moment the cab began whining its way down in low gear from St. Paul.

They told the driver to take the carpet bag back to the hôtel and then, huddled beneath the wide umbrella, they made their way toward the deserted quay. The rain thundered down upon the fabric like a hundred drummers all out of time. It took less than a dozen paces for them to decide it was futile to try to avoid puddles; the place was one giant lake and the slipway, where David was to pick them up, was a torrent.

"No sign of him yet." Standish took out his watch. "Five minutes to go — at least he won't be able to say we held him up."

"That won't stop him!"

"You're pretty hard on him, aren't you?" he remarked.

"Am I?" The thought had not occurred to Tamsin.

It was weird to be standing there amid all those shuttered houses, in a deluge of biblical proportions ... they could have been the last two people in the world. She wondered what he'd do if they were. It was an ancient daydream — castaways, alone on a tropic island. Would the old injunction, *Go forth and multiply,* seize him then, and would he love and cherish her as the only love possible?

Standish interrupted her thoughts. "If there's any doubt, he never seems to get the benefit of it from you," he said.

"Perhaps he doesn't deserve it," she replied. "I don't know. He just annoys me. He's such a *liar.*" The sudden vehemence of this denunciation surprised even her. "Well ..."

She started to retract a little but he was already responding. "Strong stuff, Tamsin! Why doth the lady protest so much? Doth the lady herself even know? Or perhaps I mean: Doth the lady even *know herself?*"

So now she had to justify her outburst instead. "He thinks he's so clever. Inventing things. And just look at the risks he takes! For what? He doesn't think of the people he'd be leaving behind. His poor father, who's already lost two sons to the sea."

"I see. So when you say 'liar' ..."

"Yes! He tells stupid lies, which wouldn't even deceive a child. About ... well, it doesn't matter."

"Lies to the Customs and Excise?" he suggested.

"No! Lies about ... you know — girls."

"Not about you, I hope?"

"About a girl who died years ago — a girl his *father* loved and lost. He just made it up ... I know very well why he did it and it was just ... *stupid!* Can't we talk about something else?"

"Yes, of course," he said in a considerate tone. "Obviously it upset you dreadfully. I'm sorry I pursued it."

"It didn't upset me at all!" she almost shouted. "He's not ... he won't win. He's not ... he's not ... *suitable!* That's all I've got to say. He's not suitable. Why are we wasting time on him? Here he is, anyway. He's just a ferryman as far as I'm concerned. We ought to be talking about important things like the Queen's."

"Yes, you're quite right," Standish said briskly. "Still, we've got several hours ahead of us if this meeting is to take place somewhere near mid-Channel."

The deep rumble of the *Merlin's* engines rose to a roar as David reversed the pitch and threw the tiller hard over, yawing the boat to a momentary halt parallel to and only a foot away from the sheer wall of the slipway. He'd become a dreadful show-off since he'd fitted that engine — throwing the boat around like that ... putting to sea in any sort of weather ...

"Jump!" he cried as the stern swung round. "I'm not stopping to tie up."

Standish just had time to collapse the umbrella before they both made their leap, side by side; the umbrella opened again, like a parachute, and clicked fast as they hit the deck, which had been about three feet below them — but wet and slippery. More by luck than anything, they landed on a falling swell, which absorbed something of their impact. Even so, they sprawled in an ungainly heap from which it took several seconds to extricate themselves, during which time, of course, their trouser legs became soaked to the skin.

"What with perspiring inside the oilskins and getting soused outside them," Tamsin said, "there's not much point in wearing clothes at all."

"All hands to the pump!" David shouted as he hit the throttle and set the pitch to forward once again. He had rigged an extra shelter of canvas aft, between the wheelhouse and the stern.

"Where?" Standish called back.

He pointed to a handle amidships, for the back-and-forth type of pump. Standish seized it and set to with vigour.

"You, maid, come and take the wheel."

"Aye *aye*, Cap'n," she replied with a sarcasm that was completely lost on him.

He piloted the *Merlin* through the narrow harbour mouth and on out through the gap between St. Clement's Isle and the Merlyn Rock — the 'Mousehole' that gives the village its name. But once they were safely into open water he set the course to 180° — due south — and handed the wheel to her.

"Aren't you glad to see us?" she asked.

But he was still smarting at the way she had cheated him (as he saw it) out of a fee for carrying Standish Coverley to safety. "I could have done it alone," he replied, "what with this wind."

True or not, a wind had, indeed, sprung up even in the short while since they had left Penzance. Or, perhaps, since it blew from the north, they had been sheltered from it, both there and in Mousehole harbour. Out here on open water, however, it was good and strong.

With Standish's help he set all the canvas she could carry — a jib, which he left loose as a spinnaker, a foresail, and a main. The tarpaulin over the stern was not one of the sails, being there to keep the rain off the engine housing, but, as they were running before the wind, it, too had some effect. Soon they were making enough way to allow David to cut the engine.

"Can we afford to do that?" Tamsin asked.

"Do I try and tell you how to run the Morrab?" he replied.

She wanted to tell him she was about to 'run' something much grander than the Morrab and so he could put that in his pipe and smoke it; but she realized she would merely be descending to his level of childishness, or churlishness, so she just maintained a dignified silence — and a course of 180°.

David next relieved Standish at the pump. He came aft, flapping his arms with relief, like a bird in slowed-down motion. "I've just realized how long it's been since I did any really hard labour," he said.

"But 'hard labour' is supposed to be what you're fleeing from," she pointed out.

He laughed. "It might have done me good — my health if not my reputation. Anyway, let's talk about the Queen's."

And so he told her what she'd need to know in order to start at the job. The chef, he said, would run the kitchen and still room entirely; he'd take orders of a general nature but would not tolerate the slightest interference in day-to-day matters.

"And suppose I just walk through the kitchen and see … I don't know — flies on exposed meat … or a chef-de-rang picking his nose. What then?"

"You tell me."

"I'd give them a ticking off. What would you do?"

"Frankly, I'd never venture into the kitchen at all. You'd be horrified at what goes on, even in the best hôtels in the world."

"Well, they're not going to go on inside the Queen's. I'll tell you that now — while you can still change your mind."

He laughed, rather bleakly, and said, "I shan't interfere but be prepared for a clash of wills. And I wouldn't start in the kitchens, if I were you. Start with the chambermaids and the standards of cleanliness in the bedrooms and other public places. Establish yourself as undisputed mistress there and then move on to the porters, pageboys, and bar. The bar is not going to be easy, either. There are so many ways to cheat customers who are already half sozzled anyway."

"Dip your finger in gin and wipe it round the rim of the glass — that sort of thing?"

He leaned over her shoulder and peered into her face. "Don't tell me you haven't worked in hôtels somewhere, sometime!"

"All right," she replied. "I won't."

"Anyway, there's the strategy I'd follow if I were you. Get every other department squirming under your rod of iron before you even stick your nose inside the kitchen door. Let your dragon-reputation go before you, breathing fire."

They continued in this way for more than an hour, hardly noticing that David had long since stopped pumping the bilge, nor even that the rain had fallen to a mere pitter-patter on the tarpaulin above their heads. Tamsin was left feeling even more daunted at the thought of all that lay ahead of her, and yet her confidence was all the greater because Standish never doubted for a moment that she could do it.

She did not really become aware of their surroundings until David came aft and, standing just outside the wheelhouse, shading his eyes while he peered into the gloom where she stood, said, "Have you noticed this wet stuff all around us, maid? It's what we call the sea! I only mention it because every now and then much bigger boats than this one make use of it, too — so it's not a bad idea to keep what we call 'a weather eye' out for them. And talking of the weather …"

"Ha ha, very funny!" she shouted back. "If I'm just a little fool, then all my weather eye can see at this moment is a much bigger one. And he's blocking the view completely."

"Shall I get out and walk?" Standish offered, stepping out from behind the wheelhouse to a position half way between them, still under the awning. "I say!" He stretched a hand out into the open. "It's stopped raining completely. And the cloud's gone over, too — it's nothing but clear sky behind. I wondered why it wasn't getting much darker."

A few moments later the trailing edge of the cloud passed clear of the sun, which was now within a few minutes of setting. As yet it showed but a thin section of its disc, but immediately everything was outlined in gold — the mast, the jib, the gunwales, the frames of the wheelhouse ... and David's head. The transformation took her unawares. As the cloud moved on and the light strengthened, so, too, did that magical aura of gold that now bathed him. How long that moment lasted was of no consequence; it was, in any case, snatched from normal Time. For that brief eternity their eyes dwelled deep, each in the other's, and something passed between them that could never be put in words — indeed, it was deeper even than thoughts, something visceral and merciless.

In a panic she tore her gaze away and turned for help to Standish. Since he was still in the shade of the awning, his eyes were hard to read. But his gesture was unambiguous. He shrugged and spread his hands with their palms toward her, as if to say, 'This is what I told you about. What can anyone do?'

No!

She was not going to let it happen. Not to her.

"David!" she called out. "Come and take the wheel. I'm tired of this."

Again he took her by surprise, placing his huge, salt-browned hands over hers, which she removed as if they were scalded.

Fighting tears of rage — or outrage, perhaps — she made her way forrard to the prow, where she caught hold of both gunwales and leaned out as far as she could. Her body spilled wind off the spinnaker, which began to flap. Far away to her right the sea was now swallowing the huge crimson orb of the sun, as oval as a rugby football.

He came and stood behind her. "Go away," she said.

"He sent me to catch you if you fell." It was not David but Standish.

"Oh, I'm sorry." She turned and gave him a brief, wan smile.

They stood thus awhile in the silence of wind and ocean, and the mewing of the single gull that had followed them thus far.

"Now you know," he said at length.

"No, I do not," she replied. "It was just a trick of the light. He's the least suitable man for me in all Cornwall. I don't have time for any of that. There's no place ... no place for ..." Her voice trailed off into a single, exasperated sigh.

"The best of luck, then," he said.

43 How David managed to make a rendezvous at dead of night, on a completely featureless ocean, with a fleet whose movements he could only guess at from long experience, was both mystery and miracle. He frequently checked the stars, but what could they tell him of the Breton fleet's movements? And several times he dipped an enamel mug into the sea, sipping it and spitting it out like a winetaster; and once or twice he poured it out where the wheelhouse light would shine through it — all of which might have told him something about the tides and the currents, or the fish that might inhabit them; but, again, how would that have led him to the French boats?

And yet, at two o'clock that night, drifting bare-masted and silent, they saw a dozen masthead lights way off to the west; and it was well within the hour when he had predicted their meeting.

"Not bad, eh!" he said to Tamsin as he hoisted a signal light and prepared to send up a maroon.

"If I'd known you were so wonderful, I wouldn't have bothered myself over you at all last week," she replied.

She had intended the words to be cutting but, somehow, they didn't emerge like that.

He rubbed the 'slatch,' as he called it, against the self-igniting fuse and stood back. There was a mighty whoosh and a shower of sparks. The well of the deck filled with smoke and the acrid tang of burned sulphur and saltpetre. They held their breaths as it drifted away, watching, meanwhile, the fiery parabola of the maroon, which burst into stars of descending crimson immediately after reaching its peak.

The Frenchmen gave an answering hoot on a klaxon, which carried faintly to them across the water.

David hoisted the mainsail again and set off in their direction. The wind had dropped considerably by now.

To Tamsin they were just so many dimly glimpsed boats, locatable only by their lights, but David seemed to know by instinct which one was Jean-Baptiste's. There was a hasty conference in a dialect she found impossible to follow beyond the occasional word, some of them none too edifying. *"Comme la vache qui pisse!"* she heard distinctly.

At one stage tots of brandy were offered all round. She declined. Eventually a price for carrying Standish was agreed. He parted with some of his francs, then turned and held out his arms to her. "It's *au revoir,* little face," he said, hugging her tight, "not goodbye."

"I wish it could be you, Standish," she said. "Not him." David must have heard but she didn't care.

"No you don't," he chided.

"I do. It would make so much more sense all round."

"Yes, well, *sense* is what aristocrats marry for. That's why their lines all become extinct. Just thank God that hot blood rules the rest of us — or those who dare follow where it leads!"

When he was aboard the lugger that was to take him to France, he called back across the ever-widening divide, "That wasn't what I meant to say at all. What I really wanted to say was that there are some people of fifty who couldn't order a daily newspaper with any conviction — and some youngsters of twenty who could order an army into battle and win. You're in that second group!"

"But I'm twenty-*one!*" she called back.

"See!" His voice only just carried to her by now. "You're ahead already!"

The tears were running down her cheeks by then, though, thankfully, she was not sobbing; she would have hated David to discover such weakness in her.

"Come-us on, maid!" he said, rubbing his hands briskly. "That's only the easy part over."

"Just tell me what to do, then," she snapped as she returned to the wheelhouse.

He was already handling the mainsail boom sheets. "Bring her about and try and steer fine to forty-five degrees. Tell me when we're there — or how near you can get. If she loses headway, ease off the helm until she picks up again."

She had to 'ease off on the helm' a couple of times before the needle settled at 45°; each time he adjusted the sheets to change the angle of the mainsail.

"And now?" she asked.

"Just hold her steady for the next four hours."

"What!"

"Sing out if you see any sort of light."

"What if it's a lighthouse?"

"It won't be — or if you see one, you'll see two. The Longships and the Wolf Rock — in which case we'll be very late into port."

"Four *hours,* you said?"

"Watch the bearing, maid. You'm too close to the wind."

She glanced down and saw that the needle had, indeed, moved; she swung the helm until the alignment was back at 45°.

"What are *you* doing?" she asked. Having to keep her eye on the lighted compass ruined her night vision. All she could see was that he was up forrard, near the reserve fuel tank.

"Working," he replied.

After a while she called out again. "Can't we start the engine?"

"No," he replied. "We're short of petrol."

"What? You've got two forty-five-gallon tanks and you haven't used any yet — except for the bit from Newlyn to Mousehole."

He appeared at her side suddenly. "How do you know we've got *two* tanks?"

"Because, when you stowed the tarpaulin, I saw a copper pipe running from the main tank, here under my feet, to somewhere up there. Doesn't it go to a spare tank, then?"

"Quite right," he said casually. "Just wondered how you knew."

"Did you get your barrel of brandy?"

"That's what I was now hiding. Listen, I was joking when I said four hours. There's a pile of nets up forrard. That'd be the softest place now. You go put your head down if you mind to." When she seemed about to argue he added, "Gusson with you! We may yet need your quick wits, so it's best you were rested."

The nets were damp and reeked of tar and barking; the deck pitched endlessly beneath her; and yet, to her amazement, she fell asleep at once and did not wake until he nudged her at just after six the following morning. "There's a cup of tea and some saffron bread aft," he said.

It was half an hour before sunrise but the sky was already a horrid shade of acid pink.

"Oh, I must look *awful!*" Tamsin cried, sitting up stiffly, yawning, and rubbing bricks of sleep from her eyes.

"You do," he agreed, "but it's nothing a good tot of brandy won't cure."

"Who's to drink it — me or you?"

He laughed and returned to the wheelhouse.

As she followed him she saw he'd rigged up a sort of tarpaulin curtain, diagonally across part of the stern. "There's a bucket there to wash your face and hands and that," he said. "And for calls of nature what you do is you slip this noose around you, under your arms, and you hold fast this sheet, and you sit as far back over the gunwale as you need."

The Cornish coast — the Land's End peninsula, she hoped — almost filled the northern horizon. She could just see occasional breakers — the high ones, she assumed, so they must be less than four miles from land.

Ten minutes later a different Tamsin joined him in the wheelhouse, ready to take on the world. Saffron bread tasted good at any time but never so good as then. And as for hot tea, sweet-sweet-sweetened with condensed milk … it was the finest beverage in all the world.

"You need a shave, David," she said, rubbing her knuckles up and down the stubble of his jaw. The alien feel of it sent shivers through her.

"If it's shaves you want, there's a close one now coming up," he replied, not taking his eye off the water ahead. "Three and a half miles out — they weren't taking any chances."

She followed his gaze and saw two long, sleek boats, navy blue in colour, patrolling back and forth, each counter to the other. Her stomach seemed to fall away inside her.

"Steam launches from Falmouth," he added with a laugh. "No expense spared!"

"How can you laugh?" she cried. "We can't possibly escape."

"They can't touch us beyond the three-mile line," he said.

"And we can't stay outside it for ever."

"No," he conceded laconically. "That's the truth. Take the wheel. It's time to start the engine."

First he struck the mainsail and then, leaving the boat to drift for a moment, he got her to hold the exhaust lift while he swung the flywheel 'up to revs.' After several goes the engine coughed into life, wavered, picked up, and then roared away.

"Right," he said, fitting the cover back in place. "A little cat and mouse before we let them catch us!"

He throttled up to maximum revs and headed straight for the
nearest Customs boat, steering to follow it wherever it went.
The other launch turned about and came steaming in at full
power to the rescue. The first launch soon found itself in a
narrowing pincer movement — unwilling to turn to port, toward
the *Merlin,* being uncertain of how reckless David was prepared
to be, and unable to turn to starboard because of the 'help'
steaming in from that quarter.

At the last minute, its helmsman realized he had no choice
but to turn away from the *Merlin,* which seemed hell-bent on
self-destruction, taking them along, too. By a miracle of
seamanship it just managed to avoid its 'rescuer' though seamen
aboard each vessel must have had a rare glance down the funnel
of the other. The *Merlin* passed close enough astern of the
second launch to see the whites of Inspector Sterne's eyes — the
terrified whites of his eyes.

"What dreadful seamanship, Mister Sterne!" David mocked,
turning a cheeky circle before speeding off again. "You don't
belong to go to sea enough — that's your trouble!"

The wild, exultant gleam in his eye frightened Tamsin — and
yet it thrilled her, too. She understood now how some men
could lead others into any sort of danger, even into certain
death. She felt it at that moment and knew she would follow him
to the end of this 'cat-and-mouse' game, as he called it, no
matter where it led.

"Wheeee!" she cried suddenly, surprising herself and startling
him into leaving a hairpin of a wobble in their wake. "Ram them
properly next time!" she added.

"Aye-aye, Cap'n!" He came about and pushed up to full
throttle once more, this time making for the second launch, with
Sterne aboard.

"No!" Tamsin yelled in his ear. "I was joking."

"Too late now!" he replied. "Hold on to your hat!"

But this time it was the *Merlin* that veered at the last moment,
after which David cut the engine to idle and set the propellor
pitch to feather.

"Enough of this fun!" he called out to the two launches.
"You're welcome aboard to search — since that's what you
seem to want."

Sterne's launch came gently alongside. A couple of seamen leaped aboard the *Merlin* and tied the two boats fast. When the Inspector made to come aboard, David even leaned over and considerately helped him — something the man did not welcome.

"What's all this?" he asked testily, shaking David's hand away.

"Just a bit of fun, sir," came the reply. "No harm done."

"Fun?" the man asked. "Call that fun?"

"Well, let's just say I had my reasons."

Their eyes met and held each other's. Sterne blinked first. "Get aboard, you men. You know what to do."

The men certainly knew what to do. In fact, they found the brandy barrel before the first minute was up.

"Oh, horror!" David cried, holding up his hands like the worst sort of strolling actor. "Who could have put that there, I wonder."

Sterne paid him no heed. "Bring it aboard," he said. "Six men! Lifting party!"

But the man who found it already had the bung out. "It's seawater, sir," he said.

"All of it?" The inspector sighed. "Tip it out."

At that moment Tamsin had an idea. David's game of cat-and-mouse had been simple high spirits, she was sure of it. But she now saw a way to make it seem part of a plan. His enigmatic words, 'I had my reasons' had put the idea into her head.

She pretended to lose interest in Sterne and his activities. "You don't mind if I get on with the washing up?" she said. And she went to the wheelhouse to take out the mugs and dip them in the sea. While she did so, she stared in what she hoped was a surreptitious manner toward the coast — toward Lamorna or Porthgwarra, if she had her bearings right. Eventually she had been at the simple chore of washing two cups for so long that the ever-suspicious Sterne came to see what she was really up to. She 'noticed' him then with a guilty start and hastily took her eyes off the distant coast.

Then, seeing that she hadn't fooled him, she said, "Very beautiful in the dawn, isn't it."

"Take a good hard look, Miss Harte," he replied. "Because when I find what I'm looking for — and I shall — there's many a dawn you'll see only on the ceiling of a prison cell. And how are you in man's trousers, anyway?"

"D'you think they'd agree to send me to a man's prison, then?" she asked.

He returned to his work without a further word.

The barrel was filled with seawater to the last drop.

"What's this, sir?" One of the men had the engine cowling up. He had noticed the pipe to the reserve fuel tank, the same one Tamsin had spotted.

"Reserve fuel," David explained. "Up forrard, for ballast, see."

He started to lead them to it but Sterne barked, "Stop him! I'll find it, don't you fear!"

"There's no trick," David said. "Just lift that decking."

They did as he directed and there, indeed, was the reserve tank — the twin of the main tank, which they had already discovered and dipped. And found to be nearly empty.

"It's got to be in there!" Sterne said delightedly. "We've looked everywhere else."

Tamsin agreed. Despite David's insouciance, she felt sure their game was now up — and jokes about prison no longer seemed quite so hilarious. Desperately clinging on to her decoy-idea, she caught hold of the mast, stepped up on the coaming of the fish-hold, and, shielding her eyes (even though the sun was rising behind her), peered even more intently toward the land.

One of the officers unscrewed the cap of the tank. Another brought forward a dipstick, a twisted strand of quarter-inch copper wire with a piece of lint trapped at the bottom.

Sterne leaned forward, ready to pounce.

David glanced anxiously at Tamsin, wondering what she was playing at.

The officer made several stabs at pushing the dipstick into the tank, thwarted by the rocking of the boat.

Sterne shouted at him and told him to get a grip of himself.

David was still far more concerned for Tamsin than the dipping of the tank.

Sterne noticed it and followed his eyes, only to discover Tamsin once again staring at the land, almost as if she expected some sort of rescue to come from that quarter.

"Got it!" The officer slipped the long rod down into the tank.

"All the way!" Sterne shouted. "We know all about tanks with false bottoms!"

His underling tapped it twice on the bottom of the tank. He pinched his finger and thumb to mark the position of the top of the filler neck and then cautiously withdrew it.

Sterne snatched at the lower end, where the lint was held, and brought it up to his nose. "Petrol!" he said in disgust. "Measure the depth."

The officer, who still had the position marked, held it level with the top of the tank and four or five heads went down to see if the end of the stick was level with the bottom of the tank.

Which, of course, it was.

They dipped it again to make sure.

But Sterne already knew he had lost — for not only was young Thorne completely unconcerned with what they were doing, he was far more interested in the antics of the Harte woman.

What *was* she doing there?

He sprang to his feet and turned to look at her properly. But at that moment she leaped lightly down from the coaming, and, with an air of immense relief, gave David a nod. And then at last she turned a broad, triumphant smile upon the Inspector.

"Quick, lads!" he shouted. " Drop all that! Step lively now — back aboard. We've been decoyed out here but, by God, we s'll catch 'em ashore!"

As he waited for his men to cross back onto the launch he said to David, "All right, young Peters. What were you doing last night? A whole tank of fuel used and nothing in the hold to show for it?"

"You should have asked me that first," David told him. "It seemed that Mister Standish Coverley had an urgent need to get to France last night. I helped him on his way, that's all."

The man frowned. "Mister Coverley — a fugitive from justice?"

"I didn't say that. I merely said he had an urgent need to get to France — just like you've got an urgent need to get to Lamorna. Oops!" He clapped his hand over his mouth and looked guilty.

"Right, cox'n! Porthgwarra it is!" He leaped back aboard the launch — this time with no offer of help. "Full speed ahead!"

David and Tamsin waited until they were well away before giving vent to cries of victory. Then she took him by the arms and danced him round and round in a wild jig on the hatch cover of the fish hold.

Louder and louder was their exultation, wilder and wilder grew their steps, until — inevitably — she stumbled and fell backward. And he, trying to hold her, fell also, half upon her, half at her side.

And there they lay, fighting for breath, their hearts beating much faster than even their exertions would warrant, their eyes locked in a full-scale audit of each other.

"All right then!" she cried angrily and pulled his face hard against hers.

Her lips were hungry for his. When they touched, it was not enough, and she wrapped her arms around his head and pulled him brutally hard against her.

He moaned and tried to pull away. But, when he half succeeded, he pressed his mouth to hers again, this time with no extra assistance from her.

In fact, she now lay back in a kind of trance, as if all her muscles had lost the will to act. Only her head moved, this way and that, to double the wonder of that magical contact between them. She broke at last, fighting to breathe, and then kissed him lightly, again and again, between gasps for breath.

Soon she was giggling, too, and so was he. And then it became a game in which she moved her lips this way and that while he struggled to follow her and trap her once more. She never made it too difficult nor forced him to pursue her for too long, though.

Eventually she flipped him over onto his back and laid her head upon his chest. "We're mad," she murmured.

"I never doubted it," he replied.

"We'll never really suit each other, you know."

"But the fun is in the trying."

"It's going to be a long courtship."

He sighed heavily. "I'm used to that."

"You liar!" She rose on one elbow and hammered his chest with her fist, half-heartedly.

"It was the truth in one respect," he said. "I was in love and it wasn't requited — or not in any satisfactory form."

"Not in any form at all! Don't give yourself airs. I still don't know why I'm doing this — falling in love with a man who could be drowned at any time."

"Ah!" he said.

"What does that mean?"

"Why d'you think I needed this two hundred and twenty-five pounds, then?"

She rose onto both elbows and looked into his eyes. "*Two hundred and twenty-five?*"

"Including the hundred Mister Coverley gave me. It's enough to refit this vessel for trips round the bay."

"Honestly?"

"Next season — you'll see. The *Saucy Sal* — trips round Saint Michael's Mount — sea trips for sporting fishermen."

"So we really have got brandy somewhere aboard! Where?"

"Come!" He struggled out from beneath her and helped her to her feet.

"Ouch!' She walked gingerly and shook her feet to make the pins and needles go away.

He led her to the reserve tank where, once again, he screwed off the lid — or, rather, she noticed, he seemed to be screwing it *on*. And now she saw that the filler neck appeared to be rising with each full turn.

And finally he pulled it off — or out. Yes — the filler neck was *two* filler necks and the inner one, inserted on a right-hand thread, screwed out to reveal itself as a pipe with a blanked-off end. He carried it gingerly to the main fuel tank and poured it in. "Waste not, want not," he said, returning with the two mugs and a cream dipper, the sort that dairymen carry on their rounds.

"I keep promising you that tot of brandy," he said. "It's high time I delivered."

It slipped down her throat like silk and came back with a sizzling afterburn.

The mugs went clattering to the deck as, once again, he put his arms around her. And now all the fight had gone out of her. All that resistance. All that common sense. What took its place was the thrill of his very being, and being *there* … the ecstasy of feeling his lips against hers, the desire for him …

The need to be his … and him, hers.

Now and for ever.